"Jerzy Kosinski has lived through—and now makes use of—some of the strongest direct experience that this century has had to offer."
—*Time*

"It is quite legitimate to see Kosinski as a spokesman for the human capacity to survive."
—*America*

"One of our most significant writers."
—*Newsweek*

"Jerzy Kosinski is one of the most important and consistently entertaining people writing today."
—*Literary Guild*

"The brutal power of Kosinski's writing derives in large part from the pure genius of his plotting."
—*Saturday Review*

"Reading Kosinski is like swimming in a placid sea and suddenly being caught in an undertow."
—*National Observer*

"Kosinski is a very Jewish writer reminding us in almost every story that human invention is in jeopardy."
—*The Washington Post*

"A strong, meaningful voice, adding something vital to the riches of the modern novel."
—*The Times*, London

"One of the foremost psychological novelists in the world."
—*Psychology Today*

THE HERMIT OF 69TH STREET

BOOKS BY JERZY KOSINSKI

NOVELS

The Painted Bird
Steps
Being There
The Devil Tree
Cockpit
Blind Date
Passion Play
Pinball
The Hermit of 69th Street

ESSAYS

Notes of the Author
The Art of the Self

NONFICTION
(under the pen name of Joseph Novak)

The Future Is Ours, Comrade
No Third Path

JERZY KOSINSKI

THE HERMIT OF 69TH STREET

The Working Papers of Norbert Kosky

SEAVER BOOKS

HENRY HOLT AND COMPANY

NEW YORK

Published by Seaver Books/Henry Holt and Company, Inc.,
115 West 18th Street, New York, New York 10011.
Published in Canada by Fitzhenry & Whiteside Limited,
195 Allstate Parkway, Markham, Ontario L3R 4T8.

Library of Congress Cataloging in Publication Data
Kosinski, Jerzy N., 1933–
The hermit of 69th Street.
I. Title.
PS3561.O8H4 1987   813'.54   87-10924
ISBN 0-8050-0611-7

First Edition

Designed by Beth Tondreau Design
Printed in the United States of America
1 3 5 7 9 10 8 6 4 2

Grateful acknowledgment is made to the following for permission to reprint
previously published material:

Oxford University Press: "How Can I Calm Myself" by Stanislaw Wyspiański,
excerpted from *Five Centuries of Polish Poetry, 1450–1970*, 2nd edition, by Jerzy
Peterkiewicz and Burns Singer, copyright © 1970. Reprinted by permission of
Oxford University Press.

Charles Scribner's Sons: Draft of Chapter One of *The Great Gatsby* is used by
permission of Charles Scribner's Sons. Copyright © 1967 Frances Scott Fitzgerald
Lanahan. Excerpts from the novel *The Great Gatsby* are used by permission of the
estate of F. Scott Fitzgerald, Charles Scribner's Sons and The Bodley Head (*Bodley
Head Scott Fitzgerald, Volume 1*). Copyright © 1925 Charles Scribner's Sons; copyright renewed 1953 Frances Scott Fitzgerald Lanahan.

Hill and Wang: Excerpts from A *Lover's Discourse* by Roland Barthes, translated by
Richard Howard. Translation copyright © 1979 by Farrar, Straus and Giroux, Inc.
Reprinted by permission of Hill and Wang, a division of Farrar, Straus and Giroux,
Incorporated, and also Jonathan Cape, Limited, and the estate of Roland Barthes.

Viking Penguin Inc.: Excerpt from *Eugene Onegin* by Alexander Pushkin, translated by Charles Johnston (Penguin Classics, 1977, with revisions, 1979). Translation copyright © 1977, 1979 by Charles Johnston. Reprinted by permission of
Viking Penguin Inc. and Penguin Books Ltd.

ISBN 0-8050-0611-7

For my wife, Katherina,

Although I conquer all the earth,
yet for me there is only one city.
In that city there is for me only one house;
And in that house, one room only;
and in that room, a bed.
And one woman sleeps there,
The shining joy and jewel of all my kingdom.

(Sanskrit)

PREFACE

Norbert Kosky left this English-language *brudnopis* (Ruthenian for work-ing papers) on *Nostromo*, an unassuming fishing junk he leased from the Manhattan Marina at the time of his untimely disappearance.

These Working Papers first came into my possession when, some few years ago, I was entrusted by the trustees of Norbert Kosky's estate with the task of bringing them to the attention of his reading public.

> A painful experience in childhood,
> a disappointing love, a cruel
> father, and numberless facts of
> personal biography may be a window
> on the work of the author, but
> notebooks such as these stand
> closer to the work than does any
> event.

writes Edward Wasiolek* and what he writes fully applies to Norbert Kosky, the Hermit of 69th Street, as he was commonly known among his friends.

—Jerzy Kosinski

---

*From the Introduction to *The Notebooks for Crime and Punishment*: Edited and translated by Edward Wasiolek (1967).

NOTE

Ever since he began writing, Norbert Kosky followed the precepts of F. L. Lucas: "In fine, there is much to be said for the principle 'Write in haste; and revise at leisure.' And revision is usually best when one has had time to forget what has been written, and comes back to it with fresh eyes." ("Methods of Writing,"*Style,* 1955, 1962, p. 259)

As this book was going to press, I discovered among Kosky's possessions a further set of footnotes and final insertions too late to incorporate in the first edition. I am assured by my publisher, however, that they will be incorporated in a later printing.

   Meanwhile, the critic and reader are inadvertently rewarded for the absence of final refinements by being offered a rare book collector's item: an incomplete *compleat* of Norbert Kosky's autofictional style.

—J.K., 1988

THE
HERMIT
OF
69TH
STREET

The present book is intended, as far as possible, to give an exact insight into the theory of relativity. . . . The author has spared himself no pains in his endeavor to present the main ideas in the simplest and most intelligible form, and on the whole, in the sequence and connection in which they actually originated. . . . May the book bring someone a few happy hours of suggestive thought. (Albert Einstein, Preface, 1916)*

At the Manfred, on Manhattan's seamy West 69th Street, all the lights and tenants have gone out—but one. Appropriately, the light comes from a two-room apartment where the single sixty-watt bulb shines above the head of one Norbert Kosky, a latter-day esoteric scribe who, pencil in hand, frenetically scribbles one word after another on various-size yellow and white six-by-nine-inch index cards spread out on his desk.

Kosky is a frenetic man whose frenzy stems primarily from his preoccupation with words, letters and numbers as much as it does with breathing evenly. Even numbers—even as well as uneven—are figures

---

*Albert Einstein, *General Theory of Relativity*, 1915. Einstein the German-Jew (most probably of Jewish-Ruthenian stock: J.K.) was a lucky man. In 1919, "observation of the total eclipse of the sun bears out Einstein's theory of relativity" (Bernard Grun, 1975), an event no novelist can ever count upon to bear out his or her view of narrative relativity—and, naturally, in 1921 Einstein gets the Nobel for "his discovery of the photoelectric effect"—most unfortunately, an effect totally foreign to literary science.

of speech to him. No wonder: an aspiring master of the Ruthenian-Jewish oral tradition and an adept of Tantric Yoga* he has been since 1965 a naturalized American, and the year 1966 saw the publication of the unexpurgated edition of his first purely fictional narrative tale, so fictional he refused to affix any biographical note to it—other than his name, first and last. Hence anything to do with the numbers nine and six—particularly when joined together in sixty-nine—is for him a top SS, with the letters SS standing here for spiritually suggestive (SS)† the key phrase to all this forthcoming literary *Mors Osculi.*‡

As everyone knows, number six often comes out of its creative closet disguised as number nine, by simply walking with its head up, while just as often number nine goes out disguised as number six—by simply walking on its own head—its preferred disguise. Inordinately fond of each other, the two numbers often meet and, by joining their opposite ends in a tight embrace they become number sixty-nine (or ninety-six, if disguised), which for Kosky, born in the sixth month of June 1933 and spiritually matured on June ninth, signifies the very best. §

SS

---

*Yogatantra—Yoga: the yoke; tantra; the loom; also the power to harness; also a manuscript of a book. See *Tantric Yoga: The Art of Primal Concentration*, by George Niskisko (Los Angeles, 1982).

†Joining the initials of spiritually suggestive (SS) words is one way through which our literary Tantrist alerts the reader's own *spiritus* (Sanskrit: prana; Greek: pneuma). "Among some of the best known SS," wrote Norbert Kosky on the margin, "is *Sesame Street*, a National Education Television program presented daily except Sunday, to an estimated audience of 6,699 preschool children and childlike adults."

‡*Mors Osculi* (death of the kiss, as opposed to *Murs Justi*, kiss of death—the ultimate state of carnal ecstasy and spinal exaltation): **One of the Hasidic texts reads: Our sages declare that there is a kind of death which is as difficult as drawing a rope through a ring set on a tall mast, and there is a death as easy as drawing a hair out of milk, and this is called the death of the kiss. (See Benjamin Walker, *Encyclopedia of Esoteric Man,* 1977.)**

§"To obtain the Jewish year, the number 3760 must be added to the corresponding year of the Common Era (A.D.) . . . To obtain the common year from a Jewish year, the same number 3760 must be subtracted. However, if the thousands are not expressed in the Jewish year, the number 1240 may be added instead, at least for all dates since the year 1240 A.D. (Jewish year 5000). (*College Yiddish: An Introduction to the Yiddish Language and to Jewish Life and Culture* by Uriel Weinreich, sixth printing, 1984, Lesson 22, p. 215)

Writes Kosky on the margin: according to every numerologist's indispensable *The Timetables of History: A Horizontal Linkage of People and Events* (by Bernard Grun, based on Werner Stein's *Kulturfahrplan*, 1975), in 1965 the Nobel Prize for Literature went to M. A. Sholokov. That's unreal, considering that it did not go to Dostoyevsky or Conrad! In that very year six former Auschwitz prison officials were sentenced to life imprisonment and not to death by dying in an oven. Just as well, since the penalty of death has already been imposed on all of us, I oppose imposition of it for a second time!

In addition, the year 1965 saw such spiritually sensational headlines as PRESIDENT JOHNSON APPOINTS ABE FORTAS TO THE SUPREME COURT. FELIX FRANKFURTER DIES. MARTIN BUBER, THE FELIX FRANKFURTER OF JEWISH PHILOSOPHERS, DIES. POPE PAUL VI VISITS NEW YORK. RALPH NADER DECLARES DRIVING A U.S.-MADE CAR UNSAFE AT ANY SPEED. HERBERT MARCUSE AND PAUL TILLICH, THE THEOLOGIANS OF THE SPIRITUAL BORDER STATE, ARE NO LONGER WITH US. SOVIET ASTRONAUT LEONOV LEAVES SPACECRAFT FOR 9.6 MINUTES (and by returning to it, refuses to choose the life of an exile: Jay Kay).

Nothing blunts and destroys taste so much as endless journeying; the poetic spirit is not the wandering Jew. (Sainte-Beuve, 1869)*

Sainte-Beuve might be wrong; nothing typifies poetic spirit better than the spirit of a wandering Jew. Particularly if the wandering Ahasuerus† happens to be wandering into himself by means of writing (defined here as writing on one's inner wall as well as an omen. PRINTER: omen not amen.), fully aware that "Death and Life are in the power of the tongue." (Proverbs 18:21)

Lost in writing, Kosky hears Hear O Israel! Another soundless sound. By resounding so resolutely in his head, the sound seems to originate in the lobe of one's inner ear—Kosky's euphemism for his heart as well as his mind, for what he calls "my sublime inner lobby."

"The sound sounds only for as long as it is heard by the physical ear," Kosky now hears his inner monk tell him. **Whatever is manifested as sound in the heart or in the ear is a power of nature. The state of**

---

*Charles Augustin Sainte-Beuve (died 1869): An inspired literary critic who, daring enough to ask *What is a classic?*, was wisely inspired not to answer such a daring question.

†"We have not yet encountered this syndrome in those of Jewish origin," write in a footnote M. David Enoch and W. H. Trethowan (op. cit., 1979).

3

decomposition of conceptual thought is beyond all form. It is divine. (Hatha Yoga Pradipika, No. 100)*

No terrestrial being can disregard the sound of life—certainly not at a time when firing of even one wrong SS—no matter how small—"can turn into a world-beheading headline or behead the world," in the words of WHM World Headline Making Channel 6 TV.

SYRIA'S SS [surface to surface] 21 MISSILES INCREASE THE RISK OF WAR. Thanks to the addition of Soviet-built SS-21 missiles to the Syrian arsenal, the Arab-Israeli conflict is now on the brink of a new era—the age of strategic missiles. (*Newsweek*)

Extinguishing the lights in his apartment (the apt. here flatly defined as 2½ rms. with 1½ bathrooms $669/month flat), Kosky goes out. The ceremony of imposing sacred sanctions (SS) on real-life is about to begin.

SS

Out on the street, walking back and forth and back again between Sixth and Ninth avenues, in front of the infamous Chamisso Towers (off Liberty Square; owner: Peter Peebles Associates), our literary numerologist† scans the urban marshland for signs of life.

Notes of busy lives in distant worlds/Beat like a far wave on my anxious ear. (Tennyson)

Suddenly, the phone rings in the nearby glass-encased empty telephone booth. The phone rings twice, three times, four. A wrong number, no doubt, but not to a numerologist. Should Kosky answer the call?

Why shouldn't he? The only part of the conduct of anyone, for which he is amenable to society, is that which concerns others. In the part

---

*In Hatha Yoga there is no real difference between the inner light and the inner sound. To a Tantric, words emanate images which talk to the eye and images are heard by the soul (as transcribed by Hans Urich Ricker, op. cit.). For the most apt rendering of such spiritual "meeting of the eyes" (Rawson), the reader is henceforth most urgently referred to the color plate No. 66 ("the twist which affects the pattern of energies in the spinal column," Nepal, eighteenth century) and the black-and-white plate No. 69 ("Couple from 'Heaven Bands'") in The Art of Tantra, by Philip Rawson, 1978.

†Numerology: a time-tested spiritual system of predicting one's fate, based on the numerical value concealed in the alphabet, and hence in one's name (as first practiced by the ancient Hebrews and codified by Alessandro di Cagliostro).

which merely concerns himself, his independence is, of right, absolute. Over himself, over his own body and mind, the individual is sovereign. (John Stuart Mill, 1859)*

A good Samaritan who believes in R.S.V.P., as much as he does in the call of life—a call so often made by an anonymous caller—Kosky rushes to the booth—and he rushes into it with the speed of John Stuart Mill bodily rushing into Mrs. Harriet Taylor on their first physical love-filled meeting of the minds. He picks up the receiver on the sixth ring. †

"Sorry! Wrong number." He utters the public domain's most public cliché.

"Don't be sorry. Not yet!" answers a man's voice. "It's the right number. You're my number now!"

"I've found you through my infrared field glasses. The infrared makes you look yellow, but I don't mind. I like what I see!" says the far-out urban ranger bent on his Binocular Pickup™, the newest far out big-town adventure.

This colossal centralization, this agglomeration of three and a half million people on a single spot has multiplied the strength of these three and a half million inhabitants a hundredfold.... But the price that has been paid is not discovered until later. (Engels)

Dumbfounded, Kosky looks up at the block upon block of hotels, hospital, apartment houses and office buildings which scraping the moon-lit sky, surround him like a multifloored domino while blocking the moonlight. The Voice-Over could be watching over him, as well as looking him over, from just about anywhere. Kosky suddenly crouches down in the phone booth as if it were a flat-bottomed canoe, thus disappearing from sight.

---

*On Liberty (1982 ed.), page 60.

†As every numerologist trained in the hieroglyphical interpretation of the Hebrew alphabet knows, number six stands for the letter W or *waw*, the sixth letter of the Hebrew alphabet, which signifies, according to *The Mysteries of the Quabalah* (1922), "the eye of man as well as the ear is the emblem of water. According to the same by-now-well-tested theory, standing for T or for *teth*, the ninth letter of the Hebrew alphabet, the number nine stands for a refuge, resistance and shelter." Finally, there is *yod*, the tenth letter, which stands for all manifested power. See also "Kabbalah" (Chapter 10) in *The Earth Is the Lord's: The World of the Jew in Eastern Europe*, by Abraham Joshua Heschel (1949–1977), pp. 69ff. (A spiritual classic like no other: Norbert Kosky, 1981)

"You can't even see me!" Kosky turns into a Jewish *waterchilde* hiding from the SS in the Pripet marshland during the war!*

"Hey! Where are you?" the Voice screams.

"Here!" Kosky says, getting up.

"Good! Tell me, why are you out so late—?"

And when he had worked for hours at a stretch, forgetting food and sleep and everything, he would rise from his desk at last and stagger forth into the nighttime streets, reeling like a drunkard with his weariness. (Thomas Wolfe)

"I'm out looking for my opposite number, preferably a dark-skinned and well-endowed bombshell," says Kosky.

"By the by," the voice intones. "Where does your Bombay accent come from?"

"Ruthenia. Ruthenia used to be part of Ruthlandia until the German bombs hit it in 1939."† **Conrad had learnt to read English long before he spoke it and he had formed wrong sound impressions of many familiar words; he had for example acquired an incurable tendency to pronounce the last e in *these* and *those*. He would say, "*Wat* shall we do with *thesa* things?" And he was always incalculable about the use of "shall" and "will." (H. G. Wells)**

"Tell me, I can't quite make it out from here—are your pants made of leather?"

"Wool."

"What about your jacket?"

"Pure cotton."

"How do you stay so trim?"

"Easy. I'm an all-around Yale stoic."‡

---

*Mare Herodotis, now known as Pripet (pron. *Preepet*) Marshes: until 1945 the most inaccessible part of Eastern Europe, as large as Holland and Belgium combined, to which, in his *Dawn of European Civilization*, Professor V. Gordon Childe attributes one of the major routes of antiquity.

†"Those Ruthenians incorporated into the Crown in 1569 obtained all the privileges already enjoyed by the Polish nobility as well as by the Ruthenian nobility on the lands earlier incorporated into the Crown by Kazimierz the Great." (*Ruthenia, Cossackdom, the Ukraine, and the Commonwealth of Two Nations*, by Andrzej Sulima Kaminski, *The Polish Review*, 1987, 93–110, p. 96)

‡The philosophy of Stoicism was most convincingly professed by Lucius Annaeus Seneca (died A.D. 65), a Roman Spaniard, in a collection of his public essays disguised as private letters. (Imperative: read again *The Stoic Philosophy of Seneca*:

"Tell me: is your widow's peak black or white? I can't quite make it out from here."

"Why do you ask?"

"Because it looks kind of *darky*. Is it a tan or skin?"

"It's a Very Superior Old Pale."

"Good. And your height?"

"Five ten. Plus my heels," says Kosky.

"Good. And your weight?"

"About a hundred and forty pounds."

"I like that!" the Voice drawls. "And your health, my friend? I bet you go through a VDOL* ordeal as often as you can!"

"I certainly do. It's the only blood ordeal as a Jew I won't refuse to go through."

"So what else do you do to keep yourself all kosher?"

"I write!" Kosky gives himself a Star of David.

"Write? What do you mean: *write*? I mean what do you *really* do?"

"I write. Really, I do."

"Do you write for movies or for TV?"

"I write books."

"What kind of books?"

"Novels. Novels which mean a lot to me."

"Good. I go for novelty," says the Voice. "What are your books about?"

"The usual surface-to-surface life spiced with astral sex," says Kosky.

"Hit me with some of your spicy titles."

Prompted, Kosky recites one title after another.

Don't think I can go on. Heart, head—everything. Lolita, Lolita, Lolita, Lolita, Lolita. Repeat till the page is full, printer. (Nabokov)

"Those titles are dry not spicy!" The Voice voices concern. "You need wet titles. Wet and hot. Don't ever confuse heat with being dry. True heat is always wet. So how many novels have you written altogether?"

Essays and Letters of Seneca, translated with an Introduction by Moses Hadas, 1958. It helps to cope. Doubleday Anchor Orig.) Yale: in Hebrew, a mountain goat (*ya'el*). See also *Yale: A Pictorial History* by Reuben A. Holden, 1967 (That's when I first saw Yale: Norbert Kosky.)

*VDOL: A little-known abbreviation for only too well-known international and interracial blood ordeal.

"Eight."

"How long did it take you to write them?"

"Over thirty years."

"You spent four dry years on a single novel. A *novel*—not even an encyclopedia?"

"That's right," says Kosky. "But these years were not dry to me even though until a few years ago, I used to fear water." **Words are like water. (Bernard Malamud)** "Besides, as the general public does not know, writers need a lot of time to write and to rewrite. They also need a lot of astral sex. Did you know that John Stuart Mill would never have written *On Liberty* without the liberties he took with Harriet Taylor?"

"Speaking of time, how old are you?"

"Over fifty."

"Over fifty? Are you pulling my leg?"

"Your leg is too far," says Kosky. "Of course I'm fifty. So what?" **At fifty—yesterday—I feel I have just begun to write. These are the best years. I spit on the grave of my awful forties. (James Thurber, 1944)** Seneca wrote his *Letters from a Stoic* at sixty-nine. What's so unusual about being over forty?" **Do you know the worst of all vices? It is being over fifty-five. (Trotsky quoting Lenin quoting Turgenev)***

"Nothing unusual," says the Voice. "In my book fifty means a port of old age. I don't go for old port—or for an old sport." The Voice hangs up on Kosky.

SS

His spell for adventure—misspelled, Kosky returns home feeling like a broken literary broker.

You don't know what it is to stay a whole day with your head in your hands, trying to squeeze your unfortunate brain to find a word. With you, ideas come very easily, incessantly, like a stream. With me it's a tiny thread of water. (Flaubert to George Sand)

At his desk, our quester now alerts the usually absent-minded reader to one finer, hence less visible thread of his narrative tapestry: the

---

*PROOFREADER TO AUTHOR: Please provide text for footnote.

AUTHOR TO PROOFREADER: Can't find it at this time. Besides, in a novel such as this one, certain quotes, like certain high-proof vodkas, automatically evoke spiritual proof No. 96.

importance of the consecutive words, each one beginning with the letter S to be noted in his forthcoming spiritual satyricon (SS). In his new book, the letters SS signify Sabbatai Sevi,* the spiritually sacred Jewish mystic who, once considered a Jewish messiah, died in 1676 at the age of fifty. At the same time the letters SS might stand for the words which either stand for all that is spiritually straightforward (SS) or for all that is spiritually sterile (SS).

Spiritual is his favorite word and for a reason: it contains the word spirit, as well as ritual. Just think of the first being who invented this word! And speaking of his favorite words, how about the word sexton? Sexton! What a word, what a profession!: Imagine having, in one word, sex, sexto (a book—and at that one formed by folding sheets into his favorite number six!) and a ton, a word which, to him clearly indicates bon-ton, a unit of measure of man's internal capacity as well as having a *"siesta*: adopted from sp. for '6th (hour)': suggested by L *sexta hora.*" (*Origins*, A *short Etymological Dictionary of Modern English*, by Eric Partridge, 1958. No. 6, p. 627). See also "Dictionaries, New and Old: Who plagiarizes whom, and why and when," by Robert Burchfeld, in *Encounter: Current Affairs-Literature-the Arts*, Sept.–Oct. 1984, p. 10–19.

There is a sequence about the creative process, and a work of genius is a synthesis of its individual features from which nothing can be subtracted without disaster. (Seneca)

By first putting all these paired letters SS in parentheses (to him, each parenthesis, no matter how closed, is a form of open para-mental prison cell) Kosky gives himself and the reader a chance to interrogate each SS at will and to decide, in the light of the available evidence, where they came from, what they stand for and whether they belong in his spiritual Storyville No. 9.†

---

*"Sabbataism was the largest and most momentous messianic movement in Jewish history. . . ," writes Gershon Sholem in his *Kabbalah.* "The figure of the man (Sabbatai Sevi) who occupied the center of the movement is one of the *most completely documented* of any Jew who played an important role in Jewish history."

†Storyville, an area in New Orleans so named not in order to honor a storyteller, but in order to honor a censor of public morals: Mr. Sydney Story. Sydney Story, or SS as he was familiarly called, was the city's morally least alerted alertman, who, alerted to the existence of the French practice of *soixante-neuf*, also known as the English vice, so popular in the bilingual, French-English New Orleans,

9

In his own storyville, our literary alertman defends narrative art and with it his entire inner thesaurus, against the onslaught of the bestial* as well as sterile with three of his most potent narrative missiles, called SS-1, SS-69 and SS-96. All these weapons are multi-headed and inward-heading SAM missiles—the word SAM standing here for the Ruthenian word *alone*, and not for SAM, the Satellite Antiballistic Missile. The SS-1 stands for Survival of the Strongest (for Kosky, No. 1 always ranks as the spiritually most inferior number). The SS-69 defends the survival of the species; SS-96, his spiritual narrative top of the narrative line, protects the safety of his spiritual survival—and the survival of those who, like him, see humans as the only spiritual species SS known to man.

SS

One way to explain why he, our selfish fish, is compelled to stay home and write his *brudnopis* (Ruth. for working paper, lit.: dirty text) instead of going, say, to the beach, is to refer the reader to one of our sopher's 1939 memory slides. On it, talking to the six-year-old Norbert, his father, Israel, points his index finger at a daily-newspaper photograph of William James Sidis, portraying him first at the age of six as "America's Greatest Child Prodigy," then at another photograph, showing him, in the words of the headline printed in large yellow letters as FAT AND FORTY AND DOING NOTHING WORTH DOING.

"Too bad Boris Sidis, Billy's father, didn't explain in time to *his seed* where Billy could find happiness," says Israel Kosky.

"Where could he?" asks Norbert.

"There. In one's own head. Only there," says his father, touching his head with his forefinger.

"How is one to look for it without getting a *kapdoloro*." (Esperanto for headache: N.K.)†

"By sitting on your ass; by reading and writing. Remember: you were

---

restricted its performance to the town's multi-tongued as well as bilingual red-light district coded by the town's police as precinct 69.

*See *Anatomy of the SS State* by Helmut Krausnick, Hans Buchheim, Martin Broszat, and Hans-Adolf Jacobsen. Appendix (6) compiled by Brian Melland. German-language edition, 1965; English-language edition, 1968.

†Esperanto: the auxiliary language invented by a Polish-Jewish eye doctor, Dr. Ludwig L. Zamenhof (1859–1917). Invented and first published in 1887 and meant

born Loewinkopf and in your name *Loew* stands for Judah Loew ben Bezalel,* a great Jewish lion born in 1609, and *kopf* stands for head. These are your traditional relations, with the word *relations* meaning a traditional narrative as well as narrative tradition. One day, if you're lucky, you might even be invited to visit the Bezalel Academy in Jerusalem!" says his father, and his image disappears just when our literary engrosser passes by Lion's Head, a well-known literary hangout and one of his favorite pit stops in lower Manhattan.

Speaking for the Romanians in Paris and, more generally, for all those who have decided to remain in the West, I said that we weren't émigrés but that we were in exile. I thought that an exiled writer should imitate Dante, not Ovid. . . . For Dante, exile was more than a stimulus; it was the very wellspring of his inspiration. (Mircea Eliade)†

One way to break out of exile left to our *homo Judens* without exiting from his hermitage is to revert to the use of his phone, but a phone poses a clear threat to his inner him, our Sidis Billy. ‡ After all, the writing process is silent: the words are silent, too. Each word carries a silent number, a number, yes; but also its own inner spiritually suggestive pushbutton tone. SPEAKING ON THE PHONE HAS ALREADY REPLACED SPEAKING FACE TO FACE AS NO. 1 MEANS OF INTIMATE COMMUNICATION, says an advertisement placed in every sixth issue of the *U.S. Phone Industry Views.*

---

for those who learned enough in their own language to know "that we must *first* find some solution to the 'language problem.' Not until we have settled this comparatively minor matter can we begin to understand one another across the frontiers and then to discuss the grave social and economic problems that face us." (*Esperanto*, by John Cresswell and John Harley, M.A., 1957, 1968, 1984, p. 9)

*Kosky is Kosky's second given name, adopted by his parents at the outset of World War II in order to replace, as well as supplement, Loewinkopf, his initial Jewish family name. **For Rabbi Loew, as for his rabbinic predecessors, the evil inclination is not evil in itself. It only becomes evil when it is misused. Paradoxically, the aspect of the soul most related to privation and matter—the evil inclination—provides man with the possibility of transcending privation and matter. The aspect of man which may lead to sin and to the enslavement of the body may free man from sin and from the corrupting influence of the body. From *Mystical Theology and Social Dissent: The Life and Works of Judah Loew of Prague*, by Byron L. Sherwin, published at 69 Fleet Street, in London, in 1982.**

†Translated from the French by Derek Coltman (1982).

‡See *The Prodigy: A Biography of William James Sidis, America's Greatest Child Prodigy,* by Amy Wallace (1986).

Such, then, are the newest phone sex ads, which scattered throughout this nation's printed pages, selflessly advertise HOOKERS' PHONE SEX while proclaiming JACKING OFF IS A CRIME. CALL FOR PUNISHMENT ON THE PHONE. MISTRESS KARA. ALL MAJOR CREDIT CARDS ACCEPTED.

However, to Kosky, to our Tantric neophyte, **the merging of mind is achieved by listening to inner sound (Hatha Yoga Pradipika),** not by listening to a lustless, invisible woman practically throwing up a stream of chosen and rehearsed sexual unconsciousness to him on the phone.

There is bound to be a way for our master oralist to be able at the same time to remain bound to his narrative tradition, yet become free of it—free only in order to dive deeper into the hidden nature of his bondage. (Here, in this narrative, *it* stands for "diving into the Freudian Id as well as into the deepest Self of our self-proclaimed literary Yid": Jay Kay.) There's bound to be such a way, and there is.

Our inventive paraphrast finds such moral *No Exit* in his use of the services of another fellow-oralist, preferably a woman who is a professionally trained expert of literary *gamahucher*—trained, as opposed to being spontaneously creative.

"She is a privately hired, part-time professional literary vulvar cleft, be it a typist, a proofreader, a line editor or even a licensed full-time galley printer—an indispensable tax deductible literary ghost every writer must employ at one time or another" in the words of Norbert Kosky, as he was quoted, for once verbatim, by *Writer's Tax*, a tax-deductible magazine, published by Jeremy Diddler Center (Kenney Place, facing South Sea port; Guido Francischini, Architect; owner: Pierre J. Proudhon, [not *proudhomme*: J.K.]).

As every writer knows, such good ghosts are hard to find. Already at the turn of the century—on August 9, 1900, to be exact—the august Henry James, a man who knew a great deal about the perils of being a public figure,* wrote to William Dean Howells, "It is not easy to concoct a ghost of any freshness."†

---

*In *The Reverberator* (1888), a novel by Henry James, George P. Flack, a corrupt newspaper reporter who writes flack and nothing but flack, is reported to be one of the two literary ghosts said to have influenced the *Right to Privacy* by Warren and Brandeis (1890). The other ghost was Steadfast Dodge, the corrupt newspaper editor who, steadfastly dodging truth, can be found in J. Fenimore Cooper's *Home as Found* (1838).

†Even those who are not into numerology must pause here to think what a

Kosky's preoccupation with number sixty-nine as a figure of speech as well as a figure from life stems from many spiritual stems as well as the history of the German occupation of Ruthenia. It stems from his coming of sexual age when, at eight, back in 1941, he first saw the figure sixty-nine acted by Ewunia and Adam, the two consenting Ruthenian minors of his age, who acted it for the first time and in one short act only on a bed made of grass, or grass which served as a bed. Equally stimulating is a vision of himself as a child, "a *vision*, not an examination, or a revisitation of a childhood" (Kosinski, 1965) reenacting at the age of nine the esthetically complex head-to-muff ritual with a girl of fourteen appropriately named Mufka.* After the war, after learning French and English sufficiently well, our Ruthenian Nabatean† also learned the obvious life-and-breath-giving benefits of *soixante-neuf*, also known to him, one who already in his Ruthenian high school was an Anglophile at Frenching and being Frenched. This was the time when, with TB rampant in the big cities as well as in the countryside, the Ruthenian health authorities (already mindful of the poisonous power of bad breath, and the dangers of catching TB via an innocent first-date first lips-to-

---

chance James—that all-time literary master of ceremonies—took by writing about *concocting a ghost* and, of all things, by writing about this to another writer! If dear Dean Howells were jealous of James, he could have easily turned things around and claimed that James was capable of writing about such a ghost only because the ghost possessed him first. "For Henry James a ghostly narrative could be neither clinical nor analytic; it had to have all the richness of life and all the terror, wonder, excitement, curiosity the mind is capable of evoking." Leon Edel in his Introduction to *The Ghostly Tales of Henry James* (1948).

*In 1948 Professor Stefan Szuman, a foremost Polish-Jewish child psychologist and educator (see his *In Praise of the Dilettantes*, 1947 and 1962), collected some 2,388 drawings in which Polish children in 1946–47 answered such questions as "What happened in your family and among your kin during the War and Nazi Occupation (1939–45)." Almost half of those who answered drew what during the War they saw most often, and now remembered most vividly: "murders and execution." (From *Ohne Mitleid: The Child in the Hitlerite System*, by Kiryl Sosnkowski [1962], page 169.)

†First incorporated as a sect in Mesopotamia, the Nabateans believe that a practice of unnatural acts (unnatural meaning not contrary to—or against—defined here as what comes to most of us naturally) invariably leads to the development of unnatural speculative spells of psychic powers.

lips kiss: Jay Kay) warned against the dangers of face-to-face sexual cohabitation. Their warning indirectly contributed to the popularity of 69 in Ruthenia.

Asanas (postures), various Kumbhakas, and other divine means, all should be practiced in the practice of Hatha Yoga, till the fruit—Raja Yoga—is obtained.[69]

End of chapter 1st, on the method of forming the Asanas. (The Hatha Yoga Pradipika, op. cit.)

His preoccupation with self-disclosure also stems from more recent American-made history. On the evening of August 9, 1969 (8-9-1-9-6-9), a lovely hamlet of Hollywood's Prince Hamlet in Destiny City, California, was invaded in the prince's absence by a Doomsday Daddy gang, composed of three American Desert Foxes disguised as passion flower holymen.

The stimulus-starved gang cut open Ophelia's silken throat with a straight razor, "and they danced on her belly until the baby she expected in a week was no longer kicking" (*The Los Angeles Transit*). They cut down the laughing Rosencrantz by knifing him many times with an army knife and they killed the slovenly Guildenstern by shooting him in the groin again and again with an American-made 6.9 caliber gun. Then, and only then, did they kill Mrs. Guildenstern. Call her Mrs. even though she and Guildenstern were not married. *

---

*See *Black Medicine: The Dark Art of Death*, by N. Mashiro, Ph.D. (The vital points of the Human Body in close combat) (1978).

14

2

Restless, still glancing through the Hot Personals—the personal ad pages of the *Hot Air Corsair*, Manhattan's notorious libertarian weekly—Kosky catches sight of Moving Finger. The Moving Finger happens to be the advertisement for Madame Wharton's Cumpany ("Cumpany, printer, cumpany!": Jay Kay), whose motto is: "If you can't come, then call." The Moving Finger offers "outcall touch-typing," and placing Mme. Wharton's reputation on the line, the ad guarantees the "typo-free *expurt* services, (expurt, printer!) having anything your Hard desires typed by one of our black and white female x-spurts."

SS

With *pneuma* in mind, our literary mover telephones the Moving Finger and talks to Madame Wharton ("Call me Edith—but call"), who then transfers his call to one Maule Hawthorne, who introduces herself to him as "a white part-time expurt touch typist." With a touch of sexual *prix-fixe* (prefix No. 69: J.K.) Mademoiselle Hawthorne offers her heavenly body's go-go services at "half rate after midnight."

Not a bit touchy, Maule assures him she can touch'n'type ("as well as touch anybody who is my type") and assures him that, in her previous job, she specialized in "writing birthday bellygrams as well as delivering and playing them person-to-person." Soon after she says it, Kosky asks her to come to his flat right away—as long as right away means after midnight.

A thousand buds swell and open . . . each disclosing . . . as at the bottom of a cup of pink marble, its blood-red stain, and suggesting even more strongly than the full-blown flowers, the special irresistible quality of the hawthorn. (Marcel Proust)

While impatiently waiting to be mauled by this tax-deductible Maule, our impatient sex patient talks back and forth to Sadhaka,* his inner Hatha Yoga Mole and he talks to him about his need for biological drama, "a prerequisite for being able to see himself as insatiably pro-creative."

"Fucking this girl will undoubtedly give you momentary exaltation—but how long will such memoryless exaltation last against your will?" Sadhaka always speaks in a spiritually soothing whisper.

"It will not last long," our Sadhaka agrees reluctantly. "But then nothing does."

"Aren't you wasting the flame of the everlasting Self?"

"Body is a candle," replies our sexual spider. "The flame cannot live apart from the candle."

The role of individuality in the struggle against evil becomes particularly conspicuous when we consider the fact that the essence of evil lies in suffering and when we recall what has been said about the role of individuality in the struggle against suffering. If evil is suffering, it is not fully communicable. (Jan Szczepanski)†

Midnight strikes. Soon after, entering the Manfred through one of six supplementary entrances that allow a visitor to bypass the main entrance and avoid the face-to-face encounter with Señor Santos, an ex–Cuban marine who's now the building's night doorman, Maule Hawthorne arrives at his door.

Our Sadhaka takes one look at her. She is a natural. As natural as

---

*Sadhaka: a yogi aspirant who follows certain heat-generating Tantric disciplines.

†"Individuality and the Elimination of Evil," by Jan Szczepanski, in *Dialectics and Humanism, The Polish Philosophical Quarterly* (Spring-Summer 1986, English-language edition) dedicated to Ethics: Science-Practice-History. ("Special issue dedicated to Marek Fritzhand, cofounder of Polish philosophy and educator of philosophers" in the words on the cover of "this most spiritual philosophical magazine:" Norbert Kosky)

Formica. Formica, not wood. As natural as, given American ability to look natural, is Lynn Shaver, a nonnaturalized American being.* Looking natural is one thing; being natural is quite another. He takes one more look at her. Her cheeks are naturally rosy. She is full of *Ros*, of *liquor vitae*, life's subtle inner dew. No wonder. She is young. Awfully young. How young is she? he asks his inner Monsieur Celan Derrida, the foremost expert of the Jewish moral drugstore.

To sustain a conviction of rape under California rule, the evidence must authorize a conclusion either that prosecutrix resisted and her resistance was overcome by force or that she was prevented from resisting by threats of great and immediate bodily harm accompanied by apparent power of execution. (*People* vs. *Lay* (1944) 66 C.A. 2d 889)

She is old enough, she tells him with the conviction of an old convict. How old? he persists with the fear of an old convict-to-be. Well over eighteen, she says speaking to him from the well of experience not to be ever confused with the inner well.† She is, also, she adds quickly, a Quick Touch™ typist—sixty-nine words per minute—a typist, not a slow decipher, not a hieroglypher, and a proofreader, but she qualifies, she can proofread only elementary texts written for elementary schools and only when they are already set by the printer. But other than that, he asks himself, is she still a virginal flower child? Is she a hawthorn, a sweet *madeleine* never touched by either Childe Roland, that brave knight,‡ or Childe Waters, that heartless lover?§ **I was immensely touched;**

---

*Profiled by *Cavalier* magazine, the nineteen-year-old Lynn Shaver "shaved her body because the G-string she wore in one of the routines was so small that she had no alternative."

†MINORS: 1. Definition. We have achieved a new definition of "minor" which will apply nationally. The term "minor," as used herein, means any performer under the age of eighteen years, except that it shall not include any such performer if: (1) the performer has satisfied the compulsory-education laws of the state governing the performer's employment; (2) the performer is married; (3) the performer is a member of the armed forces; or (4) the performer is legally emancipated. (Screen Actors Guild [SAG] and American Federation of Television and Radio Arts [AFTRA], August 1986)

‡"Childe Roland to the Dark Rower Came," a poem by R. Browning published in his *Men and Women* in 1855.

§"Childe Waters": an Old English ballad about Submissive Ellen, who serves as a page to Childe Waters, her cruel lover.

17

her youth, her ignorance, her pretty beauty, which had the simple charm and the delicate vigour of a wild flower. (Conrad)

In order to find out *Is She or Isn't She*, dressed in messy-looking though clean'nd starched pajamas—his favorite working costume, made by MittleEuropa Ltd. in Ruthenia—Kosky takes her straight to his desk where, a bit absentmindedly, his mouth open though still breathing only through his nose—a yogi prerequisite—he shows her the working papers of one chapter of his novel—which, mauled by corrections, is desperately in need of healing, i.e., of prompt retyping. It all must be retyped—in his favorite pica* before it can be read by Dustin Beach Bradley Borell, his editor—who is also the editor-in-chief of Eidolon Books, Kosky's prime-time publishers. She takes one look at him, then at the messy *brudnopis* of his chapter and asks with a smile if there is anything else she could do for him in the field of quick touch?

She certainly could, he says, and he tells her what it is that he has on his mind and what he wouldn't mind transferring elsewhere. **The male sexual function is performed in a single act: in coitus. (Franz Alexander)†** She quotes him her cut rate—cut in half after midnight, to say sixty-nine minutes of saliva sterile 69.‡

"Tell me again, how old are you?" he asks almost involuntarily. **With the passage of the Children and Young Person Act in 1933, the term "girl-child" is defined as a "girl who is over eight but under fourteen years."... This is all very interesting, but I daresay you see me already frothing at the mouth in a fit; but no, I am not; I am just winking happy thoughts into a little tiddle cup." (Nabokov)**

"My age doesn't matter. My time does," she says, glancing at him and at the room's only clock.

"Is it likely that, say, in California, you would be still considered a

---

*Pica: a unit of linear measurement for type. Also one suffering from a craving for unnatural food, such as black chalk or yellow paint, etc.

†Franz Alexander: eminent American-Hungarian psychoanalyst, author of *Buddhistic Training as an Artificial Catatonia*, *The Don Quixote of America*, *Zest and Carbohydrate*, and many other works.

‡In saliva sterile 69 safe sex, body fluids are allowed to escape each lover's body only under the strict supervision of both lovers who make certain that while their bodies do mix, their bodily fluids do not. (Norbert Kosky's *Guide to Safe Sex* [project 69], 1987)

child by law? In California, where—so I hear—they tend to easily confuse copulation with coupling and circumstances with surroundings?"

Each case involving a lustful advance upon a child must be decided by the evidence introduced and is not necessarily controlled by a previous decision. (109 C.A. 2d 189)

"I wouldn't worry if I were you," she says. "We're in New York, not California. This is the place where long before Safe Sex, you know, booby-sniffing tit-vibrations, flicking nip, and boob-lubing first started."

The body is an instrument of life; a pinnacle of being. Don't hold it a prisoner. (Tantra)

"Why aren't you in the phone sex business?" he asks while introducing her gently into the art of *kaula*.*

" 'Cause I'm not verbal. As a writer, can't you tell that I'm a Noun-Person, not a Verb-Person? Some guys like to do things, their own thing—and some like to be told what things to do. Things are nouns." She gives him a lesson in pedagogical sex technique.

Only now, with the first stage of *kaula* completed, he lets the baby quail undress and, naked, fall back onto his monastic bed. **It has been observed that in girls the occurrence of puberty is earlier in brunettes than in blondes. (J. H. Kellog, 1888)** Wanton and taut, draping one leg over the edge of the bed, she opens her thighs, offering him the sight of her flesh, then, with her fingers, stretches its delicate membranes.

But this must have been before his—let us say—nerves went wrong, and caused him to preside at certain midnight dances ending with unspeakable rites, which—as far as I reluctantly gathered from what I heard at various times—were offered up to him—do you understand?—to Mr. Kurz himself. (Conrad)

To postpone a decision, (a decision about what *not* to do) our literary cat chooses to notice the girl's oversize silver ring and bracelet, the center of each a replica of the pupil and iris of an astonishingly real-looking eye—which stares at him without so much as a blink.

---

*"The practice of *kaula* path is even more difficult than walking on blades of swords, holding the neck of a tiger or a snake in the hand. . . . This peculiar form of worship was prescribed only at a very advanced stage of spiritual development when the extreme type of self-control has been achieved, when the things that normally cause distraction could create no mental disturbance." (O. P. Jaggi, op. cit.)

"A lovely set," says Kosky, staring at her with a stare borrowed by him from a photograph of Baudelaire.* "These look awfully real!"

"They are real," says Maule. "Ante Pavelic, my jeweler, uses only real eyes. He is a kin of Pavelic—the World War II Pavelic Curzio Malaparte wrote about in something called *Kaput!* Pavelic wouldn't touch a glass eye." She glances at her ring and bracelet.

"He uses what?"

"Real eyes. Owl's eyes, catfish's eyes, dog's eyes—he likes German shepherds—as well as good-quality human eyes. The human eyes are the easiest to frame, but they are most costly. Ante even wrote a short story he called "The Glass Eye." The story came from "A Basket of Oysters," an interview in which Malaparte did Pavelic in. They weren't really oysters, nor were they made of glass, but he didn't say it," she says giggling sweetly. "All he said was that an eye is a work of art. Even an evil eye. Period." She holds out her hand. "Didn't you really know that this set comes fitted with original carefully preserved human eyes?"

"I certainly did not." Kosky backs away from the evil eye of Pavelic as invented by Malaparte.

"They look—but can they see?" Kosky often hangs on to dear life via his literary optic nerves. "Where does your Ante get these eyes?"

"He buys them from his customers. Too bad you can't lease eyes just for a year or so," she says. "That's why he believes in an eye for an eye. He pays good money for them and he always pays in cash."

"I didn't know people sell their eyes ahead of Final Blindness," says Kosky, the spiritual child of the Final Solution.

"Why not?" The body-seller is affronted. "Don't you read the "Sexy Sexton's" New Superficiality Section in the *New Worker* magazine? People sell hair and blood, don't they? They sell their kidneys and their rare parts and organs—such as, for instance, their foreskins and they often sell it ahead of time. They even accept early reservations. I read this with my very own eyes in *The Uncut Men's Magazine*."

She breathes at the ring, then polishes the lens of its eye with a finger. "When I bought my peeping Tom, the jeweler gave me a certificate that the eyes in it are real gems," she says. "I mean, that they came out of a living body—seconds after that body was no longer living in order to preserve their natural shine."

---

*"Baudelaire chose a symbolic suicide; he killed himself gradually," writes Sartre c. 1950 about his metaphysical arch-enemy Baudelaire.

"Was the living body a man or a woman? American-born or foreign? Was he or she cross-eyed?" asks Kosky, peeping at her ring. He puts his arms around her.

"That's my secret," says Maule, coyly coiling and uncoiling her girlish frame. Fondly she removes the ring, then the bracelet, and places them on the night table.

Quickly, she slips out of her immaculately white shirt and baring her bare and slim shoulders steps out of her skirt, abandons her white brassiere and her even whiter bloomers, kicks off her high-heeled shoes and rolls down her immaculately white stockings, writes Kosky for the second time, this time a bit more specifically ("he lets the baby quail undress") but still as a part of his yet-to-be rewritten narrative.

Watching the spotless frame of his Childe of Elle,* our *cherubim* Childe Harold† notices a stream of most natural-looking blood seeping onto him from her center spread.

"Is the blood real?" he asks mindful of the creative mind of Ante Pavelic. "And if it is why are you *already* bleeding?" Our *childe* molester becomes *flebile*.

Once I shaved my pubic hair and found out how comfortable and cool it was, and how neat it looked, I just decided to keep it shaved.... I wear small bikinis when I'm on the beach and I don't have to worry about pubic hair showing ... even though I know that's a turn-on for some guys. (Lynn Shaver, 1984)

"It's only my period."

"Your period? You didn't tell me you had your period."

"Yes I did," she retorts, smiling sweetly. "When you called, I told you I was coming at cut-rate because I was 'wet,' " she says, tracing with her fingers the spokes of invisible wheels on his body.

"I thought you said, 'I'm coming at cut-rate because I'm wet. Wet meaning excited. Wet meaning being fresh. Wet meaning anything, even W. E. T., the association of Writers, Editors and Translators I

---

*Childe of Elle: the subject of an Old English ballad.

†*Childe Harold's Pilgrimage*: a poetic composite Byron began in Albania in 1809. "The multi-segment poem purports to describe the outer as well as inner travels of a pilgrim who, sated and disgusted with a life of pleasure and revelry, seeks spiritual distraction in foreign lands. In the fourth canto Byron gives up the unconvincing persona of his pilgrim and continues the narrative in yet another voice disguised as his own." (Norbert Kosky, 1982)

21

once ruled over like Ahasuerus—but not a menstrual *monsoonal* known as period," he goes on since, as he has proven in his 1969 Novel No. 2, the very thought of period makes at least one of his many inner personae lose his Tantric cool and gain in sexually personalized temper so Yogi-unbecoming. "Period—a natural inner flow to which we the Jews have naturally assigned not one, but two minor tractates: the Soferim, a tractate of the writer, and Niddah, a tractate about menstrual flow." Our ha-Sofer (scribe: J.K.) talks at her, as if she were a mere semicolon, trapped in the about-to-explode canon of his sacred text. "Period." He goes on, "Chapter One in one of my favorite books, *The Well-Tempered Sentence: A Punctuation Handbook for the Innocent, the Eager, and the Doomed,* by Karen Elizabeth Gordon, published in 1983 in New Haven and in New York, my two spiritual ports as well as sports, by Ticknor & Fields," he tells the girl while ogling her like the biblical Daniel (who in 605 B.C., carried himself off into captivity: J.K.).* **In the adult, novelty always constitutes the condition for orgasm. (Freud)**

"I said I was coming to you all wet. Meaning coming with my period—at a cut rate." She smiles again. "Don't worry." She lies on the bed, drawing him closer with her arms. Then, with her hand, she guides him toward her body then into it. Under her touch, he opens up; he grows rigid; he softens again.

"I thought you weren't supposed to bleed on the job," he says firmly. "Isn't a period a curse—to a working girl, I mean?"

The consciousness that superhuman strain was no longer required had put a period to her power to continue it. (Hardy)

"No, it isn't. Touch typing is a curse. What's wrong with you? What kind of man are you?" she growls. "A lot of *foumarts* like you go bananas peeping at a girl who's riding her red pony. Haven't you heard of *The Second Sex*?"†

---

*See page 9, *From Torah to Kabbalah: A Basic Introduction to the Writings of Judaism,* by R. G. Musaph-Andriesse (New York: Oxford University Press, 1982).

†Writes Simone de Beauvoir in *The Second Sex*: ". . . It is during her periods that she feels her body most painfully as an obscure, alien thing; it is, indeed, the prey of stubborn and foreign life that each month constructs and then tears down a cradle within it; each month all things are made ready for a child and then aborted in the crimson flow." (As quoted in *Waters of Eden: the Mystery of the Mikvah,* by Rabbi Aryeh Kaplan, Second Edition, 1982.)

Looking up at the wall, Kosky catches sight of his father, who gazes down at him from a black-and-white photograph Norbert took of him shortly before he left Ruthenia. His father's lips smile, but his expression is tenderly grave, as grave as the one probably worn by Isaac Troki. (Troki, printer, not Trocki!).*

"Please be careful," says his father. "This is the time when, as perfect a creation as woman is, she is momentarily imperfect. Don't touch her, or anything that is hers. Don't let her touch you or anything that is yours." Sadly his father looks his seed in the eye. "When with her, use your senses—four of them if you must, but not the fifth. Do what Sabbatai Sevi would do under such circumstances."

"C'mon, father—please! May I at least express my true Self through her?" asks our Nathan of Troki. †

The patriarchs came into the world to restore the senses and this they did to four of them. Then came Sabbatai Sevi and restored the fifth, the sense of touch, which according to Aristotle and Maimonides is a source of shame to us, but which now has been raised by him to a place of honor and glory. (Jacob Emden, 1877)

Without a word, Israel Kosky nods as if in disbelief and turns away from his seed, who is about to be carried away by a wind of concupiscence. ‡

Free of supervision, Kosky slides his hand between her thighs, stroking her flesh. As she slides lower, he licks her breasts and now, she wraps

---

*Isaac Ben Abraham Troki (b. ? d. 1596) a Polish-Jewish Karaite scholar who wrote in Polish, Latin and Yiddish and whose *Hizzuk Emunah* was an instruction of Judaism Voltaire considered as a "masterpiece of one kind."

†In circa 1629, Zerah, born Nathan of Troki, first offered the book of Troki, Sr., for publication in Amsterdam where (not unlike Kosky's first work of fiction) it was turned down by several publishers, even though by then many of Troki's hymns were included in many Karaite books of prayer.

‡"But this all-embracing meaning of 'concupiscence' has often been reduced to a rather special meaning, namely, the striving for sexual pleasure," writes Paul Tillich, who then elaborates elsewhere: "Only a perverted life follows the pain-pleasure principle. Unperverted life strives for that of which it is in want, it strives for union with that which is separated from it, though it belongs to it. This analysis should remove the prejudice toward libido, and it can give criteria for the partial acceptance, partial rejection of Freud's libido theory." (*Love, Power and Justice.* Ontological Analyses and Ethical Applications, by Paul Tillich, London, Oxford, New York) (Timeless: Norbert Kosky)

her lips around his living flesh, then surfaces for breath. This whole world, from Brahma to a worm, is held together by the union of male and female. There is nothing to be ashamed of this when God Shiva himself was constrained by passion for a young girl to assume four faces in order to keep on looking at her. (Varahmira)*

Sliding from side to side, she glides over him, a fish wiggling up and down the stream, her shoulders, breasts, belly, thighs, hands and feet pounding, sliding, pressing. She brushes the toes of his feet against her nipples; she strokes his arms, hands, elbows, knees, ankles and heels. Her thumb and forefinger twist, grasp, and pull his toes, but no matter what she does our Tantric seed won't lose his seed or his self-control (while remaining slightly left of center of his sexual plateau: Jay Kay). As a semen I dwell in the female. (Hevajra)

His face buried in her flesh, he carries her into the tub, where the two of them bounce, splash, beat about, sway and giggle—(like two post–World War II children at play: Jay Kay).

She came safe out of his arms, without a struggle, not even having felt afraid. (Conrad)

---

*See Sagittal section of female pelvic anatomy, Plate 1, in *Sex Endocrinology*, First Edition, A *Handbook for the Medical and Allied Professions* (Bloomfield, 1945), "the very first book on endocrinology I read in English in Ruthenia circa 1947–48." (Norbert Kosky)

3

The pen is the tongue of the soul,
says Cervantes, and while writing implies the most unrestricted freedom
of inner movement and a license to go out, mentally, and otherwise,
it also implies enclosure as well as stillness **in posture and breath. (Swami
Rama)**

Mobilizing all his psychic powers by first modifying his Breath Power,
as if on cue our Raja Yogi becomes the resident of the little-known
State of Total Concentration, inhabited as well as visited mostly by
writers, artists, scientists and monks.

**My thoughts drip from my brow like water from a fountain. The
process is entirely unconscious. (Balzac)**

In such moments of creative calm our music man sees himself as a
composer, and his text as the spiritual score of his narrative opus Number
9. "If one is to absorb this music," says Karlheinz Stockhausen, "one
must take one's time: it does not carry one along with it, but leaves one
in peace; most of its changes occur very discreetly in the intimacy of
its notes *'for things that happen must have someone to happen to, someone
must stop them.'* " Add to this what Valéry says in his *Aesthetic Invention*
(page 66): "In so far as 'creation' is defined by 'order,' disorder is essential
to it. Once the universe of sound is thus defined the musician's mind
is situated, as it were, in a single system of possibilities," a single system
Valery called the Musical State.

Here, in his private mental concentration camp, he is free to first
"give head to some mindless thoughts," then, in the words of Jay Kay,
put them on paper, in order to have his head examined, preferably by

an erudite (and erotic: J.K.) proofreader who is not afraid to step out of line on her way to becoming a full-blossomed line editor.

As Balzac and Tolstoy confirm (both men rewrote their mss. many times: J.K.), the need for reliable and exact transcription of "The Harmony of Prose" (F. L. Lucas) already posed difficulties in the nineteenth century when manual labor was readily available, and "since the mere mechanical labor of a dozen rewritings is enormous" (F. L. Lucas), if transcription by hand is not manual labor, what is?

The very thought of a woman typist excites him. Whether she is black, yellow or white; whether she is nice or nasty, petty or pretty, subbornly fat or weakened by anorexia nervosa or by typing novels written in Esperanto, he cares not. At this particular creative junction, our Dr. Faustus thinks of MALE AND FEMALE CREATED S(HE) THEM (Chapter 9, p. 96, in *Women, Sex and Pornography*, by Beatrice Faust, 1980).

All monks,* as is well known, are unmarried, and hermits more unmarried than the rest of them. Not that I have anything against women. I see no reason why a man can't love God and a woman at the same time.... There is a lot of talk about a married clergy. Interesting. So far there has not been a great deal said about married hermits. Well, anyway, I have the place full of ikons of the Holy Virgin. (Thomas Merton)†

Getting out of his camp in order to secure, as well as procure, literary associations excites him the way anything to do with *Style* (1955, 1962) or *Tragedy* (1957, 1962) excited that most literary fellow F. L. Lucas. There is something quite daring in sharing his *brudnopis*, his secretly sweating manuscript with the impeccably dehydrated literary world of uptown. After all, written in the present tense his manuscript carries the secret of a writer's manu, inner script, and this for a reason. The reason is that words, whether verbs or nouns, adverbs, adjectives or even small verbal particles, are neither monks nor hermits. Words don't

---

*A monk's actual possessions are very few, and any other objects around him should be regarded by him as on loan from the Order. He has only eight Requisites: An outer double-thick "cloak," an upper-robe, an under-robe, a bowl to collect food, a needle and thread to repair his robes, a waistband for his under-robe, a razor, and a water-strainer to exclude small creatures from his drinking water so that neither they, nor himself, are harmed. (Bhikkhu Khantipālo)

†A spiritually simplified revision of the *Day of a Stranger*, by Thomas Merton (1981). (Library of Congress Number: 81-9153. "Among the highest spiritual span ratings!" says Jay Kay.)

like living alone. Like people, they like to pair and stay together; like people they often marry most unlikely partners.*

Once married to each other by a writer—or even, with or without his knowledge, by his typist, proofreader or editor—the words either stay together or dash away from one another on a dash, a dot, a colon or semicolon. In Kosky's manuscript words are usually cruelly and often grotesquely tied together—tied as in bondage. Once paired by him— paired as well as pared—his words seldom divorce; they cohabit, if often uneasily, either in a bracket or inside a parenthesis, living there in a state of constant fear of being crossed out by a politically cross-eyed— or esthetically crooked (or not constant enough: J.K.)—editor or publisher.

When the novel can no longer tell a simple tale, it becomes the mode that notes the indifference of its reader and finds the new dimensions of its fiction in the relation of that reader to the author through the object between them. (*Limits of the Novel***, David Grossvogel)†** The above quote starts a chain of reactions. First (hence, the least important) it makes him think of himself: a storyteller no longer capable of "concocting a plot of any freshness," to paraphrase Henry James. As a result, his novel No. 9 can "no longer tell a simple tale." Then David Grossvogel makes him recall Deborah Vogel who *sexpired* Bruno Schulz the way one Cathy Young inspired Kosky when she worked as his assistant at the University of Beulah School of Drama. But then the thought of life's drama—never mind drama school—makes him think of *Sarcophagus*—a play by Vladimir Gubaryev about the blow-up in the Atomic Reactor No. 4 at Chernobyl nuclear power plant and the resulting spread of radiation. (An event by comparison to which the worst earthquake in California becomes a mere local insurance company nightmare: Jay Kay.) Kosky promptly constructs his own inner reactor, then blows up its top only to reveal "The Nucleus Intellectual vs. The Nuclear State," the title of his forthcoming public lecture at the SoHo Omnibus Mini-Theater (eight seats, State Street No. 9).‡

---

*See *Word Origins: The Romance of Language*, by Cecil Hunt (1949). Also "Methods of Writing" (Chapter 11), pp. 266–99 in *Style*, by F. L. Lucas (1962).

†As quoted by Charles Newman in II. "The Anxiety of Noninfluence," *Salmagundi*, pp. 63–64.

‡According to *The Heretic Hermeneutics of Norbert Kosky*, by Kedar Kederli (1984), for years Norbert Kosky toyed with writing "Bruno and I"—a mono-drama

A book in progress brings to his mind a swimming pool still under construction: only the constructor himself must decide when the pool is worthy of water and swimmers. To a Jew, the words *pool* and *water* might signify *mikvah*—a gathering of water, not of people: gathered in a **special pool in a non-moving status, for the purpose of tvilah is ritual purification of objects and persons** as defined by Shmuel Rubenstein on page one of his *Mikvah Anthology** is synonymous with storytelling. "Water, being the prototype fluid . . . Genesis, 49:4 'unstable as water.'" page 62, in *Waters of Eden: The Mystery of the Mikvah,* by Aryeh Kaplan (1982). (The "gathering of water" consisted of the "water under the heavens" which are the "female waters" mentioned earlier. Op. cit., page 65.) Particularly so since, "In order to understand how and why a mikvah makes something ritually pure we must first know how objects or persons become 'impure' as it were." (Shmuel Rubinstein) ("Is that why one of the first Nazi laws prevented the Jews from using German public swimming pools?" asks Jay Kay, who believes that while most of the old Nazis died, most of their laws and regulations unfortunately have not: J.K.)

Given the importance of a writer's creative *mikvah*, or gathering of his narrative waters, it is only just that the writer —and only the writer who longs for a state of Inner Justice—be judged as the prime conveyor of his tale and hence the prime constructor of his narrative pool, even if his tale contains too much water, even if the pool's narrative concrete was at one time or another used to reinforce someone else's swimming pool—or another writer's creative port. "Even if the writer is Ibsen or Hardy, Zola or Proust, Rilke or Joyce—all those who, by not receiving the Nobel Prize, have ever since caused great anguish to the transmigrating soul of that explosively soulful'nd sorrowful fellow Alfred Nobel," writes on the margin Norbert Kosky, writing in handwriting not of his

---

for a man he called Bruno and a woman named Debbie, both loosely based on the romance between Bruno Schulz and his *birdie* Deborah Vogel who helped him translate Kafka's *Trial* into Polish and whom (the semisadistically inclined: J.K.) Bruno is said to have affectionately called his "seminally submissive sheers, seems and stiletto girl"—scoring eighteen hundred points on Norbert Kosky's spiritual SS scale. SSSS.

*An illustrated analysis of the construction and use of the *mikvah*. *The Mikvah Anthology* ("The Bris Milah"), by Shmuel Rubenstein, Bronx, N.Y. (5728).

own, but in a distinctly different one he created for his handwriting-conscious Jay Kay.

I am distinctly conscious of the contents of my head. My story is there in fluid—in an evading shape. . . . It is all there—to bursting, yet I can't get hold of it no more than you can grasp a handful of water. (Joseph Conrad)

There you have it: only the omnipresent writer must judge how much water he must draw from (rain, wells, natural ice and artificial ice: the four permissible sources of *mikvah*: Jay Kay). Only he must ask: Is my inner swimming pool Kosher for my reader's Immersion?

The idea of spending several additional years of his *Life-Yet-to-Be* (Israel Kosky) on writing another novel, *another*, not necessarily *new* ("and not even necessary novel"), excites him the way the very thought of a cat must excite a catfish and catching a catfish excites a cat. However, in order to start it, he must keep on questioning Jay Kay, his inner writer, who, as his potential protagonist, often will question him back in this particular literary trial by inner terror.

"What's the next novel about?" he asks Jay Kay.

"Anything or anyone that you find particularly exciting or excitable," says Jay Kay. But, lay the stress "on the incidents in the development of a soul: little else is worth study." (Browning)

"Could I perhaps write a whole book about the narrative process? About its storytelling components? About their conveyance and storage, as well as the ways of filling, heating and draining of their narrative *mikvah*?" Kosky goes on. "About freezing of the frames of the text rather than about letting them go at sixty-nine frames per minute?"

When the Jewish scribe—the sofer—sets out to copy the Torah, he must, according to religious law, take a ritual bath in order to purify himself of all uncleanness and impurity. This scribe takes up his pen with a trembling heart, because the smallest mistake in transcription means the destruction of the whole work. (Emmanuel Ringleblum, 1944)

After six hours of concentration, he steps out of his concentration camp. What a Terezin! he exclaims, when he is instantly stopped by his narrative Jewish Soul. "You're a Jew! Your Inner State must be determined by *hitlahawuth*—the Hebrew for joy—a joy of life not to be spoiled by the four letters HITL reminding you of Hitler. Then," the Soul goes on, remember that Theresienstadt (called Terezin) was one of the most perfidious Nazi–Final Solution Concentration Camps.* It housed only Jews over sixty-five (among them the German Jewish World War I veterans who had earned the Iron Cross First Class [Or even those with the Iron Cross No. 6 or 9: J.K.]) who on the way to death, left behind some four thousand drawings, as well as bits of prose and verse. These drawings gave Stefan Szuman the idea of first asking the children who survived the war about what *The War Meant to Them* (and might have contributed to the Video Archive for Holocaust Testimonies at Yale University. **"Through the original Holocaust Survivors Film Project deposit, our own videotaping, and that of our seventeen affiliates, we are now the curator of one thousand registered testimonies. We have initiated the new phrase of 'creative frame' taping to describe the experiences of special groups, such as the deaf, to explore the interaction of survivors and their children, to follow up themes from previous testimonies and to clarify the effect of time on memory. We continue, of course, to welcome every survivor or witness who wishes to be videotaped, and we plan a search for populations, such as Greek survivors, who are underrepresented in the Archive." Geoffrey H. Hartman, 1987)**

Writes Kosky on the margin: I am a writer; a wordsmith who works with words, and who loves playing with them, as much as playing with women. But while creative women still threaten me as much as, say, the noncreative ones threatened August Strindberg, words do not. They do not, except one. Each time I write the word *burn*, I feel burned. Burned—not burned out. Burned not by anyone in particular, but by the entire Western Civilization. The modern civilization which literally burned in the gas ovens so many of my people (and so many others who, spiritually akin, are only indirectly mine: Jay Kay). Yet, while I feel burned by the Holocaust, I also feel torched by it: torched not scorched. With the word *torch* signifying light and inner luminosity. **In the words of my guru, "civilization is not our religion, nor is it the religion of our problem. Judaism is the art of surpassing civilization." (Heschel)**

His writing time over, our Inner Camp Commander turns to matters of his literary property, which to our writing male means, simply, reading his mail. Kosky hates mail as much as he hates the phone (or such

---

*See *The Destruction of the European Jews*, by Raul Hilberg (1961), pp. 277–78.

30

a phrase as a final solution: J.K.). They all enter your life uninvited—and when *they* want it. "They are our life's totalitarian agents who spoil man's spiritual soil," he writes on a spare mental index card.

The management of literary property is more than the economic stewardship of a limited and wasting monopoly conferred upon an author under the copyright laws. How such literary property is exploited affects not only economic aspects of the author's works, but the esteem in which the author is held. As such, management of a literary work requires a delicate balance between economic enhancement and cultural nurture. (*New York Law Journal,* 1987)

Number six on his list is a fat envelope from Eidolon Press. Owned since 1969 by the Australian-American Salomon, Seal and Shoestring, Ltd. They are his prime American publisher because, having published him during his literary prime, they still keep on publishing him. The envelope contains a paperback version of his latest novel first published in hardcover two years earlier. Fresh from the printer it is anything but fresh: it is a cheap pocket-size printed in gray ink and on poor paper. (And then the visual horror begins: Norbert Kosky, 1979.)

The *Art Populis* cover of the book portrays an uncovered nymphette—call her Lollipop—her upper thighs show, and how!—the image of whom would make Nabokov flush. (Flush, printer, not blush!) On top of this, this little skinny girlie is shown sitting astride a polo saddle placed on top of a wooden practice horse. This is not a cover: it is a veritable cover-up—an affront to the art of Degas as much as to Rauschenberg.

Affronted, he calls Joe Kempner at Eidolon's art department and is about to start a fight over Lollipop on the Hermes saddle, when Joe disarms him by simply saying, "Please don't compare that clean-cut girl on the cover with your sixteen-year-old slut inside the book. And don't *you* dare to judge publishers by their covers."

The law of the narrative "which has no law" (Mark Twain) is one thing, a writer's ego is quite another.

His ego now checks the title page of the paperback. It contains no errors in the spelling of his first and last name. His ego sighs with relief. But then he goes into vanity shock: two of his books are not listed among his titles. As if this is not bad enough, at the end of the book he finds "ABOUT KOSKY," a four-page italicized, unsigned appendix.

Trotsky credits me with the authorship of the publicity copy accompanying the distribution of his booklet to the press. On this matter, too, much to my own vexation, I must reply to him a categoric denial. I am

not the author of this prospectus; I have had no part, direct or indirect, in composing it; I have no idea who the author is; and I do not care either. Is that clear enough? (Victor Serge, 1939)

This inflames his spiritual appendix, which gives him another shock. He dampens the heat of his momentarily monstrous ego by dumping the ego-offensive paperback on a book shelf. Only then he starts to *monstruate* (monstruation being a natural process for our literary monster: Jay Kay).

He calls John Wardle, Eidolon's publicity director. Marion Warwick, John's assistant, also gets on the line.

"What's up, Norbert?" says John.

"It's down, not up," says Kosky. "On the title page of my last novel you've listed only six titles of my eight novels. I wrote eight novels, not six." Regardless whether you keep them in print or not. (I know that six of them have been practically out of print for some three years!)

"So what?" John often pretends he is not serious.

"C'mon John, this is spiritually serious. It took me as much time to write these eight novels as Balzac needed to write seventy-four. To write them word for word, mind you, not to dictate, like Stendhal or Henry James."

"So what?" says Marion.

"By missing my two titles, you've wiped out on paper two-eighths of my past mental being—of my spiritual total state." Kosky fails to score a spiritual point.

The writer, at the point when he can be judged "successful," has served a grueling apprenticeship that can't be determined in credit hours or degrees. Willingly or unwillingly, he is a student of contemporary history and a compassionate observer of whatever struggles intrude upon society. This provides the gravity of conscience. (Roy Newquist, 1964)

"But what 'About Kosky'? I hope you like it," says John.

"What? Are you still serious? This appendix must go!" A true yogi, Kosky can't bring himself to raise his voice. **The line of demarcation between mental health and mental illness, between saneness and unsaneness, is unclear and often defined by environmental circumstances. (JAMA)*** (Unsaneness, printer, not insaneness!) By claiming I had suffered from Malic disease† it makes me potentially crazy." **No longer a**

---

*JAMA: Journal of the American Medical Association.

†Malic Malaise, the name of which is derived from the French words *mal* for

32

great man, the Author was now a nobody.[69] (Bentham, 1822, as quoted by F. L. Lucas, 1962)

" 'About Kosky' is a come-on to reading," says John.

"It's a composite," says Marion.

"It is neither biography nor fiction," says John. "Call it"—he pauses—"a biodegradable biofiction."

Already unsettled by his publishers, Kosky attempts to find solace in a handwritten letter forwarded by them from a woman reader in Brooklyn. She writes:

> Norbert: I've just finished reading your evil horse novel, and as a result I'm finished with you as a writer, and I hope you're finished as a man. Judging by what you did to the Fat Girl on page 169— simply because she was "as fit as a bass fiddle" (*Buf*), and stupid enough to fall for a man like you—you must be one of the meanest pricks on earth. Yours, Patricia Peggotty. (My friends call me Fat Pat.)

Her letter unsettles him even further. Does her hostility and resentment stem from him, from the esthetic weight of his work, or from her weight?

There's an all-out war going on right now. An all-out war declared by "Large Busted" women against gravity. Gravity pulls everything down. Gravity is the worst enemy of big tits, creating anything from bad back to sagging balloons. Large-breasted women must unite and fight this evil force.... (Juggs)

Quickly, he consults that old and wise *Guide for the Perplexed*, a magnum opus said to have been written by Moses Maimonides, "in ten years* of hard work by day and by night" in order to "save him in advanced age the trouble and necessity of consulting the Talmud on every occasion." (M. Friedlander, 1904)

---

evil and *malheur* for misfortune, is a prolonged manic condition characterized by hypothyroidism (the impaired function of the thyroid gland), due to the excessive presence or deficiency of malic acid commonly found in man. Malic acid ($C_4H_6O_5$) is derived from the apple and contained in apple cider. (*Acta Paramedica*, 1966)

*Here Kosky quickly notes that Stefan Zweig, the author of *Joseph Fouché: The Portrait of a Politician*, a book swallowed up by his entire high school, spent the last ten years of his life working on a biography of *Balzac*, his magnum opus which, choosing suicide, he failed to complete.

The *Guide* leaves Kosky even more doubtful. "The bird in its flight is sometimes visible, sometimes withdrawn from our sight," writes Maimonides on page 66. What he does not say is that in their flight such birds often become withdrawn into their own selves—that is, perplexed by the issue of their own flight, their own visibility. Would Fat Pat have written him such a hostile letter had Kosky listened to the advice of his father and kept on, throughout his life, reading books rather than writing them? Or, worse yet, stuffing himself with stuffed cabbage on the advice of some of his cabbage-bent Ruthenian friends? Still unsettled, he turns for advice to Marcus Aurelius:* 69. *To live each day as though one's last*, and this depresses his creative Self even more. [Imagine ending your life on a note from Fat Pat: J.K.]

His *brudnopis*, his working manuscript, his *forza* and *froda*, both *picaresque* and *picturesque* (Warwick Wadlington),† happens to also be fat, and it gains narrative yin-and-yang by the day. "What a madness & anguish it is," Melville wrote to Evert Duyckinck, "that an author can never—under no conceivable circumstances—be at all frank with his readers."‡ Americans love fat, his publishers assure him, and the majority of his readers are middle-aged midwesterners—after all, the Midwest is America's fat middle—most of whom are women over thirty. "And most of whom, when it comes to sex, are eerie enough to boat freely on Lake Erie," says Jay Kay.

My cheek blanches white while I write, I start at the scratch of my pen, my own brood of eagles devours me, fain would I unsay this audacity, but an iron-mailed hand clenches mine in a vise and prints down every letter in my spite. Fain would I hurl off this Dionysius that rides me.... (Melville)§

And, speaking of his own love of flesh, our skinny narrator of skin-flick fiction has for years been an avid peruser of *Buf* magazine, "the number-one magazine devoted solely to plump and heavy women," in

---

*Marcus Aurelius, who died at sixty-nine, was an educated Stoic turned Roman emperor. "To refrain from imitation is the best revenge," he wrote in maxim six of Book Six of his *Meditations*.

†See *The Confidence Game in American Literature*, by Warwick Wadlington (Princeton and London: Princeton University Press, 1975), p. 68.

‡See *The Letters of Herman Melville*, ed. by Merrell R. Davis and William H. Gilman, Yale University Press, 1960, p. 96, New Haven, Conn.

§Ibid., p. 69.

the words of its cover, as well as *Gem*, the cover of which says it is "the magazine for men who appreciate the big things of life."

There is a valid reason for Kosky's preoccupation with fat: a fat woman—one truly devoted to the pleasure of eating and growing flesh (despite what others say about it and despite what she thinks they undoubtedly think of her)—could become in his hands, precisely because of her lack of concern, an ideal *dombi*—a perfect sexual Princess *Fati*ma, turned femme *fat*ale. "—and a perfect companion for you, our American Paul Celan,"* adds on the margin of the manuscript Zero Poster, Kosky's most recently hired, sexually marginal part-time copy editor.

---

*Paul Celan, born in Romania, educated in Romanian and Yiddish, wrote his poems in German while spending most of his time in Paris. Like many other writers (Virginia Woolf, Hart Crane, and John Berryman [and, feasibly, Norbert Kosky: Ed.]) Celan died in an act of creative suffocation by water, otherwise known as drowning. Drowning, instead of blowing off one's head with a Browning.

4

Set according to the numerical guidelines of his inner calendar, first put to use circa 966 years ago (just when the duchy of Polonia had officially joined Christendom) his inner alarm clock wakes him up as it has done without fail over the years— at six minutes to nine. A bright Manhattan morning! Since in the Jewish calendar the day begins at sunset—and at sunset it ends—he likes to think he wakes up at the Jewish midday.

AUGUST 23

1349 The Black Death Persecutions reach Cologne, Germany, and the mob attacks the Jewish population. Although the Jews defend themselves, most of the Jewish community perishes when a fire breaks out. Among the dead is Rabbi Israel Thann.

1648 The Jewish population of Koric, Ukraine, is massacred by the Cossack hordes of Chmielnicki. . . .

1940 The Nazis single out 1,000 young Jewish men between 18 and 25 in Czestochova, Poland, who are sent to a forced labor camp in Ciechanov, Poland. None of them will survive. . . .

1942 The largest deportation of the 40,000 people in the Jewish quarter of Lvov, Poland (today Ukrainian S.S.R.), to the Belzec extermination camp—where they all are murdered by the SS—ends. (Simon Wiesenthal)*

Manhattan might be ready to be decoded, but our not yet extinct

---

Every Day Remembrance Day: A Chronicle of Jewish Martyrdom by Simon Wiesenthal, 1987, p. 189.

mastodon is not ready to decode Manhattan. Not yet. Not for another six hours. Engaged in decoding himself, he won't even see Manhattan today. Or tomorrow. Or even after tomorrow. He is a free man, free to see or not to see anything he chooses, remember? He is also a wordsmith: a self-employed writer.*

Writing is like Prostitution. First you do it for the love of it, Then you do it for a few friends, And finally you do it for money. (Moliere) says the advertisement in *Modern Writer* magazine—but does it tell it all?

Such vocational identity brings to his mind one dreaded word: taxes. Is it because "the purse strings tie us to our kind" (Walter Bagehot, 1879)? No, it is not. It is because "Money makes a man laugh." (John Selden, circa 1669) Because "money is a mindless text: what is imprinted on it makes no sense even to a numerologist but—just empty numbers! Look how many different things even an idiot will see in it! You see, in the eyes of the law, Kosky is a U.S. citizen first, and only then a self-employed literary masker. This means that however mobile he is as a person, his mental whereabouts are considered by the U.S. government to be American—as American as the Statue of Liberty. Hence all his creative earnings which originate there, in his mind, are considered by the U.S. government as having originated in his U.S. home, not in his mind, even if his mind is still two-thirds Jewish-Ruthenian— and even if one day he finds a new home, say, in MontCrans, a superior ski village in the Swiss Valais.

In spite of the role played by the Word both in the creation of the world and the State of the Union, Kosky's anything-but-royal writer's royalties are brutally taxed to the fullest and indeed the foulest by the federal, state and city governments. In addition, because of the word "royal," the anti-royalist, the democratic yet greedy U.S. government has recently introduced VAT (the Valor-Added Tax—valor, not value)— which, defining a writer's royalties as luxury, taxes them by an average of 6.9 percent each year. And, if all this wasn't humiliating enough, Kosky, "our foremost literary meat cutter"(*American Writer* magazine), minding his own business which resides entirely in his mind, is not allowed to depreciate from year to year his naturally diminishing mental

---

*See *The Wordsmith's Rights*, the Basic Zohar Foundation Guide to the spiritual rights of poets, playwrights, essayists, editors and novelists, by Carolina Wordsworth, Ph. D., and Jerry Swinburn, M.A., Eidolon Books, 1969.

faculties, unlike, say, a butcher who minds only his meat-cutting business.*

Won't these federal folks ever learn that **the voice is a second face. (Gerard Bauer, b. 1888)** And, above all, that **the accent of one's birthplace persists in the mind and heart as much as in speech,** in the crystally clear words of *Maxims* (written in 1665 by the one and only maximist maximus, Cardinal—or was he Comrade?—La Rochefoucauld: Jay Kay).

Tracy Pickwick Tupman, Kosky's ardent tax accountant, sensibly sensitive, who tends to fall in love with any handsome IRS tax inspector simply because, as a girl, she fell in love with Gogol's Inspector General, tells the following story each time she and Kosky get together to look over style setting, a new tax-deductible category. There she is, Tracy says, in the office of the Infernal Revenue Service (PRINTER: Infernal, not Internal) when this handsome IRS guy tells Tracy this: some half a million people in this country write for publication: call them American literary surplus and a phenomenon of *Cultural Literacy* (E. D. Hirsch, Jr., 1987). Do you know that most of them write nonfiction? Norbert Kosky is one of a handful of people who makes a living from income they derive solely from writing novels. (*Living?* You call *this* sex and subsistence SS a living?: Jay Kay) A handful!

"How full is the hand?" Tracy asks him.

"Sixty-six people," says the IRS person to Tracy. "Sixty-six people in a nation of 260 million. Yep. Sixty-six. That's all. And there are some child prodigies among them, who write full-time, six days a week, take no vacations and, in order to be protected from child molesters, write under pen names." She spells out the list of all American horrors, while brandishing in her hand a copy of *The Closing of the American Mind* by Allan Bloom, Foreword by Saul Bellow, E169.1 B653, 1987 (and these numbers tell it all!: J.K.).

---

*See *The Writer's Tax and Recording Handbook, Including Everything You Can Legally Deduct*, by William Atkinson (Chicago, 1983).

"Freelance writers are a strange lot as far as the IRS is concerned. We are 'professionals without an occupation.' Few, if any, of the examples cited in tax manuals for purposes of explaining tax law ever refer to freelance writers." (p. 9)

See also *The Jewish Aspect of Levying Taxes During the French Revolution of 1789*, by Zosa Szajkowska, in *The Journal of Jewish Studies*, 1960, p. 35.

"What? You allow children to be employed full-time?" Tracy condemns exploitation of children.

"They are self-employed! They are employees of as well as by their own Self. Have you heard the phrase 'God is my sole employer'? Well, to a self-employed writer God and Self are One."

Stirred by such visions, our hermit reluctantly lifts his fatigued frame from his cot. Writing is a self-propelled mission, as well as a most selfish emission, and this makes a writer a missionary with a mission, a revivalist no doubt but also a proselytizer, and a Healer.

I have just spent a good week, alone like a hermit, and as calm as a god. I abandoned myself to a frenzy of literature; I got up at midday, I went to bed at four in the morning. I have written eight pages! (Gustave Flaubert)

Promptly, he slides into his mental slide projector several slides showing his mother at the piano. There she is, the one and only surviving daughter of Maximilian Weinreich* (the famous chess player born in Lodz,† the most industrial town of preindustrial Poland, a town which, with no river to speak of or any other natural water of its own, allowed itself to be called Lodz—and *Lodz* means boat in Polish!: J.K.) There she is, "a piano player too bosomy to play a Jewish piano" (Israel Kosky, 1945) with a figure straight from the pages of *Girls of Double D* magazine, and his mother's intimate piano-playing bottom—reminding him of the fabulous Lotta Top—the Oklahoma-born queen of *Big'nd Busty* magazine. "Don't I look like a Gypsy?" she asks him, her three- or four-year-old suitor, as she raises and lowers her vibrant wrist above the *klaviatura* and the vibratory octaves giving him *The Sense of Beauty*: being the outline of Aesthetic Theory. (George Santayana, 1896) "My piano books tell me I must not throw my hand too far back for the hammerblow octaves, since, Yod forbid, stiffness could set in, and, there's no place in art for stiffness except at an early stage of stage fright

---

*See also *Dr. Max Weinreich's History of the Yiddish Language*, papers read by Dr. Edward Stankiewicz and Dr. Shlomo Noble at the Yivo Institute for Jewish Research, New York, 1974.

†The ghetto of Lodz was the first urban concentration of Jews established by the Nazis, which endured longer than any other wartime ghetto: 1,296 days. Its history is carefully recounted by the fifteen authors of *The Chronicle of the Lodz Ghetto* (op. cit.).

or in a man fully engrossed in the art of making love," she instructs her son already stiffened by "one of the dangers to which a modern artist is exposed: the seduction of his predecessors" (ibidem, p. 96).

Enough digressing. He looks at his *brudnopis* novel's most tentative narrative master-plan.

(I am on trial and) I will tell everything. I will write everything down. I am writing this for myself, but let others and all my judges read it (if they want to). This is a confession (a full confession). I am writing for myself, for my own needs and therefore I will not keep anything a secret. (Dostoyevsky, *Notebooks*)

Here, Kosky's *brudnopis*, his dirty slave scroll, calls for an act of digression in the form of confession. CONFESS ABOUT LILITH PIZNAI. Lilith Piznai, also known in the hardcover book business as Lililu Ardat, is his current tax-deductible manuscript-page proofreader, and one who gives good *manu* to his script. As skillful as she is, Lilith likes to be used as a roughie—a euphemism for a proofreader who proofs only the author's first rough draft. "I give great hand," she admits. Should he write about her first from memory (i.e., invent) or must he first call her, or better yet, on her?

It doesn't matter because Lilith is perfectly bad. Just think of the *Odds Against Piznai* (as the *New Worker* magazine had in June 1986); they intimated that, after "Adam" (every one in New York knows who "Adam" is, just as everybody knows "Eden") parted from his initial wife.* As a result, even her name is bad, so full of moral decomposition that even the straightforward New York social scripture (NYSS) devotes to her name no more than just one line, and yet our literary conspirator likes to be with her. A lot. What he likes to momentarily share with her is a system of reciprocal breathing maintained between two people of the opposite sex or **same-sexers (Gore Vidal)** who, sufficiently drawn to each other, are able to establish a mental rapport by synchronizing their

---

*"He was encountered by a Lilith named Piznai, who taken by his beauty. . . . (PRINTER: Rumor Self Censorship Order No. 6699. DELETE FROM HERE ON—replace with words, etc. etc. etc.) As the one who singlehandedly started the Three S Company, Sines, Sisinnios & Synodoros Proof Reading Unlimited, she would have run it until this very day, had it not been for that terrible story about her in the *Downtown Crier*. (They alleged she secretly strangled her first baby, and how can a woman ever recover from such a story?)

40

breathing rhythm.* C'mon, in your fiction, even more than in your life, you are your own boss, aren't you? he asks himself. Show the reader what it means. **Razumikhin has a very strong nature, and as often happens with such strong natures he submits completely to Dunia. (N.B.: This trait, too, is often met among people, who though most noble and generous, are rough carousers and have seen much dirt: he, for example sort of humbles himself before a woman, especially if that woman is refined, proud and beautiful. (Dostoyevsky)** Why don't you call Lilith now? Let her give you a hand! What you pay her for her honest-to-badness service is honest-to-goodness tax deductible. She gives him a sales slip for proofreading of each successive draft and besides, there's a lot of proofreading to be done on some sixty-odd raw manuscript pages retyped the other night by one Lola Gazonga, his latest part-time typist. Shouldn't these pages be checked, word for word, by Lilith before they can be eventually verified line by line by one of his (also privately procured: J.K.) out-of-line sexual line editors?

She is the one who, paid by him by the hour and asked to come to work at 9:06 in the morning, often comes to see him already at 6:09 A.M. and starts working on him long before she actually begins to work with him. This she does *not* in the second room of his two-room flat (a room he calls his office) and *not* in his bedroom (a room he calls his Ruthenian *garçonière*, rather than a Protestant bachelor's PAD), but he does it with her in his bathroom.

To a modern, big-town Tantric, such as himself, one deprived of his temple, his bathroom becomes his Gym Med, a meditational gymnasium, a minireplica of what *Walden: Life in the Woods* was for Thoreau (a smaller, more intimate version of the well-known and far better ventilated Club Med: Jay Kay), as a bathroom became, long before him, to such beings as, say, Captain John Smith. (The all-American writer who in 1616 gave us A *Description of New England*.) There, in the bathroom, it is Lilith, and only she, who assists him during his L-5, and S-1, S-2, S-3, his spine-stretching exercises, which aiming at the zones of irritation of the sacrum and the pelvis, are often embarrassing to look at—unless the assistant is a *dombi*. Working solely with her

---

*This mental resonance was called "arch-natural respiration" by T. L. Harris (d. 1906) and its intimate aspects were perfected by Laurence Oliphant (d. 1888) through the method of sexual *sympneumata*.

presence, not with her hands, she relieves the cause of but also causes, various metaphysical as well as medical and physical pressures which originate in the sacred sacroiliac joint, the address of which in the subtle body only the Tantric Buddhist knows for sure.*

Besides, shouldn't Lilith now check whether Lola, that Buf Plumper of the month straight from the pages of the *Buf Pictorial* magazine, who hits the scale at 209 pounds, missed by chance a word or a paragraph or a page while typing, then retyping, his manuscript pages? Was Lola able to follow to the letter his most intricate system of letters, numbers, footnotes—all marked by many different, and differently colored, transposition marks? For instance, did Lola notice the paragraph torn out of its rightful context on page 36, which was then flung by him all the way back to page 16—but then moved again to page 38? Did she see the single wrong word which, initially speared, was then spared and reinserted back to where it was? **The act of commerce with woman lies in refraining from ejaculation, and causing sperm to return and nourish the brain. (Cacravarti, 1963. p. 89)**†

Since our Friar Kerouac‡ still writes from the top of his head, rather than from life, spinning out stories on TV talk shows no less than in the TV-less bars and spelunks of sexual downtown, how is he to start his next chapter? "Start with your last night's dream. Latest, not midsummer's," his narrative voice tells him. Was Kosky's latest dream an esoterica—a simple illumination—such as his once recalling during his routine sleep that the wipers of his car didn't wipe? "Is your dream wet or dry?" asks an editorial in *The Astral Guide to Good Writing*. It was, of course, a wet dream. Here he was, all wet, standing alone on

---

*See also "Manual Medicine" (op. cit., 1984), Chapter 6, fig. 66 and fig. 69, both demonstrating the zones of spinal as well as spiral imitation.

†Also known as *acclivity* ("The direction of sexual energy upward toward the brain for the purpose of enlightenment and power." See page 1: *Encyclopedia of Esoteric Man*, by Benjamin Walker, 1977).

‡Typically praised for their naturalness, for their ostensibly unmediated access to experience, in fact, Kerouac's texts were routinely engendered by other texts (these, however, spoken rather than written). Kerouac encouraged the misunderstanding of his transformative enterprise by publicly eschewing rewriting and editing, which he evidently regarded as impediments to getting at the nontext of raw reality. That the reworking of his material in the form of verbal anecdotes was itself already a textualization of reality appears never to have occurred to him. (David Packman, 1984, p. 265–7)

the all-wet deck of a nameless trawler cutting across a nameless bay.

If words are indeed supposed to flow like water, and he is a floater, is water—or word—his true element? How is he to know? He, to whom, when he was a boy of six, water was first synonymous with being sparkling clean, only to become, when he was nine, a symbol of drowning and death by suffocation—the sudden absence of air. Words are also said to be pregnant with meaning and the word *pregnant* signifies life at its most wondrous. No wonder Webster's devotes almost eighteen of its page-long columns to the word *water*,* and only nine columns to the word *air*.

There is no word in Hebrew for fiction—I boycott that word. It means the opposite of truth. Prose, yes, but not fiction. I write prose. I aim at truth, not facts, and I am old enough to know the difference between facts and truth. (Amos Oz, 1985)

Is his dream a distorted memory of his fishing days oppressed by World War II, or is it their long-repressed symbol? But what was he doing in a boat? Above all, why in his dream is he wearing a bright yellow foul-weather jacket?

Yellow denotes his inner foul weather. Yellow stands for "jealousy, inconstancy, and adultery." (*Brewster's*) Yellow denotes yellowish bile. Yellow speaks of gall. Yellow was the robe worn by Diego Alonso, one of Kosky's favorite historical, real-life figures, at the auto-da-fé on the order of the Spanish Inquisition which charged him with heresy, "that dreadful crime of spiritual decomposition, and since in matters of faith decomposition means treason, the guilt of the accused must be established by the application of torture, that is torture by water, by pouring water into him—liter upon liter of, if need be yellow water, also called urine—and by making the aforesaid prisoner go through the inner Flood, that is being flooded, and if he won't confess, by being so

---

*Water: "Let the waters under the heavens be gathered together to one place, and let the dry land appear" (Genesis 1:9); Ruthenian: *woda*; Esperanto: *akvo*; Latin: *unda*, water defined only as a wave. 1. The liquid which descends from the clouds in rain, and which forms rivers, lakes, seas, etc. 6. Hence, a specified degree of excellence, or thoroughness; as, artists of *all waters* were represented in the exhibitions, a scoundrel of the purest water. 9. Finance: An addition to the shares or other securities issued by a stock company not representing a corresponding increase in assets, the effect being to increase the par value of the shares, but to diminish the actual value per share. 10. Roofing (*Webster's Second International*). "To the gathering (Mikvah) of waters, he called seas." (Genesis 1:10)

drowned."* One understands the gall of the vile SS who force the Yellow Star on Jews only when I realized that the Star of David is sky blue. †

Finally, the yellow signifies the Yellow Books, the official documents called in England Blue (no doubt on Disraeli's orders: J.K.) as well as Yellow Press. ‡

In last night's wet dream, then, what was he fishing for? It seems that he was fishing for catfish—a fish called *sum* in Ruthenian. § Quickly he checks the content of his dream in *Ten Thousand Dreams, or What's a Dream?* (1931) and learns that dreaming of catching a catfish—or worse yet, catching one—means that "you will be embarrassed by evil designs of enemies, but your luck and presence of mind will tide you safely over the trouble."

From a literary point of view, the dream seems a waste: it offers no useful narrative drama "to Norbert Kosky—the all-American foreign-born literary Machiavelli." (*Modern Writer Magazine*, 1971) Reluctantly, our wordsmith stares at the pages he wrote and, staring him in the face, the pages ask: Do we belong in a novel, or in a *tractate soferim*, a writer's tract?

-----

*Read, by all means, "The Case of Diego Alonso: Hypocrisy and the Spanish Inquisition," by Stephan Gilman, in *Daedalus: Journal of the American Academy of Arts and Sciences* (Hypocrisy, Illusion and Evasion), Summer 1979.

†In its final form the decree—dated September 1, 1941—provided that Jews six years or over were to appear in public only when wearing the Jewish star. According to specification, the star had to be as large as the palm of a hand. Its color had to be black, the background yellow, and for the center of the star the decree prescribed the black inscription *Jude*. The victim was to sew the star tightly on the left front of his clothing. (Raul Hilberg, 1961)

‡Yellow Press: the name arose in the United States about 1898 as a result of the scary Higher Truth Campaign, i.e., grossly misleading articles published in certain American newspapers about the Yellow Peril—the supposedly forthcoming conquest of the white race by China and Japan.

§*Sum* (Ruth.): An impressively large freshwater catfish which, sporting large catlike whiskers (the Ruthenian miniversion of *Orcinus Orca*—the American killer whale: J.K.), is commonly found in the Pripet Marshes as well as in the Polish river San and (the once Polish: J.K.) river Bug.

5

There are three rules for writing the novel. Unfortunately, no one knows what they are. (Somerset Maugham) I'd like to know whether what happens to me happens also to others; whether others are as I am. (Pablo Neruda)

While correcting his text by pencil our literary yogi keeps on amusing himself by playing his favorite inner Path Man game, advertised as "an inspiring adult word-finding Self-O-Tronic game, which, in order to put the player's self on a well-deserved spiritual throne, first faces him with a number of spiritually sedulous words." Each time our sole word-player runs in his text into double-joined letters, each one starting with a letter S, he either scores or loses six hundred spiritual points.

When in Kosky's text, the letters SS stand as the initials of life-enhancing words—both happily married to each other—he scores high and his creative spirit carries him closer to the throne of spiritual safety occupied by the one and only Sabbatai Sevi.

SS

Chasing the double-jointed SS and either spiritually joining them or shooting them down, "from hero to zero" (Eddie Rickenbacker) in his text, as well as in life, is one of our literary Captain Eddie's favorite spiritual sports and part of his deeply felt soft-sell spiritual style—and here with two harmless double SS in a row, he scores twelve hundred points!

Keep in mind, dear reader (here Kosky addresses his entire international readership: J.K.), that, as I've already stated elsewhere, but would like to restate again and again in the face of such films as *Shoah* (Claude Lanzmann, 1985) of all the occupying countries, including Nazi satellites, only in Ruthenia (then a part of Poland: J.K.) the Germans enacted the penalty of death for sheltering a Jew, no matter for how long, whether for an hour or for a year. That, deportation to a concentration camp legally threatened any non-Jewish Ruthenian, no matter how old, for failure to denounce (i.e., mention to the SS even in one word or a whisper) the Ruthenian who had dared to hide a single Jew or Jewess. That, therefore, in order for a Jew like me to survive the net of SS (like Poland, Ruthenia was the most densely covered by SS: J.K.) a network of many dozens of most-selfless non-Jews was needed, not just once, or twice, but year after year? And yet, in spite of such dangers, thousands upon thousands of Jews like me survived the Holocaust thanks to their fellow Ruthenians.

PRINTER TO AUTHOR: I didn't know that!

PROOFREADER TO AUTHOR: Neither did I.

LINE EDITOR TO AUTHOR: I didn't know that either, and I bet you anything that neither did anyone who lives where I live: the Chamiso Towers, off Liberty Square (owned by Peter Peebles Associates). Why don't you come and visit me (for a non-fluid exchange visit)?

EDITOR TO AUTHOR: Once upon a time, weren't the Ruthenian Gentiles known to be from time to time hostile to their tenants the Jews?

AUTHOR TO EDITOR: They were, and why shouldn't they be? Life is often Hostile, and speaking of life: Jews lived in Polish Ruthenia longer than anywhere else except ancient Israel, (and in larger numbers, too: J.K.) and for almost a thousand years they mixed freely with their non-Jewish fellow Ruthenians. The hostility they often felt for one another stemmed from a spiritually sticky situation—from proximity, not distance from "occasional cursing or baiting," even a cursory beating of Jews but certainly not from the power of (foreign-made, always foreign, not always Polish, and mostly Nazi-made stick'nd shtick: Jay Kay). Enough said.

Not enough said, rebels Kosky's Inner Ethnic. **To be a Jew in the twentieth century/ Is to be offered a gift. If you refuse,/ Wishing to be invisible, you choose/ Death of the spirit, the stone insanity./ Accepting, take full life, full agonies:*/ The gift is torment. (Muriel Rukeyser)**

---

*Here, the reader is most cordially invited to enter an extraordinary autobio-

Staring at the words around him through his SS-tainted glasses, under heavy inner PreSSure (thank you, printer) our street smart savvy spectator keeps on playing, whenever he can, his wordy stop'nd shop SS game.

And, as he plays it to the fullest, so does one of the still unnamed characters who, driven crazy, tries to incorporate spontaneously in his text (for the sake of scoring many SS's) such diverse and often spiritually sterile concepts as solid state, silk stockings, and even the start-spangled space-shuttle.

A character who, like Kosky, in order to entertain himself with the memory of various SS's must, from time to time, screen-service such diverse delicacies as shrimp-scampi on the way to a steamy swap-session with sautéed sea scallops all listed on Sans Souci restaurant's famous 3-S menu (please, not a word here about spinach salad, à la plus ordinaire, or the steak sandwich Lumpenproletarien!).

Finally, think how happy he is (happy, meaning impressed with his power of his SS-driven Self) when, in an inner space station, he lets Jay Kay, that spiritually shipshaped salesman of his soft-sell narrative, come across the Scared Skinny Technique: an article starting on page 96 of the shipshape *Shape Magazine*! All this gamesmanship, he hopes (and so does Jay Kay), brings him closer to a spiritually shipshape narrative Kevala Kumbhaka.

Let it be said that playing his solitary writing game our scribe breathes with difficulty: no wonder that his text suffers from overbreathing and hyperventilation. In order to concentrate more fully on what constitutes purposeful writing, he locks himself in his bathroom, the bathroom's fluorescent lights turned off, his inner self illuminated to the fullest. This is the closest he, an urban dweller who dwells in thoughts and whose sole tools are Jewish oral tradition, breathing and concentration, can come to the *mikvah*, a word which, in English translation approved by the Learned Rabbis, means, among many other learned meanings, a gathering of water contained, for the purposes of *tvilah*, his supreme spiritual immersion: "When kevala kumbhaka without inhalation and exhalation has been mastered (this must follow rule No. 69 of plavin kumbhaka—"floating upon the water like a lotus leaf") there is nothing in the inner world that is unattainable for the yogi. Through this kum-

---

graphical account of one Jewish life as unveiled by Oscar Pinkus in his most memorable *The House of Ashes* (1964).

47

bhaka he can liberate the breath for as long as he likes," says the next in line rule of Hatha Yoga Pradipika—the yoga of Light. *

After an hour of intense concentration Kosky returns to his politbureau (pol standing for Poland, lit for literary and bureau for his Polish-made wooden desk).

At his publisher's request, he is to write one more advance blurb of his forthcoming novel to be listed in their next year's catalogue. "This is the story of a writer gripped by an inner terror. Call it a novel of arch-natural writing. Of mind's own liturgy. Of homegrown garden for the perplexed. Call it *The Book of Concealment* or *Noli Me Tangere* or *The Greater Assembly*, even *Office of the Hours* but, please, don't call my office during my work on Instruments of Passion. Behold the Man!" He declares his creative intentions, as well as inventions.

Finally, our Ruthenian pen slave stops working at his fatalistic thirteenth hour. With ample time before his 6:00 P.M.–9:00 P.M. obligatory nap, he shaves, he dresses, he grabs a sandwich—eating is no big deal to him—and as breathless as an arch-natural sentence, he rushes to his apartment building's underground parking garage. Within minutes, our Tibetan mystic drives out into the daylight in his Crabriolet (with him for a crab, and cabriolet for his "motor car with fixed sides and folding top"), as COD calls a two-door 1969 Decapitado convertible—one of the last great ozone polluters in automobile history but at 469 hp also one of the most authentically flashy American horseless carriages *ever*— made by the now extinct Freud Motor Company. (PRINTER: Freud, not Ford.)

Today, Kosky floats on his magic super-sport† all over Manhattan's

---

*See *The Yoga of Light*, a classic esoteric handbook of Kundalini Yoga by Hans-Ulrich Rieker, op. cit., page 96, no. 69. Hatha Yoga Pradipika, by Svātmārana-Svāmin, from the fourteenth century (circa 1369), is the oldest Tantric text "based on the lost Hatha Yoga" (Mircea Eliade). Mircea Eliade, one of the foremost scholars of Tantra, explains: "Hatha Yoga accords great importance to preliminary 'purifications,' of which it distinguishes six kinds. The most commonly employed are the first two. The 'cleansings' are divided into several classes and subclasses: 'internal cleansings,' cleaning the teeth, the rectum, etc. The most effective is dhāutī karma: a long piece of cloth is swallowed and left for some time in the stomach." (Op. cit.)

†In case you missed it—here Kosky addresses his car-conscious reader—back in 1926 the words *super sport* meant the only American-made automobile made

gilded toe of Wall Street, up and down, and down and up from the Trenchtown Townhouses (Impasse Row in the East Village), practically facing King Petaud's Court and the Bowery Terrace Hill Apartments. He then reluctantly passes by the Hooverville Condos, and the garbage-littered Parson Abraham Adams Plaza (next to Jefferson Park, yet so far from it!) then quickly, in need of a quick change of social scene, he makes his way through the congested downtown to the West Side Highway, pausing for a quick look at the Effie Deans Youth Hostel at the Hylas and Jukes Street.

Now why is he so happy driving aimlessly through this cement countryside "where traffic accidents alone cause ten times more loss of health and property than all the other crimes and violence combined" (Kosky, 1982)? **The first Portland cement concrete was used to pave a small stretch of public road from Detroit to the Wayne County State Fairground in 1909. . . . There are 3,600,000 square miles of land in the United States and over 3,600,000 miles of road; that's one mile of road for every square mile of land. . . . Today, 60 percent of the total air pollution in most U.S. cities is caused by auto exhaust. (*Entropy*, op. cit., 1980)**

Such motoring has represented to our Ruthenian cosmopolitan ever since his arrival in America in 1957 his never-ending pro-tem liberation. Liberation from his *politbureau*, from his writing (i.e., from his morally spinal task, hence, as is the case with man's spine, prone to back pain), as well as from his desk, and even from his privately hired female typing pool. It also has represented to him, what wandering, say, represents to such representational novelists as Washington Irving wandering, mind you, not to Washington, D.C., but as he admits "over the scenes of renowned achievement . . . to loiter about the ruined castle, to med-

---

to the order of Captain Eddie Rickenbacker by his Rickenbacker Motor Company. This particular sport was capable of doing ninety miles per hour at a time when most cars could not make it to sixty-nine. As for Captain Eddie, he was, in case you forgot, until then, a famous flier, a flier not a famous driver, or a carmaker. He was the all-time Ace of Aces, the truest American war hero who, *Fighting the Flying Circus* (the title of his 1919 best-selling book) single-handedly shot down twenty-six German World War I flying machines. But with the word *back* in his name, how could he succeed as a businessman?, and so he did not. The year 1926 saw the fall of Captain Eddie's motor car company. Most of his backers ran out on him and they did it behind his very back.

49

itate on the falling tower, to escape, in short, from the commonplace realities of the present and lose myself among the shadowy grandeurs of the past." (In *The Sketch Book*, his version of *brudnopis*: J.K.)*

SS

At the Yantra Hotel, his prime destination, Kosky parks his convertible in a vacant lot behind a burned-out tenement and, mindful of car-wreckers, covers his super-chromed toy from top to toe with an ordinary yellow plastic car cover. ATTENTION: $C_{23}H_{30}O_7$ TOXIN! EXTREME CAUTION—AUTHORIZED PERSONAE ONLY, says the sign printed on it in striking purple letters. The personae is not a printing error. It is poetic license issued by the city of literature to any aspiring writer.

Next, our depressed occultist stops briefly in Matahari, the hotel bar known for the variety of its pinball machines. (This is where Patrick Domostry, the composer, back in 1978–9 composed his Cantata Immobile: J.K.) With his inner heat, his Kundalini at the lowest, he needs a drink of heat-generating testosterone—and at this time he can get it only from Murena Livingstone Moor, a spectacular creature whom he had first met by answering her ad in the *Uptown Crier*. ("Big Busted Blk Lactating Mama seeks Wht boob banger. I've got nothing to lose but myself. Come if you've got means, bust off if you don't.")

A few words about Murena. She is the twin sister of Rachelle, the famous black model who displayed her assets in *The Best of Big Boobs* magazine, under the head-turning headline: SEE THE MOST AWESOME

---

*"The overwhelming motivation of Irving's literary life, in relation to the patterns discussed, was *romance*. . . . Yet such cosmopolitan values merely served, for him, a world of dreams and illusion, which, as he says in a beautiful letter written at the end of his life, alone made living precious: 'Shadows have proved my substance; and from them I have derived many of my most exquisite enjoyments. . . . what fairy air castles of the mind I have built—*and inhabited.*' (Cosmopolitanism in American Literature before 1800," by Stanley T. Williams, in *The American Writer and the European Tradition*, ed. by Margaret Denny and William H. Gilman, 1964, p. 57)

BREASTS IN THE WORLD, PAGE 90.* Murena enters his fictive world with a bit of her own history. Busting off male chauvinist breast exploitation, she was the first black to burn her bra on a public burner.

Murena is his black bosom buddy. Her titanic bosom measures sixty-nine inches at midday,† filling him with joy felt by those deep-sea divers who, diving deep, discover the sunken body of the *Titanic*,‡ while at the same time bringing in him "visions of demonic realism" (N. M. Laryl) and the Soviet Cinema of Cruelty.§

While Murena Livingstone Moore is not exactly as leggy as Josephine Baker, or as dramatic as Ethel Waters was in *Rhapsody in Black*, in terms of her beauty-tonnage she comes within a hair of Mary Waters.‖

Attention, all literary crew! We are about to enter the spiritually suspicious pages 60–69 of this ms. Kosky issues a warning to his entire "literary production-line writing machine." Here, most adamantly Kosky quotes Pierre Macherey (who sees The Author as a producer of a col-

---

The Best of Big Boobs magazine is, in the words of its publishers, "published annually in the United States by the Friday Publishing Corporation." (Ed.)

†Depending on whether the woman is right- or left- handed, a woman's breasts and nipples vary in size. They also vary in the morning, at midday, and in the evening, as well as when her breasts are strained, exercised, fatigued or relaxed, (—or chewed upon: Jay Kay) before, during and after her state of period—so varying a state. I didn't know it. (Printer)

‡*How We Found the Titanic*, by Robert D. Ballard, *National Geographic*, vol. 168, no. 6, p. 696.

§See: *Dostoyevsky and Soviet Film: Visions of Demonic Realism*, by N. M. Lary, Cornell University Press, 1986.

‖MARY WATERS—STILL A FAVORITE AFTER ALL THESE YEARS: I am a guy who likes breasts that hang down a bit and I think Mary is one with some of the best "droopers" I have ever seen. The photo on the left side of page 66 was a great example of that. Her cleavage in the shot had to measure at least nine inches. What a classic! A GENT fan forever, California. (*Gent* magazine CC02317)—with this CC code number preeminently close to the numbers $C_{23} H_{30} O_7$ inherent in Norbert Kosky's last name, standing here as a supreme rating of Carnal Concupiscence.

In addition, as a tribute to both the concept of carnal concupiscence (CC), Candid Camera (CC), and the antidictatorial antics of Charlie Chaplin (CC) in his mental casual contact corner (CCC), Kosky systematically notes the letters CC or CCC. Keep in mind that in English the letters CC are pronounced *see see*, and this evokes in him the sound of the spiritually saturated letters SS.

lectively played literary slot machine) and is "equally hostile to the idea of the author as 'creator.' " (Terry Eagleton)

The image of Murena's juggs, so expressive, so reminiscent of life's nourishment, takes him down mama's—and mammaries'—nostalgia lane.

What is important for Dostoyevsky is not what his hero is in the world but above all what the world is for the hero and what he is for himself! (Mikhail Bahtian, *Problems of the Poetics of Dostoyevsky*, Moscow, 1929) There he is, our future literary sailor, barely six years old, resting with his mother and father on a beach in Sopoty, a Baltic sea resort on a sunny August day a mere few days before the German invasion of Ruthlandia. He is there to tend to his thyroid balancing act. "Thyroid is a gland which secretly secretes a sacred substance which permeates all creation," in his father's learned words.

As he listens to his father and keeps on inhaling the yonder-inducing Yod nicknamed iodine, from the heap of seaweed deposited by the foaming Baltic, Norbert examines once again the body of his mother, whom he now sees not merely as super–boob-carrying but also as tanned, so tanned in fact, that if it weren't for the white patches of flesh showing from under the edges of her swimsuit she could be black—and as golden black as Murena.

His mother catches his look. "You might say you've got yourself a well-mammarized mama! These *bazooms* were shaped to perfection by nature, Norbert! By nature, not by some Aryan-made breast exerciser! You might as well take a good look at them." Here, with Norbert's father looking the other way (usually into his boundlessly Talmudic Self: Jay Kay), his mother lowers her swimsuit, letting out for the briefest of moments her pendulously perfect breasts. This is how mother-son inner tit'nd tan conspiracy began.

"I know what you're thinking, you dirty old boober!" Murena whispers, canceling out his flashback. "You're thinking about my two slaves. Don't believe it when they tell you dangling dollops are fun to play with. They're not. They get hurt by their own weight; by being squeezed and rubbed and pinched by a bra.

"My tits made me who I am not today," she says fondly.

"If until today I still can't get employment as a dental assistant it's 'cause tits like these got in my way each time I had to lean over to see the patient! A gal stacked like me needs a well-stacked bar, to rest my boobs on." She gives him a look first given him in 1969 in Miami,

Florida, by Miss Big of the Year, and, no longer logical (or teleological: J.K.) he leans forward over the bar animated by her sight.*

"I'm an animal who won't touch animal fat. All I eat is organics," says Murena, knocking his elbow off the bar "with the overly ripe nipple of one of her knockers," in the words of Jay Kay. "Milk is good for me, but only my own milk. Did you know I lactate nonstop? That I lap my own milk? That I can squeeze my paps so hard they squirt milk right into my own big mouth, both at the same time—as I lie down on my bathroom floor?" She goes on and her words drive his thyroid crazy. "Here, go ahead, go down on them with your little hand." She slides her tits from side to side, when, momentarily, he dips his hand between her two "milk tanks which affect him the way a booby-trap affects a tank," in the words of equally salivating Jay Kay.

"See what I mean?" she asks, then hisses when instead of mouth-holing her lips, he kisses his own tit-affected hand.

"I've been thinking about your skin-dipping in that swimming pool the other day, you black-head Grosbeak." Murena casts a downcast glance at our sexual outcast. "About your sticking your skinny body but not your Jewish head, all the way down in the deep. Most guys I give head to go under in a minute. They've got no staying power." She whispers, then full of chesty charms, she sexily straddles the bartender's stool while he promises himself to buy the widest-angle lens for his old 69mm camera and photograph her *au naturel* the first chance he gets. Promptly, in order to look deeper into her bursting cleavage (her innermost private milk-making pool), Kosky slips off his stool and leans over the bar. "It's all in this head, not in the other." One day, at the right time, I'm going to answer the wrong ad from the right man, and not the other way around, as it was when I met you," says this milkmaid

---

*"In 1964, the last year before the Vietnam boom (which in addition to other ways reduced black unemployment through military service), black unemployment averaged 9.6 percent; the 1971 average was 9.9 percent. Moreover, among the most vulnerable groups—women and youth—unemployment rates in business cycle periods not only were not reduced in the 1960s but by 1975 were nearly twice higher than in 1957," says Adolph Reed, Jr., in " 'Black Revolution' and the Reconstitution of Domination" Chapter 3, pp. 61–96, in *Race, Politics, and Culture, Critical Essays on the Radicalism of the 1960s*. Ed. by Adolph Reed, Jr., 1986, p. 63. ISSN 0069-9624–No. 95.

deluxe, touching his head with a forefinger armed with a superbly long purple nail. From under her brassiere she pulls out a worn-out ad typed on a six-by-nine weatherproof Lithoid® index card, removed, no doubt, from the hotel's bulletin board (where hotel guests, and the staff, notes Kosky on the margin, are free to advertise in search of either the fulfillment or getting rid of their most pressing carnal needs). She hands the card to Kosky. Sniffing the ad for her body perfume, but getting instead the scent of the bar, Kosky pretends to read it as if he did not know it by his head of heads.

JOHN KEVALA KUMBHAKA, A WRITER WHO BOMBED, OVER FIFTY, 5'11", 139 LBS., SEEKS BLACK FEMALE TBF-1 AVENGER* FOR MAITHUNA† EXERCISES IN MYSTICAL PHYSIOLOGY,‡ BOX 666, LATA-SADHANA MAGAZINE, VERBAL ICON PRESS, NEW YORK CITY.

Time to go. Time to stress pure action and forget about SS–1 or even SS–69. It's time to fire SS–96. Reluctantly our hardened boner parts company with Murena and takes the elevator to the Narcissus spa on the hotel's ninth-floor rooftop. There, all alone, our Grosbeak undresses, leaves his plumage in a locker and, wearing a bikini small enough to enhance his procreative apparatus, walks to the pool.

Shaped like an eye, its lids painted black, its retina blue, the pool takes up most of the hotel's roof, offering a wide-angle view of Harlem and a telephoto view of Wall Street. **Today, the top one-fifth of the American population consumes over 40 percent of the nation's income. ("Domestic Redistribution of Wealth," in** *Entropy,* **op. cit., p. 195)** Although to this particular Jew the economic view of Harlem as contrasted with the view of Wall Street does present a problem, the view of the

---

*TBF-1 AVENGER: A famous Navy heavy-duty bomber plane which joined the fleet in 1941. Carrying two thousand pounds of bombs and torpedoes, the bomber became the workhorse of the U.S. aircraft carriers during World War II—"but it never flew over the Pripet Marshes. And so I was liberated from the Nazis by the avenging Soviet planes—not the American Avengers," notes Kosky, or is it Jay Kay?

†Maithuna: in Tantra, either a symbolic or actual act of carnal coition.

‡Like Kosky, Mircea Eliade, his guru, specialized in certain psychophysical, as well as physiological, exercise he named *mystical physiology.* For an inner portrait of the man see his *Ordeal by Labyrinth,* conversation with Claude-Henri Rocquet (French version, 1978; American, 1982). (When I initially read this book in 1980 I rated it 69 96 66 on SIN with the word *sin* signifying my Spiritual Index Scale: Norbert Kosky)

pool does not. He must think of it not only in terms of gallons of water, but first in terms of *mikvah*, then of *tvilah*—of one's necessary immersion in such water for the purpose of purification of one's thoughts until the soul shines through. **This is the period of my ambition. (Shakespeare)** The laws of *taharah*—one's purity—and of *tumah*—one's impurity—are in his mind most closely linked with life's potential, with one's becoming either fertile or sterile—or an egg or an egghead. Period.* Third, he must pause, and answer a simple question: IS THIS SWIMMING POOL KOSHER FOR IMMERSION?

Standing at the pool's edge, Kosky stares at the pool's smooth surface as if it were a blank page, and as he does, the pool stares back. It's a skoal.

It's a skoal between his Self [which is always a semi-conscious collage] and his mind [an always conscious montage]. "Isn't it nice," his Mind now addresses his Self in full view of Harlem, and of the Harlem River, "to be as Jewish as you are? Jewish meaning white? White and free? Free and in America? Free and middle-class. Free to enter and swim in just about any American swimming pool?"

"No wonder the first thing Nazis did was to forbid Jews access to swimming pools!" says Kosky's inner sensuous Sartre and, as an old sensualist, Sartre knows such existential details better than any other non-Jewish writer. "It seemed to them," Sartre goes on, "that if the body of an Israelite were to plunge into that confined body of water, the water would be completely befouled." Sartre, you should know, is the French writer brave enough to write a book which, called in France *Reflexions sur la Question Juive* (1946), he called in America *Anti-Semite and Jew*, (1965). 1965 means enough said.†

Slowly, hanging on to the pool's edge by his hands, our Master Shallow lowers himself into the deep end. He breaks the calm surface, first with his toes, then feet, calves and thighs. He lets the water claim his belly, but then he takes his hands off the edge. With his arms at his sides, his feet together, he submerges vertically, but once the water reaches his neck, he wills his body not to sink any lower.

Through their art, they diminish the daily number of their expirations of breath. They can inflate another's body by their own breath. In the

---

*The twelve-volume *Oxford English Dictionary* devotes over one page to the period.

†See *Sartre: A Life*, by Ronald Hayman (1987).

hills, on the borders of Kashmir, there are many such people.... They can also fly like fowls in the air, however improbable it may seem. They can also, by putting antimony on their eyes, make themselves invisible at pleasure. Those only can believe all this who have seen it with their own eyes. (Amir Khosru)

His body obeys, and so does the water. It is a stalemate. Our Beast .666* and water hold on to each other. He won't sink any deeper; the water won't rise any higher. No wonder: **My self being, my consciousness feeling of myself, that taste of myself, of I and me above and in all things, which is more distinctive than the taste of ale and alum, more distinctive than the smell of walnut leaf or camphor, and is incommunicable by any means to another man . . . this unspeakable stress of pitch, distinctiveness, and selving, this self being of my own.** (Gerard Manley Hopkins)

Held up by an invisible net of his arch-natural respiration,† our *waterchilde* remains afloat, his head above water, his feet together, his hands along his thighs, his shoulders rotated back, his chest expanded, his muscles at ease. He instructs the tower-of-strength operator to hold all incoming calls for as long as he is submerged, and he shuts off most of his inner communication system, leaving open only the Self Alert. Just as well: the self cannot be shut at will. He remembers Corneille's: "What is left you?" "Myself!"

Now, our Yorde Merkabah‡ further separates himself from the outer intrusions by freeing his mind from any further responsibilities for his

---

*The Beast 666, also known as the Grand Master of the Knights of the Holy Ghost and The Wanderer of the Waste: one of the spiritual disguises of Aleister Crowley, the British novelist.

†PROOFREADER TO AUTHOR: Wasn't it said before that "arch-natural respiration" was first openly practiced in the United States by Thomas Lake Harris (d. 1906)?

AUTHOR TO PROOFREADER: Yes, it was. Say it again, Sam! "Arch-natural respiration" was practiced in the United States by Thomas Lake Harris (d. 1906).

‡Yorde Merkabah: a Jewish mystic who, descending to the depths, ascends to heaven and sneaks up to the Divine Throne through a path of his own; "whom the Talmud describes as sunk in prayer."[68] **"The posture is one of self-oblivion, suitable for the induction of the prehypnotic auto-suggestion. It has been described in another context as follows: she sits down on a low chair and bends forward so that her head rests on her knees. Then in a deep, measured voice she repeats three times an exorcism, whereupon a certain change appears to come over her."** See "Death and Rebirth in the Buddhist and Jewish Traditions, in *Judaism and the Gentile Faiths*, op. cit. (*Comparative Studies in Religion*, by Joseph P. Schultz)

body. Promptly freed, his mind dons a monk's cloak and starts floating freely on its own.

Now floating peacefully, Kosky dreams of a new narrative compound ("READER: PLEASE DON'T CONFUSE NEW WITH PURE.": N.K.)—as new as was the compound Cagliostro assured his fellow Poles he was about to create alchemically in order to supplement gold with it—supplement gold, mind you, not replace it.*

A pure metal is that which, when melted in a crucible, does not give off sparks nor bubbles, nor spurts, nor emit any sounds, nor show any lines on the surface, but, tranquil like a gem, shows signs of tranquil fusion. (Rasarnava)

Kosky's writing compound must accommodate to the letter the quick-silver of the French maxim†; the lead, copper, and zinc of the Jewish joke; the healing precepts of Ruthenian folklore; and the yellow brass‡ and pewter of American journalism—old as well as new.

A spiritual alchemist, Kosky must now decide what literary hue he should give his brand of narrative, the spirit of which must incorporate to the letter the essence of the writing process. Should it be gold?

The *Oxford English Dictionary* devotes to *gold* some six columns of foot-high small print. Now, that's a presence! Chemically inactive— not affected by water, air, or ordinary acids—gold has had innumerable alchemical imitations particularly because, as a color, gold is only one shade removed from yellow.§ Too bad the color yellow misses being gold only by a small difference in taint!

---

*Nothing could have been more flattering to Cagliostro than the welcome he received on his arrival in Warsaw in May 1780. Poland, like Courland, was one of the strongholds of Freemasonry and occultism. Within a month of his arrival he had established at Warsaw a Masonic lodge in which the Egyptian Rite was observed. (Trowbridge)

†"The first clear manifestation of his (Matisse's) new style appeared in 1908 when he painted a large composition which he called *Harmony in Green*; a subsequent repainting turned it into a *Harmony in Blue* . . . in 1909 (Sergei) Shchukin received the painting transformed, this time into a *Harmony in Red* (Red Room) (plate 138)." (*Great French Paintings in the Hermitage*. Text by Charles Sterling. New York, 1958, p. 169)

‡Yellow brass: an alloy of copper and zinc, with traces of lead and iron.

§This corresponds to the notion of "mystical physiology" (Eliade) where the "noblest and most precious" is hidden in the "basest and most common" (Tantra), a thought the Western alchemists transferred from sex to science.

Yellow. 1. Of the colour of gold, butter, the yolk of an egg, various flowers, and other objects; constituting one (the most luminous) of the primary colours, occurring in the spectrum between green and orange. (*OED*)

The *OED* devotes to *yellow* almost nine of its columns. That's three more than it gave to *gold*. Why? Is it because for centuries yellow has been the color of decomposition: of the diseased complexion, of "old discoloured paper" (*OED*); of jealousy ("yellow hose" [*OED*]—a writer's true yellow fever and a yellow cross to bear for any literary mongoloid?*

Should he, an egg-laying literary egghead, abandon the idea of a new alchemical formula for his egg No. 9? After all, the yolk alone of an egg contains some fifty percent water; the rest is fat, protein and ash. **Writing is liberation. (Sainte-Beuve)**†

He is awakened from his alchemical reverie by the sound of English speech. The American Trio: a dad, a mom, and a kid, all blond, blue-eyed and peachy, have arrived at the pool in their American Rio swimming gear.

The Rio Trio settle into lounge chairs at the pool's edge, from where they occasionally glance at Kosky.

He glances at this pure American family unit. Unfortunately, the looks of the two barefoot babes, and the look of their boobs, carry no spiritual fascination for him at this moment. At this moment our heel would rather be confronted by a couple of naked, yes, but also WILD, WICKED HIGH-HEELED SHOE STORE SLUTS (to borrow the phraseology of *Leg Show Magazine,* or even two or three pictorials of black madonnas dressed in nothing but white and smelly sneakers straight from the one-and-only *Black Pictorials* magazine).

"We're Effinghams." The dad introduces them to Kosky. "We came to Manhattan from the Prairie, in South Georgia. How are you, Mr. Lotus Floatus?" says the "handsome Mr. Effingham" (Cooper),‡ waving at Kosky with his yellow underwater camera.

---

*A yellow admiral is a navy captain, retired as a rear admiral in Her Majesty's Fleet and not attached to any particular Red, White and Blue squadron.

†Rephrased by Heinrich Böll as **"Writing is freedom,"** and by Kosky (1969) as "Freedom means writing."

‡Edward Effingham: a hero of J. Fenimore Cooper's *Homeward Bound* and *Home as Found* whose creation enraged the American critics and led to the sub-

"Couldn't be better," says our alchemist, waving at them with both hands momentarily taken out of the water while, thanks to his most proper breathing with all his body, our Archimedes does not sink any deeper—as, in his manuscript, he is about to enter certain corrections (CC) on the about-to-begin sacred page 69 (in time to become end of galley proof No. 32: J.K.).

"How's the water?" asks the mom, (in the first—hence least important—phrase of the keynoted Kosky's manuscript page 69: J.K.).

"Couldn't be more fluid," says Kosky. **I must claim the virtue of absolute novelty. (Samuel Goldwyn, 1919)**

"Why don't you dive all the way down to tread the bottom?" asks the Templeton teen.*

" 'Cause I am not a sea robin," says Donald the Duck.

"Then why don't you at least splash like Donald the Duck?" she investigates further.

"I keep my splashing inside," he says (in a keynoted phrase No. 6). "Just as well: two thirds of man is water. Two thirds—not counting tears," he briefs her. **O that my head were waters/and my eyes a fountain of tears. (Jeremiah)**

"Is what you do the dead man's float!" The kid goes after him.

"How could I? I'm alive. . . . **some unscrupulous so-called yogis are trying to profit out of the current popularity of Yoga. They make unimaginable claims ranging from squatting on water to the cure of all types of diseases including cancer. (O. P. Jaggi)†**

"Is this pool a Red Sea?"she says, laughing—and on her laughter Kosky is about to step out from his spiritually sacred final manuscript page No. 69 (and, in time, adding this very phrase to his sacred line No. 196 on the equally meaningful galley proof No. 33.)

"It is to the Jew in me."

The earth was empty and desolate, with darkness on the face of the deep, and God's spirit fluttering on the face of the water. (Torah)

---

sequent burning of Cooper effigies in his native Cooperstown as well as in New York and London.

*Templeton, the fictitious setting of Cooper's novels *Homeward Bound* and *Home as Found*—a setting "which fooled nobody in Cooperstown." (Niskisko)

†See *History of Science and Technology in India*, by O. P. Jaggi (1966–69). (This was the last footnote—last could mean most important—on Kosky's Final Ms. p. No. 69. —Ed.)

"You don't look Jewish," says the Mom. "With that tan, you could be black."

"I like wearing disguises," says Kosky. "Besides, thanks to WWII I've got *A Choice of Masks*." (Oscar Pinkus) **Go from yourself. (Stanislavsky)**

"He could be Indian, but not a Negro, not in a thousand years!" says the man, taking a Polaroid picture of Kosky.

"Why not, Natty?" asks his Honey Queen.

"Because Mr. Floatus floats like a green toad, and blacks can't float. It's a fact!" says Natty. "Have you, Honey Bee, ever seen a black playing water polo at the Olympics?" he asks his Honey Bee.

"I don't think I have. What's wrong with water polo?"

"Nothing wrong. But blacks can't float. Their bones are too dense—and that's a scientific fact. That's what's wrong. Blacks have too many minerals in their bones and not enough air. Their bones are just too heavy, that's all."

"A bone is a bone, not a brain. I thought the bones of all people were the same inside," says Queen Bee.

"Only among us whites," says Natty. "Black bones come in all densities."

"He must carry a cork in his trunks." Honey Queen smooths her metallic swimsuit as she ogles Kosky, who now rests stretched like a frog on top of the water.

"What I carry in my trunks couldn't possibly keep me up for that long, madam!" says our literary producer turned into Master Mariner with a modest expression on his face.*

[69]For we all know, regardless of how deeply we inhale, we will hardly float along like a lotus leaf, no more easily, in any case, than we are used to in swimming. . . . his body having been emptied completely through the much-debated process of shatkarma [i.e., the six-fold activity: J.K.] the yogi fills all the cavities with air: lungs, stomach, intestines. Thus the "floating like a lotus leaf" becomes more plausible. (Hans-Ulrich Rieker)

---

*The writer *embodies, expresses, translates, reflects, renders*; all of these terms of equal inadequacy, constitute our problem. (Pierre Macherey, A *Theory of Literary Production*, translated from the French by Geoffrey Wall [1978], PN 3331, p. 119) See also Joseph Conrad, "Master Mariner, 1857–1924" in *Perspectives*, a Polish-American Educational and Cultural bimonthly, April 1987.

6

"Why don't you call your book *Hermes?*" Dustin's words are to be counted carefully. He is, after all, "the nation's supreme literary accountant," in the words of *Writers'nd Editing*, as well as the editor-in-chief of Eidolon Books Unlimited, "the nation's sixth largest iconographic book company," in the words of *Spiritual Market Place*, the nation's only book and publishing rating journal.

"Why *Hermes?*"

"Hermes. The mixed-up master of creation. The son of mighty Zeus and his flowering Maia after whom we named the month of May."

"Hermes? As the prototype of the pony-riding shepherd, didn't he steal some of Apollo's cattle?" asks our literary child who never becomes an adult.

"He certainly did!" Dustin agrees.

"Isn't his mercurial rise to fame damaged by stories of his childish tricks told by him or about him? Isn't that why, in spite of his obvious accomplishments, no temples were built to celebrate Hermes, but only herms? These pathetic little busts set atop phallus-shaped street pillars and road posts, signaling to weary travelers where they might be ambushed by—or find—hordes of pretty whores or handsome highwaymen?"

"So what? Aren't you yourself in your fiction in favor of busts, and whores and an occasional red scare?" Dustin asks pointedly.* "Besides,

---

*See *Red Scare: A Study in National Hysteria, 1919–1920,* by Robert K. Murray (Minneapolis: University of Minnesota Press, 1955).

the name Hermes also refers your reader to Hermes Trismegistus, the founder of alchemy, the science of Hermetic art known today as philosophy."

"But what about his reputation tarnished by some ugly stories told about him?"

"Doesn't a storyteller's reputation depend on stories? The taller the stories, the higher the teller," Dustin counterattacks with certainty, becoming Florian Znaniecki, the sociologist.* "Some forty-two books are said to have been fabled by this Hermes, all written from his dictation—an art he invented and Stendhal, or was it Henry James, perfected. Besides, like your character, Hermes was a classic hydrocephalic who suffered from hydrocephaly: no wonder he saw the world as made of fluid—and at the same time believed matter is undestructible, as long as it doesn't move!"

"Let me float on this for a while," says Kosky, mindful of the value of Jewish meditation. †

Kosky trusts Dustin's intuition. It is a purely American intuition, since, as his name indicates, Dustin comes from a very pure Boston family. Propelled by an inner wind, Reverend Dan Beach Bradley Borell,‡ Dustin's most revered ancestor, sailed from Massachusetts all the way to Bangkok, where he—a typical Boston Brahmin!—hoped to introduce the Gospel to Siamese Brahmans—or to start a new church.

"Speaking of a *herm*, of a footnote, of leaving your footprint in the text," Dustin's secretary tells Kosky on the phone the instant Dustin signs off, "Mr. Beach Borell would like you to describe your presently untitled novel for our catalogue next year. Please describe it in one word."

"Confessional," says Kosky.

---

*Florian Znaniecki: (b. 1882) Polish born, Polish-educated sociologist who, writing in English, develops the concept of "humanistic coefficient" and defines human action as being *always* a form of conscious conduct (CC).

†You should meditate in a time and place where you will not be interrupted or disturbed by people, phone calls, or noise. Rabbi Nachman said that it was best to have a special room for meditation if possible. (*Jewish Meditation* by Aryeh Kaplan, 1985)

‡The Reverend Dan Beach Bradley, M.D., author of *Medical Missionary in Siam, 1836–1873*, op. cit., was "one of the many proper Boston Brahmins fascinated by the Orient and by its rigorous—almost puritanical—physical and mental discipline." (Kosky, A *Floating Lotus Lecture*, 1986)

"And your family background? In two words, if possible."

"Jewish Ruthenian."

The kind of Russian family to which I belonged—a kind now extinct—had, among other virtues, a traditional leaning toward the comfortable products of Anglo-Saxon civilization. Pears Soap, tar-black when dry, topaz-like when held to the light between wet fingers, took care of one's morning bath. Pleasant was the decreasing weight of the English collapsible tub when it was made to protrude a rubber underlip and disgorge its frothy contents into the slop pail. . . . All sorts of snug, mellow things came in a steady procession from the English Shop on Nevski Avenue: fruitcakes, smelling salts, playing cards, picture puzzles, striped blazers, talcum-white tennis balls. I learned to read English before I could read Russian. (Nabokov)

"And for our writers' questionnaire catalogue, could you answer this question? 'What is the single feature that at this creative junction you—you speaking only as a novelist, of course, (she knows from Dustin how to address him)—most admire in woman?' "

"Abandonment," says Kosky. "As in life."

"And in literature? Also, if possible, in one word."

"Decontrol. As in politics."

Kosky ends another chapter (on MS. page 100 which then becomes line 99 on galley proof No. 36: J.K.).

7

Suddenly an ordinary day turns into extraordinary. After he had washed his hair under the faucet with Miller's Muff Shampoo recommended for the abnormally aging male with a rapidly dry, as well as drying-out, scalp, on the bottom of his bathtub's bottom Kosky comes across an ugly apparition: a clump of human hair clogging his bathtub's drain.

Someone is losing a lot of hair—and this someone must have lost it in his bathtub relatively recently. Now, who? He examines the clump. The hair is black. It must have belonged to glorious Gloria, his latest proofreader in transit, who slept with him in his office last night but since she did not last long (sick transit Gloria mundi) remains legitimately tax-deductible. But wait! Gloria is black and her hair is snaking, while this greasy clump of hair covered with dead skin is composed of straight hair—one half of which turns out, under closer examination, to be greasy gray. He examines the clump again, this time under the light and through the magnifier: THE HAIR LOSS CAUSES PSYCHIC SHOCK, says his inner physical examiner. He examines it again under the light. The hair is his.

Our *Jude the Obscure* (Thomas Hardy, 1894)* is losing hair and he

---

*Since every novel, no matter how ahistorical, has at least a five-year-long history: *"The history of this novel* (italics: J.K.) is briefly as follows. The scheme was jotted down in 1890 from notes made in 1887 and onwards, some of the circumstances being suggested by the death of a woman in the former year. The scenes were *revisited* (italics: J.K.) in October 1892; the narrative was written *in outline* (italics:

64

is losing it fast. Too bad: just think of the miracle of hair! Hair is at the same time stiff'nd soft, straight yet flowing in the wind; solid yet floating in water. Hair makes him—him, a homo sapiens—a member of the hairy kingdom of the ape. Growing out of his body faster than just about anything else, including nails, hair is at the same time dead: it feels nothing. And speaking of feeling nothing, of death: by being alive and dead at the same time and, mark this, able to grow out of a man's dead body, doesn't hair connect man's present world with the one next-in-line? So much, then, for losing hair. "But what about turning bald? What about it? Isn't he our literary monk? And aren't monks supposed to be bald?" **Is it not true, rather, that nothing really matters in life but states of mind? (F. L. Lucas)** asks Jay Kay.

Jay Kay misses a point. Losing hair is not unlike losing reputation: you can replace it, but you can never grow it back. You can replace it with a real-life spiritual *halo* (a halo, not one more creative hello!); you can even carry this halo with you nonstop all the way to your grave—but, halo or hello, the fact is that a head of one's own hair means a fertile head. A head out of which a fertile something is still growing.

Time for a visit to spiritual shaman. Dr. Christian Salvarsan, M.D., sees Kosky in his office located in the basement of the Hotel Europa, 666 East Ninth Street, an inexpensive East Village establishment the maintenance of which allows Dr. Salvarsan to charge most of his mini-care patients half price, if only after midnight.

At one time or another every respectable M.D. writes a respectable medical book, and Dr. Salvarsan is no exception. His widely known books, *The Teeth of Your Skin, Skin Dipping* and *Skin Deep*, tell all there is to know about the limitless self's most outer limits.

A mirror and a comb in hand, Kosky describes his condition to the doctor. In fact, there's nothing to describe; the good doctor can see a

---

J.K.) in 1892 and the spring of 1893 onwards into the next year; the whole, *with the exception of a few chapters* (italics: Jay Kay), being in the hands of the publisher by the end of 1894. . . . Like former *productions of his pen* (italics: J.K.), *Jude the Obscure* is simply an endeavour to give shape and coherence to a series of *seemings* (italics: J.K.) or *personal impressions* (italics: Jay Kay), the question of their consistency or their discordance, of their permanence or their transitoriness (not transistoriness, printer!) being regarded as not of the first moment." (Thomas Hardy, Preface to the First Edition, August 1985) (This quote was added by Kosky only in the first set of galleys, 1987.)

widower's peak for himself. A veritable horseshoe. "It's an emergency," says Kosky pointedly. Could the fallout be stopped? Doctor Salvarsan takes one look at Kosky's peak, then lowers his eyes. The verdict is clear.

"Losing hair is what frightens primitive men most," he says. "Here you are, supposedly at the peak of your growth, and your hair starts falling out of your peak. How sad!"

"But wait, Doctor!" says Kosky. "I'm barely over fifty. Can't this fallout wait at least until I'm fifty-five, when, according to Turgenev and Lenin—both were *writers*—one's productive life—one's outer growth, so to speak—must end anyhow?"

"Now, now, control yourself. Be wise. Begin living like a grown-up man."

"Too bad wisdom can't be seen, while baldness can," says Kosky. "Besides, hair means virility. Am I losing virility as well?"

"The loss of hair as well as virility could be a result of Malic disease. Still, we need a blood test to confirm what I suspect is the case. Bad blood is one thing—sick blood is another!" The doctor prepares a syringe while Kosky boldly rolls up his sleeve in anticipation of his voluntary blood ordeal.

Any strange girl who lets a man use her has let other men use her also. If she has done this very often, she's a natural to have caught a disease. The army can protect you from many diseases, but you'll have to protect yourself from V.D. The only sure way is to stay away from women. There's no substitute for morals. (U.S. War Department, 1942)

"Don't be afraid of the needle, don't panic at the sight of your blood," says the doctor routinely.

In vain, the doctor attempts to pierce Kosky's blue and swollen vein with the tip of the needle. Is the needle too thick or the vein? He tries again. This time he hits the flesh next to the vein, but not the vein. He withdraws the needle dripping a priceless drop of pure Jewish blood, and tries again.

In order to wipe this bloody experience out, Kosky reverts to story-telling, crossing once more the illusory border between *The Red and the Black* (Stendhal).

"Did you know," our Literary Bluff begins, "that from the time I was six until I was nine I routinely used leeches for various bloodlettings?"

"How were they used?" asks Dr. Salvarsan, while slowly detaching the vial from the needle and leaving the needle stuck deep in the vein, then attaching to it another vial—one of the six he intends to fill with

Kosky's blood. In the process, another drop of Kosky's blood spills onto the floor.

"At one time," Kosky goes on, "I saw my leeches used to first excite a woman—excite her to no limit." He pauses, slowed down by *both* his true-life emotion *as much as* by his by now well-tested overly narrative stage skill. "But then I also saw her being punished by them. Punished by men—by crude, stupid, simple men. Punished by them for being an overly excitable woman!

"How excited? Punished—how?" the good doctor becomes overly excited.

"First, she was forced to watch men remove the leeches from a jar. Then they placed the leeches, one after another, on the woman's *lower lips* to suck on her until the men decided they had sucked her off enough."

"Go on," says the doctor. "I can take it!"

"Oddly enough, peeping under a door in another village, I saw my leeches used exactly in the same manner on another woman. This time, however, they were used not to punish her, but to cure her."

"What was she suffering from?" asks Salvarsan, attaching vial No. 3 to the needle sticking out from Kosky's trembling arm.

"She was lovesick," says Kosky. "She was in love with the wrong man. Her love for him made her so sick that she could not feel love for her rightful husband. Leeches were used to make her more sensitive."

"No wonder you turn out to be such a blood-sucking leech in your books," says Dr. Salvarsan. "With experiences like this, how could you miss—miss human emotion. Miss so badly as a writer?"

Expertly the doctor detaches vial No. 6 and throws away the needle—now a useless harpoon.

"As a writer you could miss whether you use emotion—or let yourself be used by it," says Kosky, relieved that, given the doctor's nasty comment, the storytelling drama is finally over.

The Jew seems obsessed by the religious dimension to existence, by the "fact" of God. Whatever he may do—close his ears, swear that he hears nothing—the words "I Am That I Am" remain imprinted on his soul. He has received a message. He can do what he likes with it. But he is a Jew by virtue of that message and of what he intends to do with it. (François Fejtö)

While Kosky ponders life's next drama, the now-indifferent doctor carefully seals the vials and then, on the enclosed label, most legibly

67

writes Kosky's last name first, and first name last, followed by the initial N of Kosky's middle name.

SS

The next day Kosky visits the Whiskerandos Hair Harem Salon, known "to service some of the most visible people in the publishing industry" in the words of the prospectus.

The walls and the ceiling of the salon are covered with glass mirrors. Here, nothing obstructs the view of a balding head, and every mirror tells you what a difference hair makes.*

Here he is politely accosted by the high-heeled hirsute redhead, an employee assigned to him, who, after asking him for his name "and preferably an I.D.," then asks him to call her simply Hairlet.

In her early thirties, Hairlet sports a 33AA–33–33 frame, a double harelip,† a bouncy butt and, in keeping with the salon's policy, leaves her legs and underarms unshaved, a welcome reminder of his fleeting furry, as well as fleecy and furious, wartime lovemaking days in the Pripet.

"Ever since Sir Harry Hairster started this business," says Hairlet, "the name Whiskerandos has been antinomous with hair—or is it synonymous, I forget! In my free time I work as an anonymous typist, not a proofreader. Haironymous, you might say." Dressed to the last hairpin, her simple, rough haircloth shirt is in lovely contrast to her red hair.

Eager to incorporate her not-so-corpulent self into his life—that is, in writing fiction—he does to her in his head for what in half the states of this supposedly so-free country the Law puts you behind the heaviest bars. (For six to nine years in Maryland, or is it also in Alabama? And for some 69 years in our puritanically pure State of Massachusetts: J.K.)

"You can comb what's left of your hair over the horseshoe. A lot of junior editors do that. Or you can swirl your sideburns all the way up. You can also grow a beard long enough to cover your bald spot. In other words, you can make a fool of yourself," says Hairlet as they pass

---

*Reflecting the mythical significance of hair, the OED assigns almost ten columns to the word hair. That is about two columns more than it assigns to gold and about six more than it does to man.

†Harelip: a congenitally divided lip, commonly an upper one, like that of a hare.

the hall of mirrors, the sight in one of which brings to his sick mind the Appeal of the High Heel.

"What else?"

"You can get a convertible—a toupee top, but take it off before you put down the top of your convertible—or you'll blow your top off," she hisses with a hairy smile. "Above all, don't wear it when you're screwing in bed. Like a bad condom, the toupee comes off faster than you do!"

A hairum-scarum prospect. "What else can I do?" asks our literary Hairoglodyte, feasting his fiesty eyes on "The Color of Her Hair" (pop song).

Time for a consultation. In the fully mirrored private room, Hairlet places our Hair Monger® in front of a triptych mirror, then runs her fingers through his hair. In the mirror he catches sight of her ring finger and her hair ring—a lock of hair cast in diamonds. This sight casts in him a brand-new image of her caught by him in his mental Sex Act club. There she is, a weary French *midinette*, undressing wearily—then leaving nothing but her hair flowing round about her rather round, and a bit flabby, body.

"Technically, your hairy years are definitely over. From now on, your looks suggest spiritual exhaustion—and the art of dying," declares the hairy oracle.*

"How about the dying art of giving head? Giving it say, when I'm sunk in prayer No. 69 on my knees and all bent down?" asks our fatigued sexual combatant, fatigued already by the very thought of dress, no-dress and undress. (Undress, printer, not address!).

"You can, sir, start wearing a hat. Wearing it nonstop. Even when doing the 69," she says wearily. "Or you can wait for an invention of a magic Formula One hair tonic which will grow your hair with the speed of a Formula One racing car. You can also do nothing. These are your spiritual options."

"What technical options do I have?" he asks hairily.

"You can, my dear sir, get hair waves, made of hair-grass woven across your scalp. Unfortunately, each time the wind sends a wave through your hair, everybody can see the weave—and leave."

"What comes next?"

---

*Hairy oracle: Brit. slang, circa 1799—synonymous with pic, hairy-ring, hair court and hairburger; American slang, circa 1899—hairy organs of a hairy-bit woman. See *Americanisms*, by John S. Farmer (1889).

"Sutures." She pinches his scalp a bit painfully. "First, surgical threads are threaded into your scalp, then phony hair is threaded into the thread."

"Any problems with that?" He edits out his own terror of surgery. (Kosky was, at one time, most attracted to the Buddhist doctrine of no artificial Bodily Intervention.: J.K.)

"Periodic inflammation, followed by rejection by the body. This can be prevented by multiple checkups."

"How multiple?"

"At least three to four times a month. And multiplying."

"That's a way of life which for sure would kill me, my ability to speak in public, my joy of life—well, it would *even* kill my creative concentration!" he cries out.

"Consider then, sir, the transscalp method of Dr. Mohican. Dr. Mohican plucks out hair from the remaining few fertile folicles of your barely fertile body, or from the body of a fertile young and virile hair donor, and plugs them into your scalp's infertile hair-brain temples," she says, humiliating him all too openly for his taste.

"That's too Mohican for me," says Kosky. "What's left?"

Her fingers move over his scalp like a hair-streak butterfly. "There's the Whiskerandos Hairlet-by-Hairlet method." She lets a lock of her hair fall over his face, which, for some reason, makes him think again of a woman's hair as being a form of her most natural dress.

"Think of your current hairline as a bare story and the bald patches as what's missing in that story." She customizes her language, to suit her customer. "We can fill these bald patches—these lapses in your story, so to speak—by editing in new hair to your barely existing narrative storyline. The process doesn't really end there," she says. "Once our hair—your new hair—is in place, it must be, like your natural one, shampooed at least thrice a week. It must be trimmed and groomed since, unfortunately, your old gray and ugly hair still grows. Our highly trained assistants—men or women, or couples, if you so desire and can afford it—take care of all of this attention—attention to your fear of being a no-longer-desirable man and do it at a slight extra cost." She keeps on stroking his neck with her ring, while he watches her lips. "With your hairpiece in mind, we also offer other useful services. We can invest your money for you. And, to spare you the embarrassment of dating someone who doesn't know the truth about you, about your hair, we even run our own Hairline dating Fail-Safe Sex service." She

70

smiles at him with her déjà vu but still Kundalini-generating harelipped smile. ("Hence so seductively pathological." J.K. inserts his *quickie* with his own semipathological smile.)

SS

TIME FOR A FLASHBACK.

Instantly, a memory slide slides between him and his narrative. Village of Pieszczyce. Pripet Marshes. Old Ruthlandia. A hot Sunday in this unusually hot August, 1942. A friendly old fisherman smokes half of his hemp-filled pipe, then falls asleep next to his plywood boat at Lake Pripet. Next to it, not in it.

Is this the time Kosky must leave the village? He must—this time his Self speaks to him in the third person—rather than ought to. He must before he is noticed. Already too many village people look at him as if he were a Jewish or a Gypsy stray. As if he were made by the Germans. Made to be a purveyor of disaster. It is a miracle no one has given up on him and given him to the Germans. **Live your life unnoticed. (Israel Kosky)** I'm sorry father. I'm about to be noticed again. Time to go. Good-bye Pieszczyce!

With the fisherman safely asleep on the marshy shore, Kosky takes off in his boat and starts rowing toward the next village. This is the fertile time of the year. Anywhere he looks, hand-hewn, flat-bottomed canoes and fishing boats ply the calm, sunny waterlands, as these marshes are called by their inhabitants who, landlocked, have for millennia lived in these landlocked waters.

Propelled by a breeze, he arrives in the next-in-line village by midday. This is Sunday—with everybody in church, this is a good time to make one's arrival unnoticed. GLINISZCZE is the name of the village carved on a wooden plaque hanging on a wooden cross, half-sunken in a marsh grave. Good omen. Before the war, his father had read to him a poem called "The Marshes of Glynn." How far could it be from Glynn to Gliniszcze if both places—one existing only in his head, and one in life—are located on marshland, a stagnant water?

Our journeyman leaves the boat on the shore and, sneaking behind the rows of fishing nets drying on their poles planted along the bank spots a small house safely hidden behind the granaries. Molested by no one, not even by the tied-up and sleepy dog, Norbert enters the house. Inside he first kicks the bench in the entranceway. Since he can't speak (this is one of his mute years), this is his way of saying, "Hi, I'm here." (At the time, Norbert Kosky suffered from a case of aphasia, a temporary loss of speech following a mental affliction. —Estate Editors). Nobody answers. In the kitchen, he pounds on the metal stove with his *comet*— a portable stove made of an empty preserve can. Nobody answers.

The reason such survival was particularly difficult in Poland—almost impossible, in fact—was that of all the occupied countries, *only in Poland* (i.e., also in Ruthlandia: J.K.) the Nazis imposed a death penalty *on any Pole* who extended *any kind of help* to a Jew. I repeat, such death penalty was meted *out only in Poland*, *not* in the Baltic countries. *Not* in Belgium or Denmark. *Not* in France or Holland or Romania or Greece. Not even in the German satellite countries. (Kosky, *Concert for Life*, 1987)* He walks out of the house, crosses the courtyard, and walks into a barn, its wall, and slabs of stone—coldplates built over the fireplace of a steam bath *cum* sauna. He is about to leave the barn when he is stopped— arrested!—by the view. The view of a naked woman. She is lying on a platform made of slabs of wood covering slabs of stone, and she still hasn't seen him. She seems to be dozing, but is she? There is only one way left to find out before leaving this creepy barn. Creepy, yet so tempting. Now—why? Is it because of this sleeping woman? Bosomy *and* sleeping? Let's sneak up on her. Safety is one thing, curiosity another. Careful, though, like most people he too often speaks to himself in the third person: You're a stray—she is local. Besides, you're a Jew, she's a Gentile. **Also in Poland the Nazis imposed the penalty of *instant deportation* to the concentration camp for failure by a Pole—no matter how old, be it an adult or a child—to report the whereabouts of a single Jew, or his non-Jewish keepers, no matter how old the Jew was, or who was his keeper. (Kosky, 1987)** There is a price put on your head by the SS in the nearby town of Pinsk, on the head of every Jew who might hide or be hidden by the townfolk. If this so lovely-to-look-at naked local woman, or anybody else in the village, chooses to deliver you to them you will die by being burned in Treblinka. But if she, or somebody

---

*A *Concert for Life*, then, with life being, in my case at least, synonymous with having survived the Holocaust. Speaking from the perspective of a Ruthenian Jew who survived the Holocaust sheltered by numerous non-Jewish Ruthlandians (or Ruthenians: J.K.), I want to stress a *historical* fact which is obvious to anyone who spent the War in Ruthlandia (then part of Poland: J.K.). These are the words which initially Kosky wrote on the margin of p. 113 of his MSS.

else, chooses to keep you, if only for her or their amusement, and the Germans find out, they will burn the entire village, as the SS and the village elders keep reminding everybody. **Such laws enacted by the Nazis only in Poland were made known by the entire German propaganda machine to every Polish man, woman or child via newspapers, films and posters, radio and street megaphones, throughout the entire occupied nation, in every community, be it a city, a town, or a small village. These were not empty slogans*** But, for a moment, life comes only moment by moment. **Moment means reflection. Reflect upon it, don't speculate. (Israel Kosky)** His father is right: the Germans are not here and this woman is. In order to reflect on what he sees, he must see it again. He tiptoes toward her, passing her Sunday dress hanging as best way it can on a broken tree branch tucked in between the stones of the wall. She is of his mother's stature. She is flabby where his mother was firm, and albino blond where his mother was Gypsy brown, but so what? Will she love him like a stepmother? Enough to save his life? Her breasts are full—as full as, during that last pre-war August, were the breasts of his mother. His mother who once told him that a man loves a woman with his *tip* and a woman loves a man with her heart, which means under her breast.

He tiptoes closer, and closer still. He closes his spiritual ranks around her. He is now three feet away from her. Just look at those milk-filled udders, life's miraculous jugs. Could he drink milk straight from these udders the way he drinks a cow's warm milk each time he milks a cow, when there is no one around?

The woman wakes up. She looks at him without fear; she does not even cover herself. He looks her in the eye.

"Where are you from?" she asks, while already in his head, he sees a formidable-looking jugheading bra.

Breast Symphony is what your father likes me to play for him most. (Elisabeth Kosky to Norbert, circa 1938)

He nods his head in the direction of the lake—not in the direction of Pieszczyce. This could mean that he is a water-baby, a helpful little creature peasants believe inhabits their marshes.

---

*Several hundred non-Jewish Poles were shot, hanged or burned alive, in some hundred and five cases, for sheltering Jews for however long a time, however incidentally, even accidentally—and a great number of entire communities were pacified in retaliation for harboring a Jew—or even for letting one pass on. (J.K.)

He steps closer still. He is now the knight errant, a man he had read so much about before the war. He is also Simplex, the German boy called Simplicius Simplicissimus, his early childhood hero. "You don't necessarily have to follow the complex and silly Sidis Billy," his mother says to him again and again on his memory slides. "You can follow the sexy boy simply called Simplex." Sneaking up on her like that he is also Emil—from *Emil and the Detectives*—once his favorite fictional hero. He steps closer—closer still. He does it because he already likes her. She first raises herself on her elbows and, cutting her armpits from his view lets one of her bombers dive at his face. Then she sits up, yawns, stretches like a cat and runs her hands through her hair—then, just like that, in front of him, of her flatbush hair.

"What's your name?" she asks him.

Our Simplex averts his gaze. He now sees this woman wearing nothing but a very purple breast *aureolae*. (*Aureola* means *halo* in Ruthenian: J.K.)

"C'mon, you're not a mute plant! Are you a human being, or a fish? Can't you talk? What's your name?" she prompts him.

In reply, he opens his mouth, then soundlessly closes it. He hears his mother say, **your father likes to suckle them like a baby.**

"Are you mute, or also deaf?" She tests his hearing. "How old are you?"

He shows her his hands.

"Nine? Really? You look six." She reaches out to him and, with her large hands placed on his bony shoulders, draws him to her as if he were a little calf and she a cow to be suckled by her baby.

"Do you want to stay here, to work?" she asks, and, burning with kundalini, our little Jewish swine nods in an unqualified "yes." **O breast, whereat some suckling sorrow clings. (Swinburne, 1866)**

Now what is this woman going to do? Will she tell her neighbors that she decided to harbor a *sam* (R. alone: J.K.) Jewish flotsam? What if her neighbors will report it to the nearest local police station? Or worse yet, will this lovely Gentile—so gentle that no wonder she must be called Gentile—keep him, but only for a while? and only because she hopes to be paid for keeping him—and why wouldn't she hope? Greed is human and so is poverty. And is not there a price to be paid for taking a risk? For risking one's life—the life of this strange-looking Other? You see, what you do not see is her entire family, her many children, who with their father are this very minute in church where they pray to their Father Almighty, and not to Moses. What if one of her children, be it a little boy, or a little girl, squeals on him to one of the village elders?

Next thing you know a unit of SS might unexpectedly show up at her doorstep and, rifles in hand, ask her to show them the way to that illegally harbored Jew—that *ein kleiner Jude*.

He remembers the lesson of the Talmud his father gave him many a time: "Your life is more important than your neighbor's." End of quote. "Now, ponder this," his father would say here. "If this is what we Jews think of saving the life of another, why should we expect anyone—be it another Jew or even the nicest Gentile—to sacrifice his or her life, and risk at the hands of a Nazi the lives of an entire family, to save the life of another person, particularly if that person wasn't even their kin, and, as is your case, Norbert, does not even remotely look like a Gentile!"*

Suddenly, mindless of his safety, his peeing Tom begins to misbehave again. It begins to grow, threatening to be noticed. This threatens his safety; after all he is a Jew whose "peeing Tom must never be seen by any Gentile—particularly when he and you are both peeing together, even when peeing into the same Shibboleth, into the same river," says his mother to him on one memory slide after another. "Man's race is written not on man's face but, most unfortunately for some Jews, on man's member," his mother then says to his father and she says it as if Norbert could not hear. "You can change a family name, but you can never undo the circumcision. Never ever." In spite of such warning, his peeing Tom keeps on growing like that magic stalk growing out of a magician's transparent glass pot seconds after being planted there by the magician's voluptuously beautiful (and huge-breasted: J.K.) woman assistant—a nightclub act Norbert particularly admired as a boy of five, when he saw it first accompanied by his mother in a real, adult nightclub, mind you, not in some "overly obvious" children's circus.†

---

*Kosky's father combined the knowledge of the Buddha's Four Noble Truth and his Eightfold Path with the intimate sense of *Duties of the Heart* by that Jewish Buddhist Bahya Ibn Pakuda, conceived, or written, circa 1069, and the equally Buddhist *The Way of the Upright*, by Moses Hayyim Luzzatto (that eighteenth-century Jewish mystic. —Ed.).

†Because of her breasts, which she called "overly obvious," Elisabeth Kosky (née Weinreich: J.K.) never performed on a legitimate pianists' stage. Hence, she

The woman notices his magic act, but either it does not surprise her, or she doesn't show her surprise.

"Drop your pants," she says. "Let's peek at your peeing Tom." He obeys, and drops them promptly.

She looks at his male part as if it were a divination rod. Now she is truly surprised.

"My, my, I've never seen a skinned snake like that. Who cut you so horribly?" she exclaims, watching our Cagliostro, Jr., put on his overly tight pants with some difficulty. "What happened to you, my poor child?" she exclaims with tears in her eyes.

"Evoking real tears in an audience is a good artist's ultimate goal," Kosky hears his mother address him just before the War. "Any artist, not just a good pianist," he corrects himself. "Anybody who, for this reason or that, must play upon, or speak up from The Big Stage" (The Big Stage being his mother's euphemism for life in general).

SS

Good health is as relative as happiness; as phony as magic," Dr. Salvarsan says ominously during Kosky's return visit to his office. "You should know: aren't you the plot maker who conjures up illusion? Only the other day I saw you healthily demonstrating your sick literary wares on a talk show *Who's For or Against the Khazar Theory.** on my Cable TV."

" 'Why boys, I'm no magician. I do not do tricks. You have me all wrong. I'm just an actor!' " (Kosky quotes Frederick Tilden† as quoted by Harlan Tarbell.‡ "Never mind my magic. How is my health?"

"You're not exactly healthy. Nobody is, and that's why we all need

---

was drawn to any nightclub act which, in her words, "enhanced an independently rhythmic performance of the strippers' breasts."

*See "Six Arguments Against the Khazar Theory of the Origin of Eastern European Jewry" in *The Book of Jewish Lists*, by Ron Landau, 1984, p. 96. (While some of these arguments make some minor sense, the others are wholly unconvincing: J.K.) Here, as is often the case in the rest of this MS., these initials indicate Jay Kay, the protagonist of Kosky's never-quite-polished novel: J.K.)

†Frederick Tilden, a great stage magician, played the leading role of Alessandro di Cagliostro in *The Charlatan*.

‡Harlan Tarbell, "one of the greatest conjurers of the 20th century." (*Magic and Showmanship, a Handbook for Conjurers*, by Henning Nelms, 1969, p. 3)

doctors," says the doctor. "Just as well: Remember that, as Cioran says, 'A man of good health is always a creative disappointment to himself as well as to others, particularly to his physician.' In substance I regret to say there's nothing wrong with you." He glances offhandedly at the blood test. He smacks his lips, then says, "In reality, however, there's only one minor mental problem and this might rekindle your lost sense of life's never-ending drama."

"How minor?" Kosky asks, his lips suddenly dry. **Life doesn't pose problems. Man does. (Israel Kosky, 1945)**

"You've got the beginning of the Ganser Syndrome, so named after the guy who was the first to describe the symptoms of this whacky syndrome, and who described it as colorfully as if he were a novelist, and the syndrome invented just for him, not only by him. Today, this condition 'the pseudodementia caused by the overproduction of Malic acid' is primarily known as Malic disease—since, Malic, not Ganser, in order to make medical science more objective, the names of those doctors who often make up classysounding mental illnesses. Don't confuse it with the spiritually malignant Malison illness," says the good doctor. "Both conditions differ from each other as much as do such words as malice and malignancy—or, say, Svahili from Svengali."

"Malic disease?" our Svahili lisps.

"Yes. For some reason, your Adam's apple started to overproduce Malic acid. Heavily overproduce and for an unknown reason." He peeks into his file. "You've always had too much of it—for your age, the average norm is four to five—but it was still within the norm. Now it's over six! And nine tops the chart. To be exact, it is six point nine."

"What does Malic acid cause?"

"In most cases, it causes *Vorbeireden*, a condition defined by *Materia Medica* as an occasional need to be vague, or giving an approximate—even phony—answer rather than a yes or no—in order to improve one's image of oneself, or one's act, and by so doing forcing the spectators to believe they are witnessing an act of inspiration, not simple magic. *Vorbeireden* is commonly found among professional conjurers and artists, such as writers, who, in their act, depend on inner magic."

"Be brave, Doctor. Anything else?"

"Well, yes. In certain patients, this malaise is said to affect the working of the brain's *insula*—the peninsula of free speech, so to speak—as well as the area between the parietal and temporal lobes, the junction of the Creative Self, as we, the niggly medical psychics, call it."

77

"Anything else?"

"Malic disease can easily be considered a minor mental aberration, one which might or might not lead to Malison illness,* an illness which has nothing to do with either Malic acid or apples. 'Their malison was almost as terrible as the curse of a priest,' says G. Smith already in 1861, and he's right. Malison illness is a result of deficiency of creative estrogen which affects a person's entire being. Like anxiety, it is an illness of the spirit," the doctor goes on.

"Well?" Kosky paces the room. "How serious is my condition?"

"It depends on how seriously the sick man reacts to a healthy environment—or a sick environment to the healthy man. Both Jeanne d'Arc and Sabbatai Sevi suffered from it, and so did our own Commodore Perry and Captain Elliott, at least according to what J. Fenimore Cooper had to say about them both in his outrageous *Naval History of the United States*. (Cooper himself suffered from it: J.K.) President Andrew Johnson† was known to have contracted it. And, at the time of the Dreyfus Affair, most of Dreyfus's family, though, ironically, not Dreyfus himself." The very Dreyfus who, unimaginatively stolid, stolid, not just stoic, for a French Jew, until the end, still did not understand why he was hit: J.K.) Did you already see "The Dreyfus Affair" at the Jewish Museum?‡

"Have any writers other than J. Fenimore Cooper suffered from it?" Kosky paces the room while Dr. Salvarsan watches him calmly.

"Answer for yourself," says Dr. Salvarsan.

---

*First described circa 1320 in Sir Beaues 3969 as a malediction and curse. (*OED*)

†In 1868, had President Johnson been convicted on the strength of the voice of Stanton, that spiritual fifth-columnist, the moral voice of the American presidency would have been impeached with him. (Norbert Kosky, 1982)

‡"The Dreyfus Affair: Art, Truth and Justice," The Jewish Museum, New York, 1987. From the program: "The exhibition offers a view of the tempestuous history of the false accusation and conviction for treason of Captain Alfred Dreyfus, a French Army officer and a Jew. In 1894 Dreyfus was charged, on false evidence, of spying. He was solemnly degraded of his rank and condemned to perpetual imprisonment on Devil's Island. Four years later he was retried by appeal in Rennes, but still found guilty, this time with extenuating circumstances. Although the illegality of the first trial and insufficient evidence against him became widely known through public debate, *it was not until 1906* that Dreyfus was exonerated and subsequently reinstated in the Army with high honors."

Self-Centered Risk:

HEART ATTACK FROM THE PRONOUN "I"

Whether you focus more on yourself or upon the world outside could affect the health of your heart. Drs. Larry Scherwitz and Lewis Graham, of the UC San Francisco Medical Center, looked at the frequency with which people use self-references like "I," "me" and "my." Their findings: The less you use the first-person singular—the less self-involved you are—the lower your risk of coronary heart disease.

—*American Health*

"At this time there are no legally approved drugs for use in the diagnosis, cure, mitigation, treatment or prevention of Malic disease." Dr. Salvarsan closes Kosky's dossier. "Therefore the market is flooded with the spiritually spurious Tantric preparations." He pauses thoughtfully. "Don't be upset. You will live with this condition until you die— die not necessarily from it."

The doctor gets up and, taking Kosky by the arm, walks him to the door. Speaking about death, or even about **sex and character (Otto Weininger),** but in connection with death, even as Eros fucking Thanatos, is his way of showing his patients that, like the good life, the consultation must also eventually end.

Complete originality is rare. The most ingenious conjurer can spend a lifetime without hitting on a wholly new device or an entirely novel effect. Fresh illusions are another matter. (Henning Nelms) How true. Try, if you are a novelist, to devise a wholly new literary vice or a device, be it in a work of fiction or nonfiction; tough ticky—unless you're Dostoyevsky or Conrad, Nietzsche, Norwid, the love-obsessed Stendhal, or even Yehudah Halevi—"the greatest narrative master of them all." (Niskisko, 1982)* If through some cataclysmic catastrophe all Jewish books, from the Bible to the last Yiddish daily, were lost and only the *Book of the Kazari* remained, it would still be possible for the historian to faithfully reconstruct the diverse strands of thought and sentiment which enter into the making of the traditional Jewish mentality. (Jacob B. Agus) Tonight, wearing the hat of the Haunted

---

*Judah (or Yehudah) Halevi (or ha-Levi or Halevy, c. 1069 [or 1075]–1141): Jewish poet and philosopher born in Tudela, Spain. He is the author of the *Book of the Khazars* (or Kuzari), translated by Hartwig Hirschfeld, 1964. "The conversion of the King of the Khazars to Judaism is supposed to have taken place about the year 740, some four hundred years prior to the composition of Halevi's work (1130–1140). In Cordova, where the author lived and worked, the tale of the Khazars was a vivid reality, since a number of Jewish families in that city claimed descent from the Khazars. It was, therefore, quite natural for Halevi to relate his philosophy to the reputed triumph of the Jewish religion in the debate held at the court of Bulan, King of the Khazars." (*The Evolution of Jewish Thought from Biblical Times to the Opening of the Modern Era*, by Jacob B. Agus, London, New York 1959, pp. 260–261)

Conjurer, haunted by the Obeah Man's curse,* Kosky will experiment with switching literary routine. Tonight, right at 9:00 P.M. in one of his neighborhood's largest and fanciest mass-feeding restaurants, he will test whether an old magic disappearing act can be first adapted by him, then adopted as a literary trick.

Wearing a blond wig, a false nose and thick bifocal glasses, he chooses for the stage of his Self-test the brightly lit center table at the Elsie Venner restaurant located in tourist-infested central Manhattan.

All alone, he then waits for a waiter, building within himself a veritable wall of creative tension made of a massive dose of the magic of creating the suspension of disbelief. To him, to a "first-rate second-rate novelist," (Kosky on *David Mailman TV Show*, 1984, also in *Polityka*, 1987) such elementary, and, granted, often silly outings are as necessary as the *Heart of Darkness*. (Conrad)

This is his walking along *The Street of Crocodiles* (Bruno Schulz, also known as *Cinnamon Shops* [1934, 1963, 1985]). This is, in short, his short-cut from fiction to life and back to fiction—(a strange zigzagging between Manhattan's own folklore and East European fictional lore: Jay Kay). **The whole forest seemed to be illuminated by thousands of lights and by the stars falling in profusion from the December sky. The air pulsated with a secret spring, with the matchless purity of snow and violets. We entered a hilly landscape. The lines of hills, bristling with the bare spikes of trees, rose like sighs of bliss. I saw on these happy slopes groups of wanderers, gathering among the moss and the bushes the fallen stars which now were damp from snow. (Bruno Schultz, 1985 edition)**

Keep in mind also that such a bout with reality represents to Kosky what A *Stroll with William James* must have been to Jacques Barzun (himself a genius: Jay Kay). William James, brother of Henry, worked with Boris Sidis on the Boris Sidis theory of turning Bill into a Disraeli-like genius. Read "The Genius," a chapter in A *Stroll with William James*, by Jacques Barzun, 1983; pp. 263–302.

William James: [after whom Boris Sidis named his child. Boris Sidis was until Freud came along the best-known psychologist in the world: Ed.] a most pragmatic master and proponent of mental concentration fused with emotion. **It is impossible to conjecture what kind of psychology James would have developed if he had been an atheist like Freud,**

---

*The Obeah Man: a creature who, while inhabiting us, constantly attempts to make us look foolish by forcing us to lose our temper. (J.K.)

but it is certain—and I am devoting the rest of this book to demonstrating this argument—that if Freud had been a believer like James, he would not have developed psychoanalysis. (Peter Gay, 1987)*

The waiter shows up: an American wise guy. (Printer, don't confuse wisdom with wise: J.K.)

"Call me Smike," the wise guy says to Kosky. "What's your fancy tonight?" From some three feet away he tosses to Kosky a menu as if it were the antigravity hat.† This is Smike's magic act.

Kosky takes a look at the menu. "There's nothing on it I like," he says. "Can I have just a plate of thickly sliced North American raw onions mixed and covered with a few chunks of preferably Israeli-grown lemon?"

"Raw onions mixed with lemons? Are you nuts? That's pure acid rain! What are you going to do with all this shit?"

"It's my scurvy special," says Kosky. "I'm going to eat it! Eat it 'cause it's good for my gums." He pauses. "You see, what you can't see is that my gums were fatigued by the lack of food during World War II which, for your information, followed World War I as surely as one day World War III will follow Number Two unless something is done about it soon!"

Smike takes a long look at him. The look says, "Have it your way, nut! Nobody I know cares about the threat of war!"

The instant Smike leaves the table, Kosky bends down, as if searching for something, maybe a coin, maybe a comb, he's just dropped (He hasn't: J.K.) next to his table, the magician's purposefully audience-

---

*A Godless Jew: Freud, Atheism, and the Making of Psychoanalysis, 1987, pp. 30–31, A Godless Jew by Peter Gay does not dwell on explicit discussions of the evidence for and against Freud's theories or the efficacy of psychoanalysis while asking whether Freud's Jewish background and mature atheism determined the course of his life's work. As Freud himself once asked: "Why did none of the devout create psychoanalysis? Why did it have to wait for a completely godless Jew?"

"That such questions should fascinate Peter Gay is not surprising" writes John C. Marshall in a review under the heading "Mapping the States of Mind," Special Section of The New York Times Book Review, 1987.

†The antigravity hat: "A boy pours a cupful of liquid into a hat. This should be timed so that the magician almost catches him at it. The magician now does a number in which he wears his hat. But when he puts it on, the boy is disappointed—no water runs out." (Henning Nelms, Magic and Showmanship: A Handbook for Conjurers, op. cit., p. 69)

distracting routine. Then, when he's convinced nobody is paying any attention, to him or to his forthcoming action, our artful dodger drops out of sight—that's his act—by literally dipping under the table, the tablecloth opening for him, then closing behind, like a parenthesis. Our smoothie does it fast. Our speedy does it smoothly. No wonder! He does it the way he used to do it as a kid, except that then, doing it in the Pripet, at the sudden sight of a stranger, or of anyone who was unfriendly, or an outright enemy, he would drop out of sight, like a straw thrown into a nearby haystack, or nature-made gazebo. Doing his disappearing act, then, he was full of fear—fear of being caught by the Germans or other Nazis—while now, testing himself against an un-suspecting, (here, unsuspecting means a well-meaning audience) he's merely full of himself: of his acting, reacting and over-acting Self.

Shielded from view by the tablecloth and the chairs, our literary magician-turned-into-a-W.W.II-rare-beast-called-survivor,* remains there, all scrunched up, watching and waiting for a psychic shock— a syncopal kick, Nabokov called it—a shock as much his own as Smike's.

In the "search for oneself," in the search for "sincere self-expression," one gropes, one finds some seeming verity. One says "I am" this, that, or the other, and with the words scarcely uttered one ceases to be that thing. I began this search for the real in a book called *Personae*, casting off, as it were, complete masks of the self in each poem. (Ezra Pound)

From under the table, our minimal Selft Boy sees Smike's feet as the waiter returns to the table.

---

*Himmler had declared that it was the mission of the German people to destroy the Polish people (in what he termed a "delayed genocide": J.K.). He predicted the "disappearance of the Poles from the world." To a significant degree, Himmler's prediction came true. Besides the massive hardships endured by the Polish people under Nazi occupation, about 5,000,000 non-Jewish Poles were forced into slave labor by the Nazis. Furthermore, about 2,200,000 non-Jewish Poles were system-atically murdered.

The number of Poles—Jews and non-Jews—in German-occupied Poland was about 22,000,000. Of these, about 3,000,000 Jewish Poles and 2,200,000 non-Jewish Poles were murdered. Adding the 5,200,000 enslaved Poles, almost one of every two Poles (i.e., Polish subjects: J.K.) in Nazi-occupied Poland was either enslaved or murdered by the Nazis. (*Encountering the Holocaust*, by Byron Sherwin and David Weinberg, op. cit.)

†See Chapter Two, "The Survival Mentality," which appropriately for our nu-

"Have you seen this blond onion freak who ordered this crap from me?" Smike asks someone as, scarcely two feet from Kosky's feet-sniffing nose, Smike's feet perform another step-balancing act.

"We didn't see anyone there," says a woman at a neighboring table and you can hear the all-American sincerity in her Texas-made voice.

"I think the guy got up and left," says a man from behind and he too says the truth as he has seen it—(or has not but doesn't know it: J.K.).

"Oh, fuck that onionhead," Kosky hears Smike moan while the waiter's feet carry him and the onion platter away from Kosky's table.

If I were to reduce all my feelings and their painful conflicts to a single name, I can think of no other word but: dread. It was dread, dread and uncertainty, that I felt in all those hours of shattered childhood felicity: dread of punishment, dread of my own conscience, dread of stirrings in my soul which I considered forbidden and criminal. (Herman Hesse, *A Child's Heart*)* Just when Smike is about six feet away, our Hermann the Great† emerges from under the table as fast as a live pigeon miraculously flying out of the Magic Cauldron filled to the brim with steaming water boiling over a pigeon dummy.

"What's wrong, Smike?" Kosky calls to the waiter, and he does it sitting at his table as calmly as if he had never left it. Hearing him, Smike stops midway, then turns his head, a polo pony stopped in full gallop on a mere dime.

A strong experience in the present awakens in the creative writer a memory of an earlier experience (usually belonging to his childhood) from which there now proceeds a wish which finds its fulfilment in the creative work. The work itself exhibits elements of the recent provoking occasion as well as of the old memory. (Freud)

"Where were you?" Crying his eyes out over the platter, the waiter walks back to the table.

"What do you mean where *was* I?" asks Kosky. **When acting, play**

---

merological hero begins on page 60 and ends on page 99, in *The Minimal Self: Psychic Survival in Troubled Times,* by Christopher Lasch (1984).

*As quoted in *Prisoners of Childhood: The Drama of the Gifted Child and the Search for the True Self,* by Alice Miller (1981), p. 96.

†Hermann the Great (died 1896) adopted the Inexhaustible Bottle as well as Divination or Second Sight, both magical stage routines invented by Robert Houdin.

your point of view of the character, not the character. (Vakhtangov)

"You weren't here!" Smike puts the plate on the table. Is it the onion or anger that makes his eyes water?

"Of course I was here," says Kosky. "How did you know it was my *onion con limone* unless I was here to order it?"

"You were not! You know what I mean," says Smike warily. He watches Kosky cut a lemon, then an onion, and when Kosky eats both pieces without any change of expression, the waiter's face contorts. "How can you eat it like that?" he says, sitting down at Kosky's table, salivating like a breast-sucking infant.

"Why not? It's a great onion. Compliments to the chef."

The waiter keeps swallowing fast the rush of saliva. "That's some food! Are you into some new safe-sex food-magic?"

"How did you know?" says our idyllist, swallowing another round of round onion ring, juicily dipped in the freshly squeezed lemon. **The man is either crazy or he is a poet. (Horace)**

"The disappearing act. Not bad! Not bad at all."

"Disappearing is easy. Reappearing can be a bad lemon indeed," says Kosky. **I must run away. I must hide. (William James Sidis)**

"Where did you learn the trick?" asks Smike (starting with his question, page 96 in Kosky ms. draft no. 6).

"I learned it as a kid, running away from the Nazi SS."

"Could I learn it, too?"

"You might not want to learn it. People don't like to be fooled," says Kosky.

"Unless they know that they are," says Smike. "Then they like it."

"Quite so," says Kosky. Testing himself even further, he says pointedly to the waiter, "Each time I take off my toupee in the presence of a woman I have just met, she screams as if she was being scalped alive." Here, quite noticeably, he pats himself with both hands on his head, as if checking whether his wig is still in place. (It's such fun to be blond and so full-haired: J.K.) In spite of this, Smike fails even to look at Kosky's hair.

"Once upon a time"—Kosky keeps on testing his narrative SAM missiles—"I was invited with some other guests to the Industran Embassy in Washington, D.C., for a bash given there by the Imperator and Empress of Industran for the Israeli Ambassador Sevi-Effendi and his missus. A big bash. A lot of secret service, too. Israeli, American, and Industran's own PERSAUD not to mention many others too secret to

85

be seen or mentioned. Now, imagine the very tense moment: everybody awaits the arrival of their Royal Highnesses. No cameras or TV allowed—only tension. Suddenly, when they arrive—when the Imperator and the Empress enter the room—when everybody, even Secret Service men, turns to look at them, at this splendidly so feudal pair, I quickly slide along the backrest and under the pillows of a huge sofa. I pull the pillows over my body and there I wait, lying on my back like a lizard. I learned this trick when I was a green toad."

6: "To refrain from imitation is the best revenge." (Marcus Aurelius, *Meditations*, Book Six, #6)

"Nobody sees you?" Smike no longer minds the sight and smell of Kosky's onions. "Nobody? Not even the PERSAUD's Secret Service?"

"Nobody. I know my timing better than does PERSAUD," says Kosky, ending on this phrase his spiritually spiral page 96.

"I'm surprised. I really am. With all that Secret Service all around I still kind of can't suspend my disbelief, if you know what I mean by this."

"I do. I used to teach drama," Kosky winks at him. "But, you see, in my act, I'm pretty secret myself." What you don't see, buddy, is that **On such a night, unique in the year, one has happy thoughts and inspirations, one feels touched by the divine finger of poetry. Full of ideas and projects, I wanted to walk toward my home, but met some school friends with books under their arms. They were on their way to school already, having been wakened by the brightness of that night that would not end. (Bruno Schulz, 1934, 1985)**

"I see what you mean. Tell me what happened next." Smike swallows the narrative hook, while Kosky keeps on chewing on his Haifa-grown Israeli lemon.

"Well, then, first the Imperator sits down on the sofa; then the Empress, then the Ambassador and his wife. All these excellencies and highnesses sit propped against my body!"

"Propped against you? Against this bony bird body?" Smike chokes on the story. "I don't believe a word of this, but go on. It's too good not to be true. Tell me what happens next." He is hooked.*

"At first, nothing," says Kosky. "At first they all sit and talk—in French and in English—and have their drinks brought to them by Secret

---

*See *Hasidic Tales of the Holocaust*, by Yaffa Eliach (New York: Oxford University Press, 1982).

Service waiters and their photographs taken by Secret Service photographers. Then . . ."

Smike falls into a narrative trap. "Then—what?"

"Then, from behind the cushions—and through them—I start to nudge them. Ever so gently. First, I nudge His Excellency Ambassador Sevi-Effendi. After all, he is the guest of honor!"

"Nudge him? How?"

"By kicking his ass with my foot," says Kosky. "By kicking him once, then twice. Then three times. Nothing! He won't even budge."

"Maybe he didn't feel the kick," sys Smike, who, by saying *didn't*, shifts by his question, the question of pain—of feeling the kick—into past tense.

"The Ambassador feels it, all right," says Kosky, who keeps on testing his first-person-present-tense narration. "From under the pillow, seeing nothing and barely hearing their talk, with my mind's eye I can almost *see him feeling it*. I feel him fidgeting. He moves a bit too earnestly to the left for a rather liberal Israeli, then for an Israeli, by far too far to the conservative right, but he won't look to find out who in the center is kicking! In moments like these, being an Israeli is not enough. In moments like these you've got to be as imaginative as was that smartass of a novelist turned British prime minister, so appropriately named Disraeli.* He is, in short, a typical diplomat! trained by Sri Swami Rama."†

"I wonder why?" says the waiter. "Maybe he thought you were a secret agent assigned to protect his ass. Still, why didn't he do something? For instance, why do you suppose he didn't scream?" Smike keeps on hanging onto the past tense.

"Because he's wise enough to know how to ignore a mere kick in the ass, as long as the kick does not soil the couch." Kosky hangs on to the present.

---

*Benjamin Disraeli's father, Isaac D'Israeli, was an English critic and historian (who clearly architected his son's unprecedented march to spiritual victory: J.K.) His best-known work is *Curiosities of Literature* (6 Vol. 1791–1834) and a variety of "literary and historical anecdotes and original material." (*The New Columbia Encyclopedia*, 1975) (Wrote Kosky on Oct. 10, 1987 in the margin: Read study by J. Ogden [1969])

†See *Exercise Without Movement*, manual one, as taught by Sri Swami Rama of the Himalayas, 1984.

"I bet he did nothing, not because he was diplomatic, but because he thought he was being tested," volunteers Smike. "In any case, you were lucky. If he so much as screamed or yelled or jumped up at the sight of you, all three secret services would have pumped so many bullets into those cushions and you'd have become a cushion yourself. So tell me what happens next?" He now asks by adopting Kosky's narrative present tense.

"Well, when the Ambassador does nothing, I start to nudge—to kick, if you will—the next person in line."

"Don't tell me you kicked the Imperator himself," says Smike. "Because if you do, I won't believe one word of it."

"This is exactly the next thing I do," says Kosky. "But just for the sake of my inner public opinion poll, tell me why won't you believe me?"

"Because he doesn't call himself the almighty for nothing."

"Almighty or not, I do kick him, once twice, and when he does nothing I kick him again. He still doesn't respond. Only then do I decide to kick the lovely Empress—right in her behind. Mind you, at this time in my most personal Book of Lists she was listed as one of the world's six most beautiful women." I should have been born, your Imperial Majesty, not in Russia, but somewhere in the forests of America, among the Western colonists, there where civilization has scarcely dawned and where all life is a ceaseless struggle against wildmen, wild nature, and not in an organized civil society. Also, had fate wished to make me a sailor from my youth, I would now probably be a very respectable man; I would not have thought of politics and would have sought no other adventures and storms than those of the sea. But fate did not will either the one or the other, and my need for movement and activity remained unsatisfied. (Mikhail Bakunin to Tsar Nicholas I, 1851)

"She sure is a beauty. What a piece of ass! So what's next?"

"Well, next I kick her through the pillow once. Kick her most graciously—but, since a kick is a kick, a bit horsely. (A bit, printer, not a bet!) In writing one doesn't bet on a word; one chooses it. (Kosinski, 1982). Well, after the kick I wait for a while, and when she doesn't respond I kick her again. Once, then twice. Nothing. Finally, after a third and most final kick—by now I'm all sweat, slowly suffocating under these heavy pillows, and under the weight of the sitters, weighing upon me, I feel her twitch! Twitch, ethereally, but twitch." (Like most Ruthenians who cannot pronounce the Anglo-Saxon *th*, Kosky strains when pronouncing the word *ether*, but then, a realist by nature, he has no trouble with the word *really*.)

"You felt her ethereal ass twitch, not her," Smike corrects him, inadvertently becoming one of some 669 of Kosky's unacknowledged privately hired secretaries, proofreaders and in-line book editors.

"I feel her ass twitch," Kosky gladly incorporates the correction. "And, if this isn't enough, I feel her warmth."

"You feel her heat. Heat, not warmth. Heat from her ass, you worm!" Smike corrects him again.

"I feel her heat." A pedantic character, our literary correction officer Kosky loves corrections. "I keep feeling it spread all through the pillow. As a result I'm in heat, too."

"Maybe she thinks she's being goosed by the Israeli ambassador," Smike says. "Maybe she thinks he is making a pass at her."

"I doubt that. Anyway, I wait a minute and just as she is saying, 'We find America to be so full of surprises,' I kick her really hard and right in the middle of the sentence!" Kosky pauses. "Only then, only after she completes her thought, do I feel a response on the first period appearing on page 100 of his ms. draft no. 6. I feel something creeping under the pillow."

"Oh, no! Oh, no!" Smike moans.

"Oh, yes!" says Kosky. "It is her hand, no doubt about it. Her perfectly narrow royal hand. I feel her royal fingers creep along my leg—higher and higher."

"I bet she grabs you by—" Smike can't wait.

"She grabs me by my cuff." Here, our conjurer willingly lifts the suspension of disbelief.

"By your calf? Or by your cuff? I don't get your Punjabi accent." Smike strains.

"By my calf. Right by my ankle!" says Kosky. "And—I promise you— she digs inch-long nails into my flesh. All the way. Now I'm in pain— but I won't budge!"

"You were lucky the Empress didn't try to move her sweet little hand any higher. And root you out by your root," says Smike. "But go on— what's next?"

"Next, I start to fidget. Next, I put my hand out and very gently tap the Ambassador's back. At first, he is startled. He thinks he's being patted by the Emperor and this is my chance to survive all this little drama without being killed like the biggest fool that ever was. Just when the Ambassador starts sliding his body off the pillow that presses against my head, I squeeze my body out and crawl from under the pillows head first—crawl out, breathless, my tuxedo all messed-up and no black tie, which I lost under the pillows. The second I hit fresh air I hold up my hands in the universal sign of surrender (just think how many non-Jews surrendered during World War II!) and scream, all smiles, of course, 'SHALOM! I'M A JEW. DON'T SHOOT. THIS IS ONLY A TEST. A TEST FOR MY NEXT NOVEL.' I say, 'Shalom! I AM A JEW. Don't shoot. **It is difficult to find a single definition of a Jew. A Jew is one who accepts the faith of Judaism. That is the *religious* definition. A Jew is one who, without formal religious affiliation, regards the teachings of Judaism—its ethics, its folkways, its literature—as his own. That is the *cultural* definition. A Jew is one who considers himself a Jew or is so regarded by his community. That is the *practical* definition. (Rabbi Morris N. Kertzer)** It is only a test! This is a test—please don't shoot!', I keep on screaming. Of course now they all jump—the Imperator, the Imperatrice, the Ambassador, and the Ambassador's wife, not to mention the PERSAUD men descending on me, their guns drawn! Thank Yod that, just then, everybody starts laughing. Laughing 'cause they know me. Laughing 'cause they have seen my number before. And so I get a salvo of laughter—instead of that other salvo!"

"And so the Secret Service men all laugh, now, and they all love you all the way to dinner, right?" Smike begs for a happy ending.

"I wouldn't say love, and certainly not all the way," our Ruthenian **outcast of the islands (Conrad, 1896)** ends, cryptic at best, (his manuscript page 101.)*

---

*See "In the Kingdom of Conrad," a chapter (pp. 64–90) in *American Nights Entertainment*, by Grant Overton (New York, 1923). See also Conrad's photograph on page 65 and how "out of that uncouth time and those bizarre experiences the man Conrad has got back certain pages in *The Mirror of the Sea*, pages that we all remember" p. 69).

9

"*Helena Powska arrives in New York,*"
reads a short one-line item in the *Daily Ruthenian,* a copy of which
Kosky finds on Times Square. Her name rings an instant bell. **Słow są
bez poręczy: Words have no banisters. (Jerzy Peterkiewicz)***
Helena Powska is a Ruthenian poet, and when it comes to poetry
Kosky is a Ruthenian at heart; **poets are born, not paid. (Wilson Mizner)**
No bad man can be a good poet, said Boris Pasternak, and he was partly
right. Partly because neither can a bad woman.

> How can I calm myself—
> full of fear are these eyes of mine,
> full of terror these thoughts of mine,
> full of shudders these lungs of mine,
> full of panic this heart of mine—
> How can I calm myself?
> (Stanisław Wyspiański)

He remembers a large photograph of her he saw published on the
cover of *Today's Ruthenia,* the official English-language publication
published by the Ruthenian Ministry of Culture and distributed freely
in the free West.

---

*In *Five Centuries of Polish Poetry 1450–1970*: Second Edition, compiled by
Jerzy Peterkiewicz and Burns Singer with new translations by Jerzy Peterkiewicz
and Jon Stallworthy (1971), p. 68.

In the picture Powska poses next to a snow-capped Ruthenian *dacha* wearing a Zakopane* fur hat and a black leather sleeveless tunic which reveals the outline of her breasts, and low-heeled leather boots. "Take her poetry away from her, and—judging by her looks alone, she could be the Slavic Leg Slut, a Russian model who recently posed in various stages of sexual undress of the bimonthly Leg Show magazine under these totalitarian words: "Maybe because I am a Russian I need to dominate my men. I want them to feel like worms, like filthy disgusting dogs. I want them to feel totally worthless. Because I love them."

He knows her poetry only too well—he once tried to translate it into English but failed: only a poet who knows the value of silence can translate a poet. † **Perfect lyric poetry should be like a cast in plaster: the slashes where form passes form, leaving crevices, must be preserved and not smoothed out with the knife. Only the barbarian takes all this off from the plaster with his knife and destroys the whole. (Norwid)‡** He gets her phone number, and calls her. In Ruthenian he introduces himself to her. "It's the language of my sexual prime," he tells her. "Your Ruthenian poems talk to me with the voice of my beloved Pripet, the voice I first heard within me during my never-to-be-forgotten wartime years, an inner voice out of which came my first work of fiction," our phoney keeps whispering seductively into the phone, but Helena does not emotionally reply. **Man acts as if he were the shaper and master of language, while it is language which remains mistress of man. When this relation of dominance is inverted, man succumbs to strange contrivances. (George Steiner, 1975)**

He invites her to join him for either a "casually relaxed" lunch—or a stately, though not "totalitarian," dinner—at the American Relax—

---

*Zakopane is a Polish ski resort.

†"A contemporary translator may look back upon an old and praiseworthy tradition. Among his most remote predecessors are the Greek translators of the Old Testament, the so-called Septuagint, and Livius Andronicus, whose Latin translation of the *Odyssey* is regarded as the beginning of original Latin literature. Translators were in many epochs the first creators of national literary languages," writes Jan Parandowski in "On the Significance and the Dignity of the Translator," and as a past chairman of Polish P.E.N. he knows what he is talking about. (*On the Art of Translation* in Polish, 1955, a collection of essays by Poland's top translators delivered at seminars of Polish P.E.N., 1950–1953)

‡As quoted by Jerzy Peterkiewicz, op. cit., p. 69.

the downtown literary café, where, allegedly, in 1860, Emerson wrote his *Illusions*.

> Know the stars yonder,
> The stars everlasting,
> Are fugitive also. . . .
> Flow, flow the waves hated,
> Accursed, adored,
> The waves of mutation;
> No anchorage is.
>
> (Emerson)

Calmly, Helena turns down his invitation. "Not today," she says. "Maybe some other time." He calls again, and is again turned down. "I'm running out of time. I can't waste my time. Not today." One more call: "Would she like to go with him to the Audubon Society Birds' Calls Exhibition at the Academy of Spiritual Art at the Leo Baeck world-famous New York art gallery owned by the super-rich Ribnitzer family. Ribnitzers initially came to Ameica from Rybnice in Ruthenia and they *all* descend from Ribnitzer Rebbe who was born in 1369," our humming bird tells her humming like a Bird of Passion.

"I'm not into visual art," she tells him. "And, I'm neither a bird nor a Ribnitzer watcher."

"Don't you like bluebirds?" asks our *Barbe Bleue*. (Bluebeard: J.K.)

"I don't like bluebirds like you," she tells him straight into his ear. "Particularly, when they turn yellow."

"Is it 'cause I'm Jewish?" He does the unfair trick of implying the presence of a yellow star when there is none.

"Not at all," she snaps back. "After reading Tuwim, Slonimski and Leśmian (the names of some of the greatest poets who happened to be Polish-Jewish: J.K.) at least half of my poetic blood is Jewish and it flows with the speed of Julian Tuwim's *Lokomotywa*, which I memorized as a kid, like every Jewish and non-Jewish kid in Ruthenia. Simply, I won't go on a *randka na slepo* (Ruthenian for blind date) with you."

"Why?"

"Because, *moj drogi Pani* (my dear sir: J.K.), in my private dictionary the name Norbert Kosky is synonymous with Ruthenian renegade," she says and then hangs up on him with a smash—(on him, until now, the most smashing literary cavalier: Jay Kay)

Renegade—a harsh word even for a Ruthenian Kos*—a migrating bird of linguistic prey. As a poet, Helena chooses her words carefully. Renegade, you see, might refer to one's loyalty, not to one's capacity for betrayal. **The special loyalty of the renegade seems to me to rest on the fact that the circumstances under which he enters the new relationship have a longer and more enduring effect than if he had naively grown into it, so to speak, without breaking with a previous one. (Simmel)**

In Ruthenia, where the saber is the country's national symbol (as it is in neighboring Poland, as any Sarmatian painting will testify)† a poet is a spiritual fencer. Poetic language is Helena's saber.

Does Helena call him a Ruthenian renegade because, to her, he abandoned Ruthenia, the country of his dominant language and its 969-year-old culture and tradition? Or is he to her a renegade as a writer, because, *kos* that he is, he has migrated from Ruthlandia,‡ leaving behind the Ruthenian language, the idiom of his adolescent past, to English, the idiom of his exile?

There, in Eastern Europe, the Jewish people came into its own. It did not live like a guest in somebody else's house, who must constantly keep in mind the ways and customs of the host. There Jews lived without reservation and without disguise, outside their homes no less than within them. (Abraham Joshua Heschel)

Disguised as a Hasidic Don Quixote, with his toupee, beard, mustache and sunglasses firmly in place, Kosky waits for Helena outside her hostel. Finally she emerges and goes for a walk. He follows her for a moment. **Again and again, the Gospels resemble a palimpsest: new things have, as it were, been written over the old tidings. But on the whole it is nevertheless possible to get back to the original tradition.**

---

*In Ruthenian, *kos* means *minos polyglottos*—a mockingbird—and *kosa* means a scythe (J.K.).

†For the origins of Sarmatian paintings, see *The Polish Way: A Thousand-Year History of the Poles and their Culture*, by Adam Zamoyski, 1987, p. 196.

See also *Sarmatism and the Ottoman Empire* (ibid., pp. 189–206).

‡Throughout the text Norbert Kosky willingly confuses Ruthlandia (the official name of the Ruthenian People's Republic) with Ruthenia, which until the War, was an integral part of Poland. [Estate Editors]

(Leo Baeck, *Judaism and Christianity*, 1958) He finds her: *faultless* is the word, but how could he describe her? He often asks himself such questions. Yes, he could. He could, but only if he could find his English alchemical word compound which would combine the genius of Cyprian Kamil Norwid, his favorite Polish-language poet, with the French flavor of flawed flowers of evil found only in the "obscenely gifted."*

"You look so lovely." Speaking his *unisonized* version of the Valais Swiss-French, he modifies his inner trembling as well as his voice's volume, bass and treble. Our mini-Baudelaire blocks her path like a persistent human semicolon found on the steps of a colonnade. "As lovely as fall. Fall in Lake Tear of the Clouds on Mount Mercy. That's in the Adirondacks—not far from New York!" A foreigner himself, he enunciates like a foreigner who speaks with a French accent. **Heart— a trembling gauge so shoddily made. (Halina Poświatowska, 1966)**

"Sorry?" she replies. "Please have mercy! Don't laugh at my crooked English. When Conrad arrived in England at twenty, he knew English only barely, and look what he did with it a few bare years later! Now that's what I call concentration!† For me, English still has too many clouds too many clouds and still not enough tears. In English, I can't swim—not even in the lake of my own tears," she stammers. "But I am not so cloudy in French!"

---

*". . . It is along such a path that some investigators find similarities between Norwid and Baudelaire, or even with the French philosopher P. S. Ballanche, as well as with some others among Norwid's French and English contemporaries. We ourselves would be much more inclined to look at Norwid's models among the Italian writers of Christian Humanism beginning with Dante, to Manzoni and Mazzini. Italy was for Norwid a second homeland which was, it seems to us, a constant source of his artist inspiration," writes Olga Nedelkovic in *The Polish Review* (1986).

†"During his whole life, Conrad kept a strong foreign accent, as strong as his accent on universal principles of justice (which to him, a Briton yet a Pole of 96 percent, was feasibly synonymous with the sound of free falling water and why not: "let justice roll down like waters, and righteousness like a mighty stream" [Amos 5:24]: Jay Kay). His manners also remained quite Polish. . . . Everyone noticed Conrad's polish manners [polished—as well as Polish. —Jay Kay] writes Gustav Morf in "The English Shock," Chapter 10 of his *The Polish Shades and Ghosts of Joseph Conrad* (ISBN: 0-913994-20-0). What nobody noticed was the creative role of his wife (a British *lassie* who spiritually—spiritually, not sexually—maintained that mildly asexual Polish literary mole: Jay Kay).

"French? You speak French? Hey, that's great! *Quelle chance! Par hazard*, I speak it, too!" Our Hasidic cowboy bows gallantly, then introduces himself in French as Monsieur Georges Flotsam. "I spend most of my leisure time in Montcrans, a ski'nd golf high-mountain town in Valais, in French-speaking Switzerland. Between the medieval ruins of Sion and the famous medieval church in Raron, perhaps the two most moving sights in all the Alps." **The Acropolis does not overhang Athens in a more kingly style than these rocks frown upon the humbler town of Sion, nor do I believe that the architecture of the former, however pure and classical, is half as picturesque. [James Fenimore Cooper]***

"Flotsam?" she repeats.

"Flotsam." He catches sight of himself in a shop window. Is his South Korean toupee in place? Will the Hong Kong mustache and his goatee made in Thailand peel off in the heat of the day?

"In Ruthenian, *sam* means solo," she says in French. "In Ruthenian, *Flotsam* means one who is a solo floater. But isn't Flotsam an unusual name for a Swiss, a man of spikey mountains—not of water? Even the Swiss franc hates to float!" **Now only he began to feel, rather than see, the unequaled formation of her brow, gleaming with the whiteness of snow or of a block of Carrara marble, a brow which housed unknown thoughts, unfamiliar, subtle, beautiful, like music coming out of the darkness of night, and young as the billows of a wellspring. (Stefan Zeromski)**

"It is unusual," he admits, explaining that his own name keeps washing off him like water. And each time it does, he becomes aware of the rock underneath. He is, he tells her, a man who survived World War II saved by rock and water. Rock and water is the essence of Switzerland. "Rock'nd water *jamais pas* rock and roll!" he reassures the conservative in her.

"Explain to me by whom you were saved. By whom, not by what!" she commands him in her sudden English.

"By the most friendly, simple and Gentile people," he tells her, again fusing gentle with Gentile. "But I can't name names! You see, *made-*

---

*See also Sion, the capital of Valais. "The Beginnings of Christianity in Sion," in *Zermatt and the Valais* by Sir Arnold Lunn, 1955. (Since the Conqueror's coronation in 1066 was marred by most destructive riots, Ermefroy, Bishop of Sion, visited England in 1069, in order to crown the Conqueror again in 1070: J.K.)

moiselle," he takes her by the arm and, pressing his arm against hers, feels her warmth—a warmth emanating, no doubt, from her most moist womb, but also from her own post–World War II Stalinist wound.

"By how many people were you saved *en Suisse* during the War?" She looks him over, then looking over him, she turns one eye to history.

"This I cannot tell you, *mademoiselle.*"*

"You see, *mademoiselle,*" he goes on, "perhaps we, the Swiss, were *overly* neutral during the War, but even so, we are most humane. Because we know that *naming names* most often hurts those named and often maims them—maims, or even kills, we've substituted a number for one's name and coined a secret numbered account—a new coin indeed. Also remember that the Swiss were first to judicially declare in Sion—or was it in Bern—in 1935 that *The Protocols of the Elders of Zion* was a forgery *antisioniste!*"

"I understand—do not explain any longer," she cuts him off. "I come from Ruthenia. Like Poland, Ruthenia once was the world's biggest Commonwealth of Tolerance. Ask any Mason or Protestant," she stops him dead. "Oh, *mon dieu!*" she exclaims. "Here you tell me so much about your Swiss universal self and I forget to share with you my name."

Her name is Helena Powska, she introduces herself. And she is a published poet, she admits with pride.

She is also a member of Ruthenian P.E.N.—an ultimate honor. No wonder she writes poetry about men's penultimate fall, she says, stressing the word *pen*, a word so dear to every writer. † Only Rilke would know what she means. **We writers are in some sort trustees for human nature;**

---

*See *He Who Saves One Life: The Complete Documented Story of the Poles Who Struggled to Save Jews During World War II*, by K. Iranek Osmecki, 1987.

†An intended pen pun. P.E.N. stands for Poets, Playwrights, Essayists, Editors and Novelists. It is an international association of penultimate writers. Initially started in England by Mrs. Dawson Scott and John Galsworthy, the American Center was founded in 1922 by Robert Frost, Marc Connelly, Walter Lippmann and Eugene O'Neill. ("Booth" Tarkington was the first president of the American P.E.N. and Susan Sontag presided over this most venerable literary union at the time Kosky penned his novel No. 9: J.K.) A year sadly marred in American literary history by the death of B. J. (for Beatrice Joy) Chute, (1913–1987) the author of such splendidly crafted works as *Greenwillow*, ETC., and *The Good Woman*. "And the pen-ultimate president and chronicler of the American P.E.N. Center." (Jerzy Kosinski, 1987)

97

if we are narrow and prejudiced we harm the human race. And the better we know each other ... the greater the chance of human happiness in a world not, as yet, too happy. (Galsworthy)

"Rilke died in Switzerland," says Kosky. "He is buried at Raron, not far from Valpina, where I live. His grave has been a veritable tourist attraction. People of all languages come to it and stare at it as if Rilke was Elvis and his grave a naked pin-up girl."

Without instinct of migratory birds, we are not whole. Featherless and tardy, coercing winds, we sparkle at lagoons, without welcome. (Rilke)

"Did you know that Rilke suffered from incurable TB that made him feverish?" says Helena in English, then, catching Kosky's stare, she returns to speaking French. "That each time he even looked at a woman's breast or thigh his fever would shoot up—and, suddenly mute— mute either in German or French, the two languages his soul loved most—he would start talking in body language—and watching the body language of everybody else, as long as the everybody was a woman.* Do you know"—she changes *did* to *do* in English, then goes on in French—"that in order to avoid breathing TB germs at each other, Rilke and his lovers (and had many of them, *very many*) made love facing each other in the mirror, and not face to face. That, in the lingo of the terminally ill, I know a great deal about it," she assures him, "those healthy men and women who prey on making love to the victims of terminal illness are called hyenas? Can you imagine"—she now shifts to speaking English again as if afraid to say too much in her more fluent French—"That each time Rilke loved a woman—each time he *physically* made love to her," she corrects herself—"he knew he was, *physically* speaking, speeding up his death, his book of hours?"

They have walked for over an hour. She is pale, she is tired. But she wants to keep on walking. She wants to "know all of Manhattan before it is too late, before I'll be able to transfer what I know into words.

---

*"Sexual activity consists in speaking what we might call 'body language.' It has its own grammar, delineated by the body, and its own phonetics of touch and movement. Its unit of meaningfulness, the bodily equivalent of a sentence, is the *gesture* . . . body language is essentially expressive, and its content is limited to interpersonal attitudes and feelings." (Robert Solomon in *Sexual Paradigms*, as quoted by Janice Moulton in *Sexual Behavior: Another Position*, pp. 110–18 of *The Philosophy of Sex: Contemporary Readings*, edited by Alan Soble, 1980)

98

Words and images. Poetry is not only words, you know. Poetry is visual—it is, unlike other writings, full of inner images," she says and as she says it she sweats.

She is trembling from cold. Cold in the eighty-nine-degree heat?

Helena recites a poem of Rilke in a Ruthenian translation. Can he, a Swiss who doesn't know Ruthenian, guess by its sound which poem it is?

He listens, watchful, watching every move of her full lips. He pretends not to know. Then he asks her to recite it for him again.

"It was 'L'Étranger'—the stranger. My favorite Rilke poem," she says.

"It is my favorite because it makes me feel so universally true. And now—how about you?" For the first time she takes him by the hand, but then, too soon, she lets his hand go.

They walk again. Each time he touches her a Tantric shiver runs along his spine, and so he touches her often. Touches her with his hands, or elbows, or even with his bony hip, but this is not enough. He must be able to touch her with words. The words so well chosen she would cling to him through them. It is Kosky's turn. He recites, in his—and Rilke's—Swiss-French a few lines of Rilke's poem "Eros."

Here our hipster scores—and how! Helena listens with her eyes closed. She listens to him the way he listens to Patrick Domostroy, the pianist, playing Chopin's great A-flat Polonaise. Then, looking at Kosky attentively, she wonders aloud how good this French translation of Rilke is. After all, a German poet, Rilke wrote in German.

She is wrong, Kosky tells her. "Eros" is not a translation. It is one of several poems Rilke wrote in French. By doing so, Rilke proved that, had he wanted to, he could have been a French poet or a German-French poet. He could have, in fact, been recognized as the greatest French-language poet (French, not German!) who had ever lived. Recognized as such at least by French-speaking Valais. [After Manhattan and Beulah University in Waterbury, Connecticut, the Swiss-French speaking Valais was Norbert Kosky's favorite. Ed.] After all, Rilke spent the last years of his life in French-speaking Valais. **The only true exile is the writer who lives in his own country. (Julio Cortázar)**

Helena is surprised. She didn't know, or did she? She can't remember. Not now, anyhow. She is tired. Let's talk more. Let's talk of prose, she pleads with him. While poetry sings to the heart, prose is serious. It's all a matter of heart, you know.

"My whole life has been dramatically twisted. It feels so unnatural from within. By within I mean my mechanical body, not my ephemeral Self," she says, waving her hand aimlessly. "Ever since I was a child, my heart has threatened to stop. *To stop dead*. It has misfired ever since it first fired. Do you know that in order to slow my heart, to slow it down, I've never climbed hills? Never skied? Never swum? Never played volleyball or tennis?"

"I know what you mean. I too have a chronic problem." He dismisses her terminal story with a terminal story of his own.

"Anything serious?" She voices concern as if he too were condemned to instant death.

"Yes." Our false face produces his Hasidic act of sadness. **Tradition is not the monopoly of an elite. Each Jew is obliged to say: "Into my hands has been given the future of the entire people." Just as every person is a microcosm, so is every Jew a miniature Jewish people. He carries within him the soul of the entire people. (Abraham Joshua Heschel in *The Individual Jew and His Obligations*)**

"It's all very final. Final in a sense that, like every other being, I too am condemned to a sudden death either in the careless hands of nature or due to World War II caused by someone base living on top of the Kremlin tower or someone in the basement of the White House, someone who operates the World War III computer." He pauses thoughtfully. "Meanwhile, I learned to live with my osteoarthritis, my Zones of Irritation at the Sacrum."*

As they pass a large First Amendment NewSStand, she notices the look he gives a young woman built not unlike her and shown on the cover of *Wild'nd Wide Open* adult man's magazine.

"My mother would never let me unbutton my shirt or wear a tight sweater, high heels, or Ruthless panties. I always had to keep my skirt pulled down! I was not allowed to shave my underarms. Or my legs. She kept saying, 'You don't want anybody to get excited over you. It might excite you. Excitement can kill you.' "

She and Kosky sit down on a park bench. The sun beats down on

---

*See fig. 66: Zones of Irritation at the Sacrum, and fig. 69: Position of the supraspinous ligament and schematic representation of the interspinal muscles, among them Kosky's most painful L-5 and his most irritative SS-1 as well as SS-2 and SS-3. (Perhaps the source of his never ending irritation?: J.K.) In Chapter Six, *Manual Medicine*, by Jiri Dvorak and Vaclav Dvorak (Stuttgart–New York, 1984).

her. She breathes with effort. To let her heart calm down, she takes off her jacket. Is this an act acted out in order to keep him sexually at bay? Is she acting, reacting or overreacting? Or is she really seriously sick? Kosky keeps calling the number of his inner paramedical diagnostician, whose number remains mute. She unbuttons her short-sleeved blouse. Her underarms are shaved, and, speaking in English, in some remote fashion, he recalls for her how, as a boy of nine or older, he used to like watching "the *hairy armpits* of the peasant women." The phrase "hairy armpits"—such a cliché in English—makes her laugh when he translates it for her into French.

They are sitting at an old dock overlooking the Hudson. Above, a Carolina wren hovers restlessly. An exile from the Carolinas, she is not certain of Manhattan's climate. A Canadian warbler enviously watches American egrets having fun in the shallows. Ducking its head in the water, a pintail duck majestically floats off the docks. In the river, two schools of fish swim up and down, passing each other, one above, the other below, without as much as saying hello to each other. No wonder. Hudson is an affluent river. The salty and heavier water from the Atlantic flows at its bottom while the fresh and lighter water from the Adirondacks flows on its surface. The meeting of fluids.

Riverside Park. Here they run into a crooked-looking little bird. "Look at this poor little thing!" she says. "This bird is called *kos* in Ruthenian!" They stop to watch it and the bird watches them from the lowest branch of the tree.

"They call it mockingbird here," says our Kos, with trepidation. "Actually, it should be called a mimicbird, since clearly no animal possesses a notion of mockery, which presupposes a sense of irony and ridicule." ("Can you see yourself called Norbert Mockingbird and writing a first novel called *Who Saved the Kos?*" his incorrigible Jay Kay whispers to him.) **In our area the mockingbird has apparently always been rare and erratic north of Central New Jersey. (Stone, 1908) Until its recent comeback in the mid-1950s. (John Bull)**

For a while, they keep on walking without a word. They let nature talk.

"There, a bird called a Hermit Thrush. There goes my spiritual fellow," says Kosky, pointing at the solitary creature thrashing under the most unfriendly looking bush. "This is a most peculiar bird, you know! I know him and he knows me too," he says pointedly. "This bird knows more about wearing disguises than any other bird of its kind,

101

whether it's a painted bird or merely tainted. This bird tells you you can change disguises even after death."

"Disguise? You mean this is not the Hermit Thrush?"

"It is but only for as long as it lives. The instant the Hermit Thrush dies the color of his plumage changes so much and so unpredictably, nobody, not even his closest kin, knows who he was in life. Now how's that for leaving no traces when one day you want to disappear?"

They stand next to each other and, an old hand in such matters (and at his age not only his hand aged), he begins to sexually close in on her. (Such sexually closing-in used to be, in the good old days, a spiritually complex process which, if explained with exactness of the year, say, 1969, could cause the innocent reader of today a most guilty complex. She does not mind his transgression. Far from it, she responds to him with the ease of one brought up in the century-old tradition of Ruthenian-Polish freedom and tolerance, a tradition which, mixing the romantic and the pragmatic, became a heaven for the Jews and Protestants alike during the Reformation, then gave us the concept of—a concept and the cultural prototype of—an incurable revolutionary romantic fused with the unreally positivist pragmatic: [Jay Kay].) But it is he who now pulls away from her. He is not afraid of her tolerance; he is afraid of his overly restrictive sexual Self.

And so walking, sitting down, and nature watching dominate his mental frame now. They walk along the docks. They sit down. They watch the river. A big yellow bladder fish passes by in the water. "A man-of-war genus Fair Medusa, his bladder happens to be his sail," says Kosky. "On certain days he sails with it under full sail and on an empty bladder, and on other days it is the other way around. On some days he drifts forth, up the river; on others, he drifts back, down the river, as if lost in the mainstream of Manhattan. Follow him for some twenty-four hours and you will see him drift some ten miles down the river, then nine miles back. Is he an all-washed-up drifter? Is he going up the river—or down the drain? He is not a drifter: the Hudson River is," he concludes.

From the riverside grove Helena and Kosky watch the *Halakah*, an impressively large Israeli aircraft carrier of the Midrash class, as she inches her way into New York harbor under the gaze of the battalions of migrating jays flying overhead in tight formation. The massive bulk of the floating Red Sea fortress looms over the flotilla of welcoming tugs and small boats. The humming and buzzing of damsel flies, bumblebees and wasps drown in the sound of sirens and high-pitched whistles.

Back at the hotel, Helena invites him to her room. It offers, she tells him in addition to the Conradian and maritime view of the entire harbor, a capitalist view: black Harlem to the left, white Wall Street to the right. **Israel is now the largest recipient of any country in the world of economic and military assistance from the United States. The terms of this aid, both in the form in which it is supplied and in the flexibility of its end use, are more liberal than any other country enjoys.**

This situation is relatively new in Israel's modern history, but there is little prospect that it can change in the foreseeable future, or that aggregate American aid levels will decrease. Indeed, Israel confidently expects to shift more of its defense burden to the United States over the years to come. (Peter Grose, 1985)*

What absorbs him in her room is not the view of the most impressive Israeli-owned American-built aircraft carrier manned entirely by young Israeli Jews and Israeli-Arabs (not even the view of her taking a shower) but the Heartfelt 009—a portable electronic heart monitor placed on its own mobile stand next to her bed. She is back in the room, wearing a bra (33–23–33) and strawberry green panties. The electrocardiograph, she tells him, was installed in her room by her American doctors—she is in the U.S. in order to undergo a complex heart surgery not yet performed in Europe. The machine records her heartbeat when she is resting in her room—a record her doctors need to know.

> . . . *mieszka we mnie chwiejny chronometr*
> *serce*
> *O wadliwej konstrukcji*
> (Halina Poświatowska)

"This is where my heart paces tranquilly." She points at a volume of her poetry on the bureau. "And here it rebels!"—she clutches her chest—"though I wouldn't swear it is not the other way.

"Another atrial fibrillation, it's nothing serious." She catches his anxious stare. "The American surgeons will soon edit it out!" She looks at him. "Your face is like a bilingual test: the original and a translation— all mixed up," she says. "You look like Yankiel, that Hasid from Conrad

---

*A *Changing Israel*, by Peter Grose, A Council on Foreign Relations Book, 1985, p. 60.

transposed over Jankiel from Adam Mickiewicz." She stares at him. I can immediately tell he is a Jew: his beard is black and curly, his nose is slightly hooked, his ears stick out, he wears steel-rimmed glasses, a hat pulled down over his eyes, black clothes, his gestures are quick and nervous. (Sartre)

"It's very strange," she says. "We've just met, but I feel I've known you longer. You shape your thoughts in French the way I do mine in Ruthenian. Come to think, both of us think in a very awkward way, awkward by non-Ruthenian standards, I mean. The way Polish or Conrad did in 1909.* There's something we have in common, but I don't know what it is." She moves closer to him. She is pale, her eyes darken. The coming of fall. She draws him to her. "Kiss me," she says.

He evades her embrace. "Why did you choose this hotel?" our Secret Sharer asks, anxious to distract her. I can't say that I've fallen in love with you. In any case you're not a part of the background, but a separate complex of very intricate combinations. As such you exist in my consciousness. That's a great deal. (Witkacy)

"Jan Lechón, my favorite poet of Love and Death, lived across the street," she says.

"Do you know how Lechón died?" asks Kosky cautiously.

JAN LECHÓN DIES IN FALL FROM HOTEL. Poet and former diplomat-in-exile Jan Lechón (pen name of Leszek Serafinowicz) was killed in a dramatic fall from the roof of a hotel overlooking the Hudson River. He was fifty-seven years old. (*American Exile*)†

---

*Conrad wrote this psychological masterpiece (*The Secret Sharer*, 1909) almost a dozen years after the Congo stories. It was one of the rare works he was satisfied with. "Every word fits and there is not a single uncertain note," he wrote to E. Garnett. . . . Like the *Nigger* and the Congo stories, it is a story in an all-male world, "no damn tricks with girls there." (*The Polish Shades and Ghosts of Joseph Conrad*, by Gustav Morf, op. cit.)

†Says E. M. Cioran, that exile par excellence, "In whatever form it happens to take, and whatever its cause, exile—at its start—is an academy of intoxication. And it is not given to everyone to be intoxicated. It is a limit-situation and resembles the extremity of the poetic state. . . . It is not easy to be *nowhere*, when no external condition obliges you to do so."

Later in this text see Kosky's "Notes on Suicide," in the works of E. M. Cioran (1982).

See also *Exile*, a literary quarterly (Exile Editions, Ltd., Toronto, Ont., Canada).

"Well, yes! Lechón fell from the roof of his hotel to the street," she says. "Does it really matter whether he fell, or jumped, or was pushed down by a strange sex, dope-pushing male lover? What does matter is that he died instantly. Can you see Lechón dying slowly and in pain? Lechón, that most flamboyant and great Polish poet (Lechón was not Jewish: J.K.), whose best friend was Julian Tuwim, Poland's greatest poet, who was also a Jew?" She is surprised that he, an American-Swiss, had heard of Lechón. (With Conrad, Lechón remains the spiritually superior Polish bard that ever wrote in this Anglo-Saxon work-ethic promoting exile. Work-*ethic*, not aesthetic, clarifies Jay Kay.)

"And in spite of that you picked this street?"

"I picked it because of that. 'How else but through a broken heart may Lord Christ enter in?' says Oscar Wilde. I too might die of it," she muses somberly.

"Do you know what broke Lechón's heart?" **Equally tragic is the case of the poet. Walled up in his own language, he writes for his friends—for ten, for twenty persons at the most. His longing to be read is no less imperious than that of the improvised novelist. . . . Let us say such a man becomes—transforms himself—into an editor of such a review; to keep his publication alive he risks hunger, abstains from women, buries himself in a windowless room, imposes privations which confound and appall. Tuberculosis and masturbation, that is his fate. (E. M. Cioran)** "Do you know," he goes on, "what made him jump from the roof, him, who in Polish poetry also stood on its very roof?" Kosky paces the room, now letting his Ruthenian blood be pumped at $1.69 cents per gallon of premium by his Ruthenian-Jewish heart.

"Jump? The official *Émigré Party Organ* wrote that his fall was an accident," she says a bit uncertain. "Wasn't it? Was there any reason for suicide?"

"There was. Slander," says Kosky. "His various enemies piled on the sexual slime anywhere he turned up. Eventually Lechón couldn't take it. The roof of the hotel was his way out of that basement. A basement of sexually baseless love."

"How come you know about Lechón, a well-known Polish poet known only to well-read Poles?"

"Poetry belongs to everyone," says Kosky.

"And how!" She comes to life as if reinvented again. (PRINTER: Reinvented, not reborn. *Bardzo dziękuję.* Much obliged.: J.K.) "Too bad that most American people don't know what they've got: they've got some of the greatest poets alive. They've got the poetry of The Melting Pot!"

"And how!" he reverberates with the joy of Henry James—a creative state his brother William understood better than did Freud. (William's closest spiritual-closest *libidonistic* (non-hedonistic) friend: Jay Kay) "The Melting Pot gives American poets a new spiritual dimension. Thanks to the First Amendment (their only remaining freedom of expression: J.K.) they live in a spiritually Superior Situation, not necessarily a Spiritually Superior State." He provides his text with an additional series of SSs.

"So what else interested you about Lechón? Was it his—" Now she hesitates. "Overly abundant male-directed carnal concupiscence?" She borrows his CC, and so he eliminates it from his newest literary inventions.

"What else? Not much. Just that Lechón was born on June 13, and so was I." He dismisses her and her "pseudo-autobiographical rumor theory." (*Pseudorumor* magazine, 1982) He takes her by her hand, then by her wrist. Here our actor does it in order to take her pulse, as well as in order to touch her. "It is erratic but O.K., oscillating between 69 and 96 beats per minute." He tells her and what he says reassures him, a self-appointed doctor, more than it does her (his voluntary poet patient: Jay Kay). Slowly, from the top of the console he picks up the volume of Julian Tuwim's poetry. Slowly, for maximum effect, he opens it to his all-time favorite poem, and, at random, still slowly and still for even greater effect, he starts reading the poem. Now he reads it quickly (with a speed of rhythm he first learned, as did she, from reading Tuwim's *Lokomotywa*), just as quickly reclaiming the cadence of his mother's tongue and no longer acting or acting-out—while submerged in the poem's unhurried yet most locomotive rhythm.

From across the room, she listens to him, transfixed.

"Only one born to the language can read like that. Why didn't you tell me you too were Polish? That's not fair *Monsieur Flotsam!*" She is about to cry.

He rushes to her. "Wait—please! I'm not entirely Polish. I'm Jewish-Ruthenian American. You know that Ruthlandia was once part and parcel of Poland and so, indirectly, was I. A long, long time ago. So long, in fact, that I forgot not only my country, but also, with it, the meaning of what longing for one's country was. Dig it?" Sitting down, he draws her close.

106

Suddenly he lets her go. Quickly, in front of her, he lifts off his wig. He peels off the mustache and beard.

"Strange!" she marvels, sitting on his lap like a doll and examining his features. "It's like seeing some freaky original emerge from a perfectly decent translation." Her eyes rest on him. "Funny," she says. "You look familiar. I have a feeling I have seen you before we met under some rather pleasant circumstances. For me, *pleasant* means literary since I've got no physical pleasures—only my drives for them." She closes in on him (with all the poetic zeal and skill and samovar-made passion and tries to ridicule the scene: Jay Kay). But, where? Could it have been Ruthenia?"

She gets up and smooths out what's left of his own hair. **WOLFE DENIES HAVING PORTRAYED ASHEVILLE. (Asheville *Times*, 1929)**

"I doubt it. Not in person, anyhow."

"If not in person, then—how?" She ogles him as if from within.

"Perhaps in a photograph—a newspaper photograph," he says guardedly. "Or on a foreign book jacket," he says while ogling her, and already hoping for a 69 kiss. **For instance, there can be kisses exchanged merely in intense glances. A sort of "spiritual" kiss can pass between the adoring eyes of a pair of lovers. The hotblooded Latin races know the power of such kisses. (*The Art of Kissing*, 1977)***

"Which newspaper? What book?" Terrified, as if speaking about some foreign totalitarian terror, she is hissing at him, and dare she disregard his para-literary (literary, not military, printer!) The Art of Kissing.

"All kinds of newspapers: The Asheville *Times*, the Asheville *Citizen*, the Asheville *Daily Mail*. . . . You name it, but none of it matters." He tries to laugh it off, but can't.

"I think I know who you are," she says. "You're Norbert Kosky—the émigré writer." She drinks a glass of water.

Prostitute, n. 2. a person, as a writer, artist, etc., who sells his services for low or unworthy purposes. (*Webster's New Twentieth Century Dictionary*) "I'm no less perfect and no more than so many other writers. While Anatole France embraced France in his writing, in mine I embrace anonymous women, often not even anonymous American black women I always desired most. Anonymous means universal, as universal as jazz, the black music. A writer must be universal—and that means

---

The Art of Kissing by Hugh Morris, with Afterword by Dave Wagner, drawings by Emanuel Schongut. Dolphin Books, New York, 1977, page 69.

nonpartisan. Partisans are either white or red, as was demonstrated by World War II once and for all. In America I'm my bipartisan self. What's wrong with that?"

"Twice I told you on the phone that I didn't want to see you. If not thrice!" She raises her voice. "I think you should leave me now—and please don't come back." She is also very fatigued. Emotions fatigue.

"Haven't you heard of motion illness? Well how about emotion? Can't you give the sick original the same chance you gave the translation?" he says.

Of Mr. Cooper we desire to say but little. At all times and on all suitable occasions since the appearance of his _Home as Found_, we have described that work as grossly libelous upon our people, their manners and their customs; and of its author, as the most wholesale slanderer of our people of any man living. This is our deliberate opinion at this time; and this opinion we now repeat, in the well-grounded conviction, that there cannot be found in the United States twelve honest men who will not agree with, and justify us, in holding up to the merited scorn and contempt of his countrymen, one who has thus wantonly and recklessly traduced them. (_Courier and Enquirer_, 1943)

"Please let me stay with you—and read with you the rest of Tuwim," he pleads with the book of Tuwim in hand. This does the trick, even though it is no longer a sexual trick he is after. Oh no! he's falling in love with her—as if she were one of his most beloved Polish Flowers, a poem by Julian Tuwim, which our Diaspora Jew now reads to her with a feeling that stems from proximity, not distance. Helena lets him stay.

"This Ruthenian-made _karafka_ contains pure 69° proof Lechistan Vodka." She tells him, then pours him, and herself, a glass and— typical _inteligent_ that she is—proposes that the two of them drink a _Brüderschaft_. He agrees and they drink it as the custom requires, drinking arms intertwined. Said to be a form of skoal—a skoal carried to its logical conclusion—a _Brüderschaft_ is performed in order to allow her to abandon the customary form of addressing him as _Pan_: (a mixture of the Anglo-Saxon Sir and Mister. A Lady and a mistress for a woman. First _Pan_ Kosky, then _Pan_ Norbert, finally _Pan_ Bert (even though Bert is already a familiar, a diminutive, under such ambiguous circumstances it is and it still must be accompanied by the formal _Pan_). The _Brüderschaft_ lets him call her simply Helena or Hela. This also means that from now on they must call each other by an intimate _you_—such as the French *tu* (or *ty* in Polish or Russian)—without ever again being censored by the collective *you*, such as the English *you*. Isn't it awful, he asks her, that for some emotional reason—or error—such a familiar sexually intimate form *Ty* does not exist in English?

She dims the light, a fact significant enough to italicize. **He senses that she senses that he senses her. This is still another level of arousal, for he becomes conscious of his sexuality through his awareness of its effect on her and of her awareness that this effect is due to him. Once she takes the same step and senses that he senses her sensing him, it becomes difficult to state, let alone imagine, further iterations, though they may be logically distinct. If both are alone, they will presumably turn to look at each other directly, and the proceedings will continue on another plane. (Thomas Nagel)*** It is hot in the room, "so breathlessly hot," she complains, she could use some rest, "but please, don't leave me now. Not yet," she asks him. Would he mind if she undressed? He wouldn't. Go ahead. She undresses and, wordlessly, so does he, piling his clothes on the floor next to hers. They are both naked now. They both lie in the same king-size bed, next to each other. Their elbows touch, and so do their feet and hands. Nothing else. How is she? How is her heart? he asks her but also he asks it of the universe. A whole and wholesome universe of love which suddenly she had opened for him. A universe penetrated only once before—when he was (one who managed, at the age of, say, twelve or thirteen, to be both in love with a girl called Bożena—who saw in him only a sex-offender: Kosky) still a minor. She moves closer. "Hear for yourself, doctor!" He lays his head—face down on her breast, listens and counts. Her heart rate is high. Very high. Her heart is racing wildly. Does her excitement come from her heart or from her mind? he asks. In reply, she stretches sinuously, brushing his question away. He looks at her breast; he sees her heart.

---

*As quoted by the already quoted Janice Moulton, who writes: "Flirtation, seduction, and traditional courtship involve sexual feelings that are quite independent of physical contact. These feelings are increased by anticipation of success, winning, or conquest. Because what is anticipated is the opportunity for sexual intimacy and satisfaction, the feelings of sexual satisfaction are usually not distinguished from those of sexual anticipation. Sexual satisfaction involves sexual feelings which are increased by the other person's knowledge of one's preferences and sensitivities, the familiarity of their touch or smell or way of moving, and not by the novelty of their sexual interest." (Op. cit., p. 111)

"*Dotknij mnie proszę*. Touch me, please. Touch with your Self, not just with your eyes," she prompts him.

He won't touch her. He is afraid, can't you see? Afraid of his own panging heart. He is still a World War II kid gripped by some inexplicable, and not yet described or diagnosed, emotion.

"Touch me," she prompts, leaning against him with her hip. "Touch *ciało poetki*—poet's flesh. I read somewhere you are a yogi. Are you? Don't yogis believe in six sexual organs? Is that why the ideal Lotus grows six petals?" She watches him calmly.

"Fuck me, you stupid fuck," she laughs him in the face. "Fuck a poet who devoted two-thirds of her poetry to her own falling in love and less than one-third to her failing heart. A poet who speaks of sex as *miłość*, as love, but also as *zmysły*, as the senses, who writes of sex as a love of procreation, and of creation, sure, but also sex as love, as fucking, as *kochanie się* but also as—forgive me, sir, for *saying this in your face—pierdolenie*." (That is the most elementary form of peasant fucking another peasant the way one peasant does it to another: Jay Kay.)

She examines his face, as dormant as his flesh, while he examines his Self. Why is he put off by the word *pierdolenie*? Is it because, for some inner reason, the native word sounds perhaps dirtier to him than the Anglo- Saxon *fucking*? Is the word *pierdolenie* harsher to him because he heard it for the first time as a boy of six from a crude Ruthenian peasant girl who, clearly afraid of his menacing looks, said, "*Odpierdol się!*," meaning "Fuck off!" which could also mean she could squeal on him to the Germans (though obviously she did not: J.K.). Is this why it still sounds to him more vulgar hence, like any common phrase, eminently more accessible than the domestic *fuck off*?

A compromise is reached: our sexual con man makes her sign a sex concordat. According to it, they will make love under certain conditions. **She must not swing her arms as though they were dangling ropes, she must not switch herself this way and that, she must not shout and she must not, while wearing her bridal veil, smoke a cigarette. (Emily Post)**

Time then, for *kochanie się*, for making love, even though she hates the English phrase. "Making love sounds like a manufacturing process," she says. "I prefer the simple *pierdolenie*."

Expertly, she attaches one after another the monitor's leads to her

110

limbs and torso, their straps coiling around her like water snakes, their suction caps sucking into her skin like leeches. Briefly, most briefly, their form, their sight and feel make him think of—even see—various neck-to-waist and waist-to-wrist restraints he used to use, in some of his past fiction, either in order to sexually involve (involve, not abuse: J.K.) first himself, then the character, and finally the reader. The leads make contact with the oscillograph. The transmission begins. **"I wish I could hold you,"** she continued bitterly, **"till we were both dead! I shouldn't care what you suffered. I care nothing for your sufferings. Why shouldn't you suffer. I do! Will you forget me . . . ?"** (Emily Brontë)

On the monitor the black electric heart waves rush across the pastoral ECG screen. They rush from left to right. No wonder that, when writing in Hebrew, the language of their heart, the Jews write from right to left. The writing must not blindly follow the heart. By nature, writing is rational.

Helena draws him closer. He crawls under and in between the electrodes. He kisses her breasts; he watches the monitor. Atrial flutter is individual—as individual as one's handwriting. As individual as love. Heart is no longer to him another metaphor for the same manuscript of life—for him, it is now an instrument of love. To Kosky this is a brand new manuscript. One must read it carefully.

Glued to Helena, he monitors the monitor. On the ECG screen her heart waves come fast—too fast—a sign that the heart's own natural pacemaker cannot conduct them all. Is she going through a heart blockage? Will it be **Death: the shatterer of worlds. (Tantra)**

"I'm not excited. Not anymore," he says, and pulls away.

"You're heartless," Helena recoils. The unnatural shape of her *P* wave becomes natural. Her heart's tunnel is no longer blocked. They both lie back, elbows touching. "Kosky is a Ruthenian name," she reflects. "Were you born as Kosky—with that Semitic face? With that Jewish nose?" she asks skeptically.

"It's an ethnic pen name. My father followed the example of Israel Bael Shem Tov, a Polish-Jewish storyteller, who believed in the power of the name," says Kosky. "At the war's outset, to distract the Nazis from the shape of our noses, my parents took the name of Kosky. After the war I kept the name as an amulet of good luck: thanks to it—and thanks to countless Ruthenians who sheltered me and saved me again and again—we survived the war."

Helena cuddles next to him. Her eyes downcast, she pinches with her fingers the bulb of his *szczypior*.* Her lips are moist, her eyes watery.

"Leave the onion alone. Obey your doctors," he tells her, no longer strong enough to tell her she must obey him, the macho trick he used to perform—perform, not act out—with so many other women.

"I obey life. Like it or not, the sex instinct is the *lokomotywa* of my life and of my poetry. Get on the train!" she says. She likes the onion and particularly its tip with which she plays most inventive games of press'nd squeeze. She strokes it. She tastes it, slowly first, with her lips, then with her mouth and tongue. She takes her time. She has not tasted it for a very long time, she tells him, and at first she finds its taste too raw, though not as hard as she first thought. She is wasting a lot of her priceless energy (on trying to turn his steam-emitting stem into an empty stalk: Jay Kay), and in order to slow her down he allows himself the rare luxury of losing a drop of his spiritual spleen disguised as Hasidic-Dionysian seminal fluid. (Jay Kay) She keeps tasting it and stroking it until the bitter nectar bursts out of the hard core and the core turns soft and pliant. But even then she won't let go. She keeps on kneading it in her hands and then, to his amusement, attempts to peel its skin off.

"Our papers wrote that in your first novel you did your native country harm." She squeezes him painfully, as if testing his resistance to momentary pain. She now manipulates him verbally.

"It's been said before about Cooper and Wolfe, about Conrad and Tolstoy. About Ibsen and Pasternak," says Kosky. **"When it comes to books, I must say that this gentleman who writes novels in English nearly gave me a nervous fit. I felt, when reading about him, something slippery and disgusting coming up in my throat."** (Eliza Orzeszkowa about Conrad, 1899)

Fond of the memories,† Kosky fondles his *brit*. The *brit* responds to his touch.

She presses him hard. "You've got so much Gentile slack in you; so much loose skin."

"Maybe loosened, never loose. Please—don't make it hard on me. In Hebrew, *milah* means both word and circumcision." He defends his

---

*szczypior (Ruth.n.): a small onion without a bulb.

†Circumcision does not interrupt any vital function. It simply counteracts excessive lust. In addition, it gives all Jewish people a common bodily sign. (Maimonides)

faith in himself. "I am a Jew," he says. "I was born in Ruthenia (as were so many of our precious generations) and I was born of Jewish parents and in the strict observance of Jewish customs always respected by our non-Jewish neighbors, I set forth to leave my mother's *mikvah* and at six minutes to nine P.M. my forehead emerged, which, once the child's head is safely out of water, in the Jewish faith is considered as the actual moment of one's birth. Accordingly, I was circumcised eight days later. It was, I'm sure, a very proper Jewish ceremony attended, I have been told, by all sixty-nine members of my family. Every Weinreich, Loewenkopf and Lenkowski was there in full strength. (Just to think that by 1945 all but three of them: my parents and I, were left to attend the 1946 Jewish concert to life: clarifies Jay Kay.) The *baal brit*, the master of the circumcision ceremony, kept me on his lap in his function of *sandek*—as my godfather. I've been told, though, there even was an unoccupied chair left in the room for Prophet Elijah who, in one form or another, in order to protect the newly born, is said to attend every *brit*. I assure you I'm circumcised to the fullest. My picture could never be published in *Uncut: The Magazine of the Natural Man.*"*

"Then there's only one way to find out. Grow inside me," she says. "Grow like a living plant. I hate dead plants—they are always soft." She goes on. "Forget my heart, be hard. The life force is hard, hard enough to pump every day—so the American doctors tell me—some 1999 gallons of blood through some 69,000 miles of blood vessels. [Note to the Reader: please note the striking similarity of this blood-pumping metaphor to the one Kosky himself coined earlier. Ed.] It is a force that sends mushrooms and trees up high. Be a mushroom, if you can't grow like a tree. Be alive. Alive with me. Grow out of your self. Grow into me. I am soil. I am moist. I am hot. This trip to New York is the spring of my life: don't let me think about the fall. Stop this Slavic gloom, Norbert! And thus he does not stop. For once, he—he a monster of self-control can't control his sex, which now fuses with love—a brandnew emotion. **Reshaping life! People who can say that may have lived through a lot, but never understood a thing about life . . . they look on**

---

*"A high-quality, bimonthly magazine, *Uncut* explores every facet of the uncircumcised man with articles, features and the most lavish photo layouts of uncut men ever to appear . . . the most beautiful magazine in history devoted to foreskin," in the words of its own ad. (See also *Foreskin Quarterly* and the publications of the Uncircumcised Society of America: J.K.)

113

it as a lump of coarse raw material that needs to be processed by them.... But life is never a material, a substance ... life is the principle of self-renewal ... it is infinitely beyond your or my obtuse theories. ... (*Doctor Zhivago*, Pasternak) Did you know that until you, the only man I have seen naked all the way down was my boyfriend?

"Still, is it possible that in spite of your circumcision, you might not be Jewish? That you were circumcised, by nature—born without a prepuce or a membrane?" She kneads the *szczypior* again.

"Being born circumcised would make me the only *nolad mahul*—'one born circumcised'—found since the sacred commandment of circumcision was given to Abraham, almost four thousand years ago! Now that would make me truly unique!" **There are things, moments, that are not to be tossed to the public's incomprehension, for journalists to gloat over. No, it was not an experience to be exhibited "in the street". (Joseph Conrad)**

"Is it true that being truncated, without a foreskin to protect him, makes every man, whether he is a *Zyd** or not, end up being less sensitive as a lover?" She squeezes his flesh in a test by pain. "That as a result, every circumcised man is, by nature of the circumcision, always torn between guilt for not feeling enough and lust for feeling more?"

"How can one determine what is lust and what is feeling? What, when it comes to feeling or lust, is less or more?" asks Kosky.

"You're quite right. Only a poet can determine that," she says.

Her eyes glow. Her lips are red. "Love me, not my heart. Love me like a man. At least once. 'I must be allowed to start life everywhere,' says Rilke. And so must I."

"What about your heart?" he asks. **What for I washed my breasts/ and combed each hair in the narrow mirror?/my hands are empty/and so is my bed. (Halina Poświatowska)**

"What does the heart know!" She kisses him, opening herself to him. "My heart, my heart," she sighs. "Fuck the heart!" She draws him to her.

Exiled from the Image-repertoire   *exil*/exile   Deciding to give up the amorous condition, the subject sadly discovers himself exiled from his image-repertoire. (Roland Barthes, *A Lover's Discourse: Fragments*, trans. by Richard Howard, 1978, p. 106)

---

*Żyd—Jew, pron. *Gide*. (André Gide was the French Nobel Prize-winning controversial novelist who, as his name alone indicated, was a French Żyd.)

Hospital. Time for surgery. Escorted by nurses, Helena disappears behind a steel door. Surgery. Recovery. No visitors. Is it because the electrocardiograph says it or because her doctors don't like the sight of her—her, *their* patient, kissing Kosky in their presence? How can he know?

From afar, Kosky watches her enter the plane of Samoflot, the Ruthenian airlines. From afar, she sees him. She raises her hand. She is gone.

Jealousies, anxieties, possessions, discourses, appetites, signs, once again amorous desire was burning everywhere. It was as if I were trying to embrace one last time, hysterically, someone about to die—someone for whom I was about to die: I was performing a denial of separation. (Roland Barthes, ibid., p. 109)

A few weeks later, she writes him from Ruthenia:

Recently, I wrote 'The Blue Bird'—a short story—published this week in *Litlife*, our foremost cultural review. The story is autofiction, neither truth nor lie. It revolves around an event—neither fiction nor fact—my affair with a Ruthenian exile, whom I met in New York while waiting for my open-heart surgery. If his portrait hurts you, please remember that it is how not what I wrote about you that is my gift to you. It is a gift of language, of all the waves which come straight from my Soul and not from my American-repaired semimechanical heart. Who knows such things better than you—the mini Bruno Schulz lost amidst the American literary prairie. Only a poet can give such a gift. As for the rest? Not even the *Party Organ* can stop my heart from telling me with every beat that I love my memory of you though I am no longer in love with you.

Helena.

He reads the story, then rereads it.

"The Blue Bird" is painful. It is vicious. It is manipulative. It lies. But it is also written with malice, that marvelously creative force which propelled Swift and Pope. Where would poets and novelists, essayists, editors and translators be without malice? The Yellow Pages are written without malice. But would you ever read them for fun? For a while, to recover from the impact of her yellow pen, Kosky does not write or call her, and he returns all her letters to him unopened. Is he cruel or is he hurt? Is he yellow? But then, he misses her. She is his Lady Fall, his gossamer, his swan. She might be fully recovered, her heart ready to love and be loved without Thanatos for a witness. **To love is to escape from doubt and live in the self-evidence of the heart. (Gaston Bachelard)** One fall night he telephones the sanatorium in Ruthenia. The chief nurse is on the line. Excited, he tells her he wants to talk to *Pani* Helena Powska—and he says it in his best, most festive Ruthenian. A long pause. "Citizen Helena Powska died months ago," says citizen chief nurse, who on orders from someone stupid was asked to substitute citizen, the relatively new word for the centuries-old form of *Pan, Panna* or *Pani*.

Citizen Kosky's heart misfires. "What? Are you sure, citizen?"

Without the Other I apprehend fully and nakedly this terrible necessity of being free which is my lot: that is, the fact that I cannot put the responsibility for making-myself-be off onto anyone but myself even though I have not chosen to be and although I have been born. (Sartre)

"As sure as I am of the fall outside," says the nurse.

"But—her American surgery was a success! Why would she die?" he cries.

"Because her Ruthenian heart got broken," says the nurse. The telephone connection goes dead and so does his last connection to the People's Republic of Ruthlandia.

She is dead. Think of her as if she had never gone. Better yet, as if she had never been. Think of her as if she were a painting by Bosch. Think of her the way you think of fall in the Pripet.

Yet there is One who holds all this falling in his head, gently and without end. (Rilke) No call, no letter, no apology can bring her back. But her story is here—and so he rereads it. As a character, the Blue Bird is a dreadful man. As a story, "The Blue Bird" is lovely as any man's fall. *

---

*See also "The Blue Bird" by Halina Poświatowska (Halina Myga, died 1966). "A poet of broken heart" (Niskisko), she wrote among others, *Pagan Psalm, Under Your Slender Fingers, Love Again, My Flesh Is a Homeless Dog, Angel is My*

When I awoke stillness was all round,
Only the rain-soaked gutters louder sigh.
On the window pane I see, most clearly see
An ink black spider chase an autumn fly.

(Witkacy, 1906)

Neighbor, and *Death*, as well as her autobiographical prose:

Opowieść Dla Przyjaciela (*Tales for a Friend*) (1966). See also Jan Marx: *Poetka miłosci i śmierci* (Poet of Love and Death) 1984. Writes Marx: "Poświatowska was made (*stworzona*) for love. Sensitive, wise, educated, she was eager for love which was abundant, physiological—she wanted to be not only a muse, but also Egeria, inflamed lover, even though her flesh (*ciało*) possessed not enough strength (*energii*) to satisfy (*zadość uczynić*) her dream of love." (And here I would respectfully suggest that Mr. Jan Marx is wrong. Very wrong: Jay Kay adds his last three-cents worth.)

1 0

§ 3. *The problem of the mode of existence of the literary work*

THE FIRST DIFFICULTY WE meet is posed by the question: among what kind of objects is the literary work to be included—the real or the ideal?

The division of all objects into the real and the ideal seems to be a division that is most general and, simultaneously, most complete. One may thus believe that solving this problem will produce something conclusive about the literary work. The solution is not that easy, however. (Roman Ingarden, *The Literary Work of Art*, 1973)*

                "An ordinary suicide note is the least understood genre of undistinguished penmanship (as distinguished from distinguished literary creation), and we hope, my dear Mr. Kosky, to understand its nature better by asking you—as well as some other six hundred distinguished American fiction writers, to write for us, *pro bono publico*, one quasicide: a simulated suicide note—such as you would write if one of your fictional protagonists and not you—repeat: not you— were to consider committing suicide right now," writes Dr. Sam Hill, Jr., the author of *The Self Execution* (Felodese Press, 1986) who heads

---

*Roman Ingarden, *The Literary Work of Art*: An Investigation on the Borderlines of Ontology, Logic and Theory of Literature, with an Appendix on the "Functions of Language in the Theater." Translated from Polish with an Introduction by George G. Grabowicz, 1973. See also: *The Cognition of the Literary Work of Art* (1937) by Roman Ingarden, translated from Polish by Ruth Ann Crowley and Kenneth R. Olson, 1973.

up Thanatos Institute in Yama, California, and he writes it on the most beautifully engraved and printed a bit old-fashioned stationer.

To any serious writer, death and dying are most familiar. Death meaning Azreal. Death as "number 14 (Hebrew letter)" according to Rodale. Death as The Grim Reaper. Death as skull'nd crossbones, the deadly spiritual symbol of the Nazi SS. Death as passing (though no longer trespassing); as ceSSation and diSSolution. (Thanks, printer, for these extra SSes!) Death as extinction and extermination.

Death as self-inflicted Holocaust.

As much as the Holocaust transcends my understanding, even greater is my inability to understand the regenerating and the recreation of Jewish life, culture, religion and creativity that has emerged since the Holocaust. The demonic and the miraculous appear at least equally vexing.* (Byron Sherwin, 1986)

Death as quick as Black Horse and as silent as Quietus. Death the Great Adventure and the Grand Release. Who doesn't remember the classic scene of Nero's suicide ending in *Quo Vadis?* the novel by Henryk Sienkiewicz?† Or Farewell, my love, farewell/Don't be upset, don't furrow your brow. Dying isn't anything new in this life/And, of course, life isn't any newer," lines written by the sad Russian poet Esenin in his own hand, and with his pen dipped in his own blood, only a day before hanging himself in an anonymous room of a Leningrad hotel.

Voracious time devours everything, moves all things from their places, allows nothing to endure for long, Rivers Fail, the land encroaches on the receding sea. Mountains subside and lofty peaks collapse. Why do I speak of such petty matters? The whole most beauteous structure of the heavens will suddenly burn away in its own flames. Death demands all things. It is a law, not a penalty, to perish. A time will come when there will be no world here, says Petronius, the elegant Roman writer

---

*"Conceptions, Misconceptions and Implications of the Holocaust: A Jewish Perspective," by Byron L. Sherwin, *Shofar*, Summer 1980, p. 10.

†Henryk Sienkiewicz, a Polish most universal, yet also most domestic novelist who in addition to *Quo Vadis?*, published in this country on June 6, 1896, gave the world *With Fire and Sword*, *The Deluge* and the Polish all-time national classic, *Pan Michael*, all translated from the Polish of Henryk Sienkiewicz into English by one Mr. Jeremiah Curtain, who, born Jeremiasz Kurtynski, worked on these translations while living in—of all places!—Ilom, northern Guatemala.

forced by Nero in the year 66 to die at forty-six. And what about the already-quoted *Book of Jewish Lists* which—besides some most famous Jewish buccaneers and pirates, as well as those Jews who made it in, say, pop music—list "Eighteen Jewish Suicides" on pages 18–19, such Jewish case histories as:

1. SIMON LUX—This Czech writer shot himself in the chest in the Hall of the League of Nations in 1936 as an act of protest against the free world's appeasement and indifference toward Hitler.
3. SAMSON—The biblical strongman took his own life, along with those of thousands of Philistines, when he brought down their temple.
6. THE GIRLS OF THE WARSAW GHETTO—A letter found in Poland in 1975 tells of the abduction by the Nazis of 93 students of the Beth Yakov Religious School in 1942. Upon discovery that they were expected to become prostitutes for the SS, the entire group committed suicide by poison. The letter was written by one Chaya Friedman before she took her life. (Ron Landau, 1984)

Like all other fictional notes collected by Thanatos from the other professional writers, Kosky's quasicide note (note, as opposed to a notebook, a diary, short story, a play or a novel), he is told, "will later be scientifically matched, in terms of scientifically defined motivation," unsigned, against notes (notes, as opposed to a verse, an idyll, a love letter, etc.), each one written to the best of our knowledge by one suicidee; notes written by a hired suicide expert or ghostwriter were not considered. "As far as we were able to ascertain," the letter goes on, "none of the suicidee notes (often ink-stained prosody or villanelle written with blood drawn from one's own vein) were written by a person aspiring to be a professional knight of the quill—be it a verse, librettist or a ballad-monger, though a great number of them, it must be noted, seemed to stem from physiological reactions induced by either an overdose or underproduction of one form or another of existential despair.* ("And, I bet, of absence, in one form or another, of some good easily

---

*See: "Choice of Method for Suicide and Personality: A Study of Suicide Notes," by David Lester in *Omega*, vol. 1, 1971, pp. 76–81, and "A Psychosocial Aspect of Terminal Care: Anticipatory Grief[1]," by Robert Fulton and Julie Fulton, both of the Department of Sociology, University of Minnesota, *ibidem*, pp. 91–100.

obtainable sexual repair." Jay Kay adds his six cents' worth of words of despair.)

"Finally, let it be said that what will ultimately distinguish the suicide notes used in our study from the quasicide notes written by writers known to be masters of creative usurpation, and against which these notes will be rated, is that none of the authors of the suicide notes is still among the living. Acting promptly upon their notes, everyone of these suicidees has killed himself or herself (though it could be assumed that they might still be living in some other invisible and even unforeseeable reincarnatory form). Subsequently, their suicide notes were retrieved by the Institute from the records of medical examiners and homicide bureaus all over the country."

In him, too, as in the unthinking animal, there prevails a sense of security as a permanent state, a security which springs from the innermost conscious—that man is nature, that he himself is the world. Because of this security no man is noticeably bothered by the thought of a certain and never distant death; but everyone continues to live as if he were to live eternally. This goes so far, that one could say that no one actually has a living conviction about the certainty of his death. Otherwise there could not be such a great difference between his mood and that of the convicted criminal. (Schopenhauer)

So muses our Tantric muse.*

"A Tantric ritual: during the initiation ceremony, you are given a mirror in which you see your own image. Contemplating it, you realize you are nothing but that, i.e., nothing. To what end, so many pretenses, so many airs and graces, when it is so easy to comprehend one's insignificance?" writes the incomparable Cioran.

"Cioran is one of the most *delicate* minds of real power writing today. Nuance, irony, and refinement are the essence of his thinking. Yet he declares in the essay "On a Winded Civilization": "*Men's minds need a simple truth, an answer which delivers them from their questions, a gospel, a tomb. The moments of refinement conceal a death-principle: nothing is more fragile than subtlety,*" writes superbly supreme Susan Sontag.

---

*See introduction to *The Temptation to Exist* (1968), a key collection of essays first written in French by the Romanian-born, Romanian-educated E. M. Cioran and his *Drawn and Quartered* (1983), both translated from the French by Richard Howard.

Every one of those six hundred notes came from under the writing hand of one who, in life's fatal, as well as final, moment, even though not a writer, reached for a pen, a pen or pencil, to write words with it—words, mind you, not drawings or arabesques. ". . . for a mighty pen connects one directly with the Almighty." (Israel Kosky) Second, remember that these real-suicide notes were written for us, for the living, by hundreds of women, children and men who, whether fragile or strong, sexually subtle or living without sex at all, literally finished themselves off (ending their life as writers: J.K.). Finally, mark that those who wrote these notes, in the words of the letter from Thanatos, killed themselves by—let us be purposefully vague here—passive means, such as inhaling gas, swallowing poison, or drowning in a hot bath— as well as by active means. They were written by those most diversely universal kind of people: Gentiles and Jews, atheists. (And believe me, by a lot of depressingly depressed moronic people: interjects Jay Kay.) Among them, no doubt, by some ordinary American Tantrics who, eager, say, to die fast, rather than to fast endlessly, died by (let us spare you details) injecting themselves with poison, either directly, into their arteries with a hypodermic needle, or indirectly, via medical pills; by those who, sportsmen to the end, jumped without a chute from a plane or drowned after a jump from a bridge. Among them, there was a stripper called Joanna who, after stripping, locked herself from inside in a giant factory meat freezer—then . . . (description deleted. Proofreader No. 68 to author: Please, I can't take it anymore! I'm quitting now. —Rita Maria.) **There's nothing bad about death except the fear of it.** Someone must have said it, but who? Was it Seneca? Our vain Kosky vainly searches his secret numbered word account for the footnote. (Secret word, as well as world account, printer, not secret Swiss bank account!)

"Science tells us that those who are about to kill themselves organize their thoughts pretty much the way professional, i.e., creatively bound, writers do because a disorganized mind could never execute suicide— an act of rational self-execution," note the scientists at Thanatos. Hence, they say, the purpose of this experiment is to predict, on a blind basis, and with the help of advanced psycholinguistic methods,* which of the

---

*"These methods use the following parameters: Age. Sex. Marital status. Words per note. The use of self-centered as well as other-centered pronouns and possessives. Verbs of explicit thought or too explicit action. The ratio of rational to

"final notes" are real, i.e., written by those who killed themselves, who meant what they had scribbled down, and which were written by writers such as Kosky who, like him, contemplated suicide, but only on a written page, and only as an act of creative usurpation.

And what he so cheerfully writes about applies to everyone on this earth, whether one is cheerful or not. ("Let's then be positivist about it," writes Kosky, "and rather than romantically kill oneself by an overdose of, say, a hot bath à la Seneca, I would prefer to live and work for the laying of a foundation for the spiritual reconstruction of my Ruthenian-Jewish origins disguised by history as remnants. To let them die is to give the Nazis—the Nazis who planned the final annihilation of everything Jewish, the Nazis, not just annihilation by indifferent time—a final salute of Victory! And, WILL FELLOW AMERICAN JEWS PASSIVELY STAND BY AGAIN? screams from Kosky's imaginary grandstands his suddenly rebellious again Jay Kay.)

Whether skilled writer—or perhaps a person who had himself experienced the suicidal state without actually taking his own life—would be able to intuit the suicidal state more completely, and thereby encode the style more faithfully, we do not know. (Charles E. Osgood, 1960)

The assignment requires of Kosky, first, to imagine himself as being someone else—someone utterly different from himself. It forces him to become, if only in fantasy, fed up with life or with himself or with both that, for the first time in his life, he must feel desperate enough to kill himself. Kill himself? Voluntarily? When? *Soon.* By tomorrow. Maybe, the day after tomorrow. **All is Number. Number is the individual. Ecstasy is a Number. (Charles Baudelaire)**

In order to facilitate such mental operation he imagines himself first as one whose number is literarily up whether he likes it or not, as one, say, whose number was written for him on his skin somewhere between his wrist and elbow, written there not by merciful nature, but by unmerciful man. In his imagination, he is a World War II concentration camp inmate sentenced to die gassed to death in a Holocaust oven, anything is better than confronting again the Ghetto of Lodz. That is too close to his emotional home! No longer one of those "literary soldiers of fortune who can take the count of nine—and get up when ten is

---

irrational, or "I want to *die*" as opposed to "I want to *kill* myself" or "I wish to be killed." The use of dread-inhibitors or courage-prompters." (Thanatos)

123

heard" (Vincent Lopez, *Numerology*, 1961, p. 123), he is now, rather one of some 4,000,000 Soviet prisoners of war who were also gassed by the Germans, i.e., died up—up meaning in ashes.

This imaginary concentration camp number gives him a case of pain that he feels in his ethical tennis elbow. It is the pain of slow suffocation by gas. Slow and purposefully painful. It was suffered for the first time in history, when the Nazis exterminated their own mentally ill (euthanasia program). When those "certifiably insane" were gassed in gas chambers disguised as showers, **a dry run for the extermination (David Weinberg and Byron L. Sherwin, op. cit.)** of Jehovah's Witnesses. Of homosexuals. Of Gypsies. Of Jews. And of Poles, millions of whom perished in the Nazi-induced specifically anti-Slavic and just as barbaric clamor.*

Having found being gassed as a proper way to go, Kosky now must decide HOW MUCH YOUR LIFE IS ACTUALLY WORTH TO YOU, SINCE WHEN YOU DIE YOU ARE WORTH NOTHING.

This is easy. Now once again he imagines himself dropping dead, not as a result of suffocation caused by gas, but invaded by the most common heart attack (which kills many millions of Americans every year: J.K.). What then? *Nothing.* (Jay Kay) "There is no doubt in my mind that in my case such death would resolve all the unresolved." (Norbert Kosky, 1982)

What else could he now do to make the task of writing his last note more convincing (i.e., most realistic and life-resembling) and yet, at the same time, make it as narrative art requires, more original, (i.e., entirely invented—imagined, not copied from reality)?

---

*"In 1939 the world Jewish population stood at about 18 million, and in 1945 at about 12 million. One in every three Jews was murdered, two of every three in Europe. Four of every five Jewish scholars, schools, synagogues, and libraries were destroyed.

"Of the Poles, it is estimated that about 2.2 million were systematically murdered and about 5.2 million were enslaved. Neither the experiences nor the memory of the six to eight million non-Jewish victims of Nazi-designed and implemented systematic murder can be obscured, forgotten or minimized. Such revisionist history, in my view, should not be tolerated, especially by Jews or from Jews. Recognizing the victimization of others in no way mitigates the victimization suffered by Jews during the Holocaust," writes Byron L. Sherwin in *Shofar*, op. cit. (1986), p. 10.

I concluded my remarks to the medical professions with these words: If there is anything I can leave with you in terms of the treatment of patients with a terminal illness it is this: we are all terminal—we all must die sometime—so why should a terminal illness be different from terminal life? There is no difference. (Jacob K. Javits, 1984)

A professional literary villain, he could describe, say, in the form of a villanelle or even a villanette, the very act of killing himself in the greatest detail—then, following the description, actually kill himself. Now, how does that grab you for mixing fact with fiction, and turning a literary pseudocide into an act of nonfiction?

But depression, even a hopeless one, is one thing, suicide is quite another. Kosky believes that in his life until now he had considered suicide twice: first at the age of six (at six he was still, to himself, a child), then at nine, when, after a sudden loss of speech (of speech as much as of willingness to talk: J.K.), muted from within as well as from without, he no longer wanted to grow into a man.

Now, "our prime post-modern fictionist" (Kosky on Kafka) must try to kill himself again—once if only on a Kafkaesque roll of paper. This is the paper Kosky likes to write on, but which, in reality, is fed from its very roll into Kosky's copying machine. [Say it's copying paper. Ed. I can't. Paper does not copy. I do. Do you copy me? Author.]

From a symbolic point of view it may be thought feasible to regard the Ganser Syndrome as a state of death within life, and therefore is in some way analogous to that form of attempted suicide in which appeal for help is uppermost. (M. D. Enoch and W. H. Trethowan) Looking into the fictional mirror, he must see there not himself but another being. A ghost. A ghost of whom? Since none of his fictional characters who inhabit Fictlandia, his private fictive state, has ever committed suicide, Kosky, our literary ghost supreme, must look for one in Gravelandia—a publicly owned literary estate. After several telephone inquiries about the topic, as well as about who could be an ideal typist for his suicidal hype, he is not, by chance, invited to be a keynote speaker on the subject Intellectual vs. Suicide, one of the heavier topics of the already heavy convention appropriately named "The United States and The Soviet Union: Which one is an Ultimately Suicidal State?" He accepts on the condition that, speaking as an apolitical novelist, he sees the subject matter of his talk the way he regards suicide: as being both *either too serious—or too funny for words.*

Romain Gary, the controversial French novelist, died of an apparently self-inflicted gunshot wound. *Roots of Heaven,* one of Mr. Gary's best-known works, takes place in a German concentration camp, where its hero finds mystical comfort thinking about wildlife.

Mr. Gary used World War II as the theme of other novels. *His Dance of Genghis Cohn* tells the story of a German-Jewish nightclub comic who becomes a dybbuk of Auschwitz.

Equally fluent in French, English and Polish—he was born in Lithuanian Poland as Kacew Gary, his mother's stage name. **It is also a form of the Russian verb to burn. (*The New York Times*, July 1, 1981)** and spent his early boyhood there—Mr. Gary was at one time French consul general in Los Angeles. He wrote some of his novels in English (which he then translated into French) and some in French (which he then translated into English) at the rate of one every year. *

—*Times Square Record*

Then, of course, the Koestlers: found dead in their London flat, a bottle of barbiturates and a glass of brandy in Arthur's hand, a glass of whiskey next to Cynthia and plastic bags neatly wrapped over each one's head. Their brand of Socrates' hemlock. **The closest I could get to writing would be to work for a writer. (Cynthia Koestler)**

He examines his face in the mirror: this is the face about to be defaced by the quasicide, by his own writing something quasi, i.e. artificial; by, for once, writing it in order to imitate real life, imitate, not re-create— yet, creation, even re-creation is his business—not imitation, and not for the national class of creative writing.

Suddenly, one got an image of his own death ... of a shameful death that went out softly, dully in anesthetized oblivion, with the fading smell of chemicals on man's final breath. And the image of that death was hateful. (Thomas Wolfe)

Now, his ghost says to him, pull yourself closer to your writing desk, and Norbert, pull yourself together. You are about to become your own ghostwriter. Got it? Every writer has at least one living within one's self.

------

*See also "Jean Seberg and the Media Myth Makers," by Jeffrey Hart in *The Saturday Evening Post*, May/June 1981, and "Death of a Friend," by François Bondy, in *Encounter*, August 1981, p. 33, and "Romain Gary's Double," by François Bondy, *ibidem*, Oct. 1981, p. 42.

Ask Henry James. Or O. Henry. Ask Thomas Wolfe. Or Virginia Woolf. Ask Turgenev or Thomas Mann. Ask Sylvia Plath or Anne Frank. Ask any writer who has lived in a Secret Annex. **In the meantime, I must uphold my ideals, for perhaps the time will come when I shall be able to carry them out. Yours, Anne. (1944)*** Ask Simone Weil. †

Above all, for your current spiritual serial number consult Conrad, Celan, Cioran, your favorite bilingual literary threesome. (Author to Editor: Since I am a floater, and water is as sacred to me as my work, I'll try to say a little about Paul Celan, my narrative bilingual fellow floater who killed himself by drowning. Better yet, the Ghost continues, if writing about writer's *inwardness* is the business of your ordinary working day, in your silent moments do consult Bruno Schulz, your literary fellow foot-fetishist Consul Supreme. ‡

I am leaving life. I am lowering my head, before a hellish machine, before which I am helpless and which, has acquired gigantic power, fabricates organized slander, acts boldly and confidently. (Bukharin, 1938)§

---

*Anne Frank's *Diary* ends there. Soon after, in August 1944, the Gestapo raided the Secret Annex. In March 1945, two months before the Allies liberated Holland, Anne Frank died in the Bergen-Belsen concentration camp.

†Born in 1909, the essayist Simone Weil (*Waiting for God*) died in England (after her arrest and torture by the Gestapo in Marseilles) "as a result of voluntary starvation, for she refused any food beyond the rations allowed the French in the occupied zone." *The Essential Prose*, op. cit., p. 965.

‡Bruno Schulz, an archetypical Polish-Jewish novelist (Polish Kafka: J.K.) and graphic artist, taught art in a Polish high school in Drohobycz (then in Poland; today in the U.S.S.R.). Having the option to write in Yiddish or German, the languages he mastered as a child, he wrote instead in Polish, as did many Polish-Jewish poets and novelists in Poland (e.g., Aleksander Wat, Boleslaw Lesmian, Antoni Slonimski, Mieczyslaw Jastrun, Jozef Wittlin, Marian Hemar, Janusz Korczak, Benedykt Hertz, Roman Karst and many others: J.K.) considering Polish to be his mother tongue. The author of *Sanatorium Under the Sign of the Hourglass* and *The Street of the Crocodiles*, he died in 1942, murdered by the Nazis at the age of fifty.

A graphic artist in his own right, in his drawings Schulz often portrays an act of adoration of a female foot, usually performed by a "man seen as a 'pokraka' " (a misshapen creep), in the words of Witkacy. (St. I. Witkiewicz)

§One day before his execution in 1938, Bukharin asked his young wife, Anna Larina, during her only, and last, visit to his cell, to memorize his suicide note as he told it to her some nine hours before his execution on Stalin's orders.

"Bukharin married his third wife in 1934 when he was fifty-four; she was Anna

Now, must he start rewriting Bukharin's note as he would rewrite his own? There are so many directions in which he could go in rewriting it. But would a man who is about to kill himself bother to rewrite his— or even somebody else's—suicide note? "Is my ongoing hunger strike also against the law of subversive suicide?" asks Bukharin in *Total State*.

It depends on who such a man is. If he happens to be a simple Ruthenian-American longshoreman who, utterly discredited by the mob, wants to kill himself after he is suddenly abandoned by his entire union and deprived of his job—his job is his only craft—he might rewrite in order to name names and, by doing it, to state exactly what, and who, brought him to death. But if Kosky is to write his quasicide note as a writer, and one who is himself now writing a novel about a suicidal writer called Jay Kay, must he impersonate this other hypothetically real-life writer and write his suicide note as if he were Jay Kay or should he consider at this time of his life writing one as himself and leasing it, as it were, to the main character of his novel. What sort of writer must Jay Kay be? An all-American one, perhaps? A new Mark Twain, who, too filled with noncombustible irony, had finally decided to burn himself? Or must it be a Russian or Polish or Ruthenian émigré, an alchemical mixture of Mayakovsky with Julian Tuwim, an Esenin with Tadeusz Borowski?* **Do not blame anyone for my death and please do not gossip. The deceased terribly disliked this sort of thing. Mamma, sisters, and comrades, forgive me—this is not a way out (I do not recommend it to others), but I have none other. Lily—love me. . . . Comrades of VAPP—do not think me weak-spirited. Seriously— there was nothing else I could do. Greetings. (Mayakovsky, 1930)†**

Finally, Kosky brings himself to his writing desk and sharpens his

---

Mikhaylovna Larina: a beautiful young woman of nineteen. In 1935 she moved in with him and they began living together, though without registering the marriage. Anna came from a family of professional revolutionaries." (Roy A. Medvedev, *Nikolai Bukharin, The Last Years*, 1980)

*Tadeusz Borowski, who killed himself, wrote a book called *Good-bye, Maria*, entitled in English *This Way to the Gas Chamber, Ladies and Gentlemen*.

†From Mayakovsky's real-life suicide note he addressed "To all." Vladimir Mayakovsky, the Russian Poet-Reverberator of the post-revolutionary period, killed himself because, as he said at a writer's meeting shortly before his death, **so much abuse is being flung at me and I'm being accused of so many sins (real and unreal) that I sometimes think that I should go away somewhere for a year or two so as not to listen to so much invective.** And so he did, finally, go away.

"twice the pleasure, half the speed" Blackbird 669 pencil. A moment of concentration. Must his note open on a romantic Good-bye, Cathy! and end on a neo-realistic phrase, I'm all fucked up (or perhaps it should be the other way around?), and—presto!—his ready-made quasicide note is ready—and as full of real-life suicide stuff as the real-life suicide note which says, "Death, I'm ready!"*

The reports of my death are greatly exaggerated. (Mark Twain)

After he had written his quasicide, rewritten and written and rewritten again, (and after it was retyped two or three, or even four or five times by a different and, most often, indifferent woman typist whom Kosky would call for [calling her always his proofreader] even though, if anything, safe sex, not typing, was their prime calling: Jay Kay) Kosky puts the final text (final indeed!) into an envelope and, instead of mailing it in the Institute's SAE, sends it to Thanatos by his privately hired most-reliable messenger. Such confidentiality, and expense of the test, are justified. Just think what yellow-press hoods could do with Kosky's literary note. They could for one, pretend that they took it literally and publish it, say, first as a literary death warrant. (WRITER SAID HE WANTED TO KILL HIS SELF.) Or they could literally kill him and, planting his note in his dead hand, make the murder appear a suicide (WRITER DIES. COULD NOT SWIM IN THE DEEP LITERARY WATERS). Worse yet, they could send his note to some George P. Flack at *Rumoroid* magazine. "Just think of the best-selling headlines!" exclaims Marion, recently promoted to the all-powerful position of Eidolon's publicity director.

"It has got fins to swim with; and it has got scales, and sharp teeth.

---

*"Suicide was for several decades the favorite hunting ground of sociologists; but literary suicide, while not reducible to statistical methods of inquiry, would be a curious subject for study. A few pre-Romantic or Romantic French writers attempted it, from Chamfort to Baudelaire (perhaps), and to Charles Barbara and to Nerval, who carried out the attempt. . . . But fictional suicide has a rich history: Stendhal's *Armance*, Vigny's *Chatterton* and *Stello*, Petrus Borel's *Champavert*, Lassailly's *Les Roueries de Trialph*, Maxime du Camp's *Memoires d'un suicide*. Flaubert, Louis Bouilhet, Alfred Le Poittevin, and many young and exasperated romantics, around 1845–55, pondered over suicide. Our contemporary novelists have to resort to automobile accidents and to stoical and inordinate absorption of whiskey to replace the former means of dismissal of fictional characters, which were suicide, consumption, and general paralysis exacting the wages of sin." Henri Peyre in "The Personal Novel," in *Literature and Sincerity*, 1969, Chapter 6, p. 178.

It will be dead soon. It is going to die. It cannot stir anymore. Now it is quite dead. The fish dies because it is out of the water, and Charles would die if he was in the water." (Anna Barbauld, 1788)

SS

In the final tabulation at Thanatos, Norbert subsequently learns, the scientists guess correctly only about half of the quasicide notes—Kosky's among them—to be genuine, and about half of the real suicide notes to be fictional. To him the score proves that reality and imagination are divided by a mere toss of a coin, such a toss being a victory of the imagination, as well as chance. *

Death is the sanction of everything that the storyteller can tell. He has borrowed his authority from death. (Walter Benjamin)

---

*A propos chance and imagination: ask the reader to read, as a spiritual must, the last two strictly spiritual chapters of *Chance and Necessity*, by Jacques Monod (1971). (All the other chapters I find too technical: Jay Kay). If they are, or choose to be, technically minded, they can proceed directly to *Origins of Molecular Biology*, A Tribute to Jacques Monod, edited by André Lwoff and Agnes Ullman (Academic Press, 1979). (Jacques Monod was once the spiritual pastor as well as director of the most innovating Pasteur Institute: J.K.)

11

These days our *waterchilde* splits infinitives while spawning his watery tales, most of which flow out of his life when, during World War II, it centered on fish of the Pripet—his literary Mare.

The Führer orders that German troops are to be empowered and ordered to recognize no restrictions in the methods they employ in this struggle, even against women and children, as long as they achieve success. (Field Marshal Wilhelm Keitel, 1940)

Words are supposed to flow but, do keep in mind, he has always been troubled by the notion of flow, first, obviously, during the war, where Pripet means marshes as well as the flowing Pripet River. Then, he was troubled by the flow of desire, as well as by its often unintentional course. As an adolescent boy playing with his Self, with the flow of his semen, as well as with the flow of words which, let it be said here, have always flown out of him, as fast as water and as reluctantly as semen. *

The fear of falling into the water was the fear of falling into the vagina, which was perceived as dangerous because, once in the vagina, he would meet up with his father. And his father, in this unconscious fantasy, would say, "What are you doing here? This place belongs to me," and at that

---

*"Everybody masturbates! From infancy to old age, both consciously and unconsciously, everybody masturbates. It is a universal practice indulged in by both sexes, in all societies, and even among certain subhuman mammals. It may be defined as every sexual act that is carried out alone," writes David Cole Gordon (1968), and just as well that he does.

point, the patient would be castrated. Hence, the adult symptom of the premature ejaculation was in part motivated by having to get out of the dangerous vagina as quickly as possible. (Michael H. Sacks, 1982)*

And now, after all these years, he is still troubled by writing as one who, as a minor, had a fall resulting in a minor head injury and who, as a result, suffered from apraxia of speech muscles (his wartime speech-lessness and his post-War asphasic symptoms: Jay Kay).†

"Some of these most peculiar symptoms—their duration and manifestation—no doubt belong in your book number nine," Dustin Beach Bradley Borell, his editor at Eidolon, writes on the margin. Then, on the following day, he sends Kosky a Xerox copy of *Hughlings Jackson on Aphasia*, a classic statement on head injuries edited by—O irony of word!—Henry Head. There is a reason for this mailing: proposing a psychological approach to aphasia, Hughlings Jackson claims that "to locate the damage which destroys speech and to locate speech are two different things."

And finally, now, Kosky is suffering from it again. This time as a maker of writing as defined by the Sophisticated Synonyms of Mr. Rodale, WRITING (Literary): the muddy bilge that passed for prose; continue to turn out superannuated drivel; can stand pen to pen with; tear off an exciting mystery yarn; his compositions, filled with a twittering nebulosity; the magnum opus of his extraordinary talents; does not grace the sacred pages; some of the journalistic barbs; effusions; he pounded out two pages a day; he's published a lot of swell stuff in limp art covers with deckle edges; he is quite a hand at putting one word down after another; wore his typewriter to the bone; his veins flowed with printer's ink; their daily drivel; wrestling with the belles-lettres; the mellifluity of his line. (Rodale)‡

---

*From "Psychopathology," by Michael H. Sacks, Chapter Seven, p. 122, in *Introducing Psychoanalytic Theory*, ed. by Sander L. Gillman, Ph.D. (New York, 1982). "As you must know by now, psychoanalysis is obsessed with mental conflict," writes Lawrence Friedman in "Sublimation" (op. cit.), p. 69.

†Aphasia: here, loss of speech resulting from head injury. "In 1906 Pierre Marie's paper on cortical function and localization caused considered discussion. To Marie, speech was an intellectual function for the adequate performance of which a particular portion of the brain was set aside. . . . The degree of defect, he believed, would vary according to the intensity of the lesion and the education of the individual," writes J. M. Wepman in his *Recovery from Aphasia* (1950), p. 15.

‡See *The Phrase Finder* (Rodale Press, 1958).

There are many ways for a stubborn writer's body to burst out of his creative persona and one of them is to burst out of it with the help of another body, preferably a body belonging to a biological (i.e., non-transsexual: J.K.) woman, rather than to another writer (e.g., Dostoyevsky, see "Joseph Conrad Today," *The Newsletter of the Joseph Conrad Society of America*, July 1977, or Strindberg vs. Freud, or Ibsen vs. Kierkegaard: see *Ibsen*, by Michael Meyer, 1971, pp. 186–7).

What kind of woman? Jay Kay demands to know. Oh, I don't know, any kind, providing she is kind enough but also dramatic and tempting enough to do to me what countless women portrayed every month in *High Society Magazine* have done for their men (and often for women either in the presence of their men or in their absence). (Just another shoestore slut, Kosky fires back.)

A privately hired line editor readily comes to mind—one who, going through the text line by line, aligns the novel's narrative line pretty much the way a professional car mechanic aligns the front end of a car.

The compromise we worked out was that we would not put the clause in the contract, but that the book would be copyedited by an outside copy editor of the author's choice. It is a problem. Like most problems in author-publishing relationships, its solution depends on the amount of clout the author has.* (Authors Guild Symposium, 1982)

Well, literary comrades, the fact is that, by now, our tireless ghoul has hired, as well as gone out with (as his tax-deductions record shows most clearly) some sixty-eight different proofreaders, and line and copy editors—most of them attractive females.

Thou hast ascended on high. Thou hast led captivity captive. (Psalm 68)

While sixty-eight is a spiritually high number—consider the mindfully staggering spiritual implication of being a captivity captive,† the

---

*Quoted from the transcript of the Authors Guild symposium on "Authors, Editors, and Editing" (held in February 1982 at the New School for Social Research in New York City: J.K.). The symposium covered the author-editor relationship in all its phases; among other topics the panelists discussed the all-too-common "assigning of authors to overworked editors to their equally overworked assistants, the plight of the author whose manuscript becomes an orphan when his or her editor moves to another company or when the author no longer benefits from his latest publishing company."

†Among the followers of Sabbatai Sevi, some believe that in the phrase "captivity captive" "the captive in question," means the inner Torah "forced to dwell in the

133

number sixty-nine is a one-of-a-kind number—a number so spiritually kind (i.e., permissive: J.K.) that it must not be treated as a mere consecutive one. His sixty-ninth-in-line editor must be someone of high spiritual standing, as high as the standing of Saxe Cummings*—the editor of such diverse authors as W. H. Auden and Eugene O'Neill, of Stephen Spender and Isak Dinesen, of Faulkner and Gertrude Stein— who joined Random House on July 9, 1933, (When I was not even a month old: Jay Kay.)

Mobilizing all his existing as well as potential clout, Kosky asks Dustin to recommend a female Sexy Saxe. He describes her, vaguely, as one whom, *via his text* he could "make her enjoy my flesh through her flesh in order to compel her to feel herself flesh" in the fleshy words of that strange man Sartre. A few days later he receives a résumé of one Ann Pudeater Paterson, "a most dignified young line editor whose middle name does not give any true idea of her," in Dustin's words.

His imagination responds to his having fired his first SS–69 missile. Will he and Ann become AMERICA'S KINKIEST LITERARY COUPLE— (*The Crier*) one who will make erotic history as "a passionate pair who live the bizarre life to its fullest hungry for horny new thrills and, most of all, who don't mind telling the world about their ways"? (*Exposé* magazine, 1981)

Only time will tell. "Time—that master storyteller and the extinguisher of passion." (Jay Kay) Time and Ann Pudeater Paterson—his most recent para-literary catch. Oh? (Ann Pudeater Paterson, 1987)

Only by the discernment of its individual features can we gain a true insight into the general nature and function of language. "He who does not know foreign languages does not know anything about his own language," says Goethe. We have to penetrate into foreign languages in order to convince ourselves that the true difference does not consist in the learning of a new vocabulary, that it does not consist in a formation of words, but in a formation of concepts. To learn a new language is, therefore, always a sort of spiritual adventure; it is like a journey of discovery in which we find a new world. (Ernst CaSSirer, 1942)

---

prison cell of the material Torah." (Gershon Sholem, *The Messianic Idea in Judaism*, op. cit., pp. 117–118.)

*What Is an Editor? Saxe Cummings at Work, by Dorothy Cummings. Chicago 60637 PN 149.9.C6 C6. (The PN number—so rich in numbers six and nine and letters CC tells it all: Jay Kay)

Wearing a flannel suit, Ms. Paterson arrives in Kosky's apartment at 6:00 P.M. and she arrives dressed in, of all colors, pink. Just looking at her makes Kosky's shadow grow longer. She is tall. She is a natural redhead. She wears six-inch Stiletto Sneakers. (Dustin is right: this woman is ideal. She is an ideal literary registered nurse: Jay Kay.) Since as the color pink is said to be a diluted version of purple, this could also mean that this is her way of saying to him that, as an editor, she won't tolerate the color purple in his text. (Pink is what's left of purple when all the spunk is edited out by an editor: Jay Kay.)

Her wearing pink could also mean something else. For one, Dustin's letter recommends her as "no stranger to anything strange and certainly not to anything bizarre." The persona of *The Stranger,* in a novel by Camus, was the first literary being she was in love with, she tells him at the outset. Camus was the second, "though I am by no means a stranger to such strange sexual stratagems as the one demonstrated by Samuel Kramer in *La Fanfarlo,* the most curious novel about a literary most original imitator written by that most original of French men, one Charles Baudelaire," she assures him, strutting serenely back and forth across the room, and occasionally quietly moaning, "O world! O time!" the Lament by Shelley she has usurped as her own.

For two, Dustin states that having once gone to the Beulah University School of Drama, "Ann has acquired a sense of tragedy—in her being permanently perplexed as well as naturally complexed." So much for what Dustin has to say.

"My friends in the pub [here pub stands for publishing, as well as for public and a public pub: J.K.] tell me that you are an instinctive man, one obsessed by sex, by the crudest of life's instincts. In these days of AIDS, this alone makes you, in my eyes, at least, practically extinct." She treats him with **coldness humiliated. (Sartre)**

"I read somewhere that you're a professional levitant. A water levitant. Was this another one of your original literary lies—or was it something you said to the young reporter's microphone?" She treats him with the contempt she reserves for a man who, in her eyes, treats writing the way Sartre does women: as a sexual routine.

"A Levi, not levitant." He dismisses the issue of being profiled half-naked in the recent issue of *WaterSports* magazine.

"I like the color pink," she says without a trace of apology, just when, by sheer speculation, openly seen by her, he manages to catch sight of a small pink bird embroidered on the right leg of her seemingly seamless pale pink panties (which, crotch-revealing, are nevertheless called crotchless).

He serves her a cup of his special TeaPot® tea while she treats him to her résumé. Neatly typed on one-sixth of a page of a virginally pure bond paper, it mentions that even in high school (she went to the Simone de Beauvoir High School in Brookbridge, N.Y.) she was nicknamed Sexual Sophisticate* of her class. The résumé lists as her personal ideal Mrs. Jessie Conrad, that stigmatic wife of Joseph, and she mentions Thomas Wolfe as a writer whose work she would not mind editing.

Between Conrad's life, then, and his fiction there exists much the same relation as between the two divisions (past and present) of his life. (Edward W. Said) Enough said.

He peruses once more her résumé, then resumes his perusal of her. This Jessie Conrad excites him, the way sharing certain descriptions with Flaubert must have excited Conrad, but after all, Kosky's writing muse No. 69 reminds him, he was excited by almost every one of her in-line line-editing self-possessed predecessors.

The image of myself which I try to create in my own mind in order that I may love myself is different from the image which I try to create in the minds of others in order that they may love me. (W. H. Auden, 1956)

"Your face brings to my mind the portrait of an exquisite young Jewess drawn in pencil by William James. She was the one with whom he is said to have been hopelessly in love, and he was the very first American to point out that "in certain nauseated states the idea of vomiting will make us vomit." The idea—not just bad food or illness or half-swallowing one's index finger. "The idea, meaning the power of words and of imagination," says our master of the nauseated state. "Your résumé says you've spent six months working full-time as a literary patient of Matthew Duke, working with him on *Underneath This Sacred Armor*, his latest book," he goes on.

"Indeed I did, but my résumé tells only the most obvious professional story. Matt and I spent so much time together that in Duke's latest book the character of the nurse called Marble Juno was drawn by him straight

---

*See "The Sexual Sophisticate," in "The Struggle for Orgasm," (Chapter 6) of *The Sexually Responsive Woman*, by Phyllis and Eberhard Kronhousen; preface by Simone de Beauvoir (1964).

from me. To a shadow!" she whispers. Graciously, she leaves the length of the shadow to Duke's biographers. "Normally I prefer to take a writer's manuscript—as well as the writer—to my home, where I can concentrate on the two of them better—and not necessarily at the same time." She laughs. "Affections in me spring mostly from the mind," she says probably unaware she is literally quoting the words uttered to Jules Troubat by the dying Baudelaire, what, to Kosky, makes her even more dear. "Matthew, however, insisted that I work with him on his text, page after page and that I do it at his place every day—his wife was there most of the time—and so I did for over a year."

Ms. Paterson shifts position, and her shift, prurient as it is, could bring her in conflict with *United States of America vs. Sex.* * "Why don't you write your sex-offending books either in your native Ruthenian or, better yet, in Esperanto, which I gather, was your second tongue?" asks Ms. Paterson. "Wouldn't it be easier?"

"Anything but. In Ruthenian, I would be rated against the Ruthenian best—while here, as a writer-in-exile, I carry no ratings, I knew Esperanto as a kid. I forgot it all by now," modestly answers our vicarious literary vicar. **I hold our Polish literature in too high esteem to spoil it with my unskilled work. For the English, my abilities are sufficient and they provide me with bread. (Conrad to Wincenty Lutosławski, 1899)†**

"What's your current book about?"

"About **cosmic interior.**" (Karol Hiller)‡

"What else?"

"About half-baked ideas. About mental action and novelistic reaction," he recites while ogling her like an eagle.

"Novels are about action, not about ideas." She chills him.

United States of America vs. Sex: How The Meese Commission Lied About Pornography, by Philip Nobile and Eric Nadler, with commentaries by William F. Buckley, Jr.; Betty Friedan; John Irving; William Kennedy; and John Updike (Minotaur Press, 1986).

†Concluded Professor Lutosławski: "We are rich enough to give many such writers to all the nations of the earth, keeping for ourselves only the best who will express their souls in Polish."

‡Karol Hiller: born in Lodz in 1891, Hiller invented heliographs (paintings painted by the painter as well as by their own inner light: Jay Kay).

"My novel attempts to turn ideas into action." Our alchemist is at it once more.

"Ideas are a motley crew. Most of them tend to be uptight, not tight. Idle not wild." She threatens him (a man who back in 1957 landed at New York's airport then called Idlewild, carrying nothing but a writing pen: Jay Kay.) with her editorial pencil.

"Well, then, if a particular idea won't strike you in my novel as being particularly wild, mark it on the margin IDLE or WILD! But don't strike it out: idle or not, it is *my* idea! You see, I believe that a true intellectual is a vendor of ideas. His kiosk must be open to everyone: if he favors his buyers on the left more than those on the right or vice versa he is out of spiritual place."

"Ideas belong to everybody, but since I don't, how much will you pay me in U.S. dollars?" She dismisses his apolitical stance, a stance he has maintained for some thirty years, with her crude sell, then strikes an easy point with a grin made famous by Jessica Wilde, the young Actress of Adult cinema he saw in *The Three-Way Lovers* magazine.

"Somewhere between sixteen and nineteen dollars per hour depending on how illegible my manuscript is." He watches her as if he were at an X-rated movie called Chateau 69.

Neither financial need nor the entreaties of his publishers, who alternated between friendly reproaches and legal action, could dissuade Balzac from pursuing his expensive system. On numerous occasions he forfeited half his fee, and sometimes the whole of it, because he had to pay the cost of corrections and resetting out of his own pocket. But it was a matter of artistic integrity, and on this point he remained inexorable. (Zweig on Balzac)

"How would you want me to work? Under you, or away from you?" The lady starts a new paragraph while glancing at him with **sadistic attraction (Sartre)**, the very attraction Sartre betrays when writing about Baudelaire.

"How about with me," says Kosky. "That means next to me—or, if you prefer, across. This means in my physical, as well as spiritual, presence."

"Where do we work? In my flat or in your *church*?"

"We'll work here at my place." Modestly, he drops his gaze only to recover it in tripe size six by nine. This will give me a chance to fool around with the text while you watch the fool in me. He catches a glimpse of her underarm which makes him long for a strong antiemetic called (a perfect combination of words of "drama" and "pantomine") Dramamine.*

... from now on until they take the manuscript away from me finally and irrevocably, I have a tremendous job of work to do.... There is something final and terrifying about print, even about proof, and I want to pull myself together for this big effort and keep at it if need be until I drop. (Thomas Wolfe)

"I recognize this flat from its fictional description in one of your novels." She glances around the apartment. "Is there, by the way, a voyeuristic Nietzsche niche hidden behind a false wall, where like that cocksure guy in your cocky book you too hide at night? From where you eavesdrop on your unsuspecting mistress and her unsuspecting lover?"

"There is—but only as a mental image."

Ms. Paterson shifts position again. Leaning back, she offers an unobstructed view of her armpit.

Tempted by the sight of it (to our *erotoman*, an armpit is a tempting orifice) in order to counteract his rising passion, Kosky, our master of part-time control, starts concentrating on Ms. Paterson's birthmark, her one obvious imperfection. Her birthmark is a single smudge which smirches the lower left side of her face, and smutches it all the way onto the neck and even part of her impeccably Aryan-shaped chin.

"One day could you take me inside this niche?"

"I could, but I mustn't," says Kosky. "This is my fictional private annex. This mental niche cheers me up. It reminds me of the niches where I used to hide as a boy during World War II, as much as it does about *The Diary of Anne Frank* [the most genuine diary there ever was, accused by some fools as not being genuine enough: Jay Kay]. Hence, it reminds me of my own survival." In his little box of stage properties he kept six or eight cunning devices tricks and artifices for his savages and woodsmen to deceive and circumvent each other with, and he was never so happy as when he was working these innocent things and seeing them go. (Mark Twain about J. Fenimore Cooper)

"This is 1987, not Orwell's *1984*," says Ms. Paterson. "Now why would a grown-up man secretly spy on his own mistress, and police her lover, unless he is sick—or works for some sick private police?"

"Maybe because he loves her. Maybe because he needs her. Maybe because he can't help himself," volunteers Kosky.

---

*See *Physicians' Desk Reference* (PDR, 1986), where page 1,669 tells you all!

For man has closed himself up, till he sees all things through the narrow chinks of his cavern. (William Blake)

Ms. Paterson edits again. "In your novel, Cocksure often uses his secret knowledge to emotionally punish and sexually humiliate his various lovers."

"I guess that's where I either part company with him or with your interpretation of what he does," says Kosky. In physical things a man may invent; in moral things he must obey—and take their laws with him into his invented world as well. (George Macdonald, 1893)

"Your reader never knows whether you're a model for your character or he for you. Will I be working for you—or with him?"

"You'll decide as you go along," says Kosky. "At least you know that behind every fictional wall there might be a *gemütlich* little literary niche." What is so sparkling, so fragrant, so intoxicating, as possibility? (Søren Kierkegaard)

He hands her a freshly typed manuscript page. "A sample for you to try your hand at," he says.

Biting the dull end of her pencil, Ms. Paterson starts reading. A critical smile—her other most attractive trademark—lights up her face. She says nothing. She keeps on reading. Finally she stops.

"You must learn to italicize scientific names, such as *Urctus arctos*, European brown bear." She sends him to "Italics" (underlining) in *Punctuate It Right!* by Harry Shaw, 1964, Chap. 19, para. 6, p. 100.

"Quite right," he readily agrees. "What else?"

"Like most Slavs enslaved by their mother tongue, you too have trouble with the use of the article *the*," she remarks offhandedly.

"Trouble? What trouble?" He stares at her with his *waterchilde* starry-eyed stare.* This I think accounts for what people call the obscurity, the involved formless "style," endless sentences. I'm trying to say it all in one sentence, between one cap and one period. I'm still trying, if possible, to put it all on one pinhead. I don't know how to do it. All I know to do is to keep on trying in a new way. (Faulkner to Malcolm Cowley)

"Well"—she hesitates—"in English, the definite and indefinite ar-

---

*According to the *American Heritage Word Frequency Book*, the word *the* occurs three times as often as the word *of*, the second most common word. Among the other most frequently employed words are *and* (3), *in* (6) and *that* (9). The first most employable noun is *time* (60) followed by *people* (79) and *water* (90).

ticle are integral to the language, though I gather they don't exist in Ruthenian."

"They don't," he agrees.

"Well," she goes on, "you can't just arbitrarily drop the article 'a'— as you have done in parts of this text!"

"Why not? he inquires. "A woman, *a* dog, and *a* walnut tree, **The more you beat 'em, the better they be."**

"Well—it has a lot to do with the 'countability' of nouns. In English, common nouns are usually (though not always) countable—for instance, one book, two books; one person, two persons; one bed, two persons—sorry, two beds," she corrects herself. "But then the material nouns—nouns describing a material from which something else is made— are usually, though not always, uncountable. For instance, flesh, time, rubber. Since 'a' means 'one,' the indefinite article can appear in front of countable nouns when they are in the singular—a book, an hour, an ass—but not in front of uncountable nouns. You cannot put 'a' or 'an' in front of laughter, advice or blood."

"Nevertheless," Kosky argues, "they are used to give such nouns a sense of oneness, of singularity. For instance, a piece of ass; a pool of blood; a piece of advice about an item. A speck—or a spot—of blood."

"I understand," says Ms. Paterson. "But you've dropped the definite article 'the' from most of this page." She lifts the page—the offending article—in her fingers, then drops it on the table. "This is unpardonable, since the definite article is used to show that a noun, whether countable or uncountable, is being used in a definite and particular sense and not in a general sense. For instance, *the* bed, *the* ass, *the* rubbers." She looks at him with the saintly, yet so whorish, look of Pope's Heloise. **Oh happy state! To be my lover's whore,/ And love in liberty, by nature's law. (Pope)**

"But then, whether with the rubbers or without them, don't we say in English: 'I feel like *going to bed* with you'?" says Kosky employing the verbal italics as matter-of-factly as he can make it.

"We certainly do," she agrees. "But only to indicate that we go there to sleep. After all, in the era of safe sex, sleep, not sleeping around, is what a bed is for," she explains patiently.

"To conclude"—she puts aside the pages he gave her—"without the article 'the' this piece reads like a telegram written by a foreigner. Some-one to whom the English language is a foreign article."

"Let's see." He glances over her shoulder, sniffing her hair in the process. "I'm sorry," he exclaims. "It's my error. What you have read was not written by me—but by someone else." (He pauses.) "In fact, it is a quote from Jeremy Bentham. Bentham was the only Englishman who robbed the rich English language of most of its articles. Imagine that!"*

"Is Bentham Ruthenian?" she volunteers.

"He is not," says Kosky, handing her another page. **Advertisements, none. Bookseller did not, Author could not afford any. . . . No longer a great man, the Author was now a nobody. (Jeremy Bentham, as quoted by F. L. Lucas, in *Style*, op. cit., under "Brevity and Variety")**

Ms. Paterson scans the next manuscript page. "I am obliged to write every book about six times," Conrad said. "First I tumble out a mass of words, incoherent even to myself, but fairly bristling with ideas. Then, laboriously, I straighten them out until I have something like a skeleton to work on. Then I pull them this way and that until the events are arranged in order. Then I dive into my characters and try to bring them to life. My last two revisions are usually devoted to polishing up." (Cyril Clemens in *Perspectives*, March/April 1987)

"I read somewhere, or maybe I merely heard it from someone, that you once asked some of your American students studying English prose at Beulah University to analyze a fragment from a Joseph Conrad novel and to write a critical essay about it. When they did, and when they found all kinds of Conradian word affinities and Conradian pitch, you admitted that some two hours before the seminar, you'd bashed out the piece yourself, and given it to them in order to test them as textual critics, as well as students of Conrad."

"It's true." Kosky laughs insincerely. Insincerely because, in his own words, "it was an unfair test of literary stereotyping. Unfair, 'cause the students depend on their teacher so much here." **Nobody really knows what constitutes an ideal upbringing. (John F. O'Connor, M.D., 1984)**

Now, in order to give her a touch—a touch, mind you, not a sense—

---

*Jeremy Bentham: English philosopher and author of *Introduction to the Principles of Morals and Legislation* (1789). Bentham identified happiness with pleasure and devised a system of moral arithmetic for measuring the relative value of pleasure or pain. In his brilliant prose, Bentham, the founder of utilitarianism and stylist par excellence, carried his motto "words as few as possible" to a truly utilitarian end.

of his creative dependence on her via his sacred text (and of his need to be prompted to mental action by an image of a fallen woman—who lets herself fall down on him like a not-so-ordinary whore: Jay Kay) our *sopher* is meanwhile glancing through the pages of *Sexual Compatibility** at an angle which allows Ms. Paterson to catch sight of a diagram of female genitalia in preexcitement state and the plateau phase. †

"May I ask how, in your text, does your philosophy of action—which, I take it, has a lot to do with live sex—and your 69s square with safe sex?" this most modern woman asks him most directly.

"It does," answers our macho enigma. "I put the circle in the square."

Annoyed by the sight of him, or by the book, Ms. Paterson reads aloud: **"When I reached my wretched lovely house at West Egg I ran the car under its shed and, feeling wide awake, walked around the house and sat down on an abandoned grass roller on the lawn. It was a loud bright night with wings beating in the trees and a persistent organ sound as the full bellows of the earth blew the frogs full of life."**

"This is kind of messy," she says, striking the page with her pencil, in what he perceives as an editorially orgasmic phase. "You can tell all this was written not by an American native but by an *anxious* foreigner. And a recent one at that! You see"—she pauses tactfully—"no native American—writer or no writer, I don't care—would throw all this stuff—house, car, grass, roller, lawn, night, trees, frogs, even the organ sound, into one paragraph. All these material things mean too much to us to be easily thrown into a mere one sentence. By the way, is the house lovely or wretched? You can't have both, you know! Also, whose wings are beating what—or whom—in the trees?"

Ms. Paterson shifts position on the sofa. As she does, so does her skirt. "I hope my criticism upsets you enough to rewrite the text, but that it doesn't offend you. I'm trying to be as open as I can," she says thoughtfully, while involuntarily, no doubt, she spreads her legs with a fresh largesse. The result is a brand new vista—and, this time, an unobstructed view of her upper thighs and lower belly. And here our prurient pleasure seeker is in for a spurious shock: there's no doubt that not only does Ms. Paterson wear custom-made pink panties—a slightly fuzzy'nd furry brand known as Swiss Tease, but that on top of them

---

Sexual Compatibility: A Practical Approach to Solving Problems, by John F. O'Connor, M.D. (1984).

†Ibid., p. 69.

143

she wears—and this is the crotch of the matter—a leather corset fitted with—this is for him a moment of spurious suspense—a device known to the vice squad as a labia spreader—upon which our sexual Tantrist voluntarily opens his ejaculatory ducts.

He could, of course, assume that, knowing his books, knowing most of the voices'nd vices of his fantasy (to some fantasy is, by itself, a silent vice), she had put it on in order to put him on. Or that she had put on her corset and the spreader today the way she might have put them on every day or every other day, put them on for a reason (or a person) of her own.

"Sure you upset me but so what? You also excite me," he says openly. "If you're to become my privately hired, and paid entirely by me, line editor, I want you to be as open as you possibly can," he assures her with a firm skoal of his eyes. "Please go on. Be as rough on me as you wish: This is my ninth novel, and," he adds in galley proof No. 80, "it is also the fifty-fifth year of what I hope will be at least a sixty-nine-year-long life." I'm sure I can take it."

She reads from the text again: "**The shadow of a moving cat wavered across the moonlight and turning my head to watch it I saw that I was not alone—fifty feet away a figure had moved out from the long shadow of my neighbor's hedge and was standing with head thrown back, and eyes turned upward toward the silver pepper of the stars.**" She stops and gives Kosky a thoughtfully reproachful look. "This is awkward step by step," she says. "One: Surely the cat's shadow wavered across the moonlit grass, not across moonlight. Two: The figure had moved out . . . and was standing. 'Had moved' and 'was standing' don't go well together. Why not just 'stood,' period? Three: If the figure's head was thrown back, your character couldn't see the figure's eyes, right? Four: 'The silver pepper of the stars' strikes me as another typically Ruthenian polka-dot—a heavy-handed metaphor. I recommend you cut this whole passage. Too many Ruthenian shadows!" She laughs, then locks her thighs, in what, speaking sexually, of course, he perceives as her resolution phase.

"Is my foreign background as evident in my English prose and as bad as that?" he asks.

Nobody can doubt that Conrad's works are haunted by the shades of his Polish past. (Gustav Morf)

"It is certainly evident," she says firmly.

As she moves, her blouse pops out of her skirt, for a moment baring her belly, a visual drama which prompts our literary dramatist to tighten from within the cremasteric muscles helplessly lost in the loose skin pouch of his scrotal sac (channeling the one and only *Kundalini* from the base of his spine right into the creative part of his brain: Jay Kay), a process simply known as literary acclivity (or as the Oli techniques: J.K.).

She starts reading again. **"Something in his long scrutiny and his pocketed hands and the secure position of his feet on the lawn suggested that it was G himself—perhaps come out to determine what share was his of our local heavens.**

"I could not see his but I remembered that Miss Baker had asked me about him at dinner and I decided to speak to him. I got to my feet and was about to call out when suddenly I saw him stretch out both hands toward the sky in a curious way—as far as I was from him I could have sworn that he was trembling. Involuntarily I looked up. When I looked down again he was gone, and I was left to wonder whether it was really the sky he had come out to measure with the compass of those aspiring arms."

Lost in thought, she raises her pencil to her mouth, spreads her lips and sucks on the end, and how she does it sends Kosky's inner stock market into a frenzy of exchange of prostate gland for prostaglandins.

"This is a very, very raw text," she pronounces. "It's creatively uncooked—*saignant*, the French would call it. What's 'long scrutiny'? And why wouldn't G's feet not be secure upon the lawn unless he is drunk? Well, was he drunk or not? The text doesn't even suggest that he was."

When Kosky doesn't suggest it either, she goes on.

"A share of the local heavens? C'mon! Heavens! Also the reader might want to know what it means to stretch out one's hands in a curious way. What is 'curious'?" She laughs at him. "No, no, Norbert! Your text is too Ruthenian, though I'm sure a good American editor could easily fish out all that raw literary fish."

"Then I guess I still have to work at it," he says. "I didn't realize one could hear my accent in my prose."

"One certainly can. There's some charm in your rhythm, but it's a foreign charm. No American writer would write it like that, you see! Not in a **hundred years of solitude!"** García Márquez)

No passion in the world is equal to the passion to alter someone else's draft. (H. G. Wells) "I feel hurt, very hurt, though I appreciate your

145

comments, I really do," says Kosky. "They make me realize that every editor must feel obliged to find such errors in my manuscript—not because my manuscript sounds foreign, but because I do. Now you know why I must rely only on myself—and take precautions against overpowering editors. They simply wouldn't dare to do to Fitzgerald* or any other U.S.-born-and-made-in-U.S.A. literary Fitz or Gerald what they feel free to do to Kosky."

But now he seemed sure of what he wanted to say as he walked up and down the room. He won't need to make any corrections, I thought; the style was simple and clear. Sentences like "Deprived of the right to say 'no,' man becomes a slave" stuck in my head. (Cynthia Koestler)

"What is it exactly that you want me to do?" asks Ms. Paterson, glancing at the new page.

"Attention," he tells her taking her briefly by her hand. This is the spiritually charged ms. page no. 169.

"Let's see." Under the pretext that he wants to look at the text from her point of view, Kosky moves from the chair to the sofa and sits down next to her. By now, even his *verumontanum*† is inflamed.

"Above all," says Kosky, "what I want most as a writer is to be clear!" In a momentary act of creative surrender he spreads the test page no. 69 on the table in front of her. "Flag—or flog, if that's what turns you on—any word, any sentence, any description that doesn't make sense to you as a reader." **The limits of my language means the limits of my world. (Ludwig Wittgenstein)**

---

*AUTHOR TO READER: Please compare this earlier draft of Fitzgerald's *Great Gatsby* with Fitzgerald's published text, which begins with: "I decided to call to him. Miss Baker had mentioned him at dinner, and that would do for an introduction. . . ." and ends with, "When I looked once more for Gatsby he had vanished, and I was alone again in the unquiet darkness." These and other fragments of the pencil draft of *The Great Gatsby* as well as its published version can be found in *Write and Rewrite: A Study of the Creative Process* by John Kuehl, New York, 1967, pp. 133–66.

PROOFREADER TO AUTHOR: Why didn't you tell Ms. Paterson you were testing her with the writings of Fitzgerald?

AUTHOR TO PROOFREADER: Because the purpose of the test was to encourage me to listen to my inner editor (rather than, say, to what she had to say) and not to discourage her from saying it.

†*Verumontanum*: see schematic representation of the prostate gland in *Sexual Compatibility*, op. cit., p. 10.

"I see one already. You spelled limpid as limpet. A nasty error."

"Clearly, my typist's minor typo—not mine. As one who majors in the Jewish narrative art, I make only major errors," he admits modestly.

It must be said that Conrad was not always sure of his spelling. He made spelling mistakes in Polish, French, and English alike. In *Nostromo*, almost half of the numerous Spanish words are misspelled. A few are not even Spanish. . . . In French, he would often write *présant* for *présent*, *example* for *exemple*, and he was never sure about the endings -ance or -ence. In English, words like *although* gave him trouble, as Garnett reported in his introduction to *Letters from Joseph Conrad*. (Gustav Morf)

"I found another one," says Ms. Paterson. "You say here 'Who will, may hear Bordello's story told,' and then again, 'Who would, has heard Bordello's story told.' " She mixes her smile with a sneer. "Both sentences make no sense—regardless of what happened in that bordello!"

"Oh, I'm so sorry. Another typing error!" Kosky looks over her shoulder. "It's not bordello—it's Sordello, Browning's 'Sordello'! Otherwise the quote is correct; that is, that's the way Browning wanted these two sentences to read. One begins his famous poem, the other one famously ends it."

"Robert Browning? *The* Robert Browning?" She looks at the text with horror she initially reserved for Kosky.

"Indeed." Triumphs quietly our hero over the narrative heroin. "George Eliot claimed that while reading Browning what we took for obscurity in him was superficiality in ourselves."

"Maybe so." Undefeated, she returns skeptically to the text. She reads for a moment, then says, "I just found a wrong quote. You say here *Women are men like us.*"

"It's a quote from Proudhomme." Sniffing her natural scent, he tries to distinguish it from her sweat, as well as from her Carnal Number Sixty-Nine French perfume.

"I know it's a quote. But quote or no quote, it just doesn't make sense. No matter how perverse. (I know from your books, women are your icons of perversity.) Women are *not* men and never will be. Your enlightened women readers would find this line most offensive."

"I must keep it for the sake of the story," says Kosky. "You see, that's Proudhomme's view, not mine. The quote demonstrates what and who comes to my protagonist's mind at a different time of literary creation; this is how he thinks."

"He could think of someone else. Why must he think of—Proudhomme? What's his name? Proudhomme?"

"Possibly because, being bilingual, he is attracted to anything or anyone who is bi—split between reason and dissent; anyone who bears a bilingual name [preferably Canadian: J.K.] *Proud* is English, *homme* is French."

"Have it your way, then." Ms. Paterson glances at his manuscript again.

"Some of your quotes from other writers are all screwed up," she says, sucking sensually on the rubber-filled eraser end of her pencil.

"Screw them, or unscrew," he says. Changing position he can now view her raised skirt and thighs as if she were about to be photographed for *Open Women** magazine.

"Stylistically, some of them don't make much sense." She snatches a page from the table. " **'Whoever has not himself been on the tentacles of this throttling viper will never know its fangs (H.),' "** she reads aloud. "To start with, a viper—a viper is a snake—doesn't have tentacles," she laughs. "Then, if the viper kills its victims with coils—coils are snake's body language—then the snake doesn't carry any venom either. Besides, a person throttled by a viper (here, I assume, the word *throttle* stands for Adam's apple strangulation, not for a hand job) can't feel the viper's fangs no matter how vituperative the snake or its victim is! By the way, who is H.?"

"Adolf Hitler," says Kosky. "Hitler was once a struggling writer— struggling with the language as well as with the Jews."

"What else must I watch for?"

"Ordinary alchemical blunders." He remains vague on purpose.

"Anything else?"

I shot an arrow into the air,/it fell to earth, I knew not where. (Longfellow, 1845)

"Make sure I stay strong on verbs—in my text, verb stands for action and reaction. Also, keep strict count of all the attributive nouns."

"Wait a sec! Should I count them as nouns or as pronouns?"

"Count pronouns and adjectives as nouns because, like nouns, they often beg to differ from verbs—even when they don't," Kosky rules. "You can hardly tell them apart." **Those who judge nominal style good**

---

*Published at 6565 Sunset Boulevard, Hollywood, *Open Women* magazine features young and naked *erohostesses*, capturing them in a *casa de trato*.

do so implicitly, for the most part; nominal style is practiced more than preached. (Rulon Wells)

"Now, when sexual all-out means a sickening fallout, I imagine your sex life must be Misery Unlimited." She addresses him as if he already sought her "cruel literary favors" (Jay Kay).

"Must it?" he shoots back. "But what if I'll keep imagining that it isn't, and think for instance about you in my semi-sleep?"

"Any other things I must watch for?" She challenges him again.

"Keep my Semitic influences intact. Also, please keep in mind that, as A. Q. Morton assures us, 'Now it is true that structural linguistics has demonstrated the difficulty of formulating a completely satisfactory definition of 'sentence.' Whatever definition may be offered, exceptional and ambiguous sentences can be produced to challenge the definition.' "*

"But," Ms. Paterson repeats and, looking at him under her armcave, gives him a blank look of an **automatic sweetheart. (William James)** "If I were to follow your precepts, wouldn't your novel be at the same time too dressed up and overly bare—a bit like you?"

"There's only one way to find out," says Kosky, still transfixed by the sight of her by now perspiring armpit.

Has there ever been erected a Monument to an Unknown Poet? (Norbert Kosky, circa 1986)

Every punctuation mark has its own intonation. Treasure the spoken word. (Stanislavsky)

---

*A. Q. Morton, *Literary Detection* (1978), p. 99.

1 2

"The Hollywood Academy Awards is by far the biggest show on earth. And the slowest." Oswald Ortolan, a producer-director of the forthcoming fifty-first Hollywood Academy Awards, beams at Kosky, and he beams at him across a gold-plated table during their tête-à-tête luncheon in Monroe Stahr (PRINTER: not Star Monroe) restaurant—Manhattan's most notoriously exclusive place.

"This year, in order to boost the Oscar ratings up we've got some surprises." He lifts his index finger at Kosky. "For one, we want you, you, Norbert Kosky, to be the only Oscar presenter who will present not one Oscar—but two! Two Oscars—to two different winners, of course! One Oscar for the most original screenplay—words is your schtick, isn't it—and one for the most original adaptation of someone else's original novel or play or anything also made up of words. Now, isn't this neat? Having you, a relatively unknown, never-heard-of literary somebody, presenting two of the best-known literary Oscars in town?"

He lifts a small finger. Instantly, the servile steward materializes with a new bottle of wine.

"Six hundred million people will watch you at this year's Academy Awards and see you, a writer yourself, awarding them to other writers. To writers who—*so far unlike you*—sold out to the cinema! The Awards are fifty-one years old and so are you! You couldn't buy publicity like this for six—make it nine—million dollars!"

"Too bad most of my books are out of print," moans Kosky.

There is no prestige attached to being an author in Hollywood. An author (of standing) in London, in Paris, even in New York, enjoys a

certain distinction. He is acceptable. He is even desirable. His opinion is worth something. But when he reaches Hollywood, he finds himself curiously, unexpectedly and completely anonymous. The arrival of Joan Crawford at the Metro-Goldwyn-Mayer studios in Culver City is an event. Her lavish car rolls through the gate, onto the lot.... I may be wrong, but I do not recall ever having seen an author's car within the sacred precincts. (Mildred Cram)

"Books? Fuck the books! I'm talking fame." Ortolan leans all the way across the table. "More than fifty years have passed since Sam Goldwyn founded within his studio a writing collective he called the Eminent Authors [6/9/1919]. It's time to remind people that moving pictures must be written in words before they can start moving." He sips his wine. "Aren't you grateful to be chosen?"

"I am pleased. Of course I am," says Kosky.

"Face it, Norbert." For a gentile squire, Ortolan faces Kosky squarely. "How many obscure storytellers do you know who had instant fame delivered just like that—on a silver-screen platter in front of some six hundred million fucking spectators watching you from all over the fucking world—some of them watching you, no doubt, even while fucking?"

"I can't think of even one—except perhaps the one who wrote the initial Book of Creation," says Kosky.

"Good Lord!" exclaims Ortolan. "Even he had only a word-of-mouth for an audience—a Word, not the World. So what do you say—YES or NO?"

"I don't know, not yet," Kosky mumbles, crossing knife with a fork in the form of a cross. "You see, my father taught me that the happy life means being unnoticed; hence, according to him, only obscurity can lead to a happy life. Lead to—not guarantee it."

"I can't see how, it's all too obscure for me!" Ortolan interrupts him noisily.

"Because, as my father did say," Kosky interrupts Ortolan, "obscurity stems from the obscure verb 'to obscure'—which means to dim the luster of life, and to dim it in order to take the glare away but only in order to be able to see life better—and perhaps be able to find out what life is all about. Perhaps. That's why, while fame, reputation and no-toriety are derivative states of being (they derive from the presence of other people), only obscurity is original: one achieves obscurity quite by oneself."

"Your father obviously was not an American. Believe me, in this country fame is as good as a good reputation, maybe better, and much tougher to lose." Ortolan looks like pure Calvin Luther but speaks with an accent of Bruno Schulz the Drohobycz Casanova. "However," he goes on, "one bad headline, in even the smallest paper, can cost you your good reputation, however good, while no headline can kill fame which, made of headlines, in this country is synonymous with notoriety."

"I'm not convinced, not yet," mumbles Kosky, while Ortolan fixes upon him his crucifyingly tempting smile. "You see, in order to stay as obscure as possible, on the back cover of my books I used to list only my name and titles of my past books in lieu of a single biographical note."

"Those years are over," pronounces Ortolan. "I've just read 'On Kosky'—a special release distributed by your publishers worldwide. C'mon, Norbert, say yes to my golden offer." Ortolan breathes out the scent of caviar dipped in champagne. "Besides, aren't you a writer who is obliged by his Jewish faith—his faith being a Jewish narrative tradition—to turn anything, be it himself or Hollywood Oscars, into another spiritually inspiring story?"

"I stand convinced," says Kosky, and as he says it, his tongue—his tongue, as well as lips, suddenly turn dry. "For how long will I be on live display on the Oscar stage?" asks our Medusa Man who is already suffering from early stage fright. **What was he up to, what was he doing, what did he want? That's rather hard to tell, because he wanted so many things, but the thing he wanted most was Fame. Those were the years of his concentrated quest of that fair Medusa. (Thomas Wolfe)***

"For as long as it will take you to say a few dozen catchy words plus the name of the nominees, plus 'May I have the envelope, please'— plus handing out the Oscars! And, for the first time in recent memory, to go twice through this extraordinarily charged and tensed Oscar stage routine—and go through it without a fault! And you better do it fast: every second of the show buys thousands of dollars worth of advertising,

---

*Thomas Wolfe (who at one time starred in his own play) wrote about his manuscript *Of Time and the River*, stored in a giant wooden box: **There is an immense amount of it, millions of words, and although it might not be of any use to anyone else, it is, so far as I am concerned, the most valuable thing I have got.** (*The Letters of Thomas Wolfe*)

and thousands of advertisers all over the world buy every second of the show. Every second counts!"

It is like one of those South American palace revolutions conducted by officers in comic opera uniforms—only when the thing is over the ragged dead men lie in rows against the walls and you suddenly know that this is not funny, this is the Roman Circus, and damn near the end of a civilization. (Raymond Chandler)

The following week Kosky flies to Los Angeles for the Oscar ceremonies rehearsal.

He checks into a downtown Torquemada Inn where, trying to keep his stage fright in check, on an empty bladder he floats for hours in the bladder-shaped empty swimming pool. The stage fright is, of course, *angor animi*, an anguish of the spirit, as Anaïs Nin (his past literary colleague long since past: Jay Kay) knew only too well; it is—an illness as damaging to one's creative psyche as is that dreadful Malison illness, or thanatophilia—a death wish. He attempts to calm his turbulent inner pond by looking at himself in the calm surface of the motel's swimming pool, an obligatory confrontation between his self and Self.

Enough has been said about the BeShT* to show that his behavior as well as his relationship to nature and the supernatural was deeply influenced by his Gentile environment. It remains to add that in his appearance, too, he cultivated a resemblance to the Gentile holy men, many of whom were active in his days among the Raskol ("dissenting") peasantry of Ruthenia, Podolia, Volhynia, and the Ukraine. (Raphael Patai)

A day later he is picked up by a large limousine which, he is told by the youthful lad who is his driver, once drove some Eastern somebody such as Max Eastman—and once carried such heavy woods as Christopher Isherwood, Robert Sherwood and Marx Brothers, meaning the

---

*Born in the super-magical year 1699, Israel Bael Shem Tov "usually referred to by the acrostic BeShT" (Raphael Petai) was the founder of the Hasidic movement.

Hasidism represents one of the most significant and most original phenomena not only in the history of Judaism, but also in the history of the development of religions in general.... It did not aim at an improvement of the tenets of the faith or at a reform of religious practices; what it endeavored was something greater and deeper: the perfection of the soul. By means of exerting a powerful psychological influence Hasidism succeeded in creating a type of believer who valued the ardor of feeling higher than the observance of rites, piety and religious fervor higher than speculation and Tora-study. (Simon Dubnow, as quoted by Raphael Petai, op. cit., Chapter 8: "Jewish Dionysians: The Hasidim")

Animal Crackers Groucho, Harpo and Chico. The car takes him to the Oscar rehearsals.

As they arrive at the auditorium and stop at the entrance, a sizable crowd of screaming kids and shouting grown-ups surrounds the car. "They all want your autograph or a picture," says Allan. Our Eminent Author panics.

"What's this? I thought today was the rehearsal. Don't Oscars take place tomorrow?"

"They do," says the driver. "Tomorrow is D-Day."

"Then what are all these people here for today?"

"Today is the rehearsal for D-Day. Today they can see the celebs like yourself—a nobody suddenly turned into somebody—without paying top buck for the real thing," says the driver. "Tomorrow they can see the real thing on their TV."

Ready for extinction in the hands of the mob, Kosky extracts himself from the limo and, shaking with excitement, lets himself be photographed *en face* as well as *en profile* waving to the screaming kids as if he were an Oscar winner.

At the door to the auditorium, he is accosted by a lanky twenty-two-year-old Aryan. Appropriately for our page-turning author, the Aryan introduces himself as Kosky's official page—"assigned to guide you, sir, without fail on your part or mine throughout the events of today and tomorrow."

They enter the auditorium. Here the sight of the stage filled with people and lights—and of the enormous auditorium filled to its last seat with screaming people—gives Kosky another massive dose of stage fright.

"Why are all these people here? I thought this was a rehearsal." The author screams at his page.

"It is. That's why they're here," answers the page. "Oscars are live, aren't they?" he goes on. "So is the rehearsal."

Stretching practically the length of a city block, the giant stage is crowded with anonymous stagehands and—imagine that!—some two dozen of movieland's biggest stars, young and old men and women who now face him face-to-face and whom, until now, he faced only on the screen of the street corner's Cinema 69, as well as from on the screen of his six-by-nine TV. Now, Kosky shakes hands with Mike Wordsmith, one of the show's directors, who then leads Kosky by a hand, as if Kosky were a small-bodied boy and he a football coach, to center stage. There, in front of everybody—and what a front that is!—he places Kosky, again behind a stationary pulpit equipped with a stationary microphone carrying a hand-held mike. In a low voice he asks Kosky to start getting ready. From here and in this slot of time, rehearsing for the Oscars, Kosky will read aloud his Oscar remarks. Terrified and shaken, he is nevertheless pleased to notice that these remarks have been printed in giant block letters (so big he could read them from across a city block) on several man-sized cue cards. The cards are stacked now one in front of another, as they will be during the actual Academy Awards ceremony, next to the giant TV cameras which stand in the middle of the auditorium.

"Now, don't you say anything bad about the audience, do you hear me loud and clear?" Mike warns Kosky in a whisper and sticks a mike into Kosky's mouth.

"Why not? The bastards can't hear us, right?" whispers Kosky. "The mikes are not plugged in yet."

"Oh yes, they are! The BASTARDS can hear us—CAN'T YOU?" Mike whispers in a stage whisper into the mike and the six thousand strong audience replies in unison, YES WE CAN!, then laughs at Kosky with the loudest collective laugh.

Calm returns to the audience but not to our hero. On huge TV monitors facing the audience from under the ceiling, the collective eye of the audience can see our Trembling Bunting's hand trembling. Shaking silly, Kosky starts reading his text from the cue card. "The Bible proves to us that in the beginning was the Word . . .," he recites firmly.

"Watch out, son!" says Mike.

"Watch out for what?"

"For how you say it. You pronounce *word* as *world*. It's not the same, you know! While to Gentiles, in the beginning was the Word, to Jews it was heaven and earth—the whole world." He pauses and the audience chuckles easily. "That's like not knowing about the difference between a blue bird and The Bluebeard!" Mike goes on and gets another salvo of laughter.

Spiritually strained, Kosky now desperately attempts to temporarily censor his inner film director, his own nastiest critic. In order to achieve this, he starts thinking first about *The Secret Trial*, a little-known 1969 film about the Soviet leader Zinoviev, who was tragically implicated in 1936 by Stalin, but this does not seem to help him. Then he turns his *videothoughts®* (a word he coined in an interview in the *Media Message* magazine) to a blond woman—now what a perfect *dombi* would this one make!—who, all clad in soft and pliant leather, sits next to—wait a minute, is this lad one of the Allan Ladds?

No, he is not. He is—imagine that!—Beau Brummel, the American scene prime intellectual superstar! He is the one who only the other day was portrayed half-naked on the cover of *Sex Seduction* magazine.

Kosky wets his lips. "In the beginning was the Word," he enunciates most clearly. **The director must die within an actor. (Vladimir I. Ne-mirovich-Danchenko)**

"Careful, baby!" says Mike. "Your Word keeps coming out of you as a ward. Ward means prison! You don't want all these decent folks in Montana, Mombasa and Kielbasa to think that in the beginning was a prison, do you?" His ethnically colored remarks get "prolonged applause," as such collective reactions are often called. "Try again!" he prompts our electronic village idiot.

"In the beginning was the Word . . .," Kosky strains. **A gesture is a movement not of a body but of a soul. (Feodor Chaliapin)**

"Careful, Norbie," Mike interrupts him. "This time it came out as wart. Wart is a skin tumor—a cancer. Now, how would you like to hear someone telling you from TV that in the beginning was a cancer, eh?" The audience roars.

"In the beginning was the Word—" Kosky begins.

"Stop right there! Szloma Szmul,"* screams Mike. "This time, your Word came out as *wort*! Wort—d'you hear? Wort as in walewort, wallwort, wartwort, willowwort, or whitlowwort," he says. "As every pothead knows, a wort is a pot herb," he says, and the audience roars once more.

"I thought I came closer to worth than to wort," says Kosky. "I thought I said worth. Worth as in worthless; as in the words airworthy, blame-worthy, fameworthy, helpworthy, seaworthy. Worth, as in the nine worthies."

"Stop right there!" says Wordsmith. "You're practicing the wrong word, and you can't pronounce it either! You are not here 'cause you're worthy." He can't decide whether *wûr'thĭ* is an eminent noun, a worth-while adjective, or a worthy adverb. "You are here because you're a writer; a writer means being wordy, not just wordly, right? You're here because you're supposed to be a worthy writer—a worthy not wordy—

---

*Szloma Szmul (from Szloma Szmulewicz): a typical Ruthenian Jewish name.

otherwise why would they send me a dodo bird who can't say *word* in English?"

Kosky starts again. "In the beginning was the Word."

"It came out as *war*," Mike interrupts him. "Now, maybe *war* was at our beginning, but we don't want you to be the first to word it worldwide, do we? Try again." He chuckles, and so does the audience.

"In the beginning was the Word. . . ." Kosky shifts his weight from one foot to the other. **The soul does not like to be without its body because without the body it cannot feel or do anything. Therefore build a figure in such a way that its pose tells what is in the soul of it. (Leonardo da Vinci)**

"Try again," Mike cuts in.

"In the beginning was the Word," Kosky sweats out. **Drop your voice an octave and don't lisp . . . count to six and look at that lamp as if you could no longer live without it. (Josef von Sternberg)**

"Not bad, but now it sounds like *wourd*. What's *wourd*?" Mike roars and so does the audience.

"I don't know what's *wourd*. I've never heard that word before," says Kosky.

"Neither did we—until now!" says the director. "Give it another try, Norbert—I mean Robert."

Kosky tries again.

"Now it sounds like *worth*, like it's 'What's your worth?' I told you not to keep on saying *worth*."

"Maybe I should practice on Wordsworth, on a name?" says Kosky.

"Wordsworth?" Wordsmith rolls his hand to his ear.

"William Wordsworth." Kosky nods.

I do not ask pardon for what there is of untruth in such verses considered strictly as matters of fact. (Wordsworth)

"Go ahead, try it again on your Wordsworth." Mike Wordsmith seems offended.

Kosky mobilizes himself and in one long breath rushes the whole phrase straight through. **No feast, no performance. Our work is senseless if there is no holiday mood, if there is nothing to carry the spectators away. Let us carry them away with our youth, laughter, and improvisation. (Vakhtangov)**

"By George, he's got it!" Wordsmith triumphs. "Now let's go on with the rest of your speech. Take a deep breath. Here we go, Bert . . ."

After the rehearsals, on the way out, Kosky signs autographs and poses for pictures.

"Enjoy the last day of your privacy," says the lanky Aryan, gently escorting our Sweating Jew to the limo (as gently as only a Gentile would—adds Jay Kay with a bit of his own stage fright).

SS

Back at his hotel, Kosky rests by buoying up in the swimming pool, where he, a man who can't drown, is watched in silent wonder by two Arab children, their nannies and sand-shifting bodyguards. Tired, he goes to his room, and switching off, he switches on the TV. He watches the end of *The Picture of Dorian Gray* and the beginning of *Prophetic Pictures*. Finally, to prepare himself for what's ahead, his moving finger reluctantly guides him to another channel, on which a group of past-perfect Oscar winners debate the past Oscars imperfect. Then he falls asleep.

And by his side was that stern friend, the only one to whom he spoke what in his secret heart he most desired. To Loneliness he whispered, "Fame!"—and Loneliness replied, "Aye, brother, wait and see." (Thomas Wolfe)

He wakes up by midday. He is groggy, but not groggy enough. He knows this is his D-day. The countdown begins. In some six hours our Maverick Limerick from New York will enter the Planet Image.

A hermit once thought his oasis/The best of all possible places;/For it had a mirage/In the form of a large/And affectionate female curvaceous. (William S. Baring-Gould)

The limo picks him up on the dot, and on its way to the Oscars joins the stream of other limos.

At the CELEBS parking lot, past, present and future Oscar celebs park their cars. Here, our Jewfish* is spotted and picked up by Lanky Ayran, his tuxedoed page. Walkie-talkie in hand, the page escorts our trembling bookman to his seat in the auditorium, which, he is told in no uncertain terms, he may not leave alone and from where, a few minutes before his Oscar presentation, he will be collected by his most faithful, good-looking and well-meaning page. While his page hovers nearby, our

---

*Jewfish: a large dark-colored saltwater fish which populates the shallows of the coral heads and caves of the South Atlantic and feeds on other fish.

trembling Pollack* introduces himself to the fish in the next seat (they are among other presenters)—a prime-time Broadway Stonefly Nymph on his left, and the Black Sea Bass, a leading Hollywood male star.

The finest trout fisherman in the world dare those who are expert with symphs. (Tom McNally)

Shortly before the Grand Mass is about to begin, Kosky's stomach begins to bulge from within. Stage fright turns into stomach cramps. He is about to explode. Quick! He summons his page. He tells him he is about to blow up. His page leads him through the crowds, through the lobby, to the haven of a toilet. Thank heavens! Kosky locks himself in one of the stalls and, exploding in safety, suddenly sees his page peeping at him through the crack in the door frame.

After a moment, his page becomes aware that from within his stall, Kosky spies on him.

"I'm not allowed to leave you alone, sir! Not even for a most private moment!" he apologizes for being a spy. "If something awful happened to you, I'd have to alert the central stage—they would have to come up with a double real quick."

"What bad could possibly happen to me in a toilet?"

"You'd be surprised," the page whispers to him through the door— while watching him through the crack. "People do funny things when they're as sick from bad nerves as you are now. Things that aren't funny."

"Like what?"

"Like taking the wrong pill. Like hitting the wrong vein with a needle. Like going through 'I want to go home!' sudden scream!"

Emptied of everything but fear, Kosky gets out of the stall and the page escorts him to his seat.

No one has described fully the horror of this illness called anxiety. Worse than any physical illness, this is illness of the soul, for it is insidious, elusive and arouses no pity. (Anaïs Nin)

Back in his seat he resumes the posture of an ordinary U.S. writer who is suffering from ordinary hypotension and spiritual ischemia— neither spiritual anxiety nor literary angina pectoris.

Just then the curtain goes up, baring the largest stage in the world. Suspended over the stage, a huge banner proclaims: **LIVE spells backward into EVIL, while EROS reverses SORE. And, we should never forget the**

---

*Pollack: a medium-sized, lightly colored saltwater fish which, feeding on shrimp, wanders in schools at medium depths of the North Atlantic.

SIN in SINCERE or the CON in CONFIDENCE. Let's tighten up the slack sentimentality. (Marshall McLuhan)

The auditorium quiets down. The greatest show on earth begins, then proceeds in all its splendor.

"It's time!" says the page, motioning Kosky to follow him around on the double.

On the way to the big altar, they make a pit stop. At the pit, the lady makeup artist and her portable anti-perspiration powder kit neatly dispose of the heavily perspiring look of our literary man on the make. Too bad she can't do anything for a perspiring heart. After she is finished, the page escorts Kosky to the Green Box, the waiting room on the stage's right wing, assuring him that the stage's left side has its own Green Box. Our Green Box is full of journalists, other Oscar presenters, TV reporters and press photographers. ("Aren't they all merely a replica of my old country's village elders gathered in the sacristy of that old village church?" asks someone else: Jay Kay.)

The mass is in progress—the excitement builds. Everybody stares at the TV monitor. On it, Danny Boatman, the Oscar's least ceremonious master of ceremonies, announces the appearance of Beau Brummel, Hollywood's most secretive leading man. (Most secretive but not when it comes to having so many women. Is he, by chance vain?: Jay Kay.) Beau Brummel will present an Oscar to the best director. In a moment, BB strides out onto the right side of the stage.

Since, according to the program, Kosky must follow Brummel, with Brummel's appearance Pan Kosky panics.

The nature of anxiety can be understood when we ask what is threatened in the experience which produces anxiety. The threat is to something in the "core of essence" of the personality. Anxiety is the apprehension cued off by a threat to some value which the individual holds essential to his existence as a personality. (Rollo May, 1950)

"I'm next, right?" Kosky asks his page for the ninth time. A rhetorical question. Everybody in this room knows Kosky is next. Why? Because next comes the Oscar for the best original screenplay, to be followed by an Oscar for the best screenplay adapted from another source—"both to be presented by Norbert Kosky, a little-known writer from the East who suddenly made it big in the West," in the words of the *Hollywood Purporter*.

"You are," says the page, all terribly excited but most polite. "Beau Brummel is now presenting the Oscar on the right wing. He is presenting it on the right wing—not to the right wing, right? That's why you follow him on the left. Good luck!"

"On the *left*? What left?" screams Kosky, suffering a massive attack of instant sweat, but also a massive injection of world-wide awareness (world-wide, printer, not just word). Everyone in the world knows Oscar winners—and how well does the world know who won last year's literary Nobel? "But we are in the right wing!" Gripped by terror, but also by its drama (and drama is a precursor of joy), he can barely point out the sign above their heads. He is unable to move. Is he going to suddenly appear at the wrong end of a Hollywood stage in front of six thousand people in this auditorium and six hundred million people watching him all over the electronic world?

"No kidding!" The page becomes blank. Then, the blank page kid panics and blankly looks at everybody. Everybody nods. This is the right side, kid, say their nods. This right happens to be the wrong one for Kosky. Why? Simple. Because Kosky's cue cards happen to be stacked up in front of the lantern standing on the left side of the stage. And what about the two Oscar statuettes *and* the two envelopes containing the names of the lucky Oscar winners, which are also waiting for Kosky on the left side of the stage—where by now our unlucky man should have been long ago!

"It's my first job, and I got it all screwed up!" moans the blank page while our literary Ministrant goes through a massive attack of chest pain. Once again he sounds alarm no. 9. The pain, or perhaps only a spasm, takes place in the epigastric right upper quadrant of his chest; it radiates along his back and beneath the scapula all the way to the left precordial region and left shoulder.

The pain becomes severe, and intensifies rapidly. It is accompanied by an instant belching, sudden bloating by abdominal cramp and sudden nausea. Discreetly Kosky reaches for a handkerchief and—discreetly—discharges into it. Equally discreetly he throws the offensive handkerchief into the garbage basket—or was it someone's shopping bag? His bloating and belching reassure his inner Dr. Kosky that his one and only patient is going through not a terminal heart attack but, rather, an ordinary biliary spasm, precipitated, no doubt, by spiritual food fried in a spiritually disagreeable frying pan, a momentary illness most presenters probably go through. **All creative writers are hypochondriacs. (Harold Nicolson)**

"I got it all screwed up." There goes my next job, as an army recruiter—anything is better than an army recruit! The blank page keeps moaning, as he and Kosky start walking toward the left side. Just then the page's walkie-talkie beeps. Helplessly, he activates it.

"Where the fuck are you? Where is Kosky?" screams the voice of the stage manager.

"We're on the wrong side," moans the blank page.

"Kosky is next! Get his ass here—NOW!" screams the walkie-talkie. Now the page and the scribe start running through the back stage. The back stage is—easily—a mile long. It is, also, a labyrinth, a veritable marshland filled with stagehands, stage feet, stage toes, most of whom by now clearly suffer from stage fatigue.

"Get him here NOW!" the walkie-talkie screams again. Just then the blank page collides with a stage guard—and the shock of collision practically knocks him and his walkie-talkie down.

This time, Kosky doesn't wait for him. As if in a trance, he runs through entranceways marked FRONT EXIT and BACK ENTRY and DO NOT ENTER and EXIT ONLY and PRIVATE OFFICIALS ONLY, and STAY OUT OF MY ROOM, CHRIS! And anywhere he runs he hears the loud moans of the page and the page's walkie-talkie screaming: "We've got two minutes left! Where is Kosky? Kosky! Get here! Now!"

Kosky is running and he is running fast. This is no longer an ordinary run. This is a run for life. A save-your-face race. Already he sees the headlines: OSCAR PRESENTER FAILS TO PRESENT—NORBERT KOSKY CHICKENS OUT.

This is summer 1944. The simple one-way radio—the early-day walkie-talkie found by the village fishermen on the dead body of a German soldier—snaps the latest news. June 23: "On the Galician front the Red Army commences its last offensive against Germans on Russian soil." June 25: "The Red Army takes Vitebsk." June 28: "The Red Army takes Mogilev." July 3: "The Red Army takes Minsk." July 13: "THE RED ARMY APPROACHES PINSK."

The Germans retreat. Look at them all rushing home, this time ahead of their panzers who now protect their rears from the advancing Red Snappers (the Red partisans), and the suddenly invincible Red Army. The end of the war? Not quite, kid! You're on the home run, but not home free yet! The VLASOVITES ARE COMING. The Vlasovites are the deserters from the Red Army. They are big, strong, meaty. They ride horses bareback and barefooted. They eat meat raw, and they eat it *po Tatarsku* (à la Tartare), with their bare hands. Their pleasures are as raw as their meat or meatus. Raping men, women and children is their prime-time pleasure.

It was a terrible scene, one that will live in my memory until I die. After surrounding the villages, a command was given to burn it, together with all the inhabitants. The excited barbarians took firebrands to the houses and those who ran away were shot at or forced back to the flames. They grabbed small children from their mothers and threw them into the fire. And when the grief-stricken women ran to save their children, they would shoot them first in one leg and then in the other. Then, after such torments, they finished them off. . . . The fields behind the village were covered with the dead: here, a mother with a child in her arms, its brains splashed all over her face; there a ten-year-old boy with his *elementarz* (his schoolbook) in his hand. (witness, age 19, 1945)*

On the final stretch of his Oscar run, our Pan Kosky crosses another brook. It's full of panfish,† and every *pan* holds a walkie-talkie. "Hurry

---

*From "Experiences One Can't Forget," Chapter 6, page 266, in *Polish Children Accuse, 1939–45*. Part One: "Documents of Nazi Crimes," ed. and compiled by Jozef Wnuk; Part Two: "German Occupation Through Children's Eyes," ed. and compiled by Helena Radomska-Strzemecka. See also "Polesie Voivodeship," in *War Through Children's Eyes*, page 96, ed. and compiled by Irena Grudzinska-Gross and Jan Tomasz Gross, 1981. See also *The Voivode's Ghost*. See it preferably on stage or on a video cassette, an opera by yet another world-famous Polish-Jew, what's his name? GroSSman! Another well-known composer and organizer of musical life Ludwik Grossman (1835–1915), the author of such operas as *The Fisherman from Palermo*, staged in Warsaw and Paris, and *The Voivode's Ghost*, which became a success in Warsaw, Lvov, St. Petersburg, Vienna, and Berlin. He also wrote a number of works for the orchestra and for the piano, as well as many songs. The "Grossman salon" came down in the history of Warsaw's cultural life as a place where receptions were held in honour of music celebrities visiting Warsaw, and performances were given by famous artists. One could meet there eminent actors, musicians, painters, writers, among them Boleslaw Prus and Henryk Sienkiewicz, as well as aristocracy and rich bourgeoisie. Grossman played host to Helena Modrze-jewska (Modjeska), Peter Tchaikovsky, Anton Rubinstein, Pablo Sarasate, and many other celebrities of the epoch. In partnership with Juliusz Herman, Grossman ran a piano shop and factory, trade name Herman and Grossman. Attached to the shop was a concert hall where concerts and lectures on musical subjects were given. Grossman was for some time director of the Warsaw Opera. He was also one of the founders of the Warsaw Music Society, headed by Stanislaw Moniuszko. (*The Polish Jewry: History and Culture*, op cit., p. 69)

†Ask the man battling a bluefin tuna off Cat Cay what the first fish he ever caught

up, Kosky!" screams a Bluegill. "You've got about a minute left!" screeches the Green Sunfish. "What's wrong with you? Don't you know you belong on the left side?" screeches a Crappie. "Run, buddy, run!" shouts a Yellow Perch. "Where is Kosky? WHERE IS NORBERT KOSKY?" shrills Rock Bass.

"My, my! You must be Norbert Kosky? You're the only Oscar presenter in history who disappeared at the Oscars. May I have your autograph?" squawks a Warmouth. Another eddy. Another dam. Don't fall over this dam. Imagine: OSCAR PRESENTER BLEEDS ON OSCAR STAGE: WAS HE SICK OR BEATEN UP?

He runs through a portable plastic forest just removed from the right side of the stage. Careful now! Don't run into a tree; watch out—too late: the plastic branch hits him in the eye. WAS OSCAR PRESENTER BLINDED BY AN OSCAR? An eye for an eye.

Another corridor, another village. Another inlet. Another sandy bank. "Hurry up, Kosky," squawks a friendly crawfish. "Slow down, buddy! You still have a minute!" yellows a spindly grasshopper.

His Inner Boy starts hyperventilating. Nice, sixteen, nineteen expirations per minute! OSCAR PRESENTER HYPERVENTILATES TWO OSCARS. Instantly, his inner automatically programmed autodidact command takes over, ordering his body to start breathing at a slowed-down diaphragmatic rate. He obeys, with his glottis opened to full capacity. He is now exhaling six times per minute; inhaling, he now directs the fresh air straight to the vagus (which causes an overproduction of aceteylcholine—the friendly enzyme responsible for arterial relaxation).*

Running along, our Pan Marathonsky casts a quick glance at the TV monitor—one of many placed along his run. On it, Artur Atractor, the Oscar-winning director (who just had his Oscar handed to him by Beau

---

was. . . . To a man—or perhaps it would be more correct to say, to a boy—they will chorus that they grew up catching bluegills, sunnies and other panfish. (Tom McNally)

*"Specifically, dream frequency, self-verbalizations, and certain forms of mental imagery seemed to differentiate the best gymnasts from those who failed to make the Olympic team." ("Psychology of the Elite Athlete: An Exploratory Study," by Michael J. Mahoney and Marshall Avener, in *Cognitive Therapy and Research*, vol. 1, no. 2, 1977, p. 135.) See also the *Circulation of Literary Elites*, by Welkpfin and Niskisko, 1982 (a work openly based on the sociology of Circulation of Elites, of Vifredo Pareto [1843–1923] at one time Kosky's part-time literary favorite) (literary, not sociological: J.K.).

Brummel) continues the litany of thanks to those without whom his Oscar wouldn't be possible, without for once mentioning his force of creation. In a few seconds Atractor will leave the stage, and Danny Boatman, the ultramundane master of ceremonies, will appear, crack a typical Danny Boatman joke ("Everybody in Hollywood knows the unimportance of being a writer. Have *you* ever heard of Norbert Kosky?"), upon which he will announce the imminent appearance of Norbert Kosky, "our literary present as well as presenter." But where is Kosky?

Run, kid, run. Thank God for the long breaks in the Oscar program offered by commercials. A final sprint over a spring hole, and—presto!— our Ministrant appears in the Green Box, without a drop of saliva or a breath of his own.

"Where the fuck were you?" yowls the stage manager. "You've got less than a minute left!" He guides Kosky to the stage. "Walk up the scaffold all the way to the top," he instructs him. "Turn around. Face the audience. Face it with your true face. Your true face, do you hear? This is no time for an acting lesson!" He instructs Kosky as if he were a boxing manager and Kosky his only hi-score boxer. "Now, keep facing the people, *the people* not the TV cameras, until Danny ends his introduction. Start walking down the second the cameras turn toward you. Walk down all the way to the lectern. Walk down naturally. The same way you walked all the way to the very top. Naturally means slowly. Go slowly! Slowly and naturally! And, for God's sake, don't fall!"

OSCAR PRESENTER FALLS ON STAGE, ALLEGEDLY UPSET BY THE CHOICE OF THE NOMINEES.

"Now don't improvise. Just read straight from your cue cards as they appear," the manager goes on. "Where are your reading glasses?" He panics.

"I'm farsighted," Kosky reassures him.

"When you finish reading the names of the nominees, get the envelopes. Once you say, 'And the winners are . . .' open the winner's envelope slowly. Peel up the flap ever so gently. Don't ever tear it with anger. Let the people get excited. Once you read the names of the winners, look ever so pleased—even if you hate their guts. Don't spit. Don't sneeze. Don't laugh. Don't wink. Don't do anything that could be construed as rejection."

"Anything else?" Kosky collects himself.

"Oh, yes!" The manager scratches his head. "Speak to them in English. Don't say anything in a foreign language—particularly not in a language which doesn't have a country of its own, like Desperanto."

"Esperanto," Kosky corrects him gently. "Esperanto is a lovely and facile language."

"Nothing in Willpuke—"

"Volapük," says Kosky.

"Nothing in Kliterlingua."

"Interlingua." Kosky straightens him out.

"Remember, once the Oscar winners walk up to the stage to pick up their Oscars, it's their show, not yours. Be naturally humble, but not overly servile. Don't stand in their way. Don't do anything that might be construed as *obstructing* their path to glory, and don't do anything vulgar on stage. Their glory lasts only until next year's Oscars, and it starts the minute they pick up the statuette from you. While all you've got is your old literary routine. Now, please don't drop the Oscar. Would you drop a Bible?"

"I won't drop it. Not this time," Kosky swears. "I learned my lesson during the war. I'll hold onto it with all my strength."

"Don't." The manager grabs him by the shoulder, then lets go with reluctance. "Hold it gently, and don't close your thumb over it. You might get a numb thumb cramp. The thumb is the most flexible of all digits, but it can get locked in its own saddle joint. It's happened before. Of course"—he winks at Kosky—"some presenters like not letting the Oscar go. They enjoy standing up there, on the top of the world, in front of six hundred million people, being photographed with an Oscar in hand. Even with somebody else's Oscar."

"I'll be swift," Kosky promises. As swift as Jonathan Swift, that literary swifty.

"Don't be too swift. Be dignified. After all, it's an Oscar, not a piece of junk. Let it out of your hand slowly—but without teasing! And don't turn your back on an Oscar winner. He or she just won an Oscar—and who are you? Also, don't instigate or encourage any mouth-to-mouth kissing either: give them your other cheek to kiss, but not your hand. Brace them gently if you must, but don't embrace them."

"I'll watch out," says Kosky. "Anything else?"

On the monitor, the Seneca Industries commercial ends; the TV zeroes in on Danny Boatman. It's time to go. The stage manager pushes Kosky out into the worldwide video ring, just as Boatman begins to introduce our literary boxer, who walks up the staircase of the scaffold. He stops on the top of the scaffold. He turns and faces the sea of faces.

166

Ending his remarks, Danny Boatman surrenders the lectern to "AND NOW, LADIES AND GENTLEMEN, HERE IS NORBERT KOSKY."

Calmly, his heart even at sixty even beats per minute, the Survival Kid catches his breath as he slowly descends the grand staircase. At the lectern, with Boatman gone, Kosky takes over the boat. Another pause: another breath of time and air.

All composed, our altar boy starts reading from the cue cards: "The Bible tells us that in the beginning was the Word," he begins. Another pause. Was it *wŭrth* or *wărd*? Too late now!

Gatsby believed in the green light, the orgastic future that year by year recedes before us. It eluded us then, but that's no matter—tomorrow we will run faster, stretch out our arms farther.... And one fine morning—So we beat on, boats against the current, borne back ceaselessly into the past. (F. Scott Fitzgerald)

SS

After the ceremonies a night letter from UG-TV in Dasein, Israel, reaches Kosky at his hotel.

I SAW YOU ON ISRAELI TV GIVING OSCARS ON AMERICAN TV STOP AS A WWII SURVIVOR I REMEMBER YOU FROM THE TIME AFTER THE WAR WHEN WE WERE BOTH KIDS. STOP AND WHEN OTHER KIDS CALLED YOU MUTE AND DUMB YOU USED TO CUT OUR BICYCLE TIRES IN REVENGE STOP I'M GLAD TO SEE YOU SPEAK AND SPEAK UP AGAIN. SHALOM RACHEL.

They had parted as children, or very little more than children. Years passed. Then something recalled to the woman the companion of her young days, and she wrote to him: "I have been hearing of you lately. I know where life has brought you. You certainly selected your own road. But to us, left behind, it always looked as if you had struck out into a pathless desert." (Conrad)

I love it here.... The point is once you've got it—Screen Credit 1st, a Hit 2nd, and the Academy award 3rd—you can count on it forever ... and know there's one place you'll be fed without being asked to even wash the dishes. (F. Scott Fitzgerald)

A day like any other day—except that this one is a day after the Oscars. SIC TRANSIT GLORIA MUNDI pronounces its verdict upon this year's Oscars, the *Los Angeles Transit* in its customary post-Oscars front-page top-front headline. The phone rings.

"Is this Mr. Kosky?" asks a man, speaking with the accent of King Edward, mixed with the accent of Lord Mountbatten and Nehru.

"Speaking." Kosky rings his Ruthenian *ing!*

"Oh, hello, Kosky," says the man. "My name is Gardiner. Chauncey Gardiner. How are you?"

"I could be worse, as they say in Ruthenia. It could be as bad as could be!"

"Could it now?" Gardiner wonders. "Could it be worse than when you were doing your poor-taste number at this year's Oscars. Oscars which were numerically seen by the largest number of people *ever?*"

"What did I do wrong?" Kosky's heart goes through ventricular contractions. No wonder. As of today his heart is made of vanity.

"In your hardly original opening, you said, 'The Bible tells us that in the beginning was the War!' War instead of you know what," says Gardiner. "Also, you dared to call the Ten Commandments the world's first screenplay. What Jewish-Ruthenian chutzpah!"

"That's not what I meant," Kosky objects. "I meant that it's time to 'restore spiritual order.' "

When the universe was in complete disorder, Moses was called to the mountain. A warning bolt of lightning, an overture of thunder, the skies parted, and a mighty hand reached down to give Moses the stone tablets. In a way, that was the first script. Some critics thought it was overproduced for just ten lines—but, by following it, mankind restored order out of chaos. (Academy Awards, 1982)

"I'm calling because I just read that old book of yours and I found out that in your book you invaded my privacy." Gardiner's voice acquires a menacing tone.

"I—what?"

"You heard me: you invaded my privacy, privacy meaning my spiritual inner flame. *The Los Angeles Transit* calls you the Oscar's only Tantric intellectual squire. Or was it square? If indeed you are a Tantric then you know what inner flame means, to a man like me. A man of means who always lives with a blonde flame." (And as he says it, Jay Kay already sees him "grinning obscenely.")

"Nonsense. My stories are fiction. Fiction invades imagination, not privacy," Kosky intervenes firmly. "Besides, even though *John Doe vs. privacy* is not explicitly stated in the Constitution—in due respect, as an American, I mean our American Constitution—its humanistic interpretation clearly points at a 'zone of rights' as Justice Douglas called it." (Which means the opening of a brand-new libertarian and neoliberal ball park, rejoices the always politically balanced Jay Kay.) These story fragments come out of a lot of talk with friends or out of wandering around the streets, or sleeping . . . that's why it takes so long to write. You just have to let it go through you; you have to keep imagining. (Paddy Chayefsky)*

"All I know is that you've portrayed me as your gardener. That's bloody unfair!"

"If indeed you recognize yourself in my character—in the fictional character I created—such recognition belongs to you, not to me." Kosky raises his voice as a novelist. Where a name is used, it, like a portrait or picture, must, upon meeting the eye or ear, be unequivocally identified

---

*Paddy Chayefsky: who thought of himself as "a writer of satire," and who wrote most of his satire (*Marty, Middle of the Night, Network*) for the stage and screen.

as that of the complainant. If it is not, then, taken with the statement of the author that all characters portrayed are wholly fictional, the identity of name must be set down as a pure coincidence. (American Courts)

"Not bloody likely! Would you prefer to talk about it in a court of law?" screams Gardiner.

"I would rather confront you face to face. Confront without a front, or afront." Kosky, a pacifist at heart, remembers World War II. Kosky looks forward to testing his combat readiness.

"O.K. Why not?" Gardiner breathes. "Why don't we talk first? I'll send my hottest car for you."

"And I'll pay for the hot line's gasoline." Kosky hangs up first. Although it had been agreed not to make public the substance of these documents until the governments were ready for signature, word quickly leaked to the press. *The Washington Post* disclosed the Hot Line Agreement on the same day it was initialed in Helsinki. Not so predictably, Moscow revealed the existence and nature of the Accidents Agreement. (Gerard Smith, 1985)*

SS

Gardiner's car is a Phantom Six, the silver screen's veritable ghost. Inside the "luxuriously appointed" (*Inside Car Magazine*) back compartment the six-screen TV set stares the passenger in his face.

---

*First Agreements 1971, Chapter 9, p. 280–98, in *Double Talk*: the Story of Salt I, by The Chief American Negotiator, Gerard Smith, 1980, 1985, p. 296. "Speaking to the Supreme Soviet in July of 1969, Foreign Minister Gromyko said, 'There is another aspect of the matter that must not be overlooked in long-range policies of states. This is largely connected with the fact that weapons control and guidance systems are becoming . . . more and more independent of the people who create them. Human hearing and vision are not capable of reacting accurately at today's velocities and the human brain is sometimes unable to evaluate the readings of a multitude of instruments quickly enough. The decision made by a human being ultimately depends on the conclusion provided to him by computer devices.' . . . The Hot Line had been useful in at least one crisis. But it had weaknesses. One link used land lines in Europe. A Finnish farmer's plow had once put it out of operation. It seemed prudent to immunize the link from this kind of interruption. Having been involved in the original Hot Line proposal some ten years before, I was especially interested in this subject." (p. 28) See also "IV Arms Control and the Rule of Law," pp. 69–89 in *Gerard Smith on Arms Control*, ed. by Kenneth W. Thompson, 1987.

"What does Mr. Chauncey Gardiner do these days?" Kosky asks the driver—a nondescript conscript from the Valley.

"It's not for me to *decide*, sir. I just drive. That's all I do," says the conscript, fearfully glancing into the car's rearview mirror as he guides his Phantom Six in utter silence.

Gardiner's house in Malibu is a fusion of sunscreen with skylight, a hybrid of love boat beached involuntarily on a sand dune and space ship which crashed on landing.

A Mexican manservant escorts *Señor* Kosky through a granite hallway, offering, along the way, a peek at a screening room, a health spa, a video-game room and a library. Outside, on a croquet lawn, Kosky faces a middle-aged, middle-sized man lounging in a hammock suspended high above the terrace. Bearded and mustached, the man sports a sombrero with ultra-wide brim set low on his wide forehead, and dark glasses set high on his clearly Semitically shaped nose (shape number six or nine: Jay Kay).

"Mr. Kosky! So happy to make your acquaintance," says the man. He clambers out of the hammock. The men shake hands, then sink into a pair of hospital beds disguised as sundeck chairs. "So you're the usurper of my life," says Gardiner.

"I usurped folklore, not life. I invaded fiction, not fact," says Kosky. **There was some suggestion that the defendant published the portrait by mistake, and without knowledge that it was the plaintiff's portrait, or was not what it purported to be. But the fact, if it was one, was no excuse. If the publication was libelous, the defendant took the risk. As was said of such matters by Lord Mansfield, "Whenever a man publishes, he publishes at his peril." (Justice Oliver Wendell Holmes)**

"Are you certain you haven't trampled on my private garden?" Gardiner exhibits his smile. His smile is his exhibit A, and Kosky panics: exhibit A seems familiar. Had he, a survivor of a Nazi invasion, involuntarily invaded the life of another man? A man with a most familiar smile?

"Well—I almost did."

"*Almost?* That's not good enough for the British jury, sir! Didn't you know that we British love gardening?"

"Everybody knows that," says Kosky. "That's not an invasion."

"How about Chauncey—his name?"

"An ordinary name. American first, or last, name. As ordinary as chance itself. Ask Tennessee Williams," says Kosky.

171

"The fact is, your character, your Chauncey Gardiner, comes from life. From me. From property everybody in Yorkshire knows as Gardiner's Gardens."

Somberly, Gardiner jerks off his sombrero and he does it like a simple *hombre*, a Mexican lord of the prairie, not a British *caballero*.

"Since to me a reader knows just as much as the author about the State of Make-Believe, I believe my novel is a portrait. A moving portrait of a moving soul."

You can make an X-ray photograph of a face, but you cannot make a face from an X-ray photograph. (Arthur Koestler)

"It is also a novel about the Media. The media which, God bless its free soul, is as free to interpret my Chance's conduct as I am free to interpret his soul."

"Please stop that abstract talk and stop it now." Gardiner gets up from his orthopedic stool, then turns around but the turn pains him; like Kosky (and so many other men: J.K.) he too suffers from a spinal pain.

"Unless you tell the public I'm your ideal character called Chauncey I'm going to have you"—he pauses, and just then says,—"oh, what the hell!" and takes off his sunglasses. Then he peels off his beard and mustache and, one after another, his many other faces. There goes the face of Genghis Khan; there goes the police inspector—that closet queen!—who won't inspect his own closet. There goes the Onion Eater (thanks to his Dionysian Hasidic upbringing: J.K.) who made the simple act of eating onion with lemon spiritually synonymous with great acting.

Now, but only now, Kosky knows who this man is. He is Shaman Peters.

"I'm glad I fooled you. May I call you Norbert the Great?" Shaman Peters tries to embrace Kosky without leaving his orthopedic stool, but his movement is cut short by his sore spine. "I'm glad I fooled you. I was born to a Jewish-Russian, which then went to Britain, family, and I was born as a voluntary fool. I have fooled everyone ever since, at the age of three, I was already declared to be an acting child prodigy, and a true three-year-old *starets*," he declares, assuming a posture of a Russian *starets*.* "That's why, in your Chauncey, I recognize my inner

---

*Such was the *starets*, a man of the people who had attained the highest degree of wisdom complemented by divine grace, but one who still dwelt among the people, both in his inmost nature and in his actions. Official authorities, abbots and bishops, were often suspicious of the *starets*—he belonged to the people's religion, at once

yurodivy—a voluntary fool like me." No longer fooling, Peters orders (via one of his many servants: J.K.) a bottle of 1969 semi-sparkling champagne.

"When did you first read my novel?" asks our Eminent Author.*

"I haven't read it!" Peters admits. "Like your Chance—or Chauncey—I like to watch, remember?"

"You haven't read it?" The Author becomes perplexed. **Gradually there grew up within me a belief that the public was tiring of the star and a corresponding conviction that the emphasis of production should be placed upon the story rather than upon the player. In the poverty of screen drama lay, so I felt, the weakness of our industry, and the one correction of this weakness which suggested itself to me was a closer cooperation between author and picture producer. (Samuel Goldwyn)**

"I haven't read it not because I don't read, but because I can't read easily." His face becomes expressionless. "Letters and numbers bore me. They bore me visually, because visually they don't seem to drill into me—to bore into me easily, you might say. Still, as you can tell, I can tell stories and I'm hardly a social bore."

"Then how do you know the story?"

"George Scarab—my friend as well as yours—told me about it, then read it to me on the phone. I like what I heard. And after I heard it, I knew I was your prototypical Chauncey Gardiner, and the story of Chance is SHAMAN PETERS'S OWN STORY," he headlines.

"I saw it in my head as a moving story, and I saw it first and last, last meaning for the sixty-ninth as well as ninety-sixth time as a novel and not as a movie," says Kosky. **The task I'm trying to achieve is above all to make you see. (D. W. Griffith)**

My task which I am trying to achieve is, by the power of the written word, to make you hear, to make you feel—it, before all, to make you see. (Joseph Conrad)

" 'S far as I can see, and I can see far though I can't read, without rather silly-looking thick glasses, the printed image is an old-fashioned box camera," says Peters. "It doesn't move images fast enough. It knows

---

one of its highest manifestations and one of its wellsprings and luminaries. Pierre Pascal, *The Religion of the Russian People*, 1976, p. 44. (This ISBN-0 66 2 99 7 tells you all!: Jay Kay)

*On 6/9/1919 Samuel Goldwyn created within his film studio a spiritually select group he called his Eminent Authors.

no special effects; it cannot come with different angles. It talks of values, feelings, attitudes—things you can't show. It can't project star wars. I mean the Hollywood Star Wars—not ARMS CONTROL NEGOTIATIONS AND STAR WARS.* Only a movie can!"

"I see my novel as an inner hearing aid—not an image projector," says our Verbalizer.

"Your gardener is a spiritual enigma. Nobody knows who he really is. All he needs now is physical embodiment after you gave him, in your novel, so many spiritually valid pressure points. All he now needs is a fine initial release and good theatrical distribution," says Peters, speaking of the cinema.

"He knows who he is. That's all that matters. That's enough," Kosky intervenes.

"It's not enough," Gardiner interrupts. "The minute he opens his mouth, nobody knows what he's talking about. I don't want people to think that because he can't think straight neither can I." He starts perspiring.

This is getting tough. **"There's nothing tougher for a novelist than to talk about his novel to be made into a custom-made movie—and, if this wasn't bad enough, talking about it to a movie star for whom and to whose order the very novel is to be made by me." (Norbert Kosky)**

They are interrupted by the arrival of a youthful man, impeccably dressed in impeccable doctor's overalls, who shows up on the terrace unannounced and who brings with him a bit of *Suspense*. (Joseph Conrad, 1925)

"This is Dr. Daniel Chaucer. He is both a Ph.D. and an M.D." Peters introduces Dr. Chaucer. "He is the foremost specialist in Manual Medicine. Here in L.A. they call him a chiropractor. For years, Dr. Chaucer has been my prime collaborator since I won't make a movie without him. He is to me in acting what Ford Madox Ford was to your Slavic guru Joseph Conrad."† and this is Norbert Kosky, my new friend, who is by now known throughout the World!"

---

*"Arms Control Negotiations and 'Star Wars' (1984): Prospects for Arms Control Negotiations," pp. 101–109, a chapter in *Gerard Smith on Arms Control*, op cit., p. 1010.

†Wrote Dame Rebecca West: "The relationship began beautifully, with Ford as guru instructing the grateful Polish disciple in the refinements of English prose, and it ended with Conrad and Jessie (his wife) going frantic in their efforts to get

The doctor takes one good look at Kosky. "I saw you on TV handing out the Oscars. You walked up and down the stairs like someone suffering from *Praise of Folly*.* I could tell, however, that you were not quite yourself when reading the text: that you were acting."

"How could you tell?" marvels our literary marvel.

"Tell him how, Doctor," Peters says to Chaucer.

"Acting is movement and movement comes from the vertebral column. From our spine," says Dr. Chaucer. He places himself behind Peters and asks the actor to sit up straight in the chair.

Peters takes off his shirt, displaying his firm body. A session of manual medicine is about to begin. Standing behind him, with one hand placed on Peters's shoulder and the other one holding onto his cheek, Dr. Chaucer starts rotating the actor's head "as if it were an empty jug set on some static spire," a maneuver to which the actor submits with obvious relish.

"A necessary introductory procedure," explains the doctor, catching Kosky's surprised stare, "since this causes maximum flexion of the entire region of the cervical spine, and brings individual joints into their final, most extreme position." Dr. Chaucer keeps on palpating the actor's spinous spine.

The procedure is over. Dr. Chaucer is about to leave.

"Why don't you give Mr. Kosky a quick provocative test?" says Peters, putting on his shirt.

It's now Kosky's turn. He sits down on a stool while, standing beside him, Dr. Chaucer checks the working of his supposedly spiritually straight spine and finds it, in his own words, "substantially crooked."

As its name suggests, provocative testing provokes pain. While Dr. Chaucer performs his medical tests called provocations, Kosky becomes testy.

---

the Djinn back into the bottle" (*Sunday Telegraph*). *Djinn* was Conrad's pronunciation of *gin* (a fluid, the substantial dose of which he needed every day to be able to keep up his writing, his mind-settling spiritual routine: J.K.).

See William Amos, *The Originals. An A–Z of Fiction's Real-Life Characters* (1985), p. 65.

In Praise of Folly by Erasmus (1519) "A humanist who favored reform within the Church, Erasmus was classified by the Inquisition as an 'author of the second class,' which meant that his work could be read only if 'objectionable' parts were expurgated." (From *Censorship*: 500 years of Conflict, The New York Public Library, 1984, p. 27)

"Why do I feel pain? Anything wrong?" asks Kosky who, a bit irate, begins to feel his irate joints.

"Indeed, your *vertebra prominens* is troubled," Dr. Chaucer nods.

"I wonder why," wonders Kosky.

"Perhaps because you feel you're not prominent enough. It's understandable. After all the time devoted to the Holocaust and so many other *pogroms*, and not one prime-time TV program devoted to the illustrious chapter of East European Jewish History," he says matter-of-factly.

"What else?"

"Your Zones of Irritation of the Sacrum and the pelvis are irritated. Your sacroiliac joint is quite disturbed. Take care of your sacred sacrum without which you'll perish as a writer," says Dr. Chaucer as, ending his examination, he tactfully leaves the Actor vs. the Novelist ready to face each other in the combat zone known as literary-cinematic screen— or is it still a stage-arena?

"The fact is," says Peters, "that as long as your hero lives inside your novel, most people don't know he exists. Let me play him on a big screen and your Mr. Arboretum will live forever."

"What if you or your film gets run over by the film critics who might not know who my character is, but who know only too well who you are? Who might, by now, think you're *too great for my next role* (too great, not too small. Forgive me for sorely testing your most sore point!) Wouldn't an unknown actor—an unknown meaning 'spiritually pure'— be closer to my innocently unsinkable Fountainhead?"

"An unknown actor?" Peters grimaces. "Another John Doe? Another American version of the working class *Candide*?"

"Why not?" **If it was raining hundred-dollar bills, you'd be out looking for a dime you lost someplace. (*Meet John Doe*, directed by Capra, 1941)***

Peters gets up from the chair and paces around the terrace. "A John Doe would turn your Lotus man into Capra-corn. Besides, if your unknown Mr. Actor is, at his age, still unknown, it also means he either

---

*Meet John Doe, a film by Frank Capra, starring the utterly innocent Gary Cooper and the anything but innocent Barbara Stanwyck. In the first half of the film, everybody who meets John Doe wants to meet him again. In the second half of the film, after everybody reads what one newspaper had to say about him, nobody wants to meet him again. (George P. Flack, 1982)

can't act or afford to appear so innocent that many people might think that he can't act at all! To counteract such fear, he will act counter to the essence of the role: wisdom. Wisdom, simplicity confused with retardation or even innocence. He will try to prove that, even though he's been unknown, he sure can act—and in this most innocent story, to act means to kill."

"How would you play him?" asks Kosky.

"I wouldn't play him, I would *be* him. I would be, at the same time, a pure *being*"—he points at himself—"who, one day, must start living like a movie star—and living it there!" He points in the direction of his four-room-like bedroom," says Peters, dumbly and voicelessly. He gets up again from his chair and suddenly, mindless of pain, walks around and through the garden, ready to milk milkwood and suckle the honeysuckle.

He is incapable of any of the defense mechanisms in which we have been trained, and expects everyone to respond to the simplicity with which he has learned to express himself. He stops a bewildered matron and says to her: "I am hungry" whereat she turns and flees. When he is accosted at knifepoint by a gang of teenagers he holds out his remote-control to turn off the ugly scene. (Dr. H. C. Read, 1980)*

"Cut!" shouts Kosky, our literary offscreen director just as a very young woman steps out from the half-opened door of the bedroom carrying in her hand *How to Give Yourself Relief From Pain, by the Simple Pressure of a Finger* (Dr. Roget Dalet, 1982). **The performance of an actor anchored to and built upon an object is one of cinema's most powerful constructions. (Pudovkin)** "I stand convinced. Print that take! Printer!"

---

*"Being There—In the Image of God": a sermon delivered by the Rev. Dr. David H. C. Read on January 13, 1980, at the Madison Avenue Presbyterian Church in New York.

1 4

"Everything that reproduces the human silhouette—whether a shadow, a reflection, a drawing, or a sculpted image—is considered among the majority of peoples as being not only a simple combination of lines or an innocuous figure completely independent of the living individual. It is believed, rather, that there exists an intimate connection, both physical and psychological, between the image and the person that it calls to mind, between the figured representation and the real being."*

Before leaving for New York, our past Oscar presenter presents himself at his motel's star-shaped swimming pool where, keeping his head above the water while craning his neck like a Ruthenian crane, he hopes to present his floating act as a gift to the pool's lifeguard—a blond donna, a Slavic slut so spectacularly shaped that she evokes in him the image of Donna de Varona,† the odalisque queen who enslaves him in his dreams.

---

*M. Weynants-Ronday (1926) writes in *Les Statues Vivantes*, in the chapter "*L'Ame Portrait*" (Soul Portrait) which, starting on the spiritual significant page 66, ends with the above quote on page 96; quoted from *Disenchanted Images* (op. cit. p. 16), by Theodore Ziolkowski, who writes apropos: "The iconological question that I hope to answer is this: how did these images make their way out of magic into literature and, long after the disappearance of the faith that originally justified their supernatural powers, survive in such modern works as Cocteau's film?" (op. cit., p. 17).

†See *Donna de Varona's Hydro-Aerobics* by Donna de Varona (the two-time

Just then the phone rings at the pool's edge. The lovely donna answers it, then, reverently, brings it to him and tells him it is BEAU BRUMMEL HIMSELF WHO'S CALLING YOU. The way she hands him the phone and then discreetly walks away tells him she has finally noticed in him—a potential for a writer (and one who once was a sexual marine: Jay Kay).

"Hello, Norbert Kosky! You were great at the Oscars," Beau whispers on the phone in his Brummelian whisper.

"So were you," says Kosky modestly.

"With me it was not an accident," says Beau. **Why don't you come up and see me sometime?** he intones.

"When?" Our man of the East can't wait to meet the male Mae West.

"Anytime you choose, Mr. Kosky, but, if you don't mind, say, at six this afternoon?"

The film studio of today is really the palace of the sixteenth century. There one sees what Shakespeare saw: the absolute power of the tyrant, the courtiers, the flatterers, the jesters, the cunningly ambitious intriguers. There are fantastically beautiful women, there are incompetent favorites. There are great men who are suddenly disgraced. (Christopher Isherwood)

At six o'clock Kosky shows up at Brummel's own Brummel Annex at Parnassus Studios. Beau Brummel is not there. "He's been delayed by a young woman whom he had to see," says a secretary, a young woman whom he could last have seen naked, reaching out to him from pages 16–19 of the April issue of the "for adults only" *Live!* magazine.

Will you accept three hundred per week to work for Paramount Pictures. All expenses paid. The three hundred is peanuts. Millions are to be grabbed out here and your only competition is idiots. Don't let this get around. (Herman J. Mankiewicz to Ben Hecht)

"I'm glad you could make it on such short notice," says Brummel, injecting Kosky with a dose of Hollywood's instant ease. "The minute I saw you at the Oscars, I knew you were my man."

"I'm my own man, but I'm ready for a sacrifice," says Kosky. **The word does not express an idea, it creates it. (René Schwaeble)** He glances at the wall from where F. Scott Fitzgerald, Somerset Maugham, Mau-

---

Olympic gold-medal winner) and Barry Tarshis (1984). ("By all means see Donna. Never mind Barry!" adds the already infatuated Jay Kay.) (Sorry, Barry!: J.K.)

rice Maeterlinck and Faulkner look back at him from the photographs taken when they took to Hollywood ("and were taken": J.K.).

"Not anymore," says Brummel, following Kosky's stare. "Hollywood wants you!"

"For a screen adaptation of my next novel?" says Kosky.

"It's you! not your novel I want," exclaims Brummel. "I want you to be in *Total State*, a movie to be produced, written and directed by Beau Brummel and starring yours truly," says Brummel, modestly dropping his gaze.

"To be what?"

"To be as visible as the verb to be. To be a full-line performer, not some dialogue-replacement artist. With your own credit line on the film's masthead, placed well above the name of the film makeup artist or even myself as this film's producer—never in alphabetical order."

"Never mind the listing," says Kosky. "Tell me instead, how far below your name, as actor number one, my name will follow," asks Kosky.*

"Five lines below. How about your name being given number six? I want you to be a full-fledged American film actor, not another Ruthenian extra. I want you to win an Oscar either for your first performance or for yourself as a novelist. When did you last act in the biggest Hollywood moral epic yet? Think what such experience will do for you as a man (for one, you'll screw women nonstop) and as a writer who will also be a full-time prime-time big movie Movie Star."

"But I can't act. I can only act out."

"You certainly can reenact something you've acted out already many times in real life, even if you haven't! That's all there is to acting."

"Doing what?" Kosky becomes more eager to please.

"Something that would create a dramatic havoc."

"Doing what?" Kosky persists.

"Something that would make the audience salivate—and regardless of whether you'll make a fool of yourself as an actor and me as your director or not."

"Doing what?"

---

*Who, let it be said, has been already registered as a talk show "specialty act" with the American Federation of Television and Radio Artists (AFTRA), thanks to his book-promoting TV appearances.—Ed.

"Well"—Brummel poses while pausing—"in your case, *soixante-neuf* would be number one. But this is out, since *Total State* is about the unmaking of a revolutionary—not about making it with one. How about reenacting a scene, of, say, eating?"

"Eating whom?" ventures Kosky.

"Not whom, but what. Eating, say, onion and lemon. Something every Russian revolutionary used to eat in order to fight not only the economic disease brought upon them by the Czar but also scurvy—a terrible gum disease."

"Done," says Kosky. "I'll do anything to make you and the film's audience salivate."

"O.K., then." Brummel settles the matter. "Be prepared to eat all the onion and lemon you can eat. A lot of it. Say, some twenty-five *takes* of it?"

"What's *Total State* about?" asks Kosky.

"The 1938 Moscow Purges: That epic of doubletalk, of hypocrisy, of treason," Brummel whispers. "An epic film needs an epic budget. To make it look more epic, we'll pay your epic wages in Spanish pesetas."

"Who are the principal characters?" asks Kosky. **You don't have to keep making movies to remain a star. Once you become a star, you are always a star. (Mae Murray)**

"Andrew Delano Bullies, an American columnist covering these trials for the *Eastside Crier*. His wife, known as Red Flame. And Nikolai Bukharin. The Man on Trial." Nonchalantly, Brummel pulls from a folder a glossy black-and-white photograph—a recent copy of an old photograph—and handing it to Kosky asks, "Does this picture ring a bell?"

"It does," says Kosky. The 1935 picture, well-known to those who go to bed with history, shows TWO FRIENDS AT PLAY. The friends are Koba and Nicky, that is Stalin and Bukharin. Wearing only boxing shorts and socks, Stalin and Bukharin wrestle each other with friendly smiles on a boxing mat only three years before Stalin had Bukharin executed at fifty-two—and, by doing so had wrestled all the power from his Bukharinist opposition. **Stendhal: Beware of Abelard's fate, my young secretary!**

Kosky is about to ponder further the annals of hypocrisy when a young woman, as young and as pretty as was Anna Larina, Bukharin's wife (who was half his age), enters the room, a steno pad in hand.

181

Stunned by her beauty, Kosky calls her a stunning stenopad and wins another six hundred SS points. Silent, she will remain for the rest of the time in the room.

"What about Bukharin? How much do you know about him?" Kosky retrieves the film-acting thread. The literary man remains in essence an actor. (Nietzsche)

"Not much. Except that, judging by his last 1938 photograph, you seem to resemble him strikingly," says Brummel. "What about you? How much do you know about him?"

"Enough!" says Kosky. Bukharin's works are distinguished by faith in the new culture "beside which capitalist civilization will seem like the Waltz of the Dogs compared with the real heroic symphonies of Beethoven." . . . Using a wide range of stylistic devices—irony, sarcasm, metaphor, hyperbole, similes, and rhetorical questions—Bukharin saturates his language with expressions borrowed from living folklore, salty words and phrases drawn from the depths of working-class conversation, or on other occasions, using strings of images borrowed from the finest literature (*Literary Encyclopedia*). Bukharin, Nikolai Ivanovich, 1888–1938; spy and saboteur; the leader of the infamous Bukharin-Trotskyite counterrevolutionary gang. Sentenced to death in 1938. (*Party Encyclopedia*) Bukharin, Nikolai Ivanovich, 1888–1938; Russian editor, writer and Communist leader. (*The Random House Dictionary*) "To many members of my generation, (as well as to many members of the Communist Party: J.K.) Bukharin was and still is an officially unmentionable hero."

"Quite right." Brummel nods, pulling out several other photographs of Bukharin from his desk drawer. He hands them to Kosky. The pictures, once official party photos, show Bukharin as an editor of *Izvestia*, the State's main newspaper, addressing a Moscow workers' rally; Lenin embracing Bukharin; reviewing a military parade; Bukharin in a Moscow park kissing a beautiful teenage woman, his wife, young enough to be his daughter. Bukharin with an infant, his son, a picture taken in 1936, shortly before Bukharin's arrest; Bukharin leisurely walking with Maxim Gorky in a Moscow park; Bukharin addressing the Congress of Communist International; Bukharin with Boris Pasternak, Osip Mandelstam and Alexsei Surkov?—all photographed at the First Congress of Soviet Writers; finally Bukharin testifying in the Stalinist dock.

"My, my! Do you look like him!" says Brummel. "Now you can see why I think you should play him!"

"I was told I look more like Zinoviev,"* says Kosky.

We shall be dealing in particular with the trial of Bukharin which took place from 2nd to 13th March, 1938, (portrayed as Rubashov by Arthur Koestler in his novel *Darkness at Noon*). It is known that Rubashov has the physical traits of Zinoviev and the moral character of Bukharin. (Maurice Merleau-Ponty, 1947)

"You won't be the first writer to portray Bukharin, you know," says Brummel, "and I say it in order to encourage you, not to disillusion. Koestler did it in *Darkness at Noon.*" He and the steno slut watch Kosky in silence. "I saw you at the Oscar Awards," says Brummel. "I knew something went wrong with your timing backstage—but whatever it was that delayed you, you walked down those stairs and looked out at us with the arrogance of Bukharin. Wasn't that acting?"

"It was fear," says Kosky.

"If it was fear, then you mastered it. Master now the fear of acting. All you need to play Bukharin is to know the fear of Stalin, and the Stalinist State. All you need is to be yourself."

"I ran away from the total state out of fear. The fear of my Self becoming a collective," says Kosky. This is just what this author has experienced: as suddenly it became clear that his acclimatization was relative and not absolute; that somewhere "in the well of his soul" lay, still alive, a desire for something other than could be supplied to him by that collectivized new world. (Joseph Novak, 1962) "Why should I return to it—even if only in a movie?"

"If you're not free to act your fear out, you're still holding on to it," says Brummel. "In my movie, I want you to hold on to your very Self."

"To myself?" Kosky gets up and paces the room. He is already acting. He is Bukharin, lost in thought about mankind shortly before he will

---

*Zinoviev: Lenin's "maid for all seasons," and, after Bukharin, Lenin's other closest associate. He was tried (with Kamenev) on charges of counterrevolutionary plotting in 1936—two years ahead of Bukharin, Rykov and others—and executed, as were the others.

"On May 1, 1919, the first issue of the Comintern's official organ, the *Communist International*, came off the Petrograd press and thereafter appeared regularly in the United States. Edited by Zinoviev, the Russian Communist party's chief propagandizer, this magazine was printed in Russian, English, French and German." (From *Red Scare*, op. cit., p. 46)

be lost to mankind (thanks to the Byzantine betrayal by Stalin, with whom he was always sexually competing: Jay Kay). "I can hold on to my Self first and foremost only as a writer. I define what I write, while an actor is first defined by a script. By the timing imposed on him by the director. By the camera. By the film editor—and finally, by the studio's final cut. "Living on location with other actors would bother me least as long as I could engage them in some sort of mildly *obverse* sixty-nine sex." (Obverse, printer, not perverse!: Jay Kay) (*What's perverse?*: the Printer) **You are going to be the first "natural" actress. (David O. Selznick to Ingrid Bergman)**

"You might as well face it, the truth, not just sex," says Brummel. "Once you play Bukharin you'll be defined by my script, true, but also by your fear—the fear you know better than most. Hence you can also portray it better than, say, a native Hollywood actor who fears nothing but baldness, unemployment, old age and death.

"In my script"—politely Brummel turns to his super-stenographer— "the movie opens with Bukharin being already aware he is No. 1 on the list of Stalin's enemies, one who was, in Lenin's words, 'the Party's darling.' He knows his days are numbered for him by Stalin, and he counts them, day by day. His account is made of fear. Fear for his life, but also fear for his Party, the very Party of Lenin and Trotsky about to be topped by Stalin."

"Who plays Bullies?" Kosky asks.

"I play him," says Brummel. "Think of all this as an adventure, a study in psycho-political contrast: Bullies can no more figure out Bukharin than I could figure you."

"Will my scenes be filmed on location—in Russia?"

"Heavens no!" says Brummel. "You don't film a hanging in the hangman's house. All your scenes will be shot in Madrid."

"Madrid?" Kosky trembles. "Did you know that A. Lunacharsky [the man who published Dostoyevsky's *Notebooks*: J.K.], one of Bukharin's closest associates, was assassinated en route to Madrid?"

Indeed he did. "So was André Amalrik (the Russian writer who wrote *Will Russia Survive Till 1984?*), who died in a mysterious car crash in Spain," says Brummel.

"Will I survive as a writer till 1984?" Kosky mocks. **Nothing can injure a man's writing if he's a first-rate writer. If a man is not a first-rate writer, there's not anything can help it much. (Faulkner)**

"Not only will you survive as a writer, you'll triumph as an actor," says Brummel.

"You've just convinced me. When do we start?" **Why do they want me to sign a contract for five years when I haven't even finished my first picture? (Garbo) I feel so sorry for you. (Garbo to her fans)**

"The sooner the better." Brummel glows.

I would give a hundred Hemingways for one Stendhal. (Camus)
In Madrid, Kosky is measured, fitted and clothed as Bukharin by
three Spanish tailors, whose sense of Bukharin comes assisted by old
photographs of clothes Bukharin wore first as a revolutionary arrested
by the Czarist police; then when he was seated next to Lenin at the
Party Congress; what did he wear carrying, with Kamenev, Zinoviev
and others, Lenin's casket? Was he wearing a coat or a jacket when he
welcomed Maxim Gorky back to Russia?

"Now, why must I wear a black-leather jacket and this silly red scarf
which makes me look like a fag? Was Bukharin a fag?" Kosky asks one
of the Spanish tailors while smoking one cigarette after another—a new
habit he acquired in order to *impersonate* this Bukharin habit. (Say:
impressionate—not impersonate—meaning an attempt at making a lasting impression: J.K.)

"Bukharin a fag? Perish the thought!" answers the tailor, himself a
devout Spanish Bukharinist. "The red scarf—an insignia of the Russian
Young Pioneers—was Bukharin's amulet," he tells Kosky. "You see,
Bukharin wore it first when addressing the Young Pioneers Congress,
where, setting an example for the young, he, a chain cigarette smoker,
pledged publicly to quit smoking. Too bad! Stalin, himself a habitual
pipe smoker who did not intend to quit smoking, promptly put Bukharin
in chains and helped Bukharin quit smoking as well as life."*

---

*In *Total State* (Parnassus Films Unlimited), Kosky will wear Bukharin's trench

186

PARNASSUS UNLIMITED Production No. 16175 TOTAL STATE
Director: Beau Brummel
Screenplay: Beau Brummel
Stand in: Mr. George Niskisko for Mr. Norbert Kosky.
Scene 96:
INTERIOR/DAY/NIKOLAI BUKHARIN'S EDITORIAL OFFICE IN IZVESTIA
MOSCOW 1937

The room is large and impressive by Soviet standards, furnished with a mixture of pre-revolutionary furniture and Russian period pieces, modernistic by Soviet standards. In the corner stands a period duplicating machine. On the shelves, bound in red leather, stand the collected works of Marx, Engels and Lenin. On the shelves below are scattered a dozen or so of Bukharin's own books and pamphlets, with *The Road to Socialism* and *ABC of Communism*, his best-known works, lying on top in their original Soviet editions, as well as the American, British, German, Spanish, Japanese and other foreign-language editions of *Novy Mir (The New World)*.*

Sitting at the desk is NIKOLAI BUKHARIN. Fifty years old, of medium height, almost bald, he wears a mustache and beard and his favorite Revolutionary-style leather jacket.

Bukharin is in the process of correcting the latest galley proofs of *Izvestia* (he does not know that this will be the last issue to be edited by him). Bukharin has just corrected his own editorial, which will be the last published piece of writing to bear his name. (He does not know that either.) Bukharin rereads aloud the closing paragraph—"A network of deceit characteristic of fascist regimes"—and inserts a few corrections. The paragraph now reads, "A complicated network of decorative deceit

---

coat, Bukharin's business suit, Bukharin's red scarf and Bukharin's prisoner stripes. —Eds.

*The *Novy Mir*, edited in 1915 by no less than Nikolai Bukharin and Leon Trotsky, began preaching the Bolshevik philosophy in the United States two years before the Russian revolution even occurred; ... As a result, Bolshevik phrases like "All power to the Soviets" were soon bandied about at Left Wing Socialist gatherings and some elements even formed themselves into local communes. (*Red Scare*, op. cit., p. 38)

in words and action is a highly essential characteristic of fascist regimes of all stamps and hues." Bukharin signs the galley proof, and with a sigh of anxiety pushes *Izvestia* aside.

He stares at his desk, cluttered with galleys, books, pamphlets, various documents and a stack of letters. On a platter, an omelet served peasant-style, with caviar, rests cold and untouched. Bukharin reviews the photographs. He glances at the large portrait of Lenin hung above the desk; then below, on the desk, at a mounted photograph of Anna, a stunning young woman who only four years earlier, at nineteen, had become Bukharin's common-law wife. Another picture shows her and Bukharin, the two of them holding a small boy, their only child. Next to it stands an historic picture of all the members of the Central Committee (and one in which Stalin was not yet perceived by others in the picture as the archenemy of the Leninist yesterday—and the prime saboteur of the Communist tomorrow: Jay Kay).

In the picture, Bukharin, with a newspaper in hand, is placed in the dead center of the first row, flanked by the always impassive Stalin and by the happy-go-lucky Rykov, Bukharin's staunchest friend and political ally (also sentenced to death in 1938: J.K.).

Every revolution is paid for by certain attending evils, and it is only at that price that we can bring about the transition to higher forms of economic life of the revolutionary proletariat.... (Bukharin, 1921)

Stretching his back, Bukharin reaches for a German-Russian dictionary and opens it to a page.

BUKHARIN (murmuring to himself): The German words *Müssen, müssen*—in Russian, most clearly translate into *dolzhna*, in the sense of "should." But then the German language also has *sollen*—another word for "must," a must of a different kind. Our new public is not yet ready for such fine and subtle moral distinctions. (He lifts his head and recites into the mirror.) And here I am, Comrades, ready to oppose Comrade Stalin—and to oppose him—him, an enemy of Revolution! (He stops the public speech, then, no longer looking into the mirror, says as if speaking to someone else) And here I *ought to—ought* to or *must*? Substitute the word expose for oppose. But it is too late now. (Telephone rings. Jolted, Bukharin abruptly puts the dictionary aside and faces the phone. The phone rings again. Bukharin tenses, and remains still. Another ring. Bukharin rests his eyes on his revolver. The phone rings once more. Jerkily, Bukharin picks up the receiver.)

BUKHARIN: *Slyooshayou! Gavareet*. Bukharin! Hello, Bukharin speaking . . . (He listens to the other voice and involuntarily stands up. Bukharin's lips turn dry and he keeps on licking them.)

BUKHARIN: Yes. (Pause) Yes, I understand. (Long pause) That can't be. Comrade Roginski must be wrong! (He loses his composure.) All three of them testified I had proposed it? Yakovleva too? But how could she? She knows it's a lie. It simply never happened! Are you sure she actually said it on her own—or was she perhaps coerced into saying it? (He listens to an answer.) Yes, of course. (He collects himself.) To-morrow morning then: in your presence. (He replaces the receiver. Still rigid, Bukharin reluctantly lowers himself into the chair as if it were a bottomless well and as if the deep were about to claim him forever.)

For influence, in art, is always personal, seductive, perverse, impos-ing. . . . (Harold Bloom, 1975)

The telephone rings. Norbert Kosky, our American Red Man playing Nikolai Bukharin, interrupts his reading but hesitates to answer it: there's always time for bad news, and this time in his life, with him morally bound to his Party while being bound as bad boy to Stalin, things are bound to be bad. Bukharin picks up the receiver. "Hello? Bukharin speaking . . . ," says Bukharin. To Kosky, the phone is as dead as Bukharin but he must disregard this since, coming from Yezhov,* the head of the secret police, this telephone call was anything but dead to real-life Bukharin.

VYSHINSKY: That's what you claim. But Varvara Iakovleva says just the opposite. Does that mean she is telling a lie?

BUKHARIN: I don't agree with her, and I say that she is telling a lie.

VYSHINSKY: And is Mantsev also lying?

BUKHARIN: Yes, he too is lying. I am telling what I know, and it is up to them, their conscience, to tell what they know.

VYSHINSKY: But how do you explain the fact that three of your former accomplices are speaking against you?

BUKHARIN: See here, I don't have enough facts, either material or psychological, to shed light on that question.

VYSHINSKY: You cannot explain it.

BUKHARIN: It is not that I cannot, but simply that I refuse to explain it. (*Moscow Trials*)

---

*Newly appointed by Stalin as head of the NKVD, Yezhov "not only carried out Stalin's instructions but did so blindly and slavishly," writes Roy A. Medvedev in his *Nikolai Bukharin: The Last Years* (1980).

After a few seconds of listening to the dead phone, our Bukharin—
or is it Kosky?—hangs up the receiver and sits down. Restless, he gets
up, only to sit down again.

"CUT!" shouts Brummel, and instantly the lights go off and the
cameras stop. Brummel leaves his directorial post and walks briskly
toward Kosky. "Wow! This was good, Norbert, really good!" he says,
patting Kosky on the shoulder. "Almost a cinematic classic. Almost.
There's a definite apprehension in your picking up that receiver. Apprehension—yes, but not nervousness. Don't you think that, given
what's been going on after all, Bukharin knows he's being investigated—
Bukharin would be nervous—and not merely anxious? He knows his
whole life depends on what Yezhov tells him. Doesn't he have a right
to be worried? Let's try again."

Another take. "CAMERA. ACTION!"

The phone rings. Bukharin won't pick it up. Not yet. He's too frightened. But wait a second—Kosky concentrates on the spiritual subtext
of his acting—is Bukharin really frightened? Isn't Bukharin, by now,
rather resigned to his fate? After all, by this time in his life he knows
that he has been doomed. Either he must kill himself or be executed
as a spy and saboteur on Stalin's orders. By now, he knows who the
caller is. He knows it is Yezhov. A call from Yezhov means death. Why
must he talk to Yezhov? But then—why not? Isn't Yezhov, like everybody else, also subjected to death?

The phone rings again. And again. And again. You can almost hear
Bukharin's wishful thinking: Maybe it is not Yezhov calling. Maybe it
is Anna, Bukharin's wife? Bukharin picks up the receiver, but before
he speaks into it, Brummel screams "CUT!" and the action stops once
more.

"That was good. I don't want to lose it and so, just in case, let's do
it again, Norbert. Another take won't hurt!" Brummel speaks from
behind the camera while the makeup man powders Kosky's sweating
face.

"But—this was my sixteenth take." Kosky forgets about Bukharin.
"Did I at least look upset? As upset—even sick to my stomach—as
undoubtedly Bukharin must have been?"

"Upset—yes," says Brummel. "Restless—yes. Perhaps only upset,
only restless—still not nervous enough. The issue is: What is nervous?
You or Bukharin? Are you bothered, even worried, or concerned, about
your performance as an actor in this or the next scene, or are you

190

nervous as Bukharin? Bukharin, who now knows his life of a revolutionary leader is over—but who doesn't know what to do with his knowledge. *Ought* he to kill himself, and save his reputation, or *must* he go on for the sake of the Party unity—even if this unity depends on sacrificing one's life for—*O tempora, o mores.* Caligula Nero Stalin." He pauses. "Of course, should you chose to do it for me again, you might consider being even more nervous." He courts Kosky with all his "should" and "might." "By the time that phone rings," Brummel goes on, "Bukharin has already been interviewed many times by the NKVD, the feared secret police. This is more than you've ever gone through. He knows that he's been caught in the NKVD's net of lies and denunciations—that his days are numbered—while all you worry about, Norbert, is your sexual numerology and your favorite number sixty-nine." Brummel watches Kosky in silence, then says, "Never mind your own feelings: think of Bukharin's actions; think the Magic If: What *if* that call were real? What *if* you *were* Bukharin? What *if* Bukharin had just received the most upsetting news? How would it affect him? How would he react? *Act* Bukharin, not Norbert Kosky. Think the Magic If."

"What if I can't forget what I already know about Bukharin—and what he didn't know while answering that call? What if I can't forget the Magic If of history—of Bukharin's own magic?" **Who the hell am I supposed to be, anyhow? (Tallulah Bankhead)** asks Kosky, our magic man.

"You must forget what you know," Brummel cuts in from behind. "When that phone rings again, know only what Bukharin does. Think what you're about to do—don't think about what you feel. 'Act immediately,' says Stanislavsky. 'Proceed from yourself,' says Vakhtangov. You must transfer your temperament, as if it were blood, to Bukharin: you live within him, but the audience doesn't know it. All they see is Bukharin. You're not a method actor: in your acting, follow life, not the method. One more take then?" Brummel goes back to his post, and so does Kosky.

"Silence in the studio!" thunders Brummel. "Let my Tantric Bukharin concentrate! CAMERA—ACTION!"

191

Restless after ending his brief and mesmerizing film-acting stint, our stunt messiah keeps calling Voice Anonymous, his phone-answering service, at least twice a day, hoping for a message from some sexual messmate which would turn into a creative mess his suddenly overly orderly existence.

"You had several callers calling you, but only one of them left her name," says the anonymous answerette.

"Well?" Kosky pauses. "*Well—well—well?*" he intones.

"Well—what?" The answerette is impatient. "You had two anonymous male callers; one asked if you were in town, the other whether you were still alive. They did not seem friendly."

"Don't tell me anything without checking with me first," Kosky interrupts. "Your service and I have agreed that in view of the number of my potential literary enemies, the enmity of whom I rightly caused by appearing in *Total State* where I play that red man Bukharin (and the equally large number of my adoring female fans: Jay Kay), you would pass on to me my messages only after you first asked me for a prearranged password. Didn't your supervisor tell you, miss, that the word *well*—repeated three times—is this week's password? That without hearing it, you don't know who the caller is?"

I am made up of an intensest life—a principle of restlessness. Which would be all, have, see, know, taste, feel, all—This is myself. (Browning)

"I don't need to know your password. All I need is to hear the way you say 'well' and 'word,' and I know it's you. You just can't pronounce them well enough in English!" The answerette laughs.

"Who was the woman who called me?" asks Kosky.

"Emma Hart. She said she was calling you all the way from Salt Lake City and that, and I quote her, 'She is willing to come all the way'!" says the answerette.

"Emma Hart. Are you sure she said, 'Come all the way'?"

"That's the name. And that's what she said."

"What else did Emma Hart say?" asks Kosky.

"She said **'Ecstasy is a number. Baudelaire.'** "

"What else? Give me the rest of her message."

"She said nothing else. No, wait! She said, 'Bye-bye, *mon chère*, bibi'—and she hung up," says the answerette, and she hangs up on him.

The real catastrophe is the prospect of total moronization, dehumanization, and manipulation of man. (Herbert Marcuse)

SS

With her telephone call, Cathy reenters his life as Shakti, the divine *dombi* of God Shiva, and brings with her the **permission of the prohibited. (Judah Levi Toba)* Shiva without Shakti is a corpse. (Tantra)†**

Emma Hart—her name is a literary code—is Mrs. Catherina ("Cathy") Hamilton Young, and on Kosky's mental slides, she appears portrayed as Goethe saw her first in his *Travels to Italy*. **Standing, kneeling, sitting, lying down, grave or sad, playful, exulting, repentant, wanton, menacing, anxious—all mental states follow rapidly one after another. . . . The old knight holds the light for her, and enters into the exhibition with his whole soul. This much at any rate is certain—the entertainment is unique. (Goethe)‡**

Kosky places the phone in front of him on the desk. To call or not to call. Cathy is no longer a question: she is his spiritual sister (SS).

---

*Judah Levi Toba (Dervish Effendi): a Jewish literary "dervish" who proclaimed "Freedom is the secret of the spiritual Torah."

†For the purpose of most secret tantric sex rites, women are graded by men, and men by women, according to their spiritual, as well as ritual merit, each "spirit" sexually more advanced than the other.

‡Johann Wolfgang von Goethe, author of *Faust*, "looked upon old age as something remote, frigid and disappointing. He was only twenty-five when he began *Faust* and forty-eight when he finished it in 1807." (Simone de Beauvoir, *The Coming of Age* [*La Vieillesse*], 1972, p. 191. See also "Goethe's sexual life in old age," pp. 329–30.)

We think the act and it is done. (William James) Cathy rules his will even from afar and after some nine hundred and sixty-nine days since he saw her last; this means he is not strong enough not to call her. She is both his *devidassi*, an ideal whore, and Devi, the goddess, either one capable of drinking **potions containing the semen of an enlightened master.** (Philip Rawson) He saw her first all base, on the bas-relief on the Devi Jagadamba Temple at Khajuraho, built—appropriately for this story—in the year 969. **How could an accumulation of adjectives or a richness of epithets help when one is faced with that splendiferous thing? Besides, any *true* reader—and this story is only addressed to him—will understand me anyway when I look him straight in the eye and try to communicate my meaning. A short sharp look or a light clasp of his hand will stir him into awareness, and he will blink in rapture at the brilliance of The Book. For, under the imaginary table that separates me from my readers, don't we secretly clasp each other's hands? (Bruno Schulz, 1937, p. 1)***

Cathy is his ideal sexual samovar (SS), with the word *sam* standing, let us recall again, for the Ruthenian self, and the word *ovar* for ovaries. She is the one who, an ideal sexual alchemist, for over a year has kept him on a steady diet of most perfect acclivity, generating in him (we are talking here *day after day, night after night*: J.K.) the inner heat of the longest duration. She was an ideal *dombi*, one whose orgasms belong entirely to her, while she belongs entirely to her lover; one who has gone through all he needs for his ideal sādhana,† and who has gone . through it with zest and zeal, without a scream or a whisper. Enough said (though when he speaks of Cathy, nothing said about her seems to have been said enough. Enough said: summarizes Jay Kay).

No wonder. Cathy transcends any fixed dimension. She also transcends the very notion of *oli*, of "womb-fire." (In brief, Cathy's sexual energy is inexhaustible: clarifies Jay Kay) Her transcendentalist mother came from the bilingual Toronto, her father ("a bilingual bully," she

---

*From *Sanatorium Under the Sign of the Hourglass*, by Bruno Schulz (1937), translated by Celina Wieniewska, Introduction by John Updike, with 30 illustrations by the author, 1978.

†"The most significant rituals of Tantrik sādhana are performed with women who have been specially initiated. What this initiation consists of has usually been kept secret and its reasoning hidden. There seems to be a variety of methods, perhaps used together." (*The Art of Tantra*, No. 68, p. 89)

calls him) from the bilingual New Orleans. "My mother wanted me to be Margaret Fuller,"* she told him once, "while my father opted for a new Adah Menken"—an "actress, dancer, poet and adventuress" (as described by Jeanette H. Foster). † Should he call her at all? Should he call her and tell her that his need of her still makes him uncontrolled as well as unfree—him, the royal yogi? ("That he has never resolved whether it was he who initially gave Cathy unlimited access to himself or Cathy who opened him up to no limit," in the words of Jay Kay.)

Busying himself already with various images of Cathy performing for him her *devidesi* dance in his only inner temple named The Cathy-Devi Temple of clitoral bliss, he dials her number and gets a busy signal. (The Temple is not free.: Jay Kay.)

He tries again and it is busy again. **Man being both bound and free, both limited and limitless, is anxious. Anxiety is the inevitable concomitant of the paradox of freedom and fitness in which man is involved. (Reinhold Niebuhr)** What if Cathy has taken the phone off the hook in order to hook herself to her little man in the kayak? What if she has taken it off the hook in order to hook her husband, or if her husband took it off in order to help her remain in The Engorged State—uninterrupted—his way of taking her, or himself, off the sexual hook?

Kosky tries once again. This time the call goes through. On the ninth ring, a woman answers. "Hello, this is me. Who are you?" says Cathy. Her voice finds Kosky voiceless. Subdued, Kosky apologizes for calling her so late (but not for calling her).

Language is a skin; I knead my language against the other. It is as if I had words in place of fingers, or fingers at the tip of my words. My language vibrates with desire. (Roland Barthes)

"Oh, it's you! I hoped you would call me back," she says. (And she says it bit by bit—like a businesswoman, like a perfect Madame Salesmana: Jay Kay.)

---

*Margaret Fuller, "father-fixated" (Catherine Anthony), was the author of *Woman in the Nineteenth Century* and an intimate friend of Emerson, Carlyle and George Sand, the only woman she said she was in sexual love with.

†Adah Isaacs Menken was born either in Spain as Dolores Adios Fuertes, as her biographers claim, or in Louisiana as Adelaide McCord, as she does. A founder of the town newspaper in the town of Liberty, she contributed regularly to the *Cincinnati Israelite* and took liberties with a great number of great men of her time. She ended up her life at thirty-three—by then she was an intimate friend of Dumas, Swinburne, Gautier and Dickens. (*Pas mal!*: J.K.) (Clement Wood)

"I saw you in *Total State*," says Cathy. She sounds as if she and Kosky have simply parted recently. "You looked good, Norbert. The voice of Bukharin suits you fine. So does his suit. You were always good at giving great phone. Will you act again—a bigger role, better acting, maybe?"

"I've got dozens of typecast offers. None exciting enough," he mocks. "In my next movie, I want to play a Latin lover."

"Latin lover? With your Esperanto looks?" She chuckles.

"Never mind my looks; mind my mind. Speaking of looks: how have you been?" Kosky shifts into another spiritual gear.

"Quite well. I bet I look better now than when you saw me last, even though I'm about six pounds too heavy." Cathy does away with the passing time. "What about you?"

"I'm getting bald. Time sags."

"Really?" She is not interested. "For some three years—or was it four?—I haven't read anything new about you—or by you. Are you by chance still writing?"

"By chance I am. What else but writing could I do from eight to five—and remain decent?"

"What is your opus going to be this time? Another cabaret of cruelty?"

"Don't knock the notion of the cabaret," says Kosky. "Where would literary entertainment called novel be without American burlesque of French vaudeville?"*

"In my newest opus it's going to be derived from my past studies in sociology."

The work is in one movement. Six different timbres are used: flute-bassoon; clarinet-bass clarinet; trumpet-trombone; piano; harp; violin-cello (three different wind-instrument couples and three stringed instruments, struck, plucked and bowed). These six timbres merge into a single timbre: that of the piano (struck strings). (Karlheinz Stockhausen)

"Vaudeville? Do I hear you right?" she says. "May I quote you?" In her college days at Beulah, Cathy used to work as a free-lance reporter for *Erostratus* magazine—owned by the Scrubb newspaper chain.

"You may. The literary work is not the mere reflection of a real, given collective consciousness, but the culmination at a very advanced

---

*"The doctrine of fair use allows the author to "take"—only for the purpose of burlesque—without fear of infringement, the locale, the theme, the plot as well as the character and dialogue of someone else's copyrighted work." (Courts)

196

level of coherence of tendencies peculiar to the consciousness of a particular group, a consciousness that must be conceived as a dynamic reality, oriented towards a certain state of equilibrium." (Lucien Goldman, 1964)*

"In your faith, a quote is an extract—like poison. Isn't it?" she asks.

"It is, but not always. Not when the extract is used as a parable. † Not when it is used as a fictional footprint."

"Oh, yes. Of course," she moans in jest. "I can already see your newest protagonist: a literary hitchhiker who like that nonfictional fox Malraux, gets all that intellectual mileage at no extra cost to the reader. Speaking of extra costs: are you still a single swinging swingle?" She puts stress on "still," not on "swingle."

"Terminally," he declares.

"Still living in that stateless 69th Street buoy?"

"Isn't my apartment stately enough?" he objects.

All he wanted was to get away as far as possible from Park Avenue, from the aesthetic jungles of the lion hunters, from the half-life of wealth and fashion. (Thomas Wolfe)

"It's a canoe, not an apartment. C'mon, Norbert! The war ended over forty years ago, and you're over fifty. At your age men father children and grandchildren. They run governments and corporations. You've been listed in *LYP*‡ for years. Why don't you buy yourself a

---

Towards a Sociology of the Novel, by Lucien Goldman, 1964, translated from the French by Alan Sheridan, 1977, p. 9. Writes Goldman: "The work corresponding to the mental structure of the particular social group may be elaborated in certain exceptional cases by an individual with very few relations with this group. The *social* character of the work resides above all in the fact that an individual can never establish by himself a coherent mental structure corresponding to what is called a 'world view.' Such a structure can be elaborated only by a group, the individual being capable only of carrying it to a very high degree of coherence and transposing it on the level of imaginary creation, conceptual thought, etc." (Kosky met Goldman in 1968, when both men were fellows of the Center for Advanced Studies at Wesleyan University, in Middletown, Connecticut. Ed.)

†"A scribe must provide a distinguishing mark for the section beginning *And it came to pass when the ark set forward*, both at its beginning and at its end, because it is a book on its own." (*Tractate Soferim*)

‡*LYP: Literary Yellow Pages*, a directory of American poets, playwrights, essayists, editors and novelists published since 1960 by the American W.E.T.—the Association of American Writers, Editors and Translators.

decent place somewhere in Boxbury or Martha's Graveyard, where other literary Who's Whos live?"

" 'Cause I've got other things to do and I'm late as it is," says our mini-Seneca. "At my age, Bukharin, Lenin's darling, was executed by Stalin. Consider, for instance, a list of names of political persons who must be included among the movers and shapers of the twentieth century. In 1914 Vladimir Ilyich Ulyanov (Lenin) was forty-four years old, Joseph Vissarionovich Dzhugashvili (Stalin) thirty-five, Franklin Delano Roosevelt, thirty, J. Maynard Keynes, thirty-two, Adolf Hitler, twenty-five, Konrad Adenauer (maker of the post-1945 German Federal Republic), thirty-eight. Winston Churchill was forty, Mahatma Gandhi, forty-five, Jawarharlal Nehru, twenty-five, Mao Tse-tung, twenty-one, Ho Chi Minh, twenty-two, the same age as Josip Broz (Tito) and Francisco Franco Bahamonde (General Franco of Spain), that is, two years younger than Charles de Gaulle and nine years younger than Benito Mussolini. (*The Age of Empire 1875–1914*, by Eric Hobsbawm, 1988, p. 3.) By the time he was my age, Cagliostro was the best-known Freemason in the entire Free World."

"Careful now! Balzac died at fifty-two. So did Cagliostro," Cathy interrupts him gently. Her mood shifts. "What are your plans?"

"To finish my novel, if there's enough spiritual spice (SS) in me!"

"And if there isn't?"

"I'll get a job selling the Book of Job in Salt Lake City."

"Are you kidding?" she says. "This is a Mormon town. There are no witches in City Creek for you to go after!"*

"You are," he interrupts her gently. "You: my all-time witch."

Faithfulness refers to the peculiar feeling which is not directed toward the possession of the other . . . nor toward the other's welfare—but toward the preservation of the relationship to the other. (Simmel)

"I'm married, remember? 'It's not good to be too free.' As a faithful wife, with no child to raise, I've been busy rewriting my past—and marriage." She sighs as if in pain. "By the way, the other day some people called asking me a couple of questions about you—and me."

"I'm glad there are people who remember that you and I were a couple once. Who were they?"

---

*The first Mormons were experts in using water from City Creek, and through irrigation, they initiated most agricultural enterprises in Utah. (*American History*, 1986)

"Two free-lance walkie-talkie reporters. They said they were doing a little piece about you (a literary 'floater par excellence,' they called you) for the *Crier*—or was it the *Courier*—or some newspaper like that."

"Good. My books could use some exposure. So could their author. Particularly now that *Total State* is no longer playing around and Shaman Peters is no longer alive. What else did they say?"

"They said they've chosen you for their split-profile of the year. They said they were interested in you because you are a typical Gemini," says Cathy, the typical Virgo.

"The stars impel, but not compel," our Gemini interrupts her.

"They said they singled you out because of your split astral background. They said they've got to check everything you said. They said that you can't be trusted!"

"Of course I can't. I make things up. I'm a novelist, a *petit* Flaubert, remember? Why should the Fourth Estate care whether there is a Madame Bovary—or a madam in my life? Isn't Flaubert enough?"

"Not today," Cathy assures him calmly.

"They said that, in their piece, they were going to refer to you as the two-tongued Janus. Still, they were both very sweet," she goes on. "And speaking of Madame Bovary, they said they believe I was portrayed in one of your novels as the girl called Nameless. They asked me whether I believe what you wrote about me was true. 'Don't believe a word he says,' I said. 'His mind is a haunted tenement, stuffed with myths, not facts.' "

"Good. Very good!" says Kosky. "I hope they quote you in context."

Everything had been handed to him on a silver platter. I simply didn't like the man at all. Yet I didn't attack him; I simply quoted him. (A. J. Liebling)

"I'm sure they will. All they needed was my side of your story."

"What else did they say?"

Fictitious statements are examples of the courts' strong commitment to the principle that we should have unrestricted access to facts. If an author makes a fictitious statement or an erroneous statement, but *presents* it as factual, as the truth, the courts have ruled it must be treated as factual material, and that later authors have the right to use that material as if it really were factual. (Richard Danney, 1982)*

---

*See Authors League Symposium on Copyright, January 27, 1982, in the *Journal of the Copyright Bulletin*, August 1982, p. 621.

"That they've already interviewed two other witnesses—numbers two and three. Still and all, I was their witness number one." She keeps putting the stress on the word witness. "They are religious, too. They said the Bible says that while a single witness won't do and can't do you in, three witnesses might. And they told me that I might as well go on record, since such statements as 'she has refused to see us,' 'she suddenly stopped answering her phone,' 'she did not return our calls,' or 'she was not available for comment,' don't look good to the public. They wanted to know more about you. As you know, a typical Gemini is always a sage, or a writer."

"A typical Gemini can also be a mathematician or an astronomer," Kosky corrects her.

"All they wanted to know is how you—a typical Gemini—work," the earthy Virgo reassures the watery Gemini.

"Did you tell them that too?"

Once more: his own smithy is the only possible place for these developments—they cannot occur in the office of any editor whom Thomas Wolfe will ever know. (Bernard De Voto, 1936)

"Did I ever! I even told them"—she giggles—"how you and I had initially met. How, when I came to visit you—my professor—in your office, you said, with your European charm, 'It's quite warm in here. Why don't you take it all off, Miss Young?' "

"I only meant your coat!" says Kosky.

Stop the upward movement. Bestow power. Bring about confluence of the three currents. Take the mind to the space between the eyebrows. Settle, concentrated, inhaling balancing on the two palms, strike the ground with the buttocks. This also brings about the union of currents. Cease to breathe. Exhale. (Tantra)

"You did not."

"I did, and when, hiding my geriatric crush on you," says Kosky, "I leave the room and return in less than a minute, a bottle of beer and two glasses in hand, I find you—" **Be in favor of bold beginnings. (Virgil)**

"You find your Lady of Shalott stripped and naked by the fire—and you don't so much as blink," she goes on, laughing. "You just hand me the glass, pour the beer and say, 'Please help me through the beginning, Cathy!' And when, in the best tradition of academic inquiry, I rip off your veneer of respectability and find your naked truth, you interrupt my bare act with 'Wait a moment, Cathy!' then disappear into the bathroom only to reappear with the truth in question literally naked—

200

"I was thoughtful! I thought of your lips burnt by my burning under-bush—and roughed up as if by a brush."

It was marvellous to see Lord David dress a cock for the pit. Cocks lay hold of each other by the feathers, as men seize each other by the hair. Lord David, therefore, made his cock as bald as possible. With a pair of scissors he cut off all the tail feathers, and all the feathers on the head and shoulders as well as those on the neck. (Hugo)

"Ruthenian lip service!" she giggles, then is silent for a moment. "In truth were you ever jealous?—I mean upset by my other men—by my 'love of the parallels.' " (Aldous Huxley)

"Not really. Our parallels are part of us." **The practice in which the navel is above and the palate below—the mystic sun above and the moon below—is known as topsy-turvy. This is said to prevent** *amrita* **from the moon-reaching fire of the sun. (Tantra)**

"In the beginning I dreaded being solo with you," Cathy goes on. "I had visions of being split in half. There was so much of that upturned—dare I say epileptic?—tongue during your ecstasy; so much tension in you."

He intervenes on behalf of his *amrita*.* "Isn't sex tension?"

"Tension? I thought sex was a release." She mocks. "How silly of me!"

"What are your plans now?" he asks. **But there is also the clitorid, or sexual type of women. The whole matrix of their life is the physical and the lust for variety. (Maurice Chideckel)**

"First and foremost, to go after my divorce—my manuscript lost, so to speak. And then to finish *Manuscript Found*, my first novel—a sort of historical love story.† That is, if there's enough history or love in me," she says.

Kosky misses a heartbeat. "Divorce?"

"Well, yes, divorce!" She sounds defeated. "My rewriting of my marriage didn't work. The basic characters remain unchanged though their story is over. Over and out!"

---

*The head, the mystic moon, secretes *amrita*, which flows down in the body. As it reaches the abdomen, the fire of the mystic sun, situated near the navel, consumes it. The upturned tongue prevents the flow of *amrita*. (Tantra)

†"All one can do is to herd books into groups . . . and thus we get English literature into A B C; one, two, three; and lose all sense of what it's about." (Virginia Woolf)

"On what grounds?"

"Incompatibility. My husband has become overly orchitic.* The insecure bugger had our phone bugged and found out that I had a fling with a bartender. He couldn't take it and issued an ultimatum: either I get rid of my lover—or else. I've chosen 'or else.' I won't give up my sex life to rescue your pride, I said. Besides, good bartenders are hard to find." She laughs easily. "Who knows that better than you and I?" She livens up and goes on. "I'm separated from my husband, but I won't be free until after the divorce. Until I know where I stand—and on what."

"Do you stand alone now? Alone—I mean in a sense of not sharing your physical space with anyone. Physical space, not psychophysical," he asks tentatively.

"Yes, I do, I live alone in the house, if that's what you mean, though I know that what you mean is: do I have another lover?" She stresses "another." " 'Another' meaning a new lover who supplements my regular one? Yes, I do. By chance, he happens to be my divorce lawyer."

"That's clever!" says Kosky.

"Isn't it?" She is pleased with herself. "Who says the roles of advocate and witness are inconsistent?" She pauses. "It's good talking to you again, Norbert." She stresses "again."

"Don't go—not yet!" He stresses "don't go."

"Would you want to see me?" she asks, stressing "want."

"I miss you," he bursts out. "I miss your company. Your image, and your words keep coming back to me through various back routes. I can't stop them."

Love is the desire to prostitute oneself. There is, indeed, no exalted pleasure which cannot be related to prostitution. (Baudelaire)

"I miss you too, Norbert. I miss our fits. I miss my flood; I miss my *petit mort*. Though, in truth, I don't miss your *petit mal*!"

"And I thought my mal was grand," Kosky moans in jest. **He was quite capable of deciding when the attack was over. These moments represented, down to the minute, an unusual speeding up of self-aware-**

---

*"The orchitic man corresponds to the uterine type of woman.... Normal coitus alone appeals to them.... The phallic type of man is exactly like the clitorid woman. In both the greatest satisfaction in life is sexual congress with anyone to whom they are not married. How to prevent the mating of an orchitic man with a clitorid woman, or that of a uterine woman with a phallic man?" (Maurice Chideckel)

ness—if the condition was to be named in one word—and at the same time of the direct sensation of life in the most condensed degree. (Dostoyevsky)

"Let's say it was more grand than mal," she reassures him quickly.

"When will I see you, Cathy?"

Press the chin firmly against the chest, into the jugular notch as far as possible. Pull the spinal cord, work on the brain. (Tantra)

"I'm flying to New York for the weekend," she says. "I'll be at the Tarwater Hotel under the name Mrs. Flannery O'Connor.* Do you mind my impersonating one of your favorite American women writers?"

---

*Flannery O'Connor, "a storyteller of water and fire (Niskisko)," is the author of, among other works, *The Violent Bear It Away*. "Water is a symbol of the kind of purification that God gives irrespective of our efforts or worthiness, and fire is the kind of purification we bring on ourselves." (Flannery O'Connor)

1 7

The Ruthenian-American Institute of Culture calls Kosky, our Ruthenian-American cultural man, with an urgent message. There has been a cultural mishap, they say. For reasons of health, or domestic politics, or both, Cardinal Gregor Starowyatr, the aged primate of Ruthenia, has canceled his forthcoming trip to North America, sending in his place a lesser-known, in the U.S., youthful cardinal, Viktor Essenes (pron. *Es-en-es*). Heading the Catholic church in Redowe, Ruthenia's largest steel-manufacturing town, a gift to Ruthenia made in 1945 by the victorious Red Army, Essenes has been nicknamed the Red Cardinal, even though his stand on Church vs. State relations has been anything but red.* Could Kosky meet with the Cardinal and, as his *cicerone*, either drive or walk him around mid-Manhattan, avoiding, at all costs, "going down on Gotham," an activity they know is so dear to the heart of our amoral Petronius. † Our Petronius

---

*On the spiritually stimulating nature of the relations between the Catholic Church and the Socialist State, the reader is referred to *Christianity and Marxism* by Janusz Kuczynski and *Socialism and Atheism* by Jan Szczepanski in the issue of: *Dialectics and Humanism* (The Polish Philosophical Quarterly) vol. xiv, No. 1/1987, devoted to "The Encounter of John Paul II's Catholicism with Socialism in Poland."

†"Going Down on Gotham," Chapter 10 in *New York Unexpurgated*, by Petronius (1966), "an amoral guide for the jaded, tired, evil, non-conforming, corrupt, condemned and the curious."

agrees, since, containing double SS, the Cardinal's name already suggests a spiritual sage as well as saga.*

The thought of meeting the Cardinal face to face unsettles his mind, then calmly sets it on *Nostra Aetate 1965*—the 1965 Declaration of the Vatican on the relationship of the Church to the Non-Christian Faiths—the very extraordinary declaration which states once and for all that "searching into its own mystery the Church comes upon the mystery of Israel." (*Nostra Aetate*, 1965)† ENOUGH SAID? NOT ENOUGH!

Proofreader 101 to Kosky: What's your relationship to God?

Kosky to 101: I consider God a very close Ruthenian-Jewish relative.

I come as a pilgrim. (Pope John Paul II)

A man of imposing youthful physique, with a gentle, unaffected smile and expressive eyes, Cardinal Essenes is a vegetarian and teetotaler; he is a spiritual descendant of Cardinal John Henry Newman, that taleteller extraordinary. Whether delivering a live sermon or a talk on a TV talk show, Cardinal Essenes is a spellbinding storyteller who takes advantage of his poetic license.

We may call this speaker Pope, if we wish, but only if we remember that he always reveals himself as a character in a drama, not as a man confiding in us. (Maynard Mack)

An emotional man who understands the emotional role of the Church, Cardinal Essenes is quick to shake hands with an American union man, to kiss the forehead of a crying black child, to bless an old Hispanic woman, to console the sick and the dying. Each gesture shortens his distance from the common folks: by stepping down to them, he challenges his own spiritual charisma, and proves to himself—and others— that he is an ordinary mortal. Speaking to each other in Ruthenian, the Red Cardinal and Kosky walk through the steaming, teeming streets of New York. Since to a bilingual personality each of the two languages

---

*The Essenes, a Jewish sect in the time of Christ, were vegetarians and teetotalers. Always dressed in white and devoted to contemplation and study, they took no part in public affairs. . . . These ascetics preached voluntary poverty, community of wealth and goods, and celibacy. (J. I. Rodale)

†See also *Stepping Stones to Further Jewish–Christian Relations*, an unabridged collection of Christian Documents; Stimulus Books, vol. 1: *Studies in Judaism and Christianity*, 1977. See also "The Road Ahead for Jews and Christians" by John Pawlikowski, in *The Priest*, March 1987.

is a time machine sending the mind back in time to a different spiritual storage, whenever Kosky starts speaking Ruthenian, no matter how simple Ruthenian, at that, he instantly starts thinking in Ruthenian. Such thinking sends Kosky back in time.

In the first place we are free to express our regret that Mr. Cooper has seen fit to make his novel a vehicle for . . . promulgation of prejudice against his own country, her institutions, manners, customs, etc. (*Knickerbocker* magazine)

"I was told," says the Red Cardinal, "that the very instant you arrived in America, you discarded the Ruthenian language, your mother's favorite tongue, as if it were a useless toy, and have since written only in English—as if it were your father's favorite idiom. At least haven't you been tempted to write letters in Ruthenian?"

"Temptation isn't enough," says Kosky. "With all my blood relatives gone, I have no one to write to in Ruthenia and, given my thirty-year-long absence (a spiritual century for a man of my age) and the nature of my books all devoted to The Escape Motif, I would not dare address The Ruthenian People directly. Not yet."

When I was a child, I sometimes wanted to be pope, but a military pope, and sometimes an actor. (Baudelaire)

"If it weren't for the remnants of the Iron Curtain, would you ever consider visiting Ruthenia?"

"Sure I would: I would go there either as Cagliostro* or as the newly rehabilitated literary Bukharin," says our literary mason, for whom all this is a great dramatic moment. **Here he is, Comte de Cagliostro walking through the streets of French Strassburg. One fine day in September, 1780 . . . fresh from his triumphs in Poland where he established a number of his lodges of Egyptian Freemasonry, and had gained much fame as a necromancer and a medical empiric. And walking not alone, but with the most powerful man in France: Cardinal de Rohan. (Henry Ridgely Evans, Litt. D.)†**

---

*Nothing could have been more flattering to Cagliostro than the welcome he received on his arrival in Warsaw in May 1780. Poland was one of the strongholds of Freemasonry and occultism. (Trowbridge, 1910)

†"Fantastic stories were circulated about him. The Cardinal de Rohan selected and furnished a house for him and visited him three or four times a week, arriving at dinner time and remaining until an advanced hour in the night. It was said that the great Cardinal assisted the sorcerer in his labors, and many persons spoke of

I am an artist. I am interested in life. Bolshevism is a new phase of life. I must be interested in it. (Charlie Chaplin, 1920) Cagliostro was some time at Warsaw, and several times had had the honor of meeting Stanislas Augustus, the Polish king. One day, as this monarch was expressing his great admiration for his powers, which appeared to him supernatural, a young lady of the Court who had listened attentively to him began to laugh, declaring that Cagliostro was nothing but an impostor. (Laborde, 1781)

Cutting across Central Park the Cardinal and his ministrant stop at the Central Park zoo. There, like everyone else, they watch the baboons. Catching sight of the Cardinal's black soutane, one of the famous trio of black baboons begins to mimic him. While the Cardinal laughs his head off, the zookeeper reprimands the baboon by hitting him over the head. Understanding nothing, the black baboon begins to imitate the zookeeper—and promptly starts hitting another baboon on the head.

On the street, an old beggar with a face of a conquered conquistador—conquered by some incurable disease—asks the Cardinal for an instant cure. Unable to cure him, the Cardinal blesses him instead; weeping, the beggar kisses his hand.

Kosky and the Cardinal keep on walking. They stop on the corner of West 69th Street, at the newsstand where Kosky often buys his newspapers, and magazines. The covers of some of these very magazines stare him face-to-face.

"Such is the troubled but free sex life of our Miss Liberty," says Kosky, catching the Cardinal's troubled stare, a stare resting, most momentarily, on *Eros and Gent, High Society, Man to Man,* and *Sex and I.* "Their presence is guaranteed to us by our First Amendment," says Kosky. "The First Amendment which I support wholeheartedly, even though in my book, number one stands for A, or Aleph, for a man seen as a collective unity—and by nature I'm most anticollective."

Being is a mystery, being is concealment, but there is meaning beyond the mystery. The meaning beyond the mystery seeks to come to expression. The destiny of human beings is to articulate what is concealed. The

---

the mysterious laboratory where gold bubbled and diamonds sparkled in crucibles brought to a white heat. But nobody except Cagliostro, and perhaps the Cardinal, ever entered that mysterious laboratory." (Henry Ridgely Evans, Litt. D., in "The Conjurer and the Cardinal," in *Cagliostro, Sorcerer of the Eighteenth Century,* op. cit., Chapter 2, p. 16)

divine seeks to be disclosed in the human. (Abraham Joshua Heschel, *Who Is Man*, 1965)

The Cardinal and Kosky have just been noticed by the vendor. The man could not look more Jewish. In fact he looks like a bit younger Chairman Rumkowski* (the very Rumkowski who's been on Kosky's mind quite independently of what had been said or written about this most complex man by other luminaries of literary fiction and fictionalized history: Jay Kay). He is a chubby cherub with a round face and curly hair, always in control and a bit patronizing. He steps out from behind his stand to greet the two men as if he were a ruling Israeli monarch and they the Ruthenian-Jewish pilgrims. At the sight of the Ruthenian Cardinal and the sound of the Ruthenian language,† which, you can tell by his expression alone bring to him memories of Ruthenia and of his Ruthenian-Jewish parents, the vendor opens up like a Yiddish flower.

"My name now is Yankel Jacob, but in Ruthenia I was known as Jakób Jankiel, as Your Prominence must have guessed, and I still like Ruthenia a lot." He smiles sweetly. "Tell me, Your Eminence, in your prayers do you ever pray for us—for the Ruthenian Jews who in the year 1969 forcefully departed—like me—from my one and only Ruthenia?"

"Indeed I do. In every Mass for the Faithful Departed," says the Cardinal. "And in my prayers I quote from the two books written about Judas Maccabaeus by the original ghostwriters of the Old Testament. They constitute the sacred evidence for the existence of Purgatory—and where would Thomas More be without it?"‡

----

*Chaim Mordechai Rumkowski was the Jewish chairman of the Nazi ghetto in Lodz, Poland, a man charged with responsibility no other Jew was ever charged with. (See *The Chronicle of the Lodz Ghetto 1941–1944*, ed. Lucjan Dobroszycki, Yale University Press, 1984.)

As his name alone indicates—how can you fail with "rum" in your name?— Rumkowski has been a subject of a great many rumors.

†The primarily agricultural Ruthenians speak a dialect intermediate between Polish and Russian. "They are a sturdy people, well built and muscular." (Louise A. Boyd, op. cit., 1937)

‡More's defense of the existence of Purgatory was taken by the reformers to be exactly on a level with his description of Utopia: one was as imaginary as the other, and More lied by claiming either existed. (Robert C. Elliott, *The Literary Persona*, op. cit., p. 65)

208

"Judas the Maccabee whose name was since the year 165 the Jewish battle cry?" Yankel cries out. "The very sopher whose spectacular military victory the Talmud purposefully omits? I say: Omits, not censors."

"Indeed the one who led the Jews in their rebellion against Syrian suppression. Don't you celebrate this event through the feast of Chanukah?"

"Sure I do, your High Priestship," says the vendor. "I can even tell why Chanukah must be observed for eight days and why during that time eight lights must be kindled on the Chanukah menorah! I even know why the ninth candle, the special *shamash*, is used to light the other eight—something I bet Your Eminence might not know."

"But I also might," the Cardinal laughs heartily, while Yankel lights his inner menorah. He glances absentmindedly at the newsstand's impressive array of tabloids and magazines. The Cardinal follows his glance. Their respective glances irrespectively stop at the shameless cover of *Fatican Flesh* magazine (PRINTER: Fatican as in fat, not Vatican), on which, a shamefully sexy Ava Maria Cardinale sprawls stark naked on the steps of St. Peter's.

"Even the sanctity of an altar won't stop these incorrigible porn makers," says the Cardinal. "When will they be stopped from growing such shameless harvests?"

"Let's hope never," says Kosky.

"It's smutty stuff read only by sex-starved people who have nothing better to do with their time than stare at pictures—rather than read," says Yankel.

"Still, there ought to be a way of limiting its impact on the innocent at heart," wonders the Cardinal. "Perhaps some form of prior restraint?"

"Prior restraint is spiritual censorship. Censorship is censorship, wherever it comes from. Today we ban the organs, tomorrow the organists."*

Sexual modesty cannot then in any simple way be identified with the use of clothing.... The most we can say is that a tendency to cover the body and those parts of the body which declare it male or female goes

---

*"Organ: The introduction of the o. into the Sabbath synagogue service became a controversial issue between the Orthodox and the Reform movements in the nineteenth century. . . . The o. became usual in Reform and some Conservative services. It is also found in many Italian and French synagogues. In the West, it came to be used for wedding and other weekday services, even in Orthodox congregations." (*The Concise Jewish Encyclopedia*, op. cit., p. 412)

209

together with sexual shame but is not an essential feature of it. (Karol Wojtyla)*

September 4.
This is, for Kosky, the most troubling anniversary: a D-day marked forever in his Jewish history. This is the day when, back in 1942, turning his back on past and future history, Chairman Rumkowski, the famous (some say infamous; J.K.) Polish-Jewish chairman of the ghetto in Lodz,† addressed some two thousand of his fellow Jews over the German-made microphone. Speaking in Yiddish, Rumkowski asked his fellow inmates for a sacrifice which he considered essential to the preservation of life.
For: *Lodz Ghetto* (a film)
Sample Script: READER: NORBERT KOSKY‡
Text: Word for word as Rumkowski spoke it. (Plus'nd minus the liberties of translation: J.K.)
PRINTER: Kindly set the following text in spiritually strong caps. Break the paragraphs as often as you can, in order to leave space'nd scene for tears and choked voice and sneezing and coughing—the various, most

---

*Love and Responsibility, by Karol Wojtyla (Pope John Paul II), translated by H. T. Willets, 1981.

†Lodz (sp. Łódź, pron. woodz), Poland's second largest city, renamed Litzmannstadt by the Nazis during the War. (Litzmann was a German general: J.K.)

‡ATTENTION: All but two members of Norbert Kosky's once numerous family perished in the ghetto of Lodz. (ESTATE EDITORS) "During a visit to Lodz, Eichmann witnessed the gassing of 1,000 Jews in sealed buses." From *The Nazis: World War II*, by Robert Edwin Herzstein and the Editors of Time-Life Books, 1980, p. 145.

"In his protest Oberburgermeister (of LODZ: J.K.) Ventzki announced that he would divest himself of every responsibility for the consequences of the measure. Then he recited some reasons for his attitude: The ghetto had originally held 160,400 people in an area of 4.13 square kilometers. The population had now declined to 144,000 owing to deaths and departures to forced labor camps, but there was more than a corresponding decline of area, to 3.41 square kilometers. Density was now 59,917 persons per square kilometer. The 144,000 inhabitants lived in 2,000 houses with 25,000 rooms, that is, 5.8 persons per room.

"Within the ghetto, said Ventzki, large factories were producing vital materials needed by the Reich [figures cited], but only starvation rations were coming into the ghetto. Lack of coal had impelled the inmates to tear out doors, windows, and floors to feed the fires in the stoves." From *The Destruction of the European Jews*, by Raul Hilberg, op cit., p. 142.

210

dramatic acts of Chairman Rumkowski which break his speech. Since Chairman Rumkowski was a most effective public speaker, these were either natural acts or an artificial display.

RUMKOWSKI (addressing the ghetto inmates in front of the well-known ghetto fire station) (well known, I imagine, since I have not been in the ghetto of Lodz since the end of the War: J.K.):*

RUMKOWSKI:

THE GHETTO HAS BEEN AFFLICTED WITH A GREAT SORROW. WE ARE BEING ASKED TO GIVE UP THE BEST WE POSSESS—CHILDREN AND OLD PEOPLE. I WAS NOT PRIVILEGED TO HAVE A CHILD OF MY OWN AND SO I DEVOTED THE BEST YEARS OF MY LIFE FOR THE SAKE OF THE CHILD.

I NEVER WOULD HAVE IMAGINED THAT MY HANDS WOULD DELIVER THE SACRIFICE TO THE ALTAR.

IN MY OLD AGE I MUST STRETCH FORTH MY ARMS AND BEG: BROTHERS AND SISTERS, YIELD THEM TO ME! FATHERS AND MOTHERS, YIELD ME YOUR CHILDREN!

YESTERDAY AFTERNOON, I WAS GIVEN AN ORDER TO DEPORT SOME 20,000 JEWS FROM THE GHETTO. IF NOT, *THEY* WOULD DO IT.

THE QUESTION AROSE: SHOULD WE TAKE IT OVER, DO IT OURSELVES, OR LEAVE IT FOR OTHERS TO CARRY OUT? WE—THAT IS I AND MY CLOSEST COLLEAGUES—CONCLUDED THAT HOWEVER DIFFICULT IT WOULD BE FOR US, WE WOULD HAVE TO TAKE OVER THE RESPONSIBILITY.

I HAVE TO CARRY OUT THIS DIFFICULT AND BLOODY OPERATION.

I HAVE TO CUT OFF LIMBS IN ORDER TO SAVE THE BODY!†

---

*EDITOR: Do not change. This is the *REAL* speech. Thanks. (J.K.)

†The following paragraph[2] reads: "And thus, women to whom heathens say, 'Give us one of you that we may defile her, otherwise we shall defile you all, let them defile them all, but they shall not surrender a single soul from Israel.' It is in enlarging on this paragraph that the Jerusalemite Talmud adduces the teaching 'A company of men,' with heathens demanding a person in order to put him to death—otherwise the entire group will be expunged." (III. "The Place of the Problem in the System." 6. The teaching of about A.D. 100 as to the handing over of a woman for defilement. Pages 69–104 contained in *Collaboration with Tyranny in Rabbinic Law* by David Daube. Oxford University Press, 1965)

For further cannonade of Jewish legal arguments both for and against certain interpretation of the canon of never yielding to the requests for Jewish victims the delivery of whom would save further victims, the reader is referred to I: "The Problem and Its Main Solution," and II. "Defiance and Compromise" in the above quoted most essential work. (J.K. 1988)

I HAVE TO TAKE CHILDREN BECAUSE OTHERWISE—GOD FORBID—OTHERS WILL BE TAKEN.

I HAVE NOT COME TO COMFORT YOU. NOR HAVE I COME TO SET YOUR HEARTS AT EASE, BUT TO UNCOVER YOUR FULL GRIEF AND WOE.

I HAVE COME LIKE A THIEF TO TAKE YOUR DEAREST POSSESSIONS FROM YOUR HEARTS.

I LEFT NO STONE UNTURNED IN MY EFFORTS TO GET THE ORDER ANNULLED, BUT WHEN THIS WAS IMPOSSIBLE, I TRIED TO MITIGATE IT.

I SUCCEEDED IN ONE THING—SAVING ALL THE CHILDREN BEYOND THE AGE OF TEN.

LET THIS BE A COMFORT IN OUR GRAVE SORROW.

PERHAPS THIS PLAN IS DEVILISH, PERHAPS NOT, BUT I CANNOT HOLD BACK FROM UTTERING IT. "GIVE ME THE SICK AND IN THEIR PLACE, WE CAN RESCUE THE HEALTHY."

I COULD NOT MULL THE PROBLEM FOR LONG. I WAS FORCED TO DECIDE IN FAVOR OF THE WELL MAN.

I CAN UNDERSTAND YOU, MOTHERS, I SEE YOUR TEARS. I CAN ALSO FEEL YOUR HEARTS, FATHERS, WHO TOMORROW, AFTER YOUR CHILDREN HAVE BEEN TAKEN FROM YOU, WILL BE GOING TO WORK, WHEN JUST YESTERDAY YOU HAD BEEN PLAYING WITH YOUR DEAR LITTLE CHILDREN.

I KNOW ALL THIS AND I SYMPATHIZE WITH IT.

SINCE FOUR P.M. YESTERDAY, UPON HEARING THE DECREE, I HAVE UTTERLY COLLAPSED.

I LIVE WITH YOUR GRIEF AND YOUR SORROW TORMENTS ME.

I DON'T KNOW HOW AND WITH WHAT STRENGTH I CAN LIVE THROUGH IT.

I MUST TELL YOU A SECRET. THEY DEMANDED 24,000 VICTIMS. BUT I SUCCEEDED IN GETTING THEM TO REDUCE THE NUMBER TO 20,000, AND PERHAPS EVEN FEWER THAN 20,000.

BUT ONLY ON CONDITION THAT THESE WILL BE CHILDREN UP TO THE AGE OF TEN.

CHILDREN OVER TEN ARE SAFE.

WE WILL HAVE TO MEET THE QUOTA BY ADDING THE SICK AS WELL.

YOU SEE BEFORE YOU A BROKEN MAN. DON'T ENVY ME. THIS IS THE MOST DIFFICULT ORDER THAT I HAVE EVER HAD TO CARRY OUT. I REACH OUT TO YOU MY BROKEN AND TREMBLING HANDS, AND I BEG YOU:

GIVE INTO MY HANDS THE VICTIMS.

HAND THEM OVER TO ME, SO THAT WE WILL AVOID HAVING FURTHER VICTIMS . . . AND A POPULATION OF A HUNDRED THOUSAND JEWS BE PRESERVED.

SO THEY PROMISED ME. IF WE DELIVER OUR VICTIMS BY OURSELVES, THERE WILL BE PEACE.

SHOUTS FROM THE CROWD:

WE WILL ALL GO! MISTER PRESIDENT, *ONLY* CHILDREN SHOULD NOT BE TAKEN. TAKE ONE CHILD FROM THOSE PARENTS WHO HAVE SEVERAL!*

RUMKOWSKI:

THESE ARE EMPTY PHRASES. I DO NOT FEEL STRONG ENOUGH TO ARGUE WITH YOU. IF SOMEONE OF THE AUTHORITIES ARRIVES, NONE OF YOU WILL SHOUT.

I IMPLORED ON MY KNEES, BUT IT DID NOT WORK. FROM SMALL HAMLETS WITH A JEWISH POPULATION OF SEVEN AND EIGHT THOUSAND, BARELY A THOUSAND ARRIVED HERE. SO WHAT IS BETTER, THAT EIGHTY OR NINETY THOUSAND JEWS REMAIN, OR THAT, GOD FORBID, THE WHOLE POPULATION BE EXTINGUISHED?

ONE NEEDS TO HAVE THE HEART OF A BANDIT TO ASK FROM YOU WHAT I AM ASKING. BUT PUT YOURSELF IN MY PLACE, THINK LOGICALLY AND YOU WILL REACH THE CONCLUSION THAT I COULD NOT PROCEED OTHERWISE. †

THE PART THAT CAN BE SAVED IS MUCH BIGGER THAN THE PART THAT MUST BE GIVEN AWAY. (Here the speech ends: J.K. but it does not end the question of Jewish Elites Under German Rule [Lucjan Dobroszycki, 1980]‡)

---

*There are many fictional and nonfiction works written about Rumkowski. Whether exact or not they are all most exacting since they desperately try to account for his reign of warmth, "as well as for his pro-forma reign of terror." (Jay Kay)

†Rumkowski could proceed otherwise. Like any other regular ghetto-*dweller*, Rumkowski could have gotten rid of his job very easily. All he had to do was to improve on the example set for him on October 19, 1943, by a Jewish woman named Łaja.
Tuesday, October 19, 1943
SUICIDE ATTEMPT
On October 18, Łaja Krumholz, born in Łódź in 1920 and residing at 9 Wawelska Street, attempted suicide by swallowing a sleep-inducing drug. She was taken to the hospital by the Emergency Service. (*The Ghetto Chronicles*)

‡"Jewish Elites Under German Rule" by Lucjan Dobroszycki in *The Holocaust: Ideology, Bureaucracy, and Genocide, The San Jose Papers*, edited by Henry Friedlander and Sybil Milton, 1980.

See also "The Untold Story of the Lodz Ghetto" (edited by Lucjan Dobroszycki, 1984), an extraordinary cover story in *The New York Times Magazine*, July 29, 1984.

Having finished with this most painful text (the reading as well as correcting in the galley proofs: J.K.), which leaves him morally exhausted, Kosky annotates it with the following footnote:

Whenever Rumkowski spoke publicly in the ghetto—and he spoke publicly often—he always spoke with the authority "of a feudal lord: the first Jewish feudal lord in history!" (Jay Kay) He also spoke like one who was a *de facto* ruler of what he is said to have jokingly referred to as "my mini-Jewish State." "**I will remove the troublemakers and agitators from the ghetto and not because I tremble for my life, but because I fear for you all. You have to be protected; as for me, my hair is white as snow, I walk with a stoop—my life is already behind me!**" (Rumkowski, 1943)

In point of fact, the operation proceeded as follows—block after block was surrounded by the Jewish police and then each building surrounded by a host of police and Jewish firemen and entered by a representative of the authorities (the Gestapo). A shot was fired as the signal to assemble, and then all the residents of a given building were assembled in the courtyard, arranged in two rows, and subjected to inspection by representatives of the authorities. In the meantime, the Jewish police were searching the apartments and bringing out anyone who had been hiding or people who were ill. In the smaller buildings, this operation often took only a few minutes. (Lodz Ghetto)

While Kosky waits for his appointment with Barza Omadi, a writer, playwright and essayist from Indostran who is about to visit Kosky in Kosky's flat, Kosky is driven mad. Mad by the pain in his sacrum. Mad, because he does not know *What to Do for Your Aching Back* (*Consumer Reports*, 1987) other than lying on his back on his bathroom floor with his legs drawn up and over and around the base of the toilet bowl, "in the most effective pelvic tilt exercise available." (Jay Kay)

"Most people suffer an incapacitating backache at some time in their lives. And yes, it can come back to haunt you. Once stricken, you run a 60 percent chance of a return bout within two years," assures him the authoritative *Consumer Reports*, 1987. *Sixty* percent? Are you sex-consuming folks sure it was a straight sixty and not, say, sixty-nine percent? **What a difference a number nine makes!** revolts Kosky's inner *Consumer Reports* specialist.

Some six years earlier, Omadi, one of his country's intellectual ayatollahs, was arrested by PERSAUD, Indostran's secret service, on charges of ideological conspiracy and was kept in solitary confinement without trial. He was released recently from prison and allowed to come to the United States at the invitation of Bakunin University in Kropotkin, Hawaii.

Santos, the doorman at the Manfred, rings Kosky on the house phone to announce the visitor. Reluctantly, Kosky parts with his vibrating heating pad.

"A most strange-looking stranger is here to see you, *Señor*," he whispers, "but he won't give me his name."

"It's *his* name," says Kosky. "Why should he give it to a stranger like you? I know who he is. Ask him to come up."

In a moment, Omadi materializes at the door to Kosky's apartment, and enters it without hesitation. He, who until now was known to Kosky only by his writing—writing denoting the presence of the anarchic persona—becomes now a real-life person. The person is of middle height, middle age and the nondescript looks of a most accomplished literary conscript. While the two men resemble one another a bit—Kosky's face could feasibly belong to Omadi (though not the other way around: J.K.)—they also could not be more different. Omadi is a writer who sees himself as *engagé* on the side of the politically predefined left or right—not merely on the side of the always individually defined RIGHT OR WRONG. Kosky belongs in a bag of assorted humanistically inclined apolitical intellectuals—i.e., he is more than willing to "Establish Justice, to insure Domestic Tranquility" (Final Report of the National Commission on the Causes and Prevention of Violence, December 1969) acting and working within the Jeffersonian value system.

Omadi is a writer who, had it not been for his massive talent, could be qualified not as a writer but rather as a writing revolutionary. (Omadi is the Marxist Tolstoy fighting the Church of the Repressive State. Kosky is a Dostoyevskian version of Omadi. Enough said: Jay Kay)* A climac-

---

*See *Tolstoy or Dostoyevsky: An Essay in Contrast,* by George Steiner, 1960. (Did you know that Dostoyevsky had translated Balzac's *Eugénie Grandet*? I did not!: J.K.)

"This is a young man's book. It was written, as first books ought to be, out of sheer compulsion," writes George Steiner, in 1980, that *mimus polyglottos maximus,* in his preface to the 1960 edition. "It was my conviction that Tolstoy and Dostoyevsky tower over the art of fiction; that their pre-eminence entails certain fundamental points about western literature as a whole (so far as the Russian novel may be said to belong to this literature), and that the reader's inevitable preference of the one master over the other will define a whole philosophic and political stance. . . . Twenty-one years later, I still subscribe to these convictions, though I would now qualify them. The magnitude of the Tolstoyan and Dostoyevskian performance still seems to me unmatched. But there are in Proust categories of intelligence, of psychological acuity and philosophic discovery which make the *Remembrance of Things Past* an indispensably central act." (Op. cit., the not-numbered first page)

tic moment: seeing Kosky, Omadi bends his torso in a bow and, suddenly, grabbing Kosky by his right hand, places on it with his parched lips a dry kiss. "I should kiss your feet," he says. With effort, he walks to a chair. With effort, he sits down. With effort, he turns the table lamp toward Kosky. After so many years in solitary, he can't see well. "I want to see you better; you are my spiritual brother," he says. "I want to know you; you are the one to whom I owe the rest of my life, though I think I am about to die from the New York summer heat."

"You owe it to yourself," says Kosky. **To be free in the freedom of others—that is my whole faith, the aspiration of my whole life. I considered it my sacred duty to rebel against all oppression, no matter where it came from or on whom it fell. There was always a lot of quixotism in me, not only political but also private. I could not view injustice—to say nothing of actual oppression—with equanimity. I often interfered in the affairs of others without being asked, and with no right, and without having given myself time to think it over.... (Bakunin to Czar Nicholas I, 1851)**

"In prison, I thought of you each time when they gave me the 'ninety degrees': when they would lie me on the floor, legs up at ninety degrees, and beat my feet with a whip until either I broke, or the whip," says Omadi. "I thought of you when I signed my name to my Bakuninist 'confession.' " He breathes deeper. "I thought about you even when, for months, I had no news from my wife or children. When they gave me drugs. Even when they kept me without books, newspapers, anything to read, not a piece of literature, not even the Koran! The greatest poetic work of all!"

"The main thing is that you're alive," says Kosky. ("A dead rebel to the cause does no good to the cause, particularly when, as is the case in Industran, this cause is still very much alive." Kosky speaks here with the voice of his past presidency of W.E.T.)

Trumped-up charges of "anti-Court Marxist activities," both current and retroactive, had been leveled by PERSAUD against Barza Omadi and many prominent teachers, writers and clergy, who were sentenced without trial to spend years in PERSAUD prisons. To extract their confessions and denunciations, they were subjected to electric shocks and pushed into pits of human manure. PERSAUD had ordered public executions of several intellectuals; the deaths of many others were never

made public, but it was established that Barza Omadi was not among them. He is said to be next in line. (George Levanter to Kosky)*

"Well, since I refused to die or kill myself—how unoriginal to do by oneself what in any case will be done to all of us—they finally let me go." Omadi brightens. "One day the all-powerful prison director comes to see me. 'Who's Norbert Kosky?' he asks me.

" 'I don't know, sir,' I answer, for once truthfully, since I'd never heard of you.

" 'Don't lie,' says the director. 'That man Kosky has been for months turning the United States upside down for you. Is he an Armenian or a Ruthenian? A Jew, a Gentile or a Gypsy? Is he thoroughly insane or merely crazy? You must tell me who that man Kosky is and who he is to you.'

" 'I don't know, sir. I've never heard of him.' I say. 'If you don't believe me, give me another ninety degrees.'

"And so he does give me the ninety degrees, and after it's over, and even though I can barely breathe from pain, I still can't tell him who Kosky is. Only then he most reluctantly leaves me. But then, in a few days—or was it a few weeks or months?—by then I lost the sense of time if not my senses—he is back in my cell, and he is most upset.

" 'This is important, Omadi,' he tells me. 'This can mean your end— and a painful one, I guarantee that,' he threatens. 'The other week, that man Kosky talked about you most urgently to the Indostran ambassador at the embassy dinner in New York. What he said to him gave our ambassador a serious case of moral indigestion. To willingly cause indigestion of our high court official is a crime synonymous with the desire to poison. Why did that man Kosky want to morally poison our ambassador over you?'

" 'I don't know, sir,' I say. 'I've never heard of Norbert Kosky. But, tell me, sir,' I ask him humbly, 'why would our ambassador bother to have such a poisonous man to dinner? Can't PERSAUD these *Royal Cannibals* (Reza Barahani, 1977)† take care of that man Kosky and give him ninety degrees before they eat him alive?'

---

*George Levanter, the well-connected past president (1973–75) of the American Center of Investors International.

†*The Crowned Cannibals*: Writings on Repression in Iran, by Reza Baraheni, with an Introduction by E. L. Doctorow, 1977. "Reza Baraheni is chronicler of his nation's torture industry, and poet of his nation's secret police force," (E. L.

218

" 'We can't. Not now, anyhow,' the director says. 'He happens to be the president of W.E.T., an international association of the most established writers, editors and translators. Of the most elitist American intellectual elite. And, if that's not enough, he is a member of EON, the most exclusive American intellectual club, so exclusive it won't even admit intellectual women.' Once again, the prison director leaves me perturbed. In a few months, or may be in a year? (note that by then I no longer counted days), he's back in my cell again, this time with an official letter in hand.

" 'This is most serious, Omadi,' he tells me. 'I just heard on the official phone the other day that at an official New York reception given to honor Habeas Voyvoda, our prime minister, that man Kosky, who was among the guests, suddenly surfaced and in front of everyone he verbally attacked our prime minister for what we supposedly did to you. Of course, our prime minister assured him he had never even heard of you—and he was telling the truth. How could he hear about someone who formally doesn't exist? Today the prime minister's office called me to find out if you were still alive—and I told them that you might or might not be. Life, I said, and Omadi, are perhaps no longer synonymous—and how's that phrase for someone as uneducated as me. Now if you intend to go on living you must tell me: who are you to Kosky?' the director barks.

" 'I swear I don't know,' I cry out. 'Maybe I'm one of his spiritual servers?'

" 'There's no way to know what length that man Kosky might go to to get you out of here,' says the director. 'The man is a yogi terrorist. They say he can float on water for hours like some sickening-to-look-at crab.'

" 'If he's a floating terrorist, PERSAUD should drown him,' I propose, but this answer infuriates the director and so I get from him another ninety degrees. Afterward, the prison director leaves my cell all upset, only to come back a few weeks later. This time he is really shaken. He is unhappy. 'I was told,' he says, glancing at me harshly, 'that recently that man Kosky appealed on your behalf to all American media. Now, this is most serious. This could mean a boycott of our forthcoming Horror Film Festival to be held in our new Nirvana Palace under the

Doctorow) See also *Writer Says Ex-Premier on Trial Helped Free Iranian Intellectuals* (*The New York Times*, 1979).

patronage of the Imperial Highnesses.'* He leaves me in a fury—but forgets to give me the usual ninety degrees—a procedure, come to think, he would have invented by himself even if he would not have first seen it in some old film made by or about Hitler's Nazis. In a few weeks he returns to my cell. This time he seems pensive and most concerned for my welfare.

" 'This is no longer possible.' He bites his lip. 'Yesterday, in New York, that man Kosky talked about you in person, to'—he swallows hard—'to the imperial highnesses. To the Imperator and the Imperatrice. Imagine that!' Tears well in his eyes.

" 'But that's impossible. How could he?' I say.

" 'He could, and he did. The many court witnesses say that he must have talked to them about you for over twenty minutes. Twenty minutes. Imagine that!'

" 'I can't,' I say. 'How could he even come close to the imperial highnesses—much less talk to them even for a second? Where was PERSAUD? Why wasn't he shot on the spot?'

" 'Don't be silly, Omadi!' says the director. 'This was at a black-tie reception: the highest security this side of the Koran. In fact, before talking to the imperial highnesses, that man Kosky was seen talking to the imperial highnesses in front of Henry Grandstand, the American Secretary of State, and Konrad Walenrodzky, the past national security adviser.'

" 'But why would Kosky be invited to such a reception unless he has something to add to it?' I ask, for I still knew nothing about you.

" 'How do I know?' says the director. 'I run this prison, not a Luny Park for the intellectual lunies.' He raises his hands to the imperial sky and leaves my cell in disgust—this time despairing over his fate, not mine.

"Six hours later the director comes to see me once more," says Omadi.

" 'That's it,' he says without preliminaries. 'That's it, Omadi. It's over! The Imperatrice has just called Habeas Voyvoda, our prime minister, to find out how you are—and whether you still are. Now the prime minister called me in person. In person—' he repeats, 'and, in person, he ordered me to get rid of you. This is the end.'

" 'I swear to you I had nothing to do with all these provocations.'

---

*See *Images of Horror and Fantasy*, by Gert Schiff, 1978.

Now I plead for my life. 'Please give me another ninety degrees—make it a hundred! Anything! But let me live a bit longer.'

" 'What ninety degrees?' the director chokes. 'Can't you hear me right? It's over! This is the end! On your feet,' he commands—for the first time without using his whip.

" 'Where am I going?' I pray for my life.

" 'You're going to the great beyond,' says the director.

" 'I came from there some fifty years ago,' I say. 'I don't want to go back. Can't I stay here, in life, a bit longer?'

" 'You're going to America. The great beyond,' says the director. 'It's the only way left to stop that man Kosky from surfacing.'

"It was a miracle," says Omadi. "A pure miracle. I feel like one who no longer fears drowning. But tell me, Kosky," he says, lowering his voice. "How did you manage to get me out? What methods did you use? Blackmail? Terror? Did you ever threaten to blow them up on a ski lift?"

"I can't tell you," says Kosky. "I must protect my fictional sources."

FOREIGN JOURNALISTS TOUR IMPERATOR'S PALACE. From our Foreign Correspondent. Following the sudden overthrow of the Imperator of Indostran by the Musmarx, the coalition of Muslim muhtis and Marxists, the American journalists were offered a tour of the deposed monarch's Nirvana Palace, located high in the hills of the capital. On the night table beside the Imperator's bed were the books the monarch was reading before he escaped the ax of Musmarx. They were the memoirs of Ghandhi and Ben-Gurion; Henry Miller's *Plexus, Nexus,* and *Sexus*; the Coldcut sisters' biography of Henry Grandstand, the U.S. Secretary of State; and the works of Norbert Kosky, the American-Ruthenian novelist known primarily for his anarchic literary characters. (*Centralia*)*

Centralia: an elite literary magazine founded in 1919 during the Great Red Scare, in the small town of Centralia, in the State of Washington, and located at No. 69 on the town's notoriously radical Tower Avenue (near the headquarters of the Industrial Workers of the World [IWW], also known as the Wobblies).

"Is there, in your new book, a love affair without sexual aggression?" aggresses upon Kosky a free-lance *reporteress* at the American Booksellers Association.

A perfect head-turning mixture of Cinderella and Conchita, she comes onto him strong—straight from the pages of the head and head-giving *Oriental Adult Women* magazine.

"There is at least one carnal carnage and one love-quickie, but, unlike in my other novels," he adds quickly, "this time the quickie is verbal. It stems, to put it briefly, from the most imaginative safe-sex, save-sex known: the Verbal Art, Verbal Sign and Verbal Time,"* he states solemnly, watching her nubile Siamese hips, the sight of which would prompt Lucian Goldmann to entirely revise, even rewrite, his "Understanding Marcuse" (*Partisan Review*, 1971, No. 3), the very Marcuse who said that "the emergence of new sensibility will probably have as a first consequence the reduction of productivity," as quoted by Leopold Labedz in his "The Destiny of Writers in Revolutionary Movements Survey," No. 1 (82) Winter 1972, p. 32.

---

*See *Verbal Art, Verbal Sign, Verbal Time*, Eleven Essays by Roman Jakobson; Krystyna Pomorska and Stephen Rudy, eds.; with the assistance of Brent Vine, University of Minnesota, 1985. Born and educated in Moscow, Roman Jakobson (1896–1982) is best known for his contributions to the structuralist approach to linguistics and literature "without whom no book." (Norbert Kosky, 1982; repeated 1986) See also *Selected Writings of Roman Jakobson*.

"Is there in it a good old 1969 B.J.?" Her purple lips deliver a final blow job (called B.J. in Thai fiction) to his latest Book-of-Job.

"There is," he assures her calmly while setting his kundalini on 69° Fahrenheit degree fire by inhaling this woman's Soixante-Neuf perfume.

"And, in these days of Unsafe Sex, how does your hero define oral pleasure?"

"He defines it as **tongue lashing (Cathy Young.)** He defines it as sexually straight talk, meaning the right to use and abuse a lover by using on him or her at bedtime very bad words—bad, meaning 'far more inventive than simply obscene' (Niskisko), and using them either as the right word at a bad time, or a bad one at the right time. These bedtime-bad-words rights are guaranteed to us by the First Amendment. Today, they are the prime carriers of OTT—of Orally Transmitted Tease. Tease, printer, not disease! (No more sleaze! Please!)

SS

"You're not divorced. In this country adultery is still punishable by law. Another sex law, no doubt drafted by the old Hebrew or maybe Jewish-American Khazar*—lawyers," says Kosky, helping Cathy to unpack in the hotel room. "Was it wise to come to New York for just one day?" Our Dionysian stares her straight in her lips.

"So what?" she shoots back. "This is not exactly being 'A Girl of Six from the Ghetto Begging in Smolna Street in 1942.'† She stares at him trying to silence his carnal cacaphony by engaging him in his spiritually sad Smolna Street ritual.

This is her way of saying to him: Because of the fear of AIDS, the times became sexually insane. Times, this time not you and not I. Fluid means life. It is opposite of ash and ash means death. People fear one

---

*Khazars: "About the time when Charlemagne was crowned Emperor of the West, the eastern confines of Europe between the Caucasus and the Volga were ruled by a Jewish state, known as the Khazar Empire. At the peak of its power, from the seventh to the tenth centuries A.D, it played a significant part in shaping the destinies of medieval, and consequently of modern, Europe." (Arthur Koestler)

†A poem by Jerzy Ficowski in his A Reading of Ashes, a collection of poems translated from the Polish by Keith Bosley with Krystyna Wandycz. Foreword by Zbigniew Herbert (London, 1981), p. 10. (A spiritually superior number: Jay Kay)

another's fluid and, as a result, the corporate state sucks their civil liberties dry! Corporate state, not corporeal! With the death of a routine kiss, how can you dare to write a full novel about 69? True, we love sex—and we know this as well as we know one another, as well as Colette would know Marcel Proust. True, we are addicts: addicts of life. Life means sex. "Yes, my spiritual sweetheart, spiritual not corporal," she teases him now. "As of today you too are a member of LASA: a life-addicted-sex-addict—the past member of NASA.* A new Napoleonic Sex-Love Code is needed," raves his Khazarina. "A brand new Sensuality Code and one not at all synonymous with the Anti-AIDS State Behavioral Code recently proposed by Senator Abraham Ronald Tamerlane, that smelly skunk of a politician from Carnalia in South Louisiana."

She ends her case. What is he to do? Must he tell her about *The State of Ambiguity*,† the only state a fiction writer can comfortably inhabit, in the wise words of that publicity conscious Jay Kay?

Must he say more? Must he ask her point blank (point blank means holding a sexual revolver), Do you still love WET? With the word *wet*, for once, openly standing for *fluid-transmitted disease called* AIDS, and, for once in this text, not for WET, his favorite Writers, Editors and Translators Association? He must not. "Why not?" (Jay Kay) Because Cathy is his spiritual source; she is simply his ideal fictional being he calls a narrative whore.

"Well, was it worth it? Answer me!" and as he asks her this safe-sex-oriented question, he recalls the nubile lips of the girls from the oral Oriental *Oriental Women* magazine.

Forms, colors, densities, odors—what is it in me that corresponds with them? (Walt Whitman)

"I came to be with you. You're my Mani: my 'Jewish Christian.'" (Gilles Quispel) She looks at him most meaningfully and her look brings to his mind the entire erotic art of Tantra found in the erotic temples of Nepal.‡

---

*NASA: National Association of Sex Addicts (founded, not accidentally, at the 1969 San Francisco Counter Obscenity Convention).

†*The State of Ambiguity: Studies of Gypsy Refugees*, by Ignacy-Marek Kaminski, University of Gothenburg, Sweden, 1980 ISBN: 91-86060-00-7.

‡See "Sex and Religious Art," in *The Art of Nepal*, by Lydia Aran (Kathmandu, Nepal, n.d.), pp. 60–69.

I recognized him and understood that he was my Self from whom I had been separated. (*The Mani Codex*)*

He won't argue with her. Not now. This is the time for magic; for celebration of real-life illusion. This is the time when, in preparation for *congressus subtilis,*† for his spiritual *sādhana*, he had set in motion the Breath Magic No. 6—an entirely different kind of breath. **In love every man starts from the beginning. (Søren Kierkegaard, 1855)**

This is the time for *samarasa*, that sublime moment in which the two arrests, the arrest of semen and the arrest of breath, lead to freedom of exaltation, when **One sees the lotus seed, pure by nature, in one's own body. (Kanha)**

This is the time when the mere thought of being with Cathy **"brings him from the chill periphery of things to the radiant core." (William H. James)**

Torn between restraint and arousal, our Tantric self-master calms himself by employing an old literary trick. He begins to watch Cathy— to watch her every move—in a carnal closeup, a closeup found usually in yet another literary sex-oriented narrative art magazine.

> . . . unhurried, unobtrusive, not cold, but also not effusive, no haughty stare around the press, no proud pretentions to success, no mannerism, no affectation, no artifices of the vain. . . . No, all in her was calm and plain. She struck one as the incarnation—Shishkov, forgive me: I don't know the Russian for *le comme il faut.*‡ (Pushkin)

"Tell me again: what's your new literary orgy about?" Cathy asks offhandedly, hanging her various voluptuous Maithuna night dresses in the closet—already a secret part of their most secret Tantric voluptuary.

"About a mixture of verb and video," he says offhandedly, loading film into his camera. Holding a camera motionlessly offers him a perfect breath-holding exercise.

------

*See *Jewish and Gnostic Man*, in Eranos Lectures 3 (1986), p. 6; these lectures contain *The Birth of the Child: Some Gnostic and Jewish Aspects*, by Gilles Quispel (1971), and *Three Types of Jewish Piety*, by Gershon Sholem, a lecture originally presented at the 1969 Eranos Conference in Ascona, Switzerland (*Eranos Yearbook* 38–1969).

†*Congressus subtilis*: an intense Tantric carnal copulation carried out by a bodily present being with one whose body exists only on an astral plane.

‡Translated by Sir Charles Johnston (1977).

The Orgy is not a novel, and I hate the non-word "non-fiction." I have written other works grounded in fact: poems, biographies, films. . . . *The Orgy* is a book—whatever happened to that category?—and it is a pity your reviewer did not read it as a book. (Muriel Rukeyser)* Music mixes. So does video and film. Why can't fiction mix?"

"Tell me more about it." Seemingly somnolent and detached, she is already readying herself for coitus (in this ms. p. 269) as, seemingly attached only to her Self, she bounces around the room while he reads her as if she were a living erotic temple—full of "erotic representations. Toward the east, there are some erotic reliefs on both sides of the window on the ground floor. Some copulatory scenes are presented, while some can be found only in an embracing pose. In some cases, perverted sex or lower congress is shown." (lower congress, Printer, not lover!) Description in *Erotic Themes of Nepal* (1980–81 edition).

"In terms of its structure, my novel shapes up as a certain *genre* of *La Condition Humaine.* (Malraux) It is, really, a teleological *roman à tease,*" he teases her. Camera in hand, he follows her, one crayfish craving for the flesh of the other. "Having my own head examined is the only research I need in order to be able to write it from the top of my head." Here our literary headhunter crawls backward photographing Cathy from the point of view reserved for one about to give head,† by one who is in a position to give it.

Her impact (impact = imp + pact: J.K.) upon our literary Imp of the Perverse (Poe) forces him to recall his pact with Seneca and with the Tantric Age.‡

---

*Muriel Rukeyser: an American poet and essayist and past president of the American Center of P.E.N. ("the international association known by its initials P.E.N., which, if only in English, stand for poets, playwrights, essayists, editors and novelists," explains Jay Kay).

†Head giving: opposite of head hunting; a Tantric ritual in which the giver literally commits his thoughts to the other person almost to the point of excluding himself—or herself. Assigned number 69 on the spiritual index by *Western Tantric* magazine where, let it be repeated, number six stands for accord and nine for invention.

‡The Tantric Age, which followed the lifting of the Puritan tendencies of orthodox Buddhism, became the age of abandon, in which erotic poetry . . . and frank references to sexual practices of great finesse began to flourish in literature and other forms of art. (Lydia Aran, op. cit., p. 61) "The erotic carvings are vivid. The wood has its natural color and is not painted. The workmanship is really

This is the time when, changing the zoom's focus, he focuses on the outside lines of her outer thigh, as tempting and as suggestive as the inside of her inner thigh was only a few sensual frames ago.

"Will the book sell?" She changes her position.

"It will, I'm sure. The footnotes alone are worth the price of literary admission," says Kosky.

"Footnotes? In a work of fiction?"

"Autofiction," says Kosky.

"Go on." She urges him with her subtle body.

"Think of it as written by an autolytus (a creature which reproduces by producing at the point near the posterior end numerous new segments of literary worms, which, attached for a time, then develop into new beings: J.K.). Think of it as if it were not a novel, but, let us say, a new type of a Literary Party. In such a Party the protagonist is, clearly, a leader, and the other figures and characters are, simply, members of his Literary Party."

Slowly, Cathy begins to take off her boots. Slowly, she rolls down her lace stockings. She looks at him—and she looks at him slowly.

Quickly, he reloads his Supra Realist Soviet-made camera (the equivalent of the German Icon 69 sold over the counter at Times Square at half the price: J.K.) and with American-made super speed film, sets the camera to a manual mode just in time for another snapshot of Cathy now posing for him as a sexual sleazebag.

Camera in hand, Kosky now watches her with dual optic: one reserved for watching his subservient Self and one for the 69mm lens of his auto-focused camera. (Model: *Erotic Works: Men and Woman*, by Paul Verlaine, the bilingual English-French edition, translated by Alan Stone, 1985: adds quickly Jay Kay.) **This odious being whom I call Me. (Stendhal)**

"You still haven't changed," says Cathy. "You can't wait to fuck me right now—just as I am undressing—rather than wait for me."

"I don't have to wait for you, slut. You're my *dombi*, remember?"

"I'm your *dombi*, true—but unlike man's stalk which needs *space* to grow, female emotions need *time*. Think of them as leaves—leaves, not lips! Admit it: time is more complex than space."

Being candid about sex—sex as soma as well as spiritual matter—is as natural to Cathy as speaking a body language which, like body En-

---

excellent." See also *Erotic Themes of Nepal*, by T. C. Majupuria and Indra Majupuria, (Nepal, 1981), p. 69.

glish, she—a full-time resident of the corporeal people's republic—speaks very well. Cathy learned her refined body language, her sexual Esperanto (as well as Esperantido) already as a child, pretty much the way he learned his. However, Kosky learned Esperanto in the drawing room and from his father—with his father standing over him with a—yes!—a mental Jewish-Ruthenian discipline! Cathy learned hers in the family bathroom with her father standing over her, "with a small hard object in hand, an object made of flesh, of real male flesh, not merely some fleshy looking rubberized plastic object," she says calmly. "Imagine being hit in my face, as if it were a piece of ass, by my father with his own nondetachable six-inch-long piece of hard yet living discipline!"

" 'Are you turning our Cathy, the kid with an I.Q. of 169, into a G-spot stripper?' my mother used to say to my father. 'Do you want her to grow into another Ample Annie?' " says Cathy.

" 'I want my little Catty Cat to develop a natural appreciation of her father—I'm the stand-in for a man in her life—as well as a healthy repulsion against any man who won't treat her the way I do,' my father would then say, turning at me a full stream of his perverted attention."

Cathy unsnaps the bra, freeing her breasts. She poses for him, carrying in one hand her dress and bra, and one of her marble breasts in the other, and under her calm stare he becomes a Simple Simon—the cretinous sex maniac from the adult movie called *Scum of Kilimanjaro*.

She puts on a translucent nightdress with matching shawl and sits down on the bed, crossing her faultlessly muscular legs under her buttocks. He keeps staring at her, he, a Ruthenian *sroka*, a migrating magpie, as overwhelmed now by the sight of this American bird of paradise as he was each time he had seen her in the past.

"Don't look at me with such an obscene eye. You look like my father when you do," says Cathy.

The remote island in which I found myself situated, in an almost unvisited sea . . . the rude uncultured savages who gathered round me . . . had their influence in determining the emotions with which I gazed upon this "thing of beauty." (Alfred Russell Wallace)

While Cathy gets up and, thirsty, goes to inspect the contents of the room's bar, Kosky walks to the window and looks out at Manhattan. This is still his town, his spiritual shop (SS). This is where he feels free to be anybody—while always remaining himself. **It was towards that buzzing hive that he now looked as if already anticipating the honey he'd suck out and, grandiosely, he said, "Now it's between the two of us." (Balzac)**

228

Cathy moves between him and the window, blocking his view.

"My lawyers tell me that in order to avoid score-settling litigation, my husband might prefer to settle our differences out of court. Soon I could be free. Meanwhile let's do something." She looks at him, reading his mental quotes.

Let no-one, least of all the author, complain about infamy. (Thomas Mann)

Under her watchful eyes he undresses, leaving his clothes in a heap on the floor. (There goes the impeccable starch-guaranteed shape of his favorite ultra-white jeans: J.K.) Next, naked and, appropriately for a Tantric, semi-Self carnally conscious, our sexy spider slips under the bed sheet. She snuggles next to him. **One of the most characteristic qualities of living matter, plant or animal, is its capacity to respond to touch. The normal, first reaction of an organism is to press against any object with which it may come into contact.... (Kinsey)** Marble Juno is cold. She is, she says, still dry. She is, he says, a study of still life. (Life—nevertheless: Jay Kay) Now, our Tantric guide guides his concentration in the general direction of Cathy whom he now perceives twofold: as a physical being supreme, and as a Subtle Body.

forehead	fingers
eyebrows and eyes	hands
nose*	lower arms
cheeks	upper arms
mouth	shoulders
jaw	chest
chin	heart center†
neck	stomach
shoulders	navel region
upper arms	pelvic region
lower arms	upper legs
hands	lower legs
finger	feet
fingertips*	toes†

*†"At these places, as you proceed from the head to the toes, you may pause for two or four relaxed breaths. There are no pauses for breathing as you proceed upward from toes to head." (Sri Swami Rama of the Himalayas, author of *Exercise Without Movement* [1984])

"I know what Rilke means when he says, 'Like an arrow enduring the string only to leap out, love frees us from the one we love,' " says Cathy. "Loving you," she pauses, uncertain, "loving you makes me aware of what I need."

"Loving me or—or your inner literary production?" Hesitantly he picks up the thread while glancing at the book in Cathy's hand.*

"Loving you. What's wrong with it?"

"The form *ing*. It weakens the verb. Why can't you simply say, 'I love you, I love you': not even 'I'm in love with you'—unless you'll correct it in the galley proofs to 'I'm in love with love, not you.' " He laughs in order to throw her off.

"I say it the way I feel it." She refuses to shift to another mood.

"The other day, after I called you and left the message with your answering service, I got frightened by my own feelings. Do you know why I felt I ought to come to New York?"

"Why?" He produces the shortest sentence of his oeuvre. **I said ought to, not must. (Bukharin, 1938)**

"Because you are the only floater I know who keeps his head above the water. Wisely so, since these days waters are polluted. Have you seen that spiritual shocker documentary called *AIDS: The Century's Greatest Sexual Shocker?*"

"AIDS is a social shocker. Social, as much as sexual," he corrects her firmly.

For a moment she cuddles next to him the way, on his bookshelves, the slim *Bangkok by Night* (1981), a sixty-six-page-long photo-volume about sensuous Siam, cuddles next to *The Book of Letters* (*Księga Listow*: J.K.) of Bruno Schulz,† whose erotic drawings bring to mind the poetic images of Charles Baudelaire.‡

---

*(Title not to be listed: J.K.)

†Bruno Schulz, *Księga Listow*, ed. by Jerzy Ficowski (in Polish: J.K.) (Krakow, 1975). In it, you must see drawing no. 6 entitled by Bruno Schulz *Autoportrait with Two Women* (pencil, circa 1934).

The drawing shows the (already balding: J.K.) Bruno naked, as he crawls out from under a table only to be embraced—or bracketed—by two voluptuously naked young women.

‡*The Intimate Journals of Charles Baudelaire*, translated by Christopher Isherwood; introduction by W. H. Auden; illustrated by Charles Baudelaire (1957).

She runs to her suitcase, retrieves from it a video cassette and inserts "this modern visual suppository" (Norbert Kosky) into the videola with electrifying ease or EE. (In Kosky's vocabulary, electrifying ease always stands for the sexually electrifying Elisabeth Eve, his favorite modern *dombi*, who learns how to enjoy *watching her lover* while making love to herself.) The screen brightens, as it projects in Tantric color *The Woman and the Tongue* or *The Worship of Shakti*, an adult movie filmed entirely on location (Dasein Productions, Munich, 1969).

"My favorite sexual wheel of life," says Cathy.

"Mine, too," says Kosky. **The more depraved the woman, the more debauched, the more fit she is for the rite. Dombi is the favorite of all Tantric writers. (Mircea Eliade)**

Slowly Cathy becomes consecrated on her altar as he performs his first and foremost sacrifice, "a fluidless optically induced perfect No. 69." (Jay Kay)

"In the good old days, could you ever generate that much kundalini without your visits to the sex clubs?" she challenges him openly, at the end of their first fluidless spiritual session.

"Sex clubs were my visual education, Cathy." **Where else could you see a virgin twenty feet high, and learn how it works and looks? (U.S. Commission on Obscenity and Pornography, 1969)**

"Besides, that's where I was free to go for a very long time. Free to get hot. So hot I would often literally get overheated when I would get my sexual *regha*."*

"Didn't you notice I just did?" He presses his body against her.

"What kind of a man wrote this book? A deeply religious man, whose blasphemies horrified the orthodox. An ex-dandy, who dressed like a condemned convict. A philosopher of love, who was ill at ease with women. A revolutionary, who despised the masses. An aristocrat, who loathed the ruling class. A minority of one. A great lyric poet." (Christopher Isherwood)

*The shortest span of time, or, Hebraically expressed, the shortest perception of time, is *regha*, "a beat, or as von Orelli so suitably suggests, the pulse-beat of time. The word is not used with *ayin* (eye) either as a verb or as a noun, as is German *Augenblick* (twinkling of an eye). If, as von Orelli assumes, the movement of the eye formed the middle term of the conception, then certainly the conception is different from that in our notion, "twinkling of an eye." "In *regha* there is

"You're not just hot; you've got a fever of at least ninety-six sexy Fahrenheit degrees." She dries a wet handkerchief in a few seconds by simply placing it on his chest.

"I'm burning in my private hell. A mere transmutation of sex into heat." His Royal Yogi dismisses his royal Self. **By the same acts that cause some men to burn in hell for thousands of years, the yogi gains his eternal salvation. (Tantra)**

"Take a shower! Oops!" She corrects herself. "I know you take baths, not showers. Showers remind you of the showers of gas the Nazis first lavished on those who, like you, were pronounced by them to be certifiably insane. Of course, I say this *in light italics*." She pacifies him.

"And what does taking of a shower remind you of?" He is just about to enjoy himself in the act of watching her.

"It reminds me of AIDS," she says firmly. "Don't you know that Watching One Another Is the Only Alternative Left to Having Rubberless Safe Sex?" She quotes the headline from *Self-Sex Safe Sex*— "the only double SS title of a medical magazine." (J.K.)

"These days your sexual salvation rests in writing your sickly sex novel, not in having sick sex." She kicks him, and with him every decent American male novelist, in his sore spot. "Call your book *Hermes 69*, if you must, but don't call on anyone for 69 sex." She lets him play with her wrists and elbows, a new sensual substitution for wet sex. "Did you hear of the 1989 convention planned by the Coalition to Restrict the Land Movement of Those Afflicted with AIDS?" She pauses and so does he. "Isn't that a far cry from the 1969 Free Sex for All San Francisco Convention when even I—I who love only big and rather masculine-looking men—fell in love with another right-on woman."* She quotes from her own page 69.

"So what is left for us to do?" he asks her, reluctant to turn to another page.

When a woman falls in love with another woman, must she then be

---

originally something violent." (From *Hebrew Thought Compared with Greek*, by Thorleif Boman, translated from German by Jules L. Moreau (SCM Press, Ltd., 1960), p. 136.

*"But there is no everyday way to meet other lesbians." P. 69 in "The Necessity of the Bizarre" in *Sappho Was a Right-On Woman: A Liberated View of Lesbianism*, by Sidney Abbott and Barbara Love (1972).

made to feel that her own womanliness is in question? (Sidney Abbott and Barbara Love, 1972)*

"Reading. What's left of 69 sex is reading. Reading about sex in the Self-Sex Safe Sex Library. Today, we witness a new wetness: the *librarylization* of sex. Forget sexual liberalization." She too likes to play with words now, when, with the words and language for a lover, she can no longer play with him.

"You look troubled," says Cathy, somewhere in the midst of their verbally charged '69 lovemaking. "What troubles you? Is it the absence of voluminous sex in your newest sexual volume? Or is it the by now confirmed rumor that Kosky is said to be one of the few surviving East European Literary Khazars?† She quotes from the old Yellow Sheet magazine called *Khazar*.

"I keep ruminating about Chairman Rumkowski. The Chairman of the Lodz Ghetto, known for his ruminating in public," says Kosky, drinking the rest of his Bermuda Shorts Rum. "Against my will, I keep comparing him to Trotsky, that other great orator."

"Are you talking just *pathos*?" Cathy interrupts him while examining his most intimate part for signs of his tantrically trained Khazar past.

"What about the knowledge? The knowledge that even the King of the Khazars could not save the life of his Rumkowski's kingdom? The pathos, yes, but the pathos of knowing that within a year or two, *maximum three*, every single Jewish man, woman and child is doomed to chemical extinction simply for being Jewish, or even for bearing a Jewish first or last name?" Cathy speaks to him like a converted Khazar Lady. "There's only one way left for you to go on living, and to forget about

---

*Ibid., p. 96.

†The Kingdom of the Khazars "held its own for the best part of four centuries," says Arthur Koestler (op. cit.), and his interest in the Khazar Empire is of interest since, as a Jewish-Hungarian, he too saw himself as a descendant of the Khazars. According to Koestler the Hungarian conversion to Judaism has proven a bit of an embarrassment to those who prefer to view Judaism as a "religion which had no support from any political power, but was persecuted by nearly all," as quoted by Koestler from *The Magyar Society in the Eighth and Ninth Centuries*, by Dr. Antal Bartha (1968). Writes Koestler: "We have now progressed into the second half of the ninth century and, before continuing with the tale of the Russian expansion, must turn our attention to some vital developments among the people of the steppes, particularly the Magyars. These events ran parallel with the rise of Russian power and had a direct impact on the Khazars—and on the map of Europe" (p. 96).

the Kingdom of the Khazars and the mini-State of Rumkowski." She allows his "right-hand fingers to have a free-for-all intercourse with her left hand." (*Safe Sex*, op. cit., p. 96)

"What's The Only Way?" moans our sexual desperado.

"It is called still sex," she quickly assures him.

"What the hell is stilled sex?" asks the past master of the 69 routine.

"Still Sex, not stilled. Still sex is the newest (medically approved: J.K.) sexually dry verbal routine," she assures him.

"Will you please define the still sex for me?" He blows hot'nd dry air into her ear. "And that, Ladies and Gentlemen of the Sex, is what is left of that good old blow-job routine." (*Safe Sex*, p. 69)

"It is sex defined as a verb." She comes to his rescue. "Sex as mental action. Mental, not physical." She dares to say this to him, he a past owner of the 1969 cool sex known as sexual snow making medicine. (Jay Kay)

"It is sex as a verb, never as a noun. Sex as **one of the nine reasons for reincarnation . . . the other eight are unimportant. (Henry Miller).**

"Go on," he prompts her.

"Sex as **the warm beast. (Camus)** Sex as the lyricism of the masses!— as defined by your good friend Charlie ChanCharlie Baudelaire, the one preoccupied with sex, not masses."

"Enough about sex," he says. He, one for whom there never was enough sex, one to whom the words *sex* and *enough* simply don't go together. (Jay Kay) "Tell me about your own *roman*—is it going to be a *roman à cleft* or *à clé?*" he asks her. The question is a trap. **You must never ask the serious novelist what his novel is all about. (*TV-Talk Show Magazine*, NoHo House, 1987. See also *The Guide to the American Art of Conversation Watching*, SoHo Press, 1988.)**

"It's about religion," she says, and her "about" tells him that even though once so imaginative in staged sex, she is not a serious writer. Any serious writer knows novels are about people—people, not subject matters.

"Here." She reaches out to her traveling bag and hands him a gift she has brought him. It's *The Child in Polish Painting*,* a thoughtful gift indeed. "There, look at the pages I marked. Take a look at painting Number sixty-five—*Autumn*, by Józef Chełmoński. In this village scene,

---

*The Child in Polish Painting (a bilingual Polish-English edition, Warsaw, 1979).

234

one of the two boys making a bonfire reminds me of you! Now see painting Number sixty-six. *The Storm.* Also by Chełmoński: a small village boy terrified by the storm and the lightning. That too could be you. Aren't you afraid of storms?" She puts the down the book—and him.

"Only of sudden thunder." He licks her sweat. (Is this Loving Perspiration, the newest anti-AIDS fad? asks the always curious Jay Kay.)

"Who is your book's hero?" It is his turn now.

"Solomon Spalding." She rotates her hand, palm upward, in order to flex her biceps, but also in order to excite him, to make him hot again.* She glances at the muscle lovingly, and so does he, our writer suffering from sexual surviving syndrome.†

"After the Book of Mormon was published its author, Joseph Smith, the Mormon prophet, was accused by his detractors of appropriating it from *Manuscript Story*, an unpublished biblical novel by Solomon Spalding, a retired minister who supposedly wrote it for his own amusement. But many years later *Manuscript Story* was discovered in Honolulu and found to be in no way a basis for the Book of Mormon. Refusing to be distracted by such irrefutable proof, Smith's subsequent critics went on to claim that he had based his work on *Manuscript Found*, Spalding's second novel, the manuscript of which—however—was never found!"

He kisses her breasts. Is he smelling her salts or are they smelling salts made by House of d'Oliva? Is it her artificial aroma or her natural body perfume? He sniffs again. A whiff of something—but of what?

"One day, when I am through with my book, but not through with you, will you read my book all the way through, and tell me what you think?" Cathy asks quietly.

"I'll read it. **The more distinct, sharp and wiry the boundary line, the more perfect the work of art. (William Blake)** But frankly, I would rather be asked to review for the *National Sex* magazine having sex with

---

*"The body produces an extraordinary heat that can, as you say, dry the sheets. There is extremely reputable written evidence concerning this 'mystical heat,' or rather this heat produced by what is termed the 'subtle physiology.' The experience of the icy wet sheets drying very quickly on a yogi's body—yes, that is certainly a reality." (Mircea Eliade)

†"Is There a Survivor Syndrome?" See *Encountering the Holocaust: An Interdisciplinary Survey* (op. cit., p. 209).

you." Once more I have even lost the precise understanding of what I look for and yet I keep on looking. (Sartre)

"Our sex? Sex with you, even 69 sex, is like reading Milton," she arches her back. "It is nonpoetic. No foreplay. No rhyme."

"I'm prosaic, not poetic. Besides, rhyme restricts. I'm into free out-petaling of the lotus. Call it anti-AIDS creative bondage—which is what *Sexual Scene* magazine called it."

Significantly, there is no word for "Original Sin" in Yiddish, the language spoken by the majority of the Jewish people for nearly a thousand years. And the Hebrew term for it occurs as late as the thirteenth century, when it presumably appeared under the impact of medieval Christian-Jewish disputations. (Abraham Joshua Heschel)

"My mother told me that as a little boy I planted a pair of tailor's scissors in the breast of one Pani Teofila, my nurse."

"First, describe your mother to me," says his Emma Hart, reenacting for him in a live-sex show a photograph in *Leg Show* magazine called the Sexual Scullcrushing Woman.

"It's too much to tell," he teases his ideal leg woman. He takes in and leaves out according to his taste. He makes many a big thing small and small thing big. He has no compunction in putting into the background that which was to the fore, or bringing to the front that which was behind. In short he is painting pictures, and not writing history. (Rabindranath Tagore)*

"Only when I saw her sinuously stretched on her deathbed (my mother died at the age of sixty-nine) I realized that, until then, I always saw her not as her son but as a photographer who photographed naked not his mother, but a persona called, after Aleksander Rodchenko, 'The Artist's Mother.' " There is a constant return to sources. The portrait of Rodchenko's mother (1924) is the most striking example, for it has all the virtues of a symbol. (François Mathey, 1983)†

"You photographed your mother without clothes but with her face on? In your faith, isn't portraying a real face synonymous with defacing?" She lets him peek at her marble body's candid crack.

---

*From *Doubly Gifted: The Author as Visual Artist*, by Kathleen G. Hjerter; foreword by John Updike (1986), p. 65.

†Aleksander Rodchenko, who "created a new photographic culture" (Victor Shklovsky), is to modern photography what Eisenstein and Vertov are to cinema, and Mayakovsky and Meyerhold to theater. (J.K.)

"It all depends on the nature of the visual act, not on the nature of a face. Not at all a brand new idea!" Buried between her thighs he does another sixty-nine about-face. "In any case," he goes on, this time examining her stocking's stain, "this is the time when, on my memory slide, the great Ms. Teofila (Teofila was not her real name: J.K.) looks more like Catherine the Great, whom your little Rasputin called 'my sexual Teofila.' " Consequently, the Hebrew language formed no specific expressions for designating the outline or contour of objects and did not even need them. We shall first of all try to feel with the Israelites how they could experience the world visually and still get along without the notion of outline, form, or contour. (Thorleif Boman, op. cit., p. 156)

"Were you really her little Rasputin?" With her forefinger, Cathy makes a foray into his hollow and sexually uneventful knee hollow. ("The newest counter-AIDS fetish in town," in the words of the fetish-istically inclined: Jay Kay.)

"I was. Already then I saw myself as a waif, my first fictional persona. As a Jewish-Ruthenian–looking version of—wait, I'll show you." He picks up a copy of *The Child in Polish Painting* and guides her all the way to painting No. 6 (painter unknown). It portrays Jan, the youngest son of King John III Sobieski. He then shows her the portrait of the (already handsome: J.K.) Dominik Radziwill, as shown on painting No. 9 (painter unknown). And there is a good reason for it. Apparently (or allegedly) even then, at the tender age of four, I was already a plant of sexual-premeditation. This is, by the way, one of many of my autobiographical tit-bits told to me by my mother, I just don't remember."

"Maybe your mother made it all up in order to plant such premeditation in you?"

"Maybe," he readily agrees.

"Didn't you once tell me that your mother was sexually premeditated? What if your mother was jealous of Pani Teofila, and hoped that, if she told you such a cruel breast story, you'd become traumatized by it, and as a result, allergic. Allergic, first to women's boobs—then to women? Wasn't your mother herself a big-titted lady?"

"She was," says Kosky. "But I believe that, as stories go, her story was essentially true. And that my mother told it to me to keep me away from scissors, not breasts, particularly in view of what happened when I was twelve."

So it is not to be wondered at that this hysterical girl of nineteen,

237

who had heard of the occurrence of such a method of sexual intercourse (sucking at the male organ), should have developed an unconscious phantasy of this sort and should have given it expression by an irritation in her throat and by coughing. Nor would it have been very extraordinary if she had arrived at such a phantasy even without having had any enlightenment from external sources. . . . (Freud)

Cathy wraps herself around him. Her breasts are his again. "What happened when you were twelve?"

"I fell in love, love defined as 'the poetry of the senses' (Balzac), not yet as a 'wine of existence' (Henry Ward Beecher)," says Kosky. "I fell in love with a girl—let's give her here the name Bożena*—a skinny 24–19–22 who was either a year older or younger than me, but who, nevertheless, gave me my first premonition of 69. Premonition rather than ammunition." He keeps his sex record straight.

"Here, that's how I still see Bożena." With Cathy's head in his lap, and, regretfully, no longer between his thighs, he now guides her head headlong to painting No. 69. Called *Girl with Landscape in Background*, it was painted by Kazimierz Alchimowicz, a painter whose last name alone brands him as an alchemist. The painting shows a sinuously slender young girl who, wearing a simple one-piece dress, dips her naked foot in the unruly stream of water.

"Such a cute cuticle cutter. Who was she?" says Cathy.

"She lived in a small house separated from the house in which my family lived by a small garden and a rather fast mountain brook—or was it a man-made stream?" Here, teasing the reader, he pauses meaningfully.

In the body of every boy who has reached his teens, the Creator of the universe has sewn a very important fluid. This fluid is the sex fluid. . . . Any habit which a boy has that causes this fluid to be discharged from the body tends to weaken his strength, to make him less able to resist disease. (*The Boy Scout Handbook*, 1934)

"Across that stream," Kosky goes on, "over and over again, I would eye her and her hair. So soft. So golden. So freshly stacked. Hay ready to be sniffed and touched and braided." When I lie tangled in her hair and fetter'd to her eye. (Lovelace)

------

*Bożena: a spirited Ruthenian female name. *Boże* is a declinable form of *Bog*, Ruthenian for God. (*Boże drogi!* means *Dear God!*) The name Bożena corresponds with the Anglo-Saxon name Godetia.

"You see? This too is new sex: Isn't loving hair the Great American Shampoo Fetish Number One?" She offers him her version of shampoo sex.

"One day, after one more mute lesson in English taught to me by my erudite and infinitely patient father—I suffered from a bout of aphasia—I finally crossed that stream." Kosky goes on. "Hiding in a bush, I waited for her. And one day, the love I felt for her hair fused with a love I felt for her lips. By alchemically fusing hair with lips I got . . ."

"You got your sick love of pubic hair." Cathy interrupts him rudely. "Love which you still confuse with 69. I can see how, right then and there, you turned your passion into **a malady without a cure (John Dryden)** only to become **the bright foreigner, the foreign self. (Emerson, Journals)**"

"But"—Kosky goes on with his story—"when I stepped out and said nothing, Bożena thought I was too shy to talk. To put me at ease she talked and talked and talked to me. Finally, I just went over to her, and kissed her head, i.e., her hair. **Desire is portrayed by the caress as thought is by language. (Sartre)** Only when she didn't mind my kiss, and she embraced me with both arms as if I were her brother, I kissed her on her lips. Her lips felt wet. Wet, not dry." He pauses and kisses Cathy's lips. They feel hot. Hot, not necessarily dry. ("Is she terrified by the prospect of contracting AIDS from him?" asks Jay Kay, himself terrified that he too might have caught it from Cathy, a woman the body of whom on many occasions, he has shared with Kosky.)

ATTENTION READER: This is one of the few instances in which the relationship between Norbert Kosky and Jay Kay acquires quasi-sexual implications. IS THE AUTHOR GAY IF HER PERSONA IS NOT? CAN A LITERARY PERSONA ACQUIRE FROM THE AUTHOR THE ACQUIRED IMMUNE DEFICIENCY SYNDROME? TO WHAT DEGREE IS THE PERSONA IMMUNE TO THE DEFICIENT AUTHOR AND THE AUTHOR TO HIS DEFICIENT PERSONA? asks the reputable Byron Chillon in his "Literary Sex: Strategies for Fictional Survival," *Writer & His Work* (1986), pp. 66–69. See also the condensed six-page version in the new *Sexual Digest Magazine* (1988).

"Kissing Bożena gave me a taste of a truly wet kiss," he says.

This episode will have lived for years in his memory and even in his wonder; it had the quality that fortune distills in a single drop at a time—the quality that lubricates many ensuing frictions. (Henry James)

"Go on," urges Cathy.

"As an old village pet, all I knew was petting. A dry hand pushing up a dry hole, the village boys called it. I'd practiced it many times. But with Bożena, it was different. I wanted Bożena wet. Pretending I was wrestling with her, I made her fall to the ground where, somehow, she found herself under me."

The old dragon straddled up to her, with her arms kimboed again, her eyebrows erect, like the bristles upon a hog's back, and, scowling over her shortened nose, more than half hid her ferret eyes. Her mouth was distorted. She pouted out her blubber-lips, as if to bellow up wind and sputter into her horse-nostrils; and her chin was curdled, and more than usually prominent with passion. (Richardson, 1748)*

"And involuntarily, of course, you moved on top of her," says Cathy. "You were Lovelace and she Clarissa."

Kosky won't be provoked. **I am a machine at last, and no free agent. (Richardson)** "I kissed her, but between kisses, she wanted to talk and to be talked to. To keep her quiet, to make her think I was a kisser, not a talker, I kept on kissing her.

She struggled violently under his hands. Her feet battered on the hay and she writhed to be free; and from under Lennie's hand came a muffled screaming. (John Steinbeck) "And then I couldn't stop."

"Couldn't stop—what?" Cathy pulls away.

"Kissing her. Biting her lips. Sucking on her until I marked her until she bled."

"Biting her? With your incisors?" With her knee Cathy kicks him in the groin.

"Then she bit me too, and cut my lip open. We kept on kissing, her blood and my blood all mixed up. **The erotically excited kiss as well as the inward feeling of physical well-being, which is so difficult to describe, of a mother nursing her child at her breast, feeds on fare that is both coarse and infinitely fine and becoming finer; but all this in the sense of the primeval evolutionary fact that in the beginning the whole skin was the seat of sensual pleasure. (Wilhelm Bölsche)**

For a moment, Kosky engages Cathy in a brief sequence of sixty-six, his favorite kiss, far less engaging than *soixante-neuf*, banned by so

---

*Samuel Richardson, *Clarissa: Or, The History of a Young Lady*: a novel about deflowering—of a flower child.

many States of the Union for being "dangerously premeditated and easily persuadable." (Courts, 1986)

"What happened to Bożena?" says Cathy, biting her lips.

"Finally, Bożena panicked, although not at the sight of blood. She began to hit me with her fists as well as words. Being literally speechless, making faces and gesturing at her were the only ways I could answer and appease her, but this convinced her she had been attacked by an idiot. At one moment, she pushed me into the stream and ran away. I went home and there, when asked by my father what happened to my bleeding lip, I wrote *nothing* on my blackboard. Nothing indeed! A few hours later Bożena came to our house accompanied by her parents and two policemen. I was arrested and charged with attempted rape of one minor by another."*

That in every large community there are certain abnormal individuals who participate in lewd and lascivious acts upon or with the body of a child is a matter of common knowledge. (*People* vs. *Ash*)

"By chance, just when the police took me away, my father had his second heart attack. As a result I learned how to interpret both the Sex Crime Code and the electrocardiogram."

"Never mind the Sex Crime Code," says Cathy. "You clearly caused your father's heart attack."

"I couldn't prevent it," says Kosky. "He was my father. Fatherhood pains."

"Well," says Cathy, "the incident explains why you hate kissing me on the mouth—and why you don't mind my period."

"It explains why I love it," says Kosky. **By impersonating the aggressor, assuming his attributes or imitating his aggression, the child transforms himself from the person threatened into the person who makes the threat. (Anna Freud)**

"It explains why you love to hurt women's lips," she goes on.

"It explains why I love them."

"Do you now!" Cathy laughs his head off.†

---

*See *Sex and the Statutory Law (in All 48 States)*, Volume 9A of the Legal Almanac Series by Robert Veit Sherwin, L.L.B. (Oceana Publications, 1949)— "the first American legal manual I read in English on my father's advice before my trip across the ocean." (Norbert Kosky)

†PROOFREADER TO AUTHOR: You mean she is laughing *her* head off?

AUTHOR TO PROOFREADER: I mean she's laughing *his* head off. The adult reader

Rejected, he retires to his corner. **A writer develops the muscles of his mind. This training leaves but little leisure for sport. (Cocteau)**

"Tell me, Cathy." He undergoes another sudden mood shift. "What happened to your multiple multipack lovers—all those college wrestlers, or wrestling coaches you used to use during our days together?" He pauses in order to give her enough time to feel the hurt.

"Now, why would you remember them?"

"Will I ever forget all those guys!" Our mockingbird now mocks her openly. "All those amino-acid bodies, isolated biceps and crystalline triceps. All those protein-filled abdominals and pectorals, molded by bodywork, coated in the body shop? Could I ever forget the hegemony of their pumping iron and oxygen over my Boy Scout's fluid?" **Those who believed in the buildup of the body were on the lookout for a man of muscle who, by eating, drinking, and exercising, added size to his limbs. A big body, they believed, contained more world and took more space. Once they found a country fit to build a body, they took residence in it. (Nachman of Bratslav)**

"Now don't be facetious." Cathy presses his face down with her fat-free stomach. "You are now in America, not in Pripet. What you fail to notice," she lectures, using his chest as her lectern, "is that body-building is artistry. Bodybuilders are sculptors—sculptors who sculpt themselves the way poets sculpt their own words or good writers curb their language—unlike you! And let me tell you something, *you cruel little Jew*," she intones. (I assure you without any anti-Semitic overtones: J.K.) "In spite of all that power, as big as they are, these guys are never full of themselves. Never hard the way you skinny Jews so often are. These Gentiles—it just so happens you are my only Jew—let the woman be on top. And when she is on top of them they don't bite her, d'you hear?" Here, she bites his nipple so hard that, jerking in reflex, he almost throws her off. He panics. Will his nipple bleed? Will he contract AIDS?

"What will happen now? Will you continue seeing them?" He ventures reluctantly.

---

knows what I mean, and my books are not read by sexual adolescents.
PROOFREADER TO AUTHOR: You mean to tell me that you know your reader?
AUTHOR TO PROOFREADER: Well, I don't. Do you?
PROOFREADER TO AUTHOR: I'm not a writer. I don't have to.

"I will. But only in my head." She smiles sweetly, while looking at the photographs of handsome young men who sinuously stretch their bodies on satin sheets of *Hot Male Review*, several issues of which she keeps next to her bed. *Beware the Wetness of Your Lover's Eyes.*

"I like these big guys (guys, not goys, Printer!), and I'll tell you why. First, they don't bite. They leave a love-bite mark on a woman's neck, not a toothmark in her lips. Hence, they pass on no fluids." Reading disdain on his face, she asks. "Are you jealous, my dear Jewish Khazar?"

"Khazars were not jealous. Like Jews, they were chosen people— chosen to protect the Muslim conquest of Eastern Europe. How can one chosen be jealous? **'In Khazaria, sheep, hone, and Jews exist in large quantities.' (Muquadassi, *Descriptio Imperii Moslemici* [tenth century]),**"* says Kosky, quickly donning one of his Khazar spiritual disguises. "Jealous indeed! Didn't I drive you day after day to Horatio, the bartender at Consolazione, your favorite man of marble? The very Horatio who by now is a Still Sex Safe Sex—a double SS wonder!"

"You drove me to Horatio, all right. Emotionally," she says. "The way you drive me to him now by telling me that Horatio, that handsome shit, is *still* working at Consolazione. If I went for Horatio, it was because of the need for sexual consolation. And why do you have to tell me again and again that you are not jealous? Is this your way of making sure that, as long as I keep more than one man afloat, you won't drown in me? That, as long as I remain your *dombi*, who is free to pick up any other man?"

"Possibly it is." He attempts to pacify her.

"Forget Horatio. Bodybuilding doesn't excite me anymore," she announces. "In any case"—Cathy consoles him with her tongue—"I'm into fencing now. I fence practically every day. Every third morning you can find me dueling like crazy with Romashov, my fencing coach, at the Rosencrantz and Guildenstern Beau Sabreur fencing studios, 906 Kuprin Avenue in Salt Lake City."

---

*"It can . . . scarcely be doubted that but for the existence of the Khazars in the region north of the Caucasus, Byzantium, the bulwark of European civilization in the east, would have found itself outflanked by the Arabs, and the history of Christendom and Islam might well have been very different from what we know." *The History of the Jewish Khazars* (Princeton, 1954), ix–x. (The pages 9–10 tell you all: J.K.)

"Fencing?" says Kosky.

"Yes, fencing. A gentle sport. So gentle it replaced painful touch by a painless electric contact."

"Fencing is antiseptic, not gentle," says Kosky. "Face guards don't bleed. Neither do they betray emotion." He uncoils his foil.

"Why this constant preoccupation with emotions?" asks Cathy. "Do you believe emotions show only when one is showing them off? Can't they be safely hidden behind a face guard?" She pauses. "Fencing is reaching out to the other, with one's arm extended!"

"Fencing is keeping the other at arm's length," says Kosky.

"Fencing is a sport that won't tolerate Byzantine foul play," she retorts.

"But it glorifies a *faux pas*," says Kosky.

"Fencing is face-to-face combat."

"It's an about-face duel. There's something unnatural about generating all that gravity, all that motion without emotion."

"Look who says it," she mocks. "You're the original motion freak for whom G forces are everything." She lets him reach out to her belly. "The G-spot is all you believe in. No wonder," she puffs. "You like to ski, to ride and to float—all sports which carry you up or down by a force other than your own," Cathy sighs. "By the way, do you remember the names of those two reporters who once called me about you?"

"I know who they are," he tells her. "They often write the 'Rumors Today' column for *The Crier*. The column reflects their transmoral point of view."

"Something tells me that though both of these reporters are extra legit, their motives might not be." She lets him do a happy-foot suck show.

"How can you separate literary leit-motif from literary motive?" He performs another kinky foot feature for safe sex's sake.

"Even though in my religion spreading rumor is not a capital sin, in yours it is worse than murder, incest and idolatry combined. These two "rumor-porters" (Niskisko) have been killing literary reputations at a rate of six a week." She sprays her body with Fishnet Stocking lotion.

"I didn't know there still were any Salingers left."* Out of necessity

---

*See "The Salinger File: Fighting for his privacy, America's most elusive author is flushed from his refuge," by Phoebe Hoban, *New York* magazine, June 15, 1987.

our Bruno Schulz rapidly turns into a non-fluid-sharing solitary sole lover.

"There are. Aren't you one of them? I mean being elusive? Elusive, not just reclusive? Next thing you know, these two **wayward press pissants (A. J. Liebling)** will print all that piss!"

"So what?" he says while her nipples enjoy his expert copulative touch the way hummingbirds enjoy the touch of flower from Passion Flowers.* "A story in which another photographer took some of his pictures of physical deformity as part of the human condition might harm a photographer as great and as humane as Aleksander Rodczenko."† A claim that Hieronymus Bosch painted his copulating figures from life and not fantasy could upset a religious art dealer. I can see a Fountainhead ruined by a rumor that his architectural blueprints did not come from under the bilingual hands of Ayn Rand. But what can be said about me that, one way or another, I haven't already spilled out as my own inner dirty linen in my own narrative dirty sex spa? (Sex spa, not sex spy, printer!) Besides, didn't I admit on *The Johnny Boatman TV Show* that 'I like to watch?' That I am an addict of live sex shows? That I even like to watch *Cable Sexvision*—the deathvision of sex without 69? Doesn't this penultimate Spectacle State (Roger Gerard Schwartzenberg)‡ still know the meaning of the word *voyeur?*" He laughs the whole matter off.

---

*See Charles Sheeler: *Flower Forms 1917*, oil on canvas, in *Reflections of Nature: Flowers in American Art*, by Ella M. Foshay (1984), p. 69. "Hummingbirds and passion flowers populate the landscape in two works: *Tropical Landscape with Ten Hummingbirds* (Fig. 106) and *Passion Flowers and Hummingbirds* (p. 96). (Populate, printer, not copulate!)

†Aleksander Rodczenko (b.1891): "the first grand master of photomontage in Soviet Russia which led him along the path toward photography . . . Rodczenko believed that it was essential to nurture a more widespread love of photography by creating photographic libraries and organizing exhibitions on a much larger scale." (Grigori Shudakov) See *Pioneers of Soviet Photography 1917–1940*, by Grigory Shudakov, Introduction by François Mathey, pp. 6–9 (New York: Thames and Hudson, 1983). "A must-see reproduction of Rodczenko's photography." (pp. 60–69), counsels camera-conscious Jay Kay.

‡*L'État Spectacle: Essai sur et contre le Star System en politique*, by Roger-Gerard Schwartzenberg (Flammarion, 1977). (ISBN: 2-08-060-946-7)—"The 69 separated by a zero? That's new! That's *pas mal!*" exclaims the No. 69–conscious Jay Kay.

"They certainly can quote or misquote you a lot. And how!" says Cathy, offering him a full 69mm tele-lens closeup view of herself.

"So what? Let them quote or unquote me! This is the country of the free, and of all the entertainers a novelist is the freest!" exclaims our First Amendment Man, while his swirling tongue turns her goose bumps into sexually swirly semicolons.

The conventional media position is that the threat of legal action and its attendant heavy costs could prevent the full exercise of First Amendment rights. Any libel win, to some, could result in censorship through intimidation. Query whether the cost of libel defense should be a trade-off for loss of reputation."* (Alan J. Harnick)

"Is it? Are you sure?" Cathy moans. "Isn't the story of Joseph K one of your favorite literary capitalist horror stories?" And he translates her Anglo-Saxon moan into Jewish-Ruthenian sensual sensations.

"He certainly is," he agrees. **Someone must have been spreading lies about Joseph K, for without having done anything wrong he was arrested one morning. (Kafka)**

"These two reporters were not just free, they were plain mean," Cathy takes another tack.

"So what?" he mumbles, lost in her (fluidless: J.K.) flesh. "Aren't most writers satirists? Aren't satirists mean. Mean by the nature of satire, not by virtue of their writing habit? Ask Jonathan Swift," our Swift modestly proposes.

"This is also a country of the Fourth Estate—of the free who are free to kill the character† of one another," she says gently, pushing his head away while raising a specter of pogrom, of flying feathers. "What do

---

*"First Amendment/Libel: Should There Be Punitive Damages for Knowing or Reckless Falsity?," by Alan J. Hartnick, *New York Law Journal*, April 3, 1987 (Entertainment Section).

†"Doubtless 'character' is an inadequate word here: we are not speaking of a coherent personality or intellectual position. Rawson, who has a splendid way with language, speaks of the tale-teller as 'an amorphous mass of disreputable energies,' " writes Robert C. Elliott in his prototypical (1982) study of autofiction. Autofiction—a literary genre which, like most literary genres—was invented by the ancient Babylonian Jews, and then perfected by such notable Gentiles as Jonathan Swift in his *Tale of a Tub, The Death of Dr. Swift* and his *Panegyric on the Reverend Dean Swift* in which, pretending he is being unfairly "scrubbed" by his critics, Swift introduces "Scrub Libel." See "Swift's Satire *Rules of the Game*," in *The Literary Persona*, by Robert C. Elliott (1982).

you intend to do to protect yourself against a potential rumor?" she asks.

"Not a thing! One mustn't even come close to a rumor! Rumor is slander; slander is vitriol. This is my faith's central fact!"

"Are you talking about faith or is it your about-face?"

"My faith: everybody's got a faith, you know!"

"Everybody's got a face!" she corrects him. "And if that's the way you feel, why don't you ask your literary lawyer to put these guys on notice. He could tell them that in the process of doing a story on you, in the process of talking about you to other people, they are spreading rumor and collecting slander. That they'll be sued for libel if they continue, and so will their newspaper."

"My lawyer could also tell them that in my book rumor is listed as Rumorlit 106, the Literature of Self-Centered Rumor, a seminar I once gave at Beulah University," says Kosky. " 'Guided by their humorous instructor, the humorless students are invited to examine the humor of Swift and Mark Twain, and the satire of Orwell and Zamiatin. The freshman seminar limited to nineteen students, preferably women.' " He quotes the university catalogue from memory. "C'mon, Cathy! We're talking about free opinion expressed about a free man, by two free men," says Kosky. "You can't restrict expression unless you intend to restrict everything else as well. To be free to write, the writer must be free to write their *libelli*, as well as libels."

A defamatory act makes the plaintiff appear to other people to be worse than he really is—less trustworthy, less chaste, less competent, or merely more ridiculous. . . . There are few people whose sense of self is not affected by how others see and treat them. Reputation and self-respect are intimately related. (Emile Karafiol)

SS

At Consolazione, during their tender dinner *à deux*—this is Horatio's night off—Kosky and Cathy run into two middle-aged ladies, who, at the sight of Kosky, instantly peel off from the group of their postmenstrual peers and introduce themselves as Mrs. Pilgrim from St. Paul, Minn., and Mrs. Kohen from Zion, Miss.

"We've enjoyed seeing you in *Total State* and at the Oscars," says Mrs. Pilgrim without a glance at Cathy. "Was Beau Brummel fun to be with?"

247

"Is it true that you and Shaman Peters first kind of hit it off together—but then hit each other off?" seconds Mrs. Kohen.

"You're also a writer, aren't you?" asks Mrs. Pilgrim. "Didn't you write *The Confidence Man*?"

"Hello, ladies," says Cathy. "Am I a ghost?"

"Well, of course you're not, dearie," says Mrs. Pilgrim. "It's just that we saw Mr. Kosky on our TV—and we haven't seen you."

"Do you really enjoy such cheap accolades?" Cathy explodes the minute the ladies retreat. "Do you really need such a crude spotlight?

"I probably thrive on them the way Bruno Schulz did each time he received another *belle* letter from Thomas Mann.*

"In any case, what can I do?" asks Kosky. "I can't be myself and I can't go out wearing disguises all the time. They irritate my skin." **He sinned in public, and although he was conscious of the dreadfulness of being turned into an object by moral condemnation of his action, he prided himself in being free and creative. This turning against himself, which by necessity accompanied the sin, stopped him from truly diving into his pleasures. He was never deep enough in it to lose his senses. (Sartre)** about Baudelaire.

---

*In order to elicit (elicit, not solicit) a response from Thomas Mann, considered by many to be "the greatest straightforward storyteller of the pre–World War II decades" (George Bayerin, 1956), Bruno Schulz sent him a *brudnopsis* of "*Die Heimkehr*," the only story Schulz wrote in German. Their correspondence lasted until the war.

2 0

Returning to Salt Lake City, Cathy leaves Kosky with a catty remark she borrows from her favorite Petronius: New York is the toughest town in the world for a lady to get laid in. And you wonder why? thunders Jay Kay. That's the 1945 TB Bad Breath Epidemic all over again. Haven't you seen the headlines: AIDS EPIDEMIC WIPES OUT NEW YORK and HAS AIDS CHOKED AMERICA? She leaves him, she says, whom she still loves, but "now my love for you walks on stilts." She is eager, she says, "to return to my half-empty conjugal twin bed and try to fill the other half with a spiritually straight guy to whom it would never ever occur that sleeping nonstop with one's lover in a twin bed is particularly during the Bad Breath epidemic a sure way to sexual grotesque."

To appear sublime or grotesque—such is the alternative to which we have reduced a desire. Shared, our love is sublime; but sleep in twin beds and yours will always be grotesque. The contradiction to which this semi-separation gives rise may result in either of two situations, which will reveal to us the causes of many conjugal catastrophes. (Balzac, American translation, op. cit. 1899)

What is he to do now? How is he to prevent the inner media from headlining Cathy's departure and from showing clips of her life with him? There is only one way. It is called distraction; for him it means driving his Desperado V-6 convertible back and forth through Times Square. Filled with human antonyms—or antonyms who have found no synonyms, while our city squire ponders whether to a wandering

249

Self sexual dereliction is a way to an inner exile (Niskisko) where such self most often resides.

The tableau of urban life which opens before him diminishes in his memory to the size of the painting called *The Boy in the Manure Pit.** Times Square is a cast-off hull where *laissez-faire* turns into *"laissez-aller!"* To the storyteller in him, this is lowlife at the low ebb. Every bum is here, be it a simple stewbum or a serious stumblebum. Times Square evokes a spiritual spiral. Here, every marquee proclaims in yellow neon IMAGE VS. WORD, or VIDEO VS. PRINT.

Paradoxically, the Waterman of Thames, the famous six-story structure which since 1869 has housed the old-fashioned editorial offices of the *Times Square Record,* is also located here. The prestigious TSR (pron. TSAR) is a newspaper sporting "all the words that make the news," with a journalistic record like no other. My range is limited, I think. It embraces a half-dozen specialties like boxing, and the press, and the war, and French politics. (A. J. Liebling)

Here, inside this building, every staff writer's immediate description is instantly measured, weighed and verified many times over by a supportive staff of dozens upon dozens of other staff writers, proofreaders, editors, lawyers, word experts and other less-than-ordinary wordsmiths.

(But this is also "the place where spiritual language of the sense often surrenders to the often senselessly sterile language of civil procedure, since by placing the burden of proof on the respective parties who no longer respect each other, and not on the judge or jury, the American civil procedure is senselessly the tensest," says Jay Kay.) "Burden of proof" often means what Whigmore has called "the risk of nonpersuasion." . . . What Wigmore has called the risk of nonpersuasion is more often called "the burden of persuasion," or "the persuasion burden." (*Civil Procedure,* op. cit.)†

Here, at the *TSR,* the language of free expression is being tested,

---

*The Manure Pit: a painting by George Welkopfin which portrays a small dark-haired boy crawling out of a steaming pit filled with manure while several festively dressed Bosch-like peasant men and boys, all laughing, watch him from a distance, covering their mouths and noses with hands and white handkerchiefs, as if guarding themselves against the stench.

†See "Some Basic Concepts in the Procedural System Developed Around the Institution of Jury Trial," in *Civil Procedure,* by Fleming James and Geoffrey C. Hazard (1977), p. 241.

becoming, in the process—and out of fear of costly litigations—more and more self-controlled and censored by the collective Self.

The statement, "Here is a glass of water," cannot be (completely) verified by any sense-experience, because the universals which appear in it cannot be correlated with any particular sense-experience. (An "immediate experience" is only once "immediately given"; it is unique.) By the word "glass," for example, we denote physical bodies which exhibit a certain law-like behavior; and the same holds of the word "water." (Karl R. Popper)

To him, Times Square offers easy enlightenment of American burlesque, fused with the challenge of French vaudeville; this is a sexual videorama mixed with spiritual video drama. This is his American Place Pigalle, with the native pigs and gals galore, the world of undressing, cross-dressing and overdressing. It is a world of its own, and very much on its own, a mixed metaphor. **If she is normally developed mentally and well-bred, her sexual desire is small. If this were not so, the whole world would become a brothel, and marriage and a family impossible. It is certain that the man that avoids women and the woman that seeks men are abnormal. (Richard von Krafft-Ebing)**

Kosky parks his car at the waterfront of the Hudson River and starts walking east, toward the United Nations Plaza. Passing a pornutopia, the basest of the city's adult video sexporiums, Kosky spots a *mamarazzo*, a gay *paparazzo* who, dressed in fatigued army fatigues, untiredly takes one picture of Kosky after another—all capturing our Boy Scout standing in front of a most unwholesome sex shop. Swiveling, our sexy scout accosts the photographer. **You furnish the pictures and I'll furnish the war. (William Randolph Hearst)**

"Am I your model, boy?" asks the Boy Scout.

"Your asseroony ain't tight enough for me," says the *mamarazzo*, sweating under the weight of his camera bag.

One look at the owner's tag attached to the bag's handle tells Kosky that the bag is the property of *Quicksand*, the dry-supremacist magazine pointedly illustrated only with black or white, not black-and-white, sepia-colored photographs.

"So what's my black brother doing at *Quicksand*?—he, who, being black, should know better what he's doing," asks Kosky.

Conclusions after thirty years of research by revisionist authors:

- **The "Hitler gas chambers" never existed.**
- **The "genocide" (or the "attempted genocide") of the Jews never**

took place. In other words, Hitler never gave an order nor permission that anyone should be killed because of his race or religion.

• The alleged "gas chambers" and the alleged "genocide" are one and the same lie.

• This lie, which is largely of Zionist origin, has made an enormous political and financial fraud possible, whose principal beneficiary is the state of Israel. (Robert Faurisson, 1979)

"I ain't no brother to you, yak," says the man. "You're that white toad who claims he's as good a swimmer as a black eel. Well, you ain't!"

"Anything wrong?" asks Kosky. **The Goy does not, in fact, believe that the Jew is better than the non-Jew; the most he will admit is that the Jew is smarter at achieving worldly success. But this he ascribes to sharp practices, not to superior ability. (H. L. Mencken)**

"You are wrong. You didn't tell the black eel the truth."

"What truth?"

"The truth about your dirty water trick. Your phony inner air assembly line! What float? Other than sis Murena, only the soul-sucking Milli Brown can float like that and it ain't for nothing she is called the Unsinkable Double D.*

"Don't we know, yak, what in your faith the letter *D* stands for? It stands for a big tit, don't it?"† C'mon, paleface. Tell me the truth: you and me and the whole world know that nobody, not even Matthew Henson,‡ could float like that. You cheated her."

"I float buoyed up by my own most buoyant Self. That's all the cheat there is to it," says Kosky. "Why don't you come one day to the pool and take my floating picture!"

---

*Millicent Brown, 50DD–34–45, "a dark brown adult model, also an operatic soprano who sings the blues in nightclubs. A lot of lung power. Millicent has moved from the bedroom to a backyard pool where she puts on quite a show, proving that those big things really do float. With just the size of hers, Millicent certainly wouldn't have to fear drowning." ("Home of the D-Cups," *Gent*, April 1984, pp. 77–82.)

†In *The Mysteries of the Qabalah* the letter *D-daleth* carries arithmetical number four, and it "signifies breast, bosom. It is the emblem of the universal quaternary, that is, the origin of all physical existence. Symbolically: every nourishing substance, and abundance of possessions." (Op. cit., vol. 2, p. 8)

‡Matthew Henson, a black man, planted the American flag at the North Pole on April 6, 1909.

A photograph is a secret about a secret. The more it tells you, the less you know. (Diane Arbus)

"Oh, yeah! How about a picture with Phillis Wheatley?"* Just to show what a clean livin' pissin' pistolero you are. I'd rather show you, *Ruthlack*, greasing yourself all over this shitpool!" he says, snapping one picture of Kosky after another with at least three of his six motor-driven, Revolta 6000s as well as the newest Revolta 9000, a highly automated self-focusing camera. "As far as I'm concerned, you're a fake," the *mamarazzo* goes on between takes. "Ain't it true, massa, that to help your fuck books float around, you kinda made up those free-floating stories about how you once freed some sexual slaves? Ain't that called cheating by *Nightfog* magazine?"†

"No, it ain't," says Kosky. "These stories are my slaves. They all come from my head. My head is full of water—and if water isn't free, what is?"

"Is that so?" *Mamarazzo* becomes precocious. "A black cunt who works as a line editor at *Players* magazine told everybody on the staff that your head ain't even Jewish! She says there's nothing missing but length from your final cut. That you've got enough uncut skin for an umbrella or a cover picture in *Uncut*, the men's magazine—though not a thing for a handle!" He giggles happily.

"Something tells me somebody is doing a sexposé on me," murmurs the child of World War II. "Is it going to be distorted by you with the help of some crooked black'nd white pictures or only with some silly revisionist 'crafty tracery' (Conrad) of words?" Here, our spiritual specter speaks with sardonic satisfaction, and no wonder. After all, isn't Kosky, like Bruno Schulz, a direct descendant of the Ruthenian Polish-Jewish relations with the word, relations, signifying, as it always does in this text, a "traditional narrative as well as narrative tradition?" (Kosinski, 1965)

Words, groups of words, words standing alone, are symbols of life,

---

*Phillis Wheatley: a black woman who wrote the second book published by a black in the U.S.A. (1773). She was commended by President Washington.

†*Nightfog* magazine (formerly *Nacht und Nebel*. J.K.): "A publication of neo-Nazi nonsense called revisionist history based on its own **myth of the XXth century (Rosenberg)** that the Holocaust which killed so many millions of Jews, Poles, Gypsies and Soviet P.O.W.s in reality never took place and is a Jewish-Polish propaganda invention. (J.K.)

have the power in their sound or their aspect to present the very thing you wish to hold up before the mental vision of your readers. The things "as they are" exist in words; therefore words should be handled with care lest the picture, the image of truth abiding in facts, should become distorted or blurred. (Conrad to Hugh Clifford, 8/9/1899)

"It's going to be a sacramental jerkorama. It's going to be a tall tale of a tale-telling Jew who might not even be a Jew—a Jew who's missin' nothin.' "

"I'll show you what's missing!" Promptly, Kosky unzips his zipper, and just as promptly he starts fumbling with his shirt and underwear.

"Hey! Don't do that, d'ya hear?" shrieks *mamarazzo*. "Didn't you have enough headlines?"

"I did not," says Kosky. "All I miss is NORBERT KOSKY SHOT PEEING ON TIMES SQUARE."

2 1

On an appointed day, at the appointed time, the two reporters appointed by the *Courier** to interview him appear at the door of the apartment of our literary D.A., with D.A. standing for once for devil's advocate, and not for district attorney.

These are the two who have already talked about him to Cathy when they first called her on her purposefully rigged (by her husband: J.K.) phone.

He knows their names. One of them is Theo de Morande, the other Tom Carlyle. While Carlyle is wearing a *proletkult* pullover by Marx Brothers, Carlyle sports a Calvinist straight jacket. Let it be said at the outset that while Kosky loves the reporting profession, this reportorial duo makes him queasy. In their presence he becomes uneasy the way an *un*sane person is. (PRINTER: unsane, not insane. For the origins of this word see the already quoted *Journal of the American Medical Association* [JAMA]).

They come equipped with paper and pencils and a tape recorder, but, just by looking at them and their attitude of emotionally low al-

---

*Founded in 1823 by Stakhov and Khovanski in the small village of Velizh, in the Russian province of Vitebsk, *The Velizh Voice* was the first paper credited with starting The Velizh Affair, in which some forty-two people (all of them Jews: J.K.) "were seized, put in chains, and thrown into jail." (S. M. Dubnow, op. cit.) The paper changed its name to *Courier* when, in 1835, all those sentenced in 1826 were declared innocent and released—except several of those released during their imprisonment by merciful death.

titude, you know that what is missing is a will to know the truth, or even a will to be pleased by life and to please it.

Suspiciously, they look around and as they do, they themselves begin to look suspicious. (They look as uncomfortable as were the first two SS officers sent to interview Thomas Mann: Jay Kay)

Now, granted some of his uneasiness stems from him, and not only from them; it stems from his spiritual solitary confinement first under the Nazis, then under Stalin's yoke. Some of it stems from Jewish history. From a fellow writer Josephus, who, once a Roman commander in Galilee, wrote the famous *Bellum Judaicum*, in which Jews, with parabellum in hand, attempted, in their numerologically lucky year 66, to shake off the Roman yoke under which they had already spent sixty spiritually painful years. When the Jews failed to shake it by the numerologically even luckier year 69, the Romans finished them off. Some stems from Polish-Jewish history. From the fate of Bruno Schulz, his Polish-Jewish literary idol No. 69, shot to death in 1942 with a single revolver bullet by an anonymous SS officer, a perfect stranger, one who wasn't even aware—aware, and jealous, of his drawings as was another SS officer. *

Of the two reporters who came to see him, Kosky particularly fears the one wearing the *proletkult* pullover. Why? Because he senses that the pullover is a headline-eager para-literary beaver who feels he has been unjustly pulled over and given an unjust traffic ticket by life's highway patrol. Keep in mind that Kosky's own headline-making career began early in life. It began with the catchy, headline-making headline: A BOY OF THREE IS ALREADY AN ASPIRING ESPERANTO PRINCE. Soon after, it was: AT FOUR HE SPEAKS ESPERANTO BETTER THAN ZAMENHOF. Like Kosky's family, Zamenhof, the inventor of Esperanto, came from Lodz, and since *lodz* means boat, it means they came from the same boat.

From this, it was only one step to: IS NORBERT KOSKY, AGE FIVE, OUR BILLY SIDIS? AND IF HE IS, WHY WON'T HIS FATHER SAY IT? an article which must have spiritually stirred Israel Kosky's otherwise happy life.

---

*According to Witkacy (St. I. Witkiewicz), the literary demonology of Bruno Schulz depended on his vision of women as being spiritually sadistic and carnally masochistic, and men as being mentally masochistic while physically sadistic. This explained why, in so many drawings of Bruno Schulz, men worship women. "Some of these women are on the loose, some of the men wear a noose," comments Jay Kay.

This article was then followed by an interview with Elisabeth Kosky which, appearing in *The Jewish Piano* magazine, headlined her saying to Israel: I NAMED MY ONLY CHILD NORBERT AFTER NORBERT WIENER, WHO INVENTED CYBERNETICS—EVEN THOUGH MY HUSBAND WANTED TO NAME HIM JAMES AFTER THE AMERICAN GHOSTWRITER JAMES HENRY AND AFTER JAMES WILLIAM SIDIS—THE FAMOUS AMERICAN CHILD PRODIGY KNOWN HERE AS SIDIS BILLY. (An interview published a few days before September 1, 1939: J.K.)

"Like writing, interviewing is an art.* Let's have your side of our story," says the jacket.

"First tell me what's the gist of yours?" asks our troubled Sidis Billy.

"The gist of our story is that we keep asking ourselves why we are doing what we are doing." The pullover laughs with Stalinist charm. "Why are we writing this story about you?"

"Are you sure you're not writing it in order to do me in?" asks our charming Bukharin.

"We might call our story: HE SURE CAN TELL A FLOATING STORY— BUT CAN HE FLOAT?" clarifies the jacket, à la Vyshinsky. "Or we might call it: A FLOATER OR A SWIMMER? HE SURE CAN FLOAT BUT CAN HE SWIM? The pullover, the jacket and Kosky settle down around a coffee table covered with Kosky's old adult cinema magazines.

"Now why of all the chosen people have you chosen me?" asks Kosky.

The awareness that every word I uttered was being recorded by a cold, precise mechanism, that my life was turning around with the tape recorder, frightened me. I realized that now I was speaking of different things than I had before. I was beginning to believe that I was guilty before I even knew what I was guilty of. (FIOC)

"Because you've floated in our literary waters for over a quarter of a century now," says the pullover, stressing the word "floated," as well as "quarter of a century."

"Because you've been profiled as a swimmer, swimming,† not float-

---

*See "The Art of Interviewing" (a symposium), *Authors Guild Bulletin*, 1982.

†Swim, 1. Float on or at surface of liquid (sink or—; *vegetables -ming in butter; with bubbles -ming on it*). 2. Progress at or below surface of water by working legs, arms, tail, webbed feet, fins, flippers, wings, body, etc., traverse or accomplish (stream, distance, etc.) 3. Appear to undulate or reel or whirl, have dizzy effect or sensation (*everything swam before his eyes; my head -s; has a -ming in the head*). 4. Be flooded or overflow with or *with* or in moisture (eyes, *deck, -ming with tears*,

ing, on the April '83 cover of *SwimLife*, the American prime watersports magazine. This was already suspect since, even in your own words, you are a floater, not a swimmer," sneers the jacket.

"Because after Jean Valjean—that criminal swimmer who was released from Water Tower prison—sank the minute he entered open waters again, you said in *SwimNews*, 'We pretended he had always been a floater. He never was. He was merely a clever swimmer.' Not a nice thing to say about a fellow swimmer." He stresses the word *swimmer*.

"Because, as a swimmer, you've never said a word about how, where, or under whom you learned to swim," says the pullover.

"Because you never told anyone about the exact nature of these supposedly secret spiritual devices which keep you—not even a good swimmer—afloat," squints the pullover, and the jacket squints, too.

"All this makes us question your veracity," says the jacket.

"To clarify these doubts—these rumors—please tell us in your own unedited words—words which we and our editors will then edit—why you don't sink," says the jacket.

"Tell us in your own simple words, whether there is any truth to your claiming a unique—or shall we say spiritually sacred—relationship to water?" says the pullover.

Instantly Svāmin Svātmarama, the commander of Kosky's Spiritually Strategic Advance Team also known as SVAT, puts SS-1, SS-2 and SS-69, his entire spiritual arsenal, on yellow alert. Such alert is sounded anytime the subject of privileged position—privileged in relation to water—is mentioned. You don't want things to get out of hand, particularly when the hand holds Galilee seawater.

Now the pullover and jacket walk around, cursorily examining the bronze menorah, a gift from Döhmeh—an Israeli educational group (based in Geneva, Switzerland, and Tel Aviv, Israel: J.K.). Kosky contributes part of his royalties derived from the sale of his books in Switzerland and Israel to them—and the framed photograph of Kosky posing

---

water; -ming eyes; floor -ming in blood). 5. -ming-bath, large enough to—in; -ming-bell, bell-shaped -ming organ of jellyfish etc; -ming-belt to keep learner afloat; -ming-bladder, fish's sound; -ming-stone, kind of spongy quartz. 6. n. Spell of -ming; -ming-bladder (rare); deep pool frequented by fish in river; (fig.) main current of affairs (esp. in the- engaged in or acquainted with what is going on). (*COD*)

as Red Comrade Nikolai Bukharin. They end their search by coming face to face with Kosky, mounted on a polo pony, on the cover of *MultiSports* magazine, under the catchy title FROM BREADLINE TO HEAD LINE: DOING THE KOSKY FLOAT.

"Quite a collection of certificates!" certifies the jacket.

"Only your floating certificate is missing," says the pullover.

"No, it is not. Here it is," says Kosky. He stands up and, like a military commander, salutes his eight novels backing him up on a bookshelf in both their hardcover and downright dirty paperback editions. Anything to keep the reporters at bay—at bay, yet far from the water.

Now, in order to appease his tormentors, our author sits down behind the desk, facing the two investigating persons, who settle at the table across from him, their drinks, writing pads and tape recorders separating them from him.

The jacket begins the interview. "Mary Terentyeva,* a certified Ruthenian-American swimming coach, told us that some twenty years ago in New York she answered an ad for a swimming instructor to instruct someone how to act as a swimmer—someone who apparently could swim only with the help of a secret flotation device—an ad anonymously placed in *MultiSports*. When Mary came to answer the ad in person, she's almost sure she found you waiting alone, and looking rather abandoned, on the side of some abandoned swimming pool rented out to you by some rich fart."

"Mary, then, seems to recall your telling her that while you are eminently unsinkable as a floater, you are also eminently sinkable as a swimmer—and that to you this means no contradiction."

"In other words, you allegedly told her that since you can't swim on your own, you can't float by yourself either," says the jacket.

"Mary can't—or won't—swear it was you. But she won't deny it either," says the pullover. "She is torn by her doubt about you, not by her otherwise excellent memory."

---

*For the unfolding of the manifold role played by Mary Terentyeva and at least two others in this period of "Compulsory Enlightenment and Increased Oppression," as it was called by S. M. Dubnov, the well-known historian of Jewish affairs, the reader is referred to "6. The Ritual Murder: Trial of Velizh." (S. M. Dubnov, op. cit., vol. 2, pp. 72–84)

"I'm so glad she thought I placed such an ad, because the fact is I keep on placing such ads all the time," says our literary miser. "Misery loves company. Writing is misery. Why should misery be miserable alone? Only last week I advertised for a free-lance swimming coach—to teach me how to crawl in the Swinging Socrates swimming pool, one of my neighborhood's last remaining sex clubs, offering SAFE SEX + NO FLUID EXCHANGE. This week alone I placed three different ads for a sexually liberated female proofreader, female line editor and female translator. A translator needed to translate into English the non-English reviews my book gets in the countries the language of which I don't speak. Got it? As you know, for a writer, employing such people is tax deductible. And if it's O.K. for a union boss—or a boss of a personally owned company—to romance with such free-lancing rhabdomancers, why can't I?"

"We have talked to a great number of people—a swimming coach, a pool guard, two Ruthenian athletes, one swimming clinic instructor—who have come in touch with you at different times in your floating career," says the pullover. "Every one of them said that at one time or another during your early floating (or is it swimming?) days, he or she heard you speak of using many different secret flotation devices."

"And while supposedly a polo player, as a swimmer you're not even good enough to be a water polo goalie, without being assisted in the water by someone else," adds the pullover.

"When it comes to being assisted in the water—*in* the water, not *by* the water, 'assisted' can mean many different things," says Kosky, measuring his meaning carefully. **The conscription horrors of that period had bred the "informing" disease among the Jewish communities. They produced the type of professional informer, or *moser*.* (S. M. Dubnow)** "It can mean having some cold water splashed on one's face when one's head is too hot! Now that's hardly a blasphemy!" he goes on. "It can mean being momentarily pushed under the water in order to cool one's head off. That's not blasphemy either! It can even mean giving head or getting it from a blowfish—the one you can see swimming in so many water tanks. That's hardly a heresy either!"

"Do you mean to say that you can always float like this without any

---

*Moser: The Hebrew and Yiddish equivalent of "informer" (S. M. Dubnow, op. cit., p. 84).

assistance—or assistants? Without some auxiliary outer bladder? Without some helpful transparent fin?" The jacket assists him à la Yezhov.

"Look here," Kosky gets up from behind his desk, and our Bukharin, questioned by Yezhov, nervously paces back and forth across the room, then sits down again. He is exasperated. Just look at these two—look at their posture. Look how misshapen and out of shape they are. In spite of being already in their midfifties, both of them suffer from simple scoliosis, a condition usually found in young girls and defined by a slightly S-shaped spine.

Now how can he answer such a question? How can he explain in a few words what his spiritual stabilizer consists of—a stabilizer, not a fin! What do these sport-simpletons know of Yoga-type breathing in which the yogi may change *his* ordinary rate of six to nine respirations a minute (versus say, the ordinary 16–19) to 1.6 "and reduce his ventilation volume a great deal." (O. P. Jaggi)*

Unless he can come up with some natural answers to these unnatural questions he might either say nothing and stick to his floating craft, and with it to the No Rumor pact he signed with Israel Kosky ("tell stories about the Self but name no names"), or say something misleading enough—misleading, because instead of leading the reader to a living person or a real land, what he will say could lead everybody back to his fiction—the backyard of his *autothematical story*. (Sandauer)

"Any interview with you we come across picks up a different Norbert Kosky story," says the jacket, all buttoned up.

"I'm a writer of fiction. That's why I haven't written my biography. Meanwhile, **Do I contradict myself?/Very well then I contradict myself,/ (I am large, I contain multitudes.) (Walt Whitman)**

"It's all *Either/Or*." The tight-lipped pullover evokes Kierkegaard.

"I could also be both—or neither," says Kosky.

VYSHINSKY: **Was the material you contributed selected tendentiously?**
RYKOV: **Of course.**
VYSHINSKY: **Perhaps it was of a slanderous character?**
RYKOV: **Tendentious and slanderous, the one easily passes into the other.**

---

*See also S. Rao, "Oxygen Consumption During Yoga-Type Breathing at Altitudes of 520m and 3800m," *Ind. J. Med. Res.*, 5/5/1968, p. 56.

VYSHINSKY: That is what I am asking. Did your material pass from the tendentious to the slanderous?

RYKOV: It is difficult to draw a line between these concepts.

VYSHINSKY: In a word, it was both.

RYKOV: In an acute question like this, everything tendentious is slanderous. (*Moscow Trials*)

"Then there's the issue of your topskin." The pullover hesitates. "Topskin meaning whether or not you are Jewish."

"Do you or don't you have it?" asks the jacket.

"Now that's the unkindest cut of all. Who do you think I am: Diego Alonso?"* says Kosky. "Of course I don't have it. My *brit* is my certificate."

"In my dictionary *brit* stands for herring and sprats: the foodstuffs of our whalebone whales—or Brit, for British. I know next to nothing about the Jews or their bloody blood ordeals," says the pullover.

"And we're certainly not trying to pin a yellow Star of David on you," says the jacket, who doesn't seem to know that the Star of David is blue.

"But when was the last time you appeared on Israeli TV or visited the East View, Eldridge Street Synagogue?" (The first synagogue serving the East European Jews, who built it in 1887 on *their* beloved lower East Side.)

He is not even a Jew! He is a filthy pagan,/a renegade, the disgrace and outcast of the world,/A foul apostate, a crooked foreigner. . . ./Move on, wandering Jew. (Hugo)

"Speaking of the yellow star, where exactly were you during the War?" The pullover pulls another fast one.

"In Ruthenia. Mostly, in the place Romans called Mare Herodotis. Call it Marshes of Glynn. Why do you ask?"

"Because we have traced your pre–World War II real-life nanny,

---

*Diego Alonso, the young "blond, curly-haired bachelor lawyer of the lineage of converted Jews" (Holy Inquisition), was charged by the Inquisition with admitting to being a witness to a gust of wind blowing a piece of Host off the altar, a sacred Host, then admitting to it being nibbled at by mice, a crime of Host desecration "the very heresy my floating is about to be both praised for by the *Times Square Record* and charged with by the *Velizh Voice.*" (Norbert Kosky, 1982 persona of Jay Kay)

who told us you were always afraid of water," says the jacket. "She says you even dreaded being washed."

"We also found your onetime wartime governess!" triumphs the pull-over. "She told us she tried to teach you how to swim, but the instant she tried, you ran away."

"During the War, war was my only governess—not counting Governor General Reich Minister Frank,"* says Kosky.

"We also obtained an affidavit from one Pan Anton Kweil," says the jacket with a mysterious smile. "As your contemporary, he was your closest post-wartime pal. He recalls most vividly your pushing him into a lake instead of jumping into it yourself. He says in your high school everyone knew KOSKY WAS AFRAID OF WATER!" She headlines her words vividly. (Vividly, though not fondly: Jay Kay)

This ends the interview, and judging by their kvetchy (kvetchy, not sketchy: J.K.) expressions, Kosky can tell that the oppressive jacket and the nonstretchable pullover are most unhappy. They either have been had by Kosky, or they have had enough of him.

The reporters collect their electronic belongings—and with them all the words they need to report The Case of the Desecrated Host. Politely, our immaculate host escorts the two unhappy members of the Fourth Estate to the elevator.

"We really enjoyed this reportorial *ménage à trois*," says the jacket, while the pullover nods.

"So did I. We must do it again," says Kosky.

"We must! Let's hope all this is only the tip of the iceberg," says the pullover.

"I'm sure it is. I love ice. Ice is another form of water, and water is my element now!" Kosky rejoices.

The elevator is on the way.

The question is whether a proposition secures rational consensus because it is true, or whether it is true because it secures rational consensus. The identification of truth is analytical in the second event, truth con-

---

*General government: a part of Ruthenia incorporated into the Third Reich and administered by Reichminister Frank, Governor General, *"der deutsche König von Polen"*—the German King of Poland—as, allegedly, Frank described himself when talking to Malaparte. See Curzio Malaparte, *Kaputt*, pp. 66–69.

sisting in the ability to command consensus; it is nonanalytical in the first, truth being that which explains the attainment of the consensus. (Philip Pettit)*

The elevator opens, swallows jacket and pullover, closes its maw and starts its descent.

---

*Habermas on Truth and Justice," by Philip Pettit in *Marx and Marxism,* edited by G. H. R. Parkinson (Cambridge University Press, 1982).

2 2

On the following day, an anonymous telephone caller leaves with Kosky's Anonymous, Inc., answering service an anonymous message. The message says: "Tell him that an ugly rumor about his confused identities is floating all around literary New York."

"That's all," says the Answerette. "There was no name."

"No name? But was it a man or a woman?" asks Kosky, distraught.

"With your callers one never can tell," she says, hanging up on him.

Why would someone go to all the trouble of leaving an anonymous message about an anonymous rumor?

He is troubled. In his faith, rumor kills three people: the rumormonger, the rumor referee, and, most certainly, the rumoree, the rumor's main target. Now you know why his faith wisely rates spreading rumor on a par with murder. In his faith, even commenting upon the rumor (even a rumor about oneself inadvertently spread by oneself) with a simple "no comment" means spreading rumor.*

R: There is something impish about the pleasure you take in slightly bewildering your questioner, isn't there?

E: Perhaps that is part of a certain educational method. One mustn't provide the reader with a perfectly transparent "story." (Claude-Henri Rocquet to Mircea Eliade, 1982)

The lower-back pain† of our Pan Kosky pains so much he can barely

---

*See "Death and Life Are in the Power of the Tongue," *The New York Times*, October 9, 1986.

†"Although we often tease about the buttocks being nothing but fat, they do

265

leave his cot—or put on his tight-sleeved trench coat. With every move, a massive pain radiates from, and into, every pore of his body.

"Your sauna offers the only—albeit temporary—relief from his terrible affliction," informs *On Your Back*—the latest guide to lower-back ills and cures. But Kosky doesn't own a sauna.

In his neighborhood, the only medically safe sauna can be found in the Reading Gaol Spa—a gay bathhouse with a reputation of attracting "the safe sex with silicone-stuffed TV clientele in town." (*GayLife*).

The silicone spa is located, literally, across the street from the Manfred, from where our literary cross-dresser drags his body—crossing the street at the diagonal—one step at a time.

He finds the Reading Gaol Spa to be what its ad, routinely placed in the *Crier*, proclaims every week: THE MOST LITERARY ROMAN BATHS IN TOWN—VISIT OUR ROMAN READING ROOM, OUR BESTIARY AND THE S.S. GAOL. NO SICK SEX ALLOWED. This is indeed the kingdom of maleness where a drag queen is king.

"Boy oh boy!" exclaims our Old Boy as he enters the place through its only unmarked door. He had entered such Roman thermae—hot baths of ancient Rome—already at the age of four or five, by reading about them, and what went on inside, in a book full of graphic illustrations. The book in question was *From the Life and Culture of Antiquity.** This was the first scholarly book Norbert read. Beaming with family pride, it was written in most elegant Ruthenian and published by the famous Ruthenian Filomata Publishers, a year after Norbert was born, by no one else but Uncle Stan, Israel Kosky's so-Ruthenian-looking professional brother.

... Moreover, the creature is apparently inclined to sadism. For after a wild love dance in which the partners rear up sole to sole, rock back and forth and even exchange regular smacking kisses, the excited snail suddenly releases a dagger of chalky material from a kind of quiver and

---

contain, as you may remember from your anatomy lesson, strong underlying muscles—especially the famous gluteus maximus. The tone of this muscle is important in telling me something about the condition of your back," says Leon Root, M.D., co-author with Thomas Kiernan of their first-person narrative book, *Oh, My Aching Back* (1973), in Chapter 6 ("The Doctor's Examination") and on p. 69.

*Z życia i kultury antyku (*From the Life and Culture of Antiquity*) by Stanisław Lenkowski, Ph.D. (Filomata Editions, Lwow). Vol. 1, 1934; Vol. 2, 1935; Vol. 3, 1936.

266

drives it into the body of its mate. . . . The wounded snail visibly twitches with pain, and indeed the act seems like the prelude to a veritable sex murder. In fact the love daggers of the Roman and garden snails occasionally penetrate the lung or the abdominal wall of their partners, inflicting deadly wounds. (Herbert Wendt)

Drama is essentially revelation, wrote W. H. Auden. At Reading Gaol, revelation is drama. This is the kingdom, and queendom, of men with youthful faces and even younger looking bodies, and of old men, old enough to father—or dare he say it? even grandfather—most of these youthful looking youths. "This is the house of the media-induced panic. STAY COOL'ND CALM reads a sign above the square.

These courageous men come here (here being courageous is not necessarily synonymous with straight) straight from the pages of the Dandie Dinmont All-Male Review, as much as from *Manchild, Manscape* and *Mandate* magazines. He has seen some of them on the pages of *Stallion Weekly* (anything to do with riding attracts him no end) and in the newest safe-sex oriented *Hand to Hand Quarterly*. These males come here from many walks of life but, given the climate of *New Sexual Epidemics*, they come here in order to pursue the verb "to watch," rather than "to do"—they walk back and forth around and across the spa, in order to see and be seen—seldom to touch. Here in every corner, be it in frigidarium, tepidarium or caldarium, the frigid, tepid or downright hot lads and ladies—though never ladies—enjoy not only the reading facilities, but also the company of each other, displaying in the act the American facility for—and freedom of—expression.

At this HALF-PRICE-AFTER-MIDNIGHT time, the Reading Gaol is teeming with the lovers of self-sauna. At the Voluptuary, the guest room near the rear entrance, Kosky runs into Teleny Douster, the American slipper snail called *Crepidula fornicata*.

Overweight, "medically overburdened" (Niskisko), Teleny has enjoyed being spiritually schizoid. He is basically a very good man. One who, being on a pill, has been a pill as well. Too bad. That's why for years he has been most effective in his free-lance part-time job as divination expert in search of witching water. Recently, however, due to unemployment, Teleny's loss of income has led to a gain in weight.*

---

*"The shape of the belly can be quite variable, as can be seen in Figure 27, a series of male subjects. Of all the myriad, possible shapes, we have delineated four basic shapes: enlargement of the upper half; enlargement of the lower half; overall

Frequenting the Reading Gaol is the only way our Teleny, a physical misfat, as our misfit Kosky calls him, can afford to join the fat-free world of muscle and fitness.

Wearing only an extra-long towel wrapped around his sumptuous waist, Teleny throws his extra weight around. Too bad he can't throw all this extra flesh away. He wears it, he says, in order to protect his virtue'nd virginity, what he calls "the enamel of the soul" (Jeremy Taylor) as well as "politeness of the soul." (Balzac) The extra 169 lbs. of weight and some nine pounds of New Spiritual'nd Sexual Anxiety do him no good. As a result, the otherwise "Symbol, Myth, and Culture" (Ernst CaSSirer) oriented Teleny has turned into a brisk Merchant from Brisk,* who keeps on chewing six times a day his doctor-prescribed weight'nd anxiety reducing Super Seren pill. "Too bad it's a pill and not a slick suppository," he tells Kosky, his expression fusing pride with sadness.

I cannot bear being alone, and while the literary people are charming when they meet me, we meet rarely. My companions are such as I can get, and I of course have to pay for such friendships.... To suggest I should have visitors of high social position is obvious, and the reason why I cannot have them is obvious also. (Oscar Wilde)

"It's been six years since I've worked for you as a waiter in your literary cuisine," says Teleny, whose life accomplishment consists of his nine-page introduction to *Dowsing for Man's Cologne*, a slim tractate on the art of latter-day rhabdomancy, followed by a six-page preface to *Witching Waters*—a guide to men's after-shave lotion. "What a miracle to see you here, my Little Lord Fauntleroysky," he whispers as he and Kosky walk along the corridors, ogled by other Reading Gaol room-mating inmates.† Teleny giggles. "I heard your old lady Cathy Young is coming

---

enlargement; and flat" (p. 69 in *The Body Reveals: What Your Body Says About You*, by Ron Kurtz and Hector Prestera, M.D., 1984).

*A merchant from Brisk ordered a consignment of dry goods from Lodz. A week later he received the following letter: "We regret we cannot fill this order until full payment has been made on the last one." The merchant sent his reply: "Please cancel the new order. I cannot wait that long." (From A *Treasury of Jewish Folklore*, Nathan Ausubel, ed., 1948, p. 423.)

†"The higher frequency of orgasm in the homosexual contacts may have depended in part upon the considerable psychological stimulation provided by such relationships, but there is reason for believing that it may also have depended on the fact that two individuals of the same sex are likely to understand the anatomy

out with a book about you. I've just had an intimate talk'nd tell session about you and her with two ladies."

"Two ladies? You and the ladies? How could you come?" Kosky exclaims.

He told, that to these waters he had come/To gather leeches, being old and poor:/Employment hazardous and wearisome!/And he had many hardships to endure:/From pond to pond he roamed, from moor/to moor;/Housing, with God's good help, but choice or/chance;/and in this way he gained an honest maintenance. (Wordsworth)

"Two handsome *laddies*, not ladies." Teleny corrects him sternly. Teleny has been a spiritually confirmed bachelor. His mother ("at ninety-six my mother is almost still, but still surviving," he muses) had been his life's only lady. "To her, I'm still her little fat fart," he reminisces. "I gather Carlyle and de Morande are doing a story on you and your life in Ruritania."

"Ruthenia. Ruritania belongs in someone else's novel," Kosky corrects this prisoner of Zenda.

"They asked me about our *Cockamamie*: I mean about my working for you for one summer season as a maid for all seasons."

"Now of all people who have worked for me on my 'literary assembly line' (De Voto), why did they ask you?" Kosky wonders aloud.

Then I found that people concerned in accidents or news stories or even war are very much flattered that somebody should be interested in them. They're usually quite eager to tell you how things happened. But you mustn't ever try to tell them how things happened. This is another fault of a great many reporters; they simply go around telling the victims what hit them. (A. J. Liebling)

"I tell you why they called on Teleny, on this fatfart," says Jay Kay. "They called on Teleny because they knew they could easily extract a quote about you, and doesn't the Tractate Soferim, your sacred Jewish writer's tract, warn that 'a quote is extract—and extract is poison'?"

"They called me with some spicy questions about you because they knew bloody well that, when it comes to headline-making, the Old Teleny is as good as Efim Tseitlin, and as bad. In case you forgot"— Teleny now faces Kosky the way at Vyshinsky's KGB headquarters Tseitlin faced Bukharin—"Tseitlin was the fellow who, once Bukharin's

---

and physiological responses and psychology of their own sex better than they understand that of the opposite sex." (Kinsey)

269

follower and friend, then claimed that Bukharin had handed him a revolver (the revolver was a gift from Klim Voroshilov, the Civil War hero, to proletarian revolution leader Bukharin: J.K.) and stationing him on a certain street corner, asked him to take a shot at, and kill the about-to-be-passing-by Comrade Stalin." **A most likely story! (Joseph Stalin to Vyshinsky, circa 1936)**

"So what did you tell these two Fourth Estate mini-Stalins?" Kosky asks Teleny. (His yet another mini-Stalin: Jay Kay)

"I told them about the great time I had with your literary part—editing for you in your manuscript version 69 only the semi-inverted commas." Teleny giggles. "I told them I once sorted and snorted out various drafts of printer's proofs of your Solofloat book—your novel about the Soviet-born water polo hero. And I told them that at least on six occasions I was your swimming aid!" Teleny, who cannot swim and will not wash, shivers at the very thought of water. "That in a coup de grace, by removing, on your instructions, the word *water* from water polo I single-handedly turned your water novel into a novel about polo. That, as I said to them, without me this would have been a very watery book indeed. I told them I did for you what John Hall Wheelock did for Thomas Wolfe.* That one day I too might be stepped upon as a footnote in a story about you." Teleny giggles.

"Be careful to whom you tell such John Hall Wheelock stories," says Kosky. "Look what happened to Thomas Wolfe after some journalist wrote he was the American writer most admired by the Nazis." THOMAS WOLFE NOT SOLE AUTHOR OF HIS ACCLAIMED NOVEL *THE OCTOBER FAIR*. WOLFE'S EDITOR JOHN HALL WHEELOCK APPARENTLY CONTRIBUTED PAST TENSE TO THIS NOVEL. LITERARY WORLD STUNNED. SIM THOMAS TEMPLE.

They are interrupted. A young man passes them by. He is tall. He is blond. He is handsome. He is wearing a self-styled SS military uniform. A uniform, not a towel (here, towels are called "Cocteau-styled textiles"). The sight of the uniform, of the uniform not of the man, makes Kosky spiritually shiver and think of zyclone gas first used on

---

*John Hall Wheelock, the editor of Scribner's who had changed *Of Time and the River* from the first person, in which it was originally written, to the third person, would be awakened by the ringing of the phone at 2 or 3 A.M. to hear Wolfe's deep, sepulchral voice say, "Look at line 37 on page 487 of *Of Time and the River*. Do you see that 'I'? You should have changed that 'I' to 'he.' You betrayed me, and I thought you were my friend!" (Elizabeth Nowell)

German homosexuals by German Nazis, a shiver which Teleny confuses with a "shower of sensual desire." The SS uniform is a take-off from the one Nazi General Jurgen Stroop wore when, on the fifth day of the armed rising in the Warsaw Ghetto, he ordered his troops to "kill every soul in this ghetto with relentless artillery fire."

"Don't you worry about a thing," says Teleny. "Everything I told those two pot-headed farts about you I qualified by 'that's impossible to say.' " He saddens. "Now why have you never never responded to any of my now-or-never love letters? All written in my own unique Gaelic style? Gaelic Style—not a style readily found in Ruthenian Galicia! Now why not, my dear boy?" he moans. "After all, I delivered them practically under your door. No wonder out of despair I gave in to being ambushed." He offers Kosky a couple of ambush grapes and just then Kosky becomes ambushed by memory. What does the presence of these sauna rooms and steam showers make him think of? DID YOU KNOW, one of his many mental footnotes asks him, THAT DURING WORLD WAR II SOME FOUR AND A HALF MILLION SOVIET PRISONERS OF WAR WERE GASSED TO DEATH BY THE NAZIS in various extermination camps—and in mobile *Einsatzgruppen* killing operations, many of which utilized portable sauna-like room and steam-like gas showers?

Writing is creation. Even writing of a novel—hardly a recent genre for someone born in 1933. **The Hellenistic period saw the birth of the novel.** *The earliest complete specimen, that of Chariton, is not later than the second century of our era, and the genre is certainly earlier.* (A. D. Nock)* Be it writing Taoist slogans on a Maoist wall or writing the cartoon dialogue in "The Continuous Adventures of Dolly D-Cup," Kosky's favorite female cartoon heroine. Be it writing seen as "a lonely and private substitute for conversation" (Brooks Atkinson) or as "a vocation of unhappiness," according to Georges Simenon.

One way or another, one cannot write out of, and about, the life-consuming Self unless one first is able to skoal life. To skoal or toast it. To skoal it preferably in the sizzling Swedish fashion to be found either in Sweden or in the Swedish-American *Skoal Sex* magazine.

In order to write, a writer must skoal life even if he is a writer defined

---

*"It is an imaginary narrative based on romantic history: the specimens preserved have plots which conform closely to a type. A young married couple (in later forms a pair of lovers) are separated by circumstances, pass through a series of tragic and violent misfortunes, and are finally reunited. The misfortunes generally include some very close approximation to death, often something which to the one member of the pair appears to be in truth the other's death, and generally the flogging of one or both parties, sometimes other tortures. Throughout there is an accent of theatrical pose. One incident may suffice." (*Conversion: The Old and the New in Religion from Alexander the Great to Augustine of Hippo* by A. D. Nock, Oxford, 1933, p. 199)

as no more than "an engineer of the human soul" (Joseph Stalin) and no less than "writer, *n*. 1. penman, penner. *Sl.* pen-pusher. 2. leg man, sob sister. 3. scribe, scrivener, *Judaism*: sopher. 4. script writer, playwright, paraphrast, satirist, mythmaker"; as rated by Kosky's favorite *Rodale Synonym Finder*, i.e., a dictionary.

The reason is simple. The Swedish skoal potentiates to the ninth degree the spiritual contents of such highly charged toasters as Ruthenian *na zdrowie*, the American chin-chin, the Germanic *prosit*, the French *salut*! A properly executed spiritual skoal begins with the Tantric meeting of the eyes—an optical opening line, so to speak. The toaster sends his glance searching for a potential toastee. Searching anywhere since skoaling can be done across a king-size terrace, a Ping-Pong table, a drawing room, or even across a double bed.

To skoal or not to skoal means to see or not to see, since the sense of seeing constitutes 69 percent of a skoal, says the authoritative *Skoal!* magazine. Upon receiving the glance, the toastee responds either by "looking blandly the other way: the Swedish way of showing the other cheek," says *Skoal!* magazine, or by voluntarily establishing eye contact, "the Swedish paving of the road for a meeting of transmigrating souls," according to the *Swedish-Jewish Weekly*. (Or is it also a magazine?)

Next comes the dramatically tense raising of the glasses to eye level, first by the skoal-seeking toaster, then by the toastee, "followed by the well-timed *yet* spontaneous act of abrupt follow-through of bottoms up! to be followed up again by raising of the empty glasses—and skoaling each other again. All decent skoaling is done with the eyes locked in eye-to-I-to-I or eye-to-eye position, informs *Swedish Maiden* magazine, adding that "preferably, it should also be done without as much as a blink and absolutely without a wink." No wonder. Winking does to skoaling what hiccups do to speech: it interrupts the flow; it insinuates another meaning. In skoaling, winking is double-talk.

Question from the audience: Are you afraid of the unknown?

Kosky: Only of the known. Why should I be afraid of what I don't know? (Public Lecture, Clearwater, Florida, 1982)

It is said that the skoal—a visual language commonly spoken by all culturally versatile Swedes—finds its origin in the ancient customs of the Vikings. The clever Vikings, who invented the skoal, defined manners as a "contrivance of wise men to keep fools at a distance" (Emerson), not their answer to manners seen as a "hypocrisy of a nation." (Balzac) Suspicious, anxious to avoid an eye for an eye, and mistrustful of any eye-to-eye, the Vikings devised a skoal as a way of one man keeping an anxious eye on the eye of another. It was their way of arresting another's movements (such as reaching for a dagger) with a simple movement of one's eye. (Still the most peaceful form of arrest known to man since the days of Papa-Doc Stalin, interferes Jay Kay.)

In a hurry to skoal life, and, as a result, make it less lifeless—(lifeless, if you like adverbs, meaning "duly; inactively; languidly; inertly; lazily; torpidly; quiescently; silently; actually; heavily; passively; sluggishly; unusually; lifeless. (*Rodale*) Our life-skoaler Kosky gulps down most of his TV dinner which, made by Rutheno-American CuisinMart Corporation, contains some of the choicest chunks of Polish *bigos* (taste non-translatable: J.K.) he's ever tasted. Satiated, he then rushes out onto the street. In minutes, he can be seen entering the newly remodeled Hotel Khazar-Esplanade (owner: Onogurs & Ostyak; architect Al-Masudi and David El-Roi-Disraeli). The Khazar-Esplanade is the only hotel which has issued its own traveler's checks which bear American-Polish inscription in Hebrew lettering.*

In the hotel Kosky runs straight to its swimming pool. At this time— it's well after 9:00 P.M.—there's no one in the water. Quickly, he changes into his swim suit, and in minutes our literary mini-messiah buoys happily in the calm waters.

As soon as the convert immerses and emerges, he is like a Jew in every way. (Talmud) His mood shifts when, thanks to the involuntary shift of his sight, he sees the full-grown form of a female locked inside the pool's Lunar ultraviolet solarium, a stall separated from the rest of the room by an ill-fitting curtain of purple rubber. Safe in his waterhole, our water snake swiftly lets his inner current carry him motionless to the pool's darkest (and deepest) corner. There the snake raises his head up and, skoaling life, safely peeks through the narrow opening under

---

*"From Khazaria the Hebrew script seemed to have spread into neighbouring countries. . . . Some Hebrew letters (*shin* and *tsadei*) also found their way into the Cyrillic alphabet, and furthermore, many Polish silver coins have been found, dating from the twelfth or thirteenth century, which bear Polish inscriptions in Hebrew lettering, side by side with coins inscribed in the Latin alphabet. Pliak comments: 'These coins are the final evidence for the spreading of the Hebrew script from Khazaria to the neighbouring Slavonic countries. . . . They were minted because many of the Polish people were more used to this type of script than to the Roman script, not considering it as specifically Jewish.' " (A. Koestler, op. cit., p. 62)

the curtain. Again our literary anti-misogynist has been uniquely favored. Inside, wearing high-heeled Roman-slave sandals and nothing else, a lunar woman calmly bathes under the man-made sun.

I liked to walk up Fifth Avenue and pick out romantic women from the crowd and imagine that in a few minutes I was going to enter into their lives, and no one would ever know or disapprove. (F. Scott Fitzgerald) It is an admiration such as "those who have devoted their thoughts to the creation of beauty feel toward those who possess beauty itself," in the words of Thomas Mann.

The lunar woman is in her most sexually potent mid-twenties; a naked mermaid who has stepped down to our Samael (the Demon of the left: J.K.) from the left-panel side of Bosch's *The Hay Wagon*. The lunar woman is a creature of physical contradictions. She looks as curvy, cuddly'nd creamy as Kirsten, the green-eyed superb Swedish Sexpot Sensation from the pages of the recent *High Society* magazine, but given her swarthy and dignified look, she could also—please forgive this sudden association—be Jewish. A true Jewish beauty. One of many such beauties who, together with the 500,000 other Jews—forgive me for bringing this about!—perished, burned alive in the flames of the Warsaw Ghetto.*

"Let us hope she is Hungarian!" Jay Kay introduces her, "Imagine, a bi- or even tri-lingual Hungarian woman." (To J.K. Hungarian signifies one who knows all there is to know about life defined, in the absence of a better term, as Transylvanian Cuisine.)† For this female, for this lunar dish, our sexual cuisinier would happily serve a splendid Hungarian dish known as *Nyaradmenti Rakott Karalabe*, which translates into English as Layered Kohlrabis from Nyarad,‡ the recipe for

---

*"In order to overawe the Jews, the Nazis first tried to break the spirit of the Warsaw Ghetto by breaking into it in six tanks on the first night of Passover." From *The Battle of the Warsaw Ghetto*, published by the American Council of Warsaw Jews and American Friends of Polish Jews (New York, 1944). And in order to overawe the Nazis, the Jews from the Warsaw Ghetto sacrificed so many of themselves. But look at what price in human life? Wouldn't so many more of them have survived had they been living in the Ghetto of Lodz—that private Jewish hell'nd heaven?

†Paul Kovi's *Transylvanian Cuisine: History, Gastronomy, Legend, and Lore from Middle Europe's Most Remarkable Region* (1985).

‡NOTE: Layered kohlrabis may be served with tomato sauce if desired. Ibidem p. 69.

which is to be found in the below-mentioned book on page—you guessed it, again, reader!—number sixty-nine!

Her shiny olive skin so smooth and shiny, and her cheekbones so high and Oriental, suggest her ancestors were the sea Gypsies of Tantric Thailand. "The latter-day Hungarians." (Jay Kay) But then she is tall— and most Caucasian, which is "sexually far less elusive." (Jay Kay) This is a lunar woman through whom, providing she would become his *mudra*, "a willing yet *detachedly attached* Tantric partner" (*Tantric News*, 1988), he could heat his Self, even overheat it to at least 96° F. (with F. standing for fucking and Fahrenheit). He can almost feel the psychic currents flowing from her to him **like threads in a spider web. (Tantra)** No wonder: Tantra means a web.

Every fixation necessarily changes the hormonal status. (O. Fenichel)

His hormonal status changed, Kosky also changes his position in the water.

Mircea Eliade, since 1966 his proto-guru, tells him in no uncertain passage that "Every naked woman incarnates *prakti* ("manifests life": J.K.). Hence she is to be looked upon with the same adoration and the same detachment that one exercises in pondering the unfathomable secret of nature, its limitless capacity to create."

Promptly, his spine erect, Kosky places the right foot on the left thigh and the left foot on the right thigh; places the hands palms upward, in the lap. **Good for meditating, this Lotus pose subdues sexual arousal in men and exerts beneficial influence on the womb. (Tantra)**

Meanwhile, in the solarium, the self-timer buzzes and turns off the UV sun. The lunar woman takes off her sunglasses, flashes her all-shaved vulva,* wraps her golden frame in a sumptuous silk robe and walks **the lady whose bulk and bloom struck him to the point of admiration. (John Galsworthy)†** out of the solarium. Our staring Tom allows her enough time to take a shower, dry her hair, sit down in the lounge and order a double-size Cuba Libre from the poolside bar. Only then

---

*Woman's vulva: It is, like reputation, "the universal object and idol of men of letters." (John Adams)

†A *Stoic*, Volume 1, p. 69 in *Caravan* by John Galsworthy (The Grove Edition, 1928)

Galsworthy was Israel Kosky's favorite English-language writer and this was Israel Kosky's favorite edition of Galsworthy's collected works appropriately starting with the story called "a Stoic."

does he get out of the water, wash off the chlorine under the shower, dry in the sauna, and—clad in his solopolo robe—take a seat at the table closest to hcrs.

In slow motion, hiking her black silky robe high on her silky thighs, the lunar woman crosses one thigh over the other. This is the time for maximum realism. **At your age, and in your condition, I recommend a little prudence. Now just take my terms quietly, or you know what happens. (John Galsworthy)*** Quickly Kosky replaces his mental tele-lens by a standard one, which, offering minimum distortion, also offers a moderately accurate—and closeup—view of her exquisite posture and exquisitely posturing thighs. Simultaneously the outer writer sends her a sneaky side skoal. Again, she simply won't notice him. Dejected, but not rejected, he humbly drops his gaze and skoals her thighs. **There was nothing remarkable in the costume, or in the countenance, but the eyes, John felt, were such as one feels they wish they had never seen, and feels they can never forget. (Charles Robert Maturin)**

If he could only catch her glance—a Tantric prerequisite to catching her "by her eyes: eyes are the hair of her soul." (Tantra) Our Tantric coughs and coughs again. This is a spontaneously nervous cough; it is also his most natural. Since it easily impersonates sonorous sneezing, the cough alerts her, and for a brief moment she looks at him, (then, momentarily, into him: Jay Kay). Her glance says: Are you, buddy, suffering from COPD?†

He seizes the moment, and literally sinks his gaze into hers, then skoals her, taking precaution—just in case!—against Psychomental Poison,™‡ the curse of the evil eye.

The child said, "I am not afraid of the evil eye,/for I am the son of a great and precious fish/and fish do not fear the evil eye,/as it is written:/

---

*Ibid., p. 96.

†CIGARETTE AND PIPE SMOKERS BEWARE: chronic obstructive pulmonary disease (COPD) is "clinically significant, irrepressible, generalized airways obstruction associated with varying degrees of chronic bronchitis, abnormalities in small airways, and emphysema." (*Merck Manual*, 1982)

‡Psychomental Poison (a curse): a product of decomposition obtained by concentration. Can be intentionally projected over any distance as a curse in order to distract, interfere and, depending on its vitriolic strength, destroy the psychic mass of someone else. The strength of Psychomental Poison™ is measured in units of vitriol (from nine to one), each depressive unit containing a higher concentration. (*Materia Psychomatica*, 1966)

"They shall multiply like fish in the midst of the earth." (Genesis) This blessing includes protection from the evil eye. (The Zohar)

The lunar woman skoals him with her eyes as well as with her drink. Encouraged, he leans toward her as naturally as he can. Careful now! Leaning forward is body language; since a proper skoal depends only on the talk of the eye, using body language is against skoal's spiritual rules.

"A man should not be tame," says the Spanish proverb, and I would say: An author is not a monk. (Joseph Conrad)

Kosky gets up and walks over to her. "I wouldn't be faithful to my faith—my faith is oral tradition—if I didn't at least try to know you." He pauses. "I'm Norbert Kosky. I live next door, on West 69th Street."

"Carmita Cardobas. From St. Petersburg, Florida," she says with an open Latin smile.

Now he skoals her and her famous city. It's all in the name! Even the florid, wet and hot Florida's St. Petersburg still evokes in him thoughts of that other St. Petersburg—the one that, as capital of the Russian Empire, always cold on the surface, boiled like a virulent boil under its surface. And what a city! The city visited by the famous Alessandro di Cagliostro—the only one during his tour of European capitals in which he failed to establish a lodge of Egyptian Rite. He failed because of some unmentionable rumors circulated by Countess von der Rocke, that wreck of a *cuntess*! The rumorization of these rumors—read: their "spread"—was supported by the guild of Russian doctors who, envying Cagliostro's popularity, feared the spread of his medical doctrine.

"Please sit down. Right there, across from me." With her shapely sandaled foot, she kicks the only other easy chair in his direction as easily as if it were a semicolon, and when, a bit uneasily, our *erotoman* sits down on it, teasing him, easily she tilts back the back of her own easy chair and with it she sensually stretches her own back. Her pose sets in motion the gears of his fantasy. Now he sees her sensually stretched in front of him, lying flat on her back in his bathroom in the classic Seegra Savasana Yoga pose known as the Quick Corps. With his standing above her, suddenly, in one swift motion, she lifts her arms and legs off the floor, and balancing on her buttocks she tightens the muscles of her abdomen and diaphragm, then just as fast, manages to release them only to repeat the procedure again and again.*

---

*"Women should suspend all Yoga practices except Savasana and Nadi Suddhi

Normally, I would ask a new man in my life, 'What line of business are you in?' but I won't ask you." She tilts her torso and lets her robe open to one side.

"Why not?"

"Because you're clearly out of line! I know who you are."

"Who am I?"

"A private hotel guide? Guide not guard! You're too old to be a guard." She laughs in the face of our Magic Flute man, and her easy abandoned laughter puts another face guard No. 6 on his already masked face. Only now he becomes aware he saw this woman before.

Artemis is Freedom—wild, untrammelled, aloof from all entanglements. She is a huntress, a dancer, the goddess of nature and wildness, a virgin physically and, even more important, a virgin psychologically, inviolable, belonging to no one, defined by no relationship, confined by no bond. (Arianna Stassinopoulos, op. cit., p. 69)*

This cultural pose,† then brings to his head Bruno Schulz's drawing No. 13, an untitled *cliché-verre*; Kosky title: A *Middle-European* Erotoman *Worships a Foot of a Robe-Clad Woman*. Enough said.

"Please sit down!" she commands him firmly, and her manner brings to his fatigued mind *Undula Taking a Walk*—Bruno Schulz's drawing

---

(nerve purification: J.K.) during their menstrual period and also for two or three days afterward. . . . Those women starting Yoga practices for the first time should not do so during pregnancy or until six months after childbirth," counsels Yogiraj Sri Swami Satchidananda (whose name, most appropriately means Existence-Knowledge-Bliss absolute) in his (superbly illustrated: Jay Kay) *Integral Yoga Hatha* (Holt, Rinehart and Winston [today, Henry Holt and Company: J.K.] 1970). "An adept at Raja and Hatha Yoga, Swami Satchidananda came to New York for an intended two-day visit . . . in 1968 he was granted permanent residence visa under the category: Minister of Divine Words." (From the blurb)

*See *The Gods of Greece*, by Arianna Stassinopoulos, text, and Roloff Beny, photographs (1983). The chapter entitled "Artemis" starts on page 69; the chapter called "Hermes" begins on page 190. Just as well: 190 is a current spiritually correct number. (With nine signifying muse, and zero signifying nothing, it is a most appropriate number for our suicide-conscious and willing-to-die-at-any-time, rapidly aging hero: Jay Kay.)

†In the integral Yoga (integral Yoga is a combination of all main branches of Yoga), the Cultural Poses are practiced "mainly as an aid to gaining perfect health, and only a minimum number of such poses is required to gain the maximum amount of benefit." (See their complete listing in "Cultural Poses," Part Four, op. cit., pp. 8–11.)

No. 1. "This exquisitely executed artwork shows Undula who, all dressed up, and accompanied by another well-dressed young woman, leads on a leash our unduly foot-worshipping Bruno Schulz." (Jay Kay)

With her shipshaped calf, she now kicks in his direction the only other chair, and she does it with the contempt of a writer kicking an upstart semicolon or comma. When, a bit ill at ease, our upstart writer sits down, she ogles him with another brand of contempt—the contempt any fully clothed woman feels at the sight of a half-man, half-beast led on a leash by sex. (See Bruno Schulz's drawing No. 69 simply entitled "A Portrait of an Incurable Erotoman." Enough shown. (Enough *shown*, not enough said, Printer!) We are talking *cliché-verre*, not literary cliché!

Judging just by the length and shape of her legs, this leggy Artemis could easily compete with such leggy super-sluts as Josephine Dietrich and Baker Marlene—the two leggy sluts who seem from time to time to be making it together on the pages of the *Stained Silk Stocking Super Sex* magazine.

No wonder that, watching this wondrously leggy being, "legs, in some remote way, make him think of running, and running means freedom" (Jay Kay), which makes him also think of the leggy goddess called Artemis.

And Artemis is the primordial teenager who never moves beyond the adolescent stage into full womanhood. The nine-year-olds who left their mothers to enter the goddess's service stayed with her until it was time for them to marry and have their own children. They grew up and left; the goddess remained. Her own independence was her essential reality, not a transitional stage. (Arianna Stassinopoulos, op. cit., p. 69)

She leans over his face like a palmist over a palm. "Your face isn't exactly on open book. Now, seriously, who are you? An American con man or a French can-can artist?"

"I'm both. **Suddenly there seemed to be something sweeping into me and inflating my entire being. (William James)** I'm a writer," he exclaims while inhaling her John Profumo. **Artist: one who practices one of the fine arts, also: master, virtuoso, genius, prodigy, wizard, trickster, deceiver, cheat, fraud, swindler, confidence man, shyster, flimflam man; fox, sly dog, sharpie, horse trader. (*Writers' Directory*)**

She brightens. "You a writer? Really? That's unreal! Now, what do you write, really, now!" Her intonation dismisses.

"I write novels. Real novels. Real, that is all made up, down to the smallest fictional detail. Made up by me and "the collective consciousness (which is: J.K.)," says Kosky. **Neither a primary reality, nor an autonomous reality, it is elaborated implicitly in the overall behavior of individuals participating in the economic, social, political life, etc."** (Lucien Goldman, ibid. p. 9) Writer: one who writes, also member of the fourth estate, pen-pusher, word painter; ink spiller, quill driver, wordsmith, hack, swindler, word-slinger, potboiler; gazeteer, leg man; stringer, sob sister, scandalmonger, dirt-dealer; scribe, scrivener, recorder; copyist, sopher; scenarist; prosaist; paraphraser; mythmaker, horse trader. (Artists Guide)

"I've never heard of a writer named Kosky. You see, I read only in English or in Spanish, the two official languages of these United Hispanic States. What quixotic language do you write in?" She bares her shoulder.

"In English, what else?"*

But I experience my first three tongues as perfectly equivalent centres of myself. I dream with equal verbal density and linguistic-symbolic provocation in all three. The only difference is that the idiom of the dream follows, more often than not, on the language I have been using during the day. (George Steiner)

"What? You write in English? With that accent?" She recoils.

"I speak English with a Ruthenian–Jewish accent, but I hide my accent when I write—and I write only in my American–Jewish English," says Kosky. †

"You must be published in the British Commonwealth!" she rejoices. "The English are so much more tolerant of those who can't speak or write English well."

"Britannia no longer rules the waves of my English. No matter where I write them first, whether in Buddhistan or Calvingrad, my books are published first in America as I once pointed out most firmly in *America First* magazine," says Kosky.

"I admit I don't read books," pensively declares the lovely female

---

*"Language is this country's spiritual monarch, not an elected official. Given the growing number of Hispanics, introducing Spanish as a ruler equal to English might one day lead to the formation of the United Hispanic States—with Spanish as the only official spiritual ruler." (George Brayerin, 1986)

†See *Seeing Ease in Exile* by Edward Alexander in *Judaism* (an issue devoted to "Being a Jew and an American—Do They Mesh?") No. 127, vol. 32, No. 3, Summer, 1983, pp. 267–70.

pensador, who then offers him for a reward a deeper view of her inner thighs.

"Don't worry," says Kosky. "How could you? Over sixty-nine thousand books are published in this country every year."

She stretches, tensing the muscles of her calves. In vain, he—a yogi with almost perfect control of his Selfhood—tries to control his self-erection. He is out of control.

To break her spell, our *escritor* runs to his dressing room and returns with a copy of his latest novel—he called it his newly issued—his passport of spiritual redemption No. 8. "It's for you. I'll inscribe it to you later—if you wish," he says humbly. (A humble writer already disciplined many times by the power of the English verb and noun—the English language is his most demanding mistress: Jay Kay)

She takes the book from him. She reads its title. She glances at his photograph on the back cover, then at his face, then at the face on the cover again. (While all he can see in her as well, is himself at this moment having some kind of sex with her, no matter what kind: Jay Kay quickly clarifies for the reader.)*

"Not bad. Not bad at all. Your picture, I mean. Why don't you wear it over your face?" She smiles sweetly, then goes through his book silently, reading a few random fragments. "This is Undula, not Artemis. This is the portrait of a MAN ABOUT TO BE LASHED BY A WOMAN.

"Why don't you go into serious business, instead of telling people stories about your denatured brand of sex? Today, unsafe sex is nobody's business." She first places the book on the table, then pushes the book away. Her gesture disqualifies him as a man far more than it disqualifies his fiction.

But so what? Here he becomes purposefully corruptible. Who cares about fiction anyhow? ("Can you name one person who can't live

---

*Sex is, as any student of advertising and publishing knows, a highly intriguing phenomenon, charged with explosive possibilities and accompanied by an infinite number of strange, beautiful, and terrible ramifications. With it are involved the most intense of human emotions: love, hate, jealousy, treachery, betrayal, cruelty, sacrifice, devotion. Suicide and murder frequently take place because of it. Life is brought into being as its consequence. Lives are dramatically and drastically changed through its agency. (Gina Cerminara) in "Sex: Some Karmic Aspects of Sex," Chapter 10 in *The World Within,* pp. 101–110, 1957.

without reading fiction? I can't," says Jay Kay.) At this time in his life (this time refers to every single moment), this woman excites him like no other, "and in his head the expression *this woman* refers just about to every passing-by (or by-passing: J.K.) woman," clarifies the sexual master Jay Kay. Still, there is no need to get overcorrupted. Corruption by one's Self is one thing; quite another is corruption by the Other, particularly when, these sick-sex-obscured days, the Other is a safe sex-dispensing woman.

"Storytelling is a commodities business. A writer is a banker. A banker of Self. Self is a rare commodity, as rare as platinum. As rare as group sex," he says, and saying this he wonders whether in this age of sexual plague a woman with legs as beautiful as hers "prefers walking by just by herself," in the cryptic language of the Tantric text which also says that a "dombi's legs must beg to be watched in the act of sexual walking." (Tantra)

"Storytelling is serious business. Our fictional bank teller now tells her. **Creation seemed a mightly crack/To make me visible. (Emily Dickinson) I have no wife, no parent, child, allie,/To give my substance to. (Pope)** "As I have no family to hand things down to, I hand them down on paper. You might say, fiction is my family business."

"No family? Isn't that bad for a writer?"

"Not for this one," says Kosky.

Magic and trickery, mischief and lying, belong as naturally to Hermes' world as guiding souls to the Underworld and initiating men into the mysteries of death. Hermes is appointed messenger of the gods because he promises never to lie, but adds that "it may be necessary for him not to tell the truth in order that he may not lie.". . . Language and speech which, according to Plato, were invented by Hermes belong to the world of form. "The name Hermes has to do with speech and signifies that he is the interpreter, or messeger of thief, or liar, or bargainer; all that sort of thing has a great deal to do with language. . . . Speech signifies all things, and is always turning them round and round, and has two forms, true and false." (*The Gods of Greece*, op. cit., p. 196) "For one, my father would disapprove of my writing fiction. He wanted me to read sexy stories from John Galsworthy and Shakespeare (and Somerset Maugham: J.K.), all of whom were to him saints from the Anglo-Saxon literary Talmud—not to write my own. You might say that the Babylonian Talmud was his spiritual baby."

"You sound awfully deliberate!" She reprimands him.

"Plotting a narrative plot evolves in one's mind beforehand, long before the writing hand takes over," he says. "That's deliberate."

"You sound terribly selfish," she pronounces.

"I am. Writing comes from Self as much as it does from fish. If that's not selfish, what is?" our Jonas mentors. **I am a camera with its shutter open, quite passive, recording, not thinking. (Christopher Isherwood)**

She gives him a fresh glance. "Every Spaniard's dream is to *tenor un hijo, planter un arbol, escribir un libro*—have a son, plant a tree, write a book. And here you are: a real *escritor* planted next to me like a tree." She looks at him—and her look is a *regard*, one that stems from regard for life—life here typified by the love of oneself as well as love of the Other.

Now it's Kosky's turn. He looks straight into her eyes. This is eye-to-eye, as well as I-to-I. This is what her eye (as well as her I) say to him: They say: cut this literary shit, *Señor*. I don't give a fuck about what you write or in what language or for whom, and even if I were to give you a fuck, I wouldn't do it because you are a writer but because when I saw you drifting not so aimlessly in that pool of water, you looked awfully skinny, sad'nd smutty—a beheaded man opening his closet filled with a skeletonlike yet sexily dressed corpse in black: a true image of Death—death seen, I guess, as a supreme vice—a final ecstasy.

Without a word, without another look at her or her thighs, Kosky gets up. He steps one step away from her. Slowly he begins to take off his robe. The slowness of his disrobing is anything but a tease. He learned to disrobe like this, then to stand semi-rigid (here rigid does not necessarily imply erected) not from life and not from phantasy, but straight from *The Manly Man*, a liberal adult photograhic publication which, published bi-monthly at 6996 Highrise Highway (10th Floor!) in Manchilde Village, Eastern California, openly advocates the implicit beauty of the male animal, portraying man as "a pliable animal, a being who gets accustomed to everything" (Dostoyevsky) as well as "the arch machine." (Emerson)* The disrobing accomplished, barefooted, Kosky stands before her. Then he starts walking toward the pool.

---

*As quoted and numbered in Stein and Day's *Dictionary of Definitive Quotations*, collected by Michael McKenna (New York, 1983, p. 118). In polo, rating No. 10 is a top rating, "and a ten-rated polo player is as rare as the rarest zebra." (Jay Kay)

In the train I was tormented by a need for intercourse, and I thought of everything that has been said, written and published about dirty old swine, those poor old swine whom the little spermatic beast still gnaws with all its might. Is it our fault if nature has implanted in us such an imperious, persistent and stubborn desire for coming together with the other sex? (Edmond de Goncourt, 1888)

He shivers. If all this could only take place in St. Petersburg, Florida. If he could only be seen by her attired in his zebra-striped purple polo shirt by Zorro. If she could only see him in the saddle, wearing his ultra white Burchell's polo britches, matched by his self-styled Fabian polo boots! The size of the polo pony adding size to our *Equus burchelli.* *

Carmita watches him as he is. Her look signals spiritual surveillance, as well as surveillance of a potential Safe Sex club member. (No, not member, say a member candidate: Jay Kay)

Kosky faces the deep end. Supporting himself only on his hands, our **spermatic beast (Goncourt, as above)** lowers himself vertically into the pool under her very eyes, his feet first, letting his bony toes, bony calves, bony thighs, and bony chest slice the surface without a ripple. Pushing off, he lets the water gently engulf him up to his bony neck—but under no condition would he allow water to reach any higher. God forbid that water should ever flood his head. Head is the seat of the brain. You don't want your seat wet. Enough said.

Don't ever let the waves of the mundane flood you from within. (Israel Kosky to Norbert)

With the physical entry accomplished, the spiritual reentry begins. Peacefully, he floats. It is his sincerely yours look. **My voice, adorned/ with the marine insignia:/Above my heart an anchor,/And above the anchor a star,/And above the star the wind,/And above the wind the sail. (Rafael Alerti)**

Carmita comes to the edge of the pool. At first she looks down— down at him—but then the minute she sees what he does her *regard* becomes altogether different. Now it has nothing to do with his human size, with being above or below.

---

*Named after a British naturalist, Burchell's zebra (*Equus burchelli*) is lighter boned than any other zebra, hence able to run at thirty-five miles per hour for a long time and distance—"not unlike any well-trained all-American polo pony." (Norbert Kosky)

"I don't know any man who floats quite the way you do, though I know a woman who does," she says demurely.

"Writing is taught," she offers. "Why don't you offer courses in, say, creative floating?"

"I can't teach it. Either one knows how to generate it from within or one doesn't. It's like sexual love or a love of writing," says Kosky. As he says it he lets his inner current take him away from her.

Camita returns to her deck chair. There she starts to read and continues reading his book.

After a while he leaves the pool. Engrossed in reading she, his newest reader, does not even notice our sex-smitten author. It's a spiritual score!

"Have the things you've written about in this book really happened? 'Did you, for instance, really meet a man who was buoyed by a force he did not know and could not name?' " she asks when our Floatus sits down beside her.

"They happen in this novel."

"Well—did they happen to you or not?" She nudges his thigh with hers: flesh skoaling flesh.

"I don't answer such questions," he admits openly. "Fiction is a fetish. You'll have to decide for yourself, if it could also happen to you. If the answer is yes, you and I share the same fetish." He could get off by just watching her, say, share her slightly hairy upper thigh."

"Now, now, don't be touchy. Who cares about what happens in a novel! And to whom? So what if it happened to you."

Carmita stands up, and standing next to her, he feels like a stand-up comic. "I've been running all over New York," she says. "and I'm getting tired of this pool. Do you mind if we move this conversation to my hotel room?"

"I don't mind. Not at all," says Kosky. **This chapter, in which we shall undertake the explication of Being-in as such (that is to say of the Being of the "there") breaks up into two parts: A. the existential constitution of the "there"; B. the everyday being of the "there," and the falling of Dasein of Being There. (Heidegger)**

They part company, but they part with each other like friends about to form one. His book in hand, Carmita retires to her room in order to, in her words, make order in the room, and make herself presentable for him.

Kosky dresses quickly, then, slowing himself down, takes the express elevator to her floor—what luck! It is floor six. There, he runs to her room. He is lucky again: it is suite No. 906. She opens the door dressed in a diaphanous gown. She leads him to an easy chair, then sits down across from him. They watch each other in silence.

Silence. 1. "A heading for all ailments." (Babylonian Talmud) 9. "A conversation with an Englishman." (Heinrich Heine) 10. "Your highest female grace." (Ben Jonson)* This is the end of the eye talk. "Now look at me and trust me," he looks her trustworthily in the eye. "I am a perfect stranger *and* an unknown writer. You can tell me anything, anything at all. Tell me about yourself, or others, or even, if you've got a story-telling talent, not only a story-telling body, make up a story about you and me; a hypothetical safe-sex story. A story about how it began—or begins; the story of the two of us—we are the main characters of this story, right? Go along with each other while getting on with the story—drama is sight in action. (Kosinski, 1982)

"Talk about yourself," he says. There's nothing like desire to prevent the things one says from having any resemblance to the things in one's mind. (Proust)

"What in particular?"

"Sex. For an opening," he encourages her.

Spiritual freedom in its fullness is neither an abstraction or a transcendent flight. It is not to be conceived onesidedly as detached knowledge or supernatural devotion. (Haridas Chaudhuri)†

She looks at him and her look says: let's kill the bull. Be true to life, even if not to each other.

"The other day, after a Broadway matinee of *Hamlet*, I ran into the guy who played him," she says impassively. "Boy! Was he good looking! The body of a boyish Ben Hur. Every muscle a string, every vein a snake. A bedroom idol if I ever saw one!" She curls a lock of her hair with her forefinger. "Somehow he took me for a drink at *his* place." She leaves her hair alone and folds her hands in her lap—between her thighs. "A good talker, too. But then in bed—fumbling with his Japanese-made Yamabuki No. 3 prophylactic—he too was into the Safe Sex business"—she takes a deep breath—"he just fell apart. His part (pardon this hard-on expression: Jay Kay) turned out to be—somehow— all soft. As soft as Hamlet was supposed to be."

---

*As ranked by Michael McKenna, op. cit., p. 174.

†See *Integral Yoga: A Concept of Harmonious and Creative Living*, by Haridas Chaudhuri (1965).

She speaks of the stage Hamlet, not of the actor. She lifts a paper napkin and, as if in warning, squeezes it into a wad. "Now I wonder why."

"Why what?"

"Why I go after every actor who plays Hamlet. I wonder who's more real—or dear—to me, the role of Hamlet or the actor who fills it?" She lets her robe disrobe her calf, then her knee, then her thigh. Fixed upon her every move, he watches her, transfixed.

To Hamlet madness is a mere mask for the hiding of weakness. In the making of mows and jests he sees a chance of delay. He keeps playing with action, as an artist plays with a theory. He makes himself the spy of his proper actions, and listening to his own words knows them to be but "words, words, words." Instead of trying to be the hero of his own history, he seeks to be the spectator of his own tragedy. He disbelieves in everything, including himself, and yet his doubt helps him not, as it comes not from scepticism but from a divided will.

Of all this, Guildenstern and Rosencrantz realize nothing. (Wilde)

"Once in bed," she goes on, "I wanted to feel my Hamlet deep within—but when I couldn't feel him," she hesitates, "what I could not feel suddenly became more essential than what I could."

"Why couldn't you feel your own body?" With his erotic telesens (tele-sens, not tele-lens, Printer!) Kosky ventures deep into her sexual hamlet.

A seduction theory. Praise everything; luring a woman away from her husband and persuading her that she is decent (though indulging her in appalling obscenity). That's the contrast I'm fond of. (Dostoyevsky)

"I couldn't because he couldn't make himself *feelable*."

"Why wouldn't he?"

"Because he couldn't, not wouldn't. He was all new to that new contraceptive business, that's why," she says contemptuously.

"Maybe he wasn't sure you really wanted him that hard?" Kosky tries again. **What would he do,/Had he the motive and the cue for passion/ That I have? (Shakespeare)**

"He was quite sure," she says with the smile of Ophelia. "I made sure he did."

"Maybe he was too hard-pressed?" Kosky won't give up. **Hard-pressed males of the world, unite! (Norbert Kosky, Toronto Public Lecture, 6/9/87)**

"He wasn't. He was soft. He was a perfect Hamlet. As coherent as

Hamlet—and as incoherent. He had such lovely eyes. Eyes with pupils that stayed constantly enlarged. Too bad nothing else was."

"He is an actor," says Kosky. "Perhaps he wasn't sure he was big enough for his new safe-sex role. For some of us, it's a tough role to play. Also,"—he pauses in false grief—"he might have needed help." **Psychologically, he would be given the usual psychological treatment indicated in such cases: better home relations, remedial reading, perhaps, special tutoring in school work; various techniques of getting along better with others. (Gina Cerminara, op. cit., p. 69)**

"Perhaps you're right." Calmly, she assesses Kosky. "I can tell that you don't find his case uplifting enough," she says, and, lowering her eyes in the direction of Kosky's Lower Depths which, from her point of view, at least, might seem to be momentarily depleted of anima, she declares him soft on arrival. This glance, this obvious lowering of her eyes and, with them, of his true sexual status, raises her spiritual status in his eyes by a full point. This brings her to No. 6 on his spiritually-straight scale from one to nine (and reduces him instantly to the most impressionable age, nine or ten: Jay Kay).

In Tantric terms, all this means she is a sexually straight washer-woman: a *dombi* who, having lost everything in the water, can now afford to be truthful. She has, by now, passed the elementary sexual tests and she passed them with floating colors—floating, not flying—because this Artemis is a washerwoman and not a water-child!" says our literary Mr. Hermes, who systematically abuses his readers by washing his dirty laundry in his water-sport-oriented semi-Oriental autobiographical fiction." (*Yellow Press Review*)

Her new rating qualifies her to progress from her current S-state (S-State being the state of an electron in an atom having an angular momentum of zero) to a spiritually Solid State—one which will render her spiritually more mobile yet more contained at the same time. Why not? Carmita is spontaneously animated. Her energy emanates from her as steam does from a steamship.* To him, a universal Zen Hasid at heart, as well as at the bottom of his spine, animated means hot as well as wet. **In the Hasidic story the symbolic character of the occurrence is emphasized, whereas in the Zen story it remains concealed, and in the**

---

*With so many sleepless sailors riding her top and bottom a steamship is, out of situational necessity, always a female, says the 1969 *Naval Dicktionary*. (PRINTER: a dicktionary, that's right: as in Dickens.)

literature the meaning of the saying is discussed; it remains however almost without doubt that the washing of the dishes is here also a symbol of a spiritual activity. (Martin Buber, 1958)* Because she is hot, and animated, she makes him steamed up in his own *kundalini* (steam is the ideal mixture of air and water: J.K.), which, after Cathy's departure, has lain dormant, "a water snake sleeping flat on the top of stagnant water." (Jay Kay)

So far so good. Carmita might turn out to be Cathy's spiritual substitute, another Sadhaka, who, practicing Tantric discipline, advances, in his eyes, from her status as a discipline, advances, in his eyes, from her status as a disciple to that of the aspirant—of one, in whose presence he, Sizzling Sex Master, can aspire freely. She might turn out to be one with whom he can practice *swara sadhana* (he scores another SS on his already high score point system), the essential Tantric practice in which our self-buoyant yogi "causes the breath to flow through the left nostril from sunrise to sunset; and through the right nostril from sunset to sunrise." (Omar Garrison)

Kosky, our spiritual follower of Sabbatai Sevi, is now ready to administer to Carmita one more test which, if passed, might admit her to his inner sardonic sanctum.

He didn't even notice when and how he yielded to the dangerous sway of her eyes.... He was swept by an impulse so difficult to express ... as if confronted by the sight of a sea, suddenly uncovered and naked, a desert, or a chain of snow-capped mountains.... Now his eye did not fail to notice the thickness of the braid of hair which, without doubt, he could not have clasped with his soldier's fist.... There was something stifling in this beauty, something which stopped one's breath and made one's head swim. (Stefan Żeromski)†

Zen and Hasidism by Martin Buber, in *Zen and Hasidism: The Similarities Between Two Spiritual Disciplines*. Compiled by Harold Heifetz, 1978, p. 169.

†Stefan Żeromski, Kosky's idol ranked by him, with Stanislaw Reymont, with the highest No. 9, "was like Reymont, Poland's prime novelist, the sexuality of whom cost him a Nobel Prize, which went to Reymont." (Jay Kay) While Reymont's novel *The Peasants* influenced the subject matter of Kosky's first novel, Żeromski's novel *Ashes* influenced Kosky's notion of female beauty which, to Żeromski, was like water, always "swishing'nd shining, steaming'nd sparkling, shadowless'nd silvery, starlit'nd seething, sweltering'nd scalding, surging." (Just think of the collected

His head swimming from the overflow of seminal thoughts (they are the brain's semen: J.K.), from his shoulder bag Kosky takes out a bunch of Plot-Quote cards, "the portable table game of literary invention," in the words of the nameless inventor. Each card contains a short fragment from a certain novel. (And thanks to their use he has succeeded in a great many instances of sexual abuse: Jay Kay) **The body then becomes, as it were, a Book of Revelation. In it is condensed much of our secret history. In it are latent the necessities of our future. (Gina Cerminara, op. cit., p. 69)**

"To start with, read about women in love with women. Read *The Street of Crocodiles*,"* says Kosky, handing Carmita the cards. Now in order to assure that his still sex, his sexual objectivity, won't be soiled—

---

number of female-saturated double SS's!: J.K.)

Through water, everything is ultimately brought back to the fulfillment of God's goal. . . . The main vehicle for this is the Torah, which, as our sages teach us, is also a spiritual counterpart of water. (Rabbi Aryeh Kaplan, op. cit. p. 67)

For an extensive discussion of the literary climate the Polish-reading reader is referred to (1) Artur Sandauer: Rzeczywistość zdegradowana: Rzecz o Brunonie Schulzu (The degraded reality: A thing (rzecz) about Bruno Schulz) in his introduction to *Proza*, collected writing by Bruno Schulz; Krakow, 1964. (2) Dzieło literackie jako książka (literary work as a book) by Danuta Danek, Warszawa, 1980. (3) Problematyka symultanizmu w prozie (The question of simultaneity in prose) by Seweryna Wysłouch, Poznań, 1981.

*The Street of Crocodiles (The Cinnamon Shops, 1934) by Bruno Schulz, 1963, translated by Celina Wieniewska, 1985. Introduction by Jerzy Ficowski, Introduction translated by Michael Kandel. Unlike Żeromski, Bruno Schulz was master of the narrative dry dock, a sexually most evocative narrative style. See *Wetness vs. Dryness in the American Literary Style* (Oceanid Press, 1986). **[Bruno Schulz] was small, unattractive and sickly, with a thin angular body and brown, deep-set eyes in a pale triangular face. He taught art at a secondary school for boys at Drogobych in southeastern Poland, where he spent most of his life. He had few friends outside his native city. In his leisure hours—of which there were probably many—he made drawings and wrote endlessly, nobody quite knew what. (Celina Wieniewska) On November 19, 1942, on the streets of Drogobych, a small provincial town that belonged to Poland before World War II (and now is in the U.S.S.R.), there commenced a so-called action carried out by the local sections of the SS and the Gestapo against the Jewish population. . . . Among the murdered who lay until nightfall on the sidewalks of the little town—who lay where the bullets reached them—was Bruno Schulz. (Jerzy Ficowski)**

or spoiled—by physical touch, he moves his chair a few inches away from her knees. From now on it's strictly sexually safe literary touch and go. She takes the cards, glances at several of them, and then, seduced by the text, starts reading one of them.

Suddenly these strange books broke down all the walls around me, and made me think and dream about things of which for a long time I had feared to think and dream. Suddenly I began to find a strange meaning in old fairy tales; woods, rivers, mountains, became living beings; mysterious life filled the night; with new interest and new expectations. . . . (P. D. Ouspensky)

He keeps watching this Spanish-American Artemis through his safe sex sens SSS-96 tele-sens (no longer to be confused with his past sex lens No. 69, which combines Żeromski's literary point of view plus Reymont plus Schulz: Jay Kay).

He thinks of her as an aqueous beauty. Aqueous, not "2. sodden'nd soggy," according to the rating of the word *watery* found in his old Rodale. *

"Is this one of the word games you play with your reading star student studs?" she asks him, letting down her sensuous Sephardic Spanish jet-black hair.

He does not answer. Intrigued, she relaxes on the bed. "It could be exciting," she says, letting her calves cross each other.

"Did you ever ask a woman to do a real-sex safe-sex skit?" She picks up another card: it is a fragment from Kuprin's *The Duel*. In a pleasant sonorous voice she reads aloud, then says, "If I were to act out for you Alexandra Nikolaev, would you respond to me as her secret lover, as Romashov does in the novel, or as yourself, as a man who by reading about Romashov has learned what Romashov didn't know: that she— a woman he adored—was, spiritually speaking, a common whore."

"Definitely as Romashov," says Kosky. "I think Romashov is infatuated with Alexandra. Whore or not, she is life to him."

---

*"And what really pisses me off," wrote Norbert Kosky in 1982 in a letter to the editor of *Word Finder Dictionary*, "is that in your otherwise spiritually sparkling word finder you allow my favorite word *WET*, which stands for my Writers, Editors, and Translation Association, to be defined by such spiritually obnoxious adverbs as "soppily, swampily and strangely." (Norbert Kosky was the twice-elected president of WET—and he served the maximum two terms allowed, without incident or accident.—Estate Editors)

"Who is she really?" asks Carmita.

"Really she is a fallen woman, one who failed to raise herself to the status of a spiritual whore," he answers without a blink. "She is both one of the most desirable and most despicable women in all of literature." **They embraced and touched each other's faces. . . . But Romashov felt that something imperceptible, murky and repellent came between them and a tiny cold current ran through him."** (Kuprin)

"I wouldn't go to bed with a guy who thinks something 'murky and repellent' is going on between us. Murky and repellent. That sounds like chewing on tobacco." She then throws the card at his feet. She glances through the stack and picks up another card. It's a fragment from *The Man Who Laughs*.* Again, Carmita reads aloud: " ' "Why, it is Gwynplaine!" said Josiana, mingling pleasure and contempt. "I prefer the astounding, and you are enough to astound me. . . . The first day I saw you, I said to myself, 'It is he! I know him! He is the monster of my dreams. I'm going to have him.' That's why I wrote to you. Have you read my letter? Did you read it yourself, or did someone else read it to you?" Again Josiana fixed her gaze upon him, and continued: "I feel degraded by you, and I don't mind it! I love you. I go for you not just because you are deformed—but because you are low. A lover who is despised, mocked, grotesque, hideous, laughed at on that pillory called the stage, attracts me no end. You are probably a devil without knowing it yourself. You embody infernal mirth. You are not only ugly: you are hideous. Ugliness is insignificant; deformity is grand. You surpass everything. You are just what I want. You are the monster without; I am within. We were made for each other." ' "

Carmita stops reading. "I like this. I like it a lot. Isn't this just great?" she says. And her words change the setting of his Kundalini from No. 66 to 69. "What a perfect description of an ideal male lover. One so straight, so full of safe sex you could never find him profiled in *All-Male Jock* magazine." She loosens her belt, widening in the process the open space between the lapels of her robe. For a moment, her breasts show. The moment is long enough. Her breasts are perfectly ordinary, predictably sloopish and uneventful, without the sensual push or the

---

*Victor Hugo wrote *The Man Who Laughs* (1869) during his exile to Guernsey. The action of the novel—a fetishistic epic—takes place in the sexual-fetish-oriented seventeenth-century England, "where the English patriciate is the patriciate in the absolute sense of the word." (Hugo)

obsessional pull. Her nipples are thin, but not thin enough to constitute for him the source of attraction such hair-thin nipples exercise upon him. Her aureoles are pale, but not pale enough to disappear entirely from sight and render her fetishistically aureoleless. Somehow, he drops his gaze to her inner thighs; *somehow*, she shuts down her robe, and the way she does it headlines that *The Breast Show* is over; "the play is closed, stricken by a single bad review!" (*Times Square Record*) She gives Kosky an equivocal look. It says, unequivocally: Stop peeping, Tom! Show yourself, buddy, as you are—even if it hurts; even if it will kill you. Stop wearing the face of Romashov or the laughing mask of Gwynplaine. Read me between the lines. Forget about reading between my thighs. "If somehow—I were to become Josiana," she says, "would you make love to me—right now, right here—as Gwynplaine, or as you— as Norbert Kosky—the fella who needs to be known as a writer who made it before he can put a make on?"

"As Kosky disguised as Gwynplaine," says Kosky. He won't give up his literary disguises.

" 'It is wrong to compare flesh with marble,' " Kosky reads from another card by Victor Hugo. " 'Flesh is beautiful because it is not marble. It is beautiful because it palpitates, trembles, blushes, bleeds; because it is firm without being hard, white without being cold. A degree of beauty gives flesh the right of nudity; its own beauty is a veil!' " Kosky stops. **A little acting won't hurt. (Haggadah)** Our Actor nonchalantly lifts her robe above her knees high enough—and for long enough—for him to examine her waist and hips.

"My, my!!" he murmurs, paying her the ultimate compliment. Then, without salivating, he continues to read from the card.

" 'Josiana personified flesh. No passion tempted her, but she knew all about passion. Instinctively, she loathed its fulfillment, but longed for it at the same time. She was a virgin stained with every kind of defilement. In her insolence, she was at once tempting and inaccessible. Nevertheless, she still found it amusing to plan a fall for herself.' "

Kosky raises his eyes from the card.

"Am I supposed to fall for you now?" asks Carmita.

"It's all in the cards," says Kosky.

Carmita picks up another card. " 'Josiana was bored,' " she reads aloud from it. " 'She and Lord David carried on an affair of a peculiar kind. They did not love each other—they pleased each other. Josiana postponed the hour of submission for as long as she could; she appre-

294

ciated David and showed him off. They had a tacit agreement neither to conclude nor to break off their engagement. They eluded each other. There was a method to their lovemaking—one step forward, two back.' " Carmita lifts her eyes to Kosky. "Now you know about me and my Lord David."

"Are you going to marry him?" asks Kosky.

"I don't know. There's no rush." She throws her silky hair over her shoulders. Half-sitting, half-lying, she leans her shoulder against the wall. Stretching her legs, she *advertently* lets her robe open again. A sight for Marc Chagall!

Again she reads from *The Man Who Laughs*: " 'It's unbecoming to be married. Marriage fades one's ribbons; it makes one look old. How commonplace it is to be handed over by a notary! Marriage suppresses the will, kills the choice; turns love into dictation. Like grammar, marriage replaces inspiration by spelling; it disperses mystery; it diminishes the right of the strong or weak; destroys the charming balance of the sexes. To make love prosaically decent—how gross! To deprive lovemaking of any wrongdoing—how dull!' " She turns to Kosky, the innermost part of her inner thighs staring him in the face. It's the frontal-body skoal.

"Well?" she says. The situation becomes frontal. "Now you know why Lord David and I haven't wedded. Or—for that matter—even wetted each other."

"Perhaps that's not the real reason," says Kosky, transferring himself from his chair to the edge of her bed—and edging toward her in the process. He picks up another card and reads from it. " 'What cannot escape us, inspires us with no haste to obtain it. Josiana wanted to remain free; David to remain young; to remain without a tie for as long as possible seemed to him an extension of youth. In those crazy times, middle-aged young men abounded; they grew gray as young fops. . . .' "

He looks up at her. "I still don't see why I should fall for you," says Carmita.

Kosky reads again. " 'All her instincts impelled Josiana to yield herself wantonly, rather than to give herself legally. Pleasure is to be measured by the astonishment it creates.' " He puts the card away. This is no longer acting. He, the past master of the 1971 "I like to watch" routine, is at it again. Sixteen years later he is ready to be caught in the safe sex act—the newest sexual routine.

How absurd, at my age, still to be the prey of the spermatic beast!

295

For the last fortnight I have been trying to keep my thoughts entirely concentrated on my play, and for the last fortnight, in the dark of my closed eyes, the little brute has been presenting me with erotic pictures warmer than Aretino's. (Edmond de Goncourt)

Carmita fidgets. "Somehow—I want to know what Josiana and Gwynplaine did that night. Give me a cue—or another card."

"There is no other card," he says. **Stolen waters are sweet, and bread eaten in secret is pleasant. (Haggadah)**

"But how did they make out?" She lets her robe split open and she opens herself in the process.

"I won't tell you," says Kosky. "This is the time when our Romashov has other things on his mind. Call them thighs, not things."

Romashov was exhausted but pleasantly so. He had hardly time to undress before he was overpowered by sleep. And his last conscious impression was the delightful smell of his pillow: the smell of Alex's hair, of her perfume, of her beautiful young body. (Alexander Kuprin, 1905)*

---

*From *The Duel*, by Alexander Kuprin (1905), translated by Andrew R. MacAndrew (1961). Alexander Kuprin (1870–1938) is the author of *Moloch* (1896), *Olesya* (1898), *Breaking Point* (1900), *Captain Rybnikov* (1906), *Sulamith* (1908) and others. "But please tell him from me that he should never pay attention to anybody's advice but just keep writing in his own way" was Leo Tolstoy's advice to Kuprin.

```
┌─────────┐
│         │
│  2 4    │
│         │
└─────────┘
```

I have always considered myself a rather hermetic poet, for a certain limited audience. And what happens when this sort of poet becomes a kind of Jan Kiepura, a tenor, or a football star? Naturally, there arises a fundamental misunderstanding. (Czeslaw Milosz, 1983)

"I knew I could finally corner you for a literary tête-à-tête, my dear Jehuda Halevi!"* says a little man who bluntly accosts Kosky when, one calm evening, our calm author walks out of the Aeon Club through the only nonrevolving door left in New York. **There is a word which, when understood, wipes out the sins of innumerable aeons. (Zen saying as quoted by Martin Buber)†** The two-hundred-year-old Aeon Club is

---

*Jehuda Halevi (b. circa 1076–1141): the greatest Hebrew poet of Spain; ("and one of the profoundest thinkers Judaism has had since the closing of the canon."— Henry Slonimsky) wrote his once-celebrated book *Kuzari* (*The Khazars*) in Arabic. "*Kuzari*, written a year before his death, is a philosophical tract propounding the view that the Jewish nation is the sole mediator between God and the rest of mankind. At the end of history, all other nations will be converted to Judaism; and the conversion of the Khazars appears as a symbol or token of that ultimate event." From *The Thirteenth Tribe: The Khazar Empire and Its Heritage*, by Arthur Koestler (Random House, 1976, #98765432). See also *The Kuzari, An Argument for the Faith of Israel*, Introduction by Henry Slonimsky, 1964.

†Martin Buber (died 1965): a Jewish thinker who discovered that Jews, the Old World's Old Believers, "are the Orient's latecomers," and that "to create means to gather within oneself all elements, and to fuse them into a single structure; there is not true creative independence except that of giving form."

an intellectual reserve reserved for men-of-letters. Men, not women. "Women are belles-lettres," Jay Kay informs the reader.

"I hate the word *corner*," says Kosky. **Homo duplex has, in my case, more than one meaning. (Conrad to K. Waliszewski)**

In his sixties and impeccably attired, his gray hair pushed neatly to one side, the little man hands Kosky an ultra modern calling card. The inscription reads "Simon Thomas Temple, Sr. Textual Context Special Investigator: CLIFFORD, ASHLEY, BUCKINGHAM, ARLINGTON & LAUDERDALE, New York, Chicago."

Never mind the calling card, "a piece of working paper. Paper is patient, the reader is not." (Jay Kay) Impatiently, Kosky takes a look at the man, then at his card.

"You probably wonder what made me ask you to meet me," says Temple tentatively.

"I do," says Kosky. "I'm a wonder kid."

"Frankly"—Temple disarms Kosky with a smile—"ever since your first novel *came about*, my wife and kids call you Giuseppe Balsamo. (The man who by impersonating Cagliostro got Cagliostro into deep trouble: J.K.) But to me you are the one-and-only literary Cagliostro. Is it true what the small press says about you in capital letters?" By starting like that, Temple unmasks himself—**He is a centrifugal man (Buber)** to whom impulse becomes act.

"It's just another newspaper story. Since there's nothing I can do for you, is there anything you can do for me?" says Kosky. **Expect poison from the standing water. (Blake)**

"I can do a lot for you. Yours is a typical writer's lot," says Temple offhandedly. "You might have heard of our firm's record in helping, among others, to settle out of court the case of the estate of the late Henry James vs. the Downtown Hagiographers, Inc. who claimed that, if James indeed had written by himself *The Ambassadors* (a novel he published in 1903: J.K.) he could not have written by himself *The American* (a novel he published in 1877: J.K.), given the formidable sameness'nd saneness of James and the sudden difference in his writing style!

"He did in fact. We proved it was a stroke of genius," says Temple. "What you might not know is that back in 1867 we also advised Turgenev to clarify in writing once and for all what went on during that 1838 fire on the steamship *Nicholas I* after Prince Dolgorukov resurrected that old rumor about Turgenev's allegedly immoral conduct. As a result. Turgenev first reprimanded Dolgorukov on the pages of St. Petersburg's *Vyedomosti* (No. 186, 1868: J.K.), then, shortly before his painful death (from cancer of the spine caused, no doubt, by the pain he felt from that old rumor: J.K.), dictated in French (he, a Russian writer! writing in French on his deathbed) to his friend Pauline Viardot a story called '*Un Incendie en Mer*' ('A Fire at Sea') translated three weeks before his untimely death into Russian by another woman. This, needless to say, started yet another rumor that it was Pauline Viardot, not Turgenev, who really wrote it."*

"Now I certainly know who you really are," says Kosky, pocketing the man's calling card "as if it were a passport to the wrong kind of sexual desire." (Jay Kay) "I heard you give a talk about your Literary Indebtedness Theory."

"I used the word infringement, not indebtedness," the man corrects him sternly.

"Infringement in what sense?" Kosky won't surrender. "Was it as '1. Disobedience. Noncompliance. Violence. Infraction' [Rodale]?"

"It was infringement as '2. Encroachment. Intrusion. Inroad. Incursion.' [Rodale]" Temple does not mind literary rodeo.

"Never mind 1969," say Kosky. Only the other day I saw that flashing super-station WHM-TV headline: SCANDAL! SCANDAL! SCANDAL! SIM THOMAS TEMPLE ALLEGES JAMES JOYCE IS NOT THE SOLE AUTHOR OF MANY PURPOSEFUL ERRORS IN SPELLING, PUNCTUATION AND SYNTAX FOUND IN HIS ACCLAIMED NOVEL *ULYSSES*, THE VERY ERRORS LITERARY CRITICS CONSIDERED ESSENTIAL TO THE UNDERSTANDING OF THE GREAT NOVEL EVER SINCE IT ATTRACTED THEIR ATTENTION BY ITS OBSCENITY TRIAL. TEMPLE SAYS MANY OF THESE ERRORS WERE CONTRIBUTED TO THE NOVEL NOT BY JOYCE BUT BY MANY OF HIS TYPISTS PRIVATELY HIRED BY THE AUTHOR WHEN HE LIVED IN PARIS. TEMPLE'S ALLEGATIONS STUN LITERARY COMMUNITY."† Kosky recites from (his 69 percent

---

*Bilingual in Russian and French, Turgenev wrote in French "*Monsieur François*," a story then translated into Russian under the title "The Man in the Gray Spectacles." "A Fire at Sea" was published in English in *London Magazine* under the title "An Episode in the Life of Ivan Turgenev"—a title which, unlike "Fire at Sea," suggests an attempt at autobiography, "a far cry from Turgenev's creative intentions. (Niskisko)

†After several professional typists refused to type episodes of Joyce's novel that

recall: J.K.) memory. "That's not just a headline. That's a beheading!"*

"I'm glad you like it." Temple smiles in his own enigmatic style.

"From now on, you might say, my name will be an eternal footnote to the eternal name Joyce, and, in my book, Joyce stands for the temple of Irish Joy. That's my way of being linked to James Joyce," says Temple modestly. "You know, one could stir up quite a stink about any American or foreign writer by merely tracking him or her to their earlier typists. They are all quqs."

"What does the word *quq* stand for?" says Kosky quizzically.

"*Quq* means quote—unquote—quote. A creative association," says Temple. "By tracing what and how authors write to what and how other writers already have written, I can prove that any text (or any author), no matter how recent, new and original, is not original at all, and I can prove it beyond reasonable doubt," he stresses.

"Could you be less eternal and more specific? Where, for instance, do you trace them to?"† asks Kosky.

. . . Although the narrative mind is working in a field of free association, there is really no such thing as free association. Every story is consciously based upon some story already in existence; it adds little increments or manipulates it—reverses the situation of it and puts plus signs for minus signs. (Thornton Wilder)

---

they considered bawdy, the author's friends (as well as part-time friends: J.K.) undertook the task of typing the mammoth manuscript on borrowed typewriters. In the process, they not only added their own punctuation, but they also misspelled some words and corrected the spelling of others that the author intended to be misspelled. (*Times Square Record*)

*To understand better the notion of "extra-literary reality," see "Balzac, James, and the Realistic Novel," by William W. Stowe, in *Literature 1987* (Princeton University Press, 1987). ISBN 0-691-10196-5. (High on my spiritual scale rating: Norbert Kosky.) Arguing equally against the idea of the novel as mere imitation of extra-literary reality and against the currently more widespread notion of the realistic novel as textually elaborated literary system, William W. Stowe maintains that the most successful realistic novels refer both outward to represented reality and back to themselves, commenting on their own techniques and on the process of reading that they require.

†The more one understands an era, the more convinced one becomes that the images a given poet employed, which one assumed to be his own, in fact, were taken almost unchanged from another poet. Images are given to poets; the talent to remember them is far more important than the talent of making them anew. (Victor Schlovsky)

"To some other equally derivative literary floats, you might say."

"Wouldn't you rather try to trace the writer's spiritual origins? Better yet, go to the very source of their narrative talent?"

"Other than '1. habitual facility of execution' (Emerson) and '4. the excitable gift' (Anne Sexton),* nobody knows what talent is. However, thanks to the new wave of literary litigation, searching for quqs has become as important as searching for old-fashioned literary clues used to be."

A young Aziyade, a stowaway from the Topkapi red-light district, her miniskirt barely covering her thighs, struts toward them on a red light, smiling to an invisible video camera.

"Want company?" She mumbles at the world at large.

"No thank you. **We've got each other.**" Kosky quotes somebody.

She widens her stance. "I give good time."

"So does a Swiss watch." Kosky smiles back as he and Temple step around and pass her by as if she were a clumsily stuck quote.

"Scientists claim that Aristotle's works on marine zoology," Temple goes on, "contain detailed closeups, so detailed in fact that they can be seen only with the help of a microscope or with eyesight found in only one nearsighted person in five million. The microscope didn't come into existence until some two thousand years after Aristotle. Ergo: was Aristotle, that pupil of Plato, that tutor to Alexander the Great, a genius also lucky enough to have such rare eyesight? Most unlikely! Somebody else, somebody nearsighted, must have contributed these closeups. But who? Who was the ghost? In this country I was the first to claim that"— he twists his face to give Kosky an impression of an oracle—"ARISTOTLE DID NOT WRITE HIS WORKS ON MARINE ZOOLOGY," he headlines for everyone to hear. Two passersby give him a stunned look, but, being nearsighted, he can't see them.

To see better, Temple takes off his glasses and, blind for a moment, breathes on the lenses and polishes them with his handkerchief. His handkerchief is oily and dirties the glasses. He doesn't notice it; he can't see without glasses.

"Better than most, Aristotle knew how to concentrate, and, quite likely, he was already then a Tantric yogi who knew all there is to know about 'mental breathing.' Concentration was his special eyesight," says

---

*Number assigned according to the listing by Michael McKenna (op. cit.).

301

Kosky. "Being physically nearsighted prompted him to become spiritually farsighted, to see in the water, underwater, and through the water better than the nearsighted Greek divers who did the marine research for him. With his own inner eyes he saw such strange, wondrous creatures as the black eel which is born spontaneously—spontaneously meaning no mother, no father, no fuck—and born from what Aristotle called a superfluous dung of the marshes, his euphemism for a pit of natural manure. Nobody had seen such an 'earth gut' before him—or has seen one ever since!" **Eels are derived from the so-called earth's guts that grow spontaneously in mud and in humid ground. Such earth guts are found especially where there is decayed matter: where seaweed abounds, and in rivers and marshes near to the edge; for it is near to the water's edge that sun heat has its chief power and produces putrefaction. (Aristotle)**

Here Temple and Kosky are accosted by a stunning female stud, a faultless piece of natural British engineering.

"Two handsome men all alone? How about a one-for-two sex escort?" she says (her Gaelic accent one pitch away from the Galician Yiddish). She focuses on Temple, but Temple won't blink. Undeterred, she unsnaps her shirt and displays a pair of symmetrically shaped 38 EE cannonballs.

"I'm just a humble literary missionary," says Temple.

"And I am just his humble literary tool," says Kosky.

"I'm a missionary, too," she snaps back. "Can't you tell by my position?"

Kosky has seen this blondie at least once before but she doesn't know it. Her name is Julia Jones. She is about twenty-six years old, and, in her line of work this super-*dombi* is known as Brighton Blonde. She is the one who, under the spiffy headline FIRM FAVORITE, he had seen photographed at her office desk, next to her firm's phone, dressed in beige, his favorite color, undressing, then naked, save for her black stockings, red garter belt and black stiletto shoes. You just don't wear shoes like that to work in England, unless you work for the British *Escort* magazine—and that's where Kosky saw her first!

"Do you know," Kosky says to Temple loud enough for Ms. Jones to hear, "that these days hypnotism is used to enlarge women's tits? That, in one experiment, some sixty-nine British volunteers were ordered to fantasize about warm fluid, or a heat-lamp, warming their juggs up? That, at the end of some nine weeks, most of these women got the tits they wanted? And even more, bought a bigger bra? That's something, eh?" **Some women managed almost twice these gains.* (Gordon Rattray Taylor)**

His words do the job. Instantly British Julia Jones becomes German Brunhilde. She pulls her pullover down and lifts her skirt up, displaying—as she does in *Escort*—an exquisite crack of natural design. "Was this made by a hypnotist too?" She hypnotizes them both; then, dropping the curtain, she gets lost in the dark.

"I'm sorry Aristotle wasn't around to refute your claim that he was not the author of his zoological works," says Kosky. "Such a claim attempts to turn what's natural in book writing into illegitimate bookkeeping. I'm sure, had he been around, Aristotle could prove you wrong," says Kosky. **But the natural weakness of a great author would be different from the artificial weakness of an imitator, whereas the forger would be unable to maintain this equality in the appearance of his writings. (B. J. Jowett)†**

Temple becomes exasperated. "Oh, yeah? How?" he challenges Kosky. "Would he rent the Hollywood Bowl, invite the public and start writing his books all over again? But what if nobody showed up? Or worse, if they did, would they watch him well enough or long enough to be convinced he got no help from anybody? That there was no hidden transmitter planted in his ear? That he didn't wear special contact lenses? Would they stay watching him for all the years he took to finish his book? And would Aristotle—even he!—survive the impact of such headlines as TELL THE TRUTH, ARI—WHERE DID THE CLOSEUPS COME FROM?" Temple throws his hands in the air. "He could no more prove that he wrote his book than could any other writer!"

They stop at the Facsimile, Manhattan's largest bookshop, owned and operated by the Neo-Fictionist Writers Cooperative. In the brightly lighted window the 2001 laser beams at the first row of current and future bestsellers, while the classics of the past occupy only the far-out rear zone.

---

*It was established that such naturally progressive and lasting enlargement did not depend on the menstrual cycle or weight gain.

†*The Dialogues of Plato*, translated into English with analyses and introductions by B. J. Jowett, M.A., in five volumes, Oxford, MDCCCLXXV, vol. 1, p. 19.

"It's all literary waste," says Temple, assessing the window. "There is no writer, dead or alive, who hasn't involuntarily copied, invaded, or infringed upon the literary folklore.

"And, this I say advisedly, goes for Khazar Bulan, as well as for the *Book of the Khazars* and its author Yehudah Halevi."

"Please—don't touch Yehudah Halevi," moans Kosky. **Thus, Halevi begins by converting the Khazars to Judaism and ends by converting himself to personal Zionism. (Jacob B. Agus)*** "Halevi is my all-time favorite Jewish writer. Without his *Book of the Khazars* ("An argument for the Faith of Israel."—Henry Slonimsky) I would never attempt to write my *The Healer* much less visit the Zion."

"What's more, I can prove it!" barks Temple. "I can either prove that there was an infringement (because the text originated in the folklore), or that there wasn't, since, as most literary folks know, folklore is not original. As you can see, I can testify either for the plaintiff or for the defendant." Triumphantly, Temple, the literary crusader looks at Kosky through his still unclean glasses.

"Indeed, I can," says Kosky. "I've seen it done before."

A rather sordid, commonplace, unedifying incident is somehow transformed—not made better but seen. We are moved not because some general truth has been sounded but because something valid about life has been revealed. (Arnold Kettle)†

"It all depends on which side of the literary litigation I stand," Temple goes on. "Name a writer, and I can prove it to you!" he says. Without waiting for a reply he scans the window—his literary Pripet Marshes— for an easy kill.

"There he is!" he exclaims. "Teodor Jozef Konrad Korzeniowski listed as Joseph Conrad!"

---

*Never was a book so utterly a part of its author as the *Book of the Kuzari* was of Yehudah Halevi. The argument of the book led the author to undertake his famed journey to Zion, which was in truth an act of self-sacrifice, unique in the annals of mankind. Halevi undertook to go to the land then occupied by the Crusaders who had murdered all the Jews in Jerusalem, in order that he might "see" the "glory of God" and then die. The one moment of divine revelation would more than compensate for the death that was sure to follow. . . . Of this preparation, no element was as important as that of a personal pilgrimage to Zion. (Jacob B. Agus, op. cit., pp. 268–269)

†*Man and the Arts: A Marxist Approach*, by A. Kettle and V. G. Hanes. American Institute of Marxist Studies, Occasional Paper No. 8, p. 6.

"Where?" exclaims Kosky, his nose pressed against the window.

"There! Sixth row, right of center, under the big letter C, standing next to Dante whom, by the way, Conrad openly quoted, and next to Dostoyevsky, whom he also quoted, but never openly, and whom he certainly most often misquoted, more than willingly. Conrad, that clever Pole who wrote in English at a late age, and who knew enough than to cling to his old Polish name and be buried—in the nineteenth row!—under the letter K, somewhere between Kosciuszko and Kosinovsky and Kosinski. Besides, who can pronounce Jozef Korzeniowski? It's a tough name"—he scans the window all the way to the eighth row—"as tough as the name Jerzy Kosinski." He grins. "Now how many people can pronounce Jerzy Kosinski the way it ought to be correctly pronounced in his once native Polish?"

"I can," says Kosky modestly. "It is pronounced *Yerzhe Kosheenskyii.*"

"Sure, *you* can. Ever since Poland was officially baptized back in year 966 (a numerically lucky year: J.K.), wasn't Polish the chosen language of the Jewish-Ruthenian, as well as Jewish-Polish, middle class? Such literary giants as Julian Tuwim (1894–1953), Alexander Wat (1900–1967) and Bruno Schulz (1892–1942) wrote *only* in Polish even though everyone of them could write without difficulty at least one other European language. Too bad Conrad (Conrad was not Jewish: J.K.) abandoned his Polish, but then, had he written in Polish, who would read him either in Poland or in his ("neo-native": Jay Kay) England? The Jewish-Ruthenian middle class?" Temple agrees. "If in this country you pronounce Jerzy Kosinski's name as *Yerzhe Kosheen-skyii,*" Temple strains, "no American would know whom you mean— unless you pronounce it as *Jersey Kozensky*—the way a Jersey-clad native American from New Jersey would." He steps away from the window.

"Speaking of Conrad, that Polish-British literary duplex, by the time Conrad said, 'I do not write history but fiction, and I am therefore entitled to choose as I please what is most suitable,' " says Kosky, "he must have realized that, in order to remain creative, choosing Conrad for his regular surname and the English language for his regular writing (he was also fluent in French and in Polish: J.K.) was not a spiritual sin." I had to make material from my own life's incidents arranged, combined, colored for artistic purposes. . . . I am a writer of fiction; and it is not what actually happened, but the manner of presenting it that settles the literary and even the moral value of my work. (Conrad)

"But it sure was an ethnic error! It enraged the Poles!" says Temple.

"Look at the Conrad Affair!* Look at what one wrong interview in London did to his reputation! Look what Eliza Orzeszkowa,† the best-known Polish writer of the period, did with it at home. Single-handedly, Madame Orzeszkowa turned Joseph Conrad—the least-known of the most popular English writers—into the best-known Polish literary renegade—and all this furor *only* because Conrad chose the English language in order to best express what was inexpressible in his Polish soul!"

"There are no renegades in art," says Kosky, "and if fiction isn't art, what is?"

It is particularly true of the renegade that, because of his sharp awareness that he cannot go back, the old relationship, with which he has irrevocably broken, remains for him, who has a sort of heightened discriminatory sensitivity, the background of the relation now existing. It is as if he were repelled by the old relationship and pushed into the new one, over and over again. (Simmel)

Kosky and Temple are interrupted by an intruder—who, as if he were a ghost, insinuates himself between the two of them. The man, call him Pilpul, is a swarthy Semite whose age, here synonymous with excessive "achromatic pallor and wanness of his face, as well as with boundless wisdom" (Jay Kay), stretches from nineteen to sixty-nine.

Standing in front of a bookstore window, Pilpul resembles Israel Kosky; Norbert can almost hear him saying to his son **In a time of dehaga concern yourself with Haggadah. (R. Hayyim)‡** Suddenly Kosky becomes aware of this Pilpul in quite another way. What if?—a thought hits him like a pupil's rod—what if this Pilpul is his father? His father who has now returned from beyond the spiritual Grand Canyon, in order to check on the conduct of his seed. And if that is the case—wait, don't say *if*—it must be! It *must* be, because look what happens! The instant Kosky looks Pilpul in the eye, the blinking of the eye automatically raises the curtain in Kosky's inner theater. On stage, Israel Kosky, age

---

*For a dispassionate assessment of the Conrad Affair (1896–1910), see *The Polish Shades and Ghosts of Joseph Conrad*, by Gustav Morf (1976), pp. 89–96.

†Eliza Orzeszkowa: a Polish novelist known for her over-realistic and most sympathetic portrayal of Polish-Jewish economic misery in pre–World War I Poland.

‡Hagga (Heb.): anxiety. Haggadah (Midrash): a collection of narrative literature occurring in the Palestinian and Babylonian Talmud as well as in independent collections of narrative Midrashim.

fifty-six, and Norbert, age twelve, stand in front of a bookstore window somewhere in Ruthenia, circa 1946. Over the bookstore window, a large sign proclaims in English: WE BUY AND SELL AMERICAN AND ENGLISH BOOKS ONLY.

"The war has ended officially, but it hasn't ended really!" says Israel Kosky to his seed who is still mute. "You must get out of here. Get out the first chance you get!" As Israel Kosky says it, the theater audience must deduce from Norbert's expression (and since he is mute, only from his expression) what the boy thinks. He thinks: here is my father, a man whom I love with my innermost heart of hearts, and barely five years after he had thrown me to the dogs, he wants to send me, his only son, out again.

"When do you want me to go?" Kosky writes on his blackboard, hiding tears, as the audience weeps.

"The minute your English is good enough. Good enough always means being able to write in it. Write, not talk," he stresses. "Any idiot can speak—but how many people can give voice—a shape in words? Readers are people who don't need to hear you speak to know who you are. In America, you will find many such readers—men and women who don't care whether their favorite author was deaf, mute or even dumb—even too dumb to write in English!"*

"Why don't they?" writes Norbert.

"Because readers know that what matters is the voice with which you write—not with which you speak."

("*When will you start yapping again you speakless mute*, the villagers used to jokingly call Norbert Kosky," informs the program.) "You see, by nature, writing is mute—too bad all writers are not," summarizes his father, facing the audience. "Writing speaks," he goes on, "even if the writer remains mute, mute or muted. And, ladies and gentlemen"— his father raises his voice a bit too high—"what matters is the spiritual

---

*As a polyglot in his own right, Israel Kosky knew some six or nine foreign languages, Hebrew, Yiddish, and Sanskrit among them, and knew them well enough to write. Write—but, in accordance with his own dictum, not talk: "I hate the art of conversation, it's the least communicable art," Israel Kosky would often say to his seed. After the War, in his official rank as head of the Ruthenian Linguistic Norm Institute, Israel Kosky ranked English as much easier to learn well enough to write in well, than French, Italian, Spanish and German—not to mention Hungarian, Finnish, Polish and Russian. (Estate Editors)

307

accent of the book, not the writer's own accent. Look at that man Conrad."*

At the end of this moving scene, Israel Kosky kisses his son on the forehead. "In any case, all six doctors who examined my son agree that there's nothing wrong with his head, rated as he is now at 269 I.Q." He addresses the audience. "They say he is definitely not suffering from ordinary mutism, and certainly not from so common aphasia. †

"WHAT IS WRONG WITH ME?" says Norbert with his lips.

His father gives him a long look. "Nothing," he declares after a pause. "Like millions of other children, you were first wronged by the War. Millions of Jewish children, Polish children, Russian, Greek, Gypsy and even German children. Second, like thousands of other kids, you went *speakless* for a while. Ask Professor Stefan Szuman. He knows more silent kids silenced from within by the War—who want to write or draw—than just about anybody."‡

The East European Jews had a predilection for elliptic sentences, for the incisive, epigrammatic form, for the flash of the mind, for the thunderclap of an idea. They spoke briefly, sharply, quickly and directly; they understood each other with a hint; they heard two words where only one was said. Mentioning the more obvious of two premises was considered trite. (Heschel)

---

*(Conrad's English accent was so foreign that nobody in England—not even the foreigners—could understand what he was saying. After hearing him speak, most people who met him didn't believe for a moment that this square Polish squire could ever command *Nostromo*—a British literary vessel—alone, and in English, the only language Conrad claimed he *could* command as a writer!: J.K.)

†Aphasia: "Inability to use and understand written and spoken words" (J. F. Simpson, M.D., and K. R. Magee, M.D., 1970). "This can manifest itself by either talking too much with only a few—usually expletive—words (fluent aphasia), or by hardly talking at all (nonfluent aphasia); by either having too much to say but no vocabulary to say it, a condition usually encountered among the underprivileged, or by having too much vocabulary to express the inexpressible (Jewish aphasia), a condition usually found among victims of trauma—and Jewish survivors of WWII." Agraphia denotes a similar inability to express thoughts in writing.

‡Stefan Szuman: the psychologist of talent, was the prime literary mentor of Bruno Schulz, and assisted him in the publication of his first novel. Writes Szuman: "One day, just when I was resting alone in the hotel lobby, a young man ran into me with a manuscript in hand and told me that, impressed by my lectures, he wanted me to read it." (The young man was Bruno Schulz: J.K.)

"What if I don't want to write in America? What if I want to fish there?" writes Norbert on his blackboard.

"Fishing won't do," declares his father.

"What if I want to ride, not write, in America?" writes Norbert.

"Don't even mention riding," says his father. "Unless your name is Ben Hur and your horse is a camel. Horses and Jews don't mix. Ask Rembrandt! See his most original rendering of an Israelite about to fall off his horse [in Rembrandt's all time classic called *Paysage*: J.K.], then take a peek at his *Good Samaritan*, a painting about what happened to that Israelite who, only one painting earlier, had fallen off his horse—as well as of the painting called *Paysage!*"

"I love riding—riding, not necessarily the horses," says Norbert keeping his inner eye on his riding past: as a boy of nine he used to transport back and forth across yet another marsh of Glynn—call it Gliniszcze—a notoriously kicking mare who once kicked him, the sole navigator, out of his narrow kayak.

"How can a man not love horses?" His father keeps on nagging him.

"It all depends on a man's past, not on his horse," says Norbert (quoting in advance the legendary American sex'nd polo playboy Porfirio Rubirosa: J.K.).

Cossacks from Don told me that it was not the fact that the Jews had beaten them in an agricultural competition which had overcome their former mistrust, but that the Jews had proved themselves to be the better riders than the Cossacks. (Feuchtwanger, 1937)

"I grew up among horses, and so one day I too will be a polo player," says our prototypic Polish rider.* **There are no problem horses, only problem riders. (Mary Twelveponies, 1982)**

"Nothing to it," says his father. "As Rabbi Hayyim has proved beyond any reasonable doubt, people like animals not only because people are good by nature and look a bit like animals; they like them because animals *are* the past or future rehabilitated people! This means that if you like horses, you like their riders, too. Enough said."

My team came off better at polo than I had hoped; . . . I made two

---

*The Polish Rider: a painting by Rembrandt Harmensz van Rijn at the Frick Collection in New York—a museum which rates as No. 6 on Kosky's own list of nine best art museums in the world. "Born in the spiritually unique year of 1606 and dead by 1669, a magic year, Rembrandt had his talent handed to him practically on a numerologically perfect platter." (Israel Kosky to Norbert)

goals myself. . . . I tell you, a corpulent, middle-aged, literary man finds a stiff polo match rather good exercise. (Theodore Roosevelt)*

"I also like skiing. I could ski in America," writes Norbert.

"This, I grant you, is one spiritual activity you could do but only as a sport. And why not? After all, snow is water temporarily solidified. Skiing is floating down. And with so many Jews bled to death in the snowbound Siberia, snow and the Jews are spiritual satellites."

"I'm on very good terms with water, as you know. How about swimming, then?" Norbert now talks only with his lips. "I could be a swimmer, Father! Better yet, I could learn to stay flat on top of the water in order to lower my drag co-efficient—and swim faster than just about anyone."

"Stop talking like Billy Sidis," says his father. "And stop talking about floating. In any case, what do you need floating for?"

"To save myself again from drowning, as I almost did—in a pit of manure."

"What pond of manure? What did you say?" his father recoils. "I can't read your lips. What do you mean by 'again' and 'I almost did'? Who threw you into the pond of manure?"

"Nobody," says our little Hippocampus. † "It was just my new fairy tale."

"Then, enough said about this Cotard's Syndrome,"‡ says his father. The inner theater closes.

---

*In 1986, *Free Polo*, the official publication of the United States Underrated Polo Players Association, celebrated its ninth anniversary issue with the publication of an essay called "Norbert Kosky Solo Polo." And why not? As of this writing Kosky is "the only living author of the only full-size novel in the English language devoted entirely to solo-polo," as it was endorsed by *Free Polo* magazine. (This explains why, since 1978, our riding master, to whom playing polo means having a ball, is, theoretically, at least, entitled to the short-term use of a polo field, polo pony, a polo saddle, a mallet and [obligatory: J.K.] attendance at every polo ball, every American polo-playing social station.)

†Hippocampus: an ordinary sea horse. Also a mythical composite with the head and forequarters of an ordinary horse and the tail of an ordinary fish. Like literature, mythology is a composite. See also Northrop Frye, *Fables of Identity* (1963).

‡"8. COTARD'S SYNDROME, *Le Delire de Negation*. To be or not to be . . . Shakespeare, *Hamlet* (III,i)" (from *Uncommon Psychiatric Syndromes*, op. cit., p. 116). Cotard's Syndrome is a rare condition in which, on the one hand, the patient professes an overriding desire to exit, i.e., "to not exist," but, on the other, believes

Back on the street, the Pilpul abruptly departs without casting a single glance at Kosky or Temple. Clearly strangers are of no interest to him unless they look strange enough. He is right. Why waste time looking in the direction of people you don't want to direct? Or be directed by?

Temple gives the passing Pilpul a passing look. "A Yankiel! Another ex-Ruthenian-Jewish philosophically trained Hasid!" says Temple. "I bet he was born in Poland. Did you know that's where most of them came from?"

"Indeed I do."

Around 962, several Slavonic tribes formed an alliance under the leadership of the strongest among them, the Polans, which became the nucleus of the Polish state. Thus the Polish rise to eminence started about the same time as the Khazar decline (Sarkel was destroyed in 965). It is significant that Jews play an important role in one of the earliest Polish legends relating to the foundation of the Polish kingdom. (Koestler, op. cit.)*

"Didn't you know that since its founding in 966, Poland [and with it Ruthenia: J.K.] was Europe's original ethnic and religious melting pot?" Kosky triumphs easily. "That's where all of my ancestors resided during the last one thousand years!"†

"A lot of assimilated Khazar-Yankiels in your intellectual family, eh?" Temple brightens. "Did you know that Conrad's Yankiel came straight out of the Yankiel invented by Adam Mickiewicz? Just think of the

---

that he or she is immortal—and, *unfortunately*, might never cease to exist, or be able to exit. Here read *The Temptation to Exist* (Seaver Books, N.Y., 1986), written by "the supreme bilinguist" (Niskisko), E. M. Cioran.

*Other Khazar enclaves have survived in the Crimea, and no doubt elsewhere too in localities which once belonged to their empire. But these are now no more than historic curios compared to the mainstream of the Khazar migration into the Polish-Lithuanian regions—and the formidable problems it poses to historians and anthropologists. (Koestler, *The Thirteenth Tribe*, op. cit., p. 147)

†See also *The Reconstruction of Pre-Ashkenazic Jewish Settlements in the Slavic Lands in the Light of Linguistic Sources*, by Paul Wexler, and *Ashkenazic Jewry and Catastrophe*, by Steven J. Zipperstein in *Polin, a Journal of Polish-Jewish Studies*, Vol. One, published annually by the Oxford Center for Postgraduate Hebrew Studies (Basil Blackwell, 1986).

potential embarrassment," Temple goes on. "Think of: CONRAD STEALS YANKIEL FROM ADAM MICKIEWICZ STOP THEFT REPORTED TO LITERARY POLICE BY SIM THOMAS TEMPLE," he recites dreamily, then ponders another literary cloak and dagger. "Conrad said, 'I don't know what Dostoyevsky stands for or reveals, but I do know that he is too Russian for me!' Not true!" Temple exclaims. "Not for a moment. I was the first American to unmask Conrad by pointing out in public that in Russian, *razum* means mind and *raskol* means dissent.* From then on everything became a simple headline: CONRAD'S RAZUMOV IS DOSTOY-EVSKY'S RASKOLNIKOV. Conrad said, 'The word *Razumov* was a mere label of a solitary individuality.' Was it? Or was it derived from Razum-ikhin, another invention of Dostoyevsky?† That's a quq! Dostoyevsky has Raskolnikov say, 'Oh, no, it is not the old hag I have destroyed. It is myself!' and Razumov justifies his crime by reasoning, 'It is myself whom I have delivered for destruction.' How's that for a quq! Like Raskolnikov, his literary identical twin, Razumov, is at the same time plaintiff and defendant, literary prosecutor and literary defense attorney. Quq again!" He pauses to unquote.

Temple continues. "It's not for nothing that Thornton Wilder said, and I quote, 'I steal only from the best department stores, Your Honor,' said the shoplifter to the judge. 'And they don't miss it!' " Temple pauses, pressing the double-space bar on his mental teletype. "Think THORNTON WILDER ENDORSES LITERARY SHOPLIFTING."

"I do think about it," says Kosky. "Such literary thoughts give me the creeps!"

"Careful now! In English *creeps* also means *ghosts*!" Temple stops him by putting his hand on his shoulder: he is an arresting wapentake. "Just think about the potential headlines: GHOSTS GIVE KOSKY HIS LITER-ARY CREEPS!"

Raskol (Russian for schism or dissent) once denoted the "dissenting peasantry of Ruthenia, Podolia, Volhynia and the Ukraine." (Raphael Patai)

Raskolniks: a Russian monastic sect of the Old Believers who believed Moscow was the Third Rome.

Raskolnikov: the hermit-like antagonist of Dostoyevsky's *Crime and Punishment* (1866), the creation of whom led Dostoyevsky to write *The Idiot* (1868–69), "his most personal *opus epilepticus.*" (Niskisko)

†Please check the following: Raskolnikov, the memory of horse episode, 54, 64, 81, 90, 139, 153.

"I don't want to think about such ghosts," say Kosky. "Leave it to the creeps!"

The two men stare at the window in silence. Temple breaks in. "Only Kafka was clever enough to admit in public that his work was a quq; that all writers invade one another by means of, in his own self-incriminating words, 'boisterously or secretively or even masochistically appropriating foreign capital that they had not earned but—having hurriedly seized it—stolen.' " The change in stress indicates that Temple might be quoting Kafka rather than paraphrasing him on the spot. "Believe me, in the literary disco, Lord Jim is only one quq away from Lord Hamlet."

"The general public doesn't know that there's nothing wrong with it," says Kosky.*

"They sure don't," says Temple. "And that's where I come in. I was responsible for such headlines as A. J. LIEBLING SAYS LITERARY BOXING IS SANCTIONED RELEASE OF HOSTILITY. LITERARY WORLD STUNNED."

"I didn't know he meant being stunned by literary boxing," says Kosky.

You've got to—and this is the hardest thing of all—you've got to draw people to you and make them "spill," which is what a detective does in a nastier way. But you've got to have this little trick; it's more than a trick: You've got to have the ability to draw people out. You're happy when you know you've got it, and you're afraid of losing it. (A. J. Liebling)

"Now you do!" Temple exclaims. "How about my other headlines? EUDORA WELTY DESCRIBES HER PROBLEM IN 'WHERE IS THE VOICE COMING FROM?' LITERARY WORLD STUNNED."

"When it comes to such headlines one never knows where the voice is coming from—or even from whom," says Kosky. "Who is the Master's Voice—"

"Oh, yes, one does," Temple interrupts him. "Remember, INTERNATIONAL TEAM OF LITERARY DETECTIVES FOUND THE NAMES OF NINETY-NINE ANONYMOUS FRIENDS JOYCE ROUTINELY HIRED, FIRED AND REHIRED AS HIS PERSONAL TYPISTS AND PROOFREADERS. LITERARY WORLD STUNNED."

"Did you know," he goes on in his loud voice, "that LEO ROSTEN

---

*Writers are interested in folk tales for the same reason that painters are interested in still-life arrangements: because they illustrate essential principles of storytelling. (Northrop Frye)

313

ADMITS HE REWROTE 'CAPTAIN NEWMAN M.D.' TEN, TWENTY, FIFTY TIMES. LEO ROSTEN. LITERARY WORLD STUNNED."

"I suspected something like that—a headline made of nothing," says Kosky. If I were to tell you that chapters of *Captain Newman, M.D.* were rewritten ten, twenty, fifty times, would you believe me? But it's true. I don't mean that I changed a word of a phrase here and there—I mean totally rewritten. One chapter runs about 8,000 words and was rewritten at least fifty times, from first word to last, cut, expanded, reshaped, remolded. (Leo Rosten)

"I only wish I could interview one or two—ideally three—of those copy and line editors Stefan Zweig hired in order to help him at night to his literary bed."

"What for?" asks Kosky.

"For a series for World-Headline-Making WHM-TV Channel Six Literary News, what else? Just think," he says, raising his eyes to the sky, "CESAR BIROTTEAU (1838) GROSSES BALZAC TWENTY THOUSAND FRANCS FOR THE SERIAL RIGHTS ALONE, SAYS STEFAN ZWEIG, THE AUTHOR'S BIOGRAPHER."

"That's not fair," says Kosky. "This was the year of Balzac's financial disaster. Says Zweig (and as always in this text I quote from memory): 'The years 1836 and 1837 were years of strain for Balzac; one disaster followed swiftly upon the heels of another. By normal hazards, if anything in Balzac's life could be judged by normal standards, the year 1838 should have brought the ultimate turning point.' We know it did not."

"How about this one, then," says Temple. "ZWEIG SAYS THAT 'WHERE GOETHE AND VOLTAIRE ALWAYS EMPLOYED TWO LITERARY SECRETARIES WORKING FOR THEM AND CRITIC SAINTE-BEUVE USED A FULL-TIME LITERARY SPADE, BALZAC EMPLOYED SIX PRIVATELY HIRED LINE EDITORS.'"

"That's also not fair," Kosky objects. "I know my Zweig as well as I know Balzac.* On the same page Zweig says that 'Balzac looked after his entire correspondence and conducted all business matters all alone.' This means without a literary agent."

"How about this, then," Temple excretes. "BALZAC BIOGRAPHER (1946) SAYS QUOTE 'BALZAC DID NOT KNOW AND COULD NOT TELL WHAT HE WAS WRITING OR WHAT HE HAD ALREADY WRITTEN.'"

---

*See *Balzac*, by Stefan Zweig (1946), a book Zweig needed a full ten years to leave still incomplete. (J.K.)

"That's the lowest blow." Kosky throws his hands in the air instead of throwing them at Temple. "Says Zweig, and I quote *in good faith*, 'Everything that Balzac wrote had to be set up in print at once because Balzac in the trance-like state in which he worked did not know what he was writing or what he had already written. Even his keen eye could not survey the dense jungle of his manuscripts. Only when they were in print and he could review them paragraph by paragraph, like companies of soldiers marching past at an inspection, was the general in Balzac able to discern whether he had won the battle or whether he had to renew the assault.' End of quote!"

"Can I have one more shot at your Balzac?" Temple hopes he can make it one day to a literary ticker-tape parade. "I bet this headline would finish him off!"

"One more time!" Kosky agrees reluctantly.

This is my work, the abyss, the crater which yawns before me. This is the raw material that I intend to shape. (Balzac)

"O.K. Here I go: HAT, MAT AND GNAT, THE THREE PROOFREADERS BALZAC HIRED FOR HIS BOOK 'LOST ILLUSIONS,' SAY THEY HAVE EACH CONTRIBUTED SOME ILLUSIONS TO EITHER THE AUTHOR'S LIFE OR TO HIS WORK. I'M DISILLUSIONED BY THEM BUT NOT DISHONORED, SAYS HONORÉ DE BALZAC."

"Just as unfair," says Kosky. "Particularly when Matthew Natty, Patrick Fatty and Eleanore Batty, Balzac's most often quoted assistants, subsequently all publicly denied that they had contributed one inch of original wax to Balzac's own. Particularly after Jacqueline Lemonde demolished the whole mini-affair by the longest article in defense of a writer ever published on this side of the infamous Dreyfus Affair."

"In this country, such headlines headline a success story, not necessarily a failure," says Temple. "Is it my fault that writers like you lend themselves to—even invite!—such treatment by the Fourth Estate?"

"Let's hope that there are numerous writers who are beyond approach—approach, not even reproach!" says Kosky, buy he says it most guardedly.

"Oh, yeah? Name one, and I'll do him in in an hour!" Temple challenges.

"Flaubert, that literary suffering supreme!" says Kosky. **I'd rather die like a dog than rush my sentence through, before it's ripe (1852). I only want to write three more pages and find four or five sentences that I've been searching for, nearly a month now (1853). My work is going very** slowly; sometimes I suffer real tortures to write the simplest sentence (1852). I can't stop myself; even swimming, I test my sentences, despite myself (1876). (Flaubert)

"I knew you'd come up with him," triumphs our literary Temple. "Years ago my dispatch from Paris became a headline: MADAME GOSSIP MENSONGE, FLAUBERT'S LAUNDRESS, DECLARED FLAUBERT USED HER AS A PROTOTYPE FOR MADAME BOVARY AFTER THE AUTHOR ADMITS HE HAS PORTRAYED HIS FATHER AS DR. LARIVIÈRE. SAYS FLAUBERT: THIS ACCUSATION PAINS ME MORE THAN BOILING WATER."*

"That's most unfair," Kosky protests. "You can tell that woman bears a bitter grudge. A grudge for being asked by Flaubert, or not being asked, to pose as a *statue vivante* in his bathroom either completely naked or naked and dressed only in the furs of Madame Flaubert. Ask *mon ami* Roland Barthes.† He's the one who knows all there is to know about Flaubert."

For Flaubert . . . writing is disproportionately slow ("four pages this week," "five days for a page," "two days to reach the end of two lines"; it requires an "irrevocable farewell to life." (Roland Barthes)‡

"Barthes? I've killed him with his own words!" Temple jumps with joy. "When his book entitled *Roland Barthes by Roland Barthes* came out, with Barthes's preface saying, 'It must all be considered as though spoken by a character in a novel,' I headlined it EVEN THOUGH SUPPOSEDLY NONFICTION 'ROLAND BARTHES BY ROLAND BARTHES' MUST ALL BE CONSIDERED AS THOUGH SPOKEN BY A CHARACTER IN A NOVEL and finished Barthes in the eyes of his readers who found his words too confusing. I did the same thing to Lowell. I said LOWELL SAYS HIS 'LIFE STUDIES' WERE NOT ALWAYS FACTUALLY TRUE. THERE'S A GOOD DEAL OF TINKERING WITH FACT, HE SAID. YOU LEAVE OUT A LOT, EMPHASIZE THIS AND NOT THAT. YOUR ACTUAL EXPERIENCE IS A COMPLETE FLUX. I'VE INVENTED

---

*"Boiling water spilled by the surgeon on the writer's hand caused a permanent scar and partial paralysis. Traits of Dr. Flaubert have also been discerned in Charles Bovary," says William Amos (op. cit., p. 298).

†"Flaubert and the Sentence," in *New Critical Essays*, by Roland Barthes. Translated by Richard Howard, op. cit., p. 69.

‡"*New Critical Essays* arrives to remind us, as if in valediction, what a consummate literary critic Barthes could be. Ingenious, rigorous, epigrammatic, and genial, his essays on classic French texts are as startling and as fresh as any reconsideration since Hulme, Pound, and Eliot gave European literature their once-over." (John Updike, *The New Yorker*)

"All these made-up admissions stun only the nonliterary world," says Kosky. "The literary world knows all there is to know about the creative *Ordeal by Labyrinth*." (Eliade)

They have reached an impasse. A dark street end; no view to speak of, dim lights, no double-parked car which give signs of life, and no police. Just as well. But here, here of all places. They've got another visitor. She is tall. She is statuesquely Slavic. She wears a low-cut dress, cut below her faultlessly carved breasts. She is also wearing confidence, femininity and Heart of Darkness perfume.

"Are you guys joyfully gay?" She stirs sensuously.

"We're both readers of *Gaja Scienza*,* says Kosky. "What about you Ms. Nietzsche? What do you read?"

The Limits of our Sense of Hearing—We hear only the questions to which we are capable of finding an answer. (Nietzsche, *Joyful Wisdom*)

She glances into the store window. "I read *Two Gentlemen of Verona*—both at the same time. "Are you game?" she asks, as her sculpted breast brushes Temple's arm. It's temple to Temple.

"I'm afraid I'm not," says Temple.

"Then don't be afraid." She dismisses him and focuses on Kosky the entire inner force of her androgynous being. "What about you?"

"I play literary games; I don't gamble," says Kosky.

"It's my gamble but your loss," she says, departing into the night.

"A lovely woman," says Temple. "What breasts! Now that's what I call original. You can't improve on nature!"

"Yes, you can, though not on chromosomes. She is a Queen of Studs,"† says Kosky. " 'A New Potency,' as Philo Judaeus called it."

Expanding every possible care on their outward adornment, they are not ashamed even to employ every device to change artificially their nature. (Philo Judaeus)

They go back past the Jefferson Media Center, and the New Coliseum

---

*Book Three, #108, *New Struggles*: "After Buddha was dead people showed his shadow for centuries afterward in a cave—an immense frightful shadow. God is dead: but as the human race is constituted, there will perhaps be caves for millenniums yet, in which people will show his shadow. And we—we have still to overcome his shadow!" (F. Nietzsche, op. cit., p. 151)

†Queen of Studs: "a male who, created fatally effeminate by fate, as a result dresses and most often overdresses as a femme fatale." (Niskisko)

and, fatigued, sit down on a bench next to the monument of Byron, right in the center of—at this time abandoned—Byron Plaza.

"I made a lot of headlines—and a lot of dough, thanks to this fellow," says Temple, awkwardly facing Kosky. "My best headline was: MOVE OVER BALZAC AND STENDHAL. MOVE OVER PUSHKIN AND NIETZSCHE. DON'T HAVE ANOTHER FIT, FYODOR D. THE SPELL OF BYRON IS EVERYWHERE."*

From the painting of Delacroix to the music of Berlioz, from the poetry of Pushkin to the philosophy of Nietzsche, the spell of Byron is everywhere. Modern fiction would be miserably impoverished without the Byronic hero: Balzac, Stendhal, Dostoyevsky have all used him in crucial roles. (Northrop Frye)

---

*"The desire to see idols hurled violently from their pedestals is strong in all human beings. Byron had been one of the most successful literary men of all times. . . . He was too successful." From *Scandal!*, by Colin Wilson and Donald Seaman (1985), p. 68.

2 5

Carmita, his penultimate Artemis, has passed the test. Too bad that so soon afterward she left town. So begins another beginning of this book's mini-central Sufi-tale.

In no time she would have qualified to become one of his best, and feasibly, most faithful proofreaders—faithful to him, as much as to his text, that is. **Proofreading is perhaps the most undervalued editorial specialty. I don't know of a publishing house that has staff proofreaders; instead proofs are sent out to freelancers who receive about ten dollars an hour for their expertise.... A careless or hurried proofreader can ruin the best editing job in the world.... (Laurie Stearns, "The Importance of Copy Editing,"** *Publishers Weekly,* **1987)**

On June 1, alone and abandoned, Kosky returns from an extended no-phone, do-not-disturb Wednesday-through-Monday weekend in the sea spa of Killcats, a Kosher-yoga meditational spa for safe-sex sexual swappers: an ecstatic experience not unlike the one described by Rupert Brooke.* There, surrounded by the peaceful woods, he was brave enough to confront his newest preoccupation with Sabbatai Sevi as well as with the fear-loaded letters SS.

Then days later, on May 10, Polizeipräsident Schäfer issued the order which closed off the ghetto population from the rest of the world. "Jews," he ordered, "must not leave the ghetto, as a matter of principle. This prohibition applies also to the Eldest of the Jews [Rumkowski] and

---

*Rupert Brooke's poem "The Voice" (published in 1918) speaks of an ecstatic experience in the woods.

to the chiefs of the Jewish police. . . . Germans and Poles," he continued, "must not enter the ghetto as a matter of principle." Entry permits could be issued only by the Polizeipräsident. Even within the ghetto, Jews were not allowed freedom of movement; from 7 P.M. to 7 A.M. they were not permitted to be on the streets. (Raul Hilberg)*

Give this event a high SS mark and mark it for good. (Norbert Kosky, 1987) "This is how, where, and when, and thanks to whom I and my parents in 1939 left The Boat before it was too late. (Boat means Lodz in translation. Norbert Kosky was born and raised in the city of Lodz: J.K.) But the weekend is over, and so our potential World War II Lodz ghetto dweller harnesses his historical memory—and he harnesses it by conveniently reverting to present-tense Tantric Yoga breathing.

Our elegant Mr. Effingham† unpacks, then, at 9:00 P.M., calls his answering service. His suddenly-impressed-with-him answerette tells him that during his absence some nineteen people called. His public number is clearly up! But who were they? he asks her impatiently.

All, if not most of these calls, says the answerette, came from newspapers, news and wire services, TV networks—and radio programs, both domestic and foreign.

"What has happened to you?" the answerette asks him impressed.

"Fame, my fair Medusa," he answers the answerette flippantly. **Beware of fame. Fame means being chosen. Being chosen could mean "the deprivation of all rights NSDAP."** (Israel Kosky to Norbert, circa 1946) Instantly, his mind becomes a flooded Lodz.

October 8, 1939: Propaganda Reichminister Dr. Goebbels, "an ideal father figure to several of his ideal German children" (Jay Kay), visits the city of Lodz, the setting for the soon-to-be-constructed prototypical Nazi wartime Jewish ghetto. During his visit Dr. Goebbels is entertained by his subordinates with on-the-spot entertainment consisting of a minipogrom of local Jews during which Jewish children are thrown out of the windows into the street. After his return, the Office for Racial Policy

---

*"The creation of the ghetto is, of course, only a transition measure. I shall determine at what time and with what means the ghetto—and thereby also the city of Lodz—will be cleansed of Jews. In the end, at any rate, we must burn out this bubonic plague." (Uebelhoer, December 10, 1934)

†"Our elegant Mr. Effingham": The fictional hero created by James Fenimore Cooper in his two novels *Home as Found* and *Homeward Bound*. See *Fenimore Cooper's Libels on America and Americans* (New World).

Affairs issues the following official recommendation: ". . . Both Poles and Jews are to be kept at an equally low standard of living, and *deprived of all rights* in the political as well as national and cultural fields." (November 25, 1939)

Still excited, and very babbly, the answerette says that when calling him, his callers called him by all kinds of names, some of them—was it Mr. Wolfe or Sidis or Thurber?—said something about Mr. Cooper and about Mr. Effingham. Mr. Samuel Kramer (or Cramer) called in reference to a Mr. Cagliostro, and somebody else in reference to Mr. Bawdy Lair. Others—Mr. Edward Browne, among them—spoke about one Mr. Sabbatai Sevi, whom he also called Effendi. All his callers spoke English, she assures him, though most of them spoke with an accent.

May 3rd. The terrible uncertainty of my inner existence. (Kafka, *Diaries*)

Mindless of his hangover, Kosky hangs up in a state of excitement. *Mon cher ami*, this is fame, he tells himself.

Fame as pure and simple as only literary fame can be. This is America of the free. "Free and free-wheeling." (Jay Kay) Forget the dreadful letters SS.* Think of the Free World. Think what the Free World did for the Jews during World War II. Think fame, my friend. Think acting career. Think anything but SS.

Throughout the Second World War the Jewish people adopted the Allied cause as their own; they shut out many thoughts of their disaster and helped achieve the final victory. The Allied powers, however, did not think of the Jews. The Allied nations who were at war with Germany did not come to the aid of Germany's victims. The Jews of Europe had no allies. In its gravest hour Jewry stood alone, and the realization of that desertion came as a shock to Jewish leaders all over the world. (Raul Hilberg, op. cit., p. 671)

And wasn't it only last week that he saw on cable TV the movie he scripted: the one and only starring the one and only late Shaman Peters?

This is an important day. Remember, or learn again if you do not, that on May 3, 1791 (a Polish-American national holiday: J.K.), the

---

*SS Industries, 588–90. SS Stuma, 500. SS Units: Leibstandarte Adolf Hitler, 616; Das Reich, 616; Skanderbeg Division, 451; Totenkopfdivision, 616; 1st Brigade, 216; Kommando 1005, 225–26, 628 647; see also Einsatzgruppen. (Raul Hilberg, op. cit., Index)

Poles enacted the Polish May 3 Constitution which, following the example set by the American Constitution, was, democratically speaking, ahead of any other constitution in Europe. It dared to impose a parliamentary responsibility on each king-appointed minister, abolished *liberum veto*, and confirmed the overall protection by the entire Polish State of the Polish Jews.

No wonder then that there he is, about to march in this May 3 literary parade, so dashing in his custom-made American-Jewish-Polish literary uniform, his every move watched from the grandstands by, among others, Kazimierz Wierzynski, Aleksander Janta-Połczynski, and Aleksander Wat—the grandees of Polish-American cultural grandees.

By now every one of these grandees has defended his work, and occasionally him, against virtually every kind of literary attack. Except one attack—the one which came after all three of them were already dead.

This one took place in 1966, when a Frenchman by the name of (*mon chéri:* J.K.) Pierre Macherey formed a sort of spiritual literary Foreign Legion, which, under the dual leadership of Major Brecht and Captain Benjamin, started an all-out war against **the idea of the author as "creator." For him, too the author is essentially a producer who works up certain given materials into a new product. The author does not make the materials with which he works: forms, values, myths, symbols, ideologies come to him already worked upon, as the worker in a car-assembly plant fashions his product from already-processed materials. (Terry Eagleton)**

However, since literature is folklore, and folklore is not an exact science,* the Macherey insurgency ended as quickly as it had begun, leaving in its wake one more title our gefilte sea lion can now safely wear: the title of an assembly-line literary carburetor (Bernard De Voto,

---

*"Macherey is indebted here to the work of Louis Althusser, who has provided a definition of what he means by 'practice.' 'By *practice* in general I shall mean any process of *transformation* of a determinate given raw material into a determinate *product*, a transformation effected by a determinate human labour, using determinate means (of production).' There is no reason why this particular transformation should be more miraculous than any other" (Terry Eagleton, op. cit., p. 69)

Also, consult "Ideology, Production, Text: Pierre Macherey's Materialist Criticism," a critical review by Francis Barker in *Praxis, Art and Ideology*, starting on p. 99 and ending, appropriately, on p. 109, of part I, No. 5, 1981.

1938) producer, i.e., a maker of a book also defined as "6. the blessed chloroform of the mind" (Robert W. Chambers) and "10. spiritual repasts" (Charles Lamb).*

SS

After a bath which combines a few minutes of his intense no-motion exercises and proper change of clothes, our Second Lieutenant Kosky rushes out of his apartment and heads for the newsstand.

Now Romashov is by himself. Gracefully, dashingly, he approaches the enchanted line. His head is thrown back arrogantly and now his eyes turn left toward the general with a daring challenge. . . . And feeling himself the central object of admiration, the center of a glamorous new world, he says to himself in a sort of iridescent daydream: "Look, look, there's Romashov now!" . . . The eyes of the ladies shone differently when they looked at him. . . . One, two left. . . . At the end of the platoon, walking with supple grace, was a young second lieutenant. . . . Left, right, left. . . . (*The Duel*)

There Yankel, his old pal, greets him with a big smile, a handshake and a hug. "Congratulations!" Yankel repeats. "A small Razumikhin from Ruthenia makes it big in the U.S.A., eh?"

He kisses Kosky on his forehead, then breathing onion, he pulls from a trashcan a copy of the *Courier*, thrusts the paper into Kosky's hand, the trash—or was it the print—soiling his jacket.

"That's the paper with the bullshit about you," says Yankel. "This is your ultimate spiritual *Spectra System.*™ (Polaroid) What a story! It's a story every writer deserves to hear while still alive. Too bad so many of them hear it only in their afterlife!"

"So where's the rest of the big news?" Kosky turns to Yankel. "To start with, give me the stuff about me printed in red ink in the other newspapers."

"What other newspapers?" laughs Yankel. "So far, the *Courier* is the only one."

"Only the *Courier*?" Kosky can't hide his disappointment.

"Only the *Courier!*" Yankel keeps on laughing.

Our literary second lieutenant now moves to the left side of the newsstand and, with martial music blasting from his inner speakers,

---

*As ranked by Michael McKenna, op. cit., p. 25.

unfolds the *Courier*. On the front page he faces a black-and-white picture of himself photographed leaning against a statue of a Swiss Valais-devil. Why the Swiss Valais? Nobody knows, and who cares? He has finally made it. Finally, at fifty, he hits the front page and—rightly so—the front page news hits him right in the face.

The article occupies—"invades" is the word—half of the front page, then goes on—and on—and on inside. The headline in Malison®—a bold typeface printed in Brickbat Red®—underlined with a bold straight line printed on Obloquy yellow® literally spits at one in the face. It reads: THE PUNCTURED BLADDER—DID HE EVER SWIM BY HIMSELF?

The article is written by Theveneau de Morande with Thomas Carlyle, the fat-assed pullover and the straight jacket, two slimy spiders who came to interview him in his apartment and whose yellow-sounding names, until now, rang a bell—a ring, yes, but not an alarm. Now they do. Carlyle is an essayist turned columnist. De Morande, who also writes under the pen name of Aleksei Surkov, is a graduate of the School of Journalism in La Rumorosa, Eastern California: a literary sports reporter with no sport to call his own.

In the short preface to the main piece, Norbert Kosky is described by these two as "our literary Cagliostro; or Ruthenian Copht." He is also named "one of the American moral preservationists," a literary conservative who advocates the takeover of America's "collective soul." Who are these kids kidding? He—a literary conserve—a conservative? And since when is a human soul collective?

Their very names (and other relevant numerological data) now bring to his vanity-filled mind the unforgettable Thomas Carlyle, the British historian known not only for his "most bizarre safe-sex sexual obsessions," "admiringly adds" Jay Kay, but also for his most obsessive History of the French Revolution, not to mention his unexplained hate of Alessandro di Cagliostro. ". . . As a matter of fact," writes W. R. H. Trowbridge, Carlyle's judgment of Cagliostro "is absolutely at sea; and the modern biographers of Cagliostro do not even refer to it."

Theveneau de Morande was, on the other hand, as M. Paul Robiquet says in *Theveneau de Morande*, "from the day of his birth to the day of his death utterly without scruple." Louis de Lomenie, another historian, writes: "There was then in London an adventurer from Burgundy named Theveneau de Morande, who, finding himself without resources, dealt in scandal, and composed gross libels, in which he defamed, insulted, and calumniated, without distinction, all names, if ever so little known, which came under his pen. Among other works, he had published, under the impudent title of *The Journalist in Armor* a collection of atrocities which perfectly corresponded with the impudence of his title." (He is the one and only spiritual food critic who gave the highest Spiritual Service Award to the East Village joint called Count di Cagliostro, owned by the one-and-only Giuseppe Balsamo: J.K.)

So what does de Morande say? And why, as if afraid that he alone won't be taken seriously, must he say it *with* Carlyle?

"This is an analysis of our para-literary Alger Hiss,"[*] says de Morande with Carlyle. "This is a probe into the nature of his floating, which we believe is a crude water act—acted out with the help of a secretly worn, and by now worn-out, wet vest, not unlike one initially invented by Mr. McWaters[†] though perhaps invisible, or hidden inside his empty testicles or sore scrotum."

Writers speak a stench. (Kafka, *Diaries*)

Our fakir keeps on reading and as he swallows every word of their verbal icon—he swallows it the way a fakir swallows a knife or a burning torch—the stench of their seminal sleaze fills his lungs and begins to suffocate him, but only for a moment.

---

[*]Alger Hiss: An American intellectual whose name became synonymous with an abrupt turn in one's career. (*High School Annotator*)

[†]"THE MCWATERS METHOD: But water workouts aren't just for elite swimmers. New equipment and techniques make these soft workouts as accessible as a swimming pool. They can be ideal training for land-played sports, or can be toning and aerobics programs by themselves.

"One person who has given pool exercises some polish and sophistication is Glenn McWaters (yes, his real name), former director of Samford University's Sports Medicine and Fitness Institute in Birmingham Ala. . . . He began supplementing training programs with water workouts, having athletes cling to the side of the pool as they 'ran' like paddling ducks. The workouts were fine, but McWaters thought they could be better if the athletes were in deep water. He tried a variety of devices to position them: ski belts, life jackets, ski vests. 'There were problems with all of them,' said McWaters. 'Either they didn't offer enough flotation, or they didn't offer enough free arm movement.'

"McWaters finally designed his own 'Wet Vest,' a flotation device made of thick foam with Velcro straps to keep it closed and a Velcro crotch piece to keep it from floating up.

"Today, McWaters uses his Wet Vest to train elite athletes. . . ." (From "The Soft Solution: Weightless Workouts," by Paul Perry, *American Health*, June 1986, pp. 78–81)

Having filled the lungs completely with air, the yogi floats upon the water like a lotus leaf. This is plavini kumbhaka. (Hatha Yoga Pradipika)

Nothing else is mentioned. Nothing about health or long life, only a rather extravagant-sounding promise. For we all know, regardless of how deeply we inhale, we will hardly float along like a lotus leaf, no more easily, in any case, than we are used to in swimming. (Hans-Ulrich Rieker)

As a result, within seconds Kosky's raging hypothalamus becomes free of humoral humors, as well as vanity and rumors.*

Go on! Face other players, not yourself. Face the polo field. (Jabar Singh)† A veritable master of the Self, our Raja Yoga is now spiritually ready to stop reading and to throw the paper into the gutter, as well as to throw up. But he hesitates and this means he is not ready. Not yet, anyhow. This time he can't just float. This time—for the first time in years—his inner buoyancy act just doesn't work, and he is about to go under. Oh, yes, don't get me wrong, literary brothers! he sighs. I'm about to go under. To drown in their very words. But—wait—he already slows himself down, aren't these guys writers like you? he asks himself. Yes they are. And now they have written a fiction about your public you, he answers himself too. Still, why would they write it in the first place? Why not? Who knows why? Maybe because the *Courier* is a drag, not only a rag? It is a first-rate newspaper; first, if you recall, is lowest on Kosky's one-to-nine scale. What this means is that the *Courier* is not on the level of, say, such specialty publications as the highly technical *Swimming Pool* magazine—or the most respected *Journal of Toilet Water Safety*.

Then, as if this wasn't bad enough, these two urban swimming-pool rats, these literary bravados, chose to examine our literary waterfowl only in terms of "his self-imposed ability to float, i.e., to *almost* walk on water," an act they call a "nautical fraud."

---

*Activation of the hypothalamus may result in (1) an increased secretion of epinephrine and a subsequent stimulation of the anterior pituitary by the increased circulating epinephrine, and/or (2) the secretion of some humoral agent by the hypothalamus which is then transported to the anterior pituitary. Stimulation of the anterior pituitary results in increased production of thyrotropic hormone with a subsequent stimulation of the thyroid gland. (Mirsky)

†Maharaja Jabar Singh (d. 1986): "an Indian-born aristocrat of the human spirit, Jabar Singh was, until the day he so prematurely passed away, one of international polo's most illustrious field masters." (Kosinski)

Having said this, they now examine his "questionable" (they call it) swimming career in terms of his "questionable" (they call it) past.

"Furthermore," they assume self-righteously, "he must have grown used to such a swimming mode at the outset of his 'pre-set' career when, under the alias of Joseph Weiss-Muller, he published two essays on Swimming Collectives denouncing in them the Stalinist NKVD, and when he supposedly performed his water tricks in the swimming pools frequented by the agents of American Wildlife Agency—all of whom routinely wear secret flotation devices. If they must wear them—they, the ultra-professional swimmers—why mustn't he?" **A very good question. But why of all the people who swim, do you question me? (Norbert Kosky, 1982)**

Next, they talk about him as a writer about to be beheaded by them via their view of his writing. Here their task is all too easy. Here, in IS HE A WRITER OR PESCATOR/BRECHT-LIKE PRODUCER?, they first openly subscribe to Pierre Macherey's notion that a writer—any writer, be it Stendhal or Conrad, Harry Truman or Truman Capote—is at best a "producer."

Now these are hardly serious charges. Under normal conditions, how many normal people would believe that a man who can float can't swim? But these are not normal conditions. Our literary man is a public figure, first made public not by his books but by his public performances in the water. He was made particularly public by recently appearing stripped down to his navel on the very public cover of *MultiSports*, a magazine for which Carlyle once wrote and from which he was asked to resign.

Here, killing Kosky with quq—the made-to-order quotes from Cathy and Teleny, strained and extracted like poison—de Morande leads the reader to believe that Kosky's floating is spiritually suspect because, in de Morande's words, "in the already diluted world of swimmers and water freaks, one who floats so easily must be suspected of relying on someone else's wet vest, not an inner craft of one's own."

It is a hot day, some ninety-six degrees in the shade. It is also a hot story—it gives Kosky a sixty-nine-degree kick. The heat makes the print flow off the page, but not off Kosky. Although Kosky has read T. Carlyle—who hasn't?—he has read about Theveneau de Morande but never bothered to read him. Why bother? The man has established a definite reputation for himself.

Let us begin with one of many aspects of his novels that impress the

reader, the frequent recurrence of material to which one must apply the adjective placental. . . . The symbolism of waters is obviously important to him, and the title of his latest novel is to be that of the series as a whole. (De Voto)

As he keeps on reading, the contaminated print sweats, soiling Kosky's fingers. He begins to leave sweaty fingerprints on everything he touches—on his forehead, on his temples, on his cheeks. The article is a nightmare—grotesque, circumstantial, eager, and untrue. (F. Scott Fitzgerald)

The story continues on the back page (where, as if dropping his patron Carlyle, de Morande refers only to himself). Only now does Kosky notice that the venomous piece goes on for two more pages and that on the last page it is accompanied by a black-and-white six-by-nine photograph on which our literary floatus is photographed clearly sinking in someone else's pool, next to a sculpture of a *Demon of Exile* by Lermontov: a demon who's simply laughing! Is he laughing at Kosky, or at that black photographer sent to Times Square to take Kosky's "sinking" picture?

Kosky is not finished reading. Not yet.

What these two men write about his "literary yoga tantra ways"* has certainly little to do with Shat Kriyas, the all-too-well-known methods of body cleansing. † By daring to question his mastery over his creative breathing, they automatically question the potential mastery of anyone, be it a man, a woman or a child, who might choose to follow in the footsteps of Jay Kay, his prime autofictional character, as well as follow his Tantric footnotes, and to realize—mark this, printer, in the biggest caps you've got—BREATHING DELIVERS OXYGEN TO THE BRAIN AS WELL AS TO THE BODY. BETTER BREATHING MEANS BETTER CONCENTRATION— AS WELL AS SURVIVAL IN A CONCENTRATION CAMP.

---

*The term *yoga* has many meanings. . . . It is etymologically related to the English word *yoke*. It means to harness everything in us in order to gain more insight. Thus the situation, the tantra, in which this is the emphasis is called the Yogatantra. (Chögyam Trungpa)

†See *Integral Yoga Hatha* (op. cit.), Part Eight, called "Shat Kriyas, or the Six Purificatory Exercises," which, in the already quoted Holt, Rinehart and Winston edition, start on p. 166 and on p. 169 actually end. If, however, the Shat Kriyas photographs bother you, read the illustrious but not illustrated *Integral Yoga* by Haridas Chaudhuri (1965). "The best one-volume work on this topic." (Pitirim A. Sorokin)

The Jews, on their part, sensed what the new arrangement had in store for them. There was no hope for anyone who could not work. Only the best and strongest workers, "the Maccabees," as Krüger called them, had a chance to live; all others had to die. There was not even room in the SS-army agreement for dependents. Survival had become synonymous with work. (Raul Hilberg, op. cit.)*

Trust me. Here, Kosky addresses the invisible Public Self. I know what I'm talking about, I'm a writer to whom writing means breathing and breathing means a heavy or light form of writing. It also means avoiding a sense of doom when you realized that something written about you, ABOUT YOU, NOT EVEN BY YOU, caused one of the loudest literary scandals.

While thousands cheer, no one has yet pointed out that his exciting play is not an entirely original creation but an Americanized re-creation, thinly disguised, of James Joyce's "Finnegans Wake." Important plot elements, characters, devices of presentation, as well as major themes and many of the speeches, are directly and frankly imitated. (Campbell and Robinson on Thornton Wilder's Best Play of the Year)†

He is almost there. One more paragraph.

Finding that people would not buy his books . . . which he (J. Fenimore Cooper: J.K.) put forth as outlets for his pent-up indignation—he resorted to his old trick of novel-making, and took advantage of those forms of literature, under which he had become popular with the American public, to asperse, vilify, and abuse that public. But he has not sown the wind without reaping the whirlwind. He is the common mark of scorn and contempt of every well-informed American. The superlative dolt! Did he imagine that he was the only person in the country that

---

*The Jews were grasping labor certificates as a drowning man grasps a straw (emphasis by Norbert Kosky. "Now you know why I learned to float!" he wrote on the margin: J.K.) When, in 1943, an SS officer seized a three-year-old Jewish girl in order to deport her to a killing center, she pleaded for her life by showing him her hands and explaining that she could work. In vain." (This also via the op. cit. of Raul Hilberg: J.K.)

†On the one hand, he gives no credit to his source, masking it with an Olsen and Johnson technique. On the other hand, he makes no attempt to conceal his borrowings, emphasizing them rather, sometimes even stressing details which with a minimum of ingenuity he could have suppressed or altered. (Campbell and Robinson)

had ever traveled in Europe, so that the gross exaggeration of his sketches would not be detected? Did he suppose . . . that his lying would not be tramped under foot? (*New World,* 1843)

Now, mind you, what he reads in their piece about NORBERT KOSKY'S IRREGULAR RELATION TO WATER, and reads it supposedly about himself, pains him the way *succès de scandale* once pained Byron—"that amorous British Stendhal." (Jay Kay) It pains him because, born in Ruthenia, he is only a naturalized American, naturalized, not a natural one. Strictly speaking, this means he is an American spiritual guest, and in his book of etiquette the guest must behave better than a host (better, meaning literary reputation, even when the American hosts often happen themselves to have terrible table manners: J.K.), the two farts de Morande and Carlyle—the farthest literary cry from Byron and Stendhal." (Jay Kay)

After his first feeling of revolt he had come round to the view that only a meticulous precision of statement would bring out the true horror behind the appalling face of things. (Conrad)

Finally, their outpour of Fourth Estate venom pains him, "our venomous literary water snake" (Jay Kay) because of what others might from now on think *not* only of him, but about the nature of water. By others he means not only the learned folks, from Faulkneria, in the American Literary South, but also his new friends from south of the border, those who once left the blue-green Caribbean waters pretty much the way he left the city of Boat and "the mists of Ruthenia" (William Jovanovich, 1987), settled in the waterless Loisaiada* (American-Hispanic pron. *lowereastside*), and have since lost both access to and understanding of soul storming, "a euphemism for floating in ordinary narrative-swimming water." (Jay Kay)

The piece ends as it began: "the whole thing is not a piece of journalistic art, but a free-wheeling act of journalistic dispeller of boredom known as self-flattery." (Jay Kay) The article is not the end of the world. Not even of his world–Old World or New. Is it a case of nerves? He listens to his heartbeat and it beats some 669 words a minute. But then he also begins to listen to his own words—the words of inner defiance—

---

*"To Kosky, whom I've known since 1960, the Lower East Side always encompassed blocks formed between Avenue A and, say, Sixth and Tenth streets, with number ten already leading you out of sexually most tempting Latino-Egyptian atmosphere of Loisaiada." (Kosinski, 1987)

and no longer to their words. Says Dr. Steelheart, his inner-heart physician, "This article must mean as much to you as does the meaning of the article 'the,' which doesn't exist in Ruthenian. Nothing is *the* name of their article." **Suddenly I realized that something had happened to my voice: I tried to cry out, but my tongue flapped helplessly in my mouth. I had no voice. (1965)** Is this PAT,* speaking? PAT, his first wartime lover? Or is it BRAD, his first wartime pal?†

He reads the article again. It is, after all, not an article of faith. It is rather an imitation of "Genius Is Not Enough."‡ Reading it fast, Kosky might have missed a lot. Has he? Just then he hears the voice of the Demon of Exile. Speaking to him, the Demon of Exile always speaks of the nature of exile—never about the nature of self.

Now I had an overwhelming sense of shame greater than any I had felt before. I felt as if I had ruinously exposed myself as a pitiable fool who had no talent and who once and for all had completely vindicated the critics who had felt the first book was just a flash in the pan. (Thomas Wolfe)

Have *they* spiritually trespassed your inner home or not? the Demon asks Kosky. Yes, they have, since I write out of imagination purposefully fused with a purposefully diffused memory. This is fiction of the highest density, he replies. Are they picnicking on your father's grave? he goes on. Yes, they are, Kosky mumbles to himself, even though my father's grave is in Lodz, where in his grave, he sleeps as always, next to my mother who joined him in it exactly ten years later. **And the rumor will go on without my being any part or object of it: a semantic force, negligible and tireless, will prevail over the very memory of me. (Roland Barthes)** But then Barthes also says in his *S/Z*: **There are said to be certain Buddhists whose ascetic practices enable them to see a whole landscape in a beam.**"§ Then curse them, says the demon. Go ahead,

---

*PAT: paroxymal atrial tachycardia. In the ECG record, as a result of rapid heart rate, the abnormally shaped *P* wave becomes literally fat, by being superimposed on the preceding *T* wave.

†BRAD: sinus bradycardia may cause fainting (Adams-Stokes Syndrome) or congestive heart failure. In well-trained—and young—athletes, sinus bradycardia (heart rate below sixty) is seen as a normal manifestation. It can be deadly to literary athletes nearing fifty-five: J.K.)

‡"But works of art cannot be assembled like a carburetor. . . . ("Genius Is Not Enough," by Bernard De Voto)

§S/Z is an attempt at finding the inner Balzac (b. 1799) in the author's text—

give them what they deserve: curse them with the Bogomil curse—the most powerful curse known to a man of the word since Ben Sira,* the very one Henry James used on August 9, 1900: the only curse valid for an indefinite period.

The most flagrant evidence of his incompleteness . . . such organizing faculty . . . as have been applied to the book have come not from inside the artist, not from the artist's feeling nor form and esthetic integrity, but . . . from without, and by a process to which rumor applies the word "assembly." (De Voto) One more look at the article. It is cleverly written. Read carefully and you realize it's just another high tale. He admits that from a purely narrative p.o.v., this is all well done: fusing the few elementary facts of his life with broken fragments of his public self, first so ineptly crystallized—crystallized as well as broken—by various members of the Fourth Estate Amateur Artists Gallery. And now these two pin on him someone else's underpinnings, craftily substituting an ideological beam for a barely noticeable rafter, pulling out the groundwork from the work he had done for W.E.T. (they give him one line of credit for freeing writers from prison without even mentioning by name his prime literary rescue of Omadi) by changing the framework into a frame and calling his entire fictional *oeuvre*, his life's most delicate shell—get this—his World War II skeleton closet!

The piece does all this—and more—and it does it without ranking, evaluating or qualifying. And it does it to him. **But the unsavory notoriety Cagliostro had acquired, the hundred and one reports that were circulated to his discredit and believed, for people always listen more readily to the evil that is said of one than to the good, closed the doors to him. Instead of floating on the crest of the wave he was caught in the under-current. . . . (Trowbridge, 1910)**

"What do you think about the implications of this sinking Lotus hullabaloo?" asks Yankel, raising to Kosky a pair of Jewish eyes.

"I don't like to think about the legal implications," says Kosky. "I would rather take yet another lesson from history." **As long as there are**

---

not life. Conceived by Barthes during the 1968–69 literary seminars he conducted in Paris at the École Pratique des Hautes-Études.

Alphabet of Ben Sira: the earliest Jewish version of the legend of Bogomil, which, conceived around the year 969, was written circa the year 999 of the common era.

readers to be delighted with calumny, there will be found reviewers to calumniate. (Coleridge)

"C'mon, what do you think about it all?" asks Yankel, the street-corner Kafka.

"It's the same thing all over again," says Kosky. I had been banished from society with one stroke. (Kafka) "But, in America, it's a helluva story! But what do *you* make of it?" he asks Yankel point-blank.

Don't be afraid to make mistakes; your readers might like it. (William Randolph Hearst)

"I can't say," says Yankel. "And if I can't say, who can?" he says in his openly amoral tone.

"You can't—or you won't?" Kosky pins the amoral man down. Still pale from (involuntary: J.K.) anger, Kosky voluntarily calms down by brushing a speck of dust from his impeccably beige suit, properly paled by age.

"There's a lot of salt in what they say about you, true, even a touch of vitriol, but I'm not a SALT 69 expert. Talk to the disarmament experts, not me!" Yankel begins to look the other way.

"And I'm not armed, nor do I intend to get armed against them. I'll keep them at arm's length, that's all." Kosky ends galley proof No. 199 on line—would you believe it—lines 188–199!

"Leave me alone, 'As long as there are such things as Printing and Writing, there will be Libels. It is an evil arriving out of much greater good,' " Yankel mutters to himself, quoting from the 1733 credo from the latest issue of *The New York Weekly Journal*. He sits down on a pile of yellowing copies of the old edition of the *Sunday Times Square Record* as if it was a chair.

"Leave me alone. It's bad enough I've got to sell such base rumor-based papers and magazines. But must I talk about it?" Yankel repeats, lifting his pale eyes to the sky, then dropping them all the way to a motto scribbled in permanent red ink on the wall of his one-man free-press enterprise.

We declare for a free press and oppose arbitrary censorship in time of peace. And since freedom implies voluntary restraint . . . we pledge ourselves to oppose such evils of a free press as mendacious publication, deliberate falsehood and distortion of facts for political and personal ends. (Henry Gordon Leach)

"This is a rumor expedition fishing for more rumor," says Yankel.

"Don't touch rumor, not even with a fishing pole," he tells our literary Pole. "Let it starve. What do you think about it, Mr. Fenimore Kuperski?"

"I say: 'no comment'! And don't you dare quote me," says Kosky.

Each Jew has within himself an element of the Messiah, which he is required to purify and mature. The Messiah will come when Israel has brought him to the perfection of growth and purity within themselves. (R. Judah Zevi Streitner, 1910)

"Don't even say 'no comment,' " says Yankel. "Don't even allude to it. Saying 'no comment' to a slander is a comment—it is already spreading the slander. Today they allege you are a floating phantom—tomorrow they'll say you can't swim in the South Street Seaport and after tomorrow they will ask you to play yourself in the *Velizhskaya Drama*.* So what? Do nothing, say nothing, show nothing. Look the other way, the Jewish way of showing—not showing off—the other cheek. Showing off is a comment."

Kosky ponders the alternatives.†

After a few minutes, it was interrupted by a great tumult. Our hero had been quite aware that he was involving himself in an action which, for the rest of his life, might be a subject of reproach or at least of slanderous imputations. He had sent Lodovico into the country to procure witnesses. Lodovico gave money to some strangers who were working in a neighboring wood; they ran to the inn shouting, thinking that the game was to kill an enemy of the man who had paid them. (Stendhal)

"This piece is as phony as your own fiction—but funnier," says Yankel. "Why don't you laugh at it? In our faith, laughing at something written about oneself—even when this something is rumor—is not considered a comment. It is humor. Turning rumor into humor is the only way of making people laugh *at it* and not at yourself, providing, of course, that you've got a sense of humor."

"I write fiction, not humor," says Kosky. "Besides, I am not good at telling jokes." As a result of the great passion and sadness I felt I was all unstrung and my common sense disturbed. Not only the fact of my

---

**Velizhskaya Drama* (The Velizh Affair) by Y. I. Gessen, St. Petersburg, 1904, in Russian.

†One of which is that It's easier to cope with a bad conscience than with a bad reputation. (Nietzsche)

imprisonment but just learning about the unspeakable and abominable deed of which I am accused caused me so much anguish that I lost all sense and judgment. (Diego Alonso, 1515)

An aged matron, aged only in terms of her parched skin, the depth and length and number of her facial wrinkles, approaches the newsstand and casts a starry eye at our literary star.

"Don't I know you from somewhere?" she mumbles through her teeth, each one a knockout of dental repairs.

"Aren't you the writer who played Bachaturian—a bad Red man in the *Oval State*, that six-and-a-half-hour-long movie?"

"Yes, I was," our literary exilechik admits politely.

"He sure was. He is the American literary hedgehog, who eats Spanish fly for breakfast—and you wouldn't want to know why. But if you would, then, here, madam, read all about him," says Yankel, pushing into her hand a copy of the *Courier*.

I came to and this is what happened: A driver (of a carriage) gave me a good whack across the back with his whip, because I had almost fallen at the feet of his horses, despite the fact that he had, it seems, yelled out to me many times. The whip's blow made me so furious that, having jumped to the railings, I angrily ground and (gnashed) my teeth. ~~All around, as to be expected with wild laughter, as to be expected. But as soon as I realized what the point was (then the rage in me immediately disappeared. It seemed to me that it was no longer worth while concerning myself with that). The thought came to me instantly that it would have been a lot better (perhaps even good) if the carriage had crushed me (completely).~~ (Dostoyevsky's *Notebooks*)*

SS

---

*PRINTER: Please retain the text as written: the crossings belong to Mr. Fyodor Dostoyevsky. (Norbert Kosky)

At home, our waterfowl turns into a Blue Jay* turning bluer by the minute.

I am not trying to laugh it off, but it didn't hurt me, it doesn't rankle, I have no vengeful feelings; and in the end I may even get some good from it. (Thomas Wolfe)

He clips from the *Courier* the offensive article, then, always on the defensive, clips from other newspapers their various minuscule or maxiscule accounts of what the *Courier* wrote about him. Just look at these headlines! SWIMMER ACCUSED OF FLOATING: IS HE FLOATING OR SWIMMING? A FLOATER DENOUNCED BY HIS PEERS. WATER CHILD CHILLED. He spread the clips on the floor, then starts reading these assorted potshots usually written by pressroom potheads, each press clipping soiling his hands and further clipping his spiritual feathers.

The greater the truth, the greater the libel: If the language used were true, the person would suffer more than if it were false. (Lord Ellenborough)

The pieces grow less original with every one he reads, but, somewhere in between different "graspings" (Buddha) of his Self, a new spiritual aggregate is emerging. Jay Kay rounds this thought out. †

---

*Blue jay (*Cyanocitta crisata (cc)*): an eastern Nearctic species of race *bromia*. A "common to abundant migrant but resident as a species. Widespread breeder." (John Bull)

†"This is perhaps the most distinctive Buddhist teaching, that suffering is the product of 'the craving of the passions, the craving for existence, the craving for

I believe that art reflects morals and that one cannot renew oneself without living dangerously and attracting slander. (Cocteau)

Is it true, Carlyle and de Morande ask, that Norbert Kosky has said—or admitted—many times that he was a bad swimmer but a good floater? It is true, they admit, yet they call it a "grave contradiction." How can a "bad swimmer" admit to being a "good floater," unless he lost the very notion of water? Didn't he himself once say that his water act has more to do with being a dowser* than it does with swimming as defined by *Swim Swim*, a complete handbook for fitness swimmers by Katherine Vaz and Chip Zempel, with the editors of *Swim Swim Magazine* (1986), a book in which floating is not even listed in the index. Sunchristined swimmers, swimming speed, swimming stress and swimming strokes are. Isn't Kosky's buoyancy act a water circus trick Kosky appropriated from someone else they continue to ask? And so on. And so on. Viewing him from now on (and why not? J.K.) as one more literary P.O.W. (they promptly turn him into their literary P.O.W.) who allegedly once told "a New Yorker who refused to be named, that ever since he set foot on this Continent of the Free, Kosky set his mind on becoming as mystic as was Romain Gary."†

---

nonexistence.' It is, however, far from an obvious truth. (Hear, hear! screams J.K.) Certain cases of suffering are plainly due to craving, namely, those that are due to frustrated desires. Desires may be eased by satisfaction or extirpation; and one may allow that if one stopped desiring, it would amount to preventing all the suffering due to frustration. But this does not prove the general case. . . . Body, feelings, perception, mentality, and consciousness are separate sets of graspings. There is nothing that *does* the grasping. We are the aggregate of the graspings, not something, apart from them, that does the grasping. This is an interesting and startling thought." (Proposed in *Mysticism and Morality: Oriental Thought and Moral Philosophy*, by Arthur C. Danto, 1972, p. 67)

*Dowser: "a water witch bewitched by the presence of water." (Norbert Kosky)

†Romain Gary, a Polish-born French Jew who, while speaking Polish like a Pole, with equal ease wrote his novels either in faultless French or English prose. Gary was the only French novelist ever to win two Prix Goncourt (according to its by-laws this prize cannot be awarded twice to the same writer).

The first time Gary won it for *Roots of Heaven*, one of the novels he wrote under his own name. But then soon after his literary success turned spiritually sour, Gary began to write under a pen name that everyone thought belonged to his nephew— the most adored novelist by the name of Emile Ajar who, after having written a book called *Pseudo*, won the Prix Goncourt for his next novel, *Momo*. After Romain Gary's untimely death, his nephew announced to the world—as part of a pact with

The persistency of Theveneau de Morande's attacks, the ingenuity of his detraction, were more effective than the most irrefutable proof. His articles, in spite of their too-evident hostility, their contradictions, their statements either unverifiable or based on the testimony of persons whose reputations alone made it worthless, created a general feeling that the man whom they denounced was an impostor. Thus the world, whose conclusions are formed by instinct rather than reason, forgetting that it had ridiculed as improbable Cagliostro's own story of his life, accepted the amazing and still more improbable past that Morande "unmasked" without reservation. (Trowbridge)

Now ponder this: how can Kosky defend himself against charges that in his floating he has benefited from others when such a charge is not a charge but a compliment: show him a swimmer who had not benefited from, say, the swimming style of Tarzan, the one and only truly convincing, also known as Johnny Weissmuller, (so convincing, since we see him as he first came to us when we were very young and most impressionable: J.K.) or even from Kosky's own Still-Water float (as it was called in the cover-story pages of a back issue of *Water-Skiing Magazine*)? Still better (since, whether a snow skier or lotus water floater, I am still afraid of both snow and water; Norbert Kosky, 1982) show me a skier, be it a Swiss or a Swede, American or Russian, who has not directly benefited in his (or her: J.K.) snow schussing from **A Fascinating Turn: The Double SS Avalement. (Georges Joubert)***

---

his uncle—that all the Ajar books, including *Momo*, were written by Romain Gary. Romain Gary's very last novel, appropriately called *The Life and Death of Emile Ajar*, was published—as the old fox had planned it all along—"not too long after his Hemingwayesque suicide." (Jay Kay)

*"The technical element which has revolutionized high-level skiing in the last few years is *avalement*. I observed the first movements of this element in Jean-Claude Killy while he was only a 'hopeful' on the French National Team. . . . Since the experiment proved conclusive in 1966, we included many pages about *avalement* in the chapter on competition in *How to Ski the New French Way*. Many of the illustrations were photomontages of Patrick Russell, then a young, unknown, high school racer from the city. Today, *avalement* is known worldwide and the name I gave to it has been universally accepted because of the publication of our last book in nine languages." From *Teach Yourself to Ski*, Aspen Ski Masters Series, by Georges Joubert, translated from the French by Sim Thomas (Aspen, 1966), a spiritually superior book of learning and mastering a sport that does for a skier what

I can say that Georges Joubert taught me everything I know about skiing. Above all, he taught me to continue to search further. Even today, he is the only one capable of correcting my mistakes. Nothing escapes him. He's the wizard of skiing. (Patrick Russell, circa 1969)

Even if, to the public, throwing slime is mud boxing, an entertainment, to Kosky it is not. Much of the propagandist writing of our time amounts to plain forgery. Material facts are suppressed, dates altered, quotations removed from their context and doctored so as to change their meaning. Events which, it is felt, ought not to have happened are left unmentioned and ultimately denied. (George Orwell)

Lost in thought, at this moment—his thoughts are as dense as the Polesie forest and as murky as the Pripet Marshes—our *waterchilde* clearly hears an inner sound. The only tyrant I accept in this world is the "still small voice" within. (Mahatma Gandhi) The sound—it is a beam, not a moan—comes from the spiritual self-service center located at the center of his tower of strength.

A persona is the invoked being of the muse; a siren audible through a lifetime's wax in the ears; a translation of what we did not know that we knew ourselves: what we partly are. (R. P. Blackmur)

Instantly, Kosky eliminates all personal static. Now he can hear the beam, and he listens to it in silence. On his spiritual scale the language of silence is accorded the highest number, 69. And this time the scale is once again checked for authentic representation of his ZEN + JUDAISM + RUTHENIAN + AMERICAN UNIVERSAL (universal, not cosmopolitan, culture).

My time is nearly done. At fifty-seven the world is not apt to believe that a man can write fiction, and I have long known that the country is already tired of me. . . .

My clients, such as they are, are in Europe, and there is no great use in going out of my way to . . . awaken a feeling in this country that has long gone out. (James Fenimore Cooper)

This is the time to decide what binds you to life—whether your soul or your "embattled persona" (Robert C. Elliott) beams the beam.

Quickly, our wizard of literary Double SS skiing turns his thoughts to Alessandro di Cagliostro, whom he had always considered (next to

---

Swift did for literature and Sally Swift does for riding in her *Centered Riding*, SF 309.S995   1985. (Sorry, Sally, but I just love your book: J.K.)

Chairman Rumkowski, the Chairman of the Lodz Ghetto: J.K.) "the most maligned Freemason in modern history. (Israel Kosky)

Now, in order to escape from within the terror of his past World War II Self, he consciously turns his immediate present and past off, and turns to the *plus perfect* past—too old to be threatening. Now is an appropriate time for our maligned man of the hour to imagine not himself as a child, and certainly not as a Jewish boy of six—locked in the ghetto of Lodz, to be then surrendered to the Germans by one's own father: one's own closest kin!—but Cagliostro, that poor devil who only wanted fun and fame, sneaking out of London, his latest exile, after he was accused by Theveneau de Morande, writing in *Courier de l'Europe*, of being Giuseppe Balsamo, an Italian crook who owed money to a great number of people, and who conveniently disappeared from sight by the time de Morande wrote about Cagliostro. In such a way he can, but only through a metaphor (he speaks in metaphors, remember?). He is many things himself, remember? His self is a mixture of Bruno Schulz and Giordano Bruno, of the Zen master Martin Buber, that most spiritual Jewish dean, and Dean Martin, who last sang "the Tango Italiano, the sexy tango."

Again, one wonders why nobody who had known Balsamo ever made the least attempt to identify Cagliostro with him either at the time of the Diamond Necklace trial or when the articles published in Morande's paper brought him a second time prominently before the public. Now Balsamo was known to have lived in London in 1771, when his conduct was so suspicious to the police that he deemed it advisable to leave the country. He and his wife accordingly went to Paris, and it was here that, in 1773, the events occurred which brought them prominently under the notice of the authorities. Six years after Balsamo's disappearance from London, Comte de Cagliostro appeared in that city. How is it, one asks, that the London police, who "wanted" Joseph Balsamo, utterly failed to recognize him in the notorious Cagliostro? (Trowbridge)

Finally, if all this humiliation wasn't final enough for a man of letters—Cagliostro was, above all, a philosophical writer—imagine him and his lovely wife arrested by the agents of the Holy Inquisition, then dumped into the dungeons of the Castle of St. Angelo. Charged with the crime of heresy, supposedly contained in *Egyptian Masonry*, his first, best-known and most stirring book, he was tried and sentenced to death by the Apostolic court. Did I hear you say "heresy" or did you say "hearsay"? asks Jay Kay. How could anybody charge Cagliostro with heresy? The man was a magician, a jack of all spiritual trades, not a heretic! "He was a literary alchemist—not a polemical chemist. He was a man who, masking his Jewishness with an Egyptian-made mask, made himself the best-known self-made man in the eighteenth-century world," writes Jay Kay with passion.

(Kosky to Jacky X, his newest *dombi*like [ideal: J.K.] secretary: Jacky X [he pronounces it *eeks*. J.K.], Did you know that *Spinball Passion* [1978] is one of the two full-size novels [by full-size I mean over 96 pages] ever written in the English language about a man who is defined only as a full-time polo player? The other one, *Last Chukker*, the 79-page-long novel by J. K. Stanford [1954]—is a novel about Jeremy, an all-round polo player who, a master tapper of the ball [see page 69: J.K.], dies in a polo game, in the three-page-long chapter 10?)

According to the infamous Father Marcello, the Inquisition's official biographer-for-hire, when questioned by the Inquisitors, Cagliostro declared that he believed all religions to be equal, and that "providing one believed in the existence of a Creator and the immortality of the soul, it mattered not whether one was Catholic, Lutheran, Calvinist or Jew." As to his political opinions, he confessed to a "hatred of Tyranny, especially of all forms of religious intolerance."

When Cagliostro was in the hands of the Inquisition, his biography was written by one of its hirelings. Naturally, it protrays him simply as a scoundrel and cheat. The obvious question arises: If Cagliostro was such a contemptible rogue, how did he achieve such influence over so many people? Carlyle replies: Because he was one of the greatest cheats that ever lived. (Colin Wilson)

This statement, which Cagliostro made under oath to the Holy Inquisition, did not help him. By then the Holy Inquisition had bought at face value from Theveneau de Morande the claim that, in addition to being a crook, Cagliostro had also been a dangerous revolutionary.

Cagliostro a revolutionary? Nonsense! Don't ask him such questions. He is an artist, a fiction writer, an ordinary storyteller extraordinaire, i.e., a walking self-contradiction. **Awareness and Routines "Some things we say are done 'without conscious awareness' or 'with unconscious awareness,' the latter phrase having on the face of it the aura of self-contradiction. But, of course, we are not contradicting ourselves; but**

341

neither are we observing two quite separate senses of the same term (such as 'sense' or 'cape')." (*Artistry: The Work of Artists*, by V. A. Howard, 1980, p. 169) His only revolutionary act was to write an open *Letter to the French People*, an open letter not a project of a peace treaty or call to arms, in which he said that, even if he were permitted by Louis XVI to return to France (after having already been banned by him), he would only do so "provided the Bastille had been destroyed and its site turned into a public promenade."

And he said it as one who knew what he was talking about. As one who, only a year earlier, had spent with his wife some six cruel months and nine days locked in a cell of the Bastille (their cell was not exactly a king-size suite) awaiting trial on charges of assisting Countess Lamotte in the theft of the diamond necklace of Marie Antoinette,[*] a necklace turned into a royal noose.

On the other hand, the curiosity which Cagliostro had excited was general and anything but reverent. . . . In the drama of the Necklace Affair it was to him that the public looked to supply the comic relief. He was by common consent the clown, the funny man of the play, so to speak. He had but to appear on the scene to raise a laugh, his slightest gesture produced a roar, when he spoke he convulsed the house. (Trowbridge)

And Cagliostro said it as one acquitted of all charges by the French

---

[*]At the height of well-deserved fame and exposure, Cagliostro was implicated in the Diamond Necklace Affair by one Madame de Lamotte, who claimed that having nothing to lose but the money she made from the stolen necklace, the royal necklace disappeared during one of Cagliostro's famous "Now You See It, Now You Don't" seances. As a result Cagliostro and his wife were arrested and kept in the Bastille, and even though they were found not guilty at the trial, their estate was ruined as a result of the long imprisonment. Ultimately, this led to Cagliostro's exile from France, then from England (and his death in Italy at the hand of the Inquisition at the age of fifty-two: J.K.).

(In the final chapter of nihilistic chance: Jay Kay), "Madame de Lamotte was sentenced to be exposed naked, with a rope around her neck, in front of the *Conciergerie* and to be publicly whipped and branded by the hangman, with the letter V (for *voleuse*—a woman thief) imprinted on each shoulder. She was further sentenced to life imprisonment in the prison for abandoned women. She managed to escape from the prison to London, where she was killed by a fall from a window, arranged no doubt, by her husband, who meanwhile sold the necklace and pocketed the money." (H. R. Evans)

court, charges all trumped up, it turned out, by Countess Lamotte. He said it as one who, while testifying in court, preferred to turn himself into a voluntary fool—he was, after all, a past royal court jester!—rather than testify on behalf of the king and Cardinal de Rohan, who were among his personal party-giving close social acquaintances if not his rather close friends (as was the case of Cardinal de Rohan: J.K.). Such harmless clowning made him a hero in the eyes of the French revolutionary crowds, and an honest man in the eyes of Louis XVI, who, responding in kind, had got rid of Cagliostro by exiling him after the trial to the comforts of liberty-ridden royalist London (a fact of royal kindness missed by many anti-royalist biographers of Cagliostro: J.K.).

At the trial, Rohan and Cagliostro were acquitted, but Rohan was ruined, and Cagliostro had become a laughingstock. It was Cagliostro, the innocent bystander, who came off worst of all. And he made a ridiculous impression at his trial, "swaggering, dashing, in a gold-embroidered green taffeta coat," his hair hanging in greasy ringlets to his shoulders. When the judge asked him who he was, he replied in the voice of a ham actor: "I am a noble voyager, Nature's unfortunate child," which drew a burst of laughter. It was time to be quiet, dignified, restrained, if he wanted to emerge from this with a shred of reputation. Instead, he played the mountebank. After the trial, he went to London, banished by the King. (Colin Wilson)

Was it his fault or the fault of his *Letter to the French People* that three years after he had published it, the Bastille fell and became *une promenade publique*?

After all, it was France who fell off the track, not Cagliostro. That's a difference between story and history. Don't argue. Read instead *Heritage: Civilization and the Jews* (Abba Eban, 1984). Jews are part and parcel of their heritage. Heritage defines a Jew. Enough said. Not enough! (Jay Kay) Okay, then. Hear me, and hear me good. I come to speak to you here with a Ruthenian-Jewish voice. It is a voice of most of the Diaspora. To me, my heritage is all important. **Heritage makes a Jew. (Kosinski, 1982)** I come to speak to you not as a potential narrative mini-Disraeli. (Disraeli, printer, not Israeli!) Enough said.

Kosky gets up, kicks the clipping and, pacing back and forth across his room, evokes the past not in order to escape from the present, but in order to confront it—and to confront it spiritually armed.

Picture him, our wandering *Wunderkind*, our literary exile, our Holy

Cagliostro facing his unholy Inquisition, and wondering: will the Inquisition buy de Morande's two-pennyworth charge that Cagliostro is actually Giuseppe Balsamo—in a new disguise?*

What? Cagliostro synonymous with Balsamo? Such claim was first advanced years earlier in Paris by one Sacchi, that little rumormonger, a scrupleless swine hired by some bitter French doctors in Paris in order to discredit Cagliostro—an Egyptian Jew they called him—whose medical practice took their practices from them—they had already lost to Cagliostro Cardinal de Rohan, the Catholic primate of Catholic France— the most important patient a French doctor can have. Now de Morande, the French spy working in London, borrows this long, discrediting claim practically intact from Sacchi, then, in order to discredit Cagliostro in London, prints it intact in his *Courier*, as if it were his own discovery. †
He knows only too well that by hanging on Cagliostro and Cagliostro's wife all the dirty linen that Giuseppe Balsamo and Balsamo's wife once wore in London, he would break Cagliostro by sending after him all the money-hungry, real and self-imagined debtors of Balsamo.

When de Morande kept on repeating his claim that Cagliostro equals Balsamo, Lord George Gordon‡ publicly came to the defense of Cagliostro by writing about him in an open letter published in the *Public Advertiser*.

Now, would Lord Gordon, already so unpopular with the British aristocracy, already in trouble with His Majesty's Government and, as if this was not enough, a convert to Judaism, risk the rest of his reputation by coming to the public defense of Cagliostro, had he or the numerous members of his family and staff for a minute believed Cagliostro was Giuseppe Balsamo? He would not!

---

*Until this day, as a result of the nonsense de Morande wrote about Cagliostro some two hundred years ago, in most biographical dictionaries, Cagliostro is listed either as "Cagliostro (see: Giuseppe Balsamo)," or "Giuseppe Balsamo (see: Cagliostro)," even though there is no doubt that Cagliostro and Balsamo were two different men.—Ed.

†"Under the editorship of de Morande," says Brissot, "the *Courier* tore to pieces the most estimable people, spied on all the French who lived in or visited London, and manufactured, or caused to be manufactured, articles to ruin any one he feared."

‡Lord Gordon was the famous "Lord Crop," as he was called, the past president of the Protestant Association, charged by the British government with fomenting the famous Lord Crop riots and the pillage of London by the mob.

But, argues Kosky's inner inquisitor, to support his claim that Ca-gliostro was Balsamo, de Morande produced three witnesses. When questioned, however, they all refused to swear to it simply because, as they admitted in the court, *they had never seen Balsamo or Balsamo's wife in person!*

Still, who were these three witnesses, asks the inquisitor? And why would they so readily agree to confirm de Morande's story? They were, Kosky answers, in order of appearance, one Monsieur Sacchi, a hack writer who, a few years earlier, during the Diamond Necklace Affair, had published in Paris a libelous pamphlet against Cagliostro—so li-belous that the Parliament of Paris ordered its suppression; a man called Mr. Aylette, a rascally British attorney convicted of perjury and exposed in the pillory; and one Signore Pergolezzi, a corrupt restaurant owner. Enough said? Not enough!

Listen to the verdict of the Apostolic Court:

Giuseppe Balsamo, also known as Cagliostro, attainted and convicted of many crimes, and of having incurred the censures and penalties pro-nounced against heretics, dogmatics, heresiarchs, and propagators of magic and superstition, has been found guilty and condemned to the said censures and penalties as decreed by the Apostolic laws.

Notwithstanding, by special grace and favor, the sentence of death by which this crime is expiated is hereby commuted into perpetual impris-onment in a fortress, where the culprit is to be strictly guarded without any hope of pardon whatever.

Likewise, the manuscript book which has for its title *Egyptian Masonry* is solemnly condemned as containing rites, propositions, doctrines, and a system which being superstitious, impious, heretical, and altogether blasphemous, open a road to sedition and the destruction of the Christian religion. This book, therefore, shall be burnt by the executioner....
(1791)

A shot of Bukharinskaya Vodka 96° prepares Kosky for the rest of Cagliostro's sad story—a story of the first man "in pre–First Amendment literary history" (Jay Kay) sentenced to perpetual imprisonment for mak-ing free use of a bag of literary tricks.

This is the rest of his story:

Cagliostro, who is then forty-eight years old, is locked in the Castle of San Leo, near Montefeltro. Situated on top of the monstrously high rock, as if hermetically sealed by nature, and once the site of the Temple of Jupiter, the ruins of which gave shelter to Saint Leo, the Christian hermit canonized for his ascetic virtues, San Leo became an impregnable maximum-security prison, reserved for the everlasting seclusion of the most dangerous enemies of the Church in order to make certain that such everlasting seclusion was short-lasting indeed.

Imagine Cagliostro, the past prisoner of the Bastille, now incarcerated in San Leo! Imagine him locked up for life in the solitary six-by-nine-foot cell of the maximum security prison as an enemy of God, of the Vatican and all Papal States! How do you deal with a deal like this?

Cagliostro's imprisonment is indeed short-lived. Fearing he might be liberated by advancing troops of the French Revolution, to whom Cagliostro was a comic hero, the Inquisition decides to get rid of him.

Shortly before the Polish legion, the best-known as the bravest as well as the best-dressed foreign legion of the French Revolution, enters San Leo under the command of the Polish hero General Dombrowski (they enter it expressly in order to free Alessandro di Cagliostro, who, when he visited Poland, became a Polish underground hero), he is found dead. Dead at fifty-two, supposedly strangled by his jailer.*

Just think: Cagliostro dead at fifty-two. **He was a pretender to genuine magic and occultism, and not a prestidigitator who exploited his wares for the amusement of the public. (Henry Ridgeley Evans)** He was the first one to use a globe of pure water in order to increase his own clairvoyant powers. A globe of water, not a ball of rock crystal tricksters used to hypnotize their audience.

With another glass of Bukharinskaya Kosky skoals himself in the mirror. Did he skoal Cagliostro? He did not. He just skoaled one who, unlike Cagliostro, decided to do nothing, thus leaving the verdict to the likes of Trowbridge and Evans.

In the year 1910 a voluminous work was published in London which treats the subject of the arch-hierophant of the mysteries in an impartial manner. It is entitled *Cagliostro: the Splendour and Misery of a Master*

---

*"They thought of rescuing him," says Figuier, "and perhaps even of giving him an ovation similar to that which he had received in Paris after his acquittal by the Parliament in 1785. But they arrived too late."

Sentenced by the Inquisition to imprisonment for life, Countess Cagliostro remained confined in the convent of St. Appoloni, a penitentiary for women, in Rome, where she died in 1794, one year before her husband of twenty-two years.

of Magic, by W. R. H. Trowbridge. The author has, in my opinion, lifted the black pall of evil which has rested upon the name of necromancer for a century and more, and has shown very clearly that Cagliostro was not guilty of the hundreds of crimes imputed to him, and, on the contrary, was in many respects a badly abused and slandered man. (Henry Ridgeley Evans)

In the aftermath of what de Morande *with* Carlyle had written about him, Kosky keeps on meditating while walking back and forth across Central Park.* No wonder: nowadays there is always an anxious reporter or reporterette at his door. Meanwhile, in the McLuhanesque electronic village the headlines keep on flashing: POLISH-JEWISH CABALIST NEHEMIAH HA-KOHEN FROM LVOV ALLEGES SABBATAI SEVI IS NOT ORIGINAL JEWISH MESSIAH. † (Such headlines left Sabbatai's devoted friends from Jewish-Ruthenia stoned. Stoned, printer, not stunned.)‡

Promptly Kosky kills the impact of the headline by firing at it his SS-65 and mind-blowing SS-69 inner rockets which, filled with his own

---

*"Mindful walking is frequently used as a main exercise in *vipassanā* meditation, alternating with periods of sitting meditation. . . ." See *"Vipassanā"* ("Development of Insight"), in *Tranquillity and Insight,* by Amadeo Solé-Leris (Boston, 1986).

†For the most complete account of the tumultuous, though brief, life of Sabbatai Sevi, the reader is once again encouraged to consult at this asexual Eastern Standard Time the already referred to earlier *Sabbatai Sevi: The Mystical Messiah,* (1626–1676) by Gershon Sholem, ISBN 0-691-09916-2 "The ISBN numbers alone give this work one of the highest spiritual ratings found in the *Working Papers of Norbert Kosky, 1982* (Jerzy Kosinski).

‡Stoned, no doubt, on *kanabo* (*hemp* in Esperanto) which arrived in Eastern Ruthenia with the first Khazar settlers. See *Plants of the Gods: Origins of Hallucinogenic Use,* by Richard Evans and Albert Hoffman (1979), Plate Cannabis Sativa, p. 96.

unique brand of $C_{23} H_{30} O_7$, known a "Kosotoxi, a yellow physiologically inactive decomposition product" (*Webster's Second International*), blow away the enemy's V-1 rocket filled with mere vitriol No. 1.

These days, after listening to what so many people, friends and no-friends, have to say about him—"unlike Fyodor Dostoyevsky, he does not believe in the spiritual value of cultivating enemies" (Jay Kay)—our floating Messiah imagines himself to be Sabbatai Sevi, Jr., a mini-replica of his beloved Jewish spiritual guru. Now, the senior Sabbatai as you may recall, was the most written-about man in the entire Jewish, and possibly non-Jewish, written history. Written about ever since, at the age of six or nine, he displayed the unmistakable spiritual signs of being able to qualify one day—qualify in terms of the impact his appearances could make on the believers, non-believers and disbelievers who are the worst of them all. In other words, of becoming a potential Jewish Messiah. And if that is not enough, he was written about day by day, by full-time, part-time and certainly overtime professional Talmud-trained Jewish *sophers*, who whether friendly to him or unfriendly watched him around the clock, and who recorded every shift of his spiritual mood by writing about him in various privately kept diaries and letters as well as in official, semi-official and nonofficial secret, semi-secret and candidly confidential accounts.

Meditating in his bathroom, for once with all his inner as well as outer lights on (his bathroom, like everybody else's, at times serves as his most private Kundalini Temple),* Kosky ponders the fate of Sabbatai Sevi—the very Sabbatai Sevi portrayed in the only known likeness ever made of him: he was sketched by an eyewitness in 1666 (the sketch was first made available in print in 1669). Portrayed as a Jewish Keeper of the Book, mind you. As the one who in 1665, in Gaza, "proclaimed himself the Messiah and swept with him the whole community" (Sholem)† and not as one who, in 1666, became a Turk, after an apostasy forced upon him as a result of denunciation by Nehemiah Ha-Kohen, an apostasy which forced upon him the name of Aziz Mehemed Effendi

---

*See "Temples of Three Goddesses," Chapter Six in *Erotic Themes of Nepal: An Analytical Study and Interpretation of Religion-Based Sex Expressions Misconstrued as Pornography*, by Trilok Chandra Majupuria, Ph.D. and Indra Majupuria, M.A. (Nepal, 1981), p. 69.

†See also *The Messianic Idea in Judaism and Other Essays on Jewish Spirituality*, by Gershon Sholem (1971). A "spiritual *must*." (Must, printer, not bust!)

and a new job, that of the Keeper of the Palace Gate! And yet, in spite of such spiteful change in his career, during the spiritually seminal year of 1669 Sabbatai had "dictated a longer version of his doctrine ("entitled *Mystery of the Godhead:* J.K.) to one of his scholarly visitors, or at least induced him to write it down." (Sholem)

Now you know why the dates '65, '66 and, of course, '69 are spiritually sacred to me. (Norbert Kosky, 1982)

Otherwise, our Judah Levi Toba* carries himself not unlike Sabbatai, who at a similar time in his life, according to an Armenian poet, "was found to have relations with women, and the prose account mentions accusations of lewdness and 'debauches with women and with favorites.' These accusations, surprising and strange as they may seem, cannot be dismissed lightly."†

Such a quote implies a lot—but says nothing! What "women"? Which "favorite"? What kind of "lewd relations"? Tell us more, man, or shut up.

"Anything else worth mentioning here?" Dustin notes on the margin. "Not much, really," Kosky writes on the margin back-to-back. "Except that," he reluctantly quotes Sholem, the spiritually shameless rumor-maker, "More recently, important and weighty testimony has come to light, to the effect that Sabbatai prided himself on his ability to have intercourse with virgin women without actually deflowering them."‡

SS

A special-delivery letter from Cathy brings not a letter but a Video-matic™ video cassette. No wonder: Thanks to AIDS (no thanks!), Cathy has become a video addict and a video camera buff.

"I'm so glad you've finally left your lair No. 69 and agreed to serve as New York Library's only nonliterary Lion Fish.§ Now, with your

---

*Judah Levi Toba, also known by his Islamic name Dervish Effendi, was a Jewish writer, poet and a great Kabbalist who lived at the end of the eighteenth and beginning of the nineteenth century and "openly advocated the mystic doctrine of holding wives in common." (Sholem, 1971)

†Gershon Sholem, *Sabbatai Sevi*, op, cit, p. 669.

‡Ibid.

§Lion Fish (*Pterois volitans*): A black-and-white "nightmare fish" which, most frightening in appearance, inhabits the Red Sea.

literary teeth pulled out by all this to Swim or Not to Swim *Affaire*,* you're like every other fish," says Cathy Young, and she says it in her letter. She also says it as the Salt Lake City patroness of books, who as a lion provider, is not inviting Kosky to a Salt Lake City benefit for the Writers Censoring Writers exhibit.

"These days, all arts end up as video, not as *roman*."† She goes on. "No wonder our literary lions are in trouble! And so is the entire literary jungle," she says, sounding like a book censor. "Any day now books will be written not in words but in predigested nonverbal images called up by a writer on a personal LIC—a literary image computer."

The impact of venereal disease is greater than it seems at first. Since some of Cupid's arrows are poisoned, the relations between men and women have become unwanted, belligerent, even sinister. (Schopenhauer)

Quickly, Kosky, our Eastern anti-gadget man, eager to participate in the new sexual gadget nightmare, plugs the tape into his videotape deck attached to his Videomatic TV set. The video letter starts with Cathy. It shows her standing next to her bed in her bedroom. It shows her dressed in a Roman tunic made of rawhide, as she faces the camera or her unseen cameraman.

"Norbert, my love," says Cathy, snapping open one button of her tunic. "This is the boldest moment of your adulthood. Defend yourself against the Ultimate Threat.® By now, the Kosky Float Puzzle is no longer puzzling. **By now what you take for your life others take for fiction, and vice versa."** (Kosky to an interviewer, circa 1985)

On the screen, she moves closer to him. "In one of your books you said that **When their nonsense reaches a level where it finally becomes apparent even to the undiscerning eye, one might as well say to them: the more reckless your statements the better. (Schopenhauer)**

"Plot a real-life potboiler about all this *L'Affaire*. Plot it now in your inner boiler room," she says, splitting even higher her demi-split floor-length skirt, and under it she lets him catch sight of her black fishnet stockings and most of her black-and-white garter belt, as if he were her

---

*Ironically, in French, the word *l'affaire* "usually means something one would rather not have." (Lewinkopf, 1982)

†Ironically, in French, *roman* means *novel*, while in Ruthenian (as well as in Polish: J.K.), as long as it is written *à la Française*, and with the letter S at the end, the word means *have a sexual affair*.

sexual Lexicographer.* "The more depraved and debauched the Kaulini the more she is fit for the rite," writes Mircea Eliade, and who knows more about it than she who is, when it comes to sex, like him, herself a foremost post-modern para-literary Tantric?" (Jay Kay). Instantly, she, his ideal *dombi*, puts on what makes a great impression on him: her fish is about to be caught in her no-fluids-exchange net. "No fluids exchanged? Are you sure? What happened to partaking of wine, fish, meat, grain and *maithuna*—the Tantric sex prerequisites? What happened to his need of Vama Sadhana, most exciting as well as more dangerous sexual practice, "generally practiced only by the more advanced *kaula* initiate and usually at midnight," in the learned words of the already quoted O. P. Jaggi," as quoted by the even more learned sex student. (Jay Kay).

"Plot it anywhere you choose as long as you plot it alone—and for me alone. Aren't you a plot-master? In your book, doesn't plot mean complot? A cabal as well as a premeditated plan of action?" The sole sister (sole, printer, not soul) practically presses her stark-naked breasts against the video camera. "You're Byzantine," the toe teaser says, excitedly slashing the air in front of the camera with her foot clad in a stiletto sex shoe. "Your books are full of sensual secrets, of coded sexual arrangements." She looks at him with suspicion. "Jerzy Andrzejewski† said that a writer's life is purgatory. That only after his death is it known whether his work went to the hell of oblivion or the heaven of remembrance. By turning yourself into the best-known literary profaner— the next best thing to being a certified prophet—you could be certain that the heaven of remembrance is yours for the taking! At your age, what else is there for you to take? By now, you've quite likely gone at least twice over what most people wouldn't think of going even once! And you haven't done once many things others routinely do—like bringing up kids, for instance. Aren't you about to turn fifty-five—and

---

Lexicographer: "A writer of dictionaries, a harmless drudge . . ." And there is the famous polysyllabic definition of *Network* (probably in reaction to Bailey's definition of *Net*—he did not attempt *Network*—as "a device for catching fish, birds, etc."): "Anything reticulated or decussated at equal distances with interstices between the intersections." (*Storming the Main Gate: The Dictionary, from Samuel Johnson* by Walter Jackson Bate, 1975, p. 22)

†Jerzy Andrzejewski: author of *Ashes and Diamonds*, "a marvelously gloomy novel about post-war doom, and a doomed political assassin." (Jay Kay)

creatively turn yourself in? I love you." Cathy stops—and she keeps looking at him, eye to eye with that shrimping starlet look in the frozen shot, frozen purposefully almost until the tape ends, on a brief—all too brief—shot offering Kosky a quickie, a few-seconds-long glance at her torso—a naked torso, a marble torso of *Salt Lake City Venus*. (Or is it the torso of *The Last of the Valerii*, lost in a shoe-shopping sex spree?: Jay Kay)*

Unsettled, Kosky walks away from his desk, and giving in to the urge, he leaves his apartment en route to ponder what to do with his Self, the central issue of his life, and to ponder it where else but in Central Park?

Outside his building, Kosky is accosted by a reporter, a young, baldish man, who promptly introduces himself as **GRIDE, ARTHUR: Arthur Gride, who has an air and attitude of "stealthy, cat-like obsequiousness" and an expression that is "concentrated in a wrinkled leer, compounded of cunning, lecherousness, slyness, and avarice." (Charles Dickens).** The man says he is a free-lance attached to *The Rambler* magazine, a new literary venture devoted to literary obscurity defined as "one of the most pernicious effects of haste." (Samuel Johnson, *The Rambler*, No. 169)

"What do you say about the allegations that you can't swim all by yourself? That, in order to stay afloat, you used some secret floating devices filled with either helium or *ilium*," he mumbles. His tape recorder is already recording. His question says he is a jellyfish posing as a man-of-war.

"I say let *them* say it, particularly since I'm not the only Flotus alive," says Kosky most modestly. **Friends have been amazed at how I manage to stay afloat no matter what position I'm in. I also sleep while floating. . . . (Bunnie Ashley, *Life*, June 1984)**

"Is that all? Under the First Amendment, you're free to tell the truth, you know!"

---

*"A similar internalization of the magic permits us to establish an otherwise unlikely parallel between the two contemporaries Sacher-Masoch and Henry James. In James's early story, "The Last of the Valerii" (1874), there is no ring, and the statue is not even a Venus but a marble Juno. Yet even though James was not working directly with the medieval or Renaissance sources, we know that his story was inspired by Mérimée's "The Venus of Ille," which James had translated in the late eighteen-sixties," writes Theodor Ziolkowski in *Disenchanted Images* (1977), p. 61—"the most enchantingly perceptive study." (Jay Kay)

"The First Amendment guarantees freedom—not truth," says Kosky. "Free means exactly that—free. Free to plot your potboiler on the Upper West Side as much as free to starve to death writing your first novel in the **Trenchtown House, Impasse Row, East Village. (New York magazine)** Writers must be as free to write reporting based on fiction as I am to write my auto-fiction that reads like reporting. That's all there is to it."

It was a random shot, and yet the reporter's instinct was right. Gatsby's notoriety, spread about by the hundreds who had accepted his hospitality and so become authorities upon his past, had increased all summer until he fell just short of being news. Contemporary legends such as the "underground pipe-line to Canada" attached themselves to him, and there was one persistent story that he didn't live in a house at all, but in a boat that looked like a house and was moved secretly up and down the Long Island shore. (F. Scott Fitzgerald)

"But"—the man hesitates—"if what is written about you is not true, hasn't someone abused the public's right to know?"

"Not really. Writing is public. Writers write on public issues, and they publish what they write in public media." With his empty hand he toasts the indifferent public sky.

But we are the sum of all the moments of our lives—all that is ours is in them: we cannot escape or conceal it. If the writer has used the clay of life to make his book, he has only used what all men must, what none can keep from using. Fiction is not fact, but fiction is fact selected and understood, fiction is fact arranged and charged with purpose. (Thomas Wolfe)

"Maybe, like so many other writers, I too can't tell the difference between swimming and floating. Between . . ." Caught in between, he breathes deeply and "takes a sip of the oxygen hidden in the polluted air." (Jay Kay) "What happened to me could have happened to any floater," says Kosky.

Great writers did not invent anything . . . but merely poured their souls into traditional materials and reshaped them. (Thomas Mann)

"It could, but it didn't," says the man talking like Sergeant Fury.

"Whatever was said about me by George P. Flack or Steadfast Dodge could also be said about any parrot fish or porkfish making it in the American post–counter culture literary aquarium," boasts Kosky, **a Master Pilot of somebody else's navigational waters. (Yellow Press Review, 1988)**

354

"I doubt that," says the man. "It certainly couldn't be said about me. I know all there is to know about the composition of water."

"And I don't. I guess I'm still not mature enough," says our Ruthenian Melmoth the Wanderer. (Charles Robert Maturin) **Immature artists imitate. Mature artists steal. (Lionel Trilling)** I still can't tell the difference between the Castle of Otranto* and the Castle of San Leo."

"May I have your permission to quote you?"

"You don't need my permission. You don't even need my quote. **The place to which we are going is not subject to any law, because all that is on the side of death; but we are going to life (Jacob Frank),**" says Kosky. "I'm a public figure. A public figure is a well of news. A sort of public phone number and numbers are **the only universal language (Nathanael West),** as any Miss Lonelyhearts knows. I'm a news bargain. Half price after midnight!" Waving good-bye, our Kosotoxi Man walks away from the toxin.

At the entrance to the park, a young Damsel Fish (*Dascyllus tri-maculatus*) breezes by. Just look at her! She is mouth-watering! She sends him a sexually sleazy skoal which says to our embattled sex soldier SOLDIERS ARE RELEASED FROM THE COMMANDMENTS. †

Kosky examines the woman again. She is a perfect Princesse a l'Odeur de Poisson. ‡ A classic *dombi*. Dressed in a yellow T-shirt which braces tightly her girlish tits, a yellow miniskirt which stresses and contrasts with her dusky Thai-like thighs and yellow shoes, she is **short, blunt-nosed, dusky in color, with a conspicuous white spot on the shoulder**

---

*In his *Castle of Otranto* Horace Walpole, the inventor of the literary Gothic romance, introduced the haunted portrait—"the physical representation of a haunted human soul" (Jay Kay), and a castle patterned after the famous Castle of San Leo made infamous by the Inquisition.

†"Soldiers are released from the commandments." This paradoxical slogan also recurs among the Polish sayings of Jacob Frank, who, born in Podole (Ruthenia), took it upon himself to "complete the mission of Sabbatai Sevi" and led his followers to Esau—a symbol of the unbridled flow of life. "The motto which Frank adopted here was *massa dumah* taken to mean 'the burden of silence'; that is, it was necessary to bear the heavy burden of the hidden faith in the abolition of all law in utter silence, and it was forbidden to reveal anything to those outside the fold." (Sholem)

‡Jean Przyluski: Princes with the Fishy Smell, *Études Asiatiques II* (1925), op. cit. See also pp. 265–69 of his *La Numération vigésimale dans l'Inde*, *Rocznik Orjentalistyczny* (*Oriental Yearbook*), IV (Lwów, 1928).

and another on the forehead. Small specimens do very well in the aquarium. (Axelrod and Vorderwinkler)

Suddenly it dawns on him. This Damsel Fish is Aileen Adamite, "the most exotic looking star of the American Adult Cinema since Hypatia Lee splashed the screen in her *Canterbury Tales*,* in the words of Jay Kay. Of course she looks familiar. Eminently familiar. Familiar meaning he's been with her at least once—"been" meaning he has seen her "open wide," on the giant adult drive-in cinema screen, as he drove by it in his car on New York Thruway 69.

"I'm Aileen Adamite. I come from Altamont, near Asheville, North Carolina," she says. "You must be Norbert Kosky, the guy who floats like nobody but won't swim like everybody. Am I right? Saw you handing out Oscars. Saw you in *Total State*, but read nothing by you. Only about you. Did you really float by yourself, or is it only a newspaper story?" The Damsel Fish gives him a finger—either a sign of victory or an *up-yours!*, "an American gestural skoal" (Jay Kay), and she signs off before he has a chance to skoal her.

The questions, put to me frequently these days by others and by myself, can be summed up this way: If the press is increasingly insistent on knowing more and more about the private lives of people in public life, does it not have the ethical obligation to tell more and more about itself? (A. M. Rosenthal, 1987)†

---

*An adult cinema superstar who starred in her own Hypatia Lee's adaptation of Chaucer's *Canterbury Tales*.

†"On My Mind: Sex, Money and the Press," by A. M. Rosenthal in *The New York Times*, June 7, 1987.

Journalism is literature in a hurry.
(Matthew Arnold) The sudden avalanche of print doesn't pass unnoticed, in a town where, on every street, the First Amendment walks hand in hand with the Sixth. *

The other day, at McCarthy's snack bar, he had run after midnight into two reporters from the Liberty News Service who want to interview him on the spot. That's bad enough. But then, a mere hour later, when, high on Kundalini, he is visiting the editorial photo studios of the newly started *Safe Sex* magazine, he is spotted by—of all people—Thomas Oliver, who, nicknamed Twist, "has singularly twisted the *Six-Sixty Show* into a prime moneymaking World Headline Making TV machine" (Jay Kay), a subsidiary of the All Media MegaCartel, Inc. This is the very man who, being only half-Jewish, is also half-Jewish rumor-conscious. Hence he is also editor-in-chief of *Face*, a sexually sick TV-video magazine.

Oliver, whom Kosky has never met face-to-face, waves at our super star as if the two men had known each other for years by appearing

---

*The free press/fair trial issue is one of the most clear-cut media controversies in America today—and therefore one of the most difficult to resolve. The First Amendment to the Constitution guarantees freedom of the press, and the Sixth Amendment guarantees the right of every defendant to a trial by an impartial jury. As many observers have pointed out, the two amendments are very likely to come into conflict during media coverage of a trial. (George Rodman, *Mass Media Issues*, op. cit., p. 269)

together on *Facing the Nation TV Journal* (once called *Magazine*: J.K).

Disgruntled, Kosky returns home. This tells you! he tells himself. This country is no longer the democracy-ville de Tocqueville saw. This land has become videocracy—a star system spectacle state. (Read "Television Democracy and the Politics of Charisma," by Tim Luke, *Telos*, 1986/87.)

Lavratus Prodeo. I walk disguised. (Descartes) Live your life unnoticed. (Israel Kosky) Easily said, Pa! But it is too late! Kosky's phone does not stop ringing. He is no longer WHO? in the news. He is news. "News breeds news." (Norbert Kosky, 1982)

But then the excited answerette tells him that during his momentary absence, while he was meditating in his bathroom, one Mr. Thomas Oliver, the famous Channel Six TV producer, called him, and calling on Kosky person-to-person, he called on him, imagine—in person!

This is vanity calling!

Excited by the call, which might have something to do with Kosky's forthcoming yellowback* our media midget calls Oliver back.

"You are news," says Oliver. "People want to know you. They want to know how you think and what you think about. I want you to be interviewed on my show by Bridget Bishop" (a former Miss American Waters turned into a 6:00 A.M. newscaster: J.K.).

"People can find out how I think from my books. Preferably from *The Healer*. This is my literary catfish maximus. My life's only *summa summarum*. A book, I'm sure all critics will agree, of relentless and Bosch-like sexual invention," he brags happily.

Oliver isn't happy. "Well, yes." He pauses. "I trust that *The Healer*, your sum total, is just as good as was your performance in *L'État Total*. (I saw you in *Total State* when I was briefly stationed in France.) In French, you were dubbed by some silly sounding French actor."

"Are you sure it wasn't me?" Kosky bluffs.

"Well, no," Oliver laughs. "But I'm sure'm sure you're the man behind *The Healer*—and it's the man, not the healer, whom I want on

---

*Yellowback: A cheap novel so called in England because it was bound in cheap yellow board bindings. In France, the equivalent of it is called *roman de gare* (pron. *Romain de gare*: J.K.), meaning in French a novel one reads between catching (or changing) trains (*roman*:novel, *gare*:railroad station) (a phrase from which Romain Gary coined his name in order to replace his Polish-Lithuanian-Jewish name, and he did, just for the sake of appearing to be French.: J.K.).

my show." Again he breathes in and out heavily. "Now, keep in mind that our average TV viewer spends over one-half of his entire leisure time watching TV—that's over six hours every day! And only with a brief break for a commercial, and that's when it comes time to take a look at one's kids and wife. Six hours of TV, and—brace yourself, Kosky—six hours a year [PRINTER: a year, not a day! J.K.] for reading books [other than the Good Book and textbooks: J.K.]. In this country TV is the healer, not the book," he concludes.

"Six hours would do to read *The Healer*," says Kosky. "Three hours to read it as fiction, and three as nonfiction. Add six minutes for those who in addition to reading it would want to reflect on the narrative nature of both." **Here come I to my own again/Fed, forgiven, and known again/Claimed by bone of my bone again/And sib to flesh of my flesh. (Kipling)**

Oliver laughs smoothly. "Our spectators would prefer to read you— not your book."

"Why would they?" **Writing 1. Chicken scratch. 4. Writing on the wall. (*Synonym Dictionary*)**

"Because you're a head turner. That's why."

"That's no big deal," says Kosky. "It's so much easier to join a controversy than a country club. All this stuff is rumor. In Jewish faith spreading a rumor is a cardinal sin. A sin only a storyteller cannot commit for as long as he prefaces everything he says by saying 'this is only the narrative part of my life's story.' "

With the trials were our ancestors tried and in all of them their fate was not sealed except for the sin of slander. (Torah)

"That's news to me," says Oliver. "I bet it's also news to all those Jews who read Tongue Lashing—Herbert Lashon's syndicated tongue-in-cheek gossip column in *Rumorama* magazine.

"Shame on them!" says Kosky. "As they say in Ruthenia, they've forsaken prophets for profits!"

There is no doubt that one who makes a habit of speaking gossip has thrown off the yoke of Heaven from upon him, for he sins without any benefit to himself, and he is worse than a thief or an adulterer, for they pursue after their pleasure. (Orhot Zaddikim)

"Do you have any other interests you'd be willing to converse about with Bridget Bishop? I mean other than your writing career, which by now has become all too public?"

"Alpine skiing, for one," says Kosky.

"Too seasonal. Besides, a lot of people are afraid of the Alps."

"One-on-one polo for two," Kosky ventures.

"Too limited."

"I also play bowls.* The game of biased balls, not testicles," he interjects quickly.

"Bowls? Too British. Wait! Weren't you once exposed half-naked by *MultiSports* magazine?"

"Sure I was. I was exposed—exposed meaning shown swimming in it," Kosky corrects him. "Swimming. Meaning, I was shown levitating."

"You were what?" Oliver screams into the phone.

"Levitating. When this picture was taken, I was levitating in a Harlem hotel swimming pool."

"Levitating? You mean being suspended above the water?"

"I mean being suspended by it," says Kosky. "I mean doing for hours the dead man's float with one's head way up above the water. I mean sleeping on top of the water, above the literary golden pond, without even once, even in a dream, treading the water with either my hands or feet."

"How come?" asks Oliver. "Is your body full of air—or is your head a balloon?"

"It's neither." Kosky admits modestly. "I'm a Jew and my floating coach—his name is Judah Loew—speculates that certain Jewish bones might be filled with special minerals—with *seikhel*, rather than ordinary *nefesh*.† And then, on orders from my father, I filled my head with the buoyant thoughts of R. Hayyim (the older brother of Judah Loew who wrote such classics as *Well of Living Waters*: J.K.)."

"All these materials might be of interest to your book readers, but not to our viewers," says Oliver. "At six-sixty A.M. most of our viewers are too sleepy to follow such immaterial stuff. All they want to know is what makes you so 'bodiless in water, so ghostlike and immaterial?

----

*Bowls: an ancient game of bias, played with wooden biased balls on a plot of closely mowed greensward, with the purpose of matching the aim—and bias—of the player against that of an aimless but heavily biased ball and then to roll each ball as near as possible to a jack—a small white unbiased ball. (Ed.)

†Judah Loew believed that *nefesh*—a certain Gentile soul—originates in "being here," while *seikhel*, a soul commonly found among the Jews, comes from "being there." (J.K.)

Do you know what it is and what such ghostlike incorporeality stems from?"

"Possibly from the Word. Possibly from being installed here, on earth, as a writer. In Hebrew, I'm told that in Hebrew, a language I don't know, the word *teivah* stands for both ark and word. To the Jew in me, writing means levitating," says Kosky.

" 'Possibly' is not a definite answer," says Oliver. "By the way: after your float'nd swim exposé have you received letters from other levitationists? How many?"

"Unfortunately, not too many. Only six or nine," says Kosky. "They came from Levins, and Loews and even Lewinsky, scattered in aquatic assistance clinics in Salt Lake City and Red Sea Resorts International. Unfortunately, none of these men could levitate. Their mothers, wives and daughters could, but they could not. In any case, not right away," says Kosky. **When man considers the configuration of his body, he is able to reach an understanding of God. (Judah Loew)**

Oliver seems enlightened by talking to a Levin and why not?*

"Not a single one of them could levitate? Does this mean that as a man you're in a class all by yourself? While we would like to promote levitating as a high-class form of physical cult, we can't promote it as a sport as long as you're the only person in that class. What we've got is not a personality cult, but a one-man occult."

"Levitating could be beneficial to those who can't swim because, say, they're afraid of drowning, as well as to the millions of American water-babies† who have had at least one bad experience with water," says Kosky. "Think of those who following crippling joint accidents can no longer move their joints freely. Those who feel themselves no longer able (or willing: J.K.) to swim. Those who cannot enjoy the feeling of being in deep water. Those who fear water. Those who might like to stay suspended in water in a state of spiritual suspension."

"Go on: America is a self-proclaimed nation of self-proclaimed athletes. What about the athletes?"

"Athletes—people who run, or ride—now learned from *American*

---

*Levin (archaic Engl.): to lighten, to emit flashes of light or insight.

†*The Water-Babies*, a story by Charles Kingsley starring one greedy Tom, who's about to become an elf; one supernatural Mrs. Bedonebyasyoudid; and the lazy Doasyoulikes, who devolve from men to apes. (J.K.)

361

Health magazine that 'swimming has become known as the yin to running's yang' [Paul Perry, 1986]," says Kosky. "Think about all those runners who, following the most recent advice of their running coaches, will from now on start improving their land-running act by first running in the swimming pool water: running with their heads up and above the water and their legs under it. Those who, following their advice, do it already—but while wearing one of the many flotation devices, including a Wet Vest.

"Go on. Give me more head. Anything to do with health is good for the health of American TV." Oliver breathes out excitement.

"Well, all these people could now learn how to float in water—be it in a swimming pool or in seawater. To float by themselves. To float at will, this means for hours, without the use of any flotation device. They could do it daily, or once a week, and in the process improve their sexual stamina as well as their running."

Can you walk on water? You have done no better than a straw. Can you fly in the air? You have done no better than a bluebottle. Conquer your heart; then you may become somebody. (Ansari of Herat)

"Go on. Give me more head," says Oliver, who, Kosky can hear, keeps on tapping his thumb on his phone. ("Since we have tapped the phone, and the thumb of his privately hired secretary, we are led to believe that it is not his thumb, but hers, which does all his tapping," in the words of *The Other Village*.) (Typing, printer, typing, not tapping! Enough is enough. Please!)

"Floating makes you high. This calls for the release of the endorphins. The same ones released by a polo player, a swimmer or a marathon runner."

"What kind of high is it? Give me an example!" Oliver coaches him.

"A high felt by a man of sexual extremes. A man who loves to feel as well as to touch. A man who likes the closeup of woman's body, even an extreme closeup offered, say, by a 35mm auto-focus camera equipped with a 69–96mm zoom lens."

"Go on. A closeup of what?"

"Of her womb, of course. **'Woman's womb is mankind's sacred cow.'** " **(Tantra)**

"Just think of the entry to her womb—the entry alone is a masterwork in flesh."

"Careful now, you're getting out of hand," Oliver cuts in. "The subject is your levitation; not your floating into a woman's womb.

Besides, on our show, we don't talk about wombs no more than we do, say, about kayaks."

"Too bad then. No womb-talk, no show. I too know my narrative limits," says Kosky. "I know them only because in *The Healer* I've exceeded them all. I've tasted the flesh of the Sacred Cow. I've transgressed! Two-thirds of flesh is fluid: fluid is diluted flesh. Every athlete knows the importance of fluids—be it a woman's milk or milkatine."

One of the most frequently used methods of arresting the breath is by obstructing the cavum by turning the tongue back and inserting the tip of it into the throat. The abundant salival secretion thus produced is interpreted as celestial ambrosia and the flesh of the tongue itself as the "flesh of the cow" that the yogi "eats." This symbolical interpretation of a "physiological situation" is not without interest; it is an attempt to express the fact that the yogi already participates in "transcendence": he transgresses the strictest of prohibitions (eating cow flesh)—that is, he is no longer conditioned, is no longer in the world; hence he tastes the celestial ambrosia. (Mircea Eliade)

SS

Another telephone call. Since his answering service does not intercept it, unnerved, he does. The instant he picks up the receiver and says hello, our Mr. Trud (*trud* means *work* and *tough* in Ruthenian: J.K.) knows he is in trouble. **Séduisant, sémillant, avec ses costumes couleur vive, ses chemises à fleurs, son oeillet à la boutonnière, M. Trudeau multiplie les foucades. En déclenchant dans le public, surtout féminin, un engouement semblable à la "Beatlemania," qu'on dénomme donc "Trudeaumania." (*L'État spectacle*, op. cit., p. 69)**

"This is Dustin," says the overly familiar voice. "Are you already editing yourself out of—or into—this floating affair?"

"Good to hear you, Reverend Dan,"* says our Golden boy *triomphant*

---

*The Rev. Dan Beach Bradley, M.D., "had an impressive number of accomplishments: He played a leading role in the introduction of printing to Siam; he was the first person to perform a surgical operation in that country, and, after years of futile experimentation, in 1840 he performed the first successful vaccinations for smallpox. His was the first newspaper to be published in Siam, and it was he who printed the first royal decree (against the sale of opium) that came off a press in Bangkok. Most of all, he was a respected friend of the Siamese people, and through

(ibid.). By placing the receiver between his head and his shoulder, he frees his left hand and now trains his binoculars across the street, where, on the sixth floor of a modern co-op, lives Nana, the object of his most irrepressibly fervent interest. NANA: a twenty-some-year-old woman-child who, in white miniskirt, knee-high white leather boots, no blouse or bra, has posed for him from afar. "In the safest display of wet sex this country has ever known." (Jay Kay)

Nana knows that he is watching her: he has been watching her like this at least every other day for some time now. He is not the only one. "He knows it for a fact" (lingo) that she's been watched like this by every male tenant of the Manfred '69 who's been staring at her with the sexual intent of "The Prisoners of Camus and Stendhal" (*French Review*, XLI, 5, April 1968, pp. 649–659. Notes Kosky: "This is the very first time I have ever seen number four and number five dare to separate number six from number nine the way sexual preferences separate on Kosky's Life-Death Spiritual Scale Camus [no. 6] from the number nine he reserves strictly for Stendhal).

Let me repeat: all this has been said over and over. I am limiting myself here to making a rapid classification and to pointing out the obvious themes. They run through all literatures and all philosophies. (Camus)

Now, judging by the books Nana reads (he reads their titles splashed across her bookshelves through his binoculars), he judges her to be like good wine, **a good familiar creature if it be well used. (*Othello*)** She is no stranger to good books either (and, boy, does this turn him on: Jay Kay). On the shelf next to her favorite water chair (the newest gadget which, stemming from water beds, resembles the French-made bidet) stand such classics as Leonard Shapiro's *Russian Studies** (next to the

---

his journalistic enterprises in particular, he looked after Siam's national interest in its relations with France and England." From William L. Bradley's *Siam Then: The Foreign Colony in Bangkok Before and After Anna* (1981).

*"Stalin, whose prime concern after 1923 was to prevent the rise to power of Trotsky and his supporters, readily espoused Bukharin's doctrines. Bukharin's prestige as a theorist and as editor of *Pravda*, the fact that he had stood very close to Lenin after 1921, as well as his influence and reputation abroad through the Comintern (over which he presided) were all of inestimable value to Stalin in routing his 'left' opponents on the basis of the doctrine of 'socialism in one country.' Bukharin, for his part, gave Stalin invaluable service, using every dirty trick in the communist armoury to hasten the defeat and disgrace of Trotsky, Kamenev, and Zinoviev. . . . Yet Bukharin was, after all, a communist, reared in the communist

study about the real-life Bukharin) and *Centered Riding*, by Sally Swift (1985). He sees her as one who knows a great deal about good writing, defined by F. Scott Fitzgerald (a far literary cousin of Camus, but a million light miles away from Stendhal) in his undated letter to Frances Scott Fitzgerald as—just listen to this, please!—"2. Swimming under water and holding your breath." Nana also knows a good deal about the journals of Emerson, where—just think of another coincidence—good writing is defined and rated by the already quoted Michael McKenna, as "1. a kind of skating which carries off the performer where he would not go."

Because of the kind of books she reads, Nana knows enough about life to see that Kosky, "the man who watches her indecently and whose gestures stem from the fusion of Ruthenian sexual humor with the seriousness of purpose of Camus and Stendhal, is no longer ready to either live or die." (Jay Kay) That thanks to the restrictions imposed by AIDS on the freedom of human relations, our sexual exile is considering asking Jay Kay to commit the first sexually motivated suicide in recent literary history." (Jay Kay)

Because of this, Nana says to him—just listen to this!:

I see many people die because they judge that life is not worth living. I see others paradoxically getting killed for the ideas or illusions that give them a reason for living (what is called a reason for living is also an excellent reason for dying). (Camus)

"I get off by being stared at," Nana says sensuously, twitching her heavy lips, but since she is so far away, and the windows of her room are closed, you can't tell whether—sexily supined on her black water bed—the sexpot slut is merely silently moving her lips or saying it to our lip-reader out loud.

"Finally, I've got good news for you," says Dustin. "You're invited to appear on *Controversy!*—television's hottest literary program devoted to the illustrious literary dead. Did you get that? Did you hear that word *dead*? You're the first author to be so honored, and they don't want you to talk about 'Euthanasia and Jacques Monod.'* They want you to be

---

tradition, with little sympathy for democratic niceties." From *Russian Studies*, by Leonard Schapiro, ed. by Ellen Dahrendorf, with an Introduction by Harry Willetts, 1987, p. 296.

*"The 'Right' to Live and the 'Right' to Die: A Protestant View to Euthanasia," by Joseph Fletcher, p. 12; "A Catholic View of Mercy Killing," by Daniel C.

entirely your own free Self," says Dustin who for once calls him not from another writer's home, but from his own, from his beloved Brook Farm near Boston where he lives with his wife of thirty years.

"Why do they want me? Am I already dead to them? Already lost in *The Unbroken Chain* [Neil Rosenstein]. Or is it only in the premature postwritum depression?"* says Kosky, while watching Nana doing her *Myth of Sisyphus* dance.

"These guys say that in one month you got more multimedia attention than other writing fellows get in a lifetime. They say that, to them, as a topic you are as good as Koestler. As good as Romain Gary. As good as Kerouac. As good as Capote—all of whom are, of course, dead."

"But I'm not. I still like sex which isn't stilled. I still like *The Very Best of High Society*. (See collector's edition No. 11, September 15, 1987.) I won't go on the show," says Kosky, with the conviction stemming from Apter Rabbi. † **I had of late been much perplexed in touching the question of whether the Lord guided me in editing my newspapers. I have always asked God by much prayer to guide me, and I have believed much of the time that he would. But occasionally I have fallen into sad doubt about it, and I have felt that my labor was for naught. (Rev. Dan Beach Bradley, 1866)‡**

As if hearing him, Nana gets up from the bed and, like a cordless human doll, she slowly unwinds by taking off her miniskirt. Soon, her

---

Maguire, p. 16; and "Jewish Views on Euthanasia," by Byron L. Sherwin, p. 19. (Ethical Forum: Beneficent Euthanasia. *The Humanist*, Volume XXXIV, No. 4., July/August, 1974)

*See "Postwritum Depression, False Stagnancy and Other Ills Caused by Writing Books," by Charles Salzberg in *The New York Times Book Review*, p. 3, March 1, 1987.

†Apter Rabbi: the spiritual code name of R. Abraham Joshua Heschel from Apt, Poland (1749–1825), "one of the outstanding Hasidic leaders of his generation and a disciple of R. Elimelech of Lyzhansk. He is the ancestor of Professor Abraham Joshua Heschel (1907–1972), one of the most outstanding Jewish thinkers and philosophers. . . . His concept of religion and philosophy found expression in his most popular works in English, *Man Is Not Alone* (1951) and *God in Search of Man* (1956)." See Neil Rosenstein's *The Unbroken Chain: Biographical Sketches and the Genealogy of Illustrious Jewish Families from the 15th to the 20th Century* (New York, 1976).

‡From "Freedom of the Press," a chapter in *Siam Then*, by William L. Bradley, op. cit., p. 129.

body goes through many explicit Yogasanas postures, **practiced till the fruit—Raja Yoga—is obtained."** (Hatha Yoga Pradipika)

Ironically she does them so well that she puts to shame his brand of pleasure-oriented Tantric Yoga. She sits down, letting him, all gaping, gape at her gaping flesh, while with opera glasses in hand, she watches him, "our modern day Tarzan being watched by his first truly safe-sex oriented Tarzana." (Jay Kay)*

"Don't decide. Not yet," says Dustin. "I'll be taking the midday shuttle to New York. See you at your sunken ship," Dustin signs off, and in view of what Nana has just started to do to her own sexually selfish Self, his hanging up is a most welcome hang-up. **We have seen the gutter press in heat, making its money out of pathological curiosity, perverting the masses in order to sell its blackened paper. . . . Finally, we have seen the higher so-called serious and honest press witness all this with an impassiveness—I was going to say a serenity—that I declare stypefying. These honest newspapers have contented themselves with recording all with scrupulous care whether it be true or false. . . . (Zola)**

---

*"In a valuable study, Helmuth Plessner argues that I stand to my body in a relation that is at once instrumental and constitutive: I *have* my body but I also *am* my body. As a result I live in a state of tension with regard to my physical existence, while being at the same time wholly and completely bound to it." From *Sexual Desire: a Moral Philosophy of the Erotic,* by Roger Scruton (1986), p. 69.

367

2 9

In a worn-out fedora, Cranberry raincoat and three-piece Oxford tweed suit, Dustin enters Kosky's apartment **like a New England sailor long months outbound for China on a clipper ship. (Thomas Wolfe)**

In the apartment, Dustin carefully puts down his well-abused attaché case, no doubt a one-to-one latter-day replica of the one used by the Reverend Dan Beach Bradley, M.D., then settles down behind Kosky's desk, mindlessly usurping the place which belongs to the author—and only to him.

In violation of their tradition, a mutual tradition of like and dislike, he starts staring at Kosky with, well, a dose of enmity. (Dustin is a typical Gentile; Kosky a most typical Jew) The two of them face one another face to face (hence, never in hiding: J.K.), not unlike for centuries in Poland did The Church and The Synagogue, until the Nazis bombed them both.

"You don't look too hot," he says, scanning the face of his trembling author.

"Of course I don't," says Kosky. "I'm all stirred up. I no longer can tell water from semen." Kosky says all these hot lines with a static face carved in granite, the face of Janus, one of the most famous dramatists in history.

"Then, quite at random, Dustin starts playing with Kosky's various ball point pens. Randomness is not one of Dustin's characteristics, even though he was at one time (1968–1969) Kosky's editor at the publishing house of Radom, in Radom, New York (Radom, printer, not Random!).

In case you haven't heard, or heard from the nonscholarly herd, Radom was a small provincial town in Poland, where right after the War, in a Poland already brutalized between 1939–45, first by the Nazis, then by the Stalinists, someone started an anti-Jewish riot, brutalizing and killing in the process many of the few Jewish World War II survivors. These riots were clearly started by someone freely distributing to the local thugs the Russian-made vodka Rumorova of double strength and distributed on the double (by someone who, no doubt, was an expert in starting a riot: Jay Kay).*

"You don't look too hot," he says, scanning his author's face as if it were the existentially static face of Camus.

He then casts a glance at the loose mountain of press clippings, and the first headline: HAS KOSKY EVER LIVED IN KAFKA'S BURROW—OR WAS IT THE CASTLE KEEP OF STENDHAL?

"What medicine are you taking against all these *head-aky* head lines?" he asks his sad'nd sexy Stendhal. †

---

*For an objective assessment of the events surrounding these two most tragic events, the reader must consult the various scholarly publications of the American Foundation for Polish-Jewish Studies in Oxford, Boston, Miami, Chicago (and now, finally in New York: J.K.). Among them, *The Jews in Poland*, edited by Chimen Abramsky, Maciej Jachimczyk, and Antony Polonsky, Oxford and New York (a timeless publication) ISBN 0-631-14857-4. This most scholarly work bears on its cover *Day of Atonement*, a 1878 painting by Maurycy Gottlieb, a well-known Polish-Jewish painter (although, like the rest of the most glorious Polish-Jewish history, not well-known enough: J.K.). A painting which, today, would fetch the price, say, of a good Goya. (Goya, printer, not goy!)

Also, the reader is most encouraged to read *Them: Stalin's Polish Puppets*, by Teresa Toranska, translated from the Polish by Agnieszka Kolakowska, illustrated, 1987, and to read the review of *Them* in *Books of the Times*, May 26, 1987.

As a final assignment from this Author to the Reader, please read "Some Final Thoughts on *Shoah*," an article by Father Edward Krause, in *Perspectives* May/June, 1987, p. 580, who, in view of the barbarism of the Nazi—in Nazi-occupied Poland (1939–1945)—asks most wisely: "The fact is, during World War II, Polish Christians were murdered by the thousands along with Polish Jews. To ask why Poles did little to help Jews is rather like asking why the Jews did nothing to assist the Poles. In a world where probably death awaited anyone who contravened Nazi regulations, the Germans could always exact a measure of cooperation from the intimidated populace.... Both Poles and Jews were victims of terror and conditioned by it. (Edward Krause, 1987)

†Sexy Stendhal," as he was called by his contemporaries, was, according to his

369

"Looking at myself 'outwardly inward.' (Tantra) Looking at myself via Proust's "binocular vision"; magnifying lens, monocles, prisms, optical visions, photography, fluoroscopes, et al. (Roger Shattuck)* This, plus taking Emerson Syrup as a matter of course, but only before having intercourse—having my head blown, rather than my forehead blown off."

"Are you too going to do yourself in as Romain Gary did?" The man was something of a hero, a fabulist, a high-flyer, a showman. He thought of himself as "a lyrical clown," or sometimes as "a terrorist of humor." He tried to combine slapstick with sentiment, to mix a vision of real horrors with comic grotesqueries. Am I, with these feeble attempts at characterisation, only trying to protect my soul from his persistent influence? It could be that I am yet again failing to understand, to comprehend what it was in the mind of oldest-friend that led him to lie down on his sofa and fire a bullet into his forehead. (François Bondy, in "Death of a Friend," 1981)

The last phrase unsettles Dustin, who promptly gets up from his settle.

"Emerson?" He wants to be rescued by the example of Emerson, not by the *roman*-writing Romain Gary. (*Roman*, in French: a novel; *romans*, in Ruthenian-Polish: first leading to a sexual affair.) (Just think what a difference one letter s makes!: J.K.) "What strength?"

"*Blotting Books*. Numbers one, two, three and four,"† Kosky reassures him, curling up on his cot, his hands buried in his hair. The first remedy of any victim of defamation is self-help—using available oppor-

---

many women lovers, so preoccupied with the sex act that he crystallized it in his fiction. In his *On Love* he called this process "crystalization Number 69." (J.K.)

*See Roger Shattuck, *Proust's Binoculars: A Study of Memory, Time and Recognition* in: "A la Recherche du Temps Perdu" (1967).

†Emerson's *Blotting Books* are part of Volume VI (1824–38) of *The Notebooks of Ralph Waldo Emerson* (Belknap Press, 1966). "The reasons given for Emerson's early interest in collecting quotations are many: personal inclination, the habit of the age, the ministerial tradition of the Emerson family ('the hereditary use of a text before a discourse,' as Oliver Wendell Holmes put it), the embryonic stirrings of that 'philosophy' of quotation which he later set forth in 'Quotation and Originality.' It is clear, certainly, that Emerson pursued the habit with great diligence." (Ralph H. Orth, 1966) "This is the sort of tribute—yes, tribute!—to my spiritual work No. 9 that I love to read every working day," wrote Norbert Kosky on the margin of his ms. (Jerzy Kosinski, ed., 1987)

tunities to contradict the lie or correct the error and thereby to minimize its adverse impact on reputation. (American Courts)

"Don't you think that by now you have had enough? Shouldn't you pour some water on that silly stuff?" Dustin scores an easy SS.

"I should not. I'm a storyteller. I start inner fires, not extinguish them. Besides, I can't. In my faith, trying to extinguish rumor, even with some Holy First Amendment Wasser™ means *touching* rumor and this means cardinal sin. I'm not a cardinal: I can't afford it. Enough said."

There are four acts that a man performs, the fruits of which he enjoys in this world, while the capital is laid up for him in the world to come. They are: honoring father and mother, deeds of loving kindness, making peace between a man and his fellow, and the study of the Torah which is equal to them all.

There are four things that a man performs, for which punishment is exacted from him in this world and also in the world to come. They are: idolatry, immorality, bloodshed, and slanderous talk which is the worst of them all. (Aboth D'Rabbi Nathan)

"Of course, you know, such reportorial canard has happened before," says Dustin. "After Thomas Wolfe so lavishly dedicated *Of Time and River* to Maxwell Perkins, his editor, 'without whose devotion given to each part of it . . . none of it could have been written,' Bernard De Voto—a self-styled spiritual saboteur who wrote his own little thriller under the pen name of John August—attacked Wolfe on the pages of a literary review, claiming that in his fictional river Wolfe had not swum alone—but was assisted by his own publisher's full-time editorial assembly line called Perky Marx. Assembly line, indeed!" Offhandedly, Dustin glances at the mountain of press clippings—all freshly clipped yet already yellow—spread on his author's rolled-down roll-top desk. Offhandedly, he glances at Kosky. His glance is a reprimand: for a spiritually split second he allows himself to reprimand Kosky, his literary adopted kid, for running too fast across the American literary street—instead of running slowly along it, then for being almost run over by a runaway Tuwim's Locomotive.* As if this near-miss was his kid's fault!

He painted pictures of everything he saw . . . the sun on the sea,/a

---

*Julian Tuwim (b. 1894) was the co-founder of the Skamander literary group. "He was a Polish-Jew who, writing in Polish, has been recognized in Poland as one of the country's six greatest poets," quickly informs Jay Kay.

wind-blown tree,/some flowers in a bowl/and one picture, the best of all,/of a beautiful, brilliant, flamboyant bird./And this picture which he'd painted from his imagination/the painter loved the most. (*The Painted Bird*, by Max Velthuijs, 1971) (Children's story with illustrations: J.K.)

Offhandedly, Dustin says, "And to think that in this town, where everyone saw you float, *ad nauseam*, these two bona fide news porters would dare run around shopping for witnesses ready to testify that you can't swim, then almost run you over with Teleny-What's-His-Name? at least one too many. By now," he concludes, "more poison-pen fiction has been written by others about you and the process of writing fiction than penned by your own poison pen."

There are friendships to one who lives in society; thus our present grief arises from having friendships; observing the evils resulting from friendship, let one walk alone like a rhinoceros. (Buddha)

"I don't mind," says Kosky. "Good poison is hard to find." **The book about mescaline visions interests me a lot. (Bruno Schulz to Stefan Szuman, 1932)**

"Surely you intend to take their floating argument apart?" Dustin is ruffled. "All you have to do is to give one press conference and, with all present, give a demonstration of your Bruno Schulz float, not unlike Bruno Schulz's demonstration of what he meant in his written stories by adding his own *cliché-verre* drawings to them. As your prime-time publishers, we could easily arrange something as visually informative and even release a video-cassette titled "Kosky on Water." That's one. Two, to be on the level with your head well above the level of ordinary swimming pool water, you can then easily ask the members of the press to question you on any subject—and question you pretty much the way one adversary questions another during the American pretrial procedure known as discovery."

"I believe in creation, not in discovery," says Kosky.

S6.9 Privileged Matter

The discovery rules do not permit discovery of "privileged" matter, but they provide no definition of the applicable privileges. The definition must therefore be sought elsewhere. (Civil Procedure, 1965)*

---

*See p. 196 in the already-referred-to "Discovery and Other Pretrial Devices," Chapter Six in *Civil Procedure*, by James Fleming, Jr., and Geoffrey C. Hazard (1965).

"Look, Norbert!" Dustin settles back in the chair. "Unless you'll convince your readers that you can float the way they believe that you do, they might not sufficiently disbelieve what Comrade de Morande and Herr Carlyle said about you."

"I performed as an actor in *Total State* and that's enough," says Kosky. "I write fiction. I don't perform it. Fiction meaning invention, not convention. Fiction meaning making things up, not being made up of them. Fiction meaning a cock-and-bull story as well as a fishy-fish story. Fiction meaning canard, or a maggot. Fiction meaning a unit of spiritual SS or even an SS-run whodunit, not a mere Freudian unit of *Who's Who*. Fiction meaning my own literary crotchet. Fiction meaning my *Autoportrait with* (two naked: J.K.) *Women* (Bruno Schulz, pencil, circa 1934). (Make it a crotch, PRINTER, and call it a DD day!)

"I know what fiction means." Gently Dustin slams his fist on the table. "In case you didn't know, let me remind you that only last week we published the new annotated edition of Steinbeck's *Of Mice and Men* as well as Faulkner's *The Sound and the Fury*."

"I read in *PPN* (*Publishers Pub Newsletter*) that you turned down the new unabridged, author-anointed'nd annotated edition of Thomas Wolfe's *Of Time and the River*. How could you?" Kosky raised his accusing index finger like Vyshinsky raising it against the Total State's "accused Bukharin."

"We simply couldn't afford to publish it. Nobody likes big books anymore. Big meaning heavy. Heavy meaning tough to swim through."

"Still, you just published the six-hundred-page-long book called *Waterfront Means Stagnant Water*."

"That book was a front for a new supratechnicolor film version of *On the Waterfront*, and you know it!" He looks at Kosky thoughtfully. "Speaking of the waterfront, aren't you the waterman who writes from his experience of being—in the deep?" Standing in front of the mirror, Dustin smooths out his unruly hair, which, once a Grand Army, has now been reduced to a few units of gray legionnaires fighting and losing the battle at Alopecia* near the temples.

"I am a dowser, not an expert in hydraulics, remember?" says Kosky.

---

*Alopecia (primary and secondary): "Scarring of the scalp with consequent baldness as the result of a severe attack of favus when a child." From *The Index of Differential Diagnosis*, op. cit., Fig. 10, p. 9.

Like exercise without movement (Sri Swami Rama) **and sex magic (Louis T. Culling)** as well as the ancient practice of Safe Sex 69 known as Karezza, dowsing depends on one's internal radiation. Internal often means infernal; one stemming, as in my case at least, from one of my own novels called, for some reason (Kosky did not know why), *Aus den Feuern*—'Out of the fires,' even though I don't know German. Just as well, I feel burned out. I've been wounded by fire, and my creative juices have all dried up like Baudelaire's *Evil Flowers*. I've got no spiritual steam left in me 'cause that fire dried up my spiritual water. All I've got is semen." **Well, semen ain't water. (Mary Waters) Can't you get it, man? (Lingo)**

"Careful. Any minute now de Morande will accuse you of spreading radioactive dust." Here Dustin speaks a few years before the Chernobyl Era—the era which began with Soviet radioactive dust. (Soviet, for once, not always American: J.K.) "This brings me to the point." Quickly, Dustin blows his nose into a handkerchief as white and as pure as a wafer—and just as stiff.

"By charging that you can't float—without some hidden sea scooter or cryogenic lung* de Morande and Carlyle strike at the very heart of your accomplishment. You must strike back. What are you going to do to this Hannah Arendt ideological elephant?"†

"Nothing," says Kosky. "Nothing. I'm a Jewish-Ruthenian frog. Frog, not a subversive quail. Spiritual plankton, I live, like a frog, in a *nether* world made of literary ether and a gallon or two of preserved semen. To many Zenists (believers in Zen: J.K.), semen is one's inner water."

Behold the quail, the crow, the fly, the frog!/They slew the elephant! Behold the hatred of the haters! (*Jataka Tales*)‡

"This is no time for the Transcendental School.§ This is fall-out

---

*Sea scooter: here, a well-known device which, propelled by electric motor, pulls the underwater driver at some 6.9 knots. Cryogenic lung: a device which, worn by the swimmer, converts him into an underwater gas-breathing sea creature.

†"One of the more outstanding signs, however, is the accuracy with which elephants are able to locate underground water in times of drought, thereby indirectly serving humanity." (Robert H. Leftwich). Hannah Arendt elephant: synonymous with her spiritually (utterly untrue: J.K.) *Eichmann in Jerusalem*. (J.K.)

‡In the Jataka tale called "Quail, Crow, Fly, Frog, and Elephants," a small quail brings about the downfall of a mighty elephant who, seeking water, had trampled her offspring to death.

§Founded in 1836, New England's Transcendental School in Boston (Nathaniel

time," says Dustin, who, like Kosky, has been progressively losing his already unnaturally grayish and worn-out hair. (Regressively not progressively. There's certainly no 'progress,' and obviously no justice, here: Kosky also loses hair: J.K.)

"It's free speech fall-out," says Kosky, loading his pipe with Mantraki Gold. He lights it and slowly inhales, watching the smoke ruffle the water in the pipe as it passes through. This reminds him of piping supercooled liquid oxygen and nitrogen through an inner warming coil. While Kosky smokes his potpourri, Dustin chews his Skoal Bandits™ brand of tobacco, a habit he acquired at the tender age of nine, just about the time Kosky acquired his taste for smoking the Ruthenian-grown Kanabo while doing on someone else his favorite number sixty-nine. Thus, in their respective obsessions, both men can be, to say the least, orally inclined.

"It's a docu-slander, not a docu-drama," says Dustin. "Yet I've been told you steadfastly refuse to *flack* your detractors in public. You keep referring to your upbringing, to the ghetto, and to the terrible role rumors perform in a ghetto. You've even quoted a most scientific article on the subject about Rumors in the Lodz Ghetto. That's O.K. with the public though it is not O.K. with me. But how will you morally justify your refusal to appear on *Controversy!?*"

"I won't justify it," says Kosky. " 'Rumors are unavoidable in a society,' " he quotes Isaiah Kuperstein.* **In a sense, the sin of one who gossips about something that is true is greater than that of one who tells false gossip. For when a man tells true things about another, people believe him and the victim remains contemptible in their eyes. . . . (Orhot Zaddikim)†**

"But at least you could make fun of them. You were very funny in *Total State*, you know."

"My Hippocratic law‡ won't let me joke about this either. I'm not

Hawthorne, Ralph Waldo Emerson, and Margaret Fuller were among its illustrious students/teachers) once made Boston the spiritual capital "of this otherwise Profit-Oriented Republic.": Jay Kay.

*"Rumors: A socio-historical phenomenon in the Ghetto of Lodz," by Isaiah Kuperstein, *The Polish Review*, Vol. XVIII, 1973, No. 4.

†An anonymous Jewish medieval code of non-anonymous Jewish ethics.

‡Hippocrates treated medicine as the most noble of all arts, and was the first to suggest that the noble artists whom we call physicians take his oath, in order to make sure their patients wouldn't be mistreated.

Hannah Arendt, the writer who usurped from Conrad the notion of banality of evil," says Kosky.

"Your Hippocratic law just won't do as another banality of evil excuse,"* says Dustin.

"It's a remedy—not an excuse. These days my life is like the life of the early Judeo-Christians—a constant combat machine."

"You are your own remedy, Norbert!" Dustin heats up, but, a true Brahmin, he instantly calms himself down by channeling his attention elsewhere.

Pedantically, with his thumb and two fingers, Dustin reaches into his tobacco *pochette*, removes a small pinch of tobacco, stuffs it under his lower lip and chews upon it like a polo pony. While, as befits a man named Dustin (who can't dust his anger—anger always disguised as anxiety), he dusts his fingers just as pedantically and just as angrily, as he would anxiety. Then, and only then, he closes his *pochette* and replaces it in his tweed jacket's lower pocket. In seconds, his eyes water and, not surprisingly for a tobacco chewer who was once a tobacco snorter, unable to hide his smoking habit, he habitually sneezes some six or nine times. His paroxysm over, he continues. "Go on Controversy! with me. Let's give the noncreative world a creative lesson in your allegedly noncreative floating."

"I no longer teach creative floating," says our Abraham Abulafia (d. 1296: J.K.) quietly. "Not since I left Beulah University." **With the exception of Abraham Abulafia (1240–after 1292), the Spanish Kabbalist, and his disciples, who developed a Judaized version of yoga in which breathing techniques and rules of body posture were stressed, the Jewish mystics for the most part did not place meditative techniques at the center of their system. (Judaism and the Gentile Faiths, op. cit. p. 96)**

"If you'll allow me to quote Sophocles," says Dustin in a low voice, "you have 'too much pride for one drowned in ill fortune.' Think of J. Fenimore Cooper—one of life's early idols. Think of the Effingham

---

*"The banality of evil" (Conrad) was Hannah Arendt's excuse for the American German Jews who during World War II excused the Nazi extermination of the Polish and other East European Jews with a phrase "they went to their death like sheep." (And she dares to say it, as though not the Germans, but the Jews were sheep—by sheep she also implies the instinct of the horde: Jay Kay.) See *Eichmann in Jerusalem: a Report on the Banality of Evil* (1965).

Libels.* Like Cooper, you too must state where you stand in this matter."

"My stand is fiction. Monodrama,† not melodrama," says Kosky. "Literally speaking I stand in water. In, not upon. For obvious reasons, please don't confuse my act of standing in the water with walking upon it."

"I wish you'd reconsider. For a floater like you, there is no life outside your narrative. The narrative you keep confusing with water."

"I won't. Besides, nothing, not even this floating scandal, can separate me from water."

Zhivago is not merely a doctor, he is a poet. And to convince the reader that his poetry has true significance for mankind, you end your novel with a collection of your hero's poetry. In doing so you, Boris Pasternak, sacrifice the better part of your own poetic talent to this character you have created in order to exalt him in the reader's eyes and, at the same time, to identify him as closely with yourself as possible. (Editors of *Novy Mir* to Pasternak) (Before *glasnost:* J.K.)

"At the time Thomas Wolfe was docu-slandered by De Voto," Dustin reflects after a long silence, "Maxwell Perkins wrote the following to him: 'One night in a nervous moment when the rumors were flying thick and fast, I wrote you by hand asking you if you would be willing to write a letter saying they were groundless. But then, in the end, I tore up my letter because **I thought it was only part of the game that we should take our own medicine.**' " Dustin quotes Perkins from mem-

---

*"Mr. Cooper has libeled America, Americans, and every thing American, in a manner which should call forth the contempt and scorn of every man, woman, and child in the country possessed of the smallest portion of patriotic feeling. His libels on our people and her institutions are general; but he appears to have singled out Otsego, the county of his nativity, as the particular region of our whole country the most *boorish* and 'unprincipled,' and therefore meriting the infamous distinction of being held up in an especial manner to the contempt of Europe." (Park Benjamin, *New World*)

(Park Benjamin was editor of *The New Yorker* in 1838–39, after which he became the editor of the *Evening Signal* and the weekly *New World*.)

See also "The 'Effingham' Libels on Cooper," by Ethel R. Outland, University of Wisconsin Studies in Language and Literature (1929), p. 65.

†Monodrama: the art of staging as well as acting out a dramatic monologue— "a monotone with plenty of change and no weariness," as Tennyson called his *Maud*, was initially introduced by Rousseau in his *Pygmalion*.

ory. "Maybe Perkins was right after all." A troubled editor gives his troubled author a troubled look.

Time for literary inspection. Dustin puts on his glasses and eyes Kosky's manuscript. "How's your work on *The Hermit?*" he asks.

"I decided to call the novel *The Healer*," says Kosky.

"*The Healer?*" Dustin concentrates, looking down. "That's not bad," he exclaims, looking up. "After all, Christ was a healer and Corpus Christi, so I learned from your first fiction even you keep on denying it, is your most memorable childhood day. But what made you change the title? What, or who. Is it a new *dombi?*"

"*The Healer* seems to better reflect the art of creating fiction," says Kosky, "Besides, another writer is soon coming out with a novel called *The Hermit of 69th Street.*"

"No kidding! And who's that?"

"Kosinski," says Kosky. "That other literary Kosotoxin Man."

Dustin grins jovially. His grin ends the (inevitably creative: Jay Kay) confrontation between the author and his editor. On the way to the door he picks up the fatigued pouch of his Skoal Bandits wintergreen-flavored tobacco, his fatigued hat, his worn-out attaché case and "his pre–World War II sexually suspect mackintosh," in the words of the always sexually suspicious Jay Kay.

3 0

Autofiction means inner drama as much as it means history, and before leaving New York—the city sweats'nd steams in the Fahrenheit's high 96°—Dustin leaves on Kosky's desk the following description of one of his authors: "*Constant* preoccupation with himself, when self-love abandons him, which happens whenever danger is imminent. . . . all that is left is a typical man of letters whom a life of studies has weakened in body and soul."

"Is this supposedly you? A portrait of the spiritual you? The late August Wilhelm Schlegel, as he was described by the late Benjamin Constant?"* asks Jay Kay but only after Sexy Soula, Kosky's proofreader number 40D, left the room.†

---

*See *Mistress to an Age: A Life of Madame de Staël*, by J. Chistopher Herold (1958) p. 301. "The first almost footnote-less National Book Award biography that I really enjoyed," wrote Kosky on the margin of his ms. No. 8, p. 437. (The National Book Award is the American equivalent of the French Prix-Goncourt.— Estate Editors)

†"To start with, how many of you (adult male readers only: J.K.) think the number part of a bra measurement is the number of inches a woman measures around the fullest part of her tits? Say the bra size in question is 40D. You'd think 40 was the measurement around her tits, right? Wrong. The *number* in a bra size is actually a *band* measurement. The 'D' is the *only* part of the bra measurement that has anything to do with the actual breast size. Here's how cup size is determined. A woman meaures around the fullest part of her tits, while wearing a bra that fits her well. Then she measures around her chest *above* her tits, right under her armpits. The difference between these two measurements tells what size cup

If Dustin does mean him, then he is dead wrong. Didn't Heinrich Heine describe Schlegel as "elegance personified"? Elegance means concentration, as well as control. Now, when it comes to literary "elegance personified" whom do you trust more, say, Heine or Constant? Is not the Jewish-German Heine still one of the greatest German-language poets who ever lived in Germany? And in his spiritual judgment how constant in his corporal obsessions was the sex-obsessed Benjamin Constant? (Jay Kay) But never mind. Kosky's mind is, at this time of his life, full of pure Ashkenazian literary ash. **The Ashkenazim were not interested in writing literature; their works read like brief lecture notes. They were products, not of pure research but of discussions with pupils. . . . They wrote commentaries or notes on the classical works of olden times, books that modestly hug the monumental walls of older citadels. (Abraham Joshua Heschel, *The Earth Is the Lord's*, op. cit., p. 33)** Regardless of Kosky's character, Dustin knows only too well that all this fuss about Float or Swim is one more sterile squibble between de Morande and Kosky: "between two writers, one semi-senile and one spiritually sterile." Jay Kay offers a situational summary.

Sweating profusely—to a yogi, sweat is spiritual steam—Kosky consults the role of sweat as dealt with in books on Tantric medicine*— and, still sweating, reaches for *Hatha Yoga Kosherica*, a book of Jewish Yoga.

"You do not have to twist yourself into a pretzel in order to reach Sadhana," teach the authors of *Kosher Yoga,†* and their invitation is spiritually tempting. When it comes to autofiction, a book about an open conflict with one's Self, there is always a place for entertainment, for a new literary dimension which, oscillating between SS and CC, qualifies as CS, as a literary circus *spiritualis*.

VYSHINSKY: Accused Bukharin, did you tell Ivanov, in 1927–28, that you . . . were preparing for open battles against the Party?

BUKHARIN: Excuse me, but as a matter of fact, I was referring to

---

she wears." ("Max Facts: Truth About Bra Sizes," an editorial in *Max Magazine/* 49291, August 1987.)

*See the already quoted *Yogic and Tantric Medicine*, by O. P. Jaggi (Delhi-11006).

†See *Kosher Yoga*, by Albert L. Schutz and Hilda W. de Schaps, ISBN: 0-686-96936-7. (High spiritual content: Norbert Kosky, 1982)

open actions and not to open battles. The words "open battles" did not mean violent open battles.

VYSHINSKY: You speak of open battles, and that is what you said in your conversation with Ivanov, too.

BUKHARIN: I was not referring to violent... (dots in the text).

VYSHINSKY: ... You did refer to open battles? ...

BUKHARIN: ... We did not refer to open battles in the sense of armed insurrection.

VYSHINSKY: I am referring to open battles. (*Moscow Trials*, 1938)*

Now you see what Kosky means. He means that unless you write fiction—and you'd better make it clear that fiction it is—you are in trouble each time you open your mouth. Just think of Sismonde de Sismondi, his favorite economist, who thirty long years before Marx, wrote, "The current social order is a state of war between those who own and those who work." (1819) See also Lenin's *Characteristics of Economic Romanticism: Sismondi and our Russian Sismondists* (1896?)†

As a member of the legal opposition (legal means open), open to the scrutiny of its Stalinist opposition, Bukharin used openly to speak of open battles, and look at what Vyshinsky did with it several years later, when the liberal opposition within the Party was no longer legal and not a trace was left of the Party's old left wing, the remnants of the surprisingly rich tradition of Russian Liberalism. ‡

---

*The Moscow Purge trials (1936–38), during which hundreds of Old Party guards were sentenced to death on the strength of what they had supposedly said about what they were going to do to Lenin some thirty years earlier, with no evidence that they had actually done it, "offered a classic case of enlisting the language itself—almost the language outside its presence in history—as a witness for the fraudulent prosecution." (George Brayerin)

†At one time at a wedding dinner party in Southampton, Long Island, Norbert Kosky was heard listing Sismondi as No. 1 among the distinguished group of his other 96 literary SS saints, among them Saint-Simon ('65), Stephen Sondheim, ('66) Stefan Szuman, ('69) and Susan Sontag ('96).

‡See *Russian Liberalism: From Gentry to Intelligentsia*, by George Fischer, second edition, 1969.

"In point 6, only minor and stylistic changes were made, the final version reading as follows:

6. For the full development of the spiritual forces of the people, for a universal clarification of popular needs, and for the unobstructed expression of public opinion, it is essential to provide freedom of conscience and religion, freedom of speech

Restless, Kosky leaves his apartment (more and more often he calls it his safe sex cell No. 96 at San Leo) and makes a pit stop at Joe Doe McCarthy's, his favorite snack bar in his neighborhood which, by remaining open twenty-four hours a day, open as well as crowded, remains Kosky's ideal, "like the idea of never-ending daylight during which he writes his never-ending novel." (Jay Kay)

From behind the bar, Joe, the Sexual Simplex, steps out. Joe has been for years an equal opportunity bartender-bar-owner who does not believe in **all men are created equal (Jefferson), a short phrase so powerful that it will trouble us a thousand years. (Robert Frost).** *Trouble* means thinking. *Us* means thinking as well as book-reading and enlightened individuals, not such emotionally (hence also morally) untroubled emotional still-water monsters as Joe Doe McCarthy. Enough said? Not enough. (Jay Kay).

Like most untroubled men of his kind, "he is stupid, isn't he? Call him then by his real name," interferes Jay Kay. Joe dares to refer to **Yiddish as Hebrew in German letters (Hannah Arendt),** not knowing that the Nobel Prize for writing in Yiddish (Yiddish, not Hebrew or German) was won by Isaac Bashevis Singer, that Super Literary Polish-Jewish Wonder Yonder.

Go on. Hit the ball. Hit it "so fiercely that it will vanish into thin air. Hit with a stick in such a way that in an instant the ball would be face to face with the moon." (Jabar Singh, quoting in 1983 the Persian Shah-nameh, the author of the ninth-century polo classic)*

Joe knows the history of the Holocaust but only from television. He is the ignoramus who never understood that genocide meant mass-extermination, not only of the Jews.† He does not know that the Nazi-

---

and press, and also freedom of assembly and association." (From the Draft Resolution of the gathering of the Group of Zamstvo Constitutionalists, Moscow, 1904. ibidem, p. 183)

*Jabar Singh was a nine-goal player, and in polo a ten-goal player is absolutely tops. Having settled in the Dominican Republic, he coached Kosky in polo from at least 1971.

†"Once they were many; now they are so few. Nearly three and a half million Jews lived in Poland in 1939, and their homes, synagogues, and schools throbbed with an exuberance that made Poland a center of world Jewish culture. Then came the Holocaust. . . . In the years since, anti-Semitism has driven thousands more from Poland. Today, the remaining Jews number perhaps 5,000, nearly all of them old, scattered like withered straw across the Polish plain." (Writes Malgorzata

orchestrated genocide claimed before World War II many of the German mentally ill, as well as Jehovah's Witnesses and many other nonconforming Germans gassed en masse by the German military personal. Stress the words German military—meaning not only the Nazis! He feels no sorrow and no pity whatsoever for the fate of two out of five Poles and some half of the world's Gypsy population who perished during the War, and he is particularly not sorry for the millions of gas-exterminated Soviet prisoners of war in German hands who, before their capture, were once America's greatest military ally. (He doesn't know that either.) Sure, he has heard of Hannah Arendt's *Eichmann in Jerusalem,* but so what? Too bad he is not educated enough to read *And the Crooked Shall Be Made Straight: The Eichmann Trial, the Jewish Catastrophe, and Hannah Arendt's Narrative,* by Jacob Robinson (1965; Library of Congress Card Catalogue /CCC/ Number: 65-184666).

"Do you wear black-on-blue Punjabi underwear?" asks Joe, conspiratorially covering his mouth with his hand.

"Indeed I do, but only when I'm sexually tense," says Kosky. "Why? Is my underwear now making headlines—or is it my sexual tension?"

Joe lowers his voice. "Do you still play Strip Tac Toe with that fancy redhead who wears pink crotchless pantyhose?"

"No comment," comments Kosky. "But why do you ask?"

" 'Cause someone saw you." Does Joe tell the truth, or does the s.o.b. bluff "and bluff like Vyshinsky, the supreme master of rhetorical bluff." (Jay Kay)

"So what? having constant sex represents to me, 'the most serious sentiment of my life' as it did to my sexual prototype Benjamin Constant."* Kosky plays into his hand.

"How about playing with her open parts right on your balcony atoll?" To Joe, open parts are synonymous with Vyshinsky's open battles, and, like Vyshinsky vs. Bukharin, he too rejoices at the thought of opening more of Kosky's already overly opened inner balcony. "Didn't you, by the way, one day, photograph a velvety-smooth redhead and photograph her stark naked? Wasn't she the one who first came to work for you as

---

Niezabitowska and Tomasz Tomaszewski in "The Last Jews of Poland" in *National Georgraphic Society,* Vol. 170. No. 3, p. 363.)

*From Benjamin Constant's letter to Germaine Necker, better known today as Madame de Staël, "the opium-smoking writer, who stood neck-to-neck and necked with most famous men of letters." (Jay Kay)

an X-rated ex–pen pal after being fired from *Penmanship Magazine?*"

"Did I? What if I did not *fuckograph* (Elisabeth Kosky, 1948) her?" says Kosky.

"What if I only saw her on the cover of the April issue of the for-adults-only tax-deductible* *Velvet* magazine?"

"At your desk, at the window, do you still pull out your gray hair every morning while glancing through editions of *Slaves* and Dr. Masters Report on the use and abuse of prurient sexual paraphernalia?" (National Obscenity Commission, 1982) Joe's voice becomes a whisper.

"Sure I do. Like Kafka, I'll do anything to postpone writing, but I do all I can to speed up correcting of these galleys." (He adds for the sake of his galley-correcting time-greedy publishers.) **Another thing that pleases me is being without white hair. (Sartre)**

"Tell me." Joe won't laugh. "Do you squeeze blackheads from your nose—or is it from your dick—while squeezing words out sitting at your Dickens 669™ word processor?"

"I sure squeeze out *them* blackheads—though I don't use a word processor.† Don't and won't." He sounds as balsy as would Dickens accused of copying the writing work methods of Honoré de Balzac.

Writing is a deeply personal process, full of mystery and surprise. No two people go about it in exactly the same way. (William Zinsser, 1983)‡

"Then tell me this: do you cut your toenails—or is it your Ruthenian corns—with scissors?"

"I sure do. I'm an old limb no longer limber enough to bite them off all by myself," says our stiff Schlegel."§ "How do you know about

---

*"Since, in order to say self-employed, a self-employed author must feed his Self, the author is allowed to deduct from his income the money spent on books, newspapers and periodicals including—unless the author is a child—any adult magazine." (Unless "the child" is over the literary age of sixteen—depending on the laws of any given State of the Union, not on the state of the child.) (Tracy Tupman, writing in *The Writer's Accountant* magazine)

†Consult *Writing with a Word Processor* (1983), by William Zinsser, author of *Writing Well*.

‡Ibid.

§August Wilhelm Schlegel, a German writer known chiefly as the translator of Shakespeare and Calderón. He was one of many prominent men of letters who fell in love with Mme. de Staël and became one of her many "sexual proofreaders for hire" (Niskisko, 1982) after she was exiled from France by Napoleon and lived in the Swiss Gothic town by the name of Coppet. "He [Schlegel] tried to develop

all this? I haven't written about it—not yet, anyhow. And, as far as I know, neither did Germaine."

"Maybe you haven't but somebody else did. Or maybe someone reads what you write by using a couple of fine-print binoculars. Here, he left this for you. He didn't mind if I took a peek and so I did," says Joe, handing Kosky an open 6 x 9 mini-vanilla envelope from Manila.

"Who's somebody?"

"A little writing guy. Over fifty. Like you, strictly a creepy-crawlee."

"So what did this little guy have to say about my pen pal Germaine and about me?"

"He said that just for his own fun, he's kept you under sexual surveillance! That one night it was he who talked to you by simply calling a number of a public street phone. By calling it *not* by chance, just as you were going down on someone in that very phone booth on that notorious 69th Street."

"I was going down on someone called Chance." Kosky contributes another fictional rumor to his already fictional spiritual story.

"But never mind. What's inside the envelope?" asks our literary trader of *Slave* and Masters.

"All the sexual inside stuff. See for yourself," says Joe as Kosky opens the envelope and pours out of it six impeccably black-and-white "adult photographs of himself doing 69 to his nose as well as to the Khazar nose of Germaine, dressed only in a safe-sex leather hood and most becoming safe-sex slave collar."* (Jay Kay) Then he pours out of it an

---

his physique. He took riding lessons; he went swimming; he marched the boys on epic walks around the lake and through the Alps. Perhaps all this improved his health, but it did not change him into an athlete." (J. Christopher Herold, op. cit., p. 301) ("All this eminently applies to me—to the literary ghost Norbert Kosky," Kosky wrote on the margin of galley 231, when he was given (as was *always* the case: J.K.) the solitary task of correcting all by himself, his own sets of galleys." J.K.)

*For the shape and history of the Khazar nose, consult Arthur Koestler's *The Thirteenth Tribe* (op. cit.) from p. 190: "And yet—to return to the paradox—many people, who are neither racialists nor anti-Semites, are convinced that they are able to recognize a Jew at a single glance. How is this possible if Jews are such a hybrid lot as history and anthropology show them to be?" And see p. 196, where, starting with sub-Chapter Six you will come across this important, as well as spiritual, phrase and phase: "In any discussion of the biological and social inheritance of the Jews, the shadow of the ghetto must loom large. The Jews of Europe

impeccably typed six-page sexual-pix transcript all devoted (as the scoundrel De Voto would say) to the length and shape of his Jewish nose, shaped like—number six.

Thus the nose alone is not a very safe guide to identification. . . . An ingenious way out of this conundrum was suggested by Beddoe and Jacobs, who maintained that the "Jewish nose" need not be really convex in profile, and may yet give the impression of being "hooked," due to a peculiar "tucking up of the wings," an unfolding of the nostrils. (Arthur Koestler, op. cit., Fig. 1, Fig. 2, Fig. 3, p. 191.)

One quick glance at the pictures tells Kosky that while "a fiction writer is free to lie to the reader—call the reader Joe Doe (1982)—he must now not lie to this Joe Doe. He is upset. The truth is that these photographs laugh him in the face. After all, to start with, he is supposed to be serious, and how serious can a fiction writer be anyhow? "Particularly one who, once known for the blackness of his vision, is from now on known as a squeezed literary blackhead?" (in the self-cynical words of Jay Kay).

As for the transcript, it is no big deal. The present of the sick-sex menu he presents Kosky with is no sicker than, say, serving someone a plate of shrimp soup, followed by a sizzling skewer sirloin shish kebob supreme.

This amazing HEAR BIG parabolic microphone picks up and amplifies the smallest sounds—such as bird calls, traffic noise, and all the other secret whispers of the city, from distances of over 169 feet away. Aim the 19″ orange plastic disk and listen through the earphones. Stands 42″ high on a wooden telescoping tripod. Uses six 9V transistor batteries (not included). An ideal Christmas toy for your 6–9-year-old. U.S. $69.96 (*American Toy* magazine)

"And speaking of American society treated as a giant toy industry" (this quote comes from Jay Kay), "please read about our American consumption communities in Chapter Two (starts on page 89), part 6 ('Generalized Go-Getters: Lawyers,' particularly p. 69) and part 9 ('Democracy of Clothing,' starts on p. 91 but goes on all the way to pages 96–99)." All this and much more is to be found in a book of some 699

---

and America, and even of North Africa, are children of the ghetto, at no more than four or five generations removed. Whatever their geographical origin, within the ghetto walls they lived everywhere in more or less the same *milieu*, subjected for several centuries to the same formative, or deformative, influences."

pages called *The Americans: The Democratic Experience,* by Daniel J. Boorstin (1973). "A classic of nonfictional experience" (in the words of Jay Kay).

"So what shall I tell this cancerous guy?" asks Joe after Kosky hands back to him this sexually self-incriminating literary parabolic machine. (Jay Kay)

Says Kosky, "Tell him to take it to the literary manners police, though I won't cry, **I am finished. I trust no one, not even myself. (Stalin)** as quoted by Alex de Jonge, 1986. Tell the son of a bitch that, like most writers, I too suffer from **burrow mania (Kafka)** the literary *psychose passionelle*—a sort of sexy passion play, also known, in French, as *erotomanie,* or De Clerambault's Sexual Struggle Syndrome. And tell him, above all, that **freedom means necessity realized** (my version of Hegel), which means that, as a born voyeur, I also enjoy a great deal being watched myself."

On such merely carnal sins as gluttony and lust, the body imposes by its very nature and constitution certain limits. But however weak the flesh, the spirit is indefinitely willing. To sins of the will and the imagination, kind nature sets no limits. Avarice and the lust for power are nearly as infinite as anything in this sublunary world can be. And so is the thing D. H. Lawrence called "sex in the head." As imagined sensuality it is one of the first infirmities of the human mind. (Aldous Huxley, *The Devils of Loudon*)

```
┌─────────┐
│         │
│   3 1   │
│         │
└─────────┘
```

Had Sabbatai Sevi sat in one place—
say in Gaza!—instead of going from Smyrna, where he was born, to
Patras, then Athens, then Salonika, Constantinople, Cairo, Jerusalem,
Gaza, Aleppo and then—fatal error!—to Constantinople again all this
anecdotal life (M. Borowski as quoted by Henry Miller) he would have
written more and talked and be talked about less! All this exposure, all
this public talking, did him no good! It only contributed to the ugly
rumors spread about him and his wife, the Submissive Sarah.

For some six weeks now—was it six or nine? It doesn't really matter,
does it?—our *ba'al shem* had sat down every day for six or nine hours
at a time in one place—at his desk, no less—yet our literary yeti has
not added one meaningful phrase, not even a quote to his literary
*collectanea.**

Now, in the evening, out of boredom, washed my hands in the bathroom three times in succession. (Kafka, *Diaries*)† He hasn't even re-

---

*Like his *The Universe* and *Blotting Books*, Emerson's *Collectanea* consists
"largely of entries of some length, arranged however on a more formal plane."
(*The Journals and Miscellaneous Notebooks of Ralph Waldo Emerson*, op. cit.,
p. 3.)

†Says Henry Miller: "I must say, right at the start, that I haven't a thing to
complain about. It's like being in a lunatic asylum, with permission to masturbate
for the rest of your life. The world is brought right under my nose and all that is
requested of me is to punctuate the calamities." (*Tropic of Cancer*, op. cit., p.
145.)

written one whole page! In such stoppage a result of the permanent drying out of the well of his star—or only the temporary emptiness of his creative well? Is he, perish the thought, suffering from writer's block? A curse so grave that no creative writing course can lift it? Or is he merely trying to turn every day into a Sabbath—a day of meditation—while doing nothing—and that's O.K., since you're not supposed to work during the Sabbath—and writing is work. **June 1. Wrote nothing. June 2. Wrote almost nothing. (Kafka, *Diaries*)**

Or, like so many other lesser writers before him (e.g., Baudelaire), has he too contracted the spiritually deadly Acedia Disease?*

Finally, the welcome Sabbath arrives (and in accordance with the Jewish calendar it arrives "sooner than in most non-Jewish calendars, that is, already on Friday." (Jay Kay) No wonder. The Sabbath is the *single most important day*. It is a day of rest—of obligatory pleasure, a Jew might say. In the Jewish faith, the penalty for desecrating the Sabbath—desecrating it by not resting enough—is spiritual death.

Since this is the Sabbath, Kosky's all inner-working communication channels have been shut off for the day. All but one: the channel of meditation. **Further good evidence of authenticity in "annihilation" and divine delight in the above-mentioned concentration is the category of soul's attraction to the nearness of God during the whole day (i.e., the effect of his experience in prayer makes itself felt in the good deeds he carries out during the rest of the day—translator's note). . . . Further evidence of authenticity is that he partakes but little of the delights of the world, such as fame, clothes, good food and other coarse lusts. (Dov Baer)**

"What should I meditate about." Kosky asks Svāmin, his inner Buddhist monk whom he has recently appointed as a pro-tem head of his De-

---

*Acedia: a South American Atlantic flatfish. Acedia disease is manifested by chronic fatigue as well as stupor, torpor and sloth (one of the Seven Deadly Sins). "Like many lesser writers before and after him, Baudelaire suffered constantly from acedia, 'the malady of monks,' that deadly weakness of the will which is the root of all evil. He fought against it with fury and horror." (Christopher Isherwood)

This complaint (chronic fatigue: J.K.) is encountered with outstanding frequency. (French's *Index of Differential Diagnosis*, ed. by Arthur H. Douthwaite, M.D., F.R.C.P. [Bristol, 1954], p. 299.) "Most colorfully written and illustrated with the most splendidly sickening color pictures." (J.K.)

partment of Interior Judaism. The previous head (No. 62) was Dov Baer (also known in Brooklyn, N.Y., as Rabbi Dov Baer of Lubavitch) who, (quickly adds Kosky to galley lines number 60–66) in addition to his Tract on "Contemplation," also wrote:

62. *Tract on Ecstasy*, as stated in the following footnotes of *Judaism and the Gentile Faiths*, by the already quoted Joseph P. Schultz, on p. 100.
60. Louis Jacobs, "The Doctrine of the 'Divine Spark in Man' in Jewish Sources," in *Studies in Rationalism, Judaism and Universalism*, ed. Raphael Loewe (London: Routledge and Kegan Paul, 1966) pp. 87–103.
61. *Tanya*, pt. 1, chaps. 1–2, pp. 9–13; chap. 9, pp. 26f.
62. Dobh Baer ben Shneor Zalman of Lubavitch, *Tract on Ecstasy*, trans. and intro. by Louis Jacobs (London: Valentine Mitchell, 1963) pp. 164–65.
63. G. Scholem, *Major Trends in Jewish Mysticism*, p. 139.
64. *Kunteros Ha-Hitbonanut* (Kopust, 1820). See an English synopsis of this work in Jacobs, *Tract on Ecstasy*, pp. 188–92.
65. See "Yoga," in Hastings, *Encyclopedia of Religion and Ethics*, 12:831–33.
66. For comparative studies dealing with Hinduism and Christianity, see Ninian Smart, *The Yogi and the Devotee: The Interplay Between the Upanishads and Catholic Theology* (London: George Allen and Unwin, 1968); Mariasusai Dhavamony, *Love of God According to Saiva Siddhantā: A Study in the Mysticism and Theology of Saivism* (Oxford: The Clarendon Press, 1971); John B. Carman, *The Theology of Ramanuja: An Essay in Interreligious Understanding* (New Haven, Conn.: Yale University Press, 1974.

"Meditate about your favorite subject, as long as it does not deal with work in the ghetto. Not even in the ghetto of Lodz,* where most of

---

*"After the last resettlement there is (almost) no one in the Litzmannstadt ghetto over the age of sixty-five or under the age of ten. The hospitals have been liquidated—but does that mean there are no sick people left? September 25, 1942." From *The Chronicle of the Lodz Ghetto, 1941–1944*, ed. by Lucjan Dobroszycki (Yale University Press, 1984). But then hundreds of thousands of others are still alive. If Stalin would only speed up the Red Army offensive (after all, the Red Army was his private army!) and not wait conveniently for the sake of his own sick anti-Polish, or anti-Jewish (or both: J.K.) strategy, thousands upon thousands of

your family perished." Comes a reply. "Besides, aren't you writing about it already? Careful: writing is work."

"My favorite subject is Desire vs. Death, meaning where I came from to *here*. Meaning what kind of man am I? Am I a good being or only a fairly good one? Meaning: what is the meaning of literary goodness? Is this book No. 9 good or bad? Good 'cause I quote good people or bad 'cause I think Rumkowski was a very good man and an extraordinary working-class leader," says Kosky.

"Good but you must keep Rumkowski out of it. Rumkowski means *work*. Work even on Saturday. Work as a means of survival. Work meaning ALIVE! and *not* meaning an armed rebellion. Work meaning *chaye shoo is oykh lebn*, which means *rescue through work*.* (Rumkowski 1941; Israel Kosky, 1946, Norbert Kosky, 1987.) **That the "rescue-through-work"—perhaps a melancholic illustration of the folk saying "respite of death is also life" (*Chaye shoo is oykh lebn*)—did not work in the long run does not by itself disqualify this policy. It is only by accident of military history that a considerable part of Lodz Jews did not survive. By the end of July 1944 the Red army had reached the Vistula and established a bridgehead on its western shore, south of Warsaw. The Red army did not continue its advance, but stopped some seventy miles from Lodz. Less than a month later, in August 1944, the 68,000 Jews still alive in Lodz were "resettled." (Isaiah Trunk, *Judenrat*, 1972. p. XXIX)** That's a nicely framed subject but the frame is not specific enough. It is a cliché. Clichés stem from too much work. It won't do."

"Then simply tell me what to meditate about?" Kosky cuts his long story short, and in the process gains another point for a brand new SS configuration.

"Meditate about numbers. Numbers one to five about the freeing of

---

Jews of the Ghetto of Lodz would be liberated in time, i.e., before being shipped by the Nazis to Auschwitz ovens. See also (if the money for completing it will be found, and if it is ever released), *The Chronicle of Lodz Ghetto*, a 35mm documentary film, which as of this writing is *still* not completed, by The Jewish Heritage Writing project.

*For the sight of a rare photograph of Rumkowski officiating at a wedding in the Lodz Ghetto after all the rabbis were deported in September 1942 (as well as for a photograph of the post office in the Lodz Ghetto) the reader is encouraged to read *Judenrat· The Jewish Councils in Eastern Europe Under Nazi Occupation*, by Isaiah Trunk, Introduction by Jacob Robinson, 1972, p. 190.

the Jewish soul from bondage of the Egyptian biblical soil. Then, devote all your spiritual strength to numbers six and nine: to 996 years of your soul's *unbroken physical presence* on the Ruthenian spiritually fertile soil."

"In my book, Ruthenia is part of Poland."*

"Anything. Anything at all," beams Svāmin.

"Does the subject matter?"

"It doesn't, as long as work is not what you meditate about on the Sabbath," proclaims Svāmin. "As long as you meditate about being a spiritual being or even a nonbeing. But under no condition must you meditate about human beings in general—that is spiritually most fatiguing. As your thousand-year-old Jewish-Ruthenian undoubtedly knows, Jewish spiritual fatigue does not stem from specific spiritual work, but from being, spiritually speaking, too general. Ask any Israeli general."

"Can I meditate, say, about a woman rather than about a man?" Kosky asks.

"Indeed you can, as long as this woman is not working during the Sabbath," Svāmin agrees.

"How about meditating about a Jewish woman who is about to get married to a well-known Jew on June 13?" (June 13 was Kosky's birthday: J.K.)

"A most appropriate subject on this week's Sabbath," says Svāmin, "particularly since the times of Isaac Luria, the sixteenth-century mystic of Safed, who believed the Sabbath was a queen. Careful: here, *queen* means a bride. By the way, whom do you have in mind?"

"The one and only Mrs. Sabbatai Sevi," says Kosky. "In my novel she is the Queen of 69. Mind you, my novel deals in a Bukharinist-Jeffersonian form of liberal, safe-sex, safe yet not sex-free!"

From time to time Sabbatai Sevi's messianic fancies returned and it is probable that in one of these fits of illumination he decided to marry Sarah, an Ashkenazi girl of doubtful reputation who either had arrived

---

*See *The Polish Jewry: History and Culture*, by Marian Fuks, Zygmunt Hoffman, Maurycy Horn and Jerzy Tomaszewski (Interpress, 1982), 196 pages. "With many color and black-and-white plates which, with the text appropriately ending on page 100, start on page 101 and end on, appropriately for this numerological narrative text, on page 196—as does this most indispensable book," Jay Kay finishes the sentence (as well as: J.K.)

by herself from Italy or was brought over on his initiative when he heard rumors about her from Italian visitors. She was an orphan of the 1648 massacres in Podole and used to tell curious stories about herself and her upbringing by a Polish nobleman. . . . Rumors that she was a woman of easy virtue preceded her and were current even later in the intimate circle of Sabbatai Sevi's admirers. (Gershon Sholem)

The Sabbath ends. The minute it ends Kosky goes back to work—that is, moves behind his desk and calls for Ann Pudeater Patterson: his sixty-ninth sexual proofreader disguised as a line editor. The instant she comes—comes, not arrives—he asks her to edit a dirty letter.

"This is a sick letter, very, very, very sick letter, written by a very sick man. I won't correct a single comma," says Ann. "Here, my typewriter carriage just won't move one millimeter. My electric pencil sharpener stops here. Enough is enough."

"C'mon, Ann," pleads Kosky. "Of course it's a sick letter. It must be sick 'cause in my novel this letter comes from a man who's spiritually sick. In fact, it comes from at least two sick people: my character as he is seen by *him*, by my double, and my own double-faceted Janus-like character. This is a sick mixture of Rumkowski with Tolstoy or Victor Hugo with Machiavelli. (Or Baudelaire: J.K.) That's the only kind of letter this man can write. And while a sick one, it is also a good letter. Certainly it is not. No worse than any letter you might find in the good book called *Great Letters*."* Or a letter of Bruno Schulz to Debora Vogel, a letter filled with rather extravagant sexual drawings Bruno routinely attached to his most *intellectual* letters. (See my play *Bruno and I*: J.K.) Still, it is his letter; *his* not mine.

In the course of that working day of eight hours I write three sentences

---

*See A *Second Treasury of the World's Great Letters*, selected and edited by Walace Brockway and Barth Keith Winer (1941).

which I erase before leaving the table in despair.... I assure you—speaking soberly and on my word of honour—that sometimes it takes all my resolution and power of self-control to refrain from butting my head against the wall.... I would be thankful to be able to write anything, anything, any trash, any rotten thing—something to earn dishonestly and by false pretences the payment promised by a fool. (Conrad to Edward Garnett)*

"You wrote this letter. You not he. That sick man is you. You. You. You not *him*," Ann screams. "I've edited some pretty sick stuff, published, unpublished and never-to-be published, but I've never read anything as filthy as this first draft. I wish I had with me my *Literary Filth Dictionary.*"

"I see it as being honest, not filthy. Open and *candid*. The letter is a ribald classic! Ask Swift or Chaucer. Ask Bataille. Ask Henry Miller. Ask anyone who is spiritually speaking," says Kosky.

"Don't give me this '69 spiritually speaking speakeasy. This letter is as sick—maybe even sicker, sicker'nd slicker—than the letter Joan of Arc sent to the English.† As sick as the one Lord Nelson sent to Emma Lyon, alias Emma Hart, alias Mrs. Hamilton‡ just before his final battle. This letter belongs in a manure pit, and I won't touch it," she says, getting up from her desk. "For this kind of work you don't want an adult editor. You need an adult video star. Why don't you call your favorite Hypatia Lee!"

"Editing and sexual understanding is what I pay you for, not censorship," says Kosky calmly. The signal is clear. Ann Pudeater Paterson, his line editor No. 69, (who until now was his very best in the act of 69: Jay Kay) has just stepped out of her sexual—sexual as well as, and as much as, editorial—hot-line. Enough italics.

Vanity often coexists with an experience that at first seems like its very opposite. This is the holding back we call pride.... The terms on which men and women can secure recognition as members of groups that allow for heightened (though unequal) vulnerability and for common

---

*See "Inspired by Despair," by Louis Menand, a review of *The Collected Letters of Joseph Conrad*, Vol. 2, 1898–1902, ed. by Frederick R. Karl and Laurence Davies (New York, 1987), in *The New York Times Book Review*, 1/25/87, p. 16.

†See "Joan of Arc, before the battle of Orleans, commands the English to surrender," in *Great Letters*, op. cit., pp. 66–69.

‡Ibid., pp. 299ff.

allegiance enmesh them in power relations. Engagement in shared bondage. (*Passion: An Essay on Personality*, by Roberto Mangabeira Unger [1986. BF 698. U48 1984.])

SS

Without Ann at hand our writer suffers from creative despair. A writer cures despair by visiting a bookstore. **Every man is more or less the sport of accident; nor do I know that authors are at all exempted from this humiliating influence.** (J. Fenimore Cooper, Preface to *The Pioneers*) This time, our autofictional pioneer revisits the famous Astolfo Book Center on West 6th Street. This is where some of the city's best female proofreaders, copy editors, typesetters—and, from time to time, full-fledged literary *dombis*—hang out. But this is where only the other day, he almost ran into the Honorable Abba Eban, the master of Jewish Heritage, and the equally honorable Joan Didion, the master of American Self. Tonight, some six minutes to nine P.M., he comes here disguised as one Monsieur Julien, who, judging by how our freak of letters talks and how he is dressed tonight, can be regarded as a well-educated bona fide bookish man of letters, who has just arrived in New York from the most bookish town in America known as New Haven." (Jay Kay)*

Tonight he has topped his disguise by also picking up a new mustache as well as a new name—Julien Loti—which will match his mustache best.

Like every word, every artifact comes with its own written and unwritten language. Example: the simple detachable mustache Kosky wears tonight is made of human hair; (as detachable as language: Jay Kay) now wouldn't he want to know who was its previous wearer? Was it a he or she? Then, even though he bought it in New York, the mustache was made in Hermit Islands.

But that's not all. A replica of a mustache worn in life by such

---

*"After all, if we are dealing with maybes, the New Haven episode may have helped James Cooper's next enterprise. There by Thames and Sound the boy inland bred got his smell of saltwater and his glimpse of seagoing craft." See "Trial by Water," in *James Fenimore Cooper*, by Henry Walcott Boynton (American Classics, 1931, 1966), p. 33.

dissimilar characters as Nikolai Bukharin, * the heir to Lenin who should have been the head of the First Soviet State, but was instead murdered by it, and the very Julien Viaud, who, once known as "The Magician," became known to the world at large as Pierre Loti,† the first French writer other than Victor Hugo to be given by his country a free burial disguised as a state funeral. The man who wrote *Aziyadé*, "and the first writer who, speaking about himself, openly proclaimed to the world in capital letters: I AM NOT MY OWN TYPE."

A this time—it's almost 9:00 P.M.—the bookstore is practically empty. In the fading background, three aging female proofreaders peruse the novels of Melville and Dos Passos, their, no doubt, favorite texts. In the brightly lit left corner, an aging Gay Gaius pretends to read a novel called *Teleny*, by Anonyme, while, sly fox, he keeps his admiring eye on our literary Wild Oscar (not Oscar Wilde, printer!) who, already in panic—his panic stems from being recognized—keeps his own trembling eye on Sly Porter's sly book called *Reporter* (1982). The Gay Gaius is a proofreader. He is, as a man, so inept, inept, not banal, that, in his heyday as Kosky's proofreader No. 77 and part-time social scout he could not tell, in his own words, literary sugar from the salt of the narrative, and checking for Kosky the spelling of some profane quotes, he was not able even to quote them, but now dreams of being one day quoted himself. Given by Kosky the daily task of . . . **"The correction of typos, the striking out of hyphens at the end of lines, the indication of em dashes, together with the assigning of point size to heads and subheads,** (which as we all know only too well!: J.K.) **can no longer be**

---

*Found by Vyshinsky's court to be guilty of treason, Nikolai Bukharin was shot (in the back of his head) March 15, 1938, seconds after he had written a note to Stalin which began with the words, "Koba, why do you *need* me to die?"

†By 1892, when Pierre Loti was elected to the French Academy, he was still known to the public at large as the author of *Aziyadé*, "his first and his most personal work." (Personal as opposed to autobiographical: J.K.) "*Aziyadé* has always been surrounded by mystifications, scandals, polemics and theories as to its autobiographical verity. In 1892, referring to Loti's election to L'Académie Française, Goncourt wrote of 'this author, whose love, in his first book, was a Monsieur.' It had also been said that Loti made the transposition from feminine to masculine in the first manuscript, since he well knew the temper of Islam in any matter touching the inviolate harem," writes Lesley Blanch in her biography *Pierre Loti, the Legendary Romantic* (1983).

left to the judgment and taste of printers, because of the great variety of designs, the decline of artisanship, and the substitution of the type-writer and its offspring for the author's own hand." (Jacques Barzun, 1984)

The Gay Gaius was also hired by Kosky in order to have him check Kosky's text for Kosky against the anonymous intervention of *editorial Judenrats of the publishing house* (Kosky, 1965) Kosky's ethno-centric, egocentric and idiosyncratic diction, grammar, idiom and syntax.*

Quickly, Kosky steps away and hides behind one particular bookshelf which disturbs him most. Dedicated to MAN, it contains books about only one man. His first name, Otto Adolf, like the first names of his father KARL ADOLF, are already menacing enough, even though when he was born Adolf was not yet the name which menaced us most. But it is his last name EICHMANN, and only his last which, since May 11, 1960, has menaced Kosky most.

Secretly caught by Israeli secret agents near Buenos Aires, in Argentina [Ed. to Author: Wasn't he kidnapped? Au. to Editor: He was caught: J.K.], Eichmann was then secretly flown to Israel nine days later, and, almost a year after, openly tried in Jerusalem. Read *Justice in Jerusalem*, by Gideon Hausner (1966), the man who as attorney general of Israel calmly sat in judgment of Eichmann. Of Eichmann, not of the German people. This was not the case with Hannah Arendt, that rat! It was she who usurping the notion of **Banality of Evil (Conrad)** judged all Eastern Euopean Jews to be *rats*, only because of the few Jewish rats who, forced to cooperate with the Germans, became members of the *Judenrat*† the very name, which by combining the word *Jude* with *rat*, makes him *uneasy at home* (Leonard Dinnerstein, 1987).

Here the reader is asked to pause and see what Kosky sees: He sees Eichmann as one who captured the sentiment of the pre-atomic German military long before he himself was captured. "German military" mean-

---

*See also "Behind the Blue Pencil: Censorship or Creeping Creativity," by Jacques Barzun, in *Publishers Weekly*, 1985 (the Essay originally appeared in the summer issue of *American Scholar*).

†"*Judenrat*: acceptance of appointment to and continuance in office, 159–60; authority of over property, 162–63; basic strategy of, 160–61; cooperation "the very cornerstone" of, 321 (#1); deception of members by the Nazis, 204–6; drawing of lots, 160; elements of judgment on, 161; "enjoyment" of power by, 164–65; "enormous powers" of, 161–65. (Jacob Robinson, op. cit., index, p. 393)

ing all German World War II personnel, not merely the members of
the Nazi party and SS, so all conveniently dismissed by the computerized
view of history "as the bunch of crazy Nazis." "This is a distinction too
important to miss. This is like missing the difference between a missile
and a missal, and as far as Jews are concerned, the difference between
a child who misses at school and a permanently missing child." (Jay
Kay)

"Whom else can I ask about it?" here asks an anonymous reader.
Ask someone who knows. Someone who, preferably not Jewish, "hence
not Judaistically biased" (Jay Kay), who believes in justice the way a
simple novelist believes in sex he calls his crystalline water. Hence, ask
someone with water in his name.

When you think of the long and gloomy history of man, you will find
more hideous crimes have been committed in the name of obedience
than have ever been committed in the name of rebellion. If you doubt
that, read William Shirer's *Rise and Fall of the Third Reich*. The German
Officer Corps were brought up in the most rigorous code of obedience . . . in the name of obedience they were party to, and assisted in,
the most wicked large-scale actions in the history of the world. (C. P.
Snow, 1961, p. 24)

He picks up a book and opens it at random on a chapter called,
appropriately for him, our Concentration Man: "THE SECOND SOLUTION:
Concentration." This "objective" attitude—talking about concentration
camps in terms of "administration" and about extermination camps in
terms of "economy"—was typical of the S.S. mentality, and something
Eichmann, at the trial, was still very proud of. By its "objectivity" (*Sach-
lichkeit*), the S.S. dissociated itself from such "emotional" types as Streicher,
that "unrealistic fool," and also from certain "Teutonic-Germanic Party
bigwigs who behaved as though they were clad in horns and pelts."
(Hannah Arendt, 1963)

But then, as he proceeds reading Hannah Arendt's account of Eichmann's proceedings all the way down their own immoral way, he comes
across one passage which irks him most, and—wouldn't you know it?—
he comes across it on the spiritually sacrosanct for him page ninety-six!
Hence, he simply can't ignore her ignorance any longer. Her spiritual
ignorance as much as her view that by not being in time in the mainstream of capitalist imperialism, the East European Jewry somehow
deserved to die.

. . . In an accompanying letter, addressed to "Dear Comrade Eichmann," the writer (an SS man stationed in the Warthegan) admitted that "these things sound sometimes fantastic, but they are quite feasible." (These things—meaning a quicker way to die than the one obtained by purposeful starvation: J.K.) . . . Eichmann never mentioned this letter and probably had not been in the least shocked by it. For this proposal concerned only *native* Jews, not Jews from the Reich or any of the Western countries. His conscience rebelled not at the idea of murder but at the idea of German Jews being murdered. ("I never denied that I knew that the *Einsatzgruppen* had orders to kill, but I did not know that Jews from the Reich evacuated to the East were subject to the same treatment. That is what I did not know.") It was the same with the conscience of a certain Wilhem Kube, an old Party member and *General-kommissar* in Occupied Russia, who was outraged when German Jews with the Iron Cross arrived in Minsk for "special treatment." Since Kube was more articulate than Eichmann, his words may give us an idea of what went on in Eichmann's head during the time he was plagued by his conscience: "I am certainly tough and I am ready to help solve the Jewish question," Kube wrote to his superior in December 1941, "but people who come from our own cultural milieu are certainly something else than the native animalized hordes." This sort of conscience, which, if it rebelled at all, rebelled at murder of people "from our own cultural milieu," has survived the Hitler regime; among Germans today, there exists a stubborn "misinformation" to the effect that "only" *Ostjuden*, Eastern European Jews, were massacred. (*Eichmann in Jerusalem*, by Hannah Arendt, p. 96.)

Since this novel is a novel of ideas (here Kosky speaks with the voice of Jay Kay), and like an old invoice ideas are seldom original, let me state clearly my idea about this particular narrative right of passage. By quoting this passage in order supposedly to give us an idea "of what went on in Eichmann's head," Hannah Arendt gives us throughout her book an image of what went on in hers: "it was a contrast between her university cultured German-Jewish scholars and university professors, to what Kube calls 'our own cultural milieu' and the milieu of the 'native animalized hordes' of *Ostjuden*, meaning particularly the Yiddishly inclined Jews of Poland!" (in the words of the really angered Jay Kay).

Animalized hordes indeed! Take another look, reader, at *Polish Jewry*: ONE THOUSAND YEARS OF HISTORY AND CULTURE. At the unbroken chain

400

of Polish-Jewish relations. Relations stemming from proximity, not distance. *

Look under: *Language and Literature. Lay Learning. Mysticism. Kabbala. Messianic Movements. Art. Education. Custom and Family Life. Dress. Illness and Funerals.* Look then, just for the sheer universal fun of it, at *Polish Jewry in the 19th and 20th Centuries.* Look under *Printing.* ("My New York printer is American-Jewish," exclaims Jay Kay. "He was born here, but his parents came from Poland. Among his ancesters were two famous Polish-Jewish music composers. No wonder he is so good at style'nd type composing. Look at *Theater. Music. Painting. Education. The Press.* Read all that, reader, and then, if you are a Ruthenian or a Polish Jew, check the Polish-Jewish roots of your own family thousand-year-old Polish-Jewish *Who's Who* or in the (forthcoming, one hopes by the time of the fiftieth anniversary of the Nazi invasion of Poland in 1989: J.K.) *Encyclopedia of Polish-American Jews.* Enough said.

Tell me this now, my *liebe* Hannah: WHO WERE THE ANIMALIZED HORDES OF TWENTIETH CENTURY EUROPE? The gas-dispensing Germans or the palm-reading Gypsies? How could you forget that half of all of the world's Gypsies were gassed to death by your beloved Germans? HALF, HANNAH, IS MORE THAN ONE-THIRD. MUCH MORE. Enough said. NOT ENOUGH! And, while we are at it, what about the tragic fate of the almost 4.5 million still nameless Soviet soldiers who, initially kept in German prisoner-of-war camps by the German military (military—never mind SS!), were then all gassed to death with the help of mobile gas ovens—which worked efficiently and did the extermination job in a remarkably short period of time. IS THE FIGURE FOUR AND A HALF MILLION SO INFERIOR TO THE JEWISH SACRED NUMBER SIX? Enough said. Not enough! They were all soldiers who fought not just because Stalin ASKED THEM TO, BUT BECAUSE THEY BELIEVED I and countless millions of others like me, Jews and non-Jews and every conceivable kind of Gentile, ought to be liberated by them rather than share in the Final Solution meant to be final and which turned out to be final not only for some six million Jews but also for a staggering number of Gentiles!

---

*See "Speaking for My Self," in *Dialectics and Humanism: The Polish Philosophical Quarterly,* Vol. XIV, No. 1/1987.

And, finally, my *liebe* Hannah, since I survived the War among the Ruthenian peasants, among, as well as thanks to, let's talk about the East European peasants. Were these peasants, these Slavic folks more superstitious or less than your CIVILIZED heel-clicking, oh-so-obedient GERMANS WHO BELIEVED IN A HIDDEN DEVIL—A DEVIL HIDDEN IN EVERY JEW? The fact is, my *liebe* Hannah, that, given German behavior vs. the behavior of the Central European peasants, I would rather kiss every day the dirty feet of any Ruthenian peasant than ever again salute anything militaristically German and this goes for any Jewish intellectual Dragon Lady like you. Am I clear? Is it said enough? Not enough!

Were these peasants more cruel than their not-too-distant German neighbors? Did not the trains carrying people to their final destiny come directly from that "civilized" world of modern cities filled with the relics of a thousand years of German culture, with their electricity, broadcasting stations, broadcasting in German [German; God forbids the use of Yiddish: Jay Kay], hospitals, schools, libraries, and learned societies . . . ?

This war was not started by the peasants. Like millions of educated and "civilized" city dwellers, they became its victims. Could these peasants suddenly forget what the ubiquitous *Bekanntmachungen* (notices) perpetually reminded them about, that the penalty was death for giving shelter or aid to any Jew or Gypsy *under any circumstances whatsoever?* [A law enacted only in Poland: J.K.] This law was not conceived in the remote poverty-stricken villages of Eastern Europe. The peasants did not write this law; it came to them expressly from that "civilized" German world and was carried to them on the bayonets of the German army of occupation. Its writing and promulgation were undertaken by men educated in the centers of European culture, brought up with knowledge of the Renaissance and Enlightenment, of the philosophy of Kant, Hegel and Schopenhauer, loving the music of Bach, Beethoven and Mozart, the poetry of Goethe and Schiller, and aware of the prose of the finest minds of their generation. . . . (Kosinski, 1965)*

She knows that in today's America, they, the spiritually inspired American East European Jews, and no longer only her old "our crowd from Berlin," show guts and exude creative juices, as well as, let's face

---

*"Notes of the Author," in *The Painted Bird* (New York: 1965)

it, decently earned big money. **In the course of their troubled and frustrated history during the last two centuries, the Jews have created works of lasting genius in almost every sphere of life.** (Isaiah Berlin) Each time she runs into one of them—and she runs into at least one of them on every American spiritual street corner—she is first struck by awe, an awe a rhabdomancer feels when romancing the brackish water under the Negev Desert. But then, just as fast, she is struck by envy. By that old Iago complex: "He hath the daily beauty in his life that makes me feel ugly" (Iago about Othello). To understand her emotions better, read Shakespeare as well as *Shakespeare Our Contemporary* (Jan Kott, 1974).

Surely, you know that out of these "animalistic hordes" of East European Jews came the largest spiritual and intellectual crowd in our Jewish history. *When were you last in Brooklyn?* That it was in Eastern Europe where in ten long centuries (ten is the magic number—the number suggesting past nine and the unlimited beyond) we built our cultural and worldly pyramids—pyramids, Hannah, pyramids. Pyramids that spiritually sustained (forget, for the moment, *geo-politic*) Jews of the entire world: pyramids of art and technology, of science and technology, which populated the planet Earth, the one the Nazis planned to call Planet Gentile.

It was in Eastern Europe where we built our formidable pyramids, and not only barricades. Eastern Europe where the remnants of our cemeteries and our synagogues now stand, where our sacred parchments remain sacred, though read only by the Hebrew-speaking and Yiddish Oxford-educated Gentiles. WHERE WE, THE TIME-CONSCIOUS JEWS, let it all die in the ashes of time. Where our most sacred Torah crowns and our nuptial canopies full of our Tas, our Torah breastplates full of gilded and not-gilded silver are left tended to by the few remaining Jews and mostly by the local Gentiles. ("Enough said!" Jay Kay) Not enough. This is our past—a past composed of living religious objects: living ones, not biblical relics. For reproductions of these and many other spiritually sacred objects currently in Poland under joint Polish-Jewish custody, the reader (denomination of non) is referred to the already quoted *The Polish Jewry: History and Culture*, 1982. Read the chapter called "Conclusion," starting on page 99 and ending on page 100, then see photographs of the centuries-old Torah Scroll (p. 101); Torah Mantle with the Ten Commandments (1986), p. 106; Torah

403

Crown in silver, (1819), p. 108; and, on sacrosanct p. 109, the startling black-and-white photograph of yet another mid-nineteenth-century Torah crown in silver—all this and much more. (Enough is enough: says J.K., and he says it looking into the future—the very future which, every Jew knows, is synonymous with both the Jewish State and Jewish History. Charges concerning the ultimate ineffectiveness of the policy of "rescue through work" as a method of extending the life of the ghettos and its inmates have overshadowed the moral problem involved, a moral problem common to the Jews and to non-Jews in occupied Europe and in particular to the millions of foreign laborers in Germany employed mostly in the war effort of their enemy. The problem was a simple one: How could such service, offering considerable help to the Germans, be justified when the laborers' compatriots were engaged in a mortal fight with their employers as army regulars or *resistants*? With the Jews, the problem had a difference: the Jews had been extirpated from the economic life of the countries of their residence, and unable to create a self-sustained economy in the condition of ghetto life, the only alternative to 100 percent unemployment lay in serving the enemy employer.... The lack of any articulate reflections on this moral issue either by the Jewish leadership or by the Jewish masses is the most striking proof of the hopelessness of dealing with moral problems while facing an amoral and cruel enemy. (Isaiah Trunk, 1972)

Having said this much in his longest *enough said* yet, our author places in his mental footnote for the sake of fairness Hannah Arendt: *On Revolution* (1977); *The Abandonment of the Jews: America and the Holocaust, 1941–1945*, by David S. Wyman (1984), with a new introduction by Elie Wiesel (1985); *Hannah Arendt: Politics, Consience, Evil*, by George Kateb (1984); *Hannah Arendt*, by Derwent May (1986); and "The SS: Instrument of the Final Solution," a chapter starting on page 69 as a matter of numerological course in *The War Against the Jews, 1933–1945*, by Lucy Dawidowicz (1986). He also finds there the still-to-be-completed most important and most mass-market-oriented edition of the *1,000 Year-old History and Culture of the East European Jews*.

Having finished his spiritual business Number Nine, Kosky tends to the sixth most important business of the day. He stops at the bookshelf at PRODUCTION, THEORY OF: FROM MARX TO FREUD. Here, bypassing a whole row of raw books devoted to Stalin's Sexuality, Kosky picks up another book. This was at one time his nonfictional favorite and here is why. He opens it on page 165. (In 1965 he became a published fiction writer: J.K.) and the page reveals to him the following fluid passage which, in the eyes of Jay Kay, becomes instantly "one of the most central safe-sex-oriented passages of this entire narrative." **No one will feel inclined to dispute. I think, that the mucous membrane of the lips and mouth is to be regarded as a primary** *erotogenic zone,* **since it preserves this earlier significance in the act of kissing, which is looked upon as normal. An intense activity of this erotogenic zone at an early age thus determines the subsequent presence of a romantic compliance on the part of the tract of mucous membrance which begins at the lips. Thus, at a time when the true sexual object, that is, the male organ, has already become known, circumstances may arise which once more increase the excitation of the oral zone, whose erotogenic character has, as we have seen, been retained. (Freud on Dora)*⁶⁹**

Here, number 69 matched against 1982 sends him first back to an integral footnote—69: Freud, Sigmund, Collected Papers, 6 Vols. New York, 1959. Then, impatiently, looking all over the patient page, our pageboy comes across this: "Just as each century has its own nature, so it produces its own primitives,"†⁶⁶ and this 66 comes to him from *The Ethnological Notebooks of Karl Marx*—another lip service to his own erotogenic narrative.

Bypassing the shelf where in the past he had always found all his novels, he inspects it carefully only to discover that this time all Kosky's novels are gone. **Are all his books sold out? Where is human nature so weak as in the bookstore? (Henry Ward Beecher)**

Rejoicing at his success, he is nevertheless suspicious. Maybe all these "titles" are not only out of stock, but also out of print, particularly now when German-owned Eidolon Books lost its competitive edge to the Israeli-French-owned Mirage Pockets? Quickly, but not anxiously, Kosky approaches the shop's mustached manager, a Proustian Orlando Furioso.

---

*⁶⁹: as found in *The Production of Desire: The Integration of Psychoanalysis into Marxist Theory,* by Richard Lichtman (1982), p. 165. Bibliography: 1. Psychology-Philosophy. 2. Personality-Social Aspects. 3. Marx, Karl, 1818–1883. Marxian School of Sociology. 5. Freud, Sigmund, 1856–1939. 6. Psychoanalysis.

†⁶⁶: mask cited by Lawrence Krader, *The Ethnological Notebooks of Karl Marx* (New York, 1972, p. 6), as cited in *The Production of Desire,* op. cit., p. 164.

"I do not *trouvé* or *retrouvé* anything by Norbert Kosky. Is Kosky all sold out?" says Kosky, with an exaggerated French accent.

"He's finished, not just sold out," says Orlando. "I doubt you'll find him—or his books—in any of our company's stores."

Our Tantric pretends to be stunned. *"Pourquois pas?"* he asks.

"Because he is no more listed either under fiction or under nonfiction. That's why," says Orlando, furiously fingering the fingernails of his left-hand fingers with the fingernails of the other.

"What do you mean 'he is no more'? Is he dead?" says Kosky.

"Only as a writer. Haven't you read all these yellow rumors written about him in the yellow press?" says the manager.

"I don't read rumors. I read fiction," says Kosky.

"Then by all means you must read these rumors," says the man. "With that many real-life rumors floating about him, nobody is interested in his fiction. They are dull. Dull by comparison to the daily pieces written about him."

"A novel is to be read for its characters, not for the character of the man or woman who wrote it, no matter what the author's character," says Kosky. **A book is like a huge cemetery where on most tombs one can no longer read the blotted-out name. (Proust)**

"You're wrong, *monsieur*, quite wrong!" says Orlando, summoning emotion. "Literary characters are all alike. Often you can't tell the difference between the characters of one author and the characters of another. Unless, of course, the author is also a well-known film actor." His remark briefly unsettles our Comrade Bukharin. "Every author is a celestial freak, you know. Take a look at Sick Sartre—"a nexus of phobias and megalomania." Knowingly, or not, he quotes Scott Sullivan, writing in *Newsweek* magazine. "While their books are dead, writers never die. They reincarnate through other people's writing about them. They are still here."

"Here?" Kosky shivers at the thought of running into Pierre Loti. *"All* of them?"

"Maybe not all. Maybe just one at a time," says Orlando. "I suggest, *monsieur*, that if you still intend to look for Kosky's books, look for them in a rare book shop, that is at the literary cemetery."

"From my point of view, a rare book shop *is* a literary cemetery," comments quickly Jay Kay. Another day, another spiritual Halloween. "Halloween meaning the most erotic holiday of the year," Kosky quotes from the program of Manhattan's only still-existing S'nd M, Inc., Vault. Going out in the guise of someone else is no joke, even if you don't know who that someone could be. Often, a disguise—a toupee—might fall off right in the middle of a conversation or lovemaking, say, and what do you do when in the middle of the most ticklish 69, a man suddenly loses the tickling power of his beard? Besides, wearing disguises irritates one's skin, and nothing makes your newly met friend, be it a man, a woman or a transsexual, peel off faster than the sight of a man who has just let his mustache peel off. Let us hope none of this will happen to him while he is here, sitting in the very center of the auditorium of the Reforming Arts Center. Tonight, "disguised as a *Niebiesky Ptak* (Bluebird) (Halina Poświatowska), who after midnight will turn into a Blue Beard, or literary Yankel attends a Chopinist piano concerto with Patrick Domostroy* at the piano, sitting next to a woman who, judging just by her belle looks, looks like Regina Belle, called by *Newsweek* magazine the "Sensuous Soul Sensation."

Glancing at the evening's program, our music man learns from it that Chopin's Fantasia Impromptu was published twenty years after he had written it. Now why? Wouldn't Chopin, "the most *hidden* of all men of genius" (George Sand), an impatient man, publish it right away? Was it because Fantasia Impromptu contained episodes that closely— perhaps a bit too closely—resembled Impromptu in E-flat by Ignaz Moscheles, another composer who was among Chopin's friends? Insecure as an artist, Chopin was, probably, ashamed to openly acknowledge it as a tribute to his musically lesser rival ... **the usual dictionary definition of the term "episode"—a part of the musical structure in which "new" ideas are presented is only superficially true. There are no "new" ideas in great music; there is only one idea diversified. (Alan Walker)**

"Such a resemblance might have happened by chance," musically inclined Dustin writes on the margin, "particularly since musical motifs are, like fictional ones, limited in number, and since Moscheles's piece was published some time earlier in the very same volume that con-

---

*Patrick Domostroy: a Jewish-Ruthenian-American (born 1933), composer of "Ultima Thule" (1965), "Music of the Spheres" (1968) and other works. See *Who Are the Major American Music Men?*, by Johannes Kepler and Thomas Kempis (Kreutzer Press, 1969), footnotes on pp. 6, 13–14, and 33.

tained Chopin's Nocturnes, op. 15. Quite likely, Chopin couldn't help being influenced by the work of a man he admired." Quite likely, indeed.

During the intermission, Kosky, our anonymous face in the crowd, gets lost in a crowd, while suffering from a massive attack of stage fright. To him, stage fright is spontaneous Self alert. It alerts him to the dangers the novelist faces when facing the public. Isn't the word public enough? Why do you also need a public? was Israel Kosky's first comment when, back in March 1957 in the city of Boat he heard his son's first public lecture. As a result, even his thumbs become rigid, and so do the common carpa-metacarpal joints of all his other fingers.

What is music? What does it do? And why does it have the effect it has? They say music has the effect of elevating the soul—rubbish! Nonsense! It has its effect, it has a terrible effect—I am speaking about its effect on me—but not at all of elevating the soul. Its effect is neither to elevate nor to degrade but to excite. How can I explain to you? Music makes me forget myself, my real situation. It transports me into a state that is not my natural one. (Tolstoy).*

Suddenly, our Masked Man is accosted by a little man wearing a most unhappy expression.

"Hello, Mr. Kosky," **the sick soul (William James)** says cheerfully. "I hope you don't mind my barging in on you like this. Given your wartime past, you must hate people who chase you like the SS."

"I do, but it's too late to complain," says Kosky. "How did you recognize me?" he asks. "Who betrayed me?"

"You were betrayed by your walk," says the man. "You walk like Bukharin in *Total State*."

His cover broken, his disguises disqualified, dispirited by the invasion, Kosky leaves the concert hall and rushes to the underground garage where his wheels are. There, he accosts the garage attendant and hands him a claim ticket reinforced by a tip of an inflationary $9.69.

The attendant, a white Anglo-Saxon Viking, takes one look at our

---

The Kreutzer Sonata, by Leo Tolstoy. (The highest spiritual rating so far: Norbert Kosky.) "The appearance of this novel by the distinguished author of *War and Peace* and *Anna Karenina* precipitated one of the most violent controversies in literary history. Comparing it with other contemporary writers, Anton Chekhov said, 'It is hardly possible to find anything of equal importance in conception and beauty of execution.' "

penguin and his long *peise*—another disguise legitimately falling out in strings from under his black hat.

"What sort of a *ghetto* car is it?" he asks.

"Electra decapitado and even though her Freud V6 (PRINTER: Freud, like Freudian, not fraud) knocks, don't knock it!" says Kosky.

Hearing this, a black woman garage-cleaner, as worn out as her coat, turns to him.

"You're Mr. Kosky, *the* writer, aren't you?" she says.

He gives up. "Yes, ma'am. Too bad my disguises won't work tonight."

"What disguises?" She is full of authentic surprise.

"My hairpiece. My mustache. My beard!" he exclaims, pulling at his *peise* while scratching his nose.

Puzzled, she examines him again. "You mean *the hairs* are not yours?"

"Of course they're not! When did you see me last?"

"See you? I've never seen you," she says, full of fervor or, was it some form of terror? "No, sir! I only *heard* you. I heard you speak on my TV. You said war was the beginning of the world. You said it with some kind of foreign accent."

"Wait, wait!" says Kosky. "That was when in front of **some six hundred million videots (*Being There*, Kosinski)** I handed out Oscars one after another! I was not disguised on that show. How could I be? I was there as myself, wearing my black tie, white shirt—without all this stuff." He pulls at what's left of his beard.

"I wouldn't know what you wore," she says wearily. "See, the tube on my TV is burned out. I look at it and see no picture. It's a blind telly. All I hear is the sound. Words are music to me. I listen to words with my eyes open," she says dreamily. "That's no different than watching a TV talk show with your eyes closed."

The attendant brings his car. Kosky drives out of the garage. Careful now, *piano piano*—this is neither the time nor place for verbal speeding or verbal slowing down. His mental headline keeps on flashing: NOVELIST KILLS SIX, WOUNDS NINE. But once he drives onto the Eastway, as straight and as boring as the old Moscow-Pinsk-Warsaw highway, he depresses the gas pedal, an action which, as most speed-exceeding Americans know, helps him to open himself up.

I am sure you will hear it all in *Telemusik*—the gagaku player, that mysterious familiar of the Japanese Imperial court, music from the happy

409

island of Bali, from the southern Sahara, from a Spanish village festival, from Hungary, the Shipibos of the Amazon River, the Omizutori ceremony in Nara, in which I took part for three whole days and nights. . . . I had my hands full keeping open the new and unknown world of electronic sound for such guests: I wanted them to feel "at home" and not "integrated" by some administrative act, but rather, genuinely engaged in an untrammeled spiritual encounter. (Karlheinz Stockhausen, 1966)

33

Back into the night life safely seated in his Electra-Vapido, our life molester skirts the sidewalks of Brooklyn's Sixty-ninth Avenue, that notorious district near the hotel Milton and the infamous Mini-Paradiso House Bar. **"I will kill you, House,"** he gasped. **"Vile and accursed House, I will tear you down. I will bring you down upon all the whores and boarders. I will wreck you, House."** (Thomas Wolfe) Here, the not-so-classy nightwalkers form a class unto themselves. Here, solitary men solicit solitary women who solitarily, yet en masse, line the sidewalks for the purpose of soliciting these solitary men. Men are such whores!

Woman has performed two missions in life: love and motherhood. Writers, perhaps in error, have always regarded the first of these more interesting than the second. . . . It is the woman of love whom writers love most. (Maupassant)

Kosky brings down to 6900 rpm the air-cooled 6.9-liter engine of his air-suspension-equipped car (0–6: 9.6 seconds; not bad for being neither a Mazda nor a BMW: J.K.) (he believes in being cooled off—as well as suspended from within by air, not water, remember?) and slows down. He unlocks the roof, then, pressing the ROOF UP button, watches the car's roof unfold and become erect almost to its full size, then, as if suddenly spent, fold down and collapse on the car's rear!

We had read Flaubert and de Maupassant, so this nightlife seemed quite poetic to us. The whore under the streetlight, her pimp, and free love in general, were favored subjects to many a young poet. The

411

whore became sort of a heroine—that too was in the air. (George Grosz)

From his car, our Holy Sinner ogles the ladies of the night. "Look at me!" One of them shoots off her trap the way Vautrin shoots off to Eugene de Rastignac. **Feel your pulse. Think whether you can get up morning after morning reinforced in yesterday's purpose. If that's the case, I'll make you an offer that no one would refuse. (Balzac)*** Suddenly he becomes aware that he is being trailed by the American-made Gabriel 609, a gray sedan occupied by two men dressed in gray suits. One of them keeps blowing the horn.

Anywhere he turns, they turn. It is clear that they are after him. He does not like it and his dislike stems from an emotion called fear. Involuntarily, he steps on the gas, and so do they.

Just then, his inner Ruthenian rooster wakes him up with a piercing sound. It is RUN, MAN, RUN! It's SS-OPERATION HAWK. Also, it is Operation Fear: yesterday's World War II fear fused with the fear of World War III.

Kosky's inner emergency instructions are clear. Like a barely hatched chick, which must first go silent on hearing the cry of the hawk, he must urgently seek safety by running, and running fast. Voluntarily, he makes one fast turn, then another, and so does the gray menace. *Look down, look down, this lonesome road . . .* , he sings, while, alternating sudden accelerations with sudden braking, he manages to turn his car by some one hundred and sixty-nine degrees, a trick he learned long ago by describing it first in one of his novels, though he had never practiced it on the road. One can always learn something new, even from oneself. The trick works. He is now facing the robbers' sedan, and stepping on the gas, tires screeching, he passes it by burning rubber, only to see the sedan perform the same trick better and faster. These guys must have learned it from life, not fiction. Tires screeching, burning rubber, they are on his tail again. He takes off, but he is no match for them. The gray sedan passes him and blocks his path. The two gray men jump out, their *Nacht und Nebel* guns drawn and pointed at Kosky, who is still locked inside his car. **During the next few years no substantial anti-Jewish legislation was enacted. Instead the SS, the most prestigious**

---

*"Freud's famous dictum summarizing this is: 'Where there is id, let there be ego,' " writes David Cole Gordon, in his *Self Love and a Theory of Unification* (1968), p. 69.

and dreaded branch of the National Socialist movement, increasingly began to assert its hegemony with regard to the Jews over all state and party institutions. (Hannah Arendt, op. cit., p. 69.) Quickly, in order to turn off the engine before they will turn off forever the engine of his life, he turns off the ignition key, but frightened as he is, he first turns it the wrong way.

After the two-day delay the plenary session was reconvened. Bukharin and Rykov were summoned before it in order to hear the decision that had been reached. . . . The session was being held in the Kremlin where Bukharin lived. All he had to do was cross the yard and enter the building where the meeting was under way. The cloakroom was deserted. Rykov came in at exactly the same time as Bukharin. As they were handing in their overcoats eight men walked forward from the wall and approached Bukharin and Rykov, four apiece. This was the arrest. (Roy A. Medvedev)

"Police! Get out with your hands up! AND DON'T MOVE!" screams one of the men, flashing his police badge.

His heart overflowing with coronary blood flow—there goes his athletic heart syndrome!*—his knees reluctant to bend, he steps out of the car. "What is your maximum heart rate? An easy way to arrive at a figure is to subtract your age from 220."† To camouflage the shaking of his entire spiritual structure, our literary shakeup man attempts, in accordance with Rule Six of Good Car's Car-Ma, to shake hands with the detective. The attempt fails. Enough said. Picture our eagle spread-eagled against the car, and what you get is *Miranda* vs. *Arizona*,‡ or an American version of the arrest of Comrade Bukharin.

---

*Responding to strenuous exercise (whether mental or physical), the spiritually sound athlete voluntarily increases the volume of the heart's stroke, while the uninitiated spiritual slob increases cardiac output by increasing the heart rate. (Norbert Kosky)

†*Swim Swim: A Complete Handbook for Fitness Swimmers*, op. cit., p. 48.

‡In the *Miranda* vs. *Arizona* case decided in 1966 by the U.S. Supreme Court under Chief Justice Earl Warren, the Court ruled that the prosecution may not use statements made by a person in police custody unless certain minimum procedural safeguards were followed. Known as the Miranda warnings, these include informing arrested persons prior to questioning that they have a right to remain silent, that anything they say may be used as evidence against them and that they have a right to the presence of an attorney, either retained or appointed. No such safeguards exist for those questioned by certain investigative reporters.

Anonymous hands frisk him from behind. "He's clean," says the blue-eyed, very blond Aryan, as Kosky straightens and turns to face him, and the other man pockets his gun. The other man is a pure U.S.-made Puritan.

While the Artab checks his driver's license and car registration, the Puritan quickly peers into his car and accidentally opens the glove compartment, where, no longer accidentally, he presses the hidden button which promptly opens the car's trunk. Thus, *technically speaking*, the trunk was opened by accident, not by the Puritan without a search warrant. This prompts the Aryan to peer into the trunk. "D'you mind if I just take a look at what's inside your Jewish trunk?" he asks with a sweet smile.

"Our courts mind it; they have ruled that police cannot stop or search a car on the basis of mere suspicion," says our literary suspect. "Besides, any incriminating evidence found in an illegal search without probable cause will be dismissed by the Court."

"This is the U.S.A. This is Free America. Free of the Knesset* saloon," says the Aryan with an Eichmannesque smile.

"While the Fourth Amendment gives you the right to be secure against unreasonable search and seizure, it does not protect you against *all* search and seizure, however unreasonable, in your Diaspora," says the Puritan.

"The word 'unreasonable' is defined through judicial interpretation of probable cause, a phrase unfortunately also present in the amendment. The law protects you against unreasonable search and seizure,

---

The Knesset: The KneSSet, Israel's legislature (Israel is a parliamentary democracy, and structured according to the principle of ensuring checks and balances within the system: J.K.), took its name and fixed its membership at 120 from the *Knesset ha-Gedolah* (Great Assembly), the Jewish representative body convened by Ezra and Nehemiah in the early Second Temple period, some 2,500 years ago.

The KneSSet is a single-chamber house whose main tasks are to legislate and to oversee the workings of the executive (the cabinet), both in public plenary session and through its ten parliamentary committees. It is also charged with approving the state budget.

The KneSSet is elected every four years, but may dissolve itself and call for new elections before the end of its term.

The tenth KneSSet, which was elected on June 30, 1981, voted to hold early elections. (Press clipping, 1982)

but not against a reasonable one—and nobody has yet defined what is reasonable and what is not. So what's the hurry? Where are you going now, my son of Zion?" he asks while letting his hands go casually through the trunk, messing up all of Kosky's earthly valor.

"I'm going back to life. One never knows when one might die. That's why, to catch up with what's left, I'm always in a hurry," says our literary Zionist. **The Diaspora Jew has not only a duty to give but a right to receive as well: inspiration from Zion, faith from Zion.**

Judaism stands on four pillars: God, the Torah, the people of Israel, and the land of Israel. The loss of any one of these entails the loss of the others; one depends upon the other. And hence every Jew, wherever he may be found, is precious.

The people of Israel is a tree whose roots are in Israel and whose branches are in the Diaspora. A tree cannot flourish without roots. But how can it bear fruit without branches? Be careful with the branches! (Abraham Joshua Heschel)

"What's the white substance?" asks the Aryan, picking up a plastic bag from the trunk, "and since he has no search warrant he picks it up as if by accident." (Jay Kay)

"White substance? No kidding! Is that your Colombian connection or your family's World War II ashes?" asks the Puritan.

"The white substance is *allium cepa*," says Kosky. "The bulbs of an Asiatic plant with a characteristic *alliaceous* taste and odor. It's an onion."

"I see it's an onion," says the Aryan, glancing into the bag. "But what about this?" He pulls out a large empty two-pound coffee can suspended on a loop of wire. "What do you smoke in this?"

"It's a comet," says Kosky. "A harmless modern-day replica of a harmless relic from my harmful past." **The comet consisted merely of a one-quart preserve can, open at one end and with a lot of small nail holes he punched in the sides. A three-foot loop of wire was hooked to the top of the can by way of a handle, so that we could swing it either like a lasso or like a censer in church. (Kosinski, 1965)**

"A comet?" The Aryan lifts the can.

"A comet. A portable stove for a wartime Ruthenian Boy Scout. You can cook or broil a bird or fish in it."

"And burn Manhattan and Staten Island, too!" intones the Aryan, throwing the comet back into the car.

415

"What do you do for a living, Mr. Ruthenian?" asks the Puritan.

"I write novels," says Kosky, "I write them one at a time," he clarifies.

I think that anyone who does not *need* to be a writer, who thinks he can do something else, ought to do something else. Writing is not a profession but a vocation of unhappiness. (Simenon)*

"You write them about arson and onions?" volunteers the Puritan.

"Not about them but on them. Meaning, under their daily influence. Arson is my inner fire. Onions are my martini."

"So what do you write about," the man persists.

"I write about disinformation."

"What do we learn from a book—any book? The first answer that comes to mind is facts, information. (Thomas Fleming)†

"Wasn't there something about you recently in the papers?" says the Aryan, checking Kosky's face as if it were a *ken karte* (a W.W.II German-issued I.D.).

"There was."

"What was it?"

"A six-item list of my spiritual sins—including my not yet being to the State of Israel."‡ (Kosky planned to visit Israel for the first time in 1988: J.K.)

"Hey, I know who he is. He is a celebrity of Common Cause!"§ says

---

*Quoted in *The Muse and the Martini* by Donald W. Goodwin, M.D. in *JAMA* (*Journal of the American Medical Association*), April, 1973.

†See: *Portrait of the Novel As a Learning Experience* by Thomas Fleming, the American P.E.N., vol. 1, No. 2, Fall 1969.

‡"I shall never forget traveling with President Chaim Weizmann in Switzerland in the summer of 1949, and watching his excitement at new architecture, at new styles of apartment buildings, factories, laboratories, the landscaping of public gardens—even admiring the clean and cool typography on hoardings and display advertisements. 'You know,' he said, 'my dream is for Israel to be like Switzerland: a highly civilized country small in size, but a great power in quality of standards, civic courtesies, and above all beauty of everyday life. We shall get there,' he continued, 'within two generations. We must not falter or compromise in our quest for quality, and in our engagement, our commitment to excellence.' (The Lord Weidenfeld of Chelsea, Bezalel Academy speech, Dec. 6, 1986)

§"ABOUT COMMON CAUSE. Common Cause is a nonprofit, nonpartisan citizens' lobbying organization supported by dues and contributions. (Common Cause, June 1987)

the Puritan. "How come you are not a member of the U.S. Urban Swamp Rangers Association? (a charity for families of police officers who, often out of line, fall dead or crippled in the line of duty: J.K.) With a smell like this you sure need it. Let's leave him alone!" Laughing at him, the Aryan and the Puritan get into their gray Japanese-made Gabriel YAZDA (YAZDA: Ruthenian for an "undefined wheel movement." *Ruthenian-English Portable Dictionary*) and drive away, "trailing gray vapor of that Old World fear, the fear of another unreasonable World War." (Jay Kay)

His (happily progressing: J.K.) work is interrupted by an event that leaves him *totally* unperturbed: he is a self-employed writer, remember? With Self for an employer, how and why would he fear the 1987 market crash? His name is, after all, Kosky the Scribe, not Ivar Kreuger, the Swedish match-making King who first started the first crash of 1929, then killed himself.

BUSINESS DAY

FINANCIAL WORLD IN AN UPHEAVAL
DAY TO REMEMBER IN FINANCIAL DISTRICT

From the trading floors of the big brokerage firms to the stock exchanges to the shoeshine stands in the heart of the financial district, it was clear that yesterday would be a day etched in people's memories for years to come. . . .

Computers Strained by Deluge
At brokerage firms across the country yesterday, some traders saw their flickering green screens covered with question marks, while others watched helplessly as their terminals fell blank or hopelessly behind as more than 600 million shares were traded on the New York Stock Exchange.

U.S. Debt Issues Rise Strongly
The steep drop in rates for Treasury bills—a traditional safe haven for investors in times of uncertainty—began last week after the Treasury sold new bills at a rate of 6.96 percent.

(The New York Times, Oct. 20, 1987)

As a literary quickie, as a tribute to his own 6.9 percent story as well as History, he rereads Ayn Rand's play *Night of January 16th*, about the match King's fall, then with a sigh, SO WHAT? DON'T WE ALL CRASH?, our fictional hero peacefully retires to the niche of his fiction.

On the following day he faces the reality.

The Manfred, a rent-stabilized apartment house, has suddenly turned into a destabilized cooperative. Kosky must either buy his apartment at a royal price that would swallow most of his past, present and future royalties (two thirds of which have been "killed" by the 1987 market crash: J.K.) (including the ones accruing from the Israeli Hebrew editions* of his work), or move out.

"What are you going to do about it, Norbert?" asks R. Judah Zevi Streitner, Kosky's dispassionate lawyer friend, whose recent embrace of Kosher Yoga and Tantrism has helped Kosky save on many costly litigations.

"Moving out of an apartment in today's America is not the end of life, you know. Finding one is. Read 'How to Find an Apartment' (seriously) in the current issue of *New York Magazine*," Kosky writes to Streitner.

Do you know why I came to you? It is simply because there is no one anywhere in the whole great world I could go to. Do you understand what I say? No one to go to. Do you conceive the desolation of the thought—no-one-to-go-to? (Conrad)

But what if you've got no one to see and nowhere to go to? A man needs to have a somewhere. He needs it at the time when he's got to go somewhere. (Dostoyevsky)

On Streitner's advice, Kosky returns a call from one Samson Brin, one of the six vice-presidents of Matthew Hopkins Incorporated ("the fastest growing personal computer company this side of a jury system"), who wants to talk business with him. "Business which, in his words, will make Kosky 'a rich man in no time.'"

No sane man who's about to lose his shelter can disregard a message like this, and Kosky does not.

"I like your studio, Mr. Kosky," says Samson Brin when he arrives

---

*Here the reader is most encouraged to turn his mental energies to *I Asked for Wonder: A Spiritual Anthology*, ed. by Abraham Joshua Heschel, with an Introduction by Samuel H. Dresner, 1987.

419

thirty minutes too early for their appointment. Brin is all fast sell. He is straight to the point.

"I like the way you live. This place is full of *intellectual stench*," Brin says, looking around. "This place is clean. It's functional. And it's simple. As simple as truth. I can see you living in this place as comfortably as a character in a novel to be called, say, *Truthpit!*"

"A character occupies a novel forever. I've got to move out—and that's the sad truth."

"Truth cannot be sad," says Brin. "Truth simply *is*. I know what I'm talking about," he says. "I've been in the business of truth for over twenty-five years. Truth has been my calling! And that is why I've called on you!" He becomes a salesman of sAVONarola* calling!

"I'm in the business of fable, not truth," says Kosky. "Now tell me the truth: why did you want to see me?" Kosky asks as he and Brin sit down and face each other across Kosky's desk. THE CONSENSUS THEORY OF TRUTH. **Truth, according to Habermas, is something which a speaker implicitly claims for any assertion that he makes. In being bold enough to speak, the speaker invites us to believe that what he says is intelligible, that he is sincere in saying it, that he is not speaking out of turn, at least not in any serious sense of that phrase, and that he is speaking the truth: these are the four validity claims, as Habermas calls them, of any assertion. (Philip Pettit, 1970)†**

"Why?" Brin leans forward. "Because you need my company and because we need you. My company manufactures the most advanced line of the Time-Truth™ machines, and for some ten years now you've been one of this country's better known TV talk-show guests." He gives Kosky a pointed look. "We need you because we have followed your FLOAT-OR-SWIM accident with utmost interest: it was a classic case of public drowning—which is what great public hangings used to

---

*Fra. Girolamo Savonarola, the "Hermit of Florence," who, preaching a pure doctrine from the pulpit of the puritanical church of Santa Reparata in Florence, attempted to purify the sex-infested papacy of Alexander VI—the orgiastic Borgia— but failed.

†"Habermas on Truth and Justice," by Philip Pettit, in the *Royal Institute of Philosophy Lecture Series*: 14, Cambridge, 1982, p. 210. Also see: "Habermas's Consensus Theory of Truth," by Mary Hesse, *Proceedings of the Philosophy of Science Association*, 1978, 2 (1979). Reprinted in Mary Hesse's *Revolutions and Reconstructions in the Philosophy of Science* (Hassocks: Harvester, 1980).

be!" He pulls from his attaché case several worn-out press clippings and pedantically spreads them on the table, smoothing their rough edges.

"Like your characters, you too are a LAP—a literary accident-prone." Brin looks up. "According to our experts, a LAP is usually a writer or a poet who glorifies the incident, not the plot, particularly when they're also like you into screen-and-play writing or teaching an Art vs. Drama course. In a novel, incident is what accident is in life. As a matter of natural course—as part of their natural case-history. Many writers with the literary accident habit had very bad childhoods and bad experiences with authority. Such people invite accidents—the way the characters in your novels do. Maybe you have picked up their characteristics? In any case, your literary profile makes you an ideal LAP, you fall straight into my company's literary lap."

"Literary? Aren't you in the polygraph business?"

"We sure are. The word *polygraph* means 'multiwriting' and if multiwriting isn't literary, what is?" says Brin. "The truth is that, since the invention of polygraphs, writing—and, mind my words, the literary arts—will never be the same again."

"Neither will the truth," says Kosky. "Literary truth is a bit like *music concrete.*"*

A quiet and spaciously composed continuity of sounds is disturbed six times by a short refrain. This refrain contains glissandi and clusters, trills, bass notes (in the piano) and brief snatches of melody, elements which are absent from the first form. . . . (Karlheinz Stockhausen)

"It is said that the accuracy rate of even the best polygraph, of the latest truth machine, is no better than fifty-fifty. That's no better than chance," he goes on. "No better but very bad when it comes to finding out who's telling the truth—and who's not."

---

*In order to understand Kosky's literacy *spiel*, his narrative telemusic, the reader should have some firsthand knowledge of *musique concret*, of *Kontakte* (contacts), for electronic sounds, piano and percussion, by Karlheinz Stockhausen, WERGO 6009 (Germany), as well as Karlheinz Stockhausen's *spiel* and *kreuzspiel* (crossplay); his *Punkte* (points); Kontra-Punkte (VEGO C$_{30}$ A$_{66}$); his *Solo* (No. 19, first performed in 1966); his *Stimmung* (Attuning), written for (sexual: J.K.) sex-(SS)tet; his *Pole* (1969) (formidable: J.K.); as well as his erotic *Für kommende Zeiten* (Four Times to Come)—all part of his 1969 "texts for intuitive music." (All numbers retained for reasons of spiritual ranking: J.K.)

"Wrong. Our truth machines are certainly more reliable than chance," says Brin.

"How much more?" asks Kosky.

"It's not our company's public policy to reveal such intimate figures," says Brin.

"Why not?"

"Privileged information. This is the time of industrial spying. We've got competition, you know!"

"Would you reveal such information by answering questions posed to you by an Insight 900 Time-Truth™ machine?" asks Kosky.

Brin pulls back. "Now of all people why would I have to subject myself to taking a lie-detector test?"

"Say for the sake of a better-paid job with a better-paying company. Your potential new employer might request that you take the test as a condition for hiring you. What then?"

"Then I guess I would take it." Brin grins involuntarily.

"But what if, during the test, your privileged information about Insight 900 is detected by the examiner who, unbeknownst to you, might be working for one of your many competitors? Wouldn't that be disloyal to Matthew Hopkins?" asks Kosky.

"I guess it would, but such disloyalty is often the price for new loyalty," says Brin. "Believe me, Mr. Kosky, soon, very soon, the whole American jury system will be replaced by mass-produced lie boxes—the American-made lie-detecting devices."

"Isn't the American jury system the original, and still the best, lie-detector?" asks Kosky.

"By now it's as original as the first Ford. And as obsolete as Thomas Jefferson's attacks on the king. Where is the king today?"

"Don't you dare to say this. Even in its draft, Jefferson's Declaration is, spiritually speaking, one of the nine purest spiritual documents ever written! Enough is enough!" Kosky raises his non-yogi voice. I am . . . mortified to be told that, in the United States of America . . . a question about the sale of a book can be carried before the civil magistrate. . . . Are we to have a censor whose imprimatur shall say what books may be sold and what we may buy? Shall a layman, simple as ourselves, set up his reason as the rule for what we are to read? . . . It is an insult to our citizens to question whether they are rational beings or not. (Thomas Jefferson)

"I meant Jefferson's autobiography,* not his Declaration." Brin grins.

"His autobiography was the very first autofiction ever written, then rewritten," says Kosky. "That's why Jefferson mentions in it his brother and six sisters only by their number—NOT EVEN BY THEIR NAMES. That's why he barely mentions in it his marriage to Martha Skelton, and even her tragic death which followed ten years of his 'unchequered happiness.' "

Whatever Jefferson is eliminating from his written account of his life—his personality, his inner feelings, his private relations—he is stating, affirming, and maintaining his original authorship of the Declaration. If, as author, he had to subject himself to the revision and censorship of a deliberative body, he is nonetheless—rather, all the more—the writer contending at the end of his life for his original text. (James M. Cox, 1978)†

"Now you see what I mean," beams Brin with another grin. "Even Jefferson, the greatest American who ever lived, did not tell the full truth, and if he lied, how could one trust an ordinary American member of an ordinary American jury? Now you know why today, more and more juries rely on the polygraph—on the Time-Truth™ machine—not on assembly-line witnesses so difficult to assemble by the time the case comes before the court," Brin goes on. "In a society where nobody knows what the truth is, lying is a growth phenomenon. And so is the lie-detecting industry."

"Doesn't the outcome of your machine depend not on the truth but on 'relevancy'—on the right questions asked of a witness at the right moment by one of your many examiners?"

I . . . pray you to remember, that when two lutes or two harps, near to one another, both set to the same tune, if you touch the string of

---

*The autobiography of Thomas Jefferson is the nonoriginal title of his narrative text Jefferson initially called *Memoranda*. Subsequently, this was first published as *Memoir* by Jefferson's grandson and literary estate executor—(Ed.)

†*Recovering Literature's Lost Ground* by James M. Cox in *Autobiography: Essays Theoretical and Critical*, edited by James Olney, Princeton, 1980, p. 130. See also *Autobiographical Acts: The Changing Situation of a Literary Genre* by Elizabeth W. Bruss, 1976, and above all, *Victims: Textual Strategies in Recent American Fiction*, "Kosinski: The Problem of Language," by Paul Bruss, Chapter 10, pp. 167–238, 1981. (Textual, printer, not sexual!)

the one, the other consonant harp will sound at the same time, though nobody touch it. (Sir Kenelm Digby)

Examiners who, like the rest of us, are prejudiced out of, say, their initial unhappiness called the original sin?

"Still, the truth is that most people lie! Do you know of any better protection against uncertainty?"

"Faith. Even if it is as blind as was Feuchtwanger's.* I can't think of anything else," says Kosky.

"Then fear not the truth. Have faith in our truth-manufacturing machine," says Brin. "Did you know that the Time-Truth™ Series 900 grew out of top-secret saboteur interrogation research conducted during the Vietnam War by the American military?"

"No, I didn't. But if the military research was top secret, how did your company ferret the top secrets from the top brass?"

"I knew you'd ask," says Brin. "We got it by being on top. By using an earlier version—an Insight 600 truth machine—on some of the top research people, who, while taking our top lie-detector test, told us straight from the top of their heads the truth about their top secrets."

"Wasn't that thievery?" asks Kosky.

"Absolutely not!" Brin raises his hand as if swearing to tell nothing but the truth. "We usurped the result of their research for the sake of truth and we've made some money on the way. And speaking of truth"— he glances at Kosky offhandedly—"we think we could help you answer once and for all the question, WHAT IN YOUR LIFE IS FICTION? And how much of your fiction has made its way into your life before, during or after you wrote it? These questions are asked of you these days more often than of any other writer in our Company's long history."

"How could you?" Kosky revolts. "No writer could ever answer such a question except Cynthia Ozick, my spiritual writing cousin. **Novelists**

---

*Apropos the intellectual brand of faith (call it naïveté): "When Lion Feuchtwanger visited Moscow in 1937, he discovered there 'genuine freedom' (and wrote a book justifying the Moscow Trials), but he preferred to live his refugee life under 'formal' bourgeois freedom, first in France, then in America. . . . He wrote the following about 'confessions': If that was lying or prearranged, then I don't know what truth is.' Quoted by John Caute, *Fellow Travellers* (an unpublished Mss.), from which some of the subsequent quotations are taken," writes Leopold Labedz in "The Destiny of Writers in Revolutionary Movements," in *Survey*, No. 1 (82), Winter, 1972, p. 15.

424

invent, deceive, exaggerate and impersonate for several hours every day and frequently on the weekend. Through the creation of bad souls they enter the demonic as a matter of course. They usurp emotions and appropriate lives. (Cynthia Ozick, 1987)

"We feel that answering such a question could be of great advantage to you—as it would be to any other Bruno Schulz–type novelist," says Brin.

"And I don't think so," says Kosky, lifting an accusing finger to the sky.

"If any State agency—or an agent of the State—ever asks me such a question," Kosky declares solemnly, "I will refuse to answer it on the grounds that my answer might incriminate the entire field of imaginative literature—and with it the power of imagination."

"Once you answer this question and get the question of truth out of your way, the sky is the limit," says Brin. "You could even start a new Norbert Kosky Writers' School. You could again teach at Beulah University a course entitled 'The Church of Writing' or give a course on Spurs or your Portable Nietzsche."*

"I would refuse to answer it first only as a writer," says Kosky. "As a simple believer I prefer to believe in the power of the imaginative workshop, rather than in the productive power of the working masses. Karl Marx's *Capital*, Volume One, is the only imaginative book I can think of where number one stands for number six—or even for an ideologically qualified number nine, a number I usually reserve for 'The Production of Desire' (Richard Lichtman)."†

Spurs (and J.K.) *Nietzsche Style*, in one volume by Jacques Derrida, 1979.

†A literary stylist, trained in the Jewish narrative tradition, Marx criticized Hegel's books also for the impunity of his philosophical vintage writing style. Just listen to this: "We would draw attention here to a peculiarity of Hegel's style which constantly recurs and which has its roots in mysticism. The whole paragraph runs:

'The patriotic sentiment acquires its specifically determined content from the *various members of the organism* of the state. This *organism* is the differentiation of the Idea into its various elements and their objective reality.'	1. 'The patriotic sentiment acquires its specifically determined content from *the various members* of the organism of the state. These different members are the *various powers of the state* with their functions and spheres of activity.' "

See *Karl Marx: Early Writings*, including his 1843 essay "On the Jewish Question" (Vintage Books, 1975), pp. 66–69.

425

"But let's get to the point," Brin says. "Do you or don't you want to buy this apartment the minute your home-cum-office turns co-op?"

"Sure, I do," says Kosky. "I want it bad—but not bad enough to turn bad in order to get it. I'm into ownership of life, into co-oping life into my work and my work into art. Art, not a co-op."

"You don't have to get bad. You don't even have to write another bad book," says Brin with a grin. "You're an actor. Didn't you play Bukharin? All we want you to do is to play yourself in one of our Matthew Hopkins Incorporated TV commercials."

"What's the commercial about?"

"It's called a TRUTH DUEL. All you have to do is answer simple questions put to you face-to-face by an examiner—a professional literary critic working on the latest improved Insight Series 960 Truth Computer."

"That's all?" Kosky marvels. "What kind of questions?"

"Simple. So simple that they all can be answered by a simple yes or no. I can already see the headlines," he goes on, obviously pleased with himself. "FICTION WRITER TELLS THE TRUTH ABOUT HIS FICTION. I'll bet you'll be the first fiction writer taking a public lie-detector test to prove whether he told the truth in his fiction."

"Certainly not the first! Sixth perhaps. Maybe even ninth, but not first," Kosky says. "Saint Augustine was probably the first. He is the one who, working free-lance outside of his publisher, issued a guaranteed truth of his confessions by dedicating them to God. Each time he was asked by the hostile press whether he had told the truth about himself, he would raise his eyes and arms to His God and say, 'He knows the truth. Would I dare to lie to Him?' The second best known was, surely, Jean-Jacques Rousseau. He is the literary masturbateur supreme who improved on this 'guarantee' by claiming in his *Confessions* that on Judgment Day he would stand before the Throne with a copy of his book personally inscribed to God and swear that in his book he had told the truth about himself and nothing but the truth. And, speaking about narrative-going-down 96 (or even going-down-there 69), didn't Christopher Isherwood say in *Down There on a Visit* that his fictional character was in one sense his father and in another sense his son?"

"Those were all literary guarantees nobody took seriously in the first place," says Brin, chewing on an ice cube. "We are talking about you, a pen professional being asked for the very first time, on TV in a TV commercial—this means in front of this whole fucking country, where nobody is any longer fucking—now, seriously, Mr. Kosky, DID YOU OR DID YOU NOT BASE YOUR NOVELS ON FACT? YES OR NO?"

"What I write is first conceived by me, written by me, and then on my strict instructions, published by my publishers as straight'nd serious autofiction. Whether auto or not, fiction is a vessel that floats on a natural suspension made of make-believe," Kosky says.

A man of flesh and blood has a vessel (container); as long as the vessel is whole, he is happy with it. If it is broken, he no longer desires it. But not so the Holy One, Blessed Be He! As long as the vessel is whole, He does not wish to see it; broken, He desires it! And what is the favorite vessel of the Holy One, Blessed Be He? The heart of man! (*Proverbs* 16.5)

"That's why you're in trouble. Believe me, having dealt for so long in the make-believe, in autofiction, you may no longer know what to make of your life or of your fiction, or in what to believe. Let the Insight 960 sort it all out."

"This can be done only in a novel. I've already done this—this and so much more—in my *Healer of 96 Degrees*, my next proto-novel."

"Sort it all out—how?" Kosky despairs. **The mind is a kind of theatre, where several perceptions successively make their appearance; pass, re-pass, glide away, and mingle in an infinite variety of postures and situations. (David Hume)**

"Simple," says Brin. "Truth is an idea. An idea originates in the mind." He touches his head with his index finger. He takes a deep—not Yoga-type—breath. "Each time our examiner—think of him as an unbiased TV talk-show host—asks you a pertinent question, long before you respond to it with your YES or NO, the Insight 960 translates your brain's inaudible discharges into graphic, and if need be audible, signals."

"I don't think your Insight could do what I can't," says Kosky. **The conclusion now presents itself to us that there is indeed something innate lying behind the perversions but that it is something innate in *everyone*, though as a disposition it may vary in its intensity and may be increased by the influences of actual life. (Freud)** "I am a typical twin composed of two opposing Ruthenian-Jewish halves: as opposing and as drawn to each other as are the cold Moon and the hot Sun, as is the church and

427

Synagogue." Within him resides the stern'nd serious Jewish *mitnagdim*, an Apollonian who, full of himself, confronts with horror the other half: the polo-playing, horseshit-splashing Dionysian Hasid. ("See footnotes marked 69, 68, and 67," adds Jay Kay.)

"By their nature, words are ambivalent—their worth changes with each new word added to a sentence—and often purposefully so," says Kosky. "As ambivalent as writers when they are writing to their literary executioners." **The only thing that grieves me and makes me dance with rage is the cropping up of the legend set afloat by Hugh Clifford about my hesitation between English and French as a writing language. . . . When I wrote the first word of *Almayer's Folly*, I had already for years and years been thinking in English. I began to think in English long before I mastered, I won't say the style (I haven't done that yet) but the mere uttered speech. (Conrad to Walpole, 1916)***

"That's why you've got nothing to lose," Brin exults. "If with the help of the Insight 960 our examiner will declare that your books are all one big tall tale, that's O.K., because that's what fiction is supposed to be. Right? And it's just as O.K. if he will pronounce them all true to your life. After all, you can't be faulted for writing from your life no more than you can be for faulting Hannah Arendt. Either way, you'll get everybody—Jew, non-Jew and The Other—off your literary back. What do you say?"

"I say that I would rather fail to take such a test, than take it," says Kosky.

STOCKS PLUNGE 669 POINTS, 609 MILLION VOLUME NEARLY DOUBLES RECORD

WHO GETS HURT

DOES 1987 EQUAL 1929?

NOVELIST FAILS TO SHOW UP FOR TRUTH TEST

We have learned today that novelist Norbert Kosky has *failed* to give a reason why he has refused to take part in the Matthew Hopkins

---

*Published in 1916, Hugh Walpole's *Joseph Conrad* "literally drove the Pole up the wall" (Jay Kay). Still in all, those who believe in Conrad's Polish and French

Time-Truth Insight 960 lie-detector commercial, in which he would have been asked, for the entire nation to hear, "Did you or did you not tell the truth about your life in your novels?" Mr. Kosky *failed* to make himself available for comment, and all attempts to reach him by phone failed. Said by numerous friends to be in town, and "definitely not in hiding," the otherwise sociable and gregarious author has *nevertheless* failed to return any of our many calls to his answering service and also has *failed* to acknowledge receipt of our various letters of inquiry, some of which were pushed under the door of his apartment, some tucked inside the laundry delivered to his door, and some squeezed under the windshield wipers of his semi-antique American-made 1969 motor car. The implications of his refusal are clear. Kosky is afraid to face the truth. (*Times Square Record*)

---

ghosts claim that some passages in *The Arrow of God* and in *The Rover* were most likely thought out by him either in French or in Polish. There are others who insist that his "Amy Foster" and "The Sisters" were conceived by him first in Polish, although he has always insisted that he conceived them in English. See "Walpole, H., pp. 191, 192, 291, 292," the entire index entry to Gustav Morf's *The Polish Shades and Ghosts of Joseph Conrad*, "an excellent work of scholarly conradiana." (Jay Kay)

3 5

I think I would have raised an outcry
if I had believed my eyes. But I didn't believe them at first—the thing
seemed so impossible. The fact is I was completely unnerved by a sheer
blank fright, pure abstract terror, unconnected with any distinct shape
of physical danger. What made this emotion so overpowering was—
how shall I define it?—the moral shock I received, as if something altogether monstrous, intolerable to thought and odious to the soul, had
been thrust upon me unexpectedly. (Joseph Conrad).

Odious to the soul or not, this is the time our hero must visit The
Shrine—the imposing offices which, appropriately imposed upon 969
Fifth Avenue, house Eidolon Books—Eidolon Press and Eidolon Soft
Hardware.

At 969 Kosky goes straight to the sixty-sixth top floor of the building,
which houses Eidolon's publicity and advertising department. "In order
to understand why publishers pay so much attention to advertising, keep
in mind that in the mind of every publisher book advertising is second
in importance only to book burning, as it is in the minds of their writers,"
cryptically remarks Jay Kay. I do not wish to kill nor to be killed, but I
can foresee circumstances in which these things would be by me unavoidable. (Thoreau)

Once there, Kosky heads for the office of John Spellbound, Jr., the
publicity director. As one of nine head-giving and head-receiving hon-
chos—all vice-presidents, i.e., company muses—John is said to be the
sixth most important head man in the company, if not the ninth in the
entire publishing business. In the works of Dante and Saint Thomas

430

Aquinas, nine is an angelic number. It is the holy trinity multiplied by itself. (Vartan Gregorian)

Imagine John, a tall, baldish booby in his forties. Then, think of Marion Spitfire, his twenty-six-year-old, fiery high-performance head-giving girlfriend. She is a bookish madonna you last saw in Los Angeles in the Westwood Public Library. "A classy sex-server supplied to Eidolon courtesy of the Command Performance Agency which, in keeping with the new No-Touch policy, offers to its customers 'sexual gratification of the most intense nature without the danger of body-fluids exchange.' One way or another, she becomes in New York, a prisoner of time— and time renders her its ultimate jailer." Jay Kay pronounces the verdict.

John and Marion greet Kosky with sad skoals as our sad'nd tainted waterfowl sadly flies in.

"Welcome to a Happy Media Twister!" says John. Shaking hands with Kosky, and seeing his author's shaking hand, he is uncertain whether to laugh, cry or cheer in his author's face.

Keep in mind that, until now, our literary fakir has been unearthed at the Manfred, this Spiritual Burial place, for some months now— "ever since he was plastered by the mud first thrown at his solo water act by the infamous *Rumor Express*, and sealed by the media midgets with the seal of public abuse" (in the words of still angry Jay Kay).

John hands Kosky a mountain of press clippings, some of which Kosky—"our press martyr," Marion calls him—has already seen. "Our advertising department says you couldn't buy all this unsolicited adversity for six million bucks! As a result, you've been overexposed! And how!" he moans, noticing Kosky's semi-martyred glance.

"I never thought I'd hear any publicity director complain about his writer's media megaexposure," says Kosky. **What he had was not Fame at all, but only a moment's notoriety. He had been a seven-day wonder— that was all. (Thomas Wolfe)**

"Overexposure is one thing; notoriety is another, overexposure expires; notoriety lasts," says Marion. ("a classic New York slogan-spitter," in the words of the ever-present Jay Kay.) "Just look at this!" She takes the press clippings and spreads them out in front of Kosky.

"We want you to be Star Number One in a First Amendment Freak Show!" says John.

"Only if we call it Safe Sex Sexual Nirvana," says Kosky while he listens to the command coming to him from the command post of his inner Tower of Strength, code-named Nirvana.

"Beat it: you're a Ruthenian Jew first, a writer second. That's the way to look at it!" the decoded Nirvana says to him.

"*Extend yourself!*" comes Kosky's strictly coded Tantric reply.*

"Let's hope that what they said about you so far—so far we've got over six hundred worldwide articles—is only the tip of the iceberg," says Marion. "Let's hope there's more water to come!"

"More *come* or more water?" John rejoices at the thought. "More safe sex? More tongue-lashing from Funny, Nunny, and Bunny? More quotable quotes from Batty, Nutty and Fatty? More sex gossip *cum* gospel about your new Aziyadé.† And maybe, just maybe, another article in the *Journalistic More Review?*"

"I say it's all nothing. It's all a false alarm," says Kosky. "I bet you somewhere in my life one of the literary safety devices was inadvertently tripped by one of my sexual space intruders changing fiction to non-fiction."

"Let's hope somebody drops another rumor about you on these two drips," says Marion, her thinking cap on fire.

---

*It is not easy to define Tantrism." (Mircea Eliade) In the word *Tantra*, the word *tan* means to extend oneself beyond one's Self. (Ed.)

†"Loti is the novel's hero (even if he has other names and even if this novel presents itself as the narrative of a reality, not of a fiction): Loti is *in* the novel (the fictive creature Aziyadé constantly calls her lover Loti: 'Look Loti, and tell me . . .'); but he is also outside it, since the Loti who has written the book in no way coincides with the hero Loti: they do not have the same identity. . . ." "*Pierre Loti: Aziyadé*," by Roland Barthes (1970), in his *New Critical Essays*, translated by Richard Howard (1980), ISBN 0-8090. Highest rating! (Enough said: J.K.) "Loti's unpublished journals reveal that there were, indeed, some dark secrets in his life at this time. Loti was in the habit of marking certain dates or entries in the journals with signs bearing sinister implications. A heavily scored cross, or a double triangle, crudely drawn, as if under stress, is found beside initials or cryptic entries. There is rarely any clue or details as to their significance. An entry for 28 March 1882 is more explicit. Under a heavily inked cross he writes: 'Beginning of *Le Souverain* affair. The Admiral has warned me officially that my honour has been attacked in the most odious manner from aboard the gunnery training ship (the *Souverain*) where he wished to appoint me. I was turned down by a vote of thirty *for having lost the esteem of my fellow officers*. I understand the accusations are terrible. I don't know of what I am accused, or yet, who accuses me.' " From *Pierre Loti*, by Lesley Blanche, op cit., p. 160.

"At best it's only a literary brainstorm; at worst, a critical hot, or cold, water shower," says Kosky. "I won't kill myself over it as would Romain Gary."

"Face it," says John. "These days, with the First Amendment for an umbrella, even *Nightfog*, that revisionist anti-Holocaust rag, doesn't need to worry about getting wet. The local rumor soil is so fertile that one quote from the Literary Local Union No. 69 is all you need to make your word-of-mouth garden grow!"

"I've nothing to say." **I have finally explained myself fully. (Romain Gary)** From a bookshelf Kosky picks up a big book called, simply, *Seneca*.

"Everywhere I turn, people have something to say about you, Norbert," says Marion, barely hiding her excitement.

"I've nothing to say," says Kosky. This is the time to quote his favorite mental quote from Seneca. **Come now, don't you know that dying is also one of life's duties? Besides, since there's no fixed number of duties laid down which you're supposed to complete, you're leaving no duty undone. Every life is, without exception, a short one. As it is with a play, so it is with life—what matters is not how long the acting lasts, but how good it is. It is not important at what point you end. End it wherever you will—only make sure that you end it up with a good ending. (Seneca)**

"The media wants you," says John. "They want you bad. They call you 'Our Crowd's Portable Seneca.' They want you regardless of whether you're a swimmer or a floater. Good or bad. They've been calling us nonstop. Newspapers, magazines, the television and radio talk shows. They all say that you can talk or float, or do both on their shows. Do I have to say what such megaexposure could do for the sale of your forthcoming mega book?"

"*The Healer* is hardly a meganovel," says Kosky. "It's the simple story of one Jay Kay, a Ruthenian-Jewish safe-sex healer who is also a serious writer. A writer who's into self-recovery.* He and only he is the mega— Alpha and Omega—of this narrative story."

"This is a story of the pleasure of the text as well as the context. A story any nonwriting person could also use."

"Don't be obstinate," says John impatiently. "Reporters who want to talk to you are among the most reputable in the country. All they want

---

*Recovering: *Writing and Healing*, ed. by Joan Rodman Goulianos (Writers at Work Series, Gallatin Division, N.Y.U. 1983).

from you is your truth, so they can match your truth against their truth or the truth as others saw it."

"Look, Norbert," Marion brainstorms again. "They want justice done by the media—and seen done on the media, long before a legal case will reach a court of law. Ask Steadfast Dodge, at the *Record*. Talk to your friend Abbot Flack at the *Times*. What do you say, Norbert?"

This is the time (time always means one's current moment) when he must decide whether he intends to be known to himself or to the world. To be known to oneself means sticking to his spiritual *biblia*—and "living your life unnoticed by others." (Israel Kosky) To be known "means going out to the world, in order to beheaded by it." (Israel Kosky) This, of course, means being a guest on Channel Six, on the World-Headline-Making WHM-TV. To start with, as every bookish person knows, a new book is every writer's new start—and like any start, this could be a false one. A false start simply means the beginning of the end of the sales of his book, his life's only true bible, and no matter how good this good book is, it can also signify his end as a writer. "A tragic literary end—of a fifty-five-year-old bookish man of letters who died as a literary polo heretic" (in the words of death-conscious Jay Kay).

"I say that the First Amendment says a lot about freedom, but nothing about truth or justice. It says nothing about any Hippocratic writer's oath—the one I took in front of the Statue of Liberty shortly after I arrived in this country," says our literary Hippo. **The newspapers never missed a chance to try and prove that he was insane, or psychotic, or simply a freak. In truth, Billy was a completely normal child in every respect. (Sarah Sidis, 1952)**

"You're a writer who writes *on* patient paper, if not *for* one. Of all people you—you, the print *sopher* par excellence—can't run away from what newspapers write about you. Like it, or not, newspapers use paper too," says John.

Marion gives Kosky a worried look. "It's always better to meet the media halfway than to be met by them in your hallway."

"These stories about you have let all the water loose," says John. "After what they've read about you—they've read nothing written *by* you—the Philistine Café crowd still can't figure out whether you're a liberal, a libertine or a libertarian."

"Am I not responsible for at least some of this rumor?" Kosky sounds apologetic.

And there is no throwing off the yoke of Heaven as bad as when one

deals in gossip. Our Sages further said, "The sin of gossip is weighed equally with the sin of idolatry and sexual immorality and bloodshed" *(Arakin 15b).* (Orhot Zaddikum)

"Sure you are! In many eyes, you still are Bukharin," says John. "For a man supposedly new to acting, you played him very convincingly! Too convincingly—many of us thought you weren't acting at all, that all you did was to become yourself—the cold and cruel Norbert Kosky we have already met in your books."

"How can I best enjoy my notoriety?" asks our literary wonder-worker. **There is only one way of comprehending man's being-there, and that is by way of inspecting my own being. (Abraham Joshua Heschel)** "I call it Being There."*

"Enjoy it—but not in public. While fame brings you closer to other people, notoriety obstracizes," says Marion. "During the medieval witch-hunts, it was the artisan, the early day spiritual partisan, who was most often denounced as an accomplice."

The phone buzzes. John answers it and listens for a minute. "The Opium Eater is ready for you with his confessions,"† he says, pointing downstairs. He doesn't look too happy. "See him and face some non-fictional sales facts and figures."

Kosky, our footnote lover, descends the staircase by foot all the way down to the sixth-floor office of Tom De Quincey, Eidolon's publisher as well as president, chairman of the board, and chief executive officer. Furnished to resemble an opium eater's modern den, De Quincey's office offers our Comrade Bukharin a welcome Kremlin-like peace— "after the hustle'nd bustle world of word advertising." (Jay Kay)

"The Healer is a setback which sets us back before it is published. A setback already, long before it is even finished," says Tom, who has come a long way from selling antiaddiction books in a campus bookshop to running Eidolon Books. Once a dreamer too shy to succeed, Tom has the body of a Tartar athlete capped with an Oriental face. "He is

---

*Being There: Jerzy Kosinski's 1969 (1971) black-and-white novel and a 1979 Lorimar color movie (starring Peter Sellers, that shaman of the silver screen), about one Chauncey ("Chance") Gardiner, who becomes spiritually unsinkable in the book's beginning, and at the end of the movie based on the novel ends up walking over a lake, "the way an image is cast upon water." (Screenplay by Jerzy Kosinski, Jan. 10, 1979.)

†Confessions of an English Opium Eater, by Thomas De Quincey.

a prototypical Jewish Khazar." (Jay Kay) He exudes corporeal, as well as corporate, confidence.

"A setback for you, Norbert—and for us!" he repeats. "Like Stalin facing for the last time his once-upon-a-time friend Nikolai Bukharin." (Jay Kay)

"How far back am I set?" asks Kosky with pretended nonchalance.

The publisher glances at a folder in front of him.

"For some reason, no less than a dozen foreign publishers have called to tell us that unless you state ahead of time whether the book is fiction or nonfiction, they are not interested in publishing *The Healer of 96 Degrees*."

"Too bad!" Kosky exclaims, then goes on. "Ironically, the same thing happened several years ago to my dear friend, Evgenii Zamiatin. That's the man who wrote a novel called *WE*," says Kosky. "Even though he was a Russian, and lived in Russia, Zamiatin was bilingual in Russian and English. In fact he knew English as well as H. G. Wells, whose works he translated into Russian."*

It is that true literature can exist only where it is created, not by diligent, reliable officials, but by madmen, hermits, heretics, dreamers, rebels and skeptics. (Zamiatin)

Such is your reputation among your fellow-men that if you announce a revised edition of any of your works, even if you have added nothing new, they will think the old edition worthless. (Erasmus's publisher to Erasmus)

"But why? They've published my other books for more than twenty years. What suddenly changed their mind about *Brudnopsis*, my *working papers* of Norbert Kosky?" (STET! here *Brudnopsis*, not brudnopis, printer!) Kosky starts stretching his body up and down like a modern-day fakir.

"Judge for yourself," says De Quincey. He spreads in front of Kosky several telegrams from Kosky's foreign publishers. Still feigning nonchalance, Kosky glances at them over his shoulder, then notices a far more important souce of menace.

PANEL URGES MORE U.S. ACTION ON OBSCENITY
Working papers of the attorney general's Commission on Pornography propose citizen-action groups and database on firms ever involved in

---

*See: *The Russian Artist: The Creative Person in Russian Culture*, by Tobia Frankel (1972).

sexually oriented materials. They suggest that the federal government make prosecution of obscenity laws a priority, according to a review by the American Civil Liberties Union of documents it forced the Justice Department to release. (*First Amendment Watch,* 1987)

Finished with the clipping, De Quincey and Kosky look each other in the eye. Kosky holds on to his gaze with strength as far removed from a skoal as Leningrad is from Stockholm. Like these two diametrically opposed cities, the two skoals might look alike, but to Kosky, to one who knows both firsthand, they sure don't feel the same.

"We've also run into some troubles with community-level censorship. Suddenly, a lot of people don't seem to appreciate the literary value of some of our straight-fuck books."

De Quincey comes around from behind the desk and, facing Kosky, sits on the desktop. "Because the libel laws are more stringent abroad than in this country, the foreign publishers take what our press wrote about you very seriously. They hope you will clarify the situation the very minute you commence action."

"Action? What kind of action?" asks Kosky.

"A libel suit, of course!" says De Quincey. "Is there any better way to bury rumors?"

"Yes," says Kosky. "Doing nothing. **Whereupon true stasis without seed ensues. (O. P. Jaggi)***

De Quincey stands up and leans against the desk. "What do you mean, nothing? "Just look at this one." He shows Kosky THE BURIAL OF NORBERT KOSKY, AMERICA'S FIRST LITERARY FAKIR, the headline in the *Downtown Crier.*

"I won't do a thing about it. Not a thing. I won't say a word to it or about it. I won't even think about it. And I certainly will never write about it. I'll just ride it through." Kosky delivers his No. 69 Oratory. **"Imagine, once again, that you are the puppet hung by a string from the top of your head. The string suspends your head from the sky, while the rest of you hangs down from your head and neck. Then imagine that**

---

*"Since the yogi works on all levels of consciousness and of the subconscious (Mircea Eliade, op. cit., p. 99), stasis (Tantra) represents a spiritual stage in which, following concentration and meditation, a spiritual object of knowledge leads to a spiritual knowledge of the object." (J.K.)

you, this puppet, have a lot of wet sand stuck up in your neck, shoulders, and rib cage." (*Centered Riding*, by Sally Swift, op. cit. 99)

"So what will you do instead?" De Quincey follows him around the room.

"I might live for a year in the Sea of Sion,* my favorite topographical SS."

Imagine yourself seated in some cloud-scaling swing, oscillating under the impulse of lunatic hands; for the strength of lunacy may belong to human dreams, the fearful caprice of lunacy, and the malice of lunacy.... Seated in such a swing, fast as you reach the lowest point of depression, may you rely on racing up to a starry altitude of corresponding ascent. (De Quincey)

Resigned, De Quincey sits down. He folds and unfolds some papers in the folder. The papers happen to be part of Kosky's manuscript, semifinal version No. 99. He folds and unfolds his eyebrows with obvious aversion. He folds and unfolds his fingers. "No wonder: this is not an easy ms. to read. † "I think you're making a terrible mistake. Won't you reconsider?"

"I can't. It's a matter of conviction," says Kosky.

"Indeed!" says De Quincey. "You've been convicted in the press by one former swimming pool cleaner and one former swimming critic, and now you don't care what everybody thinks about you or your relation to water."

"I don't know—nor do I care who 'everybody' is!" says Kosky.

"You must care!" says De Quincey. "Everybody means your readers. Everybody means the media. Everybody means the public. Everybody

---

*Sion, the lovely capital of the Swiss canton of Valais. The great period of the See of Sion began in 999 ("Three nines! How's that for a happy date?" J.K.) when the childless Rudolph II of Burgundy invested the Bishop of Sion with the revenues of Valais. Early in 1070 Ermenfroy, Bishop of Sion, visited England. As the Conqueror's coronation in 1066 (double six!) had been broken by riots, Ermenfroy crowned him again in 1070 (missing 1069 by one.)

†In the newspaper and printing offices laughing throngs gathered round to examine the astonishing scrawl. The most experienced compositors declared their inability to decipher it, and though they were offered double wages they refused to set up more than *une heure de Balzac* a day. It took months before a man learned the science of unraveling his hieroglyphics, and even then a special proofreader had to revise the compositor's often very hypothetical surmises. (Stefan Zweig)

means the nobodies who bother to buy your books and pay your bills. Face it: no public means no book."

"Wrong!" Kosky sounds a moral gong. "At worst, no public means no sales. I can still write *The Healer* even without a public. Even without a publisher. I can have it published the Jankiel Wiernik* way."

"Sure you can," De Quincey mocks him. "You can also pass *The Healer* as a samizdat, and publish it on your mimeograph as your personal yellow sheet, a new version of *Affliction of Childhood*.† But where would you take it to sell—and where would it take you? Remember: a no-contest plea from you is an admission of guilt—the defendant's throwing himself on the mercy of the court."

"At best, a newspaper is a pool of public opinion—never a court. It's buoyed up by the voice of its writers, not the voice of its public," says Kosky. **When a Tantric Yogi reaches a very advanced stage of Enlightenment, he should practice the Tantric Madness or Act-of-Insanity by behaving like a lunatic, to completely emancipate himself from all conventional thoughts and habits and then reach final and perfect Enlightenment. (Garma C. C. Chang, 1977)**

"Is that your final stand?" De Quincey asks him, raising his eyes to the sky.

"As final as I can make it," says Kosky.

---

*Jankiel Wiernik (b. 1890): deported to Treblinka in 1942. Wiernik, a socialist Jew who was a building contractor, played a decisive role in the Treblinka uprising. His report about the camp—one of the first—was published in a clandestine printshop in an edition of two thousand copies, all marked "Yellow Alert."

†In his *Affliction of Childhood* (*Suspiria de Profundis*), De Quincey points out that since we don't have exact recall of our childhood—not even exact recall of what afflicted us when we were young—our childhood memories are, at best, visualizations (not revisitations or re-creations of a childhood: J.K.), a fact that seems to have escaped the attention of most reviewers who, while seemingly reviewing Kosky's novel about a child, reviewed his childhood instead. (Estate Editor)

3 6

Pre-set, the TV set in Kosky's room turns itself on at precisely six minutes to 6:00 P.M.—the time, under ordinary circumstances, Kosky turns onto his Second State. **The Second State is the antithesis of dreaming, just as is the waking state. Recognition of "I am" consciousness is present. . . . Participation is as fundamental as it is in the waking physical state. Sensory input is not limited to one or two sources. Emotional patterns are present to a greater extent than in the physical consciousness, but can be directed and controlled to the same degree. (Robert A. Monroe)***

In some six minutes, the case of Norbert Kosky will be discussed on *Controversy!*—a prime-time, high-rating TV program aired once every six days on Channel 69 prime-time cable TV. So what? Kosky says to himself again and again. Such are the spiritual **Advantages of Exile. (Cioran)**

The whole thing came to pass so abruptly without his dealing with it or uttering a word, without his giving any opinion, acquiescing or denying; events had transpired so swiftly that he continued to be dazed and horror-struck without literally grasping what was happening. (Maupassant)

---

*"Throughout the entire experimentation, evidence began to mount of a factor most vital to the Second State. Yet in all the esoteric literature of the underground, there is no mention of this, not so much as one word of consideration or explanation. This factor is sexuality and the physical sex drive." From "Sexuality in the Second State," in *Journeys Out of the Body*, by Robert A. Monroe (1977), p. 190. ISBN: 0-385-00861-9.

Meanwhile, on quite another channel, Kosky watches his favorite American movie devoted to a story of the first American-made entirely spiritual media man.

ABBAZ

"Dead, my ass! Now get this, honkie—you go tell Raphael that I ain't takin' no jive from anybody! You tell that asshole, if he got somethin' to tell me to get his ass down here himself!"

(*edges closer to Chance*)

"You got that, boy?"*

All this represents a perfect metaphor for what is about to take place on quite another TV channel, to which Kosky now reluctantly turns.

To our literary quail this will be a trying moment. To start with, *Controversy!* is watched "by some sixteen million North American viewers aged anywhere between the ages of sixteen and ninety years whose view of life, no longer dependent on reading books, has shifted to having them and their dead authors discussed live by two live'nd lively literari on the screen of their color TV," according to *Literary TV Cable*.

Like every other ghetto, the intellectual ghetto is a seat of poisonous snakes to whom concocting intrigues is the amateur's high art; among whom a fellow man's loss of reputation triggers solidarity of quiet joy— the commonest and most pleasurable of social sentiments. (Jozef Chalasinski)†

---

*During this, as Abbaz becomes more hostile (Abbaz is black; Chance is white), Chance reaches into his pocket and takes from it his remote-control TV channel changer. He points the changer at Abbaz and clicks it three times as if trying to cancel the Outer Image which came to him involuntarily thanks to objective reality (no thanks!) and switch to another channel of his inner, and so much richer, life. Instead, Abbaz immediately pulls out a switchblade knife and holds it to Chance. See also "Dead Souls on Campus" (Op. Ed. page, *The New York Times*), where, a few years earlier, this method of shunning off one's reality was first described by the Author. (Estate Editors).

†Jozef Chalasinski: One of the most distinguished Polish sociologists of culture, known for his works on the intellectual ghetto and *Kultura Amerykanska*, his magnum opus (American Culture): *The Forming of National Culture in the United States of America*, (in Polish). (Until 1957 Norbert Kosky studied sociology of culture—including the sociology of literary form—under the personal aegis of Jozef Chalasinski: J.K.)

Sixteen million North Americans is already a lot of people. Then, as if that number was not trying enough, a lot of new viewers might tune in to this segment of the show—the first one devoted to a living American. "Call him a flake who's got a lot of bad flack,* one who has steadfastly dodged the invitation to appear on the show." (Jay Kay) On top of all this, a lot of non-TV viewers might like to see the program try out a new "living" format called, ironically, DEAD ON, and in the process see Norbert Kosky being tried on it and by it, as if he were already dead.

So what? Kosky tells himself before committing his thoughts on this subject to the Self-image-conscious Jay Kay.

To the sound of "Barcarolle," Chopin's split-note nocturne, *Controversy!*'s theme song, the split-image face of Nocturnal Janus—the man who wears his straight face as if it were a crooked mask—fills the screen, filling Kosky with *The Dread of Self-Recognition*. (Frank Cusso, Jr., M.D., 1982)

I'll have no scandal in my life . . . for a scandal amongst people of our position is disastrous for the morality. (Joseph Conrad)

Just as the music subsides, a *sotto voce* voice-over announces *Controversy!* as "a show of literary popcorn for the literary eye. With us today is Dustin Beach Bradley Borell, perhaps the best known American Book Editor, as our special guest."

PA-PAM! PA-PAM! PA-PAM! On his TV, the triple electronic gong announces to the American electronic gang that *Controversy!*, "the worldwide TV show devoted to the worth of the word" (*Cable News*), is on the air.

Attired in a woolen cardigan and faded blue jeans, Watkins Tottle, the show's host, exudes hot air, mixed with an "unparalleled degree of anti-connubial timidity." (Charles Dickens) He first displays a bundle of books written by Isaac Deutscher, Mircea Eliade, Bruno Schulz, Julian Tuwim, Nabokov and Bronislaw Malinowski, as well as books by Conrad and Koestler, Thomas Wolfe, F. Scott Fitzgerald and Thornton Wilder, the literary bigwigs Eidolon Press has published over the years as part of their DADI (Dead Authors Dead Issues) series. Then—and only then—he shows the world (and his small studio audience: Jay

---

*George P. Flack: a journalist of ill-character created by Henry James (see earlier notes).

Kay) eight novels by Norbert Kosky, while our gymnosophist trembles with vanity-induced tremor.

Let us say a man writes a novel which makes him, overnight, a celebrity. In it he recounts his sufferings. His compatriots in exile envy him: they too have suffered, perhaps more. And the man without a country becomes—or aspires to become—a novelist. The consequence: an accumulation of confusions, an inflation of horrors, of *frissons* that *date*. (E. M. Cioran)

"Norbert Kosky, the author in question, is still alive," says Watkins Tottle, "even though he is not alive enough to be questioned on the show and was reported by the press to "have been emotionally and spiritually stilled. Stilled, not spilled. THE ISSUE OF NORBERT KOSKY is still not a dead issue," he goes on. "Besides," he tries his genre of ancient Greek—or was it first ancient Hebrew?—humor,* "on our show we bring the dead issues to life; in this case"—he smiles sweetly—"we will bury Norbert Kosky alive! No! No!" he protests mockingly. "Let me assure you, our volatile author is very much alive and kicking—as evidenced by this"—here the host produces several life-size photographs showing "our volatile author" either half-naked on a polo horse, or skimming the surface of some reader-forsaken Golden Pond wearing nothing but his swimsuit—"skinny *thing* that he is," says the hostess about Kosky to the host.

Ms. Dombey Tox is the show's hostess. She is a well-shaped, short-

---

*See THE WORD:

1. The Word in Ancient Oriental and Hebrew Thought—In the ancient Orient the divine Word belongs more to the physical realm, in Assyria and Babylonia as dreadful power, in Egypt as material emanation. In the Old Testament the Word of God appears as moral act; apparent exceptions, the creative word in Israel and in the rest of the Orient. Words bear the same character as their author.

2. The Word in Greek Thought:

The Word, *logos*, is not a dynamic concept but an intellectual one. In spite of this, *dabhar* and *logos* do admit of comparison because both express the highest mental function.

COLLECTIVE CONCEPTS AND IDEAS

1. The Hebrew Collective Concept

For the Hebrews the universal is more primary than the concrete particular. "Totalities are given, individual persons or things are manifestations of them." See *Hebrew Thought Compared with Greek*, by Thorleif Boman, op. cit., p. 6.

443

legged but not poorly bosomed, petite brunette in a pale blue suit, who, aiming no doubt at being a TV-documentary star, is meanwhile **the very pink of general propitiation and politeness (Charles Dickens),** but also **centrifuge of whirling hips (Julian Tuwim)** who now introduces a video clip of Kosky clipped from an old 1982—or was it even older?— Oscar TV ceremonies. She then follows it up introducing a short scene from *Total State.* There is Kosky conducting his own defense at the Moscow Trials at Bukharin, his literary counter-contra Stalin. The clip ends with Bukharin, by then a very tired man, saying to the always rested Vyshinsky, "Isn't this all at best nasty hearsay evidence?" The host now turns to Dustin Borell. He introduces him as "an *eminence grise* of American book publishing, a man eminent enough to launch, single-handedly, his Counter Authors Series—which he started, quite apropos, some thirty-three years earlier with the publication of a little-known first novel written by the then-little-known Norbert Kosky.

"How would you rate yourself as an editor, Mr. Borell?" the host asks with a rather silly smile.

"As an in-house editor who's not often in the house," says Dustin. "The kind of hassled and harassed editor *NewsTime* recently profiled in their cover piece appropriately headlined 'The Decline of Editing.' "

Now it is the hostess's turn. "And how would you rate Norbert Kosky, Mr. Borell?"

While Dustin, our impeccably attired Boston Brahmin, readies himself to answer her, a Sim Thomas Temple, Jr., Flash-Clash flashes in yellow letters which momentarily clash with the screen. LITERARY WA-TERGATE SERIES CONTINUES. MR. F. FITZGERALD, THE RENOWNED HOL-LYWOOD SCREENPLAY WRITER, ADMITS TO HAVING ALL SORTS OF OTHER WRITERS WORKING FOR HIM. "WE HAVE ALL SORTS OF PEOPLE—DISAP-POINTED POETS, ONE-HIT PLAYWRIGHTS, COLLEGE GIRLS—WE PUT THEM ON AN IDEA IN PAIRS, AND IF IT SLOWS DOWN, WE PUT TWO MORE WRITERS WORKING BEHIND THEM. I'VE HAD AS MANY AS THREE PAIRS WORKING INDEPENDENTLY ON THE SAME IDEA." HOLLYWOOD STUNNED.

"I'd also rate him as the most difficult to work with," says Dustin, his face as grave as his purpose.

The hostess brightens; by easily confusing "bright" with "light" and light with heat, she thinks the controversy might heat up. "Difficult? Why?" **For a brief moment she postures as a Satanella (Tuwim)**

"Because he's so damned serious about himself. He always complains **Oh, My Aching Back (Root and Kiernan),**" says Dustin. "Kosky acts as if one messed-up paragraph in his messed-up set of galleys could mess his life up—or put him on the gallows. He writes under pressure of **The Tremendum (Arthur E. Cohen's term for the Holocaust: J.K.)** And to make his point he hits you with his own idiosyncratic motivational nominal or verbal prose style. And, as if this were not enough, he then hits you over the head with his own *Vectors of Prose Style** reinforced by someone else's quote—the quote is his Talmudic moral weapon— and a kick in the groin with a nasty footnote."

The host glances at his notes. His notes are all messed up. "The general public would like you, Mr. Borell, to answer this question." He raises his eyes, as if the question in question came to him either from a single person called general public or from a publicly owned Wholly Ghost (wholly, not holy, since nothing so public can possibly be holy), a ghost called I AM THE MYTHMAKING CAMERA. "Isn't there something unethical about you, a book editor who's passing his or her creative wordy as well as worthy associations and wordy ideas on to an author? Any author?" He pauses for effect. "Don't you think that writing credits on the books written by most of our major and particularly minor writers should be shared on the book's cover at least with the names of their editors? For instance, *The Sun Also Rises*, by Ernest Hemingway with Maxwell Perkins; *Look Homeward Angel*, a novel by Thomas Wolfe with Maxwell Perkins; *Courthouse Square*, a novel by Hamilton Basso with Maxwell Perkins; *Tender Is the Night*, a novel by F. Scott Fitzgerald with Maxwell Perkins?" he recites.

"I don't think so. I don't see any ethical violation here," says Dustin. †

---

*"The sample of objects studied here consisted of 150 passages from various sources and styles of English prose. Each passage was chosen so as to be more or less self-contained with a little more than 300 words. By selecting passages according to categories—novels (both British and American, both nineteenth and twentieth centuries), essays, newspaper features and editorials, biographies, scientific papers, textbooks, speeches, legal documents, personal letters, and sermons were among the categories used—we hoped to include the widest possible assortment of subject matters and styles. The sample even included several relatively low-grade high-school English compositions." From "Vectors of Prose Style," by John B. Carroll, in *Style in Language*, ed. by Thomas A. Sebeok (1960), p. 285.

†There's another tremendous problem: the revolving-door policy that many publishers have with their editors. In my personal experience, I have had to cope with the turnover of three editors during the editorial process for one book. (Authors Guild Bulletin, 1982)

He reads aloud from his notes. **Writers constantly seek criticism from friends. And the question of editing was decided for all time in the collaboration between Wolfe and Maxwell Perkins, Scribner's "editor of genius," who pored over Wolfe's work, night after night, months to a book cutting, rearranging and pasting. Yet, Perkins would not have dreamed of being credited as a "writer." . . . An irony of American letters is that two of the figures who did the most to build the 20th-century American novel, namely Perkins and Edmund Wilson, critics of genius, could not themselves write a credible novel—and, in the case of Perkins, never considered trying. (Christopher Norwood)**

A Panacea™ commercial break. During it the camera zooms over time and space to a chemical laboratory in Moscow, where, circa 1866–69, we see an aged Russian alchemist lost among his pots, vials and burners. A man's voice-over—the invisible American scientific authority—announces that Panacea™ is an American-made derivative of dimethyl sulfoxide,* a powerful penetrant, first synthesized by Aleksandr S. Saytzeff, a Russian alchemist. "The clinical reports obtained during the 1960s from research by American scientists have proved Panacea™ to be the most important breakthrough since the discovery of penicillin in our fight against vicious viruses and stubborn bacterias," says the V.O. "Panacea™ is a sure publicity-tested remedy for just about any infection, from herpes to poisonous bite. But it won't fight AIDS." The commercial ends the medically sour success story.

Leaning over, the hostess seeks self-reflection by glancing at her complexion reflected in the glass top of the center stage table. "Acne is the name of her complexion, and what she does not know is that acne results from not enough water." (Jay Kay)

"Will Kosky ever clear his face of all this float'nd swim editorial acne?" she reflects on the stage on Kosky's moral complexion.

"I'm sure he will, though not person-to-person and not on Facing the Nation," says Dustin who knows his literary iconoclast.

"Then how?" The host catches up.

"By writing a novel. By writing it in the third person. And why not? Writing is his icon.† Besides"—here Dustin glances at the hostess while

---

*Dimethyl sulfoxide: also known as DMSO, is water's most serious competitor, "since it is the only fluid other than water known to penetrate any living tissue—and, to penetrate it exactly the way water does." (J.K.)

†"The icon goes with a man for the whole of his life: he receives it at baptism,

446

for some most un-American reason, the camera closes in on her acne-ridden skin—"nothing purifies the body and skin like water." (Jonathan Zizmor, 1980)*

"I wonder what he will call it?" wonders the host.

"He will call it Chlorine No. 69." Dustin pauses thoughtfully. "The title refers the reader to a swimming pool as well as to one of the female characters he calls Clorinne, not chlorine," says Dustin, who knows that when it comes to public appearance and utterance his fiction writer, who does not believe in the Jargon of Authenticity,† speaks in metaphors. "A world ends when its metaphor has died," says Archibald MacLeish.

The host exaggerates being perplexed. "It's a shame Kosky won't respond directly to what was said about him in the press or by the victims.‡ And why not?"

He is confirmed by the jargon's view of man which was at times more innocent. (Theodor W. Adorno) "I guess he's ashamed," says Dustin. "Ashamed either of himself or of the very press, as the twice-elected president of W.E.T. he used to trust most. Besides, as Paul Valéry once stated, 'There is no true meaning of a text. The author has absolutely no authority. Whatever he may have wanted to say, he has written what one can use according to his ways and means: there is no certainty of its maker using it better than anyone else.' "

"Are you sure that's the reason?" asks the hostess. "We offered Mr.

---

it is carried at the head of his wedding procession, and it goes before him at his burial. Parents use it in giving their blessing to those going on journeys, or to newlywed couples, and at the moment of departure from this life, to all those standing by," writes Pierre Pascal in *The Religion of the Russian People*, translated by Rowan Williams (1976), p. 16. ISBN: 0-662997

*See "Water and Acne," in *How to Clear Up Your Face in 30 Days*, by Dr. Jonathan Zizmor (1980), p. 40.

†Read *The Jargon of Authenticity*, by Theodor W. Adorno (1973), p. 66. Library of Congress Cat. Card (CCC) No. 72-96701, "and the numbers tell it all!" (Jay Kay)

‡See *Victims: Textual Strategies in Recent American Fiction*, by Paul Bruss (Associated University Presses, Ltd., 69 Fleet Street, London, England, 1981), Part III, Chapter 10: "Early Fiction: The Problem of Language," which, appropriately for Kosky's first work of fiction published in 1965, begins on p. 165. See also Chapter 12, "Cockpit: Games and Expansion of Perception," which starts on p. 198. (This is so far the highest rating ever: J.K.)

Kosky our show as a platform from which to rebut or rebuff his literary suitors, but, he turned us—and them—down, and he did so by not returning our telephone call."

Another Flash-Clash: IN HER MEMOIRS CYNTHIA KOESTLER REVEALS ARTHUR OFTEN "HIRED" ENGLISH-SPEAKING SECRETARIES TO TAKE HIS DICTATION. FLUENT AS A CHILD IN HUNGARIAN AND FRENCH BUT NOT IN ENGLISH, ARTHUR DID NOT BEGIN WRITING IN ENGLISH UNTIL HE MET CYNTHIA, WHO WAS ONE OF HIS ENGLISH SECRETARIES. QUERY: IN WHAT LANGUAGE DID ARTHUR DICTATE HIS ENGLISH-LANGUAGE BOOKS?

PA-PAM! PA-PAM! PA-PAM! The electronic gong summons the electronic gang back to *Controversy!*, "the program devoted tonight to a state of literary cold feet, that is to Norbert Kosky—our absentee author who is hiding somewhere in his narrative village," the host unctuates.

"Are we doing a program, or a pogrom?" laughs Dustin, and his laugh is an easy-to-spot mixture of Scandinavian skoal with a Slavic smile.

He smiles because he is polite as well as well-educated, and spiritually anything but sterile. He knows only too well the vast spiritual gap which separates a TV literary program from a para-literary pogrom but also a great deal about the programed pogrom, "a spiritually artificial pogrom. Artificial, because it was programed from above." (Jay Kay).

"Hardly a pogrom!" The hostess laughs nervously. "Mr. Kosky's bizarre horseplay and literary foolery have been known in downtown circles for as long as his love of polo, the rather silly, I must say, sport of the macro-macho."

"I beg your pardon, madam! Polo is anything but silly. Ask Theodore Roosevelt, who played it and recommended playing it to any middle-aged man of letters—and isn't Kosky middle-aged? And no wonder: of all mankind's early sports, polo is the most literary, since already in the ninth century it produced the poetic image of Syavoush as a polo player, not as a legendary Persian ruler." Defending polo, Dustin defends Teddy Roosevelt, not as a polo player, but rather as one of the authors published as part of his company's Distinguished Literary Rough Riders Series. "Like baseball and golf, polo is a stick-and-ball game; like football and ice hockey, it draws its thrill from decontrolled collision—an American fetish. Furthermore"—he turns toward her, Kennedyesque—"polo can hardly be called macho if the very sexily clad ladies of the T'ang dynasty played it on the T'ang dynasty seventh-century pottery—'the earliest surviving representations of polo.' (*Chakkar*, op. cit.) He pauses again.

"Polo might only appear macho to a clearly no polo-game playing literary woman. As Virginia Woolf pointed out, 'Women have served all these centuries as looking-glasses possessing the magic and delicious power of reflecting the figure of man at twice its natural size.' Kosky admits that he plays polo because it makes him look twice his size."

"For my part," says the host, **clean, plump and rosy (Dickens)**, tightening his tie, "I find Kosky's floating half-naked on the cover of *Water-Sports* magazine in rather poor taste. One cannot quite imagine our serious writers—say, Matthew Duke or Salome-Lou Moses—skinny-dipping in Walden Pond for the sake of the press!"

"Think of the stiff *Lord Jim* Conrad, or the Mad Ford. (She means Ford Madox Ford: J.K.) Think of our most serious great contemporaries: Salome-Lou Moses, "the best American Yiddish mind writing in English today" (Jay Kay), and Matthew Duke (the best American Literary Gentile: J.K.) who can't help writing like a Polish Jew. One can't imagine any one of them playing water polo and playing it like Kosky, for publicity alone?"

Dustin faces him squarely. "Yes, one can! When it comes to Self-image-making, writers are shameless. Whitman used a quote from Emerson's shamelessly personal letters for a shamelessly positive blurb, shamelessly reviewed his own books, interviewed himself, and practically every day shamelessly planted controversial leaves of grass about himself in the daily newspapers."

"All Kosky writes about is evil; his personal evil, never his sexual shame," hisses the hostess. "He is our—I admit I search for a perverse title—our veritable *Imp of the Perverse.*" Her love for the perverse Edgar Allan Poe shows all over her literary skin.

"I agree he is." Dustin smiles wisely straight into the camera. "These days, writing his perverse opus number nine, our Ruthenian mocking bird turns out to be quite a Poeish raven!"

"A raven indeed!" The hostess clearly doesn't like Poeish jokes or Kosky. (PRINTER: Poeish, not Polish. Kosky, not Koski) "Even *Centerfold Review*, that bastion of male illegitimate intimacy, indirectly accused him of rape." She pauses for effect and gets it. "Of raping women in his novels, one after another. Of raping them viciously, after first stripping them emotionally. Everybody knows his novels are not novels. He writes from life. Rape is all he writes about—and what he clearly cares for most.

"Hate, not rape, is what Kosky writes about," says Dustin calmly.

"The public is a thick-skinned beast, and you have to keep whacking away on its hide to let it know you're there." He ends by quoting W. Whitman. "He writes about it out of his hate and because he hates anything to do with hate, including rape—rape, to him, is an act of hate—he writes about it hatefully. It was he who wrote in one of his books—or was it an essay?—'Thus no death is granted to hate; virulent and as vital as life itself, it follows in the wake of life.' Didn't he say in an interview that 'Rape is hate turned sexual'?"

"There are better ways to learn about hate than through violence and rape," she snaps. "There are lots of women in this country—and I hope men too!—who wouldn't touch Kosky's books."

"Don't judge him by an American yardstick only," Dustin intervenes peacefully. "His 'life and art have been shaped by two of the most cataclysmic movements in the modern world: Nazism and Stalinist Communism. From the dual experience [he: J.K.] has survived with very few verities intact. . . . His capacity for the virtues most prized by Christians is limited. . . . His fiction depicts a world that is treacherous and dangerous. It is a bleak world, but one that has been experienced by many in this century. Even those who do not see it as "their world" must be sensitized to its possibility.' " He quotes Professor Lawrence S. Cunningham.* "Isn't he our Catastrophe Man?" again he asks the silent camera. "Our mini-Proust who spent his formative years from six to twelve surviving the most catastrophic period in the thousand-year-old Jewish-Ruthenian history?"

"*Holocaustian* he sure is; Proustian he is not. I find him as gross as his characters. As gross as the women he depicts while raping them mentally." The hostess delivers her bit of World War II history.

"Don't cramp me with this crap, madam." Dustin, our Boston Brahmin, loses his cool. "He is, I grant you that, a bit cracked'nd decrepit, but he was cracked and made decrepit by the Second World War. He chronicles sin, isolation and fear: his World War II nightmare fused with our own American urban nightmare. And he is not the only one. I strongly suggest that you read this, madam." In front of the camera he hands her the "short yet monumental" (Jay Kay) "Behavioral Study of Obedience."†

America, Vol. II, 1978, p. 329. (*America* is published by the Jesuits of the United States and Canada: J.K.)

†PRINTER: The following is one of the most important footnotes here. Please

"His book covers might be gross"—the host swallows hard—"but I guess we all could use Kosky's literary douche."

"What douche?" snarls the hostess. "Kosky's art is as heavy as his English."

"Joseph Conrad's accent was just as heavy," says Dustin. "Few who did not know him well could understand him at first. Even his British publishers and particularly their secretaries didn't know what he was talking about when he was talking about them."*

A station break. This is the time to get distracted. Quickly, Kosky rushes to the cabinet from where he draws *Norbert Kosky Reads Himself*—a long-playing 33 rpm recording issued by Rockwell Records as record No. 96 in their 1969 Top 100 Spellbound Series. This is a recording made by him nearly twenty years ago, on the thirtieth anniversary of the beginning of World War II, and on it you can hear him reading, in his own brand of English, "often effective, often irri-

---

print it most carefully, as it is meant to deliver to the reader a moral SSShock:

"'The Behavioral Study of Obedience," by Stanley Milgram, describes a procedure for the study of destructive obedience in the laboratory. It consists of ordering a naive S to administer increasingly more severe punishment to a victim in the context of a learning experiment. Punishment is administered by means of a shock generator with thirty graded switches ranging from Slight Shock to Danger: Severe Shock. The victim is a confederate of the E. The primary dependent variable is the maximum shock the S is willing to administer before he refuses to continue further. Twenty-six Ss obeyed the experimental commands fully, and administered the highest shock on the generator. Fourteen Ss broke off the experiment at some point after the victim protested and refused to provide further answers. The procedure created extreme levels of nervous tension in some Ss. Profuse sweating, trembling and stuttering were typical expressions of this emotional disturbance. One unexpected sign of tension—yet to be explained—was the regular occurrence of nervous laughter, which in some Ss developed into uncontrollable seizures. The variety of interesting behavioral dynamics observed in the experiment, the reality of the situation for the S, and the possibility of parametric variation within the framework of the procedure point to the fruitfulness of further study. (*Journal of Abnormal and Social Psychology*, Vol. 67, No. 4 [1963], 371–78)

*"The English critics—since I am in fact an English writer—when discussing me always note that there is something in me which cannot be understood, nor defined, nor expressed. Only you can grasp this undefinable factor, only you can understand the incomprehensible. It is *polskość* (*polonitas*), that *polskość* which I took into my work from Mickiewicz and Słowacki." (Conrad to Marian Dąbrowski, 1914)

451

tating" (Kosky, 1982), several fragments of his first "most effectively irritating, abstractly concrete novel" (in the words of Jay Kay).

My style may be atrocious—but it produces its effect. . . . I shall make my own boots or perish. (Conrad)

Quickly, he puts the record on his predigital turntable. After the table reluctantly starts to turn, he listens to his own master's voice, to his foreign accent which he is sorry to say sounds now as heavy'nd strained by the presence of so many SSs in him as it did then, some twenty years ago.

Disappointed, our Student of Obedience, who refuses to graduate, turns off the record player and returns to TV.

"TV is not his enemy; far from it." (Jay Kay clarifies the matter.) "TV launched him in 1966 and it launched him as a Ruthenian-Jew who survived the War in order to turn into an American writer. This was when the Humble Host—call him Madox Frost—asked Kosky in his first World-Headline-Making TV News program WHAT DOES IT MEAN TO HAVE SURVIVED THE HOLOCAUST and, looking him straight in the camera, Kosky answered: LIKE SUFFERING, SURVIVAL IS UNIVERSAL. MY UNIVERSAL SUFFERING MAKES ME FEEL SPIRITUALLY TALL.

Back to *Controversy!*

"Do you agree that in his novels Mr. Kosky constantly usurps Ruthenian folklore?" the hostess says with an inner **little squeaky voice (A. M. Rosenthal)** which, in her case, could have originated in a heavy-duty mare.

"Like every other writer in history, he does and he does not. A novelist can no more usurp folklore than a weatherman can usurp a storm," storms Dustin. "In *The Financier* did Dreiser usurp the folklore of Chicago? He did. And yet he did not. Or the folklore of Yerkes, the magnate whose every step he followed by following press accounts in the local press? He did, yet he did not. In *Darkness at Noon*, has Koestler usurped the folklore of the 1938 Soviet purges—or has he, by usurping their climate, re-created their spiritual terror? He certainly did—and just as certainly he did not."

Another literary Flash-Clash clashes with his words: BRITISH JOURNALIST ARTHUR MEE DECLARES THAT CONRAD ADMITTED TO HIM HE DROPPED HIS POLISH SURNAME KORZENIOWSKI SIMPLY BECAUSE HE FELT THAT BY NOT BEING ABLE TO PRONOUNCE IT THE ENGLISH WOULD NOT BUY HIS BOOKS, AND THE IMPLICATION MEANING ALL CONRAD CARES FOR IS FAME AND MONEY.

QUOTE BY ARTHUR MEE CAUSES FURY OF ANTI-CONRAD QUOTES IN POLAND AND ABROAD. ELIZA ORZESZKOWA, POLAND'S FOREMOST LITERARY FIGURE, DECLARES CONRAD A LITERARY PERSONA NON GRATA. OTHER POLES FOLLOW. SAYS ELIZA: "WHEN IT COMES TO BOOKS THIS GENTLEMAN WHO WRITES NOVELS ONLY IN ENGLISH NEARLY GAVE ME A NERVOUS FIT WHEN READING ABOUT HIM." POLISH LITERATI STUNNED. DID CONRAD USURP OR IMITATE IN *UNDER WESTERN EYES*, PETER IVANOVITCH'S SPEECHES FROM DOSTOYEVSKY'S *THE DIARY OF A WRITER*? NOBODY WILL TELL. LITERARY WORLD STUNNED.

On the screen, the host confronts Dustin. "By the time you or any other editor is finished with a writer's manuscript, isn't the manuscript *different* from what it was before you all worked on it?" He makes quite a thing out of the word *different*.

"That's not a fair question: that's an ambush," says Dustin.

"Of course I don't deny the manuscript would be *different*, but so what? Even if I touched up punctuation, broke a paragraph, caught an error in spelling, or crossed out repetitions, Kosky's manuscript, or printer's proofs, would be—technically speaking—*different* from what they were, wouldn't they? But only technically speaking!" Pensive, his eyebrows tightly drawn, he looks at his notes. "But who would want to make a thing out of it" (echoes the author Jay Kay).

"But so what?" he repeats, and then goes on. "While some writers write little and rewrite a lot, others rewrite little but write a lot—and so do their editors. For proof, take a look at the preliminary drafts of any novel. *Write and Rewrite* (John Kuehl)*

"What matters in literary matters is not the power of the author's

---

*Read *Write and Rewrite: a Study of the Creative Process*, by John Kuehl (1967). (Also published under the title *Creative Writing and Rewriting*: J.K.) "With very few exceptions, the drafts and the authors' statements [represented here by Eudora Welty, Kay Boyle, James Jones, Bernard Malamud, Wright Morris, F. Scott Fitzgerald, Philip Roth, Robert Penn Warren, John Hawkes and William Styron: J.K.] have been transcribed as they were written, including typographical errors. Drafts incorporating revisions were printed instead of drafts exhibiting revisions for several reasons. Authorial changes often involve great mechanical difficulties in attempting to transcribe and reproduce them. Indeed, in a number of cases obliteration was so efficient that any earlier state or states were undecipherable. Besides, the writing problems treated here frequently transcend simple word or phrase changes." (John Kuehl) (An absolutely indispensable indispensable work: Jay Kay)

453

editor. The story is every inch of the way the author's story—and that's all there is to it."

Once more the host rises to his task, as he rises from his chair and clumsily walks toward the camera, forcing one cameraman to stop him with a gesture of his hand. "It's just that the public at large remains quite unaware of how a novelist works," he says in a conciliatory manner.

"Most people agree they could not easily play a piano concerto, but they believe that with the help of an editor anybody could write a novel,"* says the hostess, who, pencil in hand, remains seated behind her desk.

"A good point," Dustin agrees. " 'Great editors do not discover or produce great authors; great authors create and produce great editors,' said John Farrar—a great editor."

After another station break, *Controversy!* comes alive again. First, for the benefit of the camera, the host produces another version of his engaging smile. "How often do you, as an editor, give a style to any of your writers?" He retrieves part of the old editorial thread.

"What? Clearly, you don't know what you're talking about!" Dustin snaps. "You're talking about a writer's style, not a turnstile. Ask my friend Joseph Conrad. He was the foremost Exile of style."† He winks at someone beside the camera. "A writer can't turn around in it and still come out with another novel. Why not? Because a novel is not a teapot and a writer's style not a tea bag. You can't just drop it into the pot and come up with a—you guessed it, a potboiler!"

---

*"The contract could be drawn up and signed in a day or two, and you could have the book for us, let's say, in about a year or two."

"I can't write," said Chance. (See: *The Quotations of Chauncey Gardiner*, © 1980: J.K.)

Stiegler smiled deprecatingly. "Of course you can't. But who can nowadays? It's no problem. We can provide you with our best editors and research assistants." (*Being There*) (See also, "The Importance of Copy Editing," by Laurie Stearns, *Publishers Weekly*, August 10, 1987, p. 48.

†In these circumstances you imagine I feel not much inclination to write letters. As a matter of fact I had a great difficulty in writing the most commonplace note. I seem to have lost all *sense* [italics by Conrad: J.K.] of style and yet I am haunted, mercilessly haunted by the *necessity* [italics by Conrad: J.K.] of style. And that story I can't write weaves itself into all I see, into all I speak, into all I think, into the lines of every book I try to read. I haven't read for days. (Conrad to Garnett)

"What about a thing called a writer's style?" asks the host.

"Or is a writer's style merely another style sheet he obtained from his printer, proofreader or line editor," volunteers the hostess, with an expression that would qualify her to play an SS officer in a film called *Total Obedience*.

"It is not. A writer's style is his spiritual stylus," declares Dustin. "It is as personally his as is his most idiosyncratic, often bilingual love-making. Ask Conrad. Ask Eliade. Ask Ayn Rand, or Koestler. Ionesco. Ask Beckett. Ask Gronowicz, Nabokov, or my favorite Cioran."

With these words he has been naming, most evocative words rather than naming names, Dustin closes his attaché case, a gesture designed to help Kosky, our literary attaché.

The rest is a station break followed by a spotless soap commercial. *Controversy!* is back on the air.

On the screen, the host blows his nose in a monogramed handkerchief, folds it into a neat square, and replaces it in an inner pocket of his jacket. "In the Ruthenian language, *kos* means *mimus polyglottos*, the mockingbird. Has Norbert Kosky, our mocking polyglot, finally been captured by the Fourth Estate? Will the printed birds ever let him go?" asks the hostess, while this time it is Dustin, and not the host who laughs most.

Just then, a heavy electronic curtain drops down over the electronic stage. "This is the end of our program tonight, but, we hope, not of the *Controversy!*" says the Voice Over. "The show is over." **In the long list of controversies which the student of literature is under the necessity of examining, none seem so uncalled for and so discreditable to the assailants as this. (T. R. Lounsbury, about J. Fenimore Cooper, 1882)***

---

*The most intense lover of his country, he became the most unpopular man of letters to whom it has ever given birth. For years a storm of abuse fell upon him, which for violence, for virulence, and even for malignity, surpassed anything in the history of American literature, if not in the history of literature itself. (Thomas R. Lounsbury)

3 7

First, Cathy is gone. This means that, missing Cathy, he also misses firing his spiritual missile No. 69 and "without such firing, and such spectral sex (SS), our literary missile cannot feed mistletoe berries to his literary missal No. 69." (Jay Kay)

Late evening. Something is wrong. He is fatigued, and, for once, he finds writing fatiguing. He must stop.

It is time to meditate, this time by taking his custom-made meditative walk. He walks along Ninth Avenue, but then decides to walk all the way down Seventh, even though seven is not his lucky, i.e., spiritually stimulating, number. Why is it not? Simple. While he knows a great deal about the powerful Jewish Khazars, and about the hazards of the first Khazar princes and princesses, he knows next to nothing about the Chaldeans who worshiped number seven. Unlike the Khazars, who once ruled a chunk of the non-Arab world, the Chaldeans kept on looking up from their unobstructed plains "from where, so they said, they could see a complete circle broken only by number seven." (Jay Kay)

He keeps on walking and, his inner meditative view obstructed more and more by the height of his inner American skyscrapers, he then crosses the avenue and walks into Whatever Street. There, he finds himself on the corner of a street called Gay, and a street called Christopher.

Then, suddenly, he notices he is now one of a multitude. "Think of them as a mixed Friday night shrimp'nd steak-eating young Greenwich Village mixed multi-ethnic, mostly bisexual our crowd," observes his non-Sabbath-observing Jay Kay in Jay Kay's own non-Kosher novel.

With six police cars and sirens and cops running all around, the crowd is looking up, still indifferent, still just looking. They, the young men and women of this after-midnight crowd, look at a young man "who, standing on the very top of an eighth-floor building, with his arms outstretched like a man on a cross, obviously intends to jump and kill himself."

Since the young man chose jumping as a means of suicide, Kosky, an occasional jumper himself, first looks at him in terms of: WILL HE JUMP OR NOT? screams someone in the crowd. In case you didn't notice, Kosky is also an athlete. He is athletic only in one sense: he survived World War II without ending up—as did so many Jews, Poles, Gypsies and Soviet prisoners of war—at a place called Auschwitz.*

While the young man waits, the crowd stands silent. Is their silence ugly or banal? Jay Kay promptly detaches Kosky from "the reality of the more or less typical American urban scene where suicide is the No. 2 cause of death among those under twenty-six." (Herald Eastsquare) Banal? C'mon, correct me please: shouldn't I say evil? Evil of banality, not *Banality of Evil*?

He acknowledges that the Holocaust was "an injustice absolute." Moreover, with great honesty he adds, "It was an injustice countenanced by God." Yet Berkovits's concern is to make room for Auschwitz in the Divine scheme despite the fact that it is an unmitigated moral outrage. (Steven T. Katz, 1983)†

Suddenly the young man leans forward. He then turns around, turns back again—and—wait, standing up, upright, looking first down, then up, then down again, he separates himself from the outline of the house and his body starts falling down, laid out in a perfect backward swallow

---

*See: Rethinking the Holocaust: "On Sanctifying the Holocaust: An Anti-Theological Treatise," by Adi Ophir, *Tikkun*, Vol. 2, No. 1, pp. 61–66.

†*Jewish Faith After the Holocaust: Four Approaches in Post-Holocaust Dialogues*, by Steven T. Katz (1985), p. 165. (Winner of the National Jewish Book Award, 1983.)

dive. The crowd moans with one loud moan: NO, MAN, NO PLEASE! WHAT FOR? WHAT FOR?

If then, the challenge is not unique, what have other generations of Jews, after previous Holocausts, made of Jewish martyrdom? Berkovits rejects outright, as do all the other major Jewish thinkers who deal with the Holocaust, the simplistic response that the death camps are *mi-penei hata'einu* (because of our sins). (Ibid., p. 165)

The body hits the street head on with a bang. A bang on the head, was it a bang, or a thud? He will not think about it. Not now. Instead, he thinks about *The Jewish Faith After the Holocaust*.

"Was the guy gay? Or was his name Christopher?" asks someone aloud. "I mean why would he otherwise bother to kill himself on the corner of Gay and Christopher streets?" Does it really matter? It does.

It does as we are closing in on September 1989, and the fiftieth anniversary of the beginning of World War II—beginning with the Nazi invasion of Poland on September 1, 1939. In case you do not re-member—Americans tend to easily forget—this was when the world of modern man fell apart as bloodied and as suddenly as did this young man's body.

Here, having read this, following in the footsteps—as well as foot-notes—of this text, the reader is encouraged to meditate for at least six straight minutes about such current notions as WHAT'S LIFE FOR? IS MEANING OF LIFE DEFINED BY HISTORY? IS THE FALL OF MAN SEEMINGLY INEVITABLE, AS INEVITABLE AS WAS IN THE EYES OF THIS ANONYMOUS CROWD THE FALL OF THAT YOUNG MAN?

And finally ponder, for a minute at least, by hiding his face (by *hester panim*), another penetrating headline in an East Village magazine called *Spiritual*. GOD DISPLAYS *AIDS* TO MAN.

This is the time to think about what's left of the man after he has left. What is left, other than his looks. Was he by chance a Jew? He might have been. And if that's the case, has this young man by chance died because, as a Jew, he felt he no longer had a meaningful past?

"Here a quick change of rhetorical pace and of dramatic race is in order," is suggested to Kosky, a note clearly written by his writing ghost, Jay Kay. Kosky obeys promptly. In order to ventilate his imagination soiled by a tragic act of life's drama, Kosky rushes for a human past, human as well as humane. A past which, like a human heart or brain or sex, is usually split in half. Had he had such center, a center architecturally resembling a soul, half of this center could be located in Ruthava (pop. 6,696.699: J.K.) the capital of Ruthlandia where, for the last 696 years, the Jewish soul has safely bathed in the local spiritually hot thermal baths. Bathed safely, again and again, until in five short years of World War II the Germans killed everyone inside and almost destroyed the baths. Almost—!

Or, he could turn to the other half of his soul. Call this other half a lush and green and fertile kibbutz. An Israeli kibbutz located next to the Sea of Galilee, within sight of the Hammat Gader Roman baths. He could call on these baths—today all you've got is their *reconstructed ruins*—and ponder: here, some centuries ago stood the largest thermal baths in the entire water-conscious Roman World! (And since the Romans did nothing to keep their own spirit alive, look at their baths now!)

And what if, Yod forbid, our suicidee was, also by chance, like Kosky, *a leg man* (Rodale's synonym No. 2 for: J.K.), a writer?

A writer as daring as Thomas Wolfe who dared to write *Of Time and the River* (the most daring fictional work yet!) and to follow it up with the *Story of a Novel*, which—as the most self-revealing novel yet!—provoked De Voto—that American literary A. A. Vyshinsky!—to shoot Wolfe down with a veto. DE VOTO CLAIMS WOLFE'S BOOK IS NOT EVEN A BOOK HE CALLS IT A "DOCUMENT OF PSYCHIC DISINTEGRATION." TOM WOLFE STUNNED. (Sim Thomas Temple Literary Wire Service) and who followed it up with the headline, DE VOTO WONDERS WHETHER THE PROPORTION OF FICTION TO PLACENTA INCREASES OR DECREASES IN MR. WOLFE'S NEXT BOOK. (1938)

Do you still wonder why Wolfe willed himself to die at thirty-eight: he a man born in the lucky year 1900?

It was because he took De Voto seriously. Instead of looking up to De Voto, he should have looked down at De Voto's writing and declare it, as does Rodale's Dictionary, to be synonymous with: 1. "scribble, scrabble, scrawl, scratch."

In order to ventilate his spiritually soiled soul, Kosky takes her for a drink to Consolazione—"a sexually relaxed safe-sex-oriented newest American speakeasy." (*City Guide*, 1987)

At Consolazione, our sexual seeker seeks the *body's festival* (Mayakovsky, 1916). First, casting his stare on every female body, Kosky pushes through the crowd, trying to reach the restaurant's private room without catching anyone's stare. He fails. Soon he is caught by a quick and clever skoal of Horatio the bartender. The skoal stops Kosky at the bar. Too bad: Horatio is one of the bartenders Cathy adored as much as she adored Theodor W. Adorno.

Horatio moves along the bar like a swaying swan, a steroidal atlas fused with Bacchus the hormone-eater. He does so while remaining authentically oblivious of the adoring whispers his body elicits from those at the bar.

"Hey, Norbert! That stuff about you in the press—that's a whole new nonfictional ball game for my Ph.D. dissertation on your fiction!" says Horatio, flexing his biceps while salting the rim of a glass for Kosky's Esperandido. "On the house!" he says, putting the drink in front of Kosky and still flexing his biceps while his bicep-like face betrays not a single intellectual reflex. "Good news! My adviser has finally approved you as the subject for my thesis—you, not your fiction!"

"I thought your subject was 'Lewd Letters,' not 'Norbert Kosky: Lewd Stud,' " says Kosky, licking the salt off the rim of his glass the way he used to rim it off Cathy.

No contemporary could have written his biography; that is contained in his books themselves. (Stefan Zweig about Balzac)

"Not anymore. From now on I must start asking you all kinds of questions. Also, one day soon I will ask you for quick access to your past notes about Dostoyevsky's *Notebooks*."*

"I guess I'm lucky you're still around."

"You bet. People writing their dissertations on Shakespeare's folios (folios, printer, not polio) are not as lucky. They will never know whether William suffered from polio or not. Do you know her?" asks Kosky,

---

*"The notebooks for *Crime and Punishment* first came to the attention of the general public in 1921, when a representative of the Soviet government in the presence of A. V. Lunacharsky, assistant commissar of education [without Dostoyevsky's consent and in clear violation of the author, who was long dead: J.K.], opened a white tin case left to the State Archives by Dostoyevsky's widow. Among articles, letters, and various documents was a listing by Anna Grigorievna of fifteen notebooks kept by Dostoyevsky. She had numbered each of the notebooks and briefly described its contents. The notes for *Crime and Punishment* were contained in the first three notebooks. They were subsequently published in full by I. I. Glivenko in 1931. (Edward Wasilolek, op. cit., p.3)

looking down the bar at a brazenly bleached blonde who seems ready to bare it all in a Squalor Motel.

"I don't, but I know her type." Horatio leans to Kosky confidentially. "Stay away from her, buddy. First, this kid is barely twenty-nine. Second, she is into magazines, not novels. She subscribes to *Fitness Magazine*—and reads *How to Combat Sexual Fatigue*. She won't go for a man who's been shown half-naked on the cover of *Open Fly Fishing Magazine!*"

"If she reads anything other than people's minds and palms, she's already part of my apolitical and transmoral literary magazine," says Kosky.

"She's into a javelin—not a dick. She's the one who does her own warm-ups." Horatio explodes his final myth. "She's the one who— when nobody watches!—gulps down a white powder—and I mean anabolic steroids, not cock-aine! She gets her male—via the male hormones, not via your Tantric now-you-see-it-now-you-don't Sexual Pantomine."

"Great. Self-exercise is great for Tantric sex, I know. I subscribe to *The Generation Gap* magazine! she's a self-educated woman who educated her Self, not sex." Kosky ogles the Scentful Blonde over Horatio's gigantic neck. "Nevertheless, stay away from her testosterone," says Horatio. "She could burn a pole like you with her lips alone! And a-propos pole-burning," says Horatio, who attracts our hero's attention by first pulling him with his massive hand by his shoulder. "My dissertation will be called 'Norbert Kosky,' subtitled 'Controversy or Conviction.' "

"Why the change?" Kosky keeps on glancing at the sex-starved vixen.

"Too bad! I like your previous subtitle: **Denial in Fantasy (Anna Freud).*** Kosky keeps on skoaling "the lean, muscular, fat-free but sex-starved vixen.

From under the counter Horatio retrieves a small tape recorder, places

---

*See "Denial in Fantasy," Chapter Six, starting on p. 69 in *The Ego and The Mechanisms of Defense*, by Anna Freud (New York, 1966). "As indicated in the title, this book deals exclusively with one particular problem, i.e., with the ways and means by which the ego wards off unpleasure and anxiety, and exercises control over impulsive behavior, affects, and instinctive urges," writes Anna Freud in her foreword to the 1966 edition.

it next to Kosky and turns it on—in order to turn our shy hero on.

"I want to have you on tape," he says. "I need objective proof that you actually talked to me. Then, in my dissertation, I'll profile you à la Malaparte,"* says Horatio.

"C'mon, you know very well Malaparte made up most of his interviews," says Kosky. "Just as well: otherwise, he would want to read them."

While he spoke, I gazed at a wicker basket on the Poglavnik's desk. The lid was raised and the basket seemed to be filled with mussels, or shelled oysters—as they are occasionally displayed in the windows of Fortnum and Mason in Piccadilly in London. Casertano looked at me and winked. "Would you like a nice oyster stew?" "Are they Dalmatian oysters?" I asked the Poglavnik. Ante Pavelic removed the lid from the basket and revealed the mussels, that slimy and jelly-like mass, and he said smiling, with that tired good-natured smile of his, "It is a present from my loyal ustashis. Forty pounds of human eyes." (Malaparte, 1946)

"In any case, I hope to have my dissertation about your work published in time as a work about you," says Horatio. "The more you say in it the better."

"Careful!" Kosky jokes. "After it is published I might blame what you say in it on your freedom to invent as guaranteed to us both by the First Amendment." The right against self-incrimination incorporated a protection against self-infamy. (Leonard Levy, 1968)†

"And who would believe a novelist—a professional story-maker?" Horatio laughs. "Look, Norbert, all I need from you is an interview about your views. A critical controversy over *my* work could help get me a teaching job—even tenure!"

"Whatever I have to say, I've already said it in my novels. My fiction belongs to everybody; I don't," says Kosky.

"But don't you write with a purpose?"

"I write to express the essence of my Selective Self. I'm a fictionist, not a propagandist. You can quote me on this."

---

*Curzio Malaparte (born in 1898 as Curzio Suckert): an Italian writer who, disguised as a free-lance wartime correspondent, in his books successfully obliterates the difference between reporting and fiction.

†Leonard Levy, *Origins of the Fifth Amendment* (1968).

"But aren't you responsible for the things you write about? Don't you want to steer your readers?"

"A fictional seer doesn't steer," Kosky muses, while sending the blonde Ms. Olympia another body-shaping skoal, and one which, for the sake of his muscular readers, goes out to her by way of his optic muscle, muscle, as well as nerve, straight out of his inner-body-building Health Club Home.

"If you don't, then don't blame me and others like me for putting things in your mouth," says Horatio. "For quoting you in the context of your fiction and out of context. Will you at least check my dissertation for inaccuracies and correct the spelling errors in my representation of your various contradictory spells?"

"I will check only your spelling of my name, rank and serial number. I'm not a censor, and I'm not in the business of literary approval or disapproval," says Kosky, our literary soldier temporarily captured by the critic trained, as Kosky once was himself, in a school of Socialist Realism.

The contradictions in Tolstoy's views must be appraised not from the standpoint of the present-day working-class movement and present-day socialism, . . . but from the standpoint of protest against advancing capitalism. . . . (Lenin, 1908)

"Too bad. But never mind. At least, what you've said so far I've got it all on my tape. This should already give my work your *imprimatur*," says Horatio. He turns off his tape recorder and hides it under the counter. Then he moistens the rim of a fresh glass with a wedge of lime, inverts the glass and dips it into the plate of kosher salt. He lifts the glass, shaking the excess salt off the rim. "How's Carnal Cathy these days?" he asks and pours Kosky another 'Ido.

"I don't know," says Kosky. "I'm no longer her Tantric mentor."

"She sure is a salt-rimmed dame!" says Horatio.

"Being salty is not her fault," says Kosky. **Females do not emit as males do. (Auddalika)**

"Too salty for me. I like a dame like that to be spicy, not just stirred. Spoiled, yes. Soiled, no. All Cathy likes is to be shaken up from inside out. Anything to have her G-string, her G-spot and her G-men going. If I were you, I'd leave her to the womanizing kind." Horatio leaves him on ms. page 513.

Q. Is it true that Gary Hart and his close Hollywood friend, Warren

Beatty, have both been womanized? Can you provide the name of the plastic surgeon who performed the operations?—N.R., Sante Fe, N.M. A. Hart and Beatty are as masculine as men come. They have been referred to as "womanizers," in the sense that a womanizer is a man who indulges himself in the pursuit of women. (*Parade Magazine*; from the Sunday *Daily News*, June 21, 1987, "Personalities" column)

In Consolazione's private room, Kosky finds Cesare. Cesare owns the place. He also owns a great deal of real estate, some of it real, some of it only imagined. **As I have no blood relatives left, my friends are my spiritual family, my visceral connection, you might say. (Kosinski)** Cesare was the man he was looking for. Cesare is his friend. Kosky, a man with no children, is the godfather of Polonius, Cesare's son and only child. At the sight of Kosky, Cesare puts aside his cognac and turns off the TV set.

"I was wondering what happened to you—the ultimate Polish remnant,* the night prowler turned into a wonder boy." He wraps his arms around Kosky. Some nine years younger than Kosky, a second-generation Italian-American, Cesare comes from a swarthy Italian family from Palermo. With not a drop of Jewish blood, as he often reminds Kosky, he nevertheless bears an uncommon resemblance to Kosky's father. This resemblance evokes the spiritually spontaneous warmth Kosky feels each time he meets Cesare.

"So how is all this press prostatis affecting your prostrate literary prostate?" asks Cesare, sitting down next to Kosky on a sofa.

"Occasionally, it irritates my sacral sacroiliac joint. Irritates, but not inflames."

---

*Here, Cesare is most likely referring the reader to *Remnants: The Last Jews of Poland*, photographs by Tomasz Tomaszewski, text by Małgorzata Niezabitowska, op cit. (See also their forthcoming exhibition, and a TV documentary: Jay Kay.)

"You, a yogi who used to walk straight, and who now looks like a man broken in half by arthritis."

"All they broke was news, not me. I still love to show off my floating act," says Kosky, examining the room's new black leather upholstery.

Observation is a silent process; without the means of participation, the silent one must observe. Perhaps this silence is also a metaphor for dissociation from the community and from something greater. This feeling of alienation floats on the surface of the work and manifests the author's awareness, perhaps unconscious, of his break with the wholeness of self. ("Notes of the Author," 1965, as quoted in "Men into Beasts," a chapter in *The Holocaust and the Literary Imagination*, by Lawrence Langer, op. cit., p. 169)

"As we say in Mamadossola, *Se non è vero, è molto ben trovato*. Even if it's not true, it's well made up," says Cesare, and he knows what he says.

To start with, the reason he has been invited to be part of this narrative is that Cesare is an educated and reasonable man; hence, he is a non-prejudiced one. For instance: an American capitalist par excellence, he nevertheless reads *Soviet Life* magazine, published by the Soviets for the Americans, as well as its counterpart, *America*, published by the Americans for the Soviets, because he is curious what image of each other the Soviet and American governments keep on exchanging, "while the Third World starves to death." And please don't confuse this governmentally owned and edited *America* with the *America* published by the Jesuits of the U.S. and Canada, and already quoted in this spiritually most idiosyncratic text. (Jay Kay) Another example: the traditional northern and southern Italian menu of his restaurant contains such Jewish delicatessen entrées as gefilte fish and chicken soup with matzoh balls. And then, his restaurant's Library Room features, among many other books, the *Encyclopedia Judaica* from Jerusalem and *Polin: the Journal of Polish-Jewish Studies* from Oxford, England. ("Many of our customers are American Jews who initially came from Khazaria, not the Rhineland," he explains to Kosky.) He knows Jewish history, particularly the part of it which refers him to his beloved New Testament, and he knows that his favorite phrase, "abomination of desolation,"* comes to him courtesy of the Jewish Maccabean family. He also knows that after the

---

*See "Jewish History," Chapter Seven in *The New Testament Background: Selected Documents*, by C. K. Barrett (1965), p. 107.

Mongol conquests, when the Slav villages wandered westward, the Jewish *shtetls* of Jewish Khazars went with them while **the Jews of Rhineland were caught in that winepress, which nearly squeezed them to death. (Arthur Koestler, op. cit., p. 163)*** "In order to figure out the life of a Ruthenian-Jewish *shtetl* see the amalgam of fact and fantasy in the paintings of that most alchemical painter Marc Chagall." (Jay Kay)†

"Face it." Cesare faces Kosky face to face. "By writing *with* Carlyle, de Morande drowns you in your own swimming pool. He would not have by writing it alone given his very special credibility. Just as well that they left the coffin open enough for the rest of the media to peek at the fakir, who—fakir that you are—is still very much literarily alive! To my mind, you are a literary Mr. Pompeii."

"Compared to the Jews of Mayence, Pompeii offers a most humane picture," Kosky agrees.

"Not in my picture book. Don't you think it's time for you to get up from that coffin? And when you do, what are you going to do to them?" Cesare nudges Kosky.

"Nothing," says Kosky. "They've got the green light."

"What green light? I'm not talking traffic. I'm talking face. I'm talking

---

*According to the Hebrew chronicler Solomon bar Simon, considered as generally reliable, the Jews of Mayence, faced [A.D. 1096: J.K.] with the alternative between baptism or death at the hands of the mob, gave the example to other communities by deciding on collective suicide:

"Imitating on a grand scale Abraham's readiness to sacrifice Isaac, fathers slaughtered their children and husbands their wives. These acts of unspeakable horror and heroism were performed in the ritualistic form of slaughter with sacrificial knives sharpened in accordance with Jewish law. At times the leading sages of the community, supervising the mass immolation, were the last to part with life at their own hands. . . . In the mass hysteria, sanctified by the glow of religious martyrdom and compensated by the confident expectation of heavenly rewards, nothing seemed to matter but to end life before one fell into the hands of the implacable foes and had to face the inescapable alternative of death at the enemy's hand or conversion to Christianity.' " (Arthur Koestler, op. cit., p. 163)

†"A Jewish community without a center of learning is unthinkable, and a *shtetl* of any size will have several varieties of school. . . ." See "May He Enter into Torah," Part II (starting on p. 69) of *Life Is with People: The Culture of the Shtetl*, by Marc Zborowski and Elizabeth Herzog, introduction by Margaret Mead (1952).

about being hit." Flushed, Cesare edges over to Kosky and with his right hand pats Kosky on Kosky's left cheek. His pat—pat, not slap—stings, but it's not painful. There is a common-law malaise in it, but no malice, no "wrongful intention generally" (*American Lawyer*), or "the desire to injure another person." (American Courts)

Cesare moves to the far end of the sofa; he is still breathing evenly. "You're not Mr. Little Guy," he says thoughtfully, and breathing normally, he is still able to collect his thoughts as if they were cash. "You're your own union boss. You are also my friend and the godfather of my kid! And you say you'll do nothing?" He loses a breath or two.

"There's nothing I want to do, and I already had communicated my decision to my Rabbi Byron (Byron was Kosky's favorite English-language poet: J.K.), whose child Joshua-Jason is also my God-child," says Kosky, assuming the perfect pose of a yogi. "True, that as a result of all this public mess I lost some breath-retention ability, but writing *with* Carlyle, de Morande did not break the law."

We must not confuse the state of law with the state of fact. The latter alone, or almost alone, makes an impact on social parity. (Vilfredo Pareto)

"What the fuck are you talking about?" Cesare gets up and walks back and forth across the room, zigzagging in front of Kosky. This physical exercise does him and his windpipe no good. Exhausted, he then sits down on the sofa again, collecting anger, while dusting off the small glossy glass table as if it were his glottis.

"What law?" He goes on. "I'm talking life, not 'law.' I'm talking about two fucking shits from some *undertown* rag spitting illiterate spittle in your face!"

"There's no crime to spitting literary spittle." Kosky dares to correct him, motionless like a sleeping lotus.

"Spitting is what counts, not spittle. The act of spitting. I heard about your being spat upon once—spat upon only once in your entire career—true, nevertheless once. Everybody in this whole country saw these two goons spitting at you in their paper's Float'nd Swim pages—and you talk law?"

"I talk spiritual law, Cesare!" Now Kosky assumes a symbolic Hatha Yoga meditative posture. "Spiritual Law number nine: freedom to express your Self. For some reason, in America this law is called the First Amendment (or *Glasnost* in today's Russia: J.K.). Too bad it's called First, since you know how little I think of being first. Thank you, James Madison! Thank you for your Ninth Amendment!"

"I'm talking honor and you are talking Madison and the Ninth Amendment? What's the ninth got to do with it except that most Madison Avenue models who come here expressly to see your Bukharin red face?" shouts Cesare. By shouting Cesare is no longer breathing correctly. This means he is no longer breathing enough air. Air means oxygen. Oxygen is the brain's bread. No wonder Cesare starts overheating: now his breathing is way off. He actually might go out of his own control. Too bad! ("Such inability to breathe correctly makes so many people kill each other in Palermo, Italy, and in Little Italy, Manhattan's own Palermo," says Jay Kay to Cesare in Kosky's novel, but Kosky would never dare say it: J.K.)

"These two men wrote about you, Norbert Kosky." Cesare recovers some of his breath, but not enough to calm him down.

"What the fuck has the Ninth Amendment got to do with it when you were hit over your *keppele* with the First?" By now Cesare is out of breath. He starts choking, choking on his words; choking as if by swallowing the wrong piece of bread, though, in fairness, I know people who choked on their own breadth. (Printer: Please don't confuse breath with bread. In this narrative text, bread must never replace air.)

"The Ninth* has a lot to do with it. Like Jefferson, James Madison was a literary monk." Kosky takes on deep additional emergency breath of air.

"What has being a mad monk got to do with it?" Cesare recovers some of his lost static air. "De Morande wrote all this shit about the Mad you. Not about the Mad Madison." He starts screaming again.

"Madison was as close to Jefferson as you are to me," Kosky attempts to calm him down.

"One day, during Jefferson's absence (Jefferson was in Paris), leaning over (Jefferson's original custom-built writing desk I saw in the main reception rooms at the State Department: J.K.), Madison was the first to notice that their beloved bill of rights lacked what he called latitude. Latitude standing for moral breath. Mind you," Kosky goes on, "Madison would no more confuse the sacred word *breath* with *bread* than

---

*"The Ninth Amendment ("The enumeration in the Constitution, of certain rights, shall not be construed to deny or disparage others retained by the people") was inspired by James Madison, the sixth greatest American monk. No wonder; he was, as his very name shows, a mixture of *mad* and *son*! He was sixth; Jefferson ninth." (Jay Kay calmly recycles his Tantric hot air.)

469

he would *word* with *worth*, or worse yet, *soul* with *soil*. When he wrote about it to Jefferson, Jefferson replied: 'Half a loaf was better than no bread.' " Kosky makes his point as transparent as air.

Cesare keeps on shouting. "These two schmucks wrote that your swim or float was like Shakespeare's 'To be or not to be.'* They wrote all this not in Ruthenian, and in Ruthenia, but in America—in America the Beautiful—in New York, and if New York isn't America what is? They wrote it in plain black-on-white basic English, for everybody to read again and again—and you say it's okay because of some First Amendment?"

"I say it's okay because I believe it's okay," says Kosky. "I believe in that, Cesare! To me, that law is basic oxygen, not basic English."†

"That's crap. What comes first—being a man or a writer?" asks Cesare. "They spit at you in public again and again—and you do nothing!" Leaning forward, his elbows on his knees, he hides his face in his hands. After a moment he gets up and stands in front of Kosky. "They call you names, and you do nothing. This must not go unsettled." Cesare now chokes on his own inner respiration. "It must not—for your sake, for my sake, even for the sake of our little Polonius, who one day deserves to be proud of his literary Godfather. If you do nothing, then I will make sure that they pay for what they've done to my son's Godfather **'or I'll eat my head' (Dickens),**" he says.

"You'll do what?" asks Kosky, a calm Buddha calmly ogling the raging sea. **Writing is the most barren profession. (Leopardi)**

---

*CESARE GRIMWIG, THE OWNER OF CONSOLAZIONE, THE SIX-STAR ITALO-AMERICAN RESTAURANT SO POPULAR WITH THE JEWISH-AMERICAN LITERARY ITALIANS HE CALLED LITALIANS, CHARGES THAT SHAKESPEARE'S FAMOUS "TO BE OR NOT TO BE, THAT IS THE QUESTION" IS WITHOUT QUESTION AN UNACKNOWLEDGED WORD-FOR-WORD TRANSLATION FROM THE ITALIAN "ESSERE O NON ESSERE, QUEST'E IL PROBLEMA," FOUND IN "CONSOLAZIONE," A SIXTEENTH-CENTURY COLLECTION OF ITALIAN ESSAYS SHAKESPEARE "MUST HAVE CONSULTED WHEN WRITING HAMLET." ITALO-AMERICANS STUNNED.

†Basic English, a dramatically simplified form of English. Developed as a secondary tongue between 1925 and 1932 by the English scholar C. K. Ogden, "it has a vocabulary of 869 words and an uncomplicated six-by-nine grammar. The vocabulary is composed of 666 nouns, 169 adjectives, and 99 other words that include verbs, adverbs, prepositions and pronouns," Jay Kay informs the ill-informed.

"I'll give them back what you owe them! By hitting you, these hit men hit me."

"These people are writers, not hit men," Kosky goes on. "Freedom to write is *all they've got* and they have merely used that freedom to the hilt meaning, by hitting someone known not only for his books, but for his being *sextra-literary*. That's all!"

"What are you—still a little war-kid?" Cesare walks slowly to the door. "You're the godfather of my little Polonius. That's not all." Now Cesare definitely insists on walking Kosky all the way to the door, a custom he too, like Kosky, learned from their mutual friend Dr. Salvarson. "You're the man who was first praised by Virgilia Peterson* for your moral stand and Virgilia, even though not Italian by birth, though married to a count, was the most honorable American writer that ever lived: she dared to do in her book what until then nobody did. You're giving honor a brand new pen name: DISHONOR." By now Cesare has escorted Norbert Kosky all the way to the half-opened door.

---

*See Virgilia Peterson's novel, A *Matter of Life and Death* (1961). Read also, if you're a writer, her essay "The Underprivileged Book" (*Authors Guild Bulletin*, Summer 1964).

"Face the music: as a Jew, you were born to hear, not to talk. Hear means music. Hear means 'Hear O Israel!' " says Harold Rockwell. (A man with absolute ear, a phenomenon not so rare among certain obsolete Jews: Jay Kay.) "A man's name is like his skin; it just fits him," says Goethe as quoted from Emerson in his *brudnopsis*, and are both of them right! Harold is into rock and, at fifty-two years of age, he rocks well. Besides, unlike Kosky, who, lacking anything absolute lacks the absolute ear, Harold, the musical S.O.B., speaks English with a pure English accent, but in spite of his pure Turkish-Jewish looks, the sly slob, like Kosky, is anything but pure. Sexually speaking, he is the original Man of Disgust—the very opposite of the Man of Marble, even though his family roots in Ruthenia extend all the way back to the year 1369.*

Yet ("In Kosky's prose there always is a yet" [Jewish calendar, 1982]) Rockwell is the descendant of Gershon Sirota, the Jewish cantor called "Caruso the King" by other Polish-Jewish famous cantors. Gershon Sirota, in case you didn't know, was, together with his entire family,

---

*For the unprecedented number of unprecedentally talented music-minded Jews, the reader is referred to "Music," by Marian Fuks, in *The Polish Jewry: History and Culture* (op. cit.), a chapter which, starting on page 64, guides the reader through the extraordinary long and dense roots of centuries of Jewish music in Poland. See also "Significant Contributions to Polish Music Made by Jewish Composers and Composers of Jewish Descent" (ibid, p. 69).

burnt alive in their flat at Wołynska Street No. 6 during the uprising in the Warsaw ghetto.

Rockwell is also (this too must be said) the spiritual descendant of Mordecai Gebirtig, a Polish-Jewish songster like no other, who carried his composer's task until the end, until he was shot and killed while being rounded up with other inhabitants of the ghetto of Cracov, on a railroad station in order to be deported to Belzec concentration camp while everybody sang his song, "S'brent, undzer Shtetl brent" ("Fire, Our Town Is On Fire!"). But what finally matters to the American non-Jewish reader unaware of the millennium of the Polish-Ruthenian-Jewish cultural past is that Harold Rockwell is a Jewish fiddler who, having fallen off the roof of yesterday's Ruthenia, now fiddles on an even higher American roof.

"Sure you're oral—so am I. Show me a Jew who isn't and I tell you he is not a Jew. We are all members of the Oral Tradition Club, right? And we enjoy every minute of it," he adds, chewing on his own tongue (as an overly excited polo pony often does). "But oral or not, all I care about is music. So what if it is only rock, which I call lull'nd rock music? So what if each time I speak about rock, I also must speak about the strictly sexual beauty of the rock stars?" says the old Khazar, glancing fondly at a wall display of covers of the forthcoming albums produced by Rockwell Records.

"What is the essence of music if not lull'nd roll? Lull as in lullaby, roll like in rock," he asks rolling his eyes to the indifferent sky.

"Instead of despairing as a novelist (novelist, printer, not Nobelist) this Year's Nobel went to one more American-Jewish East European!

"I'm not a commercial artist," protests Kosky. "I am an artist of creative despair."

"Then be creative! Improve the stinking craft of fiction [the trendy Harold picks up his trend of thought]. Do to it what was once done by the one and only Baudelaire."

"Do what?" A high-voltage American Voltaire confronts him. "Do you want my craft to sink—even more than I do? Or do you want me to sink it?"

"What sort of a novel are you writing? Will it be, like your first, a savage novel about a Jewish kid saved by good Samaritans in clear defiance of the German savages?" he asks Kosky.

"It will be a post-Exodus novel about a modern-day Juda Halevi traveling back into his Ruthenian-Jewish past." Kosky defends the notion of the Exodus as well as history. "It is a spiritual NOW THESE ARE THE NAMES (the first words of Exodus and a code for Jewish biblical tradition) with any real names—except names of those who, purposefully misquoted or quoted out of their context, render my book strictly fiction, hence, strictly kosher."

"Kosher meaning what?"

"Meaning pure narrative art. Pure storytelling, pure autofiction. The only spiritually foolproof narrative system in literary history."

"Sounds like a lot of heavy water. Is there anything salty in it?" Blinking meaningfully, Rockwell rocks Kosky's narrative chair.

"There's as much red-blooded sex in it as there is salt in the Red Sea," says Kosky.

"Is there any real history in it? Any real cemetery?"

"There is but not enough to reconstruct history."

"Is there any money in it?"

"Of course not! It's a novel of vivisection."

"In the beginning was the word, but the last word surely belongs to music. 'Music is Love in search of a word,' said Sidney Lanier* and he was right. These days only music brings the dough and fame. Play music for me! Be a cheerful Hasid again: play with the words as if they were music. Write song lyrics for me!"

> Were I a bird of domestic grove,
> I would not sing in any stranger's clover,
> Neither for water, nor for the forest,
> But under your window and for you alone.
> (Stefan Witwicki, 1829)

He intones Chopin's lightest mazurka, "and even though he comes from Ruthenia, he does it in his heavy-duty Hannah Arendt German-Jewish baritone." (Jay Kay)

"I play on a different key," says Kosky, glancing through the window at Harold's own Rockwell Plaza, fifty stories below. **An accompanying**

---

*Sidney Lanier, who for several years played first flute in Baltimore's Peabody Orchestra, wrote "The Symphony" and "The Marshes of Glynn," the poems "which alone would suffice to keep Lanier's name on the scroll of great American poets." (Reuben Post Halleck, 1934)

melody enlivens one's studies and endears the statutes which one learns. If such are described as not good it is because the melody is lacking. (*Tractate Soferim*)

"Writing books is composing," says Kosky. "First I compose myself. Then I record my literary music to my own inner tune."

"So what's the big deal?" Rockwell shrugs. "Chopin once said that nothing is more odious than music without hidden meaning." He quotes Patrick Domostroy (quoting Chopin in a musical movie about a burnt-out Polish-Jewish musical oddball called "Pinball": J.K.).

"Now that everybody knows you're hiding somewhere in your novels where they can easily find you, why don't you hide your sickly self in music? Write me a Scorching Song! Make it a German SS marching song, if you must. Call it the 'March of Pripet'! *March*—not *Marsh!*"

"How could I—I, a Jew who saw what the SS did to the local population, to the Jews and Poles and Gypsies—write an SS song?"

"How could you? By reading Hannah Arendt's *Eichmann in Jerusalem.* By learning from her how you can deflesh the SS and Nazi-run Germany from their historical flesh," here Harold again turns Kosky around as if Kosky were a Jewish Mr. Gandhi.

"So tell me again, how does one write a song? Any song!" Kosky ponders aloud.

"First one picks a *leitmotif.* Say a pleasant peasant mazurka straight from Polesie." Rockwell brightens. "Then, one polishes its dry square four- and eight-bar phrasing, one dampens its fourth, all so wet, one plays with the drone bass, one sidesteps the sexually dominant sevenths, one sucks on the submissive triplets, one enjoys the feminine endings, and, again and again, one repeats one bar as often as you can! But, above all, if one is serious about art, about pure music, one remembers to preface all that by saying, as Chopin did in capital letters, 'THAT'S MUSIC: IT'S NOT FOR DANCING.' Knowing very well that it is. The son of a bitch did not want to get rich at the price of disco dancing!" Rockwell is practically out of breath, but he knows how to make up for it—and so he keeps on rocking well.

"Most of our top singles are two-strophe love songs which make up in intensity what they lose in length," he goes on, no longer breathlessly. "Today Schumann'nd Schubert, Liszt, Brahms and Chopin would write rock—the music for the masses. It's simple. What else is left for you if not writing music after all that Lotus scam?"

"Silence," says Kosky. "I've been voiceless before." **Prose has no stage** scenery to hide behind. It is spontaneous but must be fabricated by thought and painstaking. Prose is the ultimate flower of the art of words. Next to music, it is the finest of all the fine arts. (H. L. Mencken)

"Your mother was a pianist and everyone knows you loved her not like her child. Now, as a result you love music. You call music your rallying cry. You were even able to write a novel about music disguised as a novel about *Le Sex Black*. That's the only one I read," the old goat goads him. (And why not. In the three decades he has been in the business of music, Harold managed such superstars as Jubal and Terpander duo. It was he who launched the pop-music raunchy launcher called Dactyli: informs the once-musical Jay Kay.)

"Kosky's readers won't mind such admission from you," says Kosky. "And my publishers would love it!"

"Just think—" Rockwell muses. "Our spiritual origins are pretty much the same. We came to this country from Ruthenia more or less at the same time, and with no money and no connections, and look at us now! Today I'm a Big Boy record producer—and who are you?"

"A novelist: a fabricant of novel tales. That's all."

"There's nothing wrong about being a fabricant," says Rockwell. "At one time wasn't your father a fabricant too?"

"He certainly was: like most mortals, he needed breath as well as bread. But he was engaged in a material enterprise only in order to pursue his studies. He saw himself as *kos*, as a *Mimus polygottos*. Ask anyone who remembers him. Ask Dr. Simon bar Solomon, the best Ruthenian-Jewish brain surgeon who, expelled from Ruthenia in 1969 for being Ruthenian-Jewish, today operates in the German Mayence, but would do anything to practice again—even for a week each year—in Ruthenia. And ask soon, since pretty soon, given our average age of sixty-nine, there won't be any World War II Ruthenian-Jewish fabricants left," says Kosky, assuming a Svastikasāna, his favorite pose of a Tantric yogi.* **There are a hundred and one arteries of the heart. Only one of these passes up to the crown of the head. Going up by it, one goes to immortality. (*Tantra Treatises*)**

"As far as I see it, music flows like water. You can listen to it in any

---

*"Svastikasāna (the svastica pose): "When this pose is properly performed, the legs and ankles assume the shape of a svastica. This āsana is said to be particularly useful for those whose feet remain unusually hot or cold or sweat too much." See *Yogic and Tantric Medicine*, by O. P. Jaggi, op. cit. p. 33.

position—even in your favorite position 69 when you're in no position to do anything else," Rockwell reflects. "But not so with reading. Reading a page, you can only move your head so much to the left or so much to the right. It's damn catatonic."

"One mustn't compare books with rock records. Rock is catatonic," Kosky objects strenuously.

"Then, smart ass, compare your record with one. Compare what your prose has earned you with what my *prosaics* have earned me! Did you know that just about every seventy seconds—make it sixty-nine—someone somewhere plays a Rockwell record? Can this compete with the booksales of your beloved Abraham Joshua Heschel?"* Here he becomes a hostile turnstile.

From a platinum musical cigarette box Rockwell extracts two impeccably rolled hemp joints—he calls them his THC No Nicotine cigarettes—and lights them both with his diamond-studded lighter.

"Here, try this." Leaning across the arm of his armchair made of red leather and black stone, he offers Kosky a neatly rolled cigarette joint. "It's a gift from Polesie."

"From whom?" Joint in hand, Kosky recoils.

"Polesie. The name of the first original Polesie rock ensemble in this country."

"Are you kidding?"

"Anything but," says Rockwell, smiling dreamily. "The members of the group all come one way or another from the Pripet in the old Ruthenian-Jewish Polesie (Polesie, not Pripyat). †

For Kosky, smoking a joint brings back a scent of war. Memories of marsh grass, of flax, of tar. Of the good old Polesie *papieros‡* rolled in paper.

"I knew you'd like it. It makes you think of sixty-nine," purrs Rockwell.

---

*For the geneaology of the Hasidic Dynasty of Heschel, which goes back all the way to the Chmielnicki Raid on the city of Vilna in 1648 (Chmielnicki was the Cossack Hitman disguised as Hetman), the Jewish-American reader is encouraged to seek his or her own thousand-year-old dynasty in *The Unbroken Chain* (Neil Rosenstein) of Jewish East European history.

†Read "Pripyat Journal: Crows and Sensors Watch over Dead City," by Felicity Barringer, *The New York Times*, 6/22/87.

‡*Papieros* (Ruth.): a cigarette. Originating from *papier*, the word *papieros* sounds so much better to a writer's ear than the Anglo-Saxon word *cigarette*.

There is positively no evidence to indicate the abuse of cannabis as a medicinal agent or to show that its medicinal use is leading to the development of cannabis addiction. . . . There is a possibility that a restudy of the drug by modern means may show other advantages to be derived from its medicinal use. (Committee on Legislative Activities of the American Medical Association, 1937)*

The poster shows a young black woman.

Soon, deep within him, the hemp cigarette works wonders. Soon, our marsh bellflower is transformed into a marsh Harrier. Floating about the room, he sees on the wall a large poster, "a fusion of Socialist Realism with Capitalist Nirvana." He has never seen a cunt like this face to face—and if he did, it was only in a sex club, forgive our returning to the pre-safe-sex past.

Writing consumes energy, energy is sexual. Result: he is sex-starved. **What he needs is a woman. (Haggadah)**

"I have never seen a black woman as good-looking as this one. Not in *Players*. Not in *Connoisseurs*. Not in *The Black Adult* magazine! I have never seen her Number nine face-to-face with my Number six. Never one-on-one." With such an opening line, he declares that his Sexual Star Search No. 69 is still very much going on—even in his detestable, full-of-contempt and one-on-one competition.

"This one is sure not just another pretty sister," says Rockwell. "Call her Symphony in Black. Call her Black Spectacle."

"Could I possibly call on her?"

"Call on *her*? Are you kidding?" Rocking in his made-to-order easy chair Rockwell now sniffs oxygen from a custom-made 6.9 liter oxygen bottle set in a gold container. "She is CARMELA LEROY—the lead singer of the Coybantes!" he headlines. "This season she is the third most successful black vocalist of the entire rock'n'roll business."

---

*In 1969, in *Evergreen*, E. Goode published the results of "an informal survey of about 200 marijuana users," in which he asked "some basic questions about the relationship of marijuana to both sexual desire and sexual activity." To the question "Is your enjoyment of sex any different high, or not?", 68 percent indicated that marijuana increased their sexual—particularly orgasmic—enjoyment. Seventy-four percent of the men and 62 percent of the women replied that marijuana increased sexual enjoyment. From *Marijuana Reconsidered*, by Lester Grinspoon, M.D. (Second Edition, Harvard University Press, 1977, p. 319).

"Music is an important muse. I write to it as well as with it. I really would love to spin with a spin," muses our literary Muzak man. (Printer: Muzak, not music).

"Then keep on writing different songs for me and I'll have her—and others like her, white or black—spin it for you any given time." Rockwell gives Kosky a calculating as well as cultivating look. "Would you like to have her?"

"I don't collect records," says Kosky. "I tape my own music, directly from a radio; from a nonprofit FM Mandala radio station in Catatonia, New York."

"I mean, would you want to have her?" Rockwell stops rocking in his chair.

"Sure I would. I'm a novelist of the Soul. I'm her soul brother. Show me a soul brother who wouldn't want her for a soul sister?"

"You can have her body anytime," says Rockwell.

"How?" **Music is sounding form in motion. (D. Hanslick, 1904)**

"As a gift from me in exchange for a promissory prosaic music note." Rockwell smiles like Doctor Faustus. "Promise me that you'll give some thought to my prosaic offer."

"And if I promise but won't be able to deliver my English prose?" says Kosky. **Within a certain recognizable structural framework, there has been a gradual evolution of sentence patterns—an evolution that, since the language is living, is still going on. (G. H. Vallins, 1956)***

"It's my tax-deductible risk, not yours," says Rockwell, while our titubant titien titubates to the poster where, his nose between Carmela's ebony thighs, he examines her ebonesque body. It is a body without a trace of bones to it or any sign of sag'nd stretch.

"If you promise I'll get Carmela to do a demo spin for you."

"I promise," Kosky dreams aloud.

"You do?" Rockwell acts surprised by the sexually fast corruption. "Just tell me when you want the demo."

"The sooner the better," says Kosky. "I'm always hard-pressed."

"Where do you want to have her?"

---

*_The Pattern of English_, by G. H. Vallins (1956), p. 96. See also Chapter Three, "The Verbal Phrase," starting on p. 66. See also the discussion about the participial phrase having an adjective function, "and by its position in the sentence [it] qualifies the appropriate noun or pronoun" (ibid, p. 69).

"At my *casa*, West 69th Street. Sixth floor, Apartment nine," mumbles our Casanova. "And since, when it comes to talking about sex I become unnaturally shy, let her come straight to the point."

Once all this is firmly grasped, the mechanism of the sexual impulse becomes easier to understand. Don Juanism, for example, becomes immediately comprehensible. The easiest means of achieving an immediate broadening of consciousness is the sexual orgasm. (Colin Wilson, 1963)*

"At what time should she deliver herself there?" asks Rockwell. "Herself and her sixty-nine rpm diskette."

"Preferably *de cinq à sept*. But ask her to stay longer, even if I won't."†
In anticipation of an evening of massive yet prolonged wants (here, synonymous with his Bruno Schulz–like—but also like Giordano Bruno: J.K.) and rather particular desires, Kosky contracts his rectal muscle.

"Done," says Rockwell. "But don't break our Golden Donna. She's already broken."

---

*In *Origins of the Sexual Impulse*, by Colin Wilson (1963). Library of Congress Catalog No. 63-9675.

†*De cinq à sept* (Fr.): Literally, from five to seven. "Traditionally, time reserved by the traditionally minded French for playing musical chairs, i.e., having sex with someone other than a member of one's family (or with a member of one's family) "as if he or she were an Other." (Bordellier, 1969) In work-conscious United States, this is the time traditionally reserved for commuting from work to home. (J.K.)

4 0

At home, still spinning, Kosky pulls down the shades and turns the phone off. He makes up his cot, but he cannot make up his mind. To sleep or to write? **In the night which surrounds us only human creation traces the way. (Karol Hiller, 1933)**

Too bad that the Self cannot become as simple as the *illusionistic perspectival.* (Hiller, Heliograph No. 69, 1933)

Too bad that **We do not live in a void. We never suffer from a fear of roaming in the emptiness of Time. We remember where we came from. (Abraham Joshua Heschel, 1949)**

Too bad that **This freedom, which is an essential part of him and from which he cannot escape, carries with it the fact that he is radically threatened. (Paul Tillich)** Too bad that, when it comes to writing, **The damned stuff comes out only by a kind of mental convulsion lasting two, three or more days—up to a fortnight—which leaves me perfectly limp and not very happy, exhausted emotionally to all appearance, but secretly irritable to the point of savagery. (Conrad) The sense of life, the consciousness of self, were multiplied almost ten times at these moments, which went on like a flash of lightning. (Dostoyevsky)**

Too bad that, in order to become creative again—creative meaning able to come up with the new associations of ideas (see A *Stroll with William James,* by Jacques Barzun, 1983) and even, if one is as uniquely gifted as was William James (the brother of Henry) to come up with brand new ideas of mental associations. While associations are easily found in any state, city or federal Directory of American Societies and

Associations, new ideas are not. Witness the directory of any American foundation—then look up Yellow Pages under Truly New Ideas. You won't find many!

By now all ideas have been appropriated many times over by those eager to rest their foundations upon at least one lasting idea. Lasting, not last, and certainly not latest!

I was pretty tired last night when I delivered the last batch of manuscript to you, and could not say very much to you about it. There is not much to say except that today I feel conscious of a good many errors both of omission and commission and wish I had had more time to arrange and sort out the material, but think it is just as well that I have given it to you even in its present shape. . . . Moreover, when all the scenes have been completed and the narrative changed to a third-person point of view, I think there will be a much greater sense of unity than now seems possible. . . . (Thomas Wolfe to Max Perkins)*

His state of mind is in a state of insurgency. On one end stands, quite united by now, a coalitionary force representing his inner government: the centrally rulling self-elected Self, the collective mind, and various other spiritual agencies all run by his Ruthenian-Jewish soul. At the other end, rebelling against him, are the countless masses of arguments united under one black banner with the BLUE STAR OF DAVID shown on it—shown as well as "Why Fucking Carmela Nonstop Is Better Than His Nonstop Writing?" written in large yellow letters. These masses are kept at bay by his inner armed forces. His armed forces, in case you missed the *pointe morale*, comprise, above all, the SS-69 missile-armed Navy: they protect the free passage of ideas and associations over his narrative waters. Then, there is the CC-96–equipped Air Force. The Air Force which, by guaranteeing the fresh and unobstructed supply of air to his lungs and oxygen to his brain (brain too

---

*Moreover, since parts of the manuscript were written in the first person, [John Hall] Wheelock was obliged to change them to the third person all the way through. There was one 'I' which might have been intended to mean 'I, the author,' and which Wheelock therefore did not change to 'he.' Wolfe discovered it after the book was published, and brooded over it for years." (Elizabeth Nowell about Thomas Wolfe)

PROOFREADER TO AUTHOR: I hope Wheelock did not claim that as a result of making such changes he had given Thomas Wolfe his third-person style.

AUTHOR TO PROOFREADER: Of course not! As a legitimate book editor, Wheelock knew the difference between contribution and creation.

means the uninterrupted flow of ideas), he justifiably calls his AIR—
Air means the spiritually supreme Force Nine. Air—not Water!

A spiritual siesta offers the only known way to postpone such con-
frontations from becoming brutal and bloodthirsty, which often lead to
his inner mass of Khazar massacres and Czarist pogroms all resulting
from and leading to a mass murder of old and new associations of ideas.
Our sexual Don now dons a black'nd white pajama and, his inner alarm
ringing, he goes to bed without setting his outer alarm clock. He has
nowhere to go but into sleep.

He falls asleep: So long, Macbeth!

**A metaphor is an invitation to an activity, ending in an impossibility.
(For you cannot *actually* think of something in terms of something else:
any metaphor must break down somewhere.) When one reads or hears
'Macbeth has murdered Sleep,' one tries to realize it in mental pictures
but gives up baffled. (This, in fact, worried an eighteenth-century editor,
who wanted to amend the line to read 'Macbeth has murdered a sleeper.')
(P. N. Furbank)**

Kosky has barely fallen asleep when the sound of the house phone
ringing in his kitchen wakes him up. Groggy, he grops his way to the
kitchen and picks up the receiver.

"*Señor* Kosky! *Señor* Kosky!" Santos, the doorman, speaks to him in
a high pitch. "There's a delivery for you, *señor*."

"What is it?"

"It's a lady."

"I don't expect a lady."

"Are you okay, *Señor* Kosky?" Santos hisses. "Carmela Leroy is here
and you don't expect her?"

"Carmela Leroy? Are you sure?" Kosky wakes up to his dream.

"Am I sure? Sure I'm sure."

"Tell Miss Leroy I expect her," says Kosky.

He rushes to the toilet where he sets a new record for fast self-service.
Just when he is finished, his door bell rings six times.

Tripping over nothing, our Man of Conflict opens the door—and
there, standing in front of him, is The Black Symphony.

Face to face with her, and alone, he is starstruck by a great Sexual
Star. He is no longer the Polish Rider, not even an ordinary classy rider
portrayed in the paintings of *The Classical Riding School** (The Wilton

---

*See *The Classical Riding School: The Wilton House Collection*, by Baron Reis

House Collection), not even a happy-go-lucky polo player straight from the social pages of the one and only *Polo* magazine, but, rather, a walking situation ethics sexual cliché.

"You must be Pamela Leroy, I mean *Carmela*," he says.

"I 'must' nothing. I am." The African Queen flashes her teeth. Would such a queen ever consider marrying a Ruthenian-Jewish Khazar?

"You look great. You are a living poster," our Khazar prince tells her. He then leads his queen to the black leather chair placed in the center of his living room.

"Would you ever marry Prince Khazar?"

"Hardly. Why would he want a wife from a poster? Besides, I'm also a working girl." The queen slides her subtle body into the easy chair—hardly a throne—with the ease of a queen facing a wild Khazar.

"Had Freddie Chopin seen you looking like this"—Kosky intones in Ruthenian—"what a black cunt mazurka he would have written!"

"Never mind Freddie," she says, understanding only one word. "How about you, Father Schulz?" She comes straight to the point—a point sharpened for her, no doubt, by Harold the Gross, "that sexually greedy follower of that foot-worshiping Baron Bruno von Schulz." (Jay Kay)

"This is morally awkward," says Kosky, fixing her an X.X.O. and himself a V.S.

"Morally awkward, or morally wrong?" the pinup girl pins him down.

"Morally ambiguous"—he tells her the truth—"while lying to himself." (Jay Kay) "Since I actually never expected to see you in person—to see or to have."

To me inspiration and creativity come only when I have abstained from a woman for a longish period. When, with passion, I have emptied my fluid into a woman until I am pumped dry then inspiration shuns me and ideas won't crawl into my head. Consider how strange and wonderful it is that the same forces which go to fertilize a woman and create a human being should go to create a work of art! Yet a man wastes this life-giving precious fluid for a moment of ecstasy. (Chopin)

Slowly, as if playing at half speed, she gets up, and, her tits still tightly wrapped, she inches into the sofa made of black leatherette, into

d'Eisenberg, introduction by Dorian Williams (1978). Library of Congress Catalogue Card No: 79-63965; ISBN O-670-22509-6. Known for his famous *Description du Ménage Modern*, a handbook of the equestrian art, and for his ménage-à-trois, the baron's favorite riding pose.

which she floats like a good swimmer—on her back. He follows her to it with the drinks.

"You didn't believe I was serious?" she breathes.

"I didn't think Harold was. He's such a floating DOM."* Kosky inhales her buoyant aroma.

"Seriously. I like to play at any speed." She toys with her drink.

Carmela gets up. Carmela walks around the apartment. Carmela tempts him step by step.

Step by step, she transforms herself into "Daphne's Tune" (1982), "the extraordinary works of graphic art (ink and casein)" and "A Tribute" (1985), "faultlessly executed by Pat Nagel, his Graphic Artist Favorite." (Jay Kay)†

Video meliora proboque; deteriora sequor says Emerson, quoting Bacon quoting Ovid's *Metamorphoses*, and indeed our hero "sees the better and approves of it, but follows the worst."

"Jokes aside," says Kosky, "why are you here?"

"You know why. I'm here to convince you Harold means business. To convince you not to corrupt you."

She places her necklace and bracelet on top of the copier. Defiantly, our moralizing Fuddy Duddy tightens the belt of his fatherly robe while she slips out of her virginal Saharan wrap, leaving on her white-lace brassiere, white-lace panties and white-lace stockings for him to stare at.

From her diamond-studded purse she extracts a small diamond-studded container. She opens it, then sniffs—then sniffs from it!—careful not to spill its shaky white content.

"Want some?" she asks, and when he shakes his head in denial, she replaces the container in her purse and throws the purse on top of the copier. She unhooks her brassiere and, freeing her breasts, lets it fall

---

*DOM (Ruth.): pron. *dom*, and means a House, but that's not what it means in New York. Says Petronius: "New York's *dirty old man* is the smartest, most elegant, best-dressed, most glamorous, cleanest, wittiest, most charming and sharpest D.O.M. in the world! And that includes London, Paris, Hong Kong and St. Petersburg. The New York D.O.M. must be fastidious, natty and stylish. Otherwise, he's just another dirty old man . . . always under suspicion and with a very limited range of operation." (1966)

†Pat Nagel illustrated for *Playboy* magazine from 1975 until his sudden death in 1984. See pp. 28–29, in *The Art of Playboy*, text by Ray Bradbury (1985).

to the floor. Her panties follow, then her stockings and shoes. A Venus of Bronze stretches on his cot.

Love, such as found in society, is no more but the exchange of two imaginations and two foreskins. (Chamfort)

If only Pan Fryderyk Szopen* could see her now! You can already hear his Stygian Scherzo, or his Cimmerian Polonaise! "Carmela is pure consumption. To be consumed by sex, you do not need TB." (Jay Kay summarizes the situation.)

"I'm ready," says the black mazurka.† "Put that needle on the record—but don't scratch it!" Needling him senselessly, she stretches sinuously while looking him in the eye.

"And so am I," says our Insatiable Man.

"I am not. Not yet—and might never be," says Kosky.

---

*Fryderyk Szopen: Ruthenian spelling of Frederic Chopin. The Ruthenian language spells out words the way they're pronounced, e.g., Szekspir (Shakespeare).

†The Black Mazurka, Chopin's most exotic work, and the one least plotted along predictable ABABA, ABCA and ABAC lines, was written in 1849, a few months before Chopin died. It was published posthumously as his opus 68. (Too bad Chopin never made it to opus 69: J.K.)

6 9

First, the bit of bad news: Dustin Beach Borell, his editor of six years and Eidolon's editor-in-chief, suddenly quit Eidolon Press and has since become the chief editor of Flotilla Press—"a large (Khazar-owned: J.K.) publishing concern which concerns itself with the mass publication of para-literary easy-to-operate sloops and ketches rather than the more complex tall ships—among them the barking barkentines of the Bruno Schulz/Norbert Kosky class," in the headline-making words of Sim Thomas Temple, Jr., speaking last June on WHM–Channel Six TV.

... what I feel is an immense discouragement, a sense of unbearable isolation ... a complete absence of desires, an impossibility of finding any sort of amusement. The strange success of my book and the hatred it aroused interested me for a short time, but after that I sank back into my usual mood. (Baudelaire)

At the Eidolon Press Office Building, our raging bantam stands up to Marion and John, facing them both in their luxuriously appointed newest ripple room publicity suite.

"How many copies of *The Healer* have actually been sold?" asks Kosky. A book is a postponed suicide. (Cioran)

"Not even ninety-six." Marion whistles a tango tune called "Poinciana."

"C'mon, tell me the truth." He is pretty certain to come back into favor. One of the surest signs of his genius is that women dislike his books. (George Orwell) (Books, printer, not boots!)

"Not even sixty-nine," says John, swallowing one of Marion's Yoni'nd Linga Multipotency Vitamins.

"Please be serious," says Kosky.

"Do you really want to know?" Marion and John ask him in unison.

"How many?" our **wanton young Levite (Congreve)** goes on. **"What I have written, I have written."** (Pontius Pilate, John 19:22)

"How many?" Threateningly, Kosky waves his own free copy of *The Healer*.

"As of this hour we haven't sold a single copy," says Marion, and this time she says it with a glow of recognition. "Not one copy sold," she repeats. "Not one copy in a nation of some sixty-nine million potential book buyers! No other book in recorded memory can claim such a performance." She raises her tainted eyebrows and almost forgets to drop them down.

"Never mind the book buyers," says John. "Would you believe that as of this morning not a single copy of *The Healer* has been borrowed in six hundred and sixty-nine libraries, to whom, by the way, it was sent gratis? That the envelope with your book inside was returned to us *unopened* even by the organizers of the 69th Street Book Festival?" He raises his index finger, and with it the indexi of American literary prohibitorum.

"What do you make of it?" asks Kosky. Color his face Alchemical Ash.

Gautier says: "In those days it was the prevailing fashion in the romantic school to have as pallid a complexion as possible, even greenish, almost cadaverous. This lent a man a fateful, Byronic appearance, testified that he was devoured by passion and remorse. It made him look interesting in the eyes of women." (G. Plekhanov, 1899)

"It's a publishing event! A publishing event like no other in the recorded or yet-to-be-written history of the book business!" says John to whom, let's face it, books are business too!

"It's a publishing event with precedence. Pure literary magic," says Marion.

"This could be proof of your healing power: maybe you've willed the entire American nation not to buy a single copy of *The Healer*—a book that could poison so many innocent minds," says John, casting a soulful glance first at a single copy of *The Healer* held by Kosky in his hand, then at the trembling hand of Kosky.

"And you've succeeded in spite of a huge bag of mixed and mixed-up reviews." Hands down, Marion hands him a fat envelope.

"Wow! That's a lot of free ink!" moans John.

"Good." **A writer is an ink-spiller. Ink is a form of water. (Israel Kosky, 1945)**

"A lot of valid criticism too," cautions Marion.

"Good. **I like criticism but it must be my way. (Mark Twain)**

Time to go. The author and his publicity commanders embrace one another. It is an awkward parting, but so is their particular situation.

On the way out, Kosky runs into De Quincey. "Did you get the latest sales figures?" says De Quincey, and he says it as The Publisher as he faces Kosky point-blank.

Kosky nods that he did. **Some there are, also difficult to please, even though they may be ascetics; on the other hand, there are also some laymen difficult to propitiate; therefore let one, not minding other men's children, walk alone like a rhinoceros. (Buddha)**

"I hope you are not upset by such upset," says De Quincey, walking Kosky out of the room, then escorting him the way a prison warden escorts a prisoner, all the way downstairs to the company's back door, the only nonrevolving door in the entire Eidolon Press Building. "This is not an accident in the industry, known to be more revolving than evolving" (Jay Kay comments wryly).

"I'm K.O.'d as an author but quite O.K. as a man," says Kosky, our Ruthenian-Jewish prototypical man-of-letters "turned into a man without a reference." (Jay Kay)

"Now why is he so upset? Can't he simply assume the upset caused by the no-sales of *The Healer* was caused by a faulty system—rather than by his so naturally and—under the circumstance—justifiably faulty novel?" (asks the no-longer-needed voice of Jay Kay). For some unexplained reason, he can't; he keeps on searching for a specific fault. Now, what went wrong? Was it perhaps wrong for his publishers to display him clad only in the briefest of swimming briefs, floating like a lotus in the center of an old Southampton swimming pool lost amidst the potato fields, the very fields which are about to become a new center of Old World polo?

Was it an overly realistic description of his novel? One which, on the back cover, called it "a spiritual autofocus" and used such terms as "calculated depth-of-field autoexposure," "self-focus priority," "low light aid-flash provided by the author himself"—all this in order to popularize his works among lovers of literary work? (Or are they all in love with an image? An image of a spiritually successful man they all know as "book author?" asks the always perplexed Jay Kay.)

Finally, was there enough 69? Enough? How can it ever be enough? Enough said, yes. Enough sex, no.

For whatever reason, like a man suffering from Malison disease, Kosky goes on to assume it is his fault, and his alone. Here he commits another grave spiritual sin. "What happened to his half anti-Marxist, half pro-Yoga I DON'T GIVE A DAMN! He becomes angry. Angry at himself, at his inner world, instead of being angry at the world at large. "And here he commits yet another spiritual sin: he turns into one who, suffering from Malison disease, is no longer able to distinguish between what is good for one's self and what is bad; between what is important and what is not, be it in a lifeless life of a living creature called Tardigrade, that super hermit which lives for some ninety-nine years without moisture, or the life of literary plankton as filled with forms of marine lower life, as he, our literary marine, is with himself" (pronounces the longest verdict yet our petty literary yeti Jay Kay).

"Now why do you think *The Healer* did not instantly sell?" asks De Quincey, with the self-assurance of a man whose ancestor wrote *Confessions of an English Opium Eater* ("the very first worldwide addiction best-seller, brilliantly translated into French by the opium-eating Baudelaire." Jay Kay saves Kosky from judging other writers as he would never dare to judge himself. Another sin to fear on his narrative Last Judgment Day).

"Why the book has not instantly buoyed up? Up to become at least number six or even nine on the *Times Square Record Best-sellers List*? Boy, it beats me!" says De Quincey.

"It also beats me," says Kosky.

"I've beaten my brains as well as my meat working on these Working Papers. By 'meat' I mean my subtle body, and not any other kind of meat," he adds quickly. "Do you suppose," De Quincey goes on, "it is because *The Healer* is not a *sensu stricto* novel. Because the time of it has not yet returned." "Returned, not come," Kosky goes on.

"You mean it's so much ahead of time?" De Quincey laughs.

"Not ahead. Behind. Way behind. It is so behind the current State of **a post-modernistic *roman* (Niskisko)** that you could say to the reader:

490

'This book comes to you from the Grand Beyond.' " **Beyond sounds better than behind.** (*Safe Sex Dictionary*, 1988)

"If it's so much grand beyond—then why doesn't it sell? Is it because, for the first time in your fiction, you stayed away from your favorite obsession with women's behind?"

"It's beyond me. Me and my behind." Kosky ends his new Literary Construction theory.

"Perhaps we should have published your novel as a 'How To' book," says De Quincey. "Not as a 'novel-note: the forthcoming stage of the modern novel.' " He quotes Alexander Wat.

"How to what?"

"As a One Man Amphibian Think Tank—I can see the headline already: *A sinking Trappist monk tells all about thinking. Read him or you'll sink!*"

"This book is not *about.*" Kosky pleads with the voice of Derrida. (See: "Derrida and the Diaspora" by Michael Greenstein, *Response*, Summer–Fall, 1986, pp. 33–41). "This novel is. See it as a literary sport of sorts. See it, say, as a case of wrestling. Wrestling, not boxing. See it as a multiple pole-vault, not gymkhana gymnastics."

"Wrestling? Why didn't you tell me this before? I would have read the goddamned footnotes more carefully! Who is this fellow, this Selfish Mr. Self-Fish, this Jay Kay wrestling?"

"He's wrestling someone as powerful as Bukharin. Bukharin—the man powerful enough to wrestle Stalin."

"And who's that?"

"His Self. Whom else could he legally deduct as a sparring partner. Now wait a moment!" Impulsively De Quincey takes Kosky by the arm in order to slow down his final exit from the building as well as from Eidolon Press. "We can still safely deduct the cost of *The Healer*. Deduct it as, for instance, our outstanding contribution to the Public Right to Know (This is Kosky speaking—not Thomas Wolfe!) Foundation. So don't be upset!"

"*Don't be upset?*" Kosky mocks him. Here, overpowered by self-venom, he voluntarily skips one breath, then another. Breathless, and as a result upset, he starts overproducing malic acid, which causes him to discharge Kosin—the deadly kosotoxin, **the poison of the procreative Self** which is the creative soul's own Super Sativa.*

---

*See "Beginner's Guide to Super Sativa," *High Times*, April 1987.

"Don't be upset! How can I not be upset?" **The end came suddenly. The end of those five years of torment and incessant productivity. (Thomas Wolfe, *Story of a Novel*)** "How can I be *not* upset?" he goes on. "*The Healer* is the story of my inner life, my *life*, d'you hear? Not another *Story of a Novel!*" (This is Kosky speaking—not Thomas Wolfe!)

"Still, while working on it, you were working also on yourself. I know you, Norbie, as well as you know your Thomas Wolfe! I know you've used the writing of the book as a means to abuse yourself; the Self-abusement being, no doubt, an end to enlarge your literary production." De Quincey knows Kosky only secondhand, the way Edgar Allen Poe was known to Baudelaire. *

"I have manipulated myself by writing, not just by sex, Thomas! Ask anyone who saw me do it. Ask the big girl called *La Géante* or the skinny one called *La Muse Vénale*. Ask *Edgar Allan Baudelaire.* †"

"Still and all, you've succeeded admirably, I mean for being foreign-born, foreign-named, foreign-educated," De Quincey says with a parting smile, as the author and his publisher (here publisher stands also for privately owned publishing company: J.K.) are about to part company. "You've willed your very publishers to publish *The Healer*, at no moral cost to your readers, and at no financial loss to us. I mean willed, not forced," he stresses. "In the publishing industry, we call such a rare act

---

*Baudelaire, Charles Pierre. See: *Encyclopaedia Britannica*, Eleventh Edition, Volume III (New York, 1910), p. 537.

"Charles Baudelaire did not live the kind of life which would have recommended him to doting fathers as a fitting companion for their débutante daughters—(although in truth, those débutante daughters would have been even comically safe with him: he was not interested in the undeveloped and immature)." (Edna St. Vincent Millay, 1935)

†*"La Géante"* ("The Giantess") and *"La Muse Vénale"* ("The Mercenary Muse"): titles of poems of Charles Baudelaire, to be found with many more in his *Les Fleurs du Mal* (*Flowers of Evil*). Why evil? Why not *Mad Flowers* or *Flowers of Seizures*? (asks the always annoyed Jay Kay).

"Baudelaire had learnt English in his childhood, and had found some of his favorite reading in the English "satanic" romances, such as Lewis's *Monk*. In 1846–47 he became acquainted with the works of Edgar Allan Poe, in which he discovered romances and poems which had, he said, long existed in his own brain, but had never taken shape. From this time till 1865 he was largely occupied with his version of Poe's works, producing masterpieces of the art of translation in *Histoires extraordinaires*. (*Encyclopaedia Britannica*, op. cit., p. 537)

an act of intellectual mercy, also known as public healing." They shake hands. Exeunt Norbert Kosky.

Isolated and withdrawn from the world, he is yet a light and a beacon to others. *Yod* is the letter of the phallus, creative power, and in terms of sexual symbolism the Hermit means masturbation—the true self has reached puberty, as it were, the magician has found the Master in himself. Complete in himself, solitary and virgin, the Hermit's plants all have white flowers, emblems of purity, uninvolvement. He is a symbol of the fertility, of absolute self-reliance. (John Cowper Powys)

SS

These days, self-quarantined, our bitter and salty American Saltykov-Shchedrin,* wild lord, has turned into an ultramarine hermit. He lives on *Nostromo*, an unassuming inboard-outboard American-Thai fishing junk of the Sea Robin class, which he has leased for six months from the Muscovy Marina in Little Siam, the colorful part of New York so close to Ellis Island. Simple living, like simple reading, comes to him most naturally. Isn't he, after all, the son of Israel Kosky (and a grandson of Max Weinreigh—pronounced "Wajnreigh" in Ruthenian—whose namesake wrote in America the monumental history of Yiddish: J.K.), who brought him up until 1939 (until he was six) according to rather strict Jewish **Sumptuary Laws, which restricted the number of people who could be invited to private parties, the types of food that might be served, the amount of jewelry one could wear, the type and number of wedding gifts one could give, and the like (See "Why Was It Necessary for Many Jewish Communities to Establish Laws Regulating Extravagance?"** *The Second Jewish Book of Why* **by Alfred J. Kolatch, 1985, p. 96)**

While—so the prospectus says—*Nostromo* can comfortably sleep six and feed nine, at this juncture in its sixty-nine years of service the junk sleeps only one: one Commander Norbert Kosky—anything but junk.

These days, Commander Kosky does not complain. These days he believes a man is a spiritual island, even an archipelago—by this he means himself since as a good Jew he does not proselytize. At a time when most people must live a fixed existence and live it on fixed incomes

---

*Shchedrin, N. (pseudonym of M. Y. Saltykov [d. 1889]: "Russian spiritual satirist of the highest revolutionary democratic class." (Jay Kay)

and at a fixed address, his fluid income combined with an exclusively fluid address adds new spiritual substance to his already fluid character (fluid, not spineless: J.K.) and modifies the meaning of spiritual solitude. "Je crois que la foule, le troupeau sera toujours haïssable. Il n'ya d'important qu'un petit groupe d'esprits toujours les mêmes et qui se repassent le flambeau." ("I believe that the crowd, the herd, will always be detestable. Nothing is important but a small group of always the same minds who pass the torch to one another.") (Flaubert to George Sand, *Correspondance, quatrième série*, 1869–1880, Paris, 1910.) To a writer, that is an advantage: it helps Kosky to concentrate, and to work, on his new work No. 10, "an alchemical dramatical compost which, temporarily entitled *Bruno and I*, will no doubt end up on some forgotten student stage as "Norbert Kosky's sexual *passion spielen*." (*Beulah Repertory*, 1981) Keep in mind that while he, the literary commander, is at bay called Solitude, others work in their company's workpool. CAREFUL: HOW MANY PEOPLE KNOW THAT TO A WRITER SOLITUDE IS SYNONYMOUS WITH CONCENTRATION AND CONCENTRATION WITH WORK? OFTEN THE HARDEST KNOWN? telecomputes his Inner Work Computer. (Work, printer, not word!) Keep also in mind that, on weekends and holidays, when technically speaking, his friends are free to see him, they can't get away from either their fixed incomes—or their homes nobody can fix. And there goes out through the door the argument that AMERICANS ARE REALLY FREE!

The embarrassing difficulty is subsequently to return to my own self for, in truth, I no longer am very clear about who I am. Or, if one prefers, I never am; I become. (Gide)

When your house shakes in all its members and sways unsteadily on its keel, you fancy that you are a sailor cradled by gentle zephyrs. (Balzac)

"Life upon water comes as easily to me as it does to a Clown fish."* writes our literary Plekhanovite to Dustin Beach Borell, his Protestant stakhanovite (Stakhanov was a Soviet Shock worker who died from too many shocks: Jay Kay). With the word "beach" in his name Dustin would surely not object to anyone floating full-time upon the water. "To start with"—Kosky goes on—"remember I'm not a literary upstart and that to 'start' means the least important position to me. But the fact is that this boat gives me freedom and comfort obtained at a third of

---

*The Clown fish: "perhaps the best known of the marine aquarian fishes." (Herbert R. Axelrod and William Vorderwinkler, 1956)

the price I used to pay at the Manfred for my apartment number sixty-nine." What he does not say is that the boat's limited space has forced him to edit out from his life "all the superfluous adverbs and adjectives and to stick to the verb and noun, to what really matters in good living as well as on a tightly written page," in Kosky's own words (as recorded for us by Dustin Beach Borrell: J.K., 1988).

Leo has run away on the spur of the moment. Awful! He says in his letter that no one is to look for him—that he has left forever his peaceful life of an old man. As soon as I had read it I ran out in my anguish and threw myself into the pond next door. (Sophia Tolstoy).

Whether in life or in literature, the forces of life come wearing different disguises. Indifference is but one of them, and what a non-indifferent difference the letters *in* can make when added to it. Suddenly, some of his friends, among them Cesare and Carmela, tell him on the phone (with no phone on his boat he calls them from a pay phone on the nearest dock) that his chartered *Nostromo* is not safe enough for them to visit. As if they could not see him outside his *Nostromo*.

Alone on his boat, Kosky circumambulates the city on a dreamy Sabbath afternoon as Melville advises him to do, going from Corlears Hook to Coenties Slip and from thence, by Whitehall, northward. By now, he has discovered that without fish, there is no Sabbath. (Haggadah) and that there is more to water than fish: there is fishing—though, since fishing is work, never on the Sabbath.

> A million people—manners free and superb—open voices—
> hospitality—the most courageous and friendly young men,
> City of hurried and sparkling waters! city of spires
> and masks!
> City nested in bays! my city! (Walt Whitman)

To test *Nostromo*, his floating junk (call all this sailing his real-life narrative), as well as himself as a sailor, who once worked as a proto-typical Jewish word-tailor (tailor, printer, not sailor!), Kosky takes her all the way up the Hudson River and past Bear Mountain, then all the way down, past Wall Street—but no farther than Liberty Island, near Manhattan, the current American address of his beloved Statue of Liberty.

With *Nostromo*'s seaworthiness tested in the smooth, as well as rough, waters, our captain pronounces her spiritually safe. As a result, he drifts on her peacefully all over and around archipelago Manhattan all through the summer and fall, through the season of the scallop. Drifting is a form of floating—and it allows him to taste the joys of the sweet and salty water fishing. Otherwise, our angling author keeps one anxious eye on the sextant,* his favorite sexual-sounding instrument, and the other on the fat envelope he received from Marion, "one which contains most of what the American Fourth Estate said about him" and his *free as a bird* (Plekhanov) literary narrative master sheet piece" (Jay Kay), *The Healer.*

Time to open Marion's envelope. But first, ahead of time, let's feed his so overwhelmingly esoteric Self with *Rotten Reviews: A Literary Comparison.* (Ed. by Bill Henderson, Stamford, Conn., 06903. Introduction by Anthony Brandt; illustrations by Mary Kornblum. Timeless and most wise!: Kosky, 1987) Time to turn to the critics. Will the waterpen critics, his craft's invisible pilots, declare his literary craft No. 9 seaworthy, ready to tackle the turbulent narrative waters, or will they restrict its seaworthiness by relegating it to a river, lake or (Thoreau, forgive me, but I must!) silver pond?

I don't think that anyone has ever satisfactorily defined the distinction between the reviewer and the critic. It was once suggested that the difference really is that a critic is a reviewer plus 10,000 words. (*Writers' Guild Bulletin*)

"Like any other pure art," writes an anonymous writer in the *Critical Review,* "what matters in literary criticism is the name of the writer, not the name of the newspaper in which the review appears. The critic is a man of his craft, not only a member of his profession, a profession which, priding itself for its high standards of conduct, by his own admission, wisely lacks (and wisely insists on lacking: J.K.) the professional standards of admission."

While reading one review after another, Kosky lets his inner censor censor his para-literary responses, and, above all, keep his breathing— breathing means emotions—in check. After all, so far each review was written by a critic who, Kosky presumes, wrote it as a rational contri-

---

*Sextant: sixth part of a circle; also an instrument used in navigation and surveying to measure angular distances; not to be confused with sextain (a stanza of six lines) or sextan, i.e., something recurring every fifth, or by inclusive reckoning sixth, day. Don't confuse with sexton, "officer charged with care of church" (COD).

bution to the art of literary criticism or to the art of fiction or even to *Art and Social Life* (Plekhanov).

He reads review No. 1. All one can say is that the novelist has mistaken his medium or fallen short of it. He is writing something that resembles Old Testament rhapsody but differs from it in not having the living core. He most certainly is not writing fiction. Perhaps his material might eventually prove to have the highest usefulness for fiction, but before it can become fiction. . . . it must stay longer in the tanning bath or the rising pan, it must be leavened—or whatever metaphor will suggest that a transformation must occur before it can acquire form. The essential thing has not yet been done to it. (De Voto)

Imagine this! De Voto is the very man who, writing in *The Saturday Review of Literature* on April 6, 1944 (Jacky X, please check the date: J.K.), dared to proclaim about all American writers of the American twenties that THEY TURNED THEIR BACKS ON AMERICA: WRITERS OF THE TWENTIES MISSED THE REAL MEANING OF THE TIMES!* Still Kosky keeps on reading. Literary criticism is Literature 999: a high-potency concentrate. Concentrate. Don't skip. In a good review, every word counts. These days words are expensive, "they crowd pictures on the advertising page." (Jay Kay)

Here, but only as a mental footnote, Norbert Kosky momentarily curses the very memory of Bernard De Voto (alias John August) with Kosky's Decomposition Curse™—the strongest VSOP Grand Reserve para-literary curse he knows, fully aware that cursing one's own memory of evil is a literary infraction—not a spiritual infarction. It is the same curse Kosky reserves for such abominators as Goebbels, Theveneau de Morande, and very few others.

Let's see, what do we have here. Oh, yes, good old D. S. Merezhkovsky criticizes *The Healer* for its "moral format" which resembles the climate of the *Notebooks of Leonardo D.V.* How can a format resemble climate? C'mon Merezhkovsky, that's unfair. Enough said.

---

*(This was the very issue in Russia and the United States which was reviewed in a book written by the most distinguished Pitirim A. Sorokin. (Sorokin, b. 1889,: a Russian-educated American sociologist who wrote in Russian *Crime and Punishment: Heroic Act and Reward* (1914) and *System of Sociology* (1919), then, writing in English, dared to introduce the concept of "Empirical Soul" which he identified with Self or Ego: J.K.)

Another review. This one is by A. A. Malinovsky (the pseudonym of the American critic Bogdanov, the guy who claims that new proletarian culture must break off all links binding it to bourgeois mankind: J.K.). He praises Kosky for "breaking away in *The Healer* even from the remotest notion of the novel," and has a few nice things to say about the novel's footnotes, which he calls "the indispensable tools of proletarian enlightenment." On the purely spiritual front, Jacob Frank, writing in the *Muslim & Christian Literary Magazine*, chastises Kosky for his use and abuse of Sabbatai Sevi but does not object to Kosky's use of Tantric Yoga as a means to "a veritable *kahal* of sensual ecstasy." He should know. He is the Polish-Jew who first connected to Islam via the Sexual Revolution, then converted to it only to become a Christian seduced by the freedom of Confession. What else? Oh, yes, a short review by Jerome Bentham, who has a few nice things to say about Kosky's abandonment of the article "the" as well as of his openness in matters of literary secrecy. **Bentham's pleas for publicity, and his claim that "without publicity, no good is permanent; under the auspices of publicity, no evil can continue," is, to my knowledge, the strongest challenge to administrative secrecy in print. (Sissela Bok, 1983)*** (It ends on the strongest challenge to fictional secrecy in print—fictional, not administrative: Jay Kay paraphrases the challenge.)

Another clipping, another lost breath. Just listen to this:

An "irresistible appeal" indeed! Doesn't Boynton know that *The Healer* is a work of art, not an appeal—not even a safe sex appeal—written by some ordinary Eugene Sue?"

Another clipping, another review. Will he let this clipping clip his creative feathers, the creative feathers of our American unholy Eugene Sue? (The one dismembered by Marx and Engels writing in *The Holy Family*.) And after reading it, will he be able to will himself, or be less willing, to take off, to fly in any direction ordinary water fowls fly—the black ducks, blue or green herons, brown pelicans and white gulls—in the direction of a literary mangrove forest. (MANgrove or womangrove, does it really matter?)

Mr. Conrad is words; . . . His style is like river-mist; for a space things

---

*"Secrets of State" Chapter 12 in *Secrets: On the Ethics of Concealment and Revelation* (1983), p. 174. See also her *Lying: Moral Choice in Public and Private Life* (1978). Above all, read "On Publicity," an essay on political tactics in *The Works of Jeremy Bentham*, ed. by John Bowring (Edinburgh, 1843).

are seen clearly, and then comes a great grey bank of printed matter. (H. G. Wells)

So what? What's wrong with printed matter? he answers the reviewer in a neutral voice. Just then, to the left of *Nostromo*, he spots a veritable high school of stripers, six or nine at one time, as these shamelessly nude fishes strip out of water and, arching into the air, seize their feed in a brief display of purple blotch against the green indigo. Meanwhile, a steady wind keeps pushing the unsteadily drifting *Nostromo*—drifting with the engine turned off closer to the shore—while, resting comfortably on his cot, Commander Kosky keeps on reading one review after another.

One more. Why not. This one calls Kosky *a politically ultraconservative* 1969 literary sex invader who invades year 1988 with his *fail-safe sex!* That's O.K. But then they also call his character a renegade. His character, not him. Now what does this say about Jay Kay, his novel's hero? In a passage, aptly entitled FACING HIS OWN FACE HE FORGOT THE ECONOMIC FACE OF THE NATION, they write:

The *renegade* exhibits a characteristic loyalty to his new political, religious, or other party. The awareness and firmness of this loyalty (other things being equal) surpass those of persons who have belonged to the party all along. In sixteenth- and seventeenth-century Turkey, this went so far that very often born Turks were not allowed to occupy high government positions, which were filled only by Janizaries, that is, born Christians, either voluntarily converted to Islam or stolen from their parents as children and brought up as Turks. (Simmel) Enough of such ethnic reflections. Just look at the newspaper's own photograph of our man Kosky taken back in 1969 as the Spiritual Man of the Year. Nothing to do with a notion of a renegade! Then, look at the pictures of yet another Norbert Kosky. That's when he practically dominated the W.E.T. spiritual annual dinner. WOW! There! A year later! In the center. His spirit uplifted by the spirit of his peers giving him a standing ovation. Him, not a renegade. There stands Norbert Kosky: the new president-elect—elected for the twice-only-allowed maximum second term. Nothing to do with the notion of a renegade! He has just delivered his speech (call it *triumphant*), during which he was interrupted by four LAUGHTER! three LONG APPLAUSE, one STANDING OVATION, and one PROLONGED APPLAUSE. Not a bad record for a literary renegade!

So far so good. Next item. A clipping from *American Egyptian Masonry* magazine. What do they have to say? They say: *"Float or Swim*

Affaire was a form of Kosky's own public meditation on the dying Art of Public Dying."

Another clip. This one from *Fictional Art* magazine. The headline: NORBERT KOSKY AND SELF-STYLED MONOFICTION. "Norbert Kosky stresses water, not air, as the main ingredient of his newest purofiction. A natural progression of a fiction writer who made a career of putting too much fiction into his life, but not enough life into his fiction."

Another little press clipping, a perfect time killer between serious reading: A BONY BIRD FRAMED IN AN EBONY FRAME,* says a headline about him in the all new safe-sex-oriented *Ovary & Mammary Adult Magazine*. Referring to his by now overly known predilection for a Black Madonna, as well as his fondness for *Ebony* magazine, the editors unanimously have chosen Norbert Kosky as their own 69 MAN OF THE YEAR.

Finally, at the bottom of the envelope, Kosky finds what he has been waiting for: a major review written by no less than *the* R. H. W. Trowbridge, the British critic and biographer known for such classics as *Seven Splendid Sisters* and *A Beau Sabreur* and published in *SALM†— Sincerity and Authenticity Literary Monthly* (No. 1910), which, at the time of this writing, has been for years the country's most prestigious para-spiritual publication "devoted to literature viewed as confession— as well as to confessional literature." Entitled, simply, *Cagliostro*, the piece occupies—indeed invades, six full pages accompanied by a large, full-page caricature of our Count Alessandro di Cagliostro, shown on its front cover, the very way the already famous Cagliostro once appeared. Ironically, the caricature is an exact replica of the famous bust made of Cagliostro, if I recall correctly, of solid bronze, or less solid marble, by either Hudini or Houdini, who was then the most famous sculptor of the decade—and made shortly before Cagliostro went bust. Some historians claimed that the bust of Cagliostro did to his reputation

---

The Ebony Frame (1910): a novel by Edith Nesbit in which a London journalist inherits a Chelsea house and two haunted portraits—one a "speaking image of himself," the other of a beautiful woman. Edith Nesbit takes up the motif of dual reincarnation and exploits it for sheer horror. (Theodore Ziolkowski, 1977)

†Founded in 1979 by Steadfast Flack, *SALM* has been steadfastly devoted to giving flack to the doctrine of literary *persona*. It promotes, instead, the author portrayed as an actor, so to speak, in his life's own drama, rather than in his dramatic role.

what the picture of Kosky did to him, the Jewish Jack Ass, posing half-naked on a Jack Ass of a polo horse on the cover of *SwimSport*, the nation's No. 1 swimming magazine. Enough said. "Will this critical piece by Trowbridge make Kosky whole again, A Man of Bronze, or will it break him into still smaller pieces of spiritual porcelain?" (writes Jay Kay, who now works for the most prestigious *Polo* magazine). *

He glances at the Trowbridge piece again. The famous critic and literary historian prefaces his essay by referring the reader to *The Healer*, "a novel, not a thinly veiled attempt at autobiography." In choosing for his subject Kosky (whom he keeps on calling Cagliostro), R. H. W. Trowbridge says he was **guided at first, I admit, by the belief that he was the arch-imposter he is popularly supposed to be. With his mystery, magic, and highly sensational career he seemed just the sort of pictur-esque personality I was in search of.**

Kosky is disappointed but not upset by what he reads.

Back to the critic.

The moment, however, I began to make my researches I was astonished to find how little foundation there was in point of fact for the popular conception. The deeper I went into the subject—how deep this has been the reader may gather from the Bibliography, which contains but a portion of the material I have sifted—the more convinced I became of the fallacy of this conception.

That's bad, very bad, Kosky complains aloud to the indifferent sky.

---

*See "The Florida Report," in *Polo* magazine, the official publication of the U.S. Polo Association. *Polo* is published ten times a year by Fleet Street Corporation. *Fleet means water.* (Israel Kosky) For the best and most inspired account of the most inspiring and exciting sport of polo (open field polo, not arena polo which is polo slowed down), the reader is invited to read *The Endless Cukker: One Hundred and One Years of American Polo*, by Ami Shinitzky and Don Follmer (Polo Publications, Inc., 1978: ISBN 0-933336-00-4).

This is a book about polo played, as rules demand, on 300 yards by 160 yards (yards, not feet printer!) *if bordered on the side (Blue Book*—i.e., *Handbook of U.S. Polo Association*: J.K.) of an open, flat and manicured field of grass. The relationship of such polo, as opposed to polo played in an enclosed arena (300 feet by 150 feet) (feet, printer, not yards!), *is considered ideal (Blue Book)* and is not unlike the relationship of a full-size Arab-thoroughbred of 16.9 hands tall to the Argentinian 9.6 inch miniature horse. Enough said!

See also: "Play as Negation and Creation of the World: An Attempt at a Philosophy of Sport," by Janusz Kuczynski, Dialectics and Humanism, No. 1, 1984.

How many readers read bibliographies? And how many bibliographies are complete? Besides, those who compile bibliographies are often as prejudiced by the subject matter as the biographers themselves: many of them probably hate books and authors and anything to do with print or maybe even with paper—and I bet you even though I don't bet as a principle, they hate it with gusto. "Such hate stemming from guts, from gusto, by the way, bothers me far less than the indifference, particularly indifference stemming from obedience to some State Bus Authority. And I don't mean cases of Self-abuse disguised as Self-obedience." (Jay Kay clarifies the matter.)

Obedience, as a determinant of behavior, is of particular relevance to our time. It has been reliably established that from 1933–45 millions of innocent persons were systematically slaughtered on command. Gas chambers were built, death camps were guarded, daily quotas of corpses were produced with the same efficiency as the manufacture of appliances. These inhumane policies may have originated in the mind of a single person, but they could only be carried out on a massive scale if a very large number of persons obeyed orders. (Stanley Milgram, 1963)

"Only the other day," Trowbridge goes on, "I looked up Charles Theveneau de Morande's entry in *Nouvelle Biographie Generale* (MDCCCLXI). What a sad man: imagine a writer who lists his profession, even if only in French, as *libellist et pamphletaire*." Here, against his better inner judgment, Kosky, the Superficial Man of the Year, rejoices over such critical voices.

Feel rather disheartened. Home looks distant. My mind still wanders homewards. I can almost jump overboard. Scrimshawing. Making canes and riding whips, and husked some coconuts. Scrimshawing."*

Time for shattering of his writing soul. Time for some fresh carvings and engravings, says to himself our Ruthenian-Jewish scrimshander, but what kind of scrimshaw† should it be?

---

*New Bedford Whaling Museum, MS. Captain Alexander A. Tripp, *Journal of a Voyage in the Atlantic Ocean on Board Bark "Globe" as Kept by John S. Coquin, Starting in the Year 1869*. Also in "All Hands Aboard Scrimshawing," by Marius Barbeau, *The American Neptune*, Vol. XII (April 1952), an old copy left on the *Nostromo* by the boat's previous owner, or the previous owner of this reddish and worn-out magazine.

†Arthur S. Watson in *Technology Review* (March 1938) calls scrimshaw "a triumphant answer to an acute problem . . . the most soul-shattering monotony

Saw nothing. Dul times. (dul, printer, not dull!) O dear O dear. (In January 31: All hands scrinshoning. (In May: All hands discouraged. The same dul times. The capt. did not whale on Sundays. Whales in sight, but of no use to us, the Capt. being saintish today. (John Sampson)

After pondering the sexual abandonment and other such tribulations suffered for months upon months (call these months 69-less!) by the American whalers, Kosky exclaims like Captain John Sampson (of the bark *London Packet*, 1840), "All hands scrimshoring!," then returns to the review. "Reading the nonsense written about the narrative nonsense Mr. Kosky wrote about himself, as well as the nonsense he wrote about himself and others," Trowbridge goes on, "reminds me of *Portraits of the Artist in Exile: Recollections of James Joyce by Europeans* (ed. by Willard Potts, 1979)."

"Time for fishing—for shattering the soul with another spiritually refreshing post-Joycean literary common sense." (Jay Kay, 1989) Time for fishing, for catching a big whale. "Time for a fresh brand of narrative, a new type of reading pleasure. A new concept of literary suspense." (Jay Kay)

A well-written life is almost as rare as a well-spent one. (Thomas Carlyle)

The rod's jig, reel and spool are ready. The fishing line shudders. A tremor passes along the rod. This is a moment of suspense. Unlike sexual suspense which, stemming from instinct of life never ends (Tantra), the situational suspense ends the moment it begins to depend on emotional response.

This situational suspense is about to end. A greedy fish pounces on the bait and heads away, dragging behind him yards of dangling line. It's a green bass! Pushing for balance into his invisible stirrups, Kosky starts to reel the line into a tight drag—but after some three seconds, the bass recovers its strength and, as if no longer hooked, sneaks under and around the boat. No wonder! In order to make sure the fish will go unharmed after being out of water Kosky employs a Phony Fish Hook.™ Molded from Fishgum 96, a substance slowly dissolving in water, the Phony Fish Hook™ is strong enough to pull the fish for two or three seconds out of the water. Enough said. He stops fishing for a moment. Time for a new entry in his Bark Journal. I have shortened

---

known to industrial pursuit"—the very words which describe the role of writing in *The Healer*. (Norbert Kosky, 1987)

a bit my literary harpoon. Thought of a new cane. It was wrought into diamonds and ridges, and squares and oblongs, like the war-clubs of the South Sea Islanders, and surmounted by the head of a grinning sea lion. (Joseph Hart)

Making coconut dippers. Scrimshawing. Time rolls on and the old year dies. (John S. Coquin)

Meanwhile, the poor bass is gone. Just think about what this bass must think about right now as it swims away so freely. The bass thinks: there is something transparently fishy about this fish-saving routine. What was I hooked by?

Was it a real hook—or was I hooked by something within me, something phony—but then my upper lip still hurts and hurt is as real as pain. How could something be phony when it causes real pain?

The bass thinks: but then, if the hook was real, why would it let me go just when I was so solidly hooked on it by my still stiff aristocratic upper lip?

Suddenly, Kosky sees an unsightly sight. The sight unsettles him and this means the end to fishing. Right next to the boat drifts a fish. It looks like any other ordinary fish, but it is not ordinary. For one, you can never see it near the top of the water. Why not? Simple. This is a bottom-dwelling flounder—Kosky's favorite fish. "My favorite, 'cause, like any sleepy writer, accustomed to lying and sleeping on one side of its body, it can only live on the flat and safe sea bottom. From there, the bottom-dwelling flounder watches the world, and skoals it with both eyes wide open. Both eyes, I might add, mounted by nature on one side of this creature's head." (1987)

Kosky has now let his *Nostromo* take him all the way uptown, down to Harlem (like up or uptown, down or downtown depends on how one looks at one's map of directions) and the picturesque Harlem River. He slows down *Nostromo* to a negligible speed of 0.6 knot and, himself tense like a knot, drifting over the Harlem Straits, "carefully guides his bark in the almost perfect dark." (Niskisko) He is here, so he tells himself, to follow an old Viking spirit. He too waits for his whale. His whale is a female, with a 45-DD bust. Call her MOBBY (a Mobby, printer, not Molly). But don't you dare to call him Dick. Is he here to struggle with himself or with God?*

Theological Review, LXIV:4 (p. 467). "As one is required to bear witness before God, so may one bear witness against God. Only after Jacob struggles with the

Now, seriously, why is he here? Isn't this a most unnatural sight, and one even the all-Ruthenian-Jewish Metro-Goldwyn-Mayer would never allow to be filmcd? Just imagine! Here is this all-Ruthenian, Jewish-American, serious man of serious letters, this serious W.E.T. president (during his presidency the local union was actually running the International) purposefully drifting alone, on a strangely shaped bark into the 69°-wide mouth of the Harlem River. "The most carnivorous river mouth known. There are so many pipes and tunnels, cable ducts and cables, buried under the bottom of this river—but not a single living bottom-dwelling flounder left. Each time anything on the bottom needs replacement or repairs, a massive and most costly trench has to be dragged across the entire stinking river bottom—in what the City Maritime Work Union calls black bottom-spanking routine," in the words of the Welkopfins' *Guide to New York*.

Our Jewish traveler carefully docks his boat at the old dock marked 1869. Says Welkopfin: "Here, back in 1869, the New York and Harlem railroads were merged by Vanderbilt into the New York Central, Harlem, and Hudson River Railroad one of the world's biggest and most profitable. No wonder with 69 in it, it was Vanderbilt's and the railroad's luckiest year."* But was it? As of 1969, the dock and the railroad stand abandoned.

He checks the significance of both Vanderbilt's success of 1869 and his own of 1969 in his inner book of spiritual records and decides that in spite of Swim or Float, he would not exchange the freedom of his enterprise for the business of the enterprise. But then, he could be wrong. Just see how many other writers were. There is always time for Another Writer's Note. †

---

divine is he called "Israel," which means "to wrestle with God." Israel is a people by virtue of its eternal struggle with God to make Him remain faithful to His law, to His covenant.

Of those in the annals of Jewish history, the individual most closely identified with reminding God to be faithful to His own justice is the Hasidic master, Levi Yitzhak of Berditchev. In this regard Rabbi Barukh, the grandson of the Bael Shem Tov, is reputed to have said, "According to Rabbi Levi Yitzhak of Berditchev the Holy One, blessed be He, has not done justice to even a single Jew."

*Renamed the New York Central Railroad, it was once the largest, most efficient and most profitable railroad in the entire world. As was the entire country too. "And look at it now!" moans Jay Kay.

†See also "A Study of the Suicide Notes," in the *New York Post*, 1974. "Many

Now look at this! At the water here! At all this shit, all this floating phytoplankton and swimming zooplankton. Look at all these dirty waters flowing from and into the lumpfish-eating Harlem lumpenproletariat and the all-white-caviar-eating Riverdale. Just think about all the amino acids which flood our environment. Don't you think that all the bacteria, fungi and other creatures here survived the poison by developing under such poison-filtering emergencies brand-new mouthpairs, gills and limbs— "as well as brand-new floating, swimming and narrative techniques?" (adds Jay Kay).

The public undeniably exists by reason of its numbers. Yet the public is not absolute if it is defined as an audience; in fact, the public at one time did not exist.

That time preceded the Renaissance. Writing and reading without the public's love or money, either one, is where we started in the modern Western world. (William Jovanovich, 1975)*

Here, our skipper skips the rest of Trowbridge's essay, and navigating *Nostromo* with one hand, with the other impatiently turns the pages of "this spiritually burning literary magazine" (Jay Kay), all the way to Trowbridge's final conclusion. It says:

The mistrust that mystery and magic always inspire made Cagliostro with his fantastic personality an easy target for calumny. After having been riddled with abuse till he was unrecognizable, prejudice, the foster-child of calumny, proceeded to lynch him, so to speak. For years his character has dangled on the gibbet of infamy, upon which the *sbirri* of tradition have inscribed a curse on any one who shall attempt to cut him down. (Trowbridge, 1910)

He takes the *Nostromo* up the Hudson River, and keeps watching from afar the shape of the city. Then he watches for an hour the wild birds of the Palisades. Enough of these images of natural beauty. He lets the boat drift all the way back toward Ocean City, as these days he calls Manhattan. Soon, you can catch him circling the *Oceania*, the

---

have to do with disposing of possessions. ('Car to Helen or Ray. Needs a tune-up. Money to Max and Sylvia. Furniture to George plus $137 I owe him.' Another one says: 'Fix the spark plugs on the car. I love you.' Imagine extinguishing the spark of your life with the thought of the spark plugs which don't work in your car!" *America, I love you!* (Norbert Kosky)

*"Writing and Reading for Love and Money," by William Jovanovich, *Publishers Weekly* (1975).

seagoing cruiser circling the Statue of Liberty, while our Intrepid ogles from below the calves and thighs of a whole school of pushy teenage Daughters of America who push each other against the boat's railing to see him, or his boat, better.

A skinny, miniskirted damsel screams at him, "Hey, Pa! Don't you like my little man in the kayak?" Another one, already in a swimsuit, shouts, "S'cuse me, sir, are you Captain Intrepid?"

Such is life on water.

A new generation of men came in—a more pushful set. I was one of them. (*The Book of Daniel Drew*, 1910)

But then there is also a sense of adventure, adventure as extension of one's Self. Adventure meaning not knowing what next and not knowing The Other.

Five days after reporting back for combat duty, *Intrepid* was almost the victim of another kamikaze attack. On March 18, 1945, she dodged a large bomber that crashed fifty yards off the starboard side. The aircraft carrier was showered with flaming gasoline and pieces of the enemy plane. (*American History*)

On the way back to the East and Harlem rivers, he brushes elbows with boastful motorboats of de Tocqueville class, and their passengers too cocky for words. **To attribute his rise to his talent or his virtues is unpleasant, for it is tacitly to acknowledge that they are themselves less virtuous or less talented than he was. (de Tocqueville)** Too fast for shaking a hand. Then he shakes hands with an obnoxious ferryboat followed by overbearing tug boats, a slick cruise yacht, "and with some ordinary dozen oil barges full of merchant marine heavies vaporing fatigue from their spiritually overinflated dinghies."

I am a hermit once again, and more than ever; and am—consequently—thinking out something new. It seems to me that only the state of pregnancy binds us to life ever anew. (Nietzsche)

Night is about to fall. Full moon! What kind of moody night will it be? Will Kosky, our incorrigible mood shifter, be in the mood to tell a tall story to a tall ship? To exchange a fast joke with a slow rowboat or a gross limerick with a delicate kayak? Will the water fowl in him offend a hydrofoil with an offer of a quickie?

Night. He lets *Nostromo* list perilously close to an out-of-town galleon of the *Intrepid* class, then he, a class by himself, discreetly exchanges passing kisses with an outclassed local sloop, while a discreet cloud hangs over the indiscreet moon. He turns down the advances of that old boy windjammer, but then, before midnight, he accepts an invitation to hop abroad *Madame*—an all-madam-manned houseboat offering offshore sex at half the price after midnight. Later, at dawn, passing by the prison at Riker's Island, he momentarily surrenders to the searchlight of the Coast Guard boat surveying him—a writer on the loose. **Who I am/holds/on all sides/of me like glass/holds even/above me as if I were/ a masked falcon held in a jar/I sing I beat/against the perimeter/of my madness/and still this thing leaves me here/with nowhere to go except alone. (Paul David Ashley)**

At dawn, the wind changes; waters calm down. A good reason to take off. In fact, anything could be the reason since, like a Trappist monk, he feels spiritually restless yet physically trapped. The roar of two jet engines which propel *Nostromo* sends shivers through the boat, but not through him. His inner waters are calm: for him, traveling no longer presupposes knowing one's destination.... **just one fishing boat, going slowly, and drawing the wind after it. (Oscar Wilde)** His destination is where he is.

Time for meditation again.

Speeding at 16.9 knots he puts *Nostromo* through a 69° turn, a clever maneuver called "sexual swerve" in *marinese*.

It would be worth the while to ask ourselves weekly, Is our life innocent enough? Do we live *inhumanly*, toward man or beast, in thought or act? To be serene and successful we must be at one with the universe.... the least conscious and needless injury inflicted on any creature is to its extent a suicide. What peace—or life—can a murderer have? (Thoreau)

Another turn. He is now slowly driving his boat at 6.9 knots into the part of the straits known as the Redfish Shallows, the kingdom of the Roaming Reds. **Not recognizing a prowling redfish when he sees one is the most common problem. (Brooks Bouldin)**

Indeed it is. Take Rilke. Rainer Maria was a typical saltwater redfish. He is the one who, first drawn to Russian women—he was in love with many Ludmillas—then learned Russian and for a while, mindless of the absence of basic comforts and his rampant T.B., even lived in Russia, all for the sake of love, and of Russian lust. Admit it, Rilke. It was Lust '69. Lust, not just sex.

He, a prototypical German, saw Russia, in his words, "as his protohomeland. . . . The Russians are people concerned only with the things that matter in life. Theirs is the atmosphere of eternity." And then again, as if this wasn't enough, he said, "All that is English, is foreign and distant to me. I do not know the language of that country and I almost do not know its art at all. I know none of its poets whereas everything pulls me steadily toward Russia. If ever something in the nature of a homeland were to be granted to me, it could only be there." Enough said? Not enough. "In Russia," wrote Rilke, "the graves are mountains and the people are its abyss. Its population is profound, somber and silent. . . . in every direction all seems boundless."

At times, when other boats and water gazers crowd the Manhattan waterways, our commodore takes his boat way out to sea, but not all the way out. He keeps it well within sight of the well-meaning Statue of Liberty from where once again he faces Manhattan: **a great don of the ocean. (Walt Whitman) A pink and white tapering pyramid cut slenderly out of the cardboard. (John Dos Passos)**

From his boat, our Ruthenian Sailfish looks the city straight in the face. For some thirty years this city has been his Fair Medusa, and, fair in its indifference, the city looks straight back at him. **The sense of being in an unfamiliar place deepened on me and as the moon rose higher the inessential houses seemed to melt away until I was aware of the old island here that flowered once for Dutch sailors' eyes—a fresh green breast of the new world. (F. Scott Fitzgerald)**

SS

One day, a most creative day full of authentic disquiet with his slowly deteriorating State of Self, Kosky takes his *Nostromo* all the way to Bistro Bay near Brighton Beach in Brooklyn. There, he docks the boat at the marina of the Hesperides Gardens, "a Ruthenian-Jewish joint serving only Central and East European (including Baltic States: J.K.) cuisine," in the words of *Ethnic Cuisine* (which replaced the venerable *Melting Pot* magazine, a publication recently replaced by *Right to Good Food* magazine.) (Food, printer. For once, food, not foot!)

Standing quietly at the bar, our heat-seeking SAM 69 missile seeks the heat-emitting priestess of High Times. "He seeks her, anxious to make up in still-life what he missed in his stilled literary sixty-nine narrative" (comments post-factum Jay Kay).

Here in this bar, most of these young men and women are, ironically, writers. They are matured by life. None of them live any longer in the *Country of the Young* (John W. Aldridge, 1969.) (*A superb performance.*

A. Alvarez.) Like him, everyone here is a dilettante, that is, **a sailor who sailed out searching for a new land but drowned on the way. (Stefan Szuman)** Mind you, Professor Szuman ranks dilettante artists on a par with great inventors, even discoverers. To him, a dilettante is one who, having been in love with Art for most of one's life, loves Art without reciprocity. One who, having subscribed since Vol. 1, No. 1, 1975, to *Joseph Conrad Today* (a newsletter: J.K.), keeps on calling Art out of the deepest calling, but always gets a busy number. One who, having left many most creative messages on Art's Answering Service, has yet to hear back from Art.

Here, at this bar, most of the writers are spiritually successful. They learned their art from life, and life from art. In fact, our Norbert Kosky is a typical example of such creative self-service. Back in 1963, he, then an essayist as anonymous as Suicide Anonymous, read *The Self-Born Art*, a very special chapter in Stefan Szuman's *On Art and Esthetic Education* (1962), beginning on page 33. (Kosky was born in 1933: J.K.) But then, as he kept on reading Szuman's spiritual *oeuvre*, he reached "The Amateur Literary Production," a chapter which—get this!—began on page 65 and ended on page 69! No wonder Kosky's first book of fiction was published in 1965, and his second got the 1969 Dilettante Fiction of the Year Award. **The rule that when a man takes a nazirite vow for an unspecified period, is derived from the word** *yihiyek* **("he shall be") in Numbers 6:5. (Sholem)** As if this were not enough, kindly note that—and this is the *pièce de résistance*—back in 1947, shortly after the war, when all German resistance ended, Kosky's father read aloud to Norbert in Ruthenian this very chapter then published by Stefan Szuman as a separate story called "In Praise of Dilettantes"* (the earlier version of *The Self-Born Art*), with the chapter in question beginning on page 60 and ending on page 69. Is it an accident then, that Kosky's first collection of essays was published—you guessed it!—in his spiritually seminal year 1960, a year during which—thank you, Professor Szuman!—he published his first nonfiction. But then, consider that in Ruthenian the word *szum* means nature's noise as well as man-made

---

*Stefan Szuman: a creator of the school of aesthetic education by which, in order to experience oneself and the world most fully, a human being must define himself and herself as an artist—a dilettante, eager to touch and to be touched by the beauty of the world. "What is Art," Szuman asks, "if not happiness-making reflection of the world's own beauty?"

rumor (as you will once again be told in the footnotes: J.K.). Now you know why so soon after his nonfictional debut Norbert Kosky, our Man of Szum, turned 69° off the nonfictional course, and with his back turned to facts, published back in 1965 his Szumanesque first work of fiction. First, mind you, ain't six—and what a far cry it is from his ninth. His first work was about being muted from within by the State of War. (Do not confuse it, please! with *The War: A Memoir*, by Marguerite Duras, 1986 ISBN: 0-394-55-236-9.) **This is invented. A passion for the little Jewish girl who was abandoned. (Marguerite Duras, op. cit., p. 173)** His ninth speaks about a writer's inner estate. **In this way** (and only in this: J.K.), **objective reality acquires for him a secondary importance; he makes use of it only to the extent to which it is already accommodated in the universe created by his imagination. It might be said that the writer takes from outside himself only what he is capable of creating in his imagination. ("Notes of the Author," 1965, p. 1)**

And now, so many years later, nearing fifty-four, nearsighted and weary, paunchy and almost entirely bald, our Dilettante Writer is suffering from biliary spasm which he tends to confuse with an imminent angina pectoris coronary. This is an attack which must be stopped— and stopped by a young and preferably spectacular looking Tatyana, looking the way Onegin first saw her. First, not last.

But novels, which she early favored,/Replaced for her all other treats;/ With rapturous delight she savored/Rousseau's and Richardson's conceits. (*Eugene Onegin*)*

Tatyana was her name . . . I grovel/That with such humble name I dare/ To consecrate a tender novel. (*Onegin*)

The reason is that our Samotnik is here on a blind date with a woman. The woman in question, and a question she is, could be anyone: a Damsel Fish† or a Good Samaritan.‡ She can be a Tatyanesque Indian,

---

*Eugene Onegin: a novel in verse, by Pushkin; a new translation of the *Onegin* stanza with an introduction and notes by Walter Arndt, 1963.

†For a color photograph of the Damsel Fish see *Saltwater Aquarium Fish*, by Herbert R. Axelrod and William Vorderwinkler (1956), p. 69.

‡In his book *On Art and Esthetic Education*, commenting upon Rembrandt's painting *Paysage* (op. cit., p. 99, ill. 98) and *Good Samaritan* (op. cit., p. 100, ill. 10), Szuman analyzes a fragment in the painting's right corner. There, a wounded rider tilts to the side as he is about to fall off a barely walking horse (op. cit., p. 100, ill. 9), while in spite of his so obviously forthcoming downfall, the kin of the wounded happily ride away in the resplendent coach! Rembrandt himself

Titanesque Black, or even Titianesque, i.e., a redhead painted by Tiziano Vecelli (also known as Titian, "the red-hair-fetish man." (Jay Kay)

"But tell me—which one was Tatyana?"/"Why, she who with an absent air,/Remote and wistful like Svetlana,/Came in and took the window chair." (*Onegin*)

She is the one who, replying to his purposefully odd newspaper ad advertising for "a spiritually sublime proofreader patterned after Pushkin's premarital Tatyana," replied by sending him a black'nd white blurry photograph of herself photographed naked while reading a copy of *Good Writing*. An affront since it was the magazine which called *The Healer* "as readable as any intellectual science fiction thriller."

With her unclear photograph in hand, unclear on purpose, our Death Dreader wanders through the crowded room, each face a new course offering from the catalogue called "The Learning Annex."

"I was flipping through 'The Learning Annex' magazine and I saw this 'Acting for Non-Actors' course. Although I didn't want to be a professional actress, it sounded intriguing so I signed up." (Frances V., "Acting for Non-Actors" graduate, April 1987)

As he stares at various women scattered around the room from corner to corner, they stare back at him. Will any one of them sign up? Says one stare: "I'm not into sex. I'm into 616: Racewalking—The Safe Exercise."

Says the stare of another: "I'm not into water. I take the 001 course in Ballooning in Hot Air." **The Learning Annex goes Hot Air Ballooning every Saturday and Sunday, sunrise or sunset. (*The Learning Annex*, July 1987)**

A gleeful Love Pawn, straight from Safe Sex Course 000: Shocking Splendor, stretches voluptuously in her chair, her hands hidden behind her back as if bound to an invisible post. Says her stare: "Don't look at me like that. I'm being chained and I bet in your sick life you must have seen a chained girl like me. I'm chained to my own bed, chained up by a lover whose name is Fear of AIDS."

He collects the last skoal from an Oriental beauty who feasibly in her past life was in Bangkok, where (he hopes) she modeled throughout the year Sexy Summer Swimwear. After all, the note from his blind date said, "Like you, I too am into Orient (into is not far from) and want to

---

must have considered this fragment of *Paysage* important enough to have it followed with *Good Samaritan*, a visual follow-up of the story.

avoid another Holocaust—meaning the killing of one part of unkind mankind by another who's even less kind." Not bad for a girl who, judging by her handwriting, could still be writing for *Junior Cavalcade* magazine. Her skoal says, "I'm all sex. Watch me while I do it." It says also, "I'm the ex-Mistress of the B. J. Beat-Off Blues!" Her luxurious Oriental body (here Oriental means straight out of water, and luxurious stems from *ex-oriente lux*) says to him, "Slip inside me, snake! **I'm the Princess of the Fishy Smell."** (Jean Przyluski) But then, just when, eager for touch, he walks over to her, her expression changes by 96°. It says now to him: "So sorry! You were misled by my Lotus-like body. I have just enrolled at The Learning Annex at this course called 1024: Introduction to Lotus 1-2-3. I'm not into body-to-body. Lotus is the name of a personal computer. Computer, not a Lotus Man."

Each one wants the other to love him but does not take into account the fact that to love is to want to be loved and that thus by wanting the other to love him, he only wants the other to want to be loved in turn. (Sartre)

ATTENTION: From Norbert Kosky (the Author) to all members of the International Good Faith International Translation Association!

RE: Your *Rule 69*. Urgent! Please approve of having English-language quote from Sartre *freshly* retranslated from English back into French— rather than to have it reinstated by the French translator in the original French written by Sartre. This must be done in *The Healer* in order to give the French reader a taste of foreignness; a taste of how it feels to read one's own work in forcign translation. This applies to all of my foreign-language quotes which, even if they originated in the original language into which this text will be originally translated, must be retranslated into it from English as if they had not existed in their original version. This is my ultimate tribute to your most necessary and by far one of the most creative Intellectual professions! Thank you all! Sincerely and devotedly, your most obedient intellectual servant, Norbert Kosky. © 1987.

Finally, with the photograph of her in hand, she finds Kosky sitting alone near the bar. To start with she is an ordinary Sweetwater Nymph. Enough said. "Not enough." (Jay Kay) While wearing no bra under her semi-transparent blouse, she is nevertheless wearing a serious expression, as well as a leatherette miniskirt and high heels as high as his expectations. She is also wearing her stereo headphones listening to music coming to her from her pocket-size tape recorder hidden in her purse or pocket. At his sight she shakes the headphones off her head, and rising to her feet—she is almost as tall as he—she kisses him lip-to-lip. Then they both sit down at a table placed in the far corner. The kiss literally tilts him over, and no wonder.

His calendar was different from that of his contemporaries. Their day was his night, and their night was his day. (Stefan Zweig about Balzac) It is a dainty kiss, full of the contemporary safe sex, eye-to-eye as well as tit-to-tit. After the kiss, Kosky pulls away from her, not in order to disengage himself from her but—far from it—to become closer to her by seeing all of her better. She is "The Temptress"* he first saw at the 1969 Vienna Biennale or was it in Bâle? Imagine a temptress no longer tempted by sex!

Breathless, she takes him by the hand. "Normally, I'm a square! I was too shy to talk to you when I first saw you at the Conlazio—Lasconsone—Zolocone—House Steak—" She seems lost for words.

"The Consolazione." He helps her out.

"At the Consolazione." She learns fast. "I'm basically a basic person. Basic not base. From what I saw of you in *Total State*, I thought that you didn't like basic people."

"I like Basic English," he says, consoling her quickly.

I even think that I think of it, and divide myself into an infinite retrogressive sequence of "I's" who consider each other. I do not know at which "I" to stop as the acutal, and in the moment I stop at one, there is indeed again an "I" which stops at it. I become confused and feel a dizziness, as if I were looking down into a bottomless abyss, and my ponderings result finally in a terrible headache. (Niels Bohr)

They toast each other with a sensual skoal. Eager to touch and be touched by life, our dilettante artist sits down at her side. He slides his hand along her perfect waist and hips all the way down to her own slide. This is life calling on life, as well as on Art. There is nothing wrong with it, ain't it so, Professor Stefan Szuman!?

He looks at her and then via her stare fixed upon him, he looks into her as if she were a transparent slide. There is nothing wrong with such a look. Slides are life's reflection. His visual touch prompts her, and she rests her most perfectly formed thigh against him. Her thigh is a work of true art. Her touch is spontaneous.

---

*"The Temptress": detail of the central panel of *The Last Judgment*, initially called by Bosch *The Ideal Fallen Woman*.

"Wow! Everyone is watching us—but talking only about you! What a pisser!" whispers the nymph, "this modern-day Tatyana." (Jay Kay)

"How do you know?" he asks her.

"Because I read lips. You probably think I'm a simple square."

"You're an original. Nature's first draft." He draws her closer.

"To me you are one of a kind," he goes on. "One straight out of course 996: How to Love Another Person and Make the Relationship Work. 'The Learning Annex Catalogue,' op. cit. One from course 900: Finding A Lover for Men and Women (ibid.). The courses I'm about to take."

"Now why is that?"

"Because words bother you and now they bother me too."

"I don't know much about books or writers. All I know is what I see on my TV." With her bare foot, she caresses his trousered calf. "Where do you work?"

"At home." He wraps his feet around her calves.

"What do you write?"

"Words. In my book words are numbers."

"Just words? Words like from the *Times Square Record* crossword puzzle?"

"Words as in a novel. A novel is a word puzzle."

"Ever since I was a kid, words have been a real puzzle for me. I could never read a vonel. I mean, *velon*," she stammers a bit.

"You mean a novel," he corrects her quietly.

"A novel." She learns fast. "Long words are worse for me. I bet it would take me longer to read a short story than it took you to write it!"

The twenty-two-year-old human plant plants a wet kiss on his neck, another on his ear, licking off his aging nectar. Just then he sees her and himself reflected in a wall mirror. To see what he sees, see J. Baldun Green's *The Young Girl and Death*, if death attracts you, as it clearly attracts him. (Him: a Man of the World with No Word of His Own: Jay Kay) See also his *Death and the Ages* at the Prado Gallery, offering the composition of disagreeable contrast. (Antonio J. Onieva)*

"My shrink says that as a result of watching some eighteen thousand TV hours by my last birthday, my mind is too fatigued to come up with anything on its own. He says that eighteen thousand hours equal being

---

*Antonio J. Onieva, *A New Complete Guide to the Prado Gallery* (Madrid, 1979).

for nine years on an eight-to-five job. Eight to five, or six to nine. What do you think?"

"I think *only* when I write. The word is my private-access cable TV," he says, unashamedly looking into her left eye, and no longer looking into her shamefully slutty decolletage. **The man who writes thinks differently when he writes than when he speaks. Among others, he writes slower than when he speaks. The written sentence has time to calmly mature in our mind. (Stefan Szuman)**

Orgasm is orgasm, however experienced. (Albert Ellis, Ph.D.)

"I once saw *Contra Versum*, a literary talk show on my TV. Once was sure enough for me!" A perfect *dombi*, she reassures the nonwriter in him.

"*Controversy!*" He attempts to stay calm.

"It was about—wait—a dead famous writer whose name was—his name was Weroll! He was a foreigner but like you, he wrote in English. He was once shown in *Life* magazine as the literary person Number one."

"Weroll? Are you sure? I don't recall any *life*-size foreign writer Number 1."

"No, not Weroll. Wait! Revol? His name had something to do with revolver. He was also into *futures*, into science fiction." She sets a puzzle for him.

"Wait—I really don't know." He is embarrassed. "Orwell," says Kosky. "You mean Orwell, even though that was not his real name. He was born as Eric Arthur Blair."

"Why would he call himself Orwell and not Blair?"

"Because Orwell is the name of a British river and he was awfully British. Also, because if you turn the letters around, you get *rewol*. As in *rewolver* and *rewolution*. Turn the letters around again and you get *lewo*, which in Russian means 'left'. It's all very Kafkaesque."

"Wasn't Kafka a writer who wrote about bugs and robots?"

"He was! He wrote *Amerika*—a book about this country, a country he had never seen."

"You mean he was a cheat? He wrote about something he never saw?"

"Not really. He wrote about Amerika—not America. Writing can be as exact as science. A change of one letter, such as changing the letter C to the letter K, can often mean invoking a different Letter of the Literary Law."

"But you said he had not seen *Amerika?*" She lets him have it.

"He saw it only in his head." He kisses on the forehead his nonliterary sexual pet. "The way we Americans will see sex when we will not be able to touch. When skoal will replace sex." He skoals her sex, while in fantasy he lets his Jay Kay show up again, and the knee jerk that he is fucks the brains out of her arabesque knee.

"I wish all words were just different colors. Colors, not numbers and letters. Just think how easy life would then be. Books make me sick." She squeezes her right hand under his right arm and she keeps it there for a moment. "I wish writers were painters—not writers."

"So do I. So do I." he says twice—and twice he sighs inadvertently.

"So who is your favorite painter?" she asks him, wearing an expression of an all-time perfect non-literary dombi.

"Lorenzo Costa," he replies without hesitation. "He is my favorite because his life was far more colorful than his paintings. Lorenzo is said to have once painted the "Last Supper"—the greatest painting that ever was—but then he destroyed it and left behind only a few uninspired works. He destroyed it after Mona Chiara, his mistress, who was the wife of Asdubale Tozzi, the local guard commander, was put to death by her jealous husband after he discovered she was unfaithful to him—" Kosky hesitates, then goes on—"and she was put to death by a certain creature, a half-man, half-wolf, in the most cruel way imagined."

"Oh, my God, don't tell me how," she moans, hanging onto him. "I don't want to know. I mean—I don't mind knowing but I can't take hearing about it from you."

"Aren't books important to you?" She keeps on moaning.

"Books are important only to those who know that reading is the only remedy known against any illness of the spirit. Still, were all the books in the world to disappear overnight, daily life on earth would go on pretty much the same—even for me, and I used to carry a literary banner."

"That's what I think too," she says. "My father—he's a farmer in Fabyan, Connecticut—reads all kinds of books. And every book shakes him up. One day he believes in sex, the next he says sex doesn't agree with him. Then he reads some stupid book about woman's lib, about that thing called bilib—dolib," she ad-libs.

"Libido," says Kosky.

"And he blames his libido." She squares with him.

517

They keep drinking in silence. To the Ruthenian-Jewish conversationalist in him, silence is not his favorite social pastime but it is hers, and who is he to argue? "Isn't she a prototypical young American?" (Jay Kay)

New York is the only place where, no matter how cautious or wary a person is, both parties can come out a loser. Often in the same affair. . . . The more psychotic the arrangement, the better its chances of survival here. (Petronius, 1966)

Soon she seems lost and apprehensive. "What does that sign actually say?" she asks, pointing to a well-lighted wall sign reading AIDS ALERT: DON'T EXCHANGE BODILY FLUIDS, and then adds, "I see the letters—but I can't put them together. What I've got is called word blindness. Word blindness is congentle and reditory," she recites.

"Congenital and hereditary." The writer corrects his ideal blind date. **Congenital word blindness, also known as dyslexia, is often accompanied by oral fantasies. (*Medicine Digest*, 1986)**

"Congenital and hereditary." She struggles with the pronunciation. "The words maul me; I can never get them straight."

"Neither can I," he says, moving closer to her in his ms. version No. 8, where he has still six pages of the text to rewrite. (The ms. has still to be polished—polished, not rewritten—in the galleys.) "Ask any of my pretty straight-line editors." **As in water face answereth to face. It is customary to have a master who desires to teach and a student who does not want to learn, or a student who desires to learn and a master who does not want to teach him; but in this case the master desires to teach and the student to learn. (*Tractate Soferim*)**

"Neither can I," he repeats, moving still closer to her. Lifting her blouse she lets his hand glide over her back, then back and forth from one breast to another, then all the way down to her waistline, and below, a territory begging to be subjected to drastic lip suction, but never to Liposuction Surgery.*

Just then, as our nymph and trout stare at each other inadvertently in the wall mirror, Kosky's stare falls upon two characters crossing the room. Passing by Kosky's table, they turn out to be de Morande, who

---

*Liposuction surgery: the removal of unsightly but only too well seen fat deposits by means of a special suction tube which, introduced through less than one-third-of-an-inch-long incision into the layer of fat, first dislodges then sucks out through its smooth nerve-and-vein serving end the useless fat lubules.

is walking arm-in-arm with De Voto, but this time several steps behind Carlyle.

Kosky watches them calmly. He watches them the way Abraham Abulafia would, by mixing yogi breathing with Jewish meditation, but also not unlike, Dalai Lama. (The one who knows how tough it is to separate Mahayana Buddhism from the Marxist Mahayana: Jay Kay.)* No longer part of his present tense (the one so brilliantly utilized by Stendhal to catch a catching moment), his recognition of these two now belongs to his past, a past best expressed in the French imperfect tense, wisely reserved by Balzac for mental states which seem to linger longer than they ought to.

Besides: the whole affair has been, for him, one great lesson in literary homeopathy,† and hasn't homeopathy been, for years, his most often prescribed remedy for just about every condition? "No wonder: the whole homeopathic potency system depends on number six, number nine, a bit of alcohol, some minerals—and lots of water." (Niskisko, 1947)

But one must rise by that by which one falls. (Tantra)

Exhaling into his ear, the sweet *waterchilde* unbuttons two more buttons of his shirt, her fingers exploring his severely sweating underarms. "When my man is a writer, what I like to read is this man's body, not his mind," she whispers, sliding her hand down his back between his pants and his shirt, well within the well of his behind. "By now everybody knows your mind. How many of your readers know your body?"

---

*See: *The Last Dalai Lama: A Biography*, by Michael Harris Goodman, 1986, p. 333.

†In homeopathic medicine, "preparation of a potentized remedy is a detailed and complicated process. Briefly stated, the first stage is to prepare a tincture of the selected plant by soaking it in a solution of alcohol and water for a certain length of time. Then one part of the tincture is diluted in 99 parts of alcohol and water and shaken many times, resulting in a '1' potency. One part of this mixture is mixed with 99 more parts of alcohol and water and again shaken, producing a '2' potency. For home prescribing, remedies made by repeating this process six to thirty times are used."

"The biochemics (tissue salts) are made by mixing and grinding the crude mineral in ten parts of milk sugar. Then, one part of this is mixed with ten parts of milk sugar again. A 6X potency is produced after six of these steps." From *Homeopathic Remedies for Physicians, Laymen and Therapists*, by David Anderson, M.D., Dale Buegel, M.D., and Dennis Chernin, M.D. (1979), p. 6.

"Not many. Not many at all," he agrees with her readily.

Just now, when I'm seventy, the napes of women's necks have a sexually arousing effect upon me, both the ones which are rounded as well as those which are fluted with that sinful little curl of hair against the glow of the skin. For the joy of looking at it, I find myself following a nape, the way other men go for a leg. (Edmond de Goncourt)

After the drinks, the dinner and the nonobligatory kisses exchanged defiantly—"such an innocent, almost dry kiss is not a passage for AIDS, certainly not *yet*" (*ProtoScience*, 1988), the nymph insists he take her to his home (*his* home, printer, not her home. She knows his home is *Nostromo*). He tells her he has nothing more to show her of himself since, by staring at each other so much, and for so long, they have already exchanged all programs available on their inner-cable memory TV, but she disagrees with him vehemently.

"I may not understand the meaning of a lot of courses offered by The Learning Annex." She keeps annexing him with her moonlit stare as they stand at the end of the dock. "But I sure have gone through Shower Singer's Workshop, No. 446, and once took a course on Self-Hypnosis, No. 338. If that's not close to your course 696: Wall Street Work-Out: Tummy and Buns, then what is?"

"My own course," he tells her truthfully, because he is tempted by aphrodisia, by the prospect of yet another fit of Galenesque *kundalini*."*

He compares the horrified conscience, which tries to flee and cannot escape, with a goose which, pursued by the wolf, does not use its wings, as ordinarily, but its feet and is caught. (Paul Tillich, writing about Luther)

The task of testing oneself, examining oneself, monitoring oneself in a series of clearly defined exercises, makes the question of truth—the truth concerning what one is, what one does, and what one is capable of doing—central to the formation of the ethical subject. (Michel Foucault)†

While his home is *Nostromo*, his address, keep in mind, is South Street Seaport where, at an old and seldom-used pier, *Nostromo* is most

---

*Galen: author of *On the Usefulness of the Parts of the Body* (Cornell University Press, 1968), one of the seminal theoreticians of aphrodisia, in whose view "it is the *pneuma* that seeks to exit violently from the body, and escapes in the sperm at the moment of ejaculation, depriving the body of its vital breath."

†From *The Care of the Self*, by Michel Foucault (1986), p. 109; see also *Self and Others*, p. 69.

safely anchored. On a clear night, the pier offers not only a view of the mouth of the East River, but also the mouths as well as other parts of the body of many Pierres and Pierrinnes who come to pct one another here.

But there is no one here tonight. The night is foggy. So foggy you can barely see the end of your outstretched hand—outstretched as in an act of a handshake, not in a military salute. Disoriented a bit—he is oozing booze—WAIT! NOT TRUE! PRINTER: he is oozing ozone, not booze! Isn't drinking air as if it were water his spiritual trademark number one?

As our Ibrahim ibn Jacob* ponders the Jewish-Ruthenian meaning of *Nacht und Nebel* (*Night and Fog*) (1939–1945) simultaneously he asks himself **What went wrong? We still have a minute, General! (Dick Cavett to the just fallen leader of South Vietnam.)** "Vietnam was America's own Khazar Empire." (Jay Kay) What went wrong is that, instead of expounding in his work upon the otherworldly, he pounded upon what's wordly. That instead of being buoyed up by **forces that flow from the hidden worlds (Abraham Joshua Heschel),** he floated within **limits of negative critique. (Trent Schroyer, 1973)**

He knows exactly where he stands and he has not lost his sense of direction. To his left stands Bellevue, the hospital for those whose inner vue is no longer belle. A bit farther towers the *belle* United Nations. "Belle only when rated against our own Disunited United States," in the words of the *City Guide*. And to his right, he realizes a bit uneasily, stretch upward the sixty-nine-story-high towers of the First Wall Street Safe Sex Sperm Saving Bank. He strikes five letter Ss while striking at "the newest financial empire based on fear of sex." (*City Guide*)

---

*Ibrahim ibn Jacob: the Jewish author of the first extensive account of the large number of followers of the Judaic faith who came to Poland from the East around 965 after the fall of the Khazar state. See "Jews in Poland Until the End of the 18th Century," by Maurycy Horn, in *The Polish Jewry: History and Culture* (op. cit.), p. 9.

The Jews of Poland were, in the words of Abraham Joshua Heschel (1947), "tenaciously adhering to their own traditions, concentrated upon the cultivation of what was most their own, what was most specific and personal. They borrowed from other cultures neither substance nor form. What they wrote was literature created by Jews, about Jews and for Jews. They apologized to no one. . . . They felt no need to compare themselves with anyone else, and they wasted no energy in refuting hostile opinions."

He saw it all, he took it all in hungrily as part of his experience, he recorded much of it, and in the end he squeezed it dry as he tried to extract its hidden meanings. (Thomas Wolfe)

The fog lifts. Across the river, the lights of Brooklyn flicker now, as they did when Vladimir Mayakovsky and Thomas Wolfe stood here. The beam from the Statue of Liberty pierces the clouds, as much now as it did then. Kosky is about to turn away from the visual *cliché verre* when somewhere behind he hears the vague sound of human footsteps. For men are wise:/They know that they are lost. (Thomas Wolfe)

Involuntarily, he turns around. He listens. Again, he hears the steps of three or four men sneaking toward him in sneakers, "like footnotes on life's last page." (Norbert Kosky, 1988)

Their presence, their hiding at night, and in the fog, does not surprise him. He suspects that these men are like him, street-smart city souls lost at night in this dark and wet urban marsh. Still, they also could be after him. Just in case they are, he could try to escape. Escape is only one step away. But which step is it?

He hears their steps again, but this time he hears them more clearly. This time the sound gives him gooseflesh. These men march with a goose step. Think what such a sound does to him, a child of World War II! *Never mind Childe Harold!*

Now does he at last realize that, like a Gypsy, he lives on the boundary of an alien world. A world that is deaf to his music, just as indifferent to his hopes as it is to his suffering or his crime. (Jacques Monod, 1969)*

> EICHMANN: With the Gypsies, as far as I remember, nobody worried in the least about any specification whatever.
> LESS: Why really did they exterminate all the Gypsies?
> EICHMANN: Herr Hauptmann, that was one of those things, I think—Führer—Reichsführer—I don't know—there were—all of a sudden it happened and the order went out—I don't know. (1960)†

---

*See *Chance and Necessity*, by Jacques Monod; "Death in Cannes," *Esquire*, March 1986. See also Diagram 11: "Ritual Links," in *The State of Ambiguity*: A *Study of Gypsy Refugees*, by Ignacy-Marek Kaminski (University of Götenburg, Sweden, 1980), p. 69.

†Transcribed exactly as spoken: *Eichmann Interrogated*, transcript from the archives of the Israeli police, p. 193.

The sound grows louder. This time as always, time spells out the inevitable. Inevitably, these somebodies march in his direction. Inevitably, there is no escape; like terminal illness, life too is final.

Motionless he waits. Sure, he could still run away from this printed page 523 and move his inner action from the Diaspora and move it to Israel.* **Judaism is neither an experience nor a creed, neither the possession of psychic traits nor the acceptance of a theological doctrine, but the living in a holy dimension, in a spiritual order, living in the covenant with God. (Abraham Joshua Heschel)**

"How about going back to Ruthenia? Ruthenia—the spiritual country you and Conrad never left?" (suggests overly desperate Jay Kay).

When Conrad once said to a Pole that wherever he traveled over the seas he was never far away from his country, or when he declared to another Pole: "The leading principle of my life was to help Poland," he was of course falling into the typically Polish habit of exaggerating. (Gustav Morf)†

Moving once again? Another country? Another language? A brand new—new and fresh—reputation? A brand new job, or should he say occupation? **Reputation, reputation, reputation! O I have lost my reputation! I have lost the immortal part of myself, and what remains is bestial. (*Othello*)**

Is it because he is lazy? Possibly, but only if by being lazy one means dragging a fallen foot of a woman all the way up to bed (a fallen foot, not a fallen woman, Printer!) (*why not?*: Printer), or a footnote on the way down the page. Lazy means easy going, and since he has been writing his opus No. 9 for almost five years, clearly he must find his writer's life most easy going—easy going, or even sea-going too.

Lazy, yes, but only as one is a bit fatigued by all this mental travel and physical vagabondry. As one who has gone by now through most of his Self's pastures and meadows, grasslands, steppes and savannahs.

He is not lazy, not really. He is exhausted. That's it! He exhausted

---

*"For a 'mysterious relationship' obtained between the Jewish people and the Jewish land, which remained throughout the ages a challenge to the Jews." (Abraham Joshua Heschel) the reader is advised to read Chapter 14: "Israel and Diaspora," in *The Insecurity of Freedom: Essays on Human Existence*, by Abraham Joshua Heschel (1966).

†*The Polish Shades and Ghosts of Joseph Conrad*, by Gustav Morf (op. cit.), p. 306.

the resources of his very Self, and why not? Self is not inexhaustible. ("Self is a fluid made of the love and hate of oneself." Niskisko, 1987) ("Tell the reader from what you are exhausted. Tell it now. Now before it is too late." Line Editor No. 96.)

Leave me alone! he tells her. I am even exhausted by writing—and now by even a damn number like you (in his despair he dares to call 96 a "damn number"—he a creature of 96!). Writing means breathing. I am exhausted from wrong breathing! he exclaims. **I feel beheaded by a force I don't know and could not name. (Niskisko, 1971)** By something I no longer care to know.

"Wrong breathing? You?" Jacky X interrupts him for the ninth time. "Aren't you the one-and-only fiction master who floats upon the water like a lotus leaf? The one who has mastered to the fullest Royal Yoga Kundalini?" she asks (she a mistress of 69 kundalini: Jay Kay).

"Mastership is exhausting." Our mini–Dalai Lama tells her. I have exhausted my own **lung power. (Shari Miller Sims)***

I'm tired, I guess, from the very holding of my breath when writing my Breathing Opus No. 9 without inhalation or exhalation. Tired from having my lungs filled. From straining my lungs with too much **Kosin. I. chem. A yellow physiologically inactive decomposition product, $C_{23}H_{30}O_7$, of Kosotoxin. (*Webster's Second International*)** and not enough of my Polin Vintage 965.

Thereupon God took a piece of Eretz Yisroel, which he had hidden away in the heavens at the time when the Temple was destroyed, and sent it down upon the earth and said: "Be My resting place for My children in their exile." That is why it is called Poland (Polin), from the Hebrew poh lin, which means: "Here shalt thou lodge" in the exile. . . . "And what will happen in the great future when the Messiah will come? What are we going to do with the synagogues and the settlements which we shall have built up in Poland?" asked Mendel. . . . "How can you ask? In the great future, when the Messiah will come, God will certainly transport

---

*"Our lungs: wonder machines. . . . Once the lungs fill with air, a process called gas exchange takes place: oxygen is drawn out of the air into blood vessels within the lungs and the waste product of body activity (carbon dioxide or CO_2) moves from the blood into the air. As the breathing muscles relax, air rushes out of the lungs, expelling CO_2 back into the atmosphere." From "Fitness Now: Breathing: Can You Improve It? Control It?" by Shari Miller Sims, *Vogue*, 1987.

Poland with all its settlements, synagogues and Yeshivahs to Eretz Yisroel. How else could it be?" (Sholem Asch, *Kiddush Ha-Shem*)*

And now you know why.

Motionless, "our literary Hippocrates waits all alone on his literary island of Kos." (Jay Kay) Maybe these somebodies are, like him, harmless kosher fellow writers? And, with *kos* and *her* present in the word *kosher* maybe they are women. "Women? What kind of women?" (prompts him impromptu Jay Kay). Who cares what women as long as they care more about sex than CARE? Maybe these women want to talk to him. "Talk face-to-face, or face it, even engage in a safely faceless safe-sex group sex" (monitors his master's voice Jay Kay).

Motionless, our Kos waits for them. Will they only mock him or peck him to death?

He could still get into his boat in time to cast off, but, for some reason, he does not rush and so he will not make it. Why not? Because, frankly, he feels fed up with this self-appointed novelistic investiture. He is almost fifty-five years old. Ever since the war ended, he had lived a tense life made of "a noncontinuous and continuous, active and passive condition perfect tense" (John Millington-Ward, Athens, London, 1953). By now, his once so distinguished World War II blaze is partly extinguished. Blaze, meaning, "1. Fire, flame, bonfire. *Obs.* Flagration, holocaust, wildfire" (Rodale, 1978). The fact is that already at the age of twenty or twenty-two, in the midst of his studies under the guru Chalasinski,† he did not expect to live long enough to be fifty-five years

---

Polin, A Journal of Polish-Jewish Studies: Institute for Polish-Jewish Studies, Oxford. (As of 1987 there are branches in Boston, Chicago, Miami and, last but not least, New York.) See also, as a follow-up, Chapter 1: "The Beginnings of Jewish Settlement in the Polish Lands," by Aleksander Gieysztor; Chapter 6: "Polish Society and the Jewish Problem in the Nineteenth Century," by Stefan Kieniewicz; and Chapter 10: "Notes on the Assimilation and Acculturation of Jews in Poland, 1863–1943," in *The Jews in Poland*, ed. by Chimen Abramsky, Maciej Jachimczyk and Antony Polonsky. (Basil Blackwell, Inc., 1986, in association with the Institute for Polish-Jewish Studies, Oxford)

†Jozef Chalasinski: A Polish master sociologist who wrote such sociological classics as *The Social Genealogy of Polish Intelligentsia* (1945) and *American Culture* (1960). "With Stefan Szum, Jozef Chalasinski ignited my longing for writing, for my inner *chalas*. After all, in Ruthenian *chalas* is as synonymous with *szum* ("as *noise* is with *rumor*." (Norbert Kosky, 1960)

old. After all, his spiritual sob brothers were dead before reaching such an age: think of Cagliostro and Balzac, Pushkin and Thomas Wolfe, Sabbatai Sevi and Romain Gary—to name only those few.

Instead, he lived long enough. Long enough to regret that, given another chance to repeat himself, he would have remained at Beulah University. **He would have taught/He would have been teaching/He would have been taught/He would have been being taught (rarely used).***

The steps near, their sound muffled by *Night and Fog* (Jean Cayrol, 1955).† He can almost hear these marching men breathe—breathe in and breathe out.

Then from somewhere, from inside the fog, a single disembodied voice says: *We've got him!* Before he can confront its source, someone from behind hits him on the head with something hard. Stunned, but conscious, he falls to the dock. **A shapeless figure bent over him, he smelt the fresh leather of the revolver belt; but what insignia did the figure wear on the sleeves and shoulder-straps of its uniform—and in whose name did it raise the dark pistol barrel?**

A second, smashing blow hit him in the ear. Then all became quiet. There was the sea again with its sounds. A wave slowly lifted him up. It came from afar and traveled sedately on, a shrug of eternity. (Arthur Koestler, *Darkness at Noon***)**

Now, picking our man up as if he were a detached handle and manhandling him a bit, two of them drag him by his feet, and by his feet alone, while the other two do nothing to him, as if assuming he was already dead, or not feeling anything anymore. He finds this a bit troubling, but not tormenting. His instinct tells him: THIS CAN NEVER BE AS BAD AS . . . **as bad as what? (Ed.) As bad as how I feel already. As bad as running out of some inner current. Do you know what I mean? (I don't, but do you? Ed.) I feel that what I need is a massive spiritual charger, rather than a new battery. But where can I find it now, at the creatively most dreaded number 55? (Kosky, 1987)**

Now, listening to the sound of his head banging against the less than

---

*John Millington-Ward, *The Use of Tenses in English* (Orient Longmans, Ltd., Calcutta/Bombay/Madras, 1955), p. 69.

†*Night and Fog*, 1955 (32 minutes), text by Jean Cayrol, directed by Alain Resnais. "Hauntingly objective. The very opposite of *Shoah*—an oral history of the Holocaust—by Claude Lanzman (1985), "who by discrediting my entire nation is no longer a *lanzman* to me" (in the words of Jay Kay).

even stones, Kosky detaches himself from what is going on. Inside his head. This is a form of voluntary nonfeeling. Call it Para Nirvana. He hears these men rasping and, both as a Yoga and Catastrophe Man, he is impressed with their sense of control, a sign of most even breathing.

They keep on dragging him all the way to the end of the pier. Being dragged face up like this is no fun—unless, of course, one thinks of being dragged over these stones face down. (It Could Always Be Worse: Israel Kosky)

They drag him now beyond the sign IMPASSE, all the way to the end of the dockyard. But what for? Does it matter, what for? What matters is life and life is a state of uneven reflection: Jay Kay.

They stop at the sign marked DEAD END, but so what? DEAD END does not mean death and as long as he is alive and allowed to breathe more or less evenly, there is no end to the sensual Nirvana.

Now, these faceless men—faceless since what matters in a tale is a moral—pick him up as if he were a doll. First, they grab him by his arms, legs and torso; then they lift him high off the ground. They stretch him a bit—then swing him back and forth, forth and back—then they toss him—toss him out of an invisible hammock suspended in the invisible air, toss him up, not down.

When I looked once more for Gatsby he had vanished, and I was alone again in the unquiet darkness. (F. Scott Fitzgerald)* He flies up like a bird, but up only for a moment so short it already seems ago—then, he starts falling down. He: the unsinkable Lotus Man disguised as the American Unsinkable Molly Brown.

The end came suddenly. (Thomas Wolfe)

---

*"Involuntarily I looked up. When I looked down again he was gone, and I was left to wonder whether it was really the sky he had come out to measure with the compass of those aspiring arms." (F. Scott Fitzgerald)

I believe I understood among other things not to disclose any trade secrets. Well, I am not going to.

(Joseph Conrad)

THIS BOOK IS WHOLLY FICTION. (JERZY KOSINSKI)

What makes all autobiographies worthless is, after all, their mendacity.

(Freud)

Persons attempting to find a motive in this narrative will be prosecuted; persons attempting to find a moral in it will be banished; persons attempting to find a plot in it will be shot. (Mark Twain)

This book is a description of what is, so far as the Author is aware, a new kind of hobby. (William James Sidis)

ABOUT THE AUTHOR

Born in Poland in 1933 of Jewish parents, novelist Jerzy Kosinski lost in the Nazi Holocaust all but two members of his once numerous Polish-Jewish family.

A student of American sociology, he left Poland for the United States in 1957, and has since become a U.S. citizen.

Jerzy Kosinski won the National Book Award for *Steps* and received the American Academy and National Institute of Arts and Letters Award in Literature. He is the author of *The Painted Bird, Being There, The Devil Tree, Cockpit, Blind Date, Passion Play, Pinball,* and other novels.

A Ford and Guggenheim Fellow, Mr. Kosinski was a Fellow at the Center for Advanced Studies at Wesleyan University, has taught American literature at Princeton, and was professor of English prose and criticism at the Yale University School of Drama. He left Yale in order to serve as the president of the American Center of PEN, an international association of writers and editors and, reelected, he served the maximum two terms. A human rights activist, Mr. Kosinski is the recipient of the American Civil Liberties Award for demonstrating the vitality of the First Amendment's right of free expression.

A Doctor of Hebrew Letters, H. C., from Spertus College of Judaica, Mr. Kosinski is also the recipient of the Brith Sholom Humanitarian Freedom Award as well as the Spertus College International Award.

As a Polish-American, Mr. Kosinski was honored with the Polonia Media National Achievement Award for his contribution to the Polish-American literary heritage.

For his screen adaptation of his novel *Being There* (which starred Peter Sellers and Shirley MacLaine), Mr. Kosinski won the Best Screenplay of the Year Award from both the Writers Guild of America and the British Academy of Film and Television Arts.

In his film-acting debut in *Reds*, Mr. Kosinski portrayed Grigori Zinoviev, the Russian revolutionary leader.

Currently (1988) Mr. Kosinski is the Chairman of the Board of the American Foundation for Polish-Jewish Studies (affiliated with the Institute for Polish-Jewish Studies at Oxford University) and a Fellow at Timothy Dwight College, Yale University.